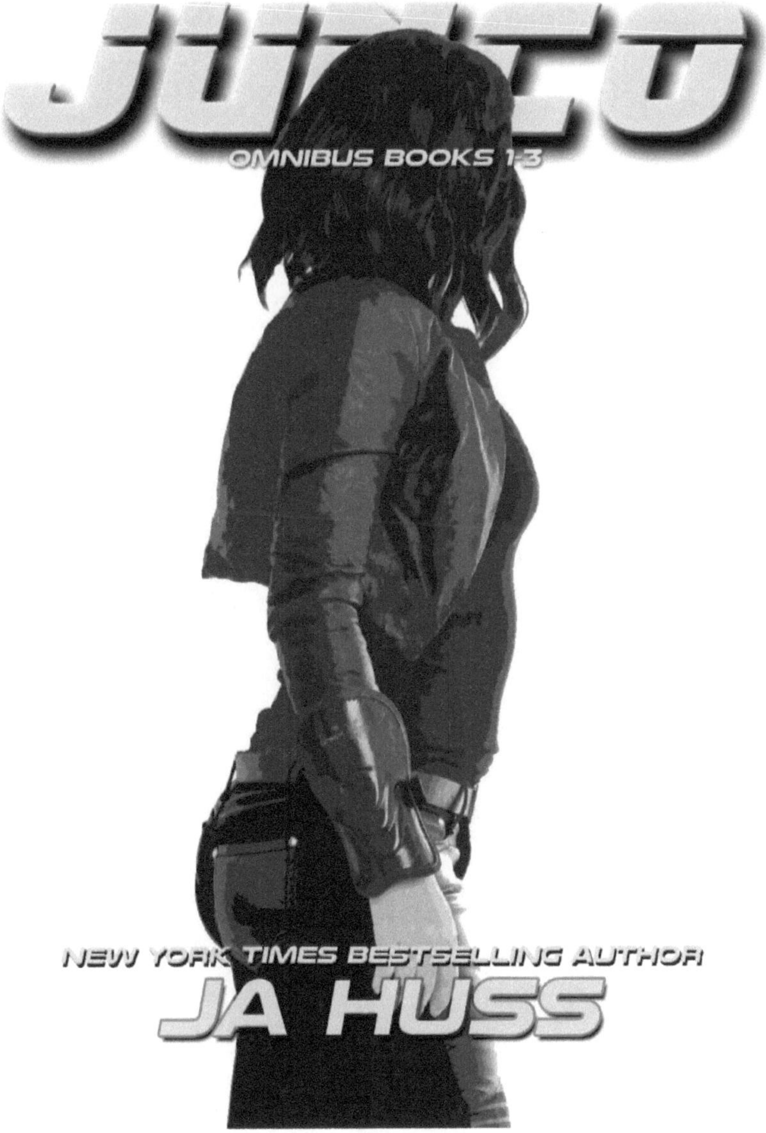
JUNCO
OMNIBUS BOOKS 1-3
NEW YORK TIMES BESTSELLING AUTHOR
JA HUSS

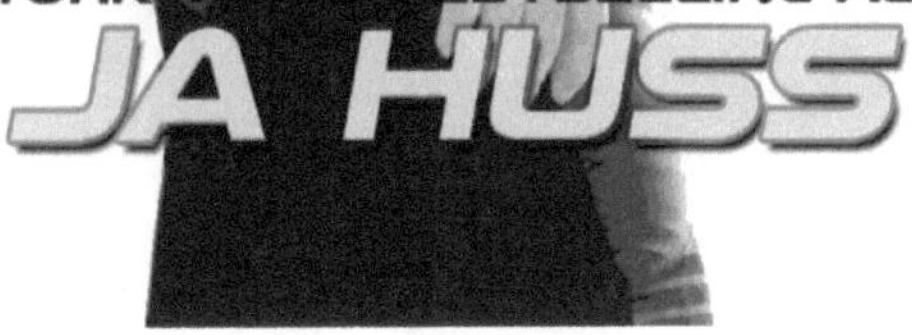

I Am Just Junco
Omnibus Books 1-3

By J. A. Huss

Edited by RJ Locksley
Cover design by J. A. Huss

ISBN-13: 978-1-950232-50-5

BOOK ONE

CLUTCH

Chapter One

Picture yourself standing on the edge of a dock...

I shake my head.

Fuck that.

I'm standing on a dirt road barefoot, exhaust from the Goat swirling dust up my funeral dress, trying to make some sense of things.

The closed stop-gate in front of me signals the entrance to the Stag, but the antlered skull in the middle of the arm spawns a moment of pause. My eyes linger on the decorations only long enough to log them. Blood-red paint on the antlers, an old wooden arrow sticking out of one of the orbits, and a crown of acacia thorns draped around the tines.

A child's prank.

The cigar slips between my lips. I cup my hand to block the wind, touch the cigar to the striker, and suck in deeply as the end glows bright orange. They stink and they make me stink, but I don't care.

Today, I don't care about much.

I slam the Goat's door and walk towards the skull, then hear the tell-tale crack of a sonic boom and turn to squint at the sun as it loses its battle with the rotating earth. Peak City has been out of my sight line for hours but I know where it should be on the horizon. I find the contrail of a suborbital coming out of the north pointing back to my home.

Turning back to the gate, I watch as the wind picks up the strip of wood hovering across the sorry excuse for a road and makes it dance. A stray magpie lands and rides the skull with a rhythm that reminds me of better days. It watches me, tilts its head to the side, and squawks, "Away!"

I flick the cigar and chase the magpie away.

There is nothing here to stop my progress into the Stag but since this is a forbidden zone in the Rural Republic, I pause before taking this final step into disobedience. Consequences tend to mean less with the loss of precious things, so they mean nothing to me now.

Reaching up, I release my long auburn hair from the tie and let it flap around my face as the wind tries to carry it across the grasslands.

If only the wind would carry me across the grasslands.

My cold toes scrunch into the dirt and I remember my funeral shoes are in the backseat, discarded hours ago. I walk over to the Goat and fish around until I pull together a pair of field boots and some black thermals. I hike the warm leggings up to my hips and then sit on the edge of my old Humvee and meticulously lace up each boot so they are snug, but not tight.

A sheathed hunting knife is in danger of dropping through the rusted-out floorboard and I rescue it, stashing it inside the boot. Then I slide my shotgun onto the front seat and drop my little pistol into the crap box along with other items one usually finds in a vehicle. The lid drops closed with a snap.

In the end I didn't need to waste all this time in front of the gate. It was never a question of if I would go. Only when. I climb back into the front seat, jam the Goat in gear and veer off the road, pressing up against the low-hanging branches of cottonwoods that have crept up from the dry riverbed. I brace myself as my vehicle bounces down into the ditch and then jolts back up. I gun it as the tires lose a little traction in the rain-softened earth, swing her around the ominous gate, and surge back onto the dirt track that still thinks it is a road.

On the other side I stop once more to check for Peak City in the distance, but all I see is the magpie, back on the skull, riding it out. I flip it off and gun the Goat again. We lurch forward, sputtering out a cloud of smoke that could get you hanged in some parts of the world.

But not here.

The Rural Republic might officially be part of the United Republics, but that's pretty much where it ends. Our national motto is quaint. *Simple Serves.* A reference to the throwback life we are supposed to be leading. But if you're not from around here and need help, (which is strictly theoretical, we're a closed campus, kids) the answer you get is disinterest. If you're lucky.

The drive out to Stag Camp is a stretch of open road, peppered with the occasional falling-down farmhouse or small herd of antelope. So I settle in, light another cigar, and slide the window down even though the warm November afternoon has given in to the cold November evening.

Nothing to do now but think about the job. My eyes track to the passenger seat, past the shotgun, and come to rest upon the thick envelope pressed into my hands as I left the funeral several hours ago.

The label on the front is machine-printed, but it doesn't say Junco. It says Dale. Resident of one Stag Camp in the middle of nowhere.

I push the funeral from my thoughts and allow the dying light to seep out of my world a little at a time. The eye-shine peering back at me from the side of the road as I take a wide turn clues me in that twilight is gone. The two glowing dots are far enough apart to estimate size and my body gives up an involuntary shiver as I run down the short list. Nightdog or prairie lion. Either one would eat me alive.

If they could catch me.

The sky is filled with stars long before I spy the dark shadow of the landmark hill in the distance. It's a slow climb that turns into a nightmare halfway up, then a flat patch to gather some steam so you can push your vehicle to its limit and struggle up the final grade that will plunge you over the other side.

I watch the approaching ridge with some trepidation. Once over it, I'll be more in than out. A sigh escapes my lips and I push the Goat until her body shakes, getting ready for the ascent.

We hit the hill going about 110, but the steep initial grade checks us and we lose speed quick. I downshift, then again, and by the time the grade evens back out for several hundred feet we are barely skimming 60. I gun it so we can gain some momentum to get over the hump and catch a little air as we clear the summit.

The buck in the road never has a chance. The Goat slams into the animal midair and the tendons and bones snap loudly in the cold night. The lower half of the deer slips under the tires, creating a slick mess of tissue and blood on the road. The head flies straight at my face and the bloodied antlers crash into the glass.

I slam on the brakes and the head loses its hold on the window and flies off out of sight. I hit a patch of greasy mud left over from the last rain and slide sideways, towards the edge of what may be a cliff, or just a gently rolling embankment.

I quickly correct, not waiting to find out, only to discover I'm now sliding backwards. I swing the wheel around, body parts flipping out from under the tires, and hit the brakes again. The Goat and I slip sideways into the ditch and I use the bounce to straighten out the wheels. When she comes down hard we're moving forward into a sparse grove of pines.

I force my foot down on the brake one more time, sliding sideways in the softened mud, and barely manage to aim between two old-growth Ponderosas as the lower branches slap against the doors.

I steer as best I can, but when you're racing a five-thousand-pound vehicle through a small forest, you tend to run out of luck sooner rather than later. A deep ditch of water erosion plunges the Goat down, but she recovers and jerks back up. My head hits the steering wheel and I feel the blood slip down my face, then taste iron as it trickles into my mouth. The Goat's front tires find another ditch and I lurch forward, cracking my head on what's left of the driver's side windshield. Finally we slam into the thick twisted trunk of a cottonwood. I have a second or two to moan, and then it all goes black.

Picture yourself standing on the edge of a dock. In front of you is a mountain lake...

The blood seeps into my mouth and I cough, then spit out a coagulated hunk of something before opening my eyes.

Shit.

I listen for noises around me and panic sets in when I hear the sharp snap of a dry tree branch off to my right. My head rolls towards the noise, not quite controlled, and I wait a few more moments to let things clear up a bit. The pain in my shoulder is like fire and the blood is hot as it trickles down the side of my head.

In front of me is a stream, not a goddamn mountain lake.

Wait.

I shake my head.

A small stream of water has materialized in the river bed from the last rain and the sound of it makes my mouth dry up immediately. I move my head slightly, allowing a moan to escape, and let my right hand reach out for the water bottle on the seat.

Of course, it's not there.

I twist my body a little so I can make a more earnest search of the cab, then grab the steering wheel with my left hand to stabilize my movement.

"Fucking shit!"

That hurts.

The pain is pulled up into every synaptic center of my brain. The resulting vertigo almost makes me heave as a thousand birds take flight from the trees and the wingbeats flare up in my ears.

And then the whispers start.

The dark whisper of a flock of starlings too long in the company of men. There is nothing more creepy than human words coming out of a starling beak and the contents of my stomach experience another moment of protest until I can push them down.

I reach into the crap box with my right hand and pull out the pistol, aiming it through the broken glass of the window in front of me. The shot rings out and the recoil travels through my body like a standing wave. When it reaches my left shoulder I cry out. This time the starlings stay silent.

More tree branch snapping hauls me back to my current situation and my eyes dart around, alert for movement. I take a deep breath and let it out slowly, but that does nothing to stop whatever is moving out in the trees.

I shoot another round off and do a better job at damping down the recoil. This time I see a shadow of a great owl fly off in the distance. It must have been hunting in the trees.

I sit there for a little longer and then swing my legs across the gear stick, scoot over to the passenger side door and release the handle. Pure determination allows me to coerce my legs into standing and then I seize my water bottle off the floor and down it in large gulps.

A thorough shuffling through dirty field clothes leads to a belt. I position it across my body and slip my arm into the loop of leather to take the weight off my injury, then sling the shotgun over my good shoulder and grab my pack to begin my walk back up the hill to the road. Looking and listening for any sign of apex predators.

The road looks like it usually does when a large deer gets mowed over by a military vehicle, so I don't dwell on it and instead walk back up to the top of the hill and try to see if there are any lights in the distance.

The Rural Republic is a chancy place to be stranded on any given day, but being alone in the Stag is exceptionally bad luck. There are no vehicles on the road, nor will there be. No one knows where I am, so no one will come looking.

I look east and see nothing but grasslands and scrub. I look west and see the same shit. That pretty much sums up the extent of what's available in terms of assistance. It makes no difference which way I go, the stop-gate back in Council 5 and the Stag Camp proper are about equal distance from the spot where I stand. I will have to winch the Goat up and out of that ravine before any other decisions can be made.

The night isn't as black as it could be and for that I'm grateful. The moon has fully risen in the time it took me to free myself from the Goat and hitch up my arm, and while it isn't anything near full, neither is it a sliver of hopelessness. Walking outside of the boundaries of the road leads me to an almost flat patch of shortgrass. I find the Big Dipper and then Cassiopeia to ease the creeping feeling of aloneness, and lower myself down on the ground, resting my throbbing head back into the palm of my hand for just a few moments.

The sounds of nature come back.

And with them are the dark whispers of starlings. They haunt me as I drift off to sleep.

Picture yourself standing on the edge of a dock. In front of you is a mountain lake and behind you is a small cabin, pristine white curtains flowing in the breeze passing through the windows. Down below the water you can see the scales of brightly colored fish reflecting the sunlight...

... and then you are in a church, looking down on a meeting.

No, wait, that's not how it goes.

I'm a piece of stained glass high up in the window. I look down at my body and see that I'm naked, but that's not the disturbing thing. Instead of feet I have long raptor talons that host a variety of knives instead of claws. From my mouth come the whispers of the starlings and the gurgling in my throat causes me to scream and break free of the glass. It shatters down to the floor where people argue. The shards of blood-colored glass kill them as they slice through their backs and then I am flying high up in the air, looking down on the Stag. I know it's the Stag because of the tall perimeter wall and the guardhouse at the gate. I land near the guardhouse, still outside the camp, and my father exits in full uniform and puts his hand up to stop me. I need to get in, Daddy, I say—even though I haven't called him Daddy since my mother disappeared when I was six. He opens his mouth and starlings fly out, screaming their whispers in my ears, and then they attack me with their long thin beaks and their wings beat against my body. I fly away, circling the Stag Camp, and then I dive down, spiraling into the gushing wind. The camp explodes and I am thrown up into the sky as a constellation where Orion hunts me like the bull for time everlasting.

And then I am warm and the starlings are gone, but the whispers are still there, making me feel safe. They are soft now, not deep and evil, but soft. And I listen to them and I say OK.

Chapter Two

The warmth of the dream fades and I wake shivering as the sweat drips off my body. A movement catches my eye across the expanse of wild grass and I sit upright in an instant, ignoring the fire in my shoulder. I have the shotgun out, propped in the dent where my hip meets my stomach, and I brace my arm on my thigh as I level the barrel on the shadow in the distance as best I can. My finger slips onto the trigger and squeezes lightly as I prepare for the shot.

It's not a prairie lion because I can see the outstretched wings back-lit by starlight as it skulks across the field. And it's obviously not an owl because it's walking on two legs.

"I wouldn't do that if I were you," it says.

I squeeze the trigger and the recoil slams me into the ground, screaming in pain.

I'm back in the blur of agony once again and fuck is coming out of my mouth at regular intervals. The black shadow stands over me now, the dark wings fully outstretched and imposing.

"I told ya not to do that."

It's a male voice.

I pull away wincing, trying to sink down into the ground to avoid him as he leans into my personal space.

"That's really going to hurt now. You humans. It's always shoot first, ask questions later."

I find my voice and snort at him. "At least a human would know better than to sneak up on a girl stranded in the middle of nowhere with a shotgun."

The avian's hypnotic green eyes brighten as he smiles at me. "Ya have a point there, darlin'."

We have a semi-serious staring contest for a few seconds and then he reaches out to me. "Ya need a hand?"

I look him up and down from my unfortunate submissive situation. His wings are a lot more imposing than I figure they should be. I've seen images of avians here and there over the years, but not enough to be any kind of expert on them.

Sighing, I consider my options as he waits. I can either roll around on my knees and try to get up—or I can get up with some dignity left intact. I shrug and extend my good arm up to him. "Sure."

He takes it and I brace for the explosion of agony that will surely come from my shoulder, but he pulls me to my feet in a smooth, gentle manner. I manage to end upright with only a few squeaks of pain escaping my lips.

"That was unlucky, eh?"

"Unlucky? I almost shot you. I figure that's pretty fucking lucky myself."

"The accident, friend. An unlucky thing to hit that animal."

I grab my gun and ignore him as I hitch my pack up on my hip and shuffle through to check my ammo supply.

"Missing something?"

I give him a long once-over and he waits patiently for me to finish. "You do realize you're trespassing, right? *Aliens are not permitted in the RR under any circumstances.*"

"You'd be surprised," he says.

I swing the shotgun on the strap so it's out in front of me, brace it on my thigh to compensate for my injured shoulder, cycle the next round into the chamber, and then point it straight at his chest. I strain to prevent the wince that really wants to spread across my face. "Look, I don't know who you are, or why you're here, but as a Farm Family Representative of Council 3, I'm asking you to leave under Regulation V.1.b—*Aliens are not permitted in the Rural Republic under any circumstances.* I have the authority to shoot and if you doubt me, I apologize ahead of time for taking your life. You are hereby legally warned."

"Look, sweetheart—"

I squeeze back and the round blasts out of the chamber but he's high above me in the air as the shot passes into the trees. The leaves rustle and the birds are wild once again. The recoil pain isn't as bad from the standing position, but I feel the blood leaking out under the skin on my hip, creating a bruise. I push the pain down. "I've been shooting since I could walk, sweetheart, and I've had a really shitty day. Do not fuck with me."

He flies off over the trees about a dozen yards away and I can just barely make him out as he lands in the cover of the brush.

"Is that how ya treat someone who saves yer life? Shoot them?"

I snort. "Saved my life? I must have missed that one while I was sleeping."

"Except ya weren't sleeping, Junco. You were unconscious."

It isn't often that I get stunned into silence, but an alien knowing my name in the middle of nowhere can do it. "How the hell do you know my name?"

Silence from him now.

The glimmer of light that was previously there is gone, and so is he.

I take stock of the mountaintop meadow. *Where are you, where are you?*

Silence.

I pivot on my heel, gun braced one-armed against my stomach to catch the recoil, and do a proper survey of the area. My good arm is tiring quick after all the adrenaline I've used up and it begins to shake. I force the bravado. "Guess you decided to take my—"

Then he is behind me, the gun is flying across the field, and he's twisted my bad shoulder just enough to make me scream out. His lips touch my cheek as he whispers, "Look, I'm not usually the type of person who abuses little girls, but you've shot at me two times now and I'm not going to stand for it. I'm here for the moment and yer just gonna have to deal with it. Ya got it?"

He eases up on my shoulder and pushes me away from him.

I rub the flaming tissue and wince. "Did you just insult me?"

He tilts his head at me. "What? Me? Ya tried ta shoot me—twice!"

"I might be little, but the way you said it implied I'm insignificant. Which I assure you, I am not. And besides, you're the one who's trespassing, right? That's you." I point my finger up at him. "I have every right to tell you to leave, I'm a fucking representative of Council—"

"3, yeah, I heard ya the first time. Who gives a shit? I'm here. Get over it."

I stare at him in the dim moonlight and quite frankly, I don't care for what I see. "You're so fucking lucky I'm injured."

"Or what?"

"Why are you here?"

"Why are *you* here?"

"Oh my fucking God, are we in playschool or what?"

"I know where you were going."

I laugh. "The road only goes one place, alien. That's not a hard deduction."

"I know what you were gonna do, as well."

That's it, I'm done. I begin walking down the hill.

"Oi! Where're ya going?" he calls.

I ignore him as he trots a little to catch up. He keeps his distance to a few paces behind as I make my way to the road and then begin the descent down the slope back to the Goat. When I finally reach it I wiggle into the back seat of the cab and lie down, trying to even out my breathing before he gets there. My eyes close as I hear him climb into the front passenger seat.

"What are you doing?" he asks.

"I'm sleeping. Get the fuck out of my Goat." My good arm slides under the seat and I allow my finger to caress the high-powered rifle tucked away for emergencies. I can't shoot it, my shoulder would never tolerate that, but it gives me comfort to know it's there.

He doesn't get out. Instead he talks.

"I saw yer headlights coming in the darkness. I didn't think much about it really, but the accident had me concerned. Ya hit yer head pretty hard, there."

Yeah, thanks for the update.

"I'm sorry for twisting yer shoulder, OK?"

My anger leaves me as I listen to his hypnotic words. I struggle to keep my eyes closed but an overwhelming force urges me to look him in the face.

"Junco, I did save your life. Ya had a bad concussion. It was a mistake to fall asleep. I was just tryin' ta help when I brought ya out of it."

This revelation jolts me out of my trance and I fight to shake off my weariness to get this story straight. "Wait," I say as I painfully push my body back up into a half-sitting position. "What? You were touching me when I was sleeping?"

He squirms a little at my tone. "No, look, it wasn't like that. You weren't sleeping, you were unconscious—I just—wrapped ya in my wings so I could bring ya back up."

"You were touching me." It's a statement this time, not a question. "In my sleep."

"Look, I saved your life, for Christ's sake!"

"How dare you swear at me! Don't you realize—"

"I'm sorry, you're right." he looks away and blows out a breath. "I shouldn't have said that. I forgot you are a pious bunch out here."

"Get out!" I snarl. I feel the blood rush to my face and the adrenaline flood my muscles as I watch him extract himself from my vehicle, stopping only to release one of his wings from the floppy seat belt as he exits the Goat.

I let myself smile after he leaves. That pious bullshit works every time on strangers. And he even heard me cussing like a soldier up on the hill. But I'm glad he's gone. I don't remember reading anything about avians having glowing green eyes before. Creepy.

When I wake my crusted-closed eyelids are the least of my worries. I struggle to force them open once I realize the sun is up. My muscles have been welded into my current sleeping orientation and no matter how hard I fight against it, they reward me with an intense shooting pain in my left shoulder with the slightest of movements.

A delicious smell meanders into the cab from outside so I force a shift in position until I can prop myself up without contorting my face into a disfigured expression. I ease my head up just enough to peer out the window and see the avian poking a stick at a roasting bird over a small campfire.

He looks up at me and smiles.

Dammit. So much for stealth. I should be ashamed of myself.

"Hungry now?" His accent is something different than mine, but I can't place it. "Still not talking, eh? Well, I made breakfast," he points to the smoking fowl, "so that should buy me some goodwill."

I wrestle around frantically for a second, trying to find an extraction route that won't cause me to scream, but I can't see it.

"So, how long do ya *young ladies* typically pout out here in the wilds, then?" he calls. "Can ya give me an estimate?"

I struggle again, pulling on the seat belt that hangs limply behind the driver's seat to get some leverage, but the aging bracket attaching it to the headliner snaps off from my weight and I give up and lie back with a sigh.

He appears at the broken window on the passenger side. "I can't believe you slept back there in that tiny space." He laughs at me, and I have to admit, he's got a nice look to him, plus his green eyes are bright in the sunlight and they are no longer glowing, so the creep factor has been dialed down a bit.

His large black wings are tucked tight against his back and the tips cup over the top of his shoulders, so I can't see much of them. A few loose arcs of dark hair tumble off his forehead and fall around his eyes. He's wearing some kind of foreign get-up that might be the alien equivalent of black jeans and t-shirt, but they are cut to his specific body modifications and made out of some kind of heavy canvas. It has the look of light armor, something we might wear for war games. His skin is light, but not fair. Like fall has stolen most of the golden tan of summer away.

"That's nice. Short jokes. Very funny." My voice sounds as cranky as I feel.

He lets off a little laugh. "Need some help out?"

I scowl and try to think up another way. But I can't. "Yeah, sure. Just come around here to the other side of the Goat and get in so you can push me up a little." Then I add, "Please."

He smiles at my manners, which make his eyes twinkle a little. Not glow, but still. The creepiness is just under the surface.

The old door creaks as he opens it and I try to turn and look at him but the shoulder flares up at my attempt. I feel his hands reach under me to my good arm and I struggle not to laugh, but it bursts out anyway. I wriggle away from his touch before he pulls back in hesitation.

"Now, what the hell was that?"

"I'm ticklish, so kill me. You can't just slip your hands into someone's pits and not expect them to laugh."

"Can I push you up or not?"

"Yes, push. Just don't stick me in my pits."

He does push and I flail around like a turtle on its back for a few embarrassing seconds, then find myself upright and looking out the window facing the campfire. It smells wonderful.

"Whew, that's better," I say as I turn my whole body so I can see him properly. "Thanks, I really appreciate it." I even manage a smile, which in turn allows him to offer me one back.

"Would you like some help with that shoulder before ya eat?"

"What's that mean?" I ask, looking at him sideways.

"The wings, darlin'," he says, pointing a thumb towards his shoulders, "they heal, remember?"

Of course I remember but I'm not even remotely interested in letting him get a hold of me again, so I lie instead. "No, I'm fine. Really." And just to prove it I scoot over to the door and flip the handle with my good hand, then smile back at him as I push it open.

His hand goes to my good shoulder and stops me before I can make my hasty exit. "Relax, Junco. I can fix it. We aren't going to get far with ya like that, anyway."

"I don't know what you mean by we, but in case you haven't noticed my legs are just fine."

"Yeah, I see that. But we won't be walking out of here. That would take days."

I laugh a little and send him a crooked smile. "The Goat has a winch, so don't you worry about me."

"Sorry, darlin', you won't be winching anything if you don't let me take care of that shoulder."

My lips involuntarily form a snarl and my eyes narrow in anger. "What's with this darling bullshit? Stop calling me that."

He just smiles. "Fine, Junco. Come here, I'll fix the shoulder. Think of it as a gift."

"No." I move to get past him but his eyes catch mine and begin to glow. I'm drawn in and I can't stop looking at him.

"I said come here, Junco."

In my mind I say no. But my body is already wrapped up in his wings and my head begins to spin. I can hear him whisper in my ear, and his breath dances across my cheek.

"Does it feel good?" he asks.

"Mmmmhmmmm, yesss," I say, slurring my words a bit. The heat from his body exchanges between us and my shoulder is sucking it up like a vacuum. My thoughts twist around in an incoherent mess as we sit, melded together. He stays that way for several minutes and my mind is carried away with the effects of his body.

Then I am high above looking down on the Stag. I see a few straggling antelope and watch the wind caress the grass as I begin to float away. "Stop, no flying."

In an instant the heat is gone and the avian has twisted me around to see my face. "What did you just say?"

My shoulder doesn't hurt anymore but my head is really fuzzy, like I'm drunk, so I don't even remember what I said.

He shakes me a little to jar my memory. "Junco? What are you talking about?"

I think hard and squint. "Flying? Did I say flying?"

"What about flying?"

"The Stag is burning," I say as I try to open my eyes.

I feel his chest collapse as he exhales. "What?"

"Just a dream," I say, forcing myself to concentrate. "It was just a dream. Didn't make any sense."

We sit there as I recover. He's still got his arms around me, but his wings never return to make their addictive cocoon of healing. I stay still as the world comes back to me a little at a time. Then our closeness gets weird and I push him off. He hops out and comes over to my side of the door to help me out.

"I'm starving. Can I have some of that?" I point over to the browned bird strung up over the coals.

"Help yourself, there's water too."

"Aren't you going to eat?" I ask. But he just walks away and busies himself with his pack.

"More for me then. And hey," I call out, "thanks, I guess. Shoulder really does feel better."

Chapter Three

He's leaning up against a twisted cottonwood trunk on the other side of the now-dead campfire and I'm gulping down the last of the filtered water from the stream just below us on the hill. "You do realize that you're in a lot of trouble for this," I say, pointing to his uneaten portion of grouse on the spit. "Prairie chickens aren't in season and strangers aren't allowed to hunt in the RR. And aliens are totally forbidden." I stick that in to remind him that he's still a trespasser.

He looks up just long enough to insult me with a dirty look and then goes back to his tech device, his black hair dropping down to cover his forehead and hide his eyes. Ever since I told him about my dream he is acting different and it makes me uneasy, so I talk.

A lot.

"You're a good cook though," I continue. "Not many people can pluck all the feathers out of such a small bird." He doesn't even look up this time.

The tech isn't anything I recognize, but that's not saying much since Farm Families aren't supposed to have much tech in their regular life. My father wasn't in any way obsessive or extreme in his adherence to the doctrine, plus we're military and that comes with certain privileges in the tech department, but I only had a few personal tech items as a kid. I wasn't allowed any communication devices and I wasn't allowed to have programmed learning. I had to read books and study the old-fashioned way.

"So, what do you have there? Some sort of phone or computer?" I ask.

He looks over and laughs. "A phone, eh? Earth must've entered the 22nd century while you were out planting corn or something." His head returns to the device in his hand.

"Mmmmhmmm. Yet another insult. That must be your default setting. And for your information we produce horses, not corn."

He looks up and lets out a deep sigh, shaking his head at me slightly, then holds up the thing in his hand to let me see it. "Sorry. It's a tracker."

I look at it intensely until I can make out a small map with some blinking lights. I'm almost afraid to ask but I do anyway. "What's it tracking?"

"Me, maybe? Not sure yet," he replies as he bows his head once more.

I let out a little "Oh," and then get up. "Well, thanks for breakfast and the healing stuff." I try to think of a word to call it so it doesn't sound like I'm being flippant or rude, but I can't find one. "I'm gonna get going now." I gather myself up and walk back over to the Goat where my shotgun is propped up against the mangled front end.

"Oh, and thanks for retrieving my shotgun," I say as I turn around to find him directly behind me, his wings slightly uplifted, like he's on the verge of something. I never even heard him move and the creepiness from last night is back out in full force. "Wow, you're quite quick and silent when you want to be."

"I think we should stick together, Junco. In fact I was thinking I can help get ya back to safety. Ya know, help ya get the Goat back up on the road. Even though yer healed, yer still pretty—" He hesitates.

"I'm pretty?" I ask.

He laughs a little and shakes his head, which pisses me off for some reason. "No, I was going to say pretty weak, ya know. From yesterday's crash. But then I wondered if ya would take that as an insult as well."

I roll my eyes and try to push past him to get the winch hooked up to a tree, but he leans his hands on either side of the Goat, essentially boxing me in. I shoot him a nasty look and he drops his hands to let me through.

"Thanks for all your help," I call back to him, "but I'm going to take it from here. And I won't report you, so don't worry about that. Just get the hell out of the RR before anyone else sees you." I turn to see how he's taking the news but he's not there. When I turn back he's in front of me again.

He shakes his head at me.

I shake mine back and raise my eyebrows.

"You'll refuse my help?"

"Look," I huff, "you have those people tracking you and neither of us is supposed to be out here in the first place, so let's just cut our losses and move on. Separately."

He looks down to the tech that is still in his hand. "They can't see anything here. Some sort of shield."

"Right. That's called a defense system. The deeper you go into the

Stag, the thicker the shields. So why don't you just fly over to the Mountain Republic where they probably can track you?"

He lifts the device to illustrate his point. "In case ya haven't figured it out yet, these people aren't my ride home."

"So why are they tracking you?"

His eyes twinkle and I know what's coming and push past him at a full run. He's on me before I can take more than half a dozen strides and pulls on my shirt until I slip in the mud and go down hard on my back.

"Stop!" I scream, but instead of stopping he pins my arms down and sits on top of me as I wriggle and kick. His legs twine around mine, essentially cutting off any thoughts of getting him off me that way. Then his eyes are glowing again and his lips are touching my cheek, whispering for me to settle and be calm.

To my surprise, I do settle. I can't help it. I realize too late that the soft words brushing past the sensitive skin on my cheek are controlling me. I can feel the sound waves trickling into my ear canal, making their way to the nerve pathways that control my muscles, and I bring my shoulders up to try and get his face away from me. His lips remain next to my ear and I am just about to fully give in when the tech device, forgotten and left on the ground during our struggle, sounds off an alarm. He loses his concentration and the words stop for half a moment, but that's all I need.

I take my opportunity and flip myself over so that I'm on my belly. This takes him by surprise and for a split-second he is off balance. I flip back around and use my right arm to knock him in the throat as my body turns. He goes reeling off of me and I'm up and running down into the little creek.

A boot goes flying just past my head, but I don't stop and wonder at this weird turn of events. I run as hard as I can, over the opposite bank, out of the small grove of cottonwoods, and into the tall flowing prairie grass. I'm short, so the leftover husks slap me in the face as I run, blurring my vision.

The wings descend and he's swooping down upon me. I look up to see talons where his boots were just a few minutes ago and they latch onto my shoulders, puncturing my skin and making me scream. His grip tightens and I fall. I roll in practiced regulation fashion and pop back up, booking it again without missing a beat.

One second I'm hauling ass towards the open prairie, the next he's on the ground in front of me and we're on a collision path. I plan my move and let him get to within a few strides of me and then I flip into the air and land on the other side of him. He misses a step and I take advantage of it, turn and deliver a hook kick to his jaw. His head snaps to the side and he stumbles over sideways a little.

I run hard for a few seconds and don't look back. Off in the distance I hear the roar of a hovercopter and a few seconds later I feel the effects of the prairie grass wind tunnel it creates from the blades, but still I push my way through the now wildly swaying grass until I come upon the alien again.

His lip is bleeding and his jaw is slightly red from my kick. I stop in my tracks, bent over and panting hard.

He's not even out of breath.

"I'm not the enemy, Junco," he screams above the roar, "and if you know what's good for ya, you'll run like hell because if those guys from the Mountain Republic get you, you'll end up in the same messed-up place as your father."

He flies off, disappearing in the tallgrass before I can even string together a sentence.

But his words stay with me. Dead like my father is not something I want to be so I follow his advice. I run until the MR soldiers blast me with a plasma bolt and I fall to the ground unconscious.

Picture yourself standing on the edge of a dock. In front of you is a mountain lake and behind you is a small cabin, pristine white curtains flowing in the breeze passing through the windows. Down below the water you can see the scales of brightly colored fish reflecting the sunlight and up above in the sky you see the eagles as they soar, free from terrestrial boundaries. The planks on the deck are warm under your feet and you're wearing a long thin white shirt, open in the front, that barely covers your body. The waves lap against the dock and you reach over and drag your fingers through the water. It folds against your wrist and smells like blood...

The blood on my bound wrists has hardened, making them itchy and painful at the same time. I take a deep breath in, wince, then cough as my lungs protest in earnest at the expansion.

"Plasma blast will do that to you." The voice originates a few paces off to my left and I open my eyes to take in the interior of a military plane. I manage to move my head just enough to log a look of concern on Aren's face.

... up above in the sky you see the eagles as they soar, free from terrestrial boundaries...

I mentally shake the image out of my mind and cough before I answer him. "I know"—the cough comes back up as I try to croak out some words, so I start again—"I know that. Asshole."

Aren lets out a prolonged sigh. "What do you want from me, Junco? I had my team set their rifles to stun. They wanted to fucking kill you—and even after I told them how small you were, they still had their rifles dialed up for fully armored tactical. I saved your ass."

I spit out some blood and take a moment to wonder what might be bleeding inside me to cause it, but my mind is blank. I drop it and turn in his general direction, wincing at the throb this simple change in perspective creates in my head. "What are you doing here? You cut and run from the Mountain Republic too? Or is treason something you reserve only for the Rural folks?"

He's bending down a few paces off, to stay eye level with me I guess, but my comment makes him stand. "You're such a fucking bitch, you know that?"

I nod and my coughing takes on a whole new level.

"Will you be rational? Or do I have to keep you bound?"

I don't answer, I just continue to cough, my chest searing in pain with every desperate inhalation of air.

He comes over, slits the bindings with a knife, and pulls me to my feet, then bends me over and whacks me on the back good and hard. Harder then he should, actually.

I take a large gasp of air, wince, and then spit more blood out towards his boots. "Fuck, Aren—mind the damn plasma burn, will ya?"

He stops and leaves me to it, then turns away as I straighten up. "We were sent to get you."

"Bullshit," I say, wiping the spit off my lips, "since when do we let MR soldiers in the Stag?"

"Since you went AWOL yesterday and were tracked to a certain alien who killed more than two dozen scientists out at the Camp. Not to mention a whole shitload of corporate executives from all over the United Republics for the past two years."

I don't react, except for a little cough that I can't tuck down, but internally I'm privately stunned. My dream comes back to me and I roll this new fact over in my mind. "So what's he got to do with me?" I look up at him now. He looks like shit. But I suppose he's thinking the same thing about me.

"You tell me and then we'll all know."

I shake my head, then take another second to catch my breath. "I wrecked my Goat, Aren. Hit a fucking tree and went unconscious. He was there and helped me out. That's it."

He walks away to the far end of the mini-drop plane so that he can stand on the edge of the ramp and look out across the tallgrass. I follow him over there, still trying to remember what it's like to breathe without the sting of residual plasma burns. When I get to the edge he grabs me by my arm and holds me so I can't go down the ramp.

"Try again, Junco," he says, exhaling a deep sigh. I look at him and see my best friend for just a moment. His face is one I know so well I could recognize it in the dark with just my fingertips. His blue eyes are still the same—deep and soulful. But they harden as I study him and then the old face is gone and it's just the asshole who left us to join the other team.

"They want to string you up for that last stunt you pulled."

I shake my head, not understanding, but he squeezes my arm a little tighter and I look back up in his eyes. "I gotta restrain you, Junco. We're still searching for him, so it'll be a while before I can take you home." He pulls me by the arm and we stomp down the ramp together, our boots clanking on the steel until we hit the grass.

Outside there is regulated bedlam as the base camp is established and I figure I was out for several hours by the look of their progress. A wiry little soldier barely out of his teens comes up as we exit and Aren hands me off to him without saying another word. The guy introduces himself as CP and tugs on my arm. I follow him to a recently fabbed bubble about the size of a small house. It's your typical on-the-fly covert-op motor pool. There are three prairie buggies parked inside and CP leads me over to one and then produces a first-aid kit, slaps some numbing antibacterial on my wrists, wraps them, and then thumbs the biometrics on the bracelet as he attaches it to my wrist and points to the passenger seat of the buggy.

"This is your guardhouse?" I let out a little laugh, then regret it when the coughing comes back. If he thinks being tethered to a prairie buggy is an inappropriate substitute for a regulation holding cell, he doesn't show it. Instead, he just points to the passenger seat again and scowls.

I get in and he attaches my new piece of jewelry to a matching tether connected to the roll bar above my head. "You're kidding me, right?"

He walks off and leaves me there.

The garage fab is not quite soundproof, but almost, and the outside world is reduced to muffled tones that are not even close to intelligible once the door slams behind him.

The bucket seats in the buggy are quite comfortable for military grade and I spend the next several minutes looking over what they have in here. Much of it is the same as what we have in our prairie buggies, but they have different aftermarket equipment.

I'm busy sifting through the contents of a case wedged between the driver and passenger seats when a blast of sound from outside disrupts my quiet world, making me turn.

"Find anything useful?"

I shrug. "I'm just passing time, Aren."

"You ready to tell me something?"

"Do I look like I'm fucking interested in chatting you up? Am I a prisoner of the MR, or what's going on here?"

He smiles. "I told you, we were sent to get you. You're being held under the direct orders of RR Command."

"Which is who exactly?"

His face turns away and I regret my outburst. It took me a little longer than usual, but I've finally crossed a line.

"Who are you these days?" He turns back towards me, his face a mixture of anger and disgust. "I heard you didn't even stay for his funeral. Just lit up in that deathtrap and left right in the middle of the ceremony."

"I stayed for most of the ceremony. Not that it has anything to do with this."

He laughs. "No? You tell me then, what the hell are you doing, Junco? What did you think you'd accomplish out there at Stag Camp?"

"I had a message to deliver."

"Yeah, like the bullshit you pulled last week?"

I shake my head. "What the hell—"

The garage doors roll up and soldiers file in, grabbing keys and jumping in the buggies. Aren walks over to CP and they whisper so I can't hear. Then CP comes over. "Gotta move now, Junco. They got a track on the alien's hiding place and they need all the buggies." I watch his thumb connect with the tether mechanism and it releases from the roll bar. "Jump out and come with me."

Aren barks orders at everyone as they fill the vehicles and he jumps into the buggy near me. "I'm gonna get your friend, Junco."

I shrug and answer back as I dutifully follow CP into another room. "Like I care."

Chapter Four

"You're chaining me to the head?"

"Sorry," CP says. "This is our most secure building. So. Nothing I can do."

At least the tether is long.

He spies me looking at it. "I gave you enough room to move around and—"

"And what?"

"Well, you know. You look like shit."

"Gee, thanks for the compliment." He shrugs and closes the door and I'm alone again.

I'm afraid to look in the mirror, so I use the facilities to prolong the agony, but that doesn't make the sight of my reflection any less shocking.

"Oh, my sweet Jeremiah!"

That face cannot belong to me. I have a giant gash that runs from my scalp and down to my right ear that has leaked blood all over one side of my hair, plastering it into a half helmet-like configuration.

Since I'm a prisoner locked in a bathroom I take advantage of what I have and fill the entire reserve water tank with the hand pump and gulp down long drinks of water. Then I stick my head into the basin and rinse as much of the blood out as I can.

When I'm done I look around and soak it all up, one square inch at a time.

And I smile.

The handle of the latrine isn't locked and opens when I push it down. I expect CP, but I get another guy. Bigger. Meaner. He's looking out a small window in the door and speaks before turning around. "Who's sweet Jeremiah?" he asks.

"What?"

"You called his name, in there. A while back." He turns, waiting for my answer.

"It's no one. It's how RR people who prefer not to swear say holy shit or something to that effect. Hey, uh," I begin, trying out a smile

24

on him, "I'd like to change into one of these clean jumpsuits hanging in here. Will you please remove the tether so I can slip my arm through the sleeve?" He shrugs and walks over towards me.

I ease back into the bathroom and grab the jumpsuit as he follows me in.

"Just so you know, I can't leave you in here untethered. So you're gonna have to change in front of me."

"Whatever." I slip out of my thermals then step into the jumpsuit and pull it up to my waist. "I'm pretty sure you've seen everything I've got. If you want to gape at me, go right ahead."

To my surprise he turns his head away.

"Honey, I'm damn sure I've never seen a naked avian before."

He says it like it's nothing. I stare at him hard, then shake my head. "You care to elaborate on that statement?"

He stares back. "Which part? The part about what kind of girls I've seen naked? Or the part where I break the news that you're a freak?"

"Is that a joke?"

"Do I look like I'm joking?"

He doesn't.

He's a big guy, not just in height, but also in muscle and weight. Easily a hundred and thirty pounds heavier than me. I play my card and strip off my dress, letting it hang off the tether, and stand there naked in front of him.

"There you go, take a good look." I even lift my hands up in the air and twirl around so he can see my back. "Not a wing in sight. Satisfied?"

He looks, long and hard even, but I can tell his only interest is in my nonexistent wings. "Put your damn clothes on, Junco."

"Oh, have we met before—?"

He grunts. "Cole."

"Cole. I don't recall your face. Are you an RR deserter as well?"

"You gonna change or what?"

"I'm ready to go. Just waiting on you." I shake the dress that's hanging off my tethered arm and smile. I'm not really the seductive type, so whether or not this even interests him is over my head. But I only need him to underestimate me, not be interested. This would never work on RR soldiers. They *all* know me and an RR guard would never even get this close to me, let alone fall for this bullshit I'm trying to pull right now.

25

But this guy? He looks a little dumb and if there's one thing I've learned about being small, it's that big guys like this don't even want to *think* about the possibility that I might kick their ass.

I watch as he bends down and my world slows down. In between these fractions my eyes dart around looking—

His thumb moves closer and closer to the release pad.

— for the long plumber's wrench propped up against the water reservoir. I track his thumb and the second he releases the tether I grab the wrench and swing.

I laugh a little as he goes down, then reach over and use his thumb to release the other bracelet, slip my clothes back on, and slide the jumpsuit over them. I roll up the pants and poke my head through the bathroom door to see if anyone is outside.

Clear.

I twirl my hair up on top of my head and grab his cap, then rush over to the motor pool door. The window he was looking through wasn't built for short girls so I just open the door and walk through.

Into utter chaos.

I slide into the fray and walk like I've got somewhere to go as people rush around shouting orders, receiving orders, and generally doing everything soldiers do when *something's up*. I pick up a stray gas can as I walk and weigh my possibilities. I'm typically a quick decision maker but my pant legs are coming uncuffed, fucking up my concentration.

A thick bank of shrubs provides cover as I slip out my knife and begin hacking away at the length of extra fabric draping down my leg. I'm just about done when I spy CP walking with an RR officer.

That little traitor. Aren wasn't lying. They are here under RR orders. I briefly consider how uncomfortable I'd be if I had a joint mission with the army I walked out on and shiver a little.

CP turns to respond to something and I see that the RR officer has a gun to his head. He pushes CP forward and yells so loud I can pick out the words. "You tell your boss that he doesn't get the prize, and there better not be a damn thing wrong with her, soldier, or I'll have your brains splashed across this whole goddamn hillside."

Huh.

Nice to know at least someone cares.

I wait until they enter the motor pool and walk back out in the activity. I've got about ten seconds before they find Cole and sound an alarm so I dash into the trees and book it towards the river.

26

My ten seconds are absolutely up when it hits me. There is no ravine, no small trickle of a stream, and no Goat. I am on the wrong side of the road.

Shit.

There are only two choices, keep going out in the Stag alone with just my boot knife, or go back for the gun and make a run for it from there.

Off in the distance I hear the howling and make up my mind. I'd rather be caught and crucified than running in the tallgrass at night with no gun.

I walk down the hill until the activity breaks off, then make my way across the road, over to the stream, and begin the walk back up.

The little bit of chrome that's left on the bumper of my Goat twinkles at me like a Christmas star and I feel a sense of relief.

Until the screaming starts.

The first scream isn't even remotely human but I know exactly what's making it. The ones that follow are, and I can hear the savage pain he is inflicting on them. My stomach clenches for a moment and I almost pee my pants. I stand there for a little longer, indecisive, my eyes searching the trees and the black sky, then climb in the Goat and reach for the rifle.

My hand slips in under the back seat and comes back empty.

I just stare at my open palm, a little dumbfounded.

"Looking for this?" says the snarling voice in the darkness on the other side of the open front door. I push myself up and peer out. Cole has a look of death on his face as he holds up my rifle. Another blood-curdling scream erupts just off to the left of where we are and a plasma bolt lights up the air a fraction before the crackle of discharge catches up with it. The flash dances across Cole's face and his expression says he's not fucking around.

"Cole, look, I'm sor—"

He lunges into the back seat and I scramble away towards the passenger door. He forces his body over the middle console and begins to pull me back by my legs. I kick and scream. "Stop it!" One foot lands squarely on his head and he is still for a moment. I reach over and open the door and tumble out on the ground head-first. He flings himself after me through the cab faster than I could ever imagine a guy that size moving, landing on top of me.

"You bitch! I will fucking kill you!" Cole's fist is raised high, ready to plunge down onto my face, when the talons appear out of nowhere.

I scream as the head is snatched from the body. He falls forward and the hot sticky blood shoots out from his decapitated neck and drenches everything around me. I scramble backwards, push him off, get to my feet, and turn to run when the avian appears.

"Get away from me, goddammit!" I run the other direction but he takes flight. I look back at the bear-sized claws reaching down to grab me when a plasma bolt hits him in the chest. He screams so loud I have to stop and hold my ears to dampen down the pain, and then I hear the distant beat of wings as he retreats.

"Come on, Junco, we gotta get the hell out of here! That won't stop him for long." Aren grabs me by my arm and throws me in the passenger side of a buggy face-first. I scramble to upright myself for a few seconds, then watch him shout orders to CP as he jumps in. We speed off up the ditch, out onto the road, and then head down deeper into the Stag.

Alone.

In an open-topped buggy.

And the nightdogs howl a hungry welcome up to the sky.

28

Chapter Five

The buggy bumps and jerks as we travel off-road but my eyes are trained on the tallgrass that surrounds us, looking for signs of apexers. In between my private panic attacks I rewind and watch Cole's head being ripped from his body. Aren, to his credit, says nothing. And that's OK with me. I'd rather not have to keep up my end of a hostile conversation at the moment.

After what seems like hours of driving my heart begins to slow down and the rhythm of the bucking prairie lulls me into stillness and I sleep.

When I wake we're not moving. Aren's seat is empty, but I can hear him trying to get someone on the comms. The moon is gone, so it must be almost morning.

I get out of the buggy and walk over to Aren. "Anyone out there?"

He shakes his head, looks me up and down, then turns his attention back to his device as he talks. "We'll make a little camp over there for the day," he says, pointing southwest, "and hole up until the comms come back online."

I nod and climb back in the buggy and let Aren find us a camp for the day. He unpacks some gear as the sun begins to rise.

"Here, catch." He throws me a packet of food. It's a military ration, so I don't get too excited. "It's blueberry pancakes, your favorite."

I smile a little because he remembers, then open the ration and squeeze it into my mouth until the packet is flat. I wash it down with water.

Aren is still busy, but I chance a conversation anyway. "Did you see what he did, Aren?"

He looks up from his task and stares at me. I know him well enough to see the wheels spin as he replays it, but he only grunts and goes back to his work.

"I have no idea who he is. None."

29

This time he doesn't look up, but he does talk. "I find that hard to believe, Junco. I mean, it looks real bad the way you took off to the Stag. What were you doing?" He drags his eyes off his hands and finds my face. "And no bullshit. It's just me."

"I told you already. I had to deliver something."

"To Stag Camp, Junco? That makes no fucking sense."

"I have a"—I blow some air out my mouth and it causes my unruly hair near my chin to go flying—"family friend there. I went out there all the time with my father, Aren, so don't pretend like you know me that well."

"Not my fault you never took me home to Daddy."

His words come out jaded and I laugh. "I never took anyone home to Daddy, Aren."

His end of the conversation is now over and all I can do is watch as he gets busy laying down a sleeping bag. There is only one, and when it's all laid out he gets in, boots and all. I watch him and shiver a little as I think about how badly I want to climb in and be close to someone.

He looks at me, smiles, then pats the ground next to him. "Come on, get in."

I smile back but shake my head. "No, thanks. I'm all bloody."

"Jasus, Junco. Just get in the bag."

I give in. Why play the game? He knows I want to sleep in there, I know I want to sleep in there. Screw it. I take off the disgusting jumpsuit and get in, boots, mud, blood and all.

I settle into his chest and he pulls me close and puts his arms around me. We're warm and it doesn't feel terrible.

"You know damn well I didn't desert you, Junco. So quit fucking saying that shit. You left me, remember?"

I think about this for a minute and then shrug. "I don't deal well with ultimatums, Aren. And you gave me one. I had a life outside of cadets, you know. But you never understood that and then you just up and left. That never made sense to me. So why?" I turn a little and try to see his face over my shoulder. "Why did you leave the RR?"

Silence.

I sigh and stay still. Waiting.

A few minutes later he gives it a shot. "A discipline action. I fucked up after your graduation. They wanted to kick me out. Make me go back home."

This sounds like a lie but I'm not really interested in making a big deal of it. "So you left the RR? That's a little excessive, don't you think?"

"Junco, I don't know what your childhood was really like since you never did talk about it, but I lived with some raging fucking assholes when I was a kid and we didn't live in Council 3 where practically everyone's got special status. My house was a shit hole. I couldn't wait to join the military and get the hell out of that place. I figured I had enough field experience to do something else, so I took my skills to the highest bidder. And frankly, I'm having a hard time swallowing this fucking holier-than-thou attitude you seem to have about it. You and I aren't that different."

I elbow him in the ribs. "Get off me," I say, disgusted. He removes his arms and turns over without saying another word and after a few minutes of silence our mutual exhaustion takes over and we fall asleep.

When I wake the sun is already setting, Aren is gone, and I'm a hot mess of sweat-caked filth. I've never felt so disgusting in my life, even when I had to spend months out in the tallgrass on maneuvers. At least then I didn't have another man's blood peeling off my body. I struggle out of the bag and look around in what's left of the daylight, then fish out a ration from the pack nearby. I squeeze pot roast into my mouth, gag, and try not to notice the film that's grown over my teeth.

Aren is down by the buggy messing with the comms.

"Are they up yet?" I yell as I walk down to him.

"Hey, beautiful, have a nice sleep?"

"Shut the hell up."

He shrugs and lets the insult slide off. "No. No comms yet."

"Why are they still down?"

"You fuck up the mission, you get penalized. Or maybe they figure it's just as easy to let us get eaten out here by the nightdogs. Who knows?"

"So this mission was to come get me. Why?"

"You'll have to ask them, Junco. I'm just the delivery boy."

"Why did Cole think I was an avian, then?"

He looks up at me and shakes his head as a pissed-off expression spreads across his face. "Fucking Cole."

"Why, Aren?"

He shakes his head again. "Dunno, Junco. I really don't. But everyone seems to think you are. They all want you."

"All who?"

"Us, them, the avians."

I let out a deep sigh, sick of the games. "Who is us and who is them, Aren?"

He shoots me a dirty look, then comes over and pokes me in the chest, hard enough to send me back a step, and then pokes his own as well. "Us," he clarifies. Then he waves his hands up in the air and says, "Them."

I don't have the energy to point out there is no us, so I drop it. "That makes no sense, Aren. The RR wants me for what? I've been living here my whole life, I was the commander's daughter, I—"

I stop myself, unsure of what I was just going to say. Aren doesn't pick up on it but I start to have a small panic attack until he starts talking again.

"I couldn't tell you. I'm only privy to what the MR is doing and we were hired to extract you and take you back with us."

"Hired? To take me back where?" I'm starting to sound like an idiot with my questions, but screw it.

"I can't say any more, but I will say that it is somewhere safe."

"And I'm supposed to believe that?"

He just shrugs.

"Am I an avian?" I know it's not possible, but I want to hear it from him.

"As far as I know, yes."

I choke on my own spit for a minute. "You're joking, right?"

I can tell he's tired of this subject by his extra-long huff of exhaled air. "Do I look like I'm fucking around, Junco?"

My feet are moving before I even process what's happening and I walk off into the tallgrass. *Picture yourself standing on the edge of a dock...*

I shake my head.

No.

I am Junco Coot, aged nineteen. Born in the Rural Republic in 2133. My mother is Carolinia Coot, maiden name Sutter. My father was Rural Republic Commander, Johann Coot, son of Wilhem Coot. I live in Council 3, I went to sniper school when I was seventeen, I play piano, collect books and guns, and last year I was the world's mounted aerial aerobatics grand champion.

... In front of you is a mountain lake...

No. In front of me is a crapload of tallgrass filled with sleeping prairie lions.

... and behind you is a small cabin, pristine white curtains flowing in the breeze passing through the windows...

No.

No.

NO.

That shit needs to go back down now, Junco!

The sun is hanging on by a sliver when I look to the west, thankful that some of the sweat on my sticky body has dried up. The cool wind chills me as it whisks the heat from my exposed arms. If I was brave I'd just keep walking. Forget about Aren, the avian, my father, my farm, my life and everything that happened over the past forty-eight hours.

But I'm not brave. So I can do nothing but sit on a rock and stare out across the plains.

Sometime later Aren comes up and joins me.

"Shit, Junco! I was calling your name, didn't you hear me?"

"Yeah, I heard you."

"So, now you're just going to ignore me? Because I told you what I know?"

I get up furious and look him in the eyes as I poke him in the chest. "You told me what you wanted me to know, so save your bullshit for someone else."

"What do you want me to do, break my security clearance?"

"It wouldn't be the first time."

"Right back at you, Junco. You're mucking around in the same shit I am, so fuck you."

I hoof it back to the buggy and search for some water and gulp it down. I'm hungry again, but since I don't know how long we'll have to be out here, I don't take another ration. Instead I plop down in the passenger seat and prop my chin up with my hand, staring up at the sky. My old friends are still up there. But not all of them are visible since the moon is only just now rising.

The comms begin to crackle and it almost makes me jump out of my seat. "Aren!" I yell. "Aren, the comms are back!"

I hear his boots running towards me and he stops by the driver's side door and reaches in for the handset, then walks off in the dark, talking.

More secret stuff about Junco, I'm sure. I go back to my skydream and find the Big Dipper, Little Dipper, and then the North Star.

Aren returns, a look of relief on his face. Probably so happy to get the hell away from my moody ass he can't contain himself. "They're on their way. Be here in about an hour."

"Airlift, then?" I ask. But I already know that means the RR has given them permission to fly in our airspace. He doesn't confirm it either way. "So what happens to me now?"

"We take you in and that's it."

"That's it? You guys just take me in and then what? Throw me a party? Take me home? Bring my father back to life? What? What happens when you take me in?"

He doesn't answer so I decide to push my luck. "Maybe they'll dissect me?"

"Don't be an idiot."

"I'm an idiot now? Because I'm the subject of a multinational, shit, multi-species manhunt, and I'm scared about what's going to happen and where I'm going to end up?"

"You're completely overreacting."

"Am I? Oh, well, phew! For a minute there I wasn't sure. Maybe I leave right now and you don't take me in at all? How 'bout that?"

"You're not going anywhere, Junco. Just sit quietly and stop acting like a raving crazy person—"

I am out of the buggy and hoofing it before he has a chance to finish his sentence. I book it hard and I feel the calories melt off my muscles and know that I won't get far. Still, I hear him yelling at me to come back and the pebbles his feet throw up as he chases me make my day. I slip into the tallgrass and I know that I could get away, if I really want to.

Do I really want to?

I stop because I'm not sure, then pant a little as I stand on my tiptoes and poke my head up to see if he's around. I don't see anything so I walk, parting the over-ripe stalks of wild wheat in front of me, while still keeping an eye out.

"Had enough yet, Junco?"

I turn to find the avian less than a pace behind me and I open my mouth to scream, but nothing comes out because he's got his hand clasped over my lips.

Tight, I might add.

"I see yer friends have ya completely strung out." I blink at him, partly because he seems to want a response and partly because that's all I can do. "If I remove my hand, will ya keep quiet then? For a moment of chat?" I nod and he removes his hand, but I'm true to my word and stay quiet.

"Now, then. Shall I present yer options? Or will ya just come along quietly?"

I shrug.

"You're coming with me, regardless of what ya choose, let's just get that straight right now."

I close my eyes like I'm tired, or bored. "So, why bother me with choices?"

"The choice is whether or not ya want yer little loverboy over there to keep his head."

Shit. Now I've done it. "Please don't kill him. He's a good guy and he's just following orders."

"Good guy, eh? I think not, Junco Coot. Ya have no idea what kind of guy he is. None at all."

I grunt. "Yeah. You're probably right about that, but hey, this is coming from someone who tears people's heads off for fun."

He squints down at me, like he's insulted or something. "The man was on top of ya, ready to throw a punch."

"I didn't need your help, alien. I practically killed him with a plumber's wrench ten minutes before you decided to decapitate him and spill his filthy blood all over me." I point to my dress as exhibit A.

"So what's the problem? I finished the job."

"I didn't want him dead, I only wanted him hurt. What you did was excessive. You're like an animal or a monster."

"Now we're getting somewhere. Sure, I'm a monster. But not any more of one than you are."

"I'm not one of you," I hiss.

He ignores my comment. "I'm willing to take you right now and leave everyone else alive. The question is whether or not you accept that proposal."

My face is suddenly hot and the frustration I feel is overwhelming. The tears escape and slip down my cheeks as I slump to the ground.

He bends down with me and leans in to part my hair away from my neck, like he's going to bite me or something. I pull back, but he's got a hold of my shoulder and keeps me still.

"This posture looks like an acceptance to me, Junco, but you're quite impulsive and wild," he croons in my ear, "and I want to be sure of your decision." I can feel the words travel into my ear canal and I put up an imaginary wall and rub my hand over my ear to brush them away.

"Learning tricks, are ya? No matter, Junco, all I need is a yes and this nightmare will end. Yes, then?"

"Her answer is no, alien." Aren's timing couldn't be worse.

I quickly reach for the avian's hand that still rests on my neck, and whisper, "Yes." Then he's gone.

I stand up and whirl around to see the avian has Aren by the throat. "You promised!" Aren is choking and his hands are frantically clutching the avian's hands. I look down and see Aren's plasma rifle and scoop it up, then point it straight at the alien's head. "Stop! We had a deal!"

The avian throws Aren down on the ground and he lies there sputtering. I drop the weapon and kneel down next to him. "Shit! Aren, are you OK?"

The avian stands over us with the plasma rifle. "He's fine. Just making a big scene is all. Come on, let's go."

"Wait," Aren croaks. "Wait! I have a message for you, Tier!"

We both turn. "Who's Tier?"

"I'm Tier. What message?" Tier asks.

"My front pocket," Aren chokes. "Junco, help me up!"

I do, and he fishes the letter from his pants pocket and hands it over. The alien takes it and walks a few paces away for privacy.

"What is it, Aren?"

He shrugs. "Dunno. I can't read their language."

"Well, where the hell did you get it? Try that one."

The alien is back so Aren doesn't answer me. "Well? What the hell does it say?" He scowls and hands it over to me. All I see is gibberish.

"Apparently," Tier begins, "we have an agreement between parties."

"English, please," I snap.

"That was English."

I throw up my hands. "What does it mean?"

"Seems yer friend there needs to grant me permission ta remove ya from custody. Though it's an old document and my plans have been recently revised. So I'm not sure I need to honor it anymore."

"You're not taking her," Aren growls.

"You have no say in that, boy. None whatsoever. She has already agreed to come."

They both look over at me and my eyes move from one to the other. Tier's tell me nothing, but Aren's speak loud and clear in their silence. "He says he won't kill you if I go."

"Goddammit, Junco, how fucking gullible can you be? Every fucking time I get you—" He stops and starts again. "Listen, Junco, he's not going to kill me. Can't kill me, OK?"

Tier laughs. "I can and I will."

"Fine," I shrug. "You want to fight over me, knock yourselves out."

Tier remains calm and looks Aren in the eyes. Aren meets his gaze and nods his head. Then the alien's face changes before my eyes and I step back and trip over a rock as I try to get away. "Aren, I'll just go—"

Aren spits on the ground and winces as he draws in a breath. "This dirty fucking avian can take his permission, his bullshit, and his ugly giant buzzard wings and get the FUCK OFF MY PLANET!"

I don't even have time to wince at his insults before Tier is on him.

Chapter Six

There is blood everywhere within seconds, but to my surprise it's not Aren's. He's got a laser knife in his hand and he's cut the avian across his chest. Tier looks down and I can see his green eyes glow with rage in the darkness.

"Stop!" I scream it as loud as I can, but they don't even hear me.

They are both in a crouched fighting position now, slowly circling each other. The blood is pouring out of Tier's chest as he speaks. "Ya have no chance against me human. None at all."

Tier actually bares his teeth and I feel my stomach clench. "Stop, you guys!"

Aren answers me this time, his eyes locked on the avian. "Junco, start running and don't stop."

"No!" I scream. "I'm not leaving you guys here to fight like children! I said I'd go, Aren, just stop! I don't want him to kill you!"

Tier is silent through this, and even though there is a lot of blood, he doesn't seem fazed or slow, or even slightly distracted. The look on his face is one of a predator about to take down a kill.

"He's not even close to killing me, Junco, he knows he can't kill me."

"W-w-what?" I stutter.

Tier answers this time. "Your loverboy here thinks he's got tricks up his sleeve, but he's wrong, Junco. I've got more tricks than he can even begin to imagine. And if you don't want to watch his head roll through the grass you'll run away like he said. I'll pick you up when we're done."

"Like hell you will," Aren snaps back.

Tier makes his move then. He's definitely not as fast on the ground as he is in the air, but his arms are almost long enough to reach out and grab Aren right where he stands. Almost. Aren ducks and catches his wing and twists it until the alien is forced to roll in the air with it or face an injury I can't stomach the thought of. He does twist and then he's free, but Aren attacks with the laser again, cutting another gash down the side of his leg.

Tier lifts off the ground like he's going to finish the job. My hands grasp around for the weapon I know is there and when I find it I hit the charge button. Aren is on the ground now and his head is bleeding. The alien hovers in the air just above him. They are talking but I'm too distracted by the charging whine of the plasma rifle to pay attention. Tier dives in for the kill, landing on top of Aren's chest. At the same time the rifle's charge button goes green and I blast the alien in the back for a full ten seconds.

He falls off to the side with a look of shock on his face.

Aren jumps to his feet and grabs my hand and we run, hard. "Is he dead?" I ask. But Aren doesn't answer me. "Is he dead, Aren?"

"Run! Just run!"

He pulls on me as I start to drop back behind him, forcing me to keep up with his pace, and we break for the buggy. When we get there he jumps in and has it started and in gear before I can even settle in my seat and we are moving across the prairie grass.

"What's happening? Is he dead, Aren?" I scream it over the raging wind that pierces my ears, but Aren is looking up in the sky and doesn't answer.

"He's coming, isn't he?" The words aren't even out of my mouth when I hear the hard beat of giant wings overhead.

Aren jams the buggy into the next gear and we go faster, but we both know that there is no way to outrun the monster circling above us.

Tier swoops down and comes straight for the buggy. "Duck!" Aren screams. I do, just as the giant talons reach out to grab me. I feel my skin open up as the sharp claws skim across my shoulders and the hot blood spills out and down my arm. The beating stops for a minute and my head goes woozy. I look over at Aren and his mouth is moving but the words don't make any sense and my world starts to blur.

I bounce as the buggy jumps the rough prairie terrain and my muscles are no longer able to compensate for the movement, causing me to slump over against the door.

Blood is flowing down my shirt and pooling around my hips. I snap back to reality a bit, just enough to realize we've stopped. Aren is dragging me out of the buggy by my arms when the monster returns and snatches me away.

Off in the distance I hear the chaos of war and feel the heat of plasma rifles as they crackle across the grassland. My senses return just enough to understand that Tier's talons are piercing my waist, his arms clasping me to his chest. We are flying.

I feel the wind across my face and try to open my eyes, but I can't. The heat of plasma fire blasts past me and it's only then that I realize we're being shot at by the soldiers who were supposed to pick Aren and me up.

A bolt of plasma hits Tier and then I am falling. It feels wonderful to be free of those claws. My bliss is interrupted as the powerful talons reach out and jerk me back into the confines of my captor and the world goes dim.

We fly until we stop, which seems soon to me, but the world is still blurry. Not as bad as it was back in the buggy, but I'm not completely coherent and I can't move my body very well. Tier drops to his knees as he lands, taking me with him. I feel the shelter of his wings as they scoop me up and I lose interest in anything else except for the warmth. I know he is talking because I feel the vibrations on my neck, but I can't hear anything. His eyes glow faintly in the darkness and I am mesmerized. It feels like we stay that way for a long time, but it could have been seconds for all I know. I have lost all sense of being.

I slip in and out of consciousness, but I do hear the soldiers off in the distance each time I come up for a gulp of reality. I can't tell exactly how far away they are, but if they are close, Tier is not worried. He never moves. I squirm until he releases my arms but not my body.

He speaks and now I can hear him. "Why do ya have to be such a troubled one, Junco?"

I'm the first to admit that I'm a fairly fucked-up person, but I'm not sure how he'd know any of that, so I say nothing.

"Why don't ya just do what yer told?" he prods.

I find my voice and croak out some words. "So, in your culture everyone does what they're told?"

"The little girls generally do, darlin'."

I manage to shake my head in frustration even though his wings are wrapped around me. "Well, maybe this will help," I croon up to him in my throaty new voice, "I'm a human, get it? And human girls around my age are quite temperamental and emotional. You must not have had very much training in human culture if that simple fact mystifies you. I feel better now, so let go of me."

He does and is crouching down as he watches me struggle to prop myself up on my elbows. I hear the soldiers off in the distance again. "They're getting closer. Why did we stop here?"

He smiles and his eyes have a faint glow to them as he answers, "Because I poisoned ya by mistake and without the antidote you'd be dead within minutes. Healing ya was necessary for the mission to continue."

I scramble up on my hands and knees and wait there as my head clears. He makes no move to help me, but I don't ask for help. So it evens out.

When the dizziness subsides I sit back on my butt and look up at him. "So, you're not allowed to kill me? That's part of the mission?" I feel a little relieved at this revelation. At least my head won't be rolling in the grass like Cole's.

"I have no plans to kill ya yet, darlin'."

"What the fuck does that mean?"

"I'm going to be honest with ya right now, Junco. I don't care for yer filthy mouth."

Wait. What? I laugh. "You're worried about me swearing? Unbelievable. How about trying to be honest about your orders to kill me as well?"

"I told ya, I'm not gonna kill ya."

"Yet. You said yet," I growl.

"Correct, I'm not gonna kill ya yet. Perhaps I will one day. Perhaps that day will never come. But right now I'm interested in keeping ya alive."

"And that's OK with you?"

"Yes, I'm OK with not killing ya. Yet."

I get up to stomp off but he grabs my ankle and I fall to the ground face-first. "Not so fast. There are soldiers right over there, sweetheart. If ya want them to live, you'll stay quiet and still."

"Where did you learn to talk to women? Lounge lizard school for the utterly stupid?"

"So, ya want them all to die? Because that can be arranged."

I shake my head and feel bad. "No, I don't want them to die."

"Then shut yer mouth and lie still so they can move on to the next search sector."

I do lie still but they do not move on. After several minutes it's clear that they know we are here, but they don't advance. "They see our heat signatures," I say.

"Yes, that's unfortunate."

"Unfortunate for whom?" I ask, but I don't want to know the answer. Whatever happens tonight, he's made one thing clear. We are leaving and if people have to die in order to accomplish that, so be it.

Aren's amplified voice crosses the distance. "Let her go, Tier. If you let her go we'll back off and let you leave."

I hear Tier snort at the stupid offer and I feel sorry for Aren because he might be dead in a few minutes if he keeps this up.

Tier stands and pushes down on my shoulder at the same time so I stay on the ground. Unlike me, he is much taller than the tallgrass and I'm sure he makes for a very good target. But no one shoots him and that makes me think they are afraid and are waiting for him to make the first move.

He speaks instead. "You have five minutes to clear out. After that, the carnage begins. If ya advance on us, I will personally eviscerate each one of ya and leave ya for the prairie lions to devour."

After that there is silence for several seconds and I am hopeful. But that hope is shattered as a bolt from a plasma cannon fires down upon us. Tier leans down casually and covers me with his wings as the heat incinerates the grass around us. When the initial burst is over, he pushes me down to the ground and I burn my palms on the smoldering remains of vegetation. I gasp when I see his face, partly because of the soot that chars his skin, but mostly because his rage produces a bright green light that actually seeps out of his eyes. Then he is gone.

I listen to the sounds of pain around me and I know that he's killing them, just like he said. In a few hours the prairie lions will follow the stench of death and eat them, bones and all, erasing any evidence of what is occurring here tonight.

When he returns I don't even recognize him. His entire body is plastered with blood: his clothes, his hair, his face, and most of all his hands. Except they are not hands anymore, they are talons like his feet. I stare at him in horror and he follows my gaze down and retracts the razors.

I want to ask about Aren but I already know the answer and I don't think I could take hearing it out loud so I just sit there and say nothing.

He doesn't console me, apologize, or even say he warned them and they asked for it. Instead he takes flight, grabs me with his talons, lifts me up into his arms that wrap around me tight, and we fly away from the glow of fire beneath us. From the air I can see the carnage we leave behind and I have yet another horror to fill my dreams the next time I fall asleep.

Chapter Seven

We fly for a long time. I'm not sure of the direction because I can't see the sky above me. The alien blocks my view. The entire core of my body hurts from his tight grasp and my face starts to feel chapped from the wind. But at least I am warm. His body radiates heat and it exchanges easily between us.

He sets me down in the darkness and I stumble a few paces before tripping and falling over. The palms of my hands sting as I reach out to try and catch my fall, but only succeed in slamming down on the ground. I realize I'm on a rock and after I adjust to the starlight I look up and find the Milky Way. Instantly my eyes are drawn down to the beacon of hope that dominates the western horizon. Peak City has never looked so beautiful and I smile as I realize where we are.

"You ever go there?" Tier asks me casually as I stand back up, like we're just a couple of friends taking in the view.

I snort out a grunt. "I grew up twenty miles from the border, of course I go there." Peak City is the capital of the Mountain Republic. The western edge of the Rural Republic bucks up against the planet pad where the suborbitals land. Technically the pad belongs to us, as it's inside our border, but since we're such a small country and very few of our citizens will ever require a suborbital, we lease the land to the MR for a tidy sum that pays for our exceptional military.

"So it's not forbidden for you to leave yer Republic?"

"Where'd you ever get that idea?" I scowl at him. People think that just because we don't have certain modern amenities that we're backwards. It's really only the entertainment shit we renounce and it's beyond ignorant to believe that people who shun screens are backwards. We simply have better things to do than sit around watching strangers do stuff, then try to convince ourselves it's fun.

He shrugs. "You Farm Families seem to have a lot of rules."

"Yeah, we do. But we're not prisoners. If you're not Farm you can even work in the MR. Lots of people in our Council do. But if you're Farm, then," I shrug, "your job is here taking care of your land and making it productive. The city is just a nice place to visit and that's pretty much it."

"Do you resent that?"

"What kind of crap is this? Some third-degree on my political leanings?"

"From what I can tell, you seem to resent quite a bit about following rules."

"Well, you don't even know me, so how the hell would you know anyway?"

"So, all the trouble you've caused over the past few months is—what? A strange coincidence?"

"For your information I went into the Stag to see if a friend was OK," I lie. "My father just died and Dale didn't show up for the funeral. So I was—worried."

"OK. Let's just pretend that's true. What about all the other stuff?"

I look back at him. He's standing with his feet apart, arms crossed over his chest, and his wings are not quite closed tight against his body, but neither are they in any way extended. Relaxed, maybe? The wing tips sneak out from behind his body in an upturned lift, like they cross somewhere at the small of his back.

I stop myself from staring. "What other stuff?"

His head nods up and down as he grits his teeth, which makes his jaw muscles tighten. But he doesn't answer me. Instead, he turns his back and walks away. I can see his wings first-hand now, and they do cross over each other, but they also seem to have a life of their own—like the ears on a horse—rotating and lifting in reaction to external stimuli.

He stops at a dark shadow along the edge of the mountain. It's about three feet long and two feet high. There are thick roots from the tall conifers that dominate the side of the mountain branching over it, half concealing it from view. If I didn't see Tier approach it, I might never have noticed the little opening. He bends down and sticks his feet in the hole, then pushes back the woody tree roots and slips inside, leaving me alone in the darkness.

I wait for several seconds but he doesn't come back so I get to my feet and walk over to see what he's up to. I try to see in the little hole, but it's too dark. His head pops back out and I scream in surprise, covering my mouth as he looks up at me, startled. "Why are ya just standing there?"

I shrug. "What do you want me to do?"

He grabs my ankles and pulls, making me fall on my ass. Then he's dragging me under the ground into the dark hole, my dress rolls up and the rocks are scraping against my plasma-burned back. Once inside I kick him hard in the shoulder and he lets go. "Get off me, you jerk!"

He puts his face right up to mine and I feel my heart jump. "I'm tired of playing games with ya, girl. If you see me go somewhere, ya follow. Understand?"

I consider saying something nasty back to him, but his eyes are glowing again and I take that as a sign that his patience is running on empty. So I just nod.

He turns and begins to slide down the rocky hill inside the mountain and I follow, trying my best not to let loose an avalanche of stones on his head. The only light we have is from a lightstick that is the same color as his eyes. In fact, I'm not entirely sure that his eyes aren't actually providing some light as well.

When we get to the bottom of the hill we stop and then he disappears into another dark shadow in the ground, taking the lightstick with him so I'm left in complete darkness.

Again his head pops back up when I hesitate. "Jump down, Junco."

"No. I'm not jumping into some dark hole, you're crazy. If you want to take me somewhere go ahead, but you're not stuffing me down into a hole."

"Jump in the hole, Junco. Or I'll leave ya here and you'll wander around in the dark until the nightdogs get a hold of yer scent and eat ya alive."

Fuck.

I climb in after him, ignoring the stench of guano, the spiderwebs that flit against my cheeks, and the noises that echo off the walls. It isn't really a hole, more like a rooftop entrance into a larger cavern which opens up into a series of tall terraced steps that takes us further and further into the belly of the mountain. Eventually it morphs into a fairly well-defined tunnel.

The terraced steps are flat, which hints that someone shaped this passageway, but the sides of the tunnel are absolutely man-made. Even in the extremely dim light I can see the toolmarks left from when it was drilled. There must be more entrances, larger entrances, that can accommodate heavy machines.

We walk on like this for a while. It's hard to tell how long. All I know is that I am exhausted from tripping over various small objects that seem to present themselves under my feet at every opportunity.

We cross a small stream, thankfully not too deep, and then I spot a faint light source up ahead. Tier grabs my hand and pulls me towards it. The width of the tunnel expands with the growing light until it empties into a spectacular wide-open cavern filled with so many different types of cave formations that it takes my breath away.

"All this time I've been living next to this place and I never knew it."

"You barely know anything, Junco." He takes my hand again and pulls me to the center of the cavern, spins me around a few times, and lets go.

"Hey, what the hell?"

"Look around."

I pivot on my heel and frown at what I see.

"You'll think twice about running off then, eh?"

I nod and find a seat at a camp table set up in the center of the room and the exhaustion takes over as I survey my new surroundings. He won't need to bind me or stick me in a hole here because there are three identical openings leading into the cavern, each one equidistant to the next. I have no idea which one we just came through.

"How long have you been here?" I ask as I take in the mounds of supplies layered around the central clearing.

He's pulling some stuff out of a container and piling it on the floor beside him. "Long enough for it to feel like home."

My mouth makes a little O shape as I spy a sleeping bag on the ground. I crawl over to it and sink into the surprisingly soft and buoyant blankets, watching him as he prepares some sort of food. "What's that?"

"Nutrition," is all he comes back with.

I yawn. "Doesn't look very good."

"Then don't eat it."

"I won't, believe me." And then my eyes close and I drift off.

The planks on the deck are warm under your feet and you're wearing a long thin white shirt, open in the front, that barely covers your body. The waves lap against the dock and you reach over and drag your fingers through the water. It folds against your wrist and slaps up the side of your arm. The drops bead against your oiled skin, pool together, then spring forth into a trickle which takes the liquid back to the source. The mountains are high and imposing and then they crowd in and consume you as the sunlight disappears...

No. That's not what happens.

I wake up and know immediately I am alone. There is a bowl of cold food sitting next to me and a note written in some gibberish. Did he really just do that? Write me a note in a language that I can't read? I toss it and smell the food as I consider how hungry I am.

Not enough to eat that shit.

I stand and stretch, taking in the room again. This time my head is much clearer, but my back is creaking from sleeping on the cold cave floor. I have no idea how long I was out but I feel pretty well-rested.

The chamber is large, about fifty feet long and maybe thirty feet at its widest point. It narrows where a massive stalactite and stalagmite meet to form a column the width of a sequoia trunk.

The roof of the cave is adorned with thousands of breathtaking stone icicles and there are large white crystals growing out of every crevice. My eyes follow the cave wall to the end and see hundreds of drapery formations hanging from the ceiling. Water flows down the curving rock and deposits into a small pool.

The floor is almost smooth, but there are soft mounds of rock which makes me think of flowing lava. This pitches the ground up and down like rolling hills as I walk.

I stand in the middle, half in awe of this cave being here in the first place, and half in awe because I am actually standing in it.

There are three wide tunnels that lead to this central room. That they are man-made I have no doubt. Whether they are enough to keep me from escaping is another story.

I study the three exits with a critical eye. They aren't all the same; they just looked that way at first because I was in a new place and I was exhausted. But now I can see subtle differences.

If you stand inside one there is a long dark column obstructing the view into the cave as you enter. I know I didn't see that as we passed through, so I knock that one off the list right away. Now there are only two, and if I take a chance, I have a fifty-fifty shot of picking the right one and walking right out of here and back to my house.

I study them a little more and walk a few paces into each one to see if there are other landmarks. The walls of one has a formation near the entrance that I remember from school. Moonmilk. I think I would have noticed that, even if I was delusional.

I walk over to the remaining cave and search for anything that might strike it off the list, but there is nothing there to make me hesitate. Then I search through Tier's supplies and find some flares, stuff some disgusting food into my boot, and grab some rope because rope is something you should probably have in a cave.

I take one last look around and then head into the dying light that semi-permeates the tunnel.

Chapter Eight

Finding my way back out to the world is child's play. I throw down the supplies and take in the view. First I look over at PC. It has a hold on me, that city. Not the kind that makes you move there. Something else. It draws me in. Makes me feel safe when I see it. Even from here, which is easily sixty miles from the ziggurat, I can see the terraces that swirl up the side of the mountain. It's not the tallest mountain in North America, but it's one of the most famous.

At night it's lit up like Vegas and I can say from personal experience that landing on the suborbital planet pad in Peak City beats Vegas as far as thrills go. Hands down. As if on cue a deafening boom announces an arrival as the suborbital plane breaks the sound barrier and comes in for a landing. My eyes follow the fluorescent pink contrail left over from atmosphere re-entry. I sort of have a thing for planet pad watching. Like stargazing, it's part of me.

I've landed on almost every planet pad on Earth and none of them have the same draw as the Peaks. Maybe everyone who lives by a pad feels that way, but somehow I doubt it. London's pad is crap—an afterthought, just like everything else in that old decaying city. Jersey and LA aren't much better. Only Vegas, with the open flat desert and the brilliance of the Strip creeping up alongside it, Tokyo, with its kamikaze landing pad floating out on the ocean five miles offshore, and Dallas, which built an entire city on top of a city to accommodate their pad, can come close to matching the landing in Peaks.

I turn my attention back to my own small world. If I stand on my tiptoes I can see faint lights through a break in the pine trees to the north. I continue my gaze northeast and see a line of tall pines that give way to a clearing that might be my ranch. It's not close enough to see anything in detail, so I'm not really sure, but it's in that general direction.

Definitely close enough to walk to.

But I hesitate.

I could go home. Very easily. But he'd just come get me again. There is no chance this hiding place with its proximity to my home is a coincidence. I could make a run for it to one of the closer neighbors, probably Mr. and Mrs. Baumer from what I can tell. But that would just be a death sentence for them. He's killed several dozen people in the past few days, what's one old couple on a cattle ranch?

I could try and look in the cavern for a radio and get in touch with my Council Elder, let him know where we are. Maybe they can mount a defense? This sounds more like a dream than a reality. Even after all these people have been killed, the RR defenses have yet to show up.

My last idea is to just stay put and do what I'm told. I laugh at that, a small chuckle that develops in my throat and bubbles up to a full-blown snicker.

And yet I do stay put. I could be halfway down the mountain by now if I wanted. In the trees, hiding and moving in silence.

Getting away.

Easily.

If—and this is a big if—Aren was telling the truth, then they all want me, including the RR. They gave the MR sky privileges, for fuck's sake.

To come get me. Because I'm not human.

Again I get the urge to laugh, but it's just not funny.

Picture yourself standing on the edge of a dock...

Fuck.

Enough already, Junco.

I stare up at the sky for a long time and find Cygnus, then up to Draco, and finally over to Cassiopeia. I wish I was a constellation, high up in the sky. And everyone would look at me in the night and marvel at how beautiful and untouchable I was. In ancient times the Gods only made you a constellation if they were mad at you, or if you were too beautiful to die. So it was either a reward or a punishment, depending on your predicament. It's funny how the very same circumstance can be eternal life for one and eternal damnation for another. It makes no sense, but it does teach a lesson in perspective.

I have a stray thought as I lie there under the Milky Way, but I push it away before it can fully form.

Maybe I just need some perspective?

Maybe I'm being brainwashed?

Or maybe I just can't think straight because of all the injuries I've sustained?

Or maybe those weird alien healing chemicals are interfering with my thought process?

It doesn't matter because the idea that wants to form slips into my head anyway. Maybe it doesn't make sense because I don't know the whole story?

Maybe I'm being lied to?

And maybe I'm lying to myself.

I hear the heavy beating of wings and know that Tier is back. He lands behind me in the small clearing and walks the few paces toward my prone body.

"What's going on?" he says as he approaches.

The question hangs between us as I tip my head back as far as I can so I can see his upside-down face in the starlight. "Having a pity party. You're invited."

He lies down next to me. "Am I now?"

I force a smile and look at him. His eyes have just a faint green glow, but it doesn't bother me anymore, probably the brainwashing kicking in. His loose mop of black curls is a mess from flying in the wind and I wonder briefly at my own hair. I push that thought away quickly. His clothes are still stained with blood, as are my own. Funny how it doesn't even register even though some of it is Cole's.

That brainwashing is some powerful shit, I really need to cut back.

"What pity are we celebratin', then?" he asks.

I exhale deeply but stay quiet. He doesn't push, but instead waits patiently and looks up at the sky. "How many did ya see?"

I don't know how I know, but I know. "None," I reply.

"That's weak. I see one right now." Then he points and I find the shooting star at the end of his fingertip.

I look at him again, and give another smile and shake my head as the tears threaten to burst out.

"So what have ya been doin' out here?" He's prying now and his accent is a little thicker as well. Like he's reverting back to how he normally talks.

I let out another heavy sigh, but keep my silence.

"Is this yer human temperament and emotions coming out?"

I let out a small laugh and then the tears ride down my cheeks. I feel him turn towards me, propped up on his elbow, and then swipe a finger down my face to remove the ribbons of water.

"Do avians cry?" I ask, turning my head away to avoid his gaze.

"We do," he whispers. He leans back into the grass and leaves me that way for several seconds. "We do," he says again, but this time he's talking to himself.

Then he gets up and grabs my hand. I fly up towards him like I weigh nothing and he pulls me close. "Come on," he says. "I have something that will make us both feel better."

I let him tug me back into the cave and we make the descent back to the cavern.

The walk back is uneventful and when we reach the vaulted room I plop down on the camp chair as he fools around looking through his supplies, stuffing things in a pack as he goes.

"Are we going on a trip?" I ask.

He smiles as he pokes his head up and looks over a cave formation. I smile back at him despite myself. Is it wrong to smile when so many people are dead? I definitely think it is.

"Oh, I almost forgot," he says as he walks toward me, pulling a small bag from his coat pocket. "Human food. In case you're hungry." He hands me the little white bag and I take it. I am famished. Is it wrong to be thankful for the food a killer gives you? I definitely think it is.

He goes back and begins to mess with a collection of tech and comm devices that sit on a ledge as I peek inside the crumpled bag. It's a smashed chicken sandwich from Chick-Chick-Chicken in Peak City. It's pretty cold, but I stuff it into my mouth and it tastes wonderful. Between bites I manage to talk. "How did you get a chicken sandwich from the Peaks anyway?" I look down into the empty bag and secretly wish for the fries that normally go with it. I chew and wait for his answer, but the info never materializes.

When I'm finished he comes back over and sees the empty bag and smiles. "Ya were starved then?"

I nod.

He holds up the pack that's almost bursting with supplies. "I've got something in here you'll like." Then he grabs my hand and pulls me up. "Come on."

"Where are we going?" I ask. But he just grins back at me and pulls me along behind him. We enter another tunnel and begin walking down the slope, which eventually ends in a path lined with strikingly beautiful folia formations. I recall from school that means all of this was under water, probably for thousands of years, before this tunnel was made. It's not long before he stops and turns. I look at his expression and I can tell he thinks he's pretty clever, but can't imagine I will be as excited as he is when he shows me what's beyond the next corner. My doubts must be written all over my face.

"Ye of little trust, I see."

I let out a little laugh before I can stop it.

"Darlin', this will put an end to all of yer temperamental emotions, at least for a little while."

"Really? Well, whatever it is you're going to show me, it must be really fucking spectacular."

He pushes me in front of him and we walk forward into another large cavern that looks almost exactly like the one we came from. I'm about to say something rude when I see it.

"Oh, yeah. That is definitely good." I look up and laugh at his bright smile.

"There's not much a nice hot bath won't fix. Even if it's just temporary."

Sweet Jeremiah, he is so right.

The hot spring is actually a flowing stream at one end with a fairly strong trickle of water that empties into it. The basin is surrounded by flowstone rock, which allows the water to collect there before gently spilling over and continuing along through the cave system. The steam coming up from the basin makes the cave humid and this makes me think of home.

Tier is unpacking towels, clothes, and some bottles as I spy shampoo and almost moan with longing. Some prisoner I make. Right now I would totally spill every secret I have just to wash my hair.

I wait and we approach the springs together and then he throws a few lightsticks into the water so it glows green from below. I look at him, unsure what to do next. He nods.

"You don't need to tell me twice. But I have no clean clothes."

"I won't let ya walk around naked. Go ahead. Get in." And then he turns around and busies himself with the pack.

I untie my boots and my knife spills out. I slip out of the thermals and whip the dress over my head. And then I am standing in my shorts. I feel ashamed that I am about to bathe with this killer, but I'm not about to give up a bath on that principle.

I check over my shoulder to see if Tier is looking, but he's still busy with the pack, so I strip off my shorts and walk towards the pool naked. I dip my toe in and give a little gasp, then look back to check on Tier and he's laughing at me. "Get in already, will ya."

I sit on the edge of the pool, then lower myself into the steaming water and find that it's deep enough so that I sink in up to my neck. A sublime moan escapes my lips.

"Your turn."

He begins peeling off his many layers of clothes and I'm fascinated, unable to pull my eyes away. He removes his coat and shirt by unsealing the seams that run under his arm and then pulling them over his head, being careful of his wings.

I see his real shape for the first time. Wings are like another set of limbs that jut out of the clavicle. It makes his upper back bulge with the extra muscle, but aside from the wings, he looks completely human. Especially when he's got them plastered flat against his back. I study his physique like a scientist, but then my eyes travel across his body to the scars. They are white, like they've been there a long time. And they are numerous. He begins to tug on his pants and I dunk my head under to shake the filth off my hair.

I try to wait underwater until I hear him get in, but I run out of breath and surface, stealing a glance at his naked form as he enters the pool. His dark curls are covering his eyes, so my intrusion goes unnoticed until he's in up to his waist and looks directly at me. He swims over and takes my hand as my heart pounds in my chest.

Chapter Nine

He pulls me towards him and I melt at his contact even though his hands have been touching me on and off for the past two days.

"Come here," he says in a low voice.

I do.

Of course he's pulling me so if I wanted to resist I probably couldn't.

But anyway, I don't resist.

He pulls me into his chest and spins me around and I feel something cold dribble onto my head and it smells like flowers. His hands move to my scalp and begin massaging as I smile. "I could almost love you right now for doing this, you know."

"That's pretty much the point, Junco."

I don't have anything to say to that, so I keep still and quiet and his fingers dance along the length of my hair like he's massaging the shampoo into each individual strand. Finally, my entire head is frothy. He turns me around again and says, "Rinse."

I dunk under and shake my head, then pop back up. As soon as I surface he's pulling me again, and this time he leads me over to the small rushing waterfall. "Go ahead, stick your head under," he says with a smile. I do, and the shock of cold water snaps me out of my fog. I gasp for breath and rake the droplets across my lashes to clear the blurriness.

I look over at him and shake my head, but I can see a real smile underneath his pretend innocence. "Here, catch!"

I do catch and find hair conditioner in my palm. "OK, shampoo I can understand, but conditioner? You must bring all the girls down here for a midnight bath."

He laughs at that and begins to shampoo his own hair. "Right, because there are so many avian girls to choose from on Earth."

I watch him in silence for a few minutes, thinking about what he said. "How long have you really been down here?"

He dunks under to rinse out the bubbles, then bobs back up and runs his fingers through his black hair as the water trickles down his chest. "Here? About two years."

"Two years? What the hell have you been doing here for two years?"

He scowls at my cursing but answers my question. "Watching you, Junco."

"That's really creepy."

"Yeah, well. I guess it is what it is."

"Why not just leave me alone? Why do anything?"

"Because if you're avian you belong with your own kind."

"If. If I'm avian? But I've been raised human, I'm human. And I don't even have wings, so how can being avian even be a possibility?" We float there, looking at each other and his eyes slip down to my chest just below the surface of the water, making me blush and avert my eyes.

"You haven't even matured yet, Junco."

"Ouch," I say, looking up at him. "That stings. I might fight like a boy, but I'm not shaped like one."

He shakes his head, says "I'm not talking about that," and then laughs a little. I think I just made him blush.

My mouth forms a little O.

"Avians grow much like humans do, up to a point. Then we go through a second maturation process and that's when your wings form."

"You aren't born with wings?" This fascinates me. "Does anyone else know this about your race?"

"I dunno," he confesses. "Probably some of them do. The ones responsible for this... mess we're in now certainly must."

"Then why are you telling me?"

"Because in all likelihood, Junco, you are avian. At least," he pauses, "in part."

"What does that mean, in part?"

"It means that you might not be one hundred percent pure avian, but might have human blood mixed in."

"Maybe that's what I am then, part human and part avian."

"I hope not."

His words come out too quick and sting me into silence. But then I shake it off and ask the obvious. "Why?"

He leans his head back and floats there in the steam for a few seconds, thinking. "Isn't it better to be one or the other?"

"I don't know, is it?"

He laughs. "It definitely is."

"What do you want me to be?"

He smiles at me. "I want ya ta be yerself." I'm just about ready to think that's the perfect answer, but then he continues. "As long as yer one or the other."

"Oh." I can't hide my disappointment and he can't take back the words, so he moves toward me, grabs my hand, and pulls me over to the other side of the pool. "Here," he says as he takes my hand and places it on a flat rocky ledge under the water. "Sit." His smile is back, but now that I've seen the real thing, it looks superficial.

I sit and he sits next to me. Then he pulls me to his chest and wraps his arms around my stomach. His wings curve in, and cradle us both. "You want to know what I think, darlin'?"

His words come out soft and he even makes the darlin' part sound sexy, but my mind is thinking about what I am. "Sure," I say halfheartedly.

"I think yer one hundred percent avian and I think that in the end, it will be something you'll come to love about yerself."

"Yeah, maybe," is all I have to say to that. I recall the scars on his upper body and turn to look at them. "What's all this?" I ask.

His eyes track down to the scar my finger is tracing on his chest. He turns me back around and his fingertip traces a scar on the fleshy muscle midway between my neck and my shoulder, but at the same time his other hand slips to the skin just below my belly button and finds the raised horizontal line across my lower stomach. "What's all this?"

I shake off the hand on my shoulder and force his other hand up higher so it can't touch the scar. "You're in my personal space, Tier."

I feel him shrug and we move on. "So, Junco Coot. Why did ya not just walk home when ya got out of the cave earlier?"

I sigh as his hands wrap a little tighter around my middle and I try and pry them loose, but don't succeed. "Would you have come gotten me from my home, if I did?" I ask, looking back at him. He studies my face and nods. "So, there was no point then, right?"

"And?" he prods me along.

"And—" I'm not sure, but he's waiting. "I dunno. What am I gonna do in that house by myself?"

"So, yer lookin' for company?"

"Jasus, Tier. I don't know. I'm looking for answers, I guess. Just drop it."

He moves his hand up to my neck and strokes the ugly scar on my shoulder and I feel a wave of heat rush up into my face. His hand continues, then slips over to my chin and he gently turns my face toward him and reaches down to kiss my neck. I gasp and he takes this as encouragement. His mouth reaches up to meet mine and for a moment I let him.

But then I pull away. "Don't—do that."

My words come out low and deep because I can't hide my desire, and I look into his eyes but see only sadness. He smiles again, then releases my head and I am once again facing forward.

"Do ya want me to give ya the answers yer looking for, then?" he asks.

I pull my legs up onto the rock shelf and rest my head on my knees as I hug them to my chest. Then I tilt my head enough so I can see his face behind me. "Do you have them?"

"I'm not sure. Some. Maybe."

I don't say anything to that, just sit and think.

His hand tracks to my exposed back and his fingertips trace a line down my spine into the water. I buckle at his touch.

"Does that hurt?" he asks.

"A little, why?"

"Plasma burn on yer back. When did that happen?"

"The MR. They stunned me when I was running in the tallgrass."

"Why?"

I shrug. "Who knows."

"Ya know why, so tell me. Why did they stun you, Junco?"

I look sideways at him. "Back off, OK? It's none of your fucking business."

He lets out a little burst of air and transitions into neutral territory. "How about a story, then?"

I stay silent for a moment, lost in the shiver that bursts from his dragging touch up and down my back. "What's it about?"

"The goddess, our greatest goddess, Inanna."

I look back at him, interested now, and he begins.

"We have two parental deities, the God Old Crag, and the Goddess Inanna. Old Crag is just your regular pantheon figurehead. He's pretty laid-back and he only has a few hard and fast rules for his children to follow. Nothing too extraordinary.

"But Inanna, she's something else altogether." He smiles at my smile, and then continues. "She's never satisfied, like most women." I grunt at his jab, but let it slide.

"She's already the ruler of all heaven and earth, all space and sky, and all the world's water. But there's one place where she can never go, and that's the world down below. This really ticks her off, so she conspires with her faithful servant, the magpie."

I groan at the mention of the trouble-making bird and he reads my mind. "Aye, you'll never make the right choice if ya conspire with a magpie, they're always up for trouble. But anyway, she tells the magpie that she's going to the world down below to demand that the ruler, who happens to be her sister, Eresh, submit the final realm to her and Old Crag. So she dresses in her finest attire to tempt the seven gatekeepers who guard the path to find Eresh."

His fingers are still tracing a pattern across my back and I realize with a start that he is drawing wings.

"And then off she goes.

"Inanna approaches the first gate and demands, as goddess of heaven and earth, all space and sky, and all the world's water, to be let in, but the gatekeepers demand a gift of power.

"As a token of her power she leaves her lapis rod and goes forward to the second gate. There the gatekeeper demands a token of humility, and so she strips off her gown and goes forward naked.

"At the third gate the keeper demands a gift of beauty, so she takes off her royal beads and drapes them over the skeleton of bones as she passes through.

"At the fourth gate the demand is for treasure, so she takes off her jewel-encrusted wedding ring and hands it over.

"At the fifth gate the keeper wants service, and so Inanna, goddess of heaven and earth, all space and sky, and all the world's water, bows her head and bends down to wash his feet in a tub of warm water.

"At the sixth gate she's asked to give wisdom, so she recites the prayer of protection that Old Crag uses to keep the whole world safe.

"She finally reaches the seventh gate and there the keeper is a large angry spirit who has been sent to the underworld as punishment by Old Crag. His demand is the truth.

"Inanna, who is not privy to the secret council kept by her husband, cannot provide the truth he is looking for, so she improvises and casts a spell that will reflect the world back to him in the gazing pool, and then tells him his truth is in the mirror.

"Finally, stripped of everything she has and standing naked in the unbearable heat of the sun burning the world down below, Inanna reaches her sister Eresh, sitting on her throne, and demands that her sister submit."

Tier pulls me back against his chest and begins to whisper in my ear, the magic of his words dancing across my cheek to make their way into the depths of my head, and I shiver with anticipation.

"Eresh looks at her visitor in all her nakedness and says, 'Sister, there is no reason to beg for my realm. You are my blood. And now that you have come here I think you should stay, and feel the heat of the darkness, while I shall go up and feel the glow of the light.'

"Inanna is about to disagree when Eresh takes her prisoner and traps her inside a dark trunk. Then she takes her leave of the throne room and one by one, on her way past each gate, collects Inanna's personal items so that when she comes up from the world down below she is wearing Inanna's wedding ring, her royal beads, and her dress, and has her all powerful lapis rod.

"Nins, that's the magpie's name, is tricked into thinking Eresh is Inanna by all her royal garb, and is astounded that she has made her way back and plans a great party. Later, after the party is over, Eresh is lying next to her new husband feeling satiated and glowing with excesses of food and drink.

"But Inanna, in the world down below, is plotting her return. She is well on her way to escaping the trunk, and soon, she is well on her way to escaping the Seven guards at the gates. She is the Goddess Inanna, blessed by her uncle, the god of all that is known, with more gifts than one woman would ever need.

"But her greatest gift is that of decision-maker. No other gift makes her so powerful or so feared. And her Sister, though she does possess an entire world, cannot prevent Inanna from making the decision to leave.

"Inanna crosses back over the first six gates that bind her to her sister's realm, but at the Seventh, she is instructed to provide her proxy. You see, you cannot leave the world down under unless there is someone to take your place.

"Inanna, being a goddess of love and battle—among many other things—promises a suitor to stand in for her and then she makes her way back to her home. When she sees Old Crag in bed with Eresh she is crazed with jealousy. She snatches them both up and drags Eresh back to her realm and leaves her there. To punish Old Crag, she makes him stand for her at the Seventh Gate for half the year, while her suitor will stand for the other half.

"From that day on Inanna is also given the title of Goddess of Retribution. Eventually Old Crag does get out of his commitments, but only because Inanna feels guilty and helps him trick another suitor into taking his place."

Tier stops and waits to see if I say anything. But I don't. I just lie against his chest for several minutes counting each time it moves in and out.

"Junco," he says finally, turning me to look at him. "Do ya see?"

I let out a long exhale. "Yeah, I get it. Don't be a victim."

He laughs. "Yeah, that's one way to see it. Don't let life happen ta ya, decide how it will go. We all have the power of decision, unless yer a slave." He lifts my chin up from his chest. "And yer not a slave, Junco."

I smile. "No."

And then Tier pushes me off him, stands up, gets out of the pool and walks away. "I'll get our clothes."

Chapter Ten

True to his word, he does have something for me to wear, but it's one of his outfits that was never made for humans. The soft, thick black shirt is tailored to fit a being with wings. It's really more like a vest that fits over the head and there are seals which hold it together under my arms. The thick, black, canvas-like jacket is made the same way. The pants, also black and made of the same material as the jacket, are way too long, but he cuts them with a knife, just like I did a few days ago with the jumpsuit.

Everything is over-sized in an exaggerated manner, but it feels good anyway. I have to wear my old boots because his are made for talons, and would never work for human feet, even if he had my miniature size, which he doesn't.

When we are finally dressed in the clean clothes the dreamy feeling in the hot springs pool is gone and I feel warm and fresh. He looks me up and down, then smiles and takes my hand as we walk back the way we came.

Tier halts abruptly and I slam into him in the dark. "Hey," I say in a joking tone, "what's the deal?"

He turns to face me and I see his eyes are glowing bright green. "Shhhhh," he says.

I'm quiet, more curious than worried, and stand behind him as he waits, maybe listening. Or maybe his eyes see in the dark. I'm not really sure which.

After a long several minutes, he looks back, his eyes still bright, and tugs me forward with him. "What is it?" I whisper again. But he just squeezes my hand and stays silent as we continue to make our way in the blackness. I figure we are about halfway back to the main cavern.

My arm is jerked as Tier ducks into a small side tunnel. He pulls me in close so he can whisper in my ear. "There's a pack of nightdogs ahead."

"What?" I whisper back. "Where did they come from?" My heart beats faster with each second.

"Junco," he says so softly that I can barely hear him. "This entire mountain is a major breeding den for them. They're everywhere."

"You mean I could have been eaten alive when I left the cavern?" His eyes glow as he looks down at me, but he doesn't say anything, so I take that as a yes.

We wait there for several minutes and I can feel him straining to hear any sign that they are either still around, or are gone. He grabs for my hand, but instead of leading me out into the main tunnel, he continues down the side shaft. I have no choice but to follow him and spend a lot of time looking back over my shoulder. This is a futile gesture be-cause it is pitch black and I don't have glowing night-vision eyes.

We both hear the haunting vocalizations at the same time and the hair on the back of my neck stands on end, charged with the chill that seeps out through my skin.

We freeze and listen. The howl begins low and ever so gradually grows in pitch and intensity, until finally it is a blood-curdling chorus of screams that makes my stomach shift in terror. They are very close but I cannot tell if they are ahead in the small tunnel or behind us in the main corridor. I trust Tier to keep their location straight and just try to keep my breathing under control, but I am not having much luck. Tier squeezes my hand again and moves forward, then stops and pushes me into a crack in the wall.

"Go to the end of this crevice, it will be tight, but you'll fit, I promise. Then use the formations on the side of the rock to climb up." His green eyes look up and I follow his gaze. "There's a ledge up there. Get to it and don't move until I come get ya."

He pushes me in as I nod my head and I begin to move forward into the narrow passageway. I have both arms stretched out so I can feel for the rock formations on either side as I make my way deeper and deeper into the crevice, all the while Tier is getting farther and farther away from me.

About thirty paces in I begin to doubt him and almost turn back when the passage becomes so narrow that I have to squeeze sideways. I scrape against the rough rock and am thankful for the thick alien clothes to protect me from the ragged edges. I continue to force myself to move forward, even as the rock presses up against my chest so hard my lungs are pushed in.

There is some shuffling behind me and I stop and con-sider calling out to Tier when the screaming starts. I panic and begin forcing my body into an opening that continues to get thinner and thinner. The sound of bones breaking echoes through the caverns and I can hear the nightdogs snarling and howling. The screams are etched into my brain, but I cannot tell if they are avian or canine.

Then everything falls silent.

I wait, panting so hard that I'm afraid I will begin to hyperventilate and I will Tier to call out for me to tell me that it is safe and I can come out.

But he doesn't. Instead I hear the insane snarling of a nightdog and it grows in intensity as I realize it's charging towards me. I imagine the teeth that will tear into my body and squirm into the crevice as far as I can.

The dog attacks and grabs my coat. I hear a great rip as the fabric gives way to the razor-sharp teeth and I remember my knife, tucked securely back in my boot after I dressed in the hot spring cavern. I am wedged tight between the rocks and have no way to reach it so I force myself to squeeze even further into the crevice, hoping that the end is near and it will open up into a passage that will lead me to the rock formations on the side of the wall, and ultimately to safety.

The dog attacks again. This time it grabs my leg and I feel the skin lift up and off of my calf in a sickening squishy tear. I scream with all my breath and kick wildly where I think its face might be. After a few unsuccessful attempts I connect and the dog cries out and backs off. I suck in my stomach and squeeze my shoulder a little farther, praying to God that I'm not just making myself a nice trapped dinner meal for a pack of wild animals. My shoulder scrapes hard against the rock and even through the strong alien canvas coat I can feel the gash that opens in my skin, and then the warm spill of blood as it runs down my sleeve.

The dog makes another attempt to eat me and lunges once again, but my shoulders break through the obstruction and half of my body is free. I fall down as my leg is grabbed by the snapping jaws beyond the slim crevice and I kick hard one more time to free myself. It lets go and I scramble to my feet, feel for the rock formations, and climb as fast as I can. I lose my grip on the calcium deposits slippery with trickling water, and the first dog makes its way into the small crevice where my legs were just seconds before. I regain my grip and climb again, and when I reach the top I fall over and choke as I inhale like I'm breathing water and not air.

Both dogs are snapping below me now, but I get to my knees and begin to crawl back towards Tier. It takes me for-ever because I can't see anything and I'm afraid of falling down once I reach the edge. I hear some occasional snapping up ahead and for a moment my mind sees Tier being eaten alive. I push this gruesome thought aside and move faster and faster until I reach the edge.

I see Tier's green glowing eyes stare up at me when I peek over the edge, and my heart sinks. The area is illuminated just enough for me to pick out the eye-shine surrounding him, and I count three sets all attacking and retreating, trying to overwhelm and take the upper hand. I slip the knife from my boot, stand up as far as I can without hitting my head on the sharp stalactite formations, and jump down on top of the raging animal that has taken hold of his arm, plunging the knife into its side.

The wild dog bawls in pain as I twist the knife and puncture the lung, then remove it in one swift motion. It lets go of Tier's arm and I'm knocked down by his sudden free-dom. In a moment we have reversed positions, he is up and I am down, and the remaining two dogs come in for another attack.

One grabs Tier by his wing and I hear an anguished scream erupt from his throat that makes my skin crawl. His eyes burst with color that almost illuminates the entire passageway and I can finally get a good look at what we are facing. The scruffy mane of fur that lines the wild dog's throat protects the jugular from almost all attacks, the canine teeth are almost three inches long, and they possess the claw length and sharpness of a grizzly bear.

The light isn't enough to inhibit their attacks, but it sure scares the hell out of me. The sheer size of them causes me to scoot backwards into the side of the jagged rocks of the corridor. Tier is breathing hard and circles around behind them so that his internal light source keeps my field of vision illuminated. "Stay put there, Junco." His breathing is labored but his voice is remarkably calm. "Don't do anything else, I got this."

"Like hell you do!" I scream and then they are upon us. I hear the swoosh of wings and then another avian screech comes up from Tier's throat as his powerful talon reaches out and snatches the dog closest to him. His wings beat hard trying to give him lift to attack with both feet, but the confined space inhibits this move.

I am fixated on his futile attempt to fly inside the corridor when the other dog attacks. My knife is still in my hand and I lunge forward to meet it halfway, trying to put it off balance. It knocks me backward and I feel another tear across my calf, then the sharp clang of the knife as it falls from my hand. The animal is on top of me before I can even process the events and it pulls back before striking at my throat.

I block automatically to thwart the attack and its teeth pierce my left hand and rip. For a moment time stands still and I wonder if I still have all my fingers, and then Tier's light fades and the dog is upon me as I pass out.

I come to, probably just seconds later because the dog is right next to me and Tier has it pinned down with one of his massive talons. Then I witness the second living creature beheaded by the powerful avian claws in as many days and I shut my eyes to the hot, sticky horror that spills out of the neck and splatters across my body.

The cave goes silent.

"Junco! Hey, ya OK?"

I feel him pick me up but I'm either in shock or going blind because even though I know he is moving, my vision blurs in and out of focus. He carries me and we travel for several minutes, in which direction I have no idea because the world goes dark.

Tier is peeling off my clothes as I try to object, but his fingers touch my lips and I remain silent. Soon after he lowers me into the hot spring water once again and I feel his wings cradle me into a deep, healing sleep.

When I regain consciousness we are back in the central cavern and I am warm and dry. But I see the nightdog attacking me and I thrash around wildly and sit up. Tier bends down and gently takes my hands. "Yer OK, Junco. The dogs won't come this far into the light."

I know that. They can barely tolerate the full moon, and this cavern is lit up like the Sun. But I can't shake the feeling of the attack and I try and take a deep breath but only succeed in coughing.

"Do I still have fingers?" I finally gasp.

He smiles but doesn't answer. "Tier," I sputter and cough again.

"Am I OK?"

"You're OK. Just relax." He pushes me back lies down next to me. "Just relax for a little longer, then we can talk about yer scorecard." His smile is gone but his attention makes me feel a little better.

"Are you OK?"

"Didn't I just tell ya to relax?"

"I can't help it, I need to know."

"We're both OK. Trust me, all right?"

I want to believe him, but I don't. He must see this in my expression because he looks into my eyes, and the glimmer soothes and calms me as he begins to talk in a soft, sad, voice.

"You'll never miss them, Junco. I promise ya, you'll never even know they're gone."

And I try to say, I do trust you, Tier, but the weary darkness creeps in and overtakes all my conscious thoughts.

Chapter Eleven

I sleep until I wake, and I have no idea what day or time it is, or how long I've been tucked away in this cave, but I have an urgent need to crawl out and become one of the living again.

I wait to hear Tier's admonishing voice, but then realize I am alone. Just getting uncovered from the blankets wipes out most of my energy, but I force myself to sit up and look around. I spy some water bottles near the bank of comm devices Tier has displayed on a makeshift shelf.

I pad over there in my socks and gulp a full bottle down in seconds, then reach for another. When I've had my fill I look down at my bandages and almost retch it back up. The skin wrap is high-quality and stretched tight over my hand and between my fingers so I can see the outline of what's left. Most of my pinky and ring fingers on my left hand are just gone. I wonder if the nightdog ate them or left them on the floor of the cave.

The devices on the shelf suddenly come alive with light and then I hear words in a language I don't understand fill the cavern. "Tier," I call, just in case he's nearby, but get no response. I stand up on my tiptoes to get a better look at the comms. They are little rectangle cards with smooth data displays. They show a map, much like the one I saw on that first day with Tier, and I wonder if they are trackers. Does the little beeping sound mean they've found us? I recall Tier's words a few days ago, that these people who were tracking him weren't his people. I pick one up and watch the little blinking light and listen to the foreign language. To my surprise, I can pick out a few intelligible words.

Then the talking stops and the device in my hand goes quiet, just as another one blinks and beeps, then settles back to sleep. Getting woozy standing there, I grab them all and take them over to the sleeping bag and drop them into the soft tumble of blankets. I look at them, one by one, but now they are all silent and the blinking has stopped. The one that was speaking is definitely alien tech, because I don't recognize the language. I pick that one up and tap it in various places on the screen, but it doesn't respond.

There are about five others that appear to be Mountain Republic standard issue. He must have taken these off soldiers that he killed over the past few days. This brings up ugly memories that I wish I could forget. It's difficult to merge the two versions of Tier: one as alien out to kill everybody and the other as the kind guy with wings who washes my hair and tells me stories.

All of the MR devices have a transparent "out of range" warning splashed across their screens except one. And this one does look like a tracker. I don't dare touch it, in case it activates our location. I stop cold when I realize that I just grouped Tier and me into us and the MR soldiers into them.

If Aren had still been alive would I still feel this way?

I don't have time to answer because Tier swoops into the cavern and lands next to the sleeping bag. His eyes are wild as he sees me holding the MR tech. "What did ya do?" he demands.

"Nothing, here," I say as I hand it over.

"Did ya touch it?"

I shake my head.

"Tell me exactly what happened."

"It flashed and beeped. That's it." I wait for his eyes to say he believes me, but I'm a little put back when I don't find the trust. "That one," I say, pointing to the avian device, "was talking."

He plucks it off the blanket and looks at it in earnest. "Tell me what it said, Junco."

I'm almost ready to tell him I don't know, but I realize that I do. "It gave positioning coordinates for a pick-up window. I didn't catch it all, that's all I know."

"Was it in English then?" he asks, even though we both know damn well it was not in English.

I shake my head.

"Then how do ya know what it said?"

I shrug. "I have no idea," I say as a long heavy sigh erupts. But he smiles, apparently happy about this development.

"You know because it's imprinted inside of ya. The language and culture of the avians. Just being around us draws it out."

"Is that good?"

"Better than the alternative."

I'm afraid to ask, but I do anyway. "What's the alternative?"

He doesn't answer, just stoops over to pick up the comms and carries them back to where they should have been on the wall.

"Did ya try and read the letter, then?"

I'm about to say what letter when I spy the crumpled piece of paper I tossed aside before leaving the tunnel. I look up at Tier, but he's no longer interested in our conversation, so I crawl off the sleeping bag and reach out for the ball of paper with my good hand, and begin to peel it open and smooth it out.

The writing is thick and decorative. I'm not sure if all their writing is this way, or Tier just has stunning penmanship, but I am impressed by how beautiful it looks to my amateur eye. I study each line, willing myself to understand, but I get all the way to the end of the full page document before anything clicks. It's my name, but not in English, so that's some progress. I stare at the lines that spell out Junco and I am in love with how it looks on paper. And written by Tier.

"Translate it to me, please!"

"That would defeat the purpose of the letter, Junco," he answers under his breath.

"What's that supposed to mean?" But he ignores me and goes back to inputting something into one of the devices.

I take another look at the writing and find that Tier's name also stands out to me as intelligible in the markings at the end, like a signature. My mind goes directly to the absurd and I wonder if it could be a love letter. I blush at my thoughts and glance up to see if Tier is looking at me, but he's not even close to being interested.

No, it's probably not anything like that since he wrote it before all the hot springs stuff happened.

My mind swings to the polar opposite: what if it explains things I don't want to know? This strikes me as the more real possibility.

I smooth the letter out a little more, then fold it neatly into quarters and search out a pocket in my alien canvas pants, and slip it inside. That's when it hits me. "Shit! The papers." It comes out louder than I expected and Tier glances over with a quizzical look on his face.

"Everything OK?" he asks.

I'm not sure, really, so I hesitate. I never opened the envelope. I was just taking it to Dale. Old Ben Wassing pushed it into my hands as I was rushing out of the funeral that day I hit the deer. He mumbled something about the estate and Dale. Then winked at me like a dirty old man and said it was private.

Which to me translates to secret.

"Hello?" Tier asks. This time he's got a look on his face and is starting to get up.

"My horses," I finally blurt out, not wanting to share something I'm not quite sure about just now. "My horses are alone back at the farm."

"Should I care what this means?"

His attitude ticks me off and I'm not in the mood to talk anyway. "Forget it."

Instead of going back to his business, he comes over to me instead. "Yer papers and yer horses? I don't see the connection."

Apparently someone hears everything, regardless of how he answers you. "Nothing, just some documents my father left for Dale. I really was just driving them out to him that day, ya know."

He winces his disagreement. "And the horses?"

I shrug. "Our barn manager, Michael, quit several months ago, so no one's taking care of them because I picked up the slack."

Tier looks away then, and I am just about to turn as well when he says, "I don't mean to be harsh, Junco, but yer not going to need to worry about yer horses anymore."

His directness stuns me. "What's that supposed to mean?" I ask, irritated at how little my life means to him.

"There are no horses in space, darlin'."

The whole situation hits me then, and even though I knew his objective was to take me somewhere the idea of leaving Earth never even entered my mind. I am stunned silent. And then he walks back over to his tech devices as I stand up, furious. "You're going to take me off the planet?" Just uttering the words makes me feel absurd.

He stops and turns and the look on his face tells me everything I need to know, but the words that come out in his thick accent bite just the same. "Junco, I'm a soldier and I have a mission. So, yes. I will be ripping ya from yer little horse, yer flying acrobatic tricks, and yer quaint little Council. You can huff all ya want over there," he continues, "but the simple truth is that yer imaginary life as a Farm Family daughter who lives in Council 3 of the Rural Republic, in the United Republics of Earth—is now over. The sooner ya accept that, the easier it will all be from here on out."

"You don't even know if I'm one of you. I'm not avian and I'm not leaving Earth."

"Everything has a consequence, Junco. Just remember that."

I slump back down on the sleeping bag and turn away from him. He seems satisfied with the outcome of his sharp words because I hear his footsteps as they cross the cavern to where his previous business is waiting.

But if he thinks I will just fall into his clutches without a fight and leave my whole life behind, he will make the same mistake Cole did. Underestimate me at your own risk, birdman.

Chapter Twelve

Picture yourself standing on the edge of a dock...

I'm not fucking standing on that piece of shit dock!

In front of you is a mountain lake...

I'm in a cave—

... and behind you is a small cabin...

Not.

... pristine white curtains flowing in the breeze passing through the windows...

Going.

... Down below the water you can see the scales of brightly colored fish reflecting the sunlight...

Back.

My dreams are unsettled as I sleep away my anger. In this one I am a small child and we are somewhere far away, skiing in the mountains, but not our mountains, or even the mountains of the MR because we never ski there. I'm too little to know where exactly, but I sense the people are different. I am fixing a wrinkle in my sock that is making my ski boot uncomfortable and then the three of us head off to the lifts. The dream surges ahead, and we are back down at the bottom of the mountain, on the side of a road. My breath is labored and has the stench of vomit. I feel like I will pass out. My parents are arguing and all the air rushes out of my body as I fall to the ground. They both run over, and my father is still angry. My mother pushes him and lifts me up and slips me into a large silver car. She stays angry, and they continue to argue. We end up in a cabin and then the police come and my mother is taken away and I never see her again.

I wake to the sound of Tier's voice whispering across my cheek and I put the wall up immediately to stop the gentle charm. My eyes remain closed, my breathing deep, and my body motionless. If he suspects my ruse, he doesn't show it, and I let the words he spoke sink in.

More orders.

I am inclined to stay put, as he so eloquently phrased it, but not because he told me to. Leaving the safety and light of the cavern isn't even close to being on my agenda. Teaching myself to read avian and snooping around in his personal stuff, is.

I wait for a few minutes to see if he'll come back and check to see if I'm making trouble, but I'm anxious to start my task and I spill out of the sleeping bag and sit up. He's put a bowl of 'nutrition' next to me, but I swat it away and the spoon goes reeling, clanking across the rock floor.

I think I've figured out the secret to learning the avian language thanks to Tier's offhanded comment the day before. He said that the mere exposure to avian things triggers something inside me and creates a learning experience. Well, that's my interpretation of what he said anyway, and I'm basing my planned actions on it whether it's a hundred percent correct or not.

I make my way over to the shelf that houses the tech devices. They are all on screen-lock today. It doesn't matter, I have no interest in them. I'm looking for history that I know must surely be here if this has been his home for the past two years. I figure I can multi-task as I snoop; learn the avian language and figure out what the real situation is regarding my past, present, and future without having it filtered through him first.

There is nothing in any of the various stacks I sift through first that appears useful—only food, water, clothes, and medical supplies. This last bit stops me cold for a second and I wonder if I should check my missing fingers to see what they look like. My stomach protests at the thought and I skip the medical examination, I wouldn't want to undo all the avian bandages and try to figure out how to wrap it back up. Not when I already have the use of my left hand the way it is.

I leave that bundle of stuff and make my way over to some more weathered crates and immediately hit the motherlode with a reading device. As a kid this was one of the few tech items I could have—books and reading were always encouraged. I'm not sure of the model, it doesn't look like anything I had, but it's human so I know it can't be that difficult. I try the switch but it does nothing. Maybe it's got a biometric lock? My reading tech never had biometrics, but I have a pad on my bedroom doorknob, so I search the cover looking for a place where a fingerprint might fit, or maybe a retinal scanner. Unless it is very well hidden, I don't see a security precaution.

Maybe all it needs is a battery charge? I place it on the charge pad with all the other tech devices and continue my search as I wait.

The next crate has astromaps in it. Lots and lots of astromaps. Some of them are of Earth, and some not. Places I've never seen or heard of before. One is a ship schematic.

None of them are in English, and none of them have any markings that look remotely familiar. Not a circle around a planet or star, not a symbol, nothing. I put them aside as I continue my search, but after turning over several more crates, bundles, duffel bags, and backpacks I come to the conclusion that none of this shit is of any use to me. I don't know where he conducts all his business, but apparently it isn't here in this cave.

The reading device beeps and snaps me back to attention.

I retrieve it and then thumb the little pad that looks like it might be an on switch. It blinks to life.

"Welcome, Iliana. It has been 407 days since your last access. Would you like to update now?"

Hmmm. Would I? Why not? "Yeah, OK. Do the update."

"Updating—" it says in a pleasant voice. "Update complete. Would you like to open the most recent delivery?"

I'm really snooping now, but fuck it. "Sure." I watch the screen as the sphere is accessed and have a brief moment of panic. Fuck, what if they can track this device? I am about to turn it off when I see the lock icon in the upper left corner that flashes the word secure.

A letter written in the avian language opens.

"Translating—" the pleasant voice says once again.

That was easy.

"Would you like me to read the document, Iliana?"

I laugh. "Please do!"

"Date October 1, 2151 — all communications from this device will cease. End of message."

Well that sucks. "Are there any old messages?"

"All messages have been erased, Iliana. Would you like to see your bookshelf?"

"Yeah, sure." A table of contents flashes but it's all in avian. "Why is it in avian?"

Silence from the device.

"Can you translate this?"

"This is a graphical image and cannot be translated on the screen. Would you like me to read it to you in English?"

"Yeah, do that."

"*The Seven Siblings: Excerpts from Avian Mythology — Part One…*" The device highlights the images as it speaks and this allows me to follow along.

"Seven siblings of the aftermath
Seven wandering spirits are they
Seven siblings created by death
Seven spirits of universal sway
Six avian children of light
All are guilty of the fall
The seventh castaway in flight
Mixing blood perpetual
Making monsters that transcend
Until the seventh brings the end."

The device goes silent.

"That's it? That's the whole myth?"

"The selection is titled Excerpts, Iliana. It is not the complete myth."

"Oh. Well, what's it mean?"

"In avian mythology the Seven Siblings are punished for creating discord among the higher species of Earth. They are cast out to create genetic instability, thus shifting the gene pool towards mutation. When their punishment is over they will come back to Earth and be reborn so that the Seventh Sibling can choose which of the higher species will live."

"Will live? Why can't both of them live?"

"The prophecy says the Seventh is a mixture of both species and must choose. And the avian will be destroyed."

"That sucks. Why would they even bother reading this stupid story?"

The device doesn't have an answer for that. It must not be sentient.

I look over the myth again and find I can read some of it myself. I repeat this several times and then fish Tier's letter out of my pants and unfold it slowly. To my surprise my heart is thumping with the thought of knowing what he wrote.

It doesn't make sense at first, at least not all of it. But my mind knows. It's weird.

Is this what it's like to have programmed learning?

I shake my head. Stupid father. I never got to learn shit this quick, I had to study like an idiot.

I focus back to the letter and my brow bunches up in frustration as I put the words together. But it's not anything I want to hear. I turn back to the myth and the acid in my stomach makes me nauseas as I take in my new information.

What do I really know about this avian, anyway? Beyond the fact that he has no aversion to murder? Nothing. That's what. I know nothing about him. My entire body is suddenly hot. Why didn't I leave last night?

Jasus, Junco! You fell for the oldest fucking trick in existence. A man!

"No, fuck—calm down. I don't fall for anyone, let alone an alien."

Shit, what the fuck am I doing here? Am I in some sort of trance? Are all those healing chemicals screwing with me?

"Goddamn it—there's no problem here. I'm on top of it."

I get up and pace the floor, wondering if I should chance it in the tunnel and leave now before he comes back. I give it some serious thought, but then I look down at my hand, at my missing fingers. They don't hurt, which is just more evidence that there are drug-like factors running through my bloodstream, dulling my senses. But even more powerful than that observation is the reality of the nightdogs. I physically shudder just thinking about them and I have real doubts that I can make that walk back outside knowing this is a breeding nest. There are a few iffy spots that would have me in a panic and I don't even have my knife. It was left back in the tunnel where we were attacked.

I hear footsteps in the tunnel and know he's on his way back. *So much for taking action, Junco.* I pick up the reading device and the letter in my good hand and wait for the confrontation.

He slips into the bright light of the cavern and walks quickly over to the tech devices and supplies to rummage around, paying no attention to me at all.

So I wait.

"Can I help ya, Junco?" he asks, but does not turn or stop looking through the supplies.

"I—" I begin, but the words get lost before they come out of my mouth.

Apparently finding what he is looking for, he turns, "Ya what?" His eyes dart down to my good hand and they lock there, briefly studying the reading tech and the letter, then lift upward to meet my own gaze. "Well?" he says walking briskly towards me, the top of his wings a little higher up behind his back than they usually are. "What's on yer mind?"

I look down, switch the letter to my injured hand, and then hold each one up as he approaches me, but the words are still stuck. He looks at both, then finds my eyes once more. "Don't believe everything you read, eh?"

My whole face squints up at him in annoyance. "What does that mean?" He ignores me and instead grabs my jacket and shirt and pulls so that they slip down to reveal the bare skin of my shoulder. "What are you doing?"

When his eyes find mine, I step back a little in fear. He grabs my shoulder tightly and pulls me toward him, so close that when I tip my face up to question him, his mouth is only a few inches away. "What the hell are you doing, Tier?"

His eyes glow briefly and I am transfixed for the second it takes for him to extend his razors, slash open my upper arm, and tear into my skin. The hot blood begins to seep out before I can even understand what's happening, and by then he's already plucked out a small flexible mesh of metal. He shakes me—hard. "What is this, Junco?"

I twist and jerk until I rip myself free from his grip and my anger grows as the blood travels along the length of my arm and drips slowly out of my jacket sleeve and onto the floor. "My health tracker, you asshole!"

"A health tracker? You do realize what Republic ya live in, correct? Ya remember, the one that shuns technology?"

"We don't shun technology, you idiot! We use it when it's necessary, and when a baby is sick and requires monitoring, we monitor them. I was very sick as a child so I have a health tracker, so fucking what?"

He flicks the small piece of tech across the room, grabs me by the arm, and pulls my shirt and jacket down once more. "Get off me." I wiggle and push him back. His grip is firm and I hear my shirt rip as he forces it down to reveal my torn skin. Then he slaps a membrane over the wound and releases me with a little push.

"We're leaving right now. If there is something ya want to take with ya," he says, eyeing the letter and the reading tech, "get it now."

He turns back to his supplies and continues to pull things out of storage and shove them in the sack.

"No," I say weakly from my motionless position in the center of the room.

He turns. "No, what?"

"I'm not going with you, Tier. Whatever's coming down that tunnel that's got you freaked out, I'm not going."

He turns back to his task and ignores me.

"I'm not going, Tier. I mean it. I want to go home now."

I watch him finish packing the small sack and seal it up. And then he walks calmly toward me and the anger in his eyes escapes as light. "Yer coming, OK. I'm not asking ya. I'm telling ya."

He grabs me by the jacket once again and pulls me with him towards the tunnel I've yet to travel through. I drop my letter and reading tech as I pull away. He lets go and trains his eyes on mine. "That health tracker, Junco? It was tracking something all right, but not yer health. It was tracking you. All these years. Everything ya did. Every. Single. Thing. And ya know what we call that, in the avian world, Junco?"

I shake my head, still locking eyes with his.

"Spying. Now, let me explain to ya exactly why we're leaving, and I do mean we. Yer precious government, who by the way, has never used this tracking on any other member of the RR, sick or not, is in collusion with the Mountain Republic and every other god-forsaken pseudo-government on this continent."

My heart skips a beat, then balances out with a series of short staccato thumps that force me to take a deep breath to calm myself.

"They were coming for ya, Junco, and only yer little impulsive flicker of teenage rebellion, and my timely appearance, has saved ya from a life of poking and prodding so they can figure out just exactly how to use ya to further their agenda."

I bring my hands up to my head and close my eyes. "Tier, I don't know what you're fucking talking—"

"And another thing, that filthy little mouth ya have is really starting to piss me off."

The last few words come out as a growl and I slink back a micro-step before pushing it down.

"Ya seem to think your Republic is just and good, that ya rural people are somehow better than the rest of them, more moral with all yer rules and traditions, a little higher, a little mightier. But yer vile mouth is all the proof I need that yer just another pathetic human pretender who follows the rules when it suits ya, and disregards them when it doesn't. Have a little self-respect, Junco. If ya believe in the founding principles of the RR, at least have the self-respect to follow the rules yer parents taught ya!"

I pick up the letter and shove it into his chest and let it go. "You'd know all about following rules, wouldn't you?"

He glares down at me. "Don't even pretend like ya know me, Junco." His eyes are not kidding and his face screams back off. "You have no idea who I am beyond being a soldier, a soldier who is trying to do the right thing. So, don't look at me like I'm something I'm not."

My anger bleeds out of me. "So what I think is the right thing doesn't matter? You're just allowed to come in here and totally fuck up my life?"

"Jasus Christ, Junco. Ya fucked yer life up plenty good without my help. Get a grip, will ya! It's over!" He reaches out and thunks a finger against my head. "Think!"

What's over? I drop my guard for a moment and turn when I hear noise coming from the tunnel.

"They're here now, and we're leaving." He grabs the letter and the reading device and quickly stashes them inside the small pack and reseals it. Then he takes my hand and pulls me with him into the hazy light of the tunnel.

And we flee.

Chapter Thirteen

My thoughts of standing my ground disappear with the light and the only thing on my mind now is the darkness. And the nightdogs.

I flick my missing fingers absently as we move, and I realize, even after everything that's happened over the past few days, I'm more terrified of those animals than I am of anything else right now. Every step into the black we take makes my panic grow and I know that it will overtake me soon. I will be helpless.

In my mind I hear the snapping of my flesh and feel the cool air as the vicious animal rips off pieces of my body. I hear whimpering and it takes me a minute to realize that I'm actually crying.

Tier stops abruptly and I think it is because the dogs are up ahead. A sob escapes my mouth and the tears stream down my face. He jerks my arm and his angry whisper briefly snaps me out of it. "Shut up, Junco!"

I do. I hold it in and wait for him to pull me along again. I can hear more noise behind us now. The soldiers have found our cavern. They will follow, probably send a team into each of the two possible escape routes, and they'll use lanterns of course. The jerky light attracts the nightdogs and will bring them out in force.

This makes me hyperventilate, and Tier stops again. "What the hell is the matter with ya?"

"The dogs, Tier! They're gonna use lights to find us and the dogs will come!"

He pressed his hand over my mouth to stop the words, but his glowing eyes soften as they search my face in the dark. "I know where the dogs are, don't worry. They're not here, OK?" I just look at his eyes, but say nothing as I try to decide if this makes it better.

He removes his hand. "OK?" he asks again. I nod, and he must be able to see me because he turns and begins to pull again.

We don't travel on the main tunnel, but take a series of side passages and when I realize I would never be able to find my own way out if something happened to Tier, the panic sets in again. He catches it before I get out of hand, and pulls me close and whispers, "Yer OK."

Our pace slows after that and I don't hear any more noises from behind. Unless they have this place mapped somehow, I don't see how they will ever find us. It feels like we've been wandering forever, twisting through small passages and crawling through low tunnels until I am helplessly turned around—I don't even know which way is up. "We're lost." The words come out before I realize I'm talking and Tier stops.

"We're not lost, Junco. Just relax, will ya?"

We begin a long descent and I slip and fall so many times my hands begin to bleed from reaching out in the dark, only to find the things I'm clasping onto are sharper than the rocks below my feet. We finally end up in a place where I can hear water dripping close by.

Tier cracks a lightstick and the room is immediately illuminated with the glowing green light that reminds me of his eyes.

I search the cavern frantically, looking for any signs of the nightdogs. He catches my panic and pulls me into his wings. "It's OK. No dogs, all right?"

I nod as I press my face into his coat, but I don't trust myself to say anything. I stay there. And he lets me.

"What did ya think of the myth you read?" he asks out of nowhere.

"The Seven Siblings? How did you know I read—"

"You updated the reader, Junco. I get updates too."

"Oh. Is it fake or is it true?"

I feel a shrug. "It's a myth."

"Is it a common myth," I ask, "with the avian?"

"A bedtime story," he replies, "recited to every young clutch many times as they grow."

"Is that how you raise your young? In a clutch?"

He doesn't answer right away, and I'm just about ready to think he's gonna dodge the question when he takes a breath and begins. "It's complicated, really. We don't come from eggs, maybe you didn't know that, but we're not birds. And we don't have our young naturally, because we're—"

His sentence drops off and I wait for him to find the words.

"We're not able to have them." The explanation sounds truncated, but I really don't care about the reproductive habits of avians right now. I only want to get the fuck out of this dark cave.

When he continues I'm a little surprised.

"You know sometimes there's little grains of truth to a myth? Like the places the Greeks built and where they say the gods and goddesses appeared and did all those things?"

I nod.

"Well, there is some truth to the myth."

I step back from him as the fear leaves as quickly as it came and I look up and see his face. "Which part?"

He smiles at me, and I wonder if this was all a plot to get my mind off the dogs. "We're an engineered race, Junco. We don't reproduce naturally because, well, it can't happen that way. It's all very sterile and nothing like the families ya have here on Earth."

"Oh," I say. "That's kinda sad. I loved my family."

"Did ya, now?" he says in a low voice.

"Yes. They gave me everything and loved me back. And kept me safe, and healed me when I was sick, and trained me to take care of myself. And I really miss them." I feel my face heat up and my throat aches with the pain of my recent loss. The tears well in my eyes, but I force them to stay put, not willing to descend back into that moat right now.

"They did a wonderful job, darlin'. A truly wonderful job." He hugs me tighter and we stay that way for a while, even after it becomes weird. "There's a little more to it, Junco. Just know that I wouldn't tell ya right now if it wasn't necessary. It's necessary, OK? That ya know."

I look up at him and wait for it.

"Those Seven Siblings from that myth ya read? They're here on Earth. Right now. And I'm beginning to think you're one of them."

I halfheartedly snort out a breath. "That's stupid. You guys are all gonna feel so dumb when you figure out I'm just another human and this shit has nothing to do with me. I'm not an avian or a sibling of anyone. I'm just Junco and that's it."

"OK, well — you can believe me or not. It doesn't matter. I'm taking you with me and we'll sort that part out afterward."

I let out a small exhale and push that last statement away for later. "How are we gonna get out of the cave?"

He tilts my chin up so I'm looking at him. "I'm very glad that yer parents did such a wonderful job raising ya. And yer highly trained, Junco, to handle stressful situations. Whether ya—" he stops for a second—"whether ya realize it or not. So I'm gonna ask ya to do something now. And ya need to trust me so we can get the hell out of here and see the stars again."

"I don't think I can do it, Tier," I say matter-of-factly as I look away.

He laughs. "But ya don't even know what it is I'm asking!"

"It doesn't matter. I recognize the speech. If you need to talk me up with shit like that before telling me, then I know I'm not gonna like it."

He brings my attention back to his eyes. They aren't glowing since the lightstick is the same color, but they are serious. "It is, Junco. I won't lie to ya. It's bad. But if you trust me, I promise that you will be fine."

I shake my head and the tears I was holding back spill silently down my cheeks. "No, I can't do it anymore. I'm done."

"Aye. But you weren't done earlier in the cavern when you told me off, were ya?"

I stay quiet and make the tears stop. I wouldn't exactly call *that* one of my stellar moments of bravery, but I let it slide.

"We don't have a choice, Junco. There are only two ways out at this point. Go back, which we know we cannot do. Or go through there."

I follow his arm and he lifts it to point to a shimmering spot of light across the small room. For a moment I don't recognize it for what it is. And then it hits me and I shake my head and blurt the words out. "No! No, no, no! I can't even swim, I swear I can't swim!"

He just laughs at me. "Of course ya can swim, Junco. Do ya take me for a fool? Ya have a pool in yer house!"

I sniffle and look up at him. "Look, if you know so much about me, then you know I only swim in that pool when they make me and it's not even close to being fun."

Shut that shit off, Junco. Now.

"Did ya hear me ask for your trust, eh?" When I don't answer he asks again. "Did ya?"

I nod.

"Either you trust me, Junco, or you will die. OK?"

I shake my head this time and look down. "I can't. That's too much, we have to find another way. We'll wait here until they go away and then we'll leave the way we came."

"No, Junco. That's never going to happen. We have about thirty minutes before they find this cavern and then they'll kill me and take you to a place you really don't want to go."

"That's not possible, they will never find this place, not after all those twists and turns we made."

"Junco, they have scenthounds. It's only a matter of time. Thirty minutes might even be pushing it."

And the sounds I've been absently logging for the better part of our trip manifest in my forward consciousness. I can hear them. The hounds. Not the screaming of the nightdogs, but the distant baying of a dog on track. And he's right. They are not that far off.

"It's time now. I have two things to tell you before we do this." He takes my hand and we walk towards the water together. He lights a stick and throws it down into the water so I can see the bottom of the pool. The water is amazingly clear and lights up beautifully. I feel myself relax a little.

"What are they? The two things?" I ask, turning back to him.

"When I tell ya, take the deepest breath you can, deeper than any breath you've ever taken before. You won't have to swim, I'll do all the swimmin' for both of us. Just keep hold of my hand, OK?"

I take a practice breath, and nod.

He removes my jacket and takes his off as well, tying the little sealed bag of stuff from the cavern to a loop on his pants. He kicks off his boots and I do the same, then he ties them to another loop. I'm going to be cold on the other side, but that's better than being drowned from heavy clothing. I stand there in my bare feet and torn shirt with the gaping sides and look up to him, already shivering with cold, or maybe fear. "What's the second thing?"

He pulls me into the cold water with him and my teeth immediately start to chatter. Then looks me straight in the eyes and I think he's going to tell me not to panic or act stupid once we're under the water. But he softens. "I need you to trust me, Junco. Can you do that?"

He pulls me close and takes my face in his hands. They are rough and calloused, but his touch is tender. My eyes are fixated on him and I almost get lost in the green. He leans down towards my lips and I feel his breath tickle my cheek and slide across to my ear. I know what he's doing but I'm in bliss and instead of putting up the wall, I imagine a flood of water sweeping up their tenderness and rushing them through raging rapids to my brain. I feel the slightest tingle against my lips and I moan. Then his mouth covers mine and I feel a rush of warmth flood through my entire body as he presses against me, his breath heavy. The kiss melts me into his arms and I whisper, "I can do that."

We hear the baying of the scenthounds as we pull apart and he tugs me further into the pool of water. "I won't be dropping any more lightsticks. If I do they'll just get through the passage all that much quicker."

I hesitate at this revelation. "Oh, come on. You're just doing this on purpose now." I shake my head at him in the dim light. "Those things are probably in there, Tier."

He laughs. "Things? Help me out here, Junco."

"Those cave river things they found a few years ago over by Ramah. They dragged a kid off when he was playing—"

"Oh, for fuck's sake, Junco. Yer afraid of fish now too? Nightdogs, prairie lions, fish—anything else I should know about?"

"Ya know what? Fuck you. I've been *chased* by prairie lions. Regularly, in fact, all growing up. Have *you* ever outrun a raging lion?"

He sighs. "Junco, on the other side we will be at the bottom of a very deep cavern with an exit straight up through the top. I'll have to fly us both out and with your extra weight it will be very difficult to make that ascent. If I leave the lightsticks as a trail, they'll catch us."

"But they can't fly, they won't be able to get past the water with anything that will help them catch us."

"They can fly, at least one of them can, anyway. And they most certainly can catch us. No lights."

I nod at that unexpected revelation. The dogs are definitely closer now.

"We have to go. On three, take that deep breath, OK? And whatever you do, don't let go of my hand."

I swallow hard, and nod. "OK."

"One. Two. Three!"

I take the deepest breath I can and go under with Tier, but something goes wrong and I sputter out half of it in a choke of bubbles. I'm just about to bob back up and take another one when I am tugged away from the surface. I let him take me and we swim down towards the lightstick. I am hoping that he will pick it up and take it with us so I can see, but he stops before we get to the bottom and slips sideways into a passageway, pulling me along with him. I scrape and bump against the hard, sharp sides and cuts open up on my bare arms. I feel strong currents of water flow past me and I realize he's using his wings to swim.

The passageway gets narrower and the darkness is absolute as we move along and my frantic heartbeat begins to increase. Soon the fast current from his wings is still and we are moving very slowly, like he is clawing his way along the rock. My chest begins to constrict with the pressure that comes from being underwater and my head throbs from holding my breath. An almost undeniable urge to puff out all the carbon dioxide building up in my bloodstream takes over my thoughts, poisoning my body from the inside out. But I push the instinct down and concentrate on keeping hold of his hand.

I feel a small tingle on my back where his avian shirt is open to the water and try to ignore it, but the tingle turns into a burn and I realize something is biting me. I push it down because I can see a small glimmer of light up ahead and I concentrate on not puffing out my cheeks and releasing the foul air that is the only thing preventing me from taking a big breath of water into my lungs.

Suddenly I am jerked backwards by my pant leg and I lose my grip on Tier's hand. The light begins to fade and I let out all my bubbles in a silent underwater scream. Water rushes into my mouth and I try against hope to prevent the inevitable inhalation of water that I know is coming. I kick at my attacker and feel it let go, then grab onto the rocks on the side of the narrow passage and begin pulling myself faster and faster back towards the light, back towards Tier, and back towards the world outside.

My lungs ache with pain and now that the expired air is no longer taking up room inside my body I struggle against the instinct to draw in the water. I see the light ahead, getting brighter and brighter, and I tell myself I am going to make it when my mouth opens and desperately draws in a false breath. The water floods my lungs and I stop swimming in shock, gasping as I choke. The world gets fuzzy and green.

Then Tier's face is in front of me and he takes my hand and pulls. I float along helplessly, knowing that I am dying and there is nothing I can do about it. Moments later, the circle of light that beckons me to safety grows larger and larger until finally I surge out of the water, gasping for air.

And that's when the nightdog attacks us.

Chapter Fourteen

The massive nightdog grabs hold of Tier's wing and they struggle. My heart beats against my chest and I try to scream, but no air will come out, only water bubbling up through my windpipe causing me to choke and go below the surface once more. My hands flail around, searching blindly for the edge of the pool, as I fight my way back up into the air that must enter into my body soon, or I know I will die. I struggle until I reach out and feel a rock, then pull myself up and over the barrier of water.

I am on the far side of the pool, and I cling there choking and coughing until Tier's strong hands grab me and pull me out, lying me on my side so I can retch up the water from my lungs.

After a few seconds I try to talk. "Where—where is the night—" I cough and sputter and can't finish my sentence.

Tier removes a heat blanket from the sealed pack and covers me and then shoves my boots on my feet but keeps his tied to the loop on his pants. "Dead, darlin'. Nothing to worry about."

"Th-th-th-there might be m-m-m-more," I manage to say through chattering teeth.

"Shhhh, no. There's only this bitch here. And she's dead. She's dead."

I stay there, shivering from both cold and adrenaline, until my eyes wander down to the floor behind him. "Y-y-y-you're bl-bl-bleeding, T-Tier!"

"Just a cut, Junco. Are you ready for the last leg of our great escape?" he asks.

I nod.

He hovers, giant smoky black wings flapping, and I can see that the bite from the bitch has affected his flight, but he squints down the pain and his talons reach out and grab me by the waist. I gasp as one pierces my skin, and then he swings me up and stabilizes my upper body with his arms, all the while his wings frantically beating to lift us both straight up towards freedom..

It's nothing like the quick flights we've taken together before and I begin to panic as I see bubbles on the surface of the water below us.

"They're coming, Tier!" I shout over the deafening sound of his powerful wing thrusts, then whisper to myself, "Holy shit, they're coming!"

The lightstick Tier used to pull me from the pool is still lying on the floor next to the dead nightdog and I can see everything. The surface becomes turbulent and I hold my breath, waiting for what will emerge. We are almost halfway now, but our progress is slow.

My eyes strain to see the water below, and then the thing breaks the surface. I gasp. "Tier," I whisper, but I know he can't hear me over his own labored breathing and thunderous undulation of his tertiary limbs. "Tier, it's..." But the words have a hard time forming because it can't be true. "It's an avian."

He doesn't answer me, so I scream it. "Did you hear me?"

Tier ignores me again, but the thing below me doesn't. "I hear you!"

Faster, I pray. Faster! But Tier's wings are starting to beat slower, and our progress creeps along. I panic for a second when it occurs to me that we might not even make it to the top, not because of the thing below, but because Tier simply won't be able to get us over the ridge of the cavern and out into the air where we can catch the wind.

"We're gonna make it, Junco, don't look down," he says as if reading my thoughts. I want to close my eyes, but they strain to see the avian in the dim green of the lightstick below. He is huge, even from this distance, and his eyes glow red, instead of green.

"Junco!" Tier screams. "Don't look at him!" I close my eyes and pray to God that we can make it out. I don't hear any wings flapping below, and we are almost to the top when I start to hope that everything will be OK. And then I feel the new current as the giant wings of the alien below force the air to part as he makes his rapid ascent.

"Holy shit, he's coming! HE'S COMING!"

I look up and the opening is right there, but our movement is like slow motion through mud, while the thing shooting up towards us is fast and quick.

We breach the rim of the underground canyon and immediately pick up the wind, allowing us to be swooped up and out over a cliff towards the vast grassland.

I turn to look around and the thing grabs me right out of Tier's arms, fumbles as Tier corrects his flight path, and then I am falling.

The ground rushes up to meet me so fast that I gasp for air, and then I am yanked from death by a pair of sharp talons around my waist. My body feels like it will snap in two as I am carried back up to the cliff where the cavern entrance is.

And then I realize who has me and I begin to scream.

"Let me go!" I swing my legs around and try to throw him off balance, but he's strong and his grip is true. Tier comes up beside him and knocks him sideways and he drops me. I fall about ten feet to the ground, roll a few times and come to a stop with my head hanging over the side of the cliff.

I scamper away in a panic as the stranger lands next to me. I turn over and lie there looking up at him.

He smiles. "Well, that was something, wasn't it?" His accent isn't avian, it's local, and his eyes aren't red, they're orange.

Tier lands in front of me, blocking my view of this new creature in a way that I find a little possessive. "Back off, Moju," he snarls.

He has a name.

Moju smiles again and steps forward. "Go fuck your-self, Tier. I'm here to talk to her."

I squint at him as I pull myself together and get up off the ground, my wet clothes covered in dirt and dry grass. "Shit," I say in my most nonchalant voice, "you don't have to throw me off a cliff to get a word in, ya know. Obviously you two know each other, so just spit it out and let's get the hell off this mountain."

"Junco," Tier snaps at me. "Go wait over there." He points to a place several yards away, as if I am a dog to order around.

"He said," I snap back, "he wanted to talk to me. So why don't you go wait over there." I motion to the same place with my head and he hands me a look that almost makes me want to pee myself.

But I don't, I suck it back in and look past him. To the new guy. "What do you want?"

This time his smile reveals dimples and his eyes twinkle. Literally twinkle. Somehow he makes it charming instead of creepy and I can't help myself, so I smile back. It's real too. And that takes me by surprise. "Who are you?"

He glares over to Tier, who shrugs like they're sharing some private mental conversation. Moju redirects his attention back to me.

"How much has he told you about the Seven Siblings?" he asks.

“I read a poem or myth about them, that's it, really." I look sideways at Tier and he's frowning. Then back towards the new guy to see where this is going. "You want to contribute to my severely lacking body of knowledge, or you wanna just stand there glaring at Tier?"

Apparently that's funny, or cute, or whatever, because he laughs. "I'm one of the Seven Siblings, and you are too, from what that asshole over there says. So there you have it, Junco. It is what it is."

I shrug. "So what if I am. What's it to you? Aren't you working for the MR? Sent to capture us?"

"Yeah. So? They should know me better by now. Like I'm gonna bring them back my sister. What a bunch of dumbasses."

The word hangs in the air between us. Sister.

Apparently Tier has heard enough because he steps be-tween us again. "Get to the point, Moju. Or I'll knock your ass off the cliff and you'll never get another chance."

Moju steps forward and they chest-bump themselves into a standoff. They are a lot alike from my perspective. Both about the same height, although Moju might be an inch or so taller. Tier is a bit thicker in the chest and shoulders, but that's probably because he's a few years older than us.

Us.

That takes me back a minute. It's a lot harder than it seems to get this simple characterization to line up with my current situation. Who is us and who is them? Why is it so hard to figure that out?

Both avians have black hair, Tier's is longer than Moju's, and more wavy. Moju has a more traditional military crop. And they both have a crapload of scars criss-crossing the exposed portions of their bodies.

I let out a deep sigh at their time-wasting bullshit and look up into the sky for my friends as they do the whisper fight between clenched teeth. It's a dark night, the moon must be coming up near new, and the clearness of the Milky Way astonishes me as I tilt my head upward. I make a slow spin and find each of the circumpolar landmarks: Big Dipper, Little Dipper, Polaris, Cassiopeia, and Perseus. My spin is complete when I notice the silence. They are both staring at me.

"What the hell are you two looking at?"

Tier frowns again, but Moju smiles and spills it all out. "I know where Dale is hiding, Junco. That rat-bastard, sonofabitch got away. He wasn't at the Stag camp when Tier blew it up. If it's answers you want, he's the guy that's got them. You wanna come with me to get some answers?"

Tier is growling but I just shrug, like this is the most natural thing in the world. "Sure."

He turns his back to me. "Hop on."

So I do.

Tier is still frowning as we leap off the cliff and my screams are pushed back down my throat by the impaling wind.

I hug Moju's shoulders as he sweeps me across the plains, but then, carefully, move my grip from around his neck to around his chest. His right hand reaches out and fans across the top of the dry wild wheat as we pass over. I let go of one of my hands and try to mimic his motion, but I can't quite reach. Then his body lowers, practically into the grass, and suddenly I feel them flicking against my fingertips as we move. I laugh and I can feel through his chest that he is laughing too. Probably at how easy I am to entertain.

I glance over to my left and see that Tier's annoying frown has become his default expression. I want to scowl at him for killing my happy buzz, but I smile and lift my disfigured hand into a quick wave instead. He shakes his head at me and does a quick salute with two of his fingers and smiles back.

The wind is cold as it passes over my wet clothes, but just as it was flying underneath Tier, the heat from Moju's body radiates outward and warms me.

Flying on top is far better than being clutched in the grip of razor-sharp talons, and not only for the obvious reasons. For one, I can see everything. I lay my cheek down on Moju's back and take in the southern view of rolling hills, then switch over and look north, past Tier's body, to see flatlands, which if followed long enough will lead you right into the Bread Basket.

Second, I can relax in knowing that I won't be dropped or slip through his talons. If there is one thing I excel at, it's balancing on the back of something moving very fast. I al-most feel lazy for not standing up for a few quick flips as we move through the air.

And best of all, it feels like I'm really flying and not just a passenger. If I am an avian then that means I will, at some point I suppose, have wings. I feel my heart beat a little faster as I think about what it would be like to be so in control and free from the confines of human transportation.

Wings and flying. These are the only slightly positive things that might come out of this crazy trip.

I lean down so that my lips are close to Moju's ear. "Don't freak out, I'm gonna flip over!"

He shoots me a thumbs-up, but when I look over at Tier, his scowl is back. I hold up one finger to him, the universal give-me-a-minute signal, then flip my body over so that I'm lying on my back. Tier is instantly next to me, holding on to my arm, and I look over and laugh at the look on his face. Moju lets out a roar that makes my heart skip, and then I look up.

It is amazing. The stars flying by from the back of a bird. Only God knows what this feels like. Well, God and me. As if reading my mind Tier flips himself over too, his powerful wings let him soar into the wind with little difficulty, even when upside down, and then we are flying together. Time stops for me and all I can see is us. He flips back to maintain his thrust and resumes his position off to Moju's left side.

I find my favorite constellations once more and then flip back over to press my cheek into Moju's back and slip my hands under his wings and feel his powerful muscles. There are two distinct sets, those which power the wings and those which power the arms, and from this vantage point I can almost see them working together in my mind. He is extraordinary, capable, commanding, and mighty and I instantly love him, whether he turns out to be my brother or not.

We fly this way for a little while and then I feel Moju's body drop into a more vertical position so he can land. I gauge the distance to the ground, match it to his slowing speed, and jump off—rolling forward into the grass and then popping back up to fling my arms in the air like I'm waiting for the dismount applause.

The guys land next to me and Tier is clapping. They are both smiling and this makes my heart happy for some reason.

"Gah! You didn't have to jump off, Juncs!" Moju is beaming down at me. His face has a bit of a wind burn to it, but I can feel the energy pent up inside him. Carrying me for a few dozen miles has not even begun to tap his reserves.

I shrug. "I'm a show-off."

He grabs me and pulls me in so he can rough me up a little and I feel it. I feel the connection. It swells within me and I hold on to it, like something precious.

Tier breaks the spell. "So, where the hell is Dale? He's hiding in the woods?"

We are on the edge of a clearing where the long grass tapers in to meet a pine forest that rolls up into a steep cliff. There is an old house on top with a crazy slanted roof and I know where we are.

"He's up there?" I ask, pointing up to the house.

Tier screws up his face. "He's not up there. That place has been abandoned for a hundred years."

He's right. I know that because that old house is a fairly common party spot for RR cadets, but I'm not sure that he should know that. It makes him feel local.

"Nah," Moju says. "We're gonna spend the day here so we don't have to fuck with the security until after we rest. He's about three miles southeast still, Juncs. We can't just bust in there, he's not totally unprepared."

Tier lets out a long breath and I can see the argument coming. "If yer taking us to where I think yer taking us..."

Moju cuts him off. "Tier, will you shut the fuck up al-ready? You know exactly where we're going, so stop with the bullshit."

Tier just stares him down. "So we're gonna sleep where? Here?" he says, pointing to the ground. "You want Junco to sleep in the pine needles?"

I open my mouth to say something but Moju beats me to it. "She's a fucking field soldier, Tier. I'm sure she's slept outside before."

"Yeah," I nod, "I'm a soldier. I've slept outside billions of times."

Tier turns to look at me. "Are ya now? A soldier, I mean?" His look is far more serious than is warranted for this stupid conversation.

"Tier, you know—"

He puts a hand up and cuts Moju off. "Are ya sure about that, Junco?"

"Of course. I was on scrubs maneuvers all summer."

He smiles at me then, as if relieved. "Well, I guess we're sleeping on the ground then."

We truck up the north side of the hill to find a flat area that can still provide us cover from any aerial reconnaissance and lie down, Tier on one side of me and Moju on the other. Tier is not a big talker, but Moju is because he's asking me a million questions about my life. I answer each one patiently until Tier has had enough and growls for us to go to sleep like a couple of kids. We laugh at him and cover our mouths and generally act like children. Tier is lying flat out on his stomach, his hands tucked under his forehead like a pillow, looking at me. But when Moju pulls me into his wings for sleep, he turns his back and I feel shunned for being happy.

Chapter Fifteen

... and up above in the sky you see the eagles as they soar, free from terrestrial boundaries...

Finally, something that's actually true.

But I'm still not going back.

So get the fuck out of my dreams...

... because they are a restless garble of incoherent imagery that make no sense. I'm walking the streets of some dirty Old E-Bloc city one minute, then competing as an aerialist in the next. Twisting and turning in the air like a bird flying into the wind. My feet are bare except for the footwrap tape which binds along the ball and heel. The white powdery rosin makes them sticky as they search for the sweet spot that exists on the back of every horse at full gallop. There is no sound except for the tick-tick of a clock in the background. Even in my dream I realize this means time's a-wastin'. At first I'm frantic, but after a while the ticking fades into the background and finally, after what seems like an endless barrage of me slinking about in dark clothes, in even darker cities, it fades so far into the background that I can only hear it if I strain myself.

I come to the end of a dark tunnel and there is a man waiting for me there. I know who he is before he even turns around. Mr. trigger-happy commander from the motor pool. I absently wonder if he ever got the chance to shoot CP in the head, but then he speaks. This is the first sound in the whole dream besides the clock, so I lean in to pay attention. But all he squeaks out is one ominous statement. "It's all lies, Junco. Better come back to reality quick."

My eyes fly open and I reach over for Moju, but he's gone. Tier opens his wings so I can move. When I realize what just happened I'm angry. "You were in my dreams again, weren't you?" In the fading daylight I can see his face screw up as he gets ready to deny it, but I turn my back to him and push his wings off me to let the cool autumn air in.

He sighs. "Whatever happens in yer dreams, Junco, it has nothing ta do with me."

I let the anger from my dream fade away and we both stay silent for a few seconds. "Where did Moju go?"

"Top of the hill, ta find the landmark for the entrance."

"Entrance to what?" I feel like an over-sleeping mountain man, completely out of the loop after what should have been a short rest.

He props himself up on his elbow and turns me back to get my attention before answering. "The tunnel where Dale is hiding."

I lie there looking at him. His eyes are just plain green now, no glow. Nothing to make him look different. And his wings are drawn back tight against his back, the tips cupped over his shoulders. He almost looks like a human.

He studies me back and it makes me smile and blush.

"Can I ask ya something?"

I look up into his eyes as they search me for some elusive answer. "Go for it."

"How is it that ya know him for mere minutes and ya already have the look of complete trust in yer eyes?"

"Who? Moju?" I shrug. "I dunno. He just feels genuine."

"But me? I'm just lying about everything, right?"

A huff escapes my lips. "I never said that."

"Ya didn't have to. Ya tried to kill me."

He's got a point there. I feel a little reality panic coming on and begin to babble. "You came out of nowhere, Tier. I'd never even seen an avian in person before you. When he came up that tunnel I was already in the rabbit hole, ya know? I've just acclimated to strange stuff since that night on the hill. It's not that I don't trust you. Didn't I say I did before we went for that little swim back there in the caves?"

"Sure," he says, but I can tell he's not sure at all and the silence hangs. Besides, I roll back the memory and I know damn well I never actually said I trusted him. I said *I could do what he asked*. He probably remembers it correctly too.

"OK, you want to know the difference between you and Moju?" I ask. "As far as I can tell, he doesn't want anything from me. There, I said it. You want to take me to your leader, or *whatever*. Away from my home and my life. And I've got to tell ya, I'm not really interested in leaving my planet. Call me crazy, but I'm a little attached to it."

"How could you be? That's the part I don't understand."

I turn my head away. "Wow, you really are an alien. You have no clue at all." I turn back to see his expression, but it's blank. Nothing.

"What kind of childhood did you have anyway? Oh, yeah, I forgot... you guys don't have families. I guess that explains things. I may not know very much about Moju, but from what I can tell at least he understands love."

Tier sneers at me. "*Love*? You think that monster understands love? You mean like yer pal Aren? That traitor ya think is such a good guy? Shit, Junco, you really have some great intuition going there, a regular Mystic Martin. Do ya pick all yer friends this way? Hell, no wonder we're in this fucking mess."

His anger tells me that I've crossed the line somewhere, but I'm not really clear on where that line was drawn, so I'm irritated. "Whatever."

He turns then, muttering under his breath. "What's that?" I ask.

He doesn't turn back, but he repeats the words anyway. "I said, yer just so lost ya can't even see what's right in front of ya."

I discard this comment completely. "I have no idea what you're talking about, Tier."

"Then ya better pay closer attention to those dreams, darlin'. Yer having them for a reason."

He starts to get up. I tug on his arm and he stops, but doesn't look me in the face. "Wait. We're not done yet."

He lies back down and looks up at the pine trees as he speaks. "I'm tryin' ta help ya, Junco. That's all. Just help ya. And all ya do is fight me." He turns to me then. His face is blank but his eyes want to say more.

"The thing is, Tier," I smile a little to settle him, make him listen, "things have just been off since you came into the picture. I mean, everything was fine up until I wrecked the Goat and saw you on the hill and you dragged me down this stupid rabbit hole."

His lip goes up in a snarl. "Me? I'm the one who dragged you down the rabbit hole?" He huffs out some air and shakes his head.

"See, this is what I mean. You seem to be under the impression that I am the problem here. And that makes no sense to me. If I've done something to you, why don't you just tell me what it is?"

"Here, how about this, Junco. Have I ever done anything to you? Anything?"

"You killed Aren."

"He was not who you think, Junco. You don't know what I know."

I sigh. Do I want to know what he knows about Aren? No. Not

right now. "You poisoned me with your claws."

"That," he huffs, "was an accident. And I healed ya right afterward. A small scare, no damage whatsoever."

"You abducted me."

"Really? You made yer escape quite quickly from my recollection. I found ya outside in a jumbled mess, remember? You could have left. I never tied ya up, I never threatened ya, I never did anything. So the truth is, yer here of your own volition. I never abducted ya."

I feel my heart quicken because he's right about that. I could've left lots of times.

"Besides, *Junco*," he drawls out my name and I tuck down a grin, "you shot at me twice, chopped me in the throat, kicked me in the jaw, and stunned me with a plasma rifle for an extended period of time."

I sit up and laugh. "It was on stun!" I knock myself in the head with the palm of my hand. "I did not understand how you could have survived ten full seconds of plasma fire." I look down at his face and then control my laugh because he is not amused.

I lie back down and change the subject quickly. "Well, you threw a boot at me. Could've hit me in the head. It was touch and go there for a second."

He smiles and then it turns into a laugh as he shakes his head, but this time I hold mine back. "And you slashed open my arm and pulled out my fucking health tracker. You're lucky I don't really need it anymore, otherwise I'd be pissed off. Plus, I have a huge gash that will probably be a scar."

"So you'd prefer to be in the custody of people who would keep ya against yer will?"

I click my tongue in frustration. "Says you!"

"Yeah, says me. And let's just take a look at the *gash* I left, OK?" His eyes meet mine as he leans his upper body over my chest to check the wound on the arm farthest from him. He looks down and gives me a smug grin and pulls gently on the corner of the membrane that he slapped over it before we fled the cavern. I can't help myself and I crank my head to the side so I can watch. He peels it back a fraction at a time, like he's trying to take care not to pull on my skin, but it doesn't hurt at all. The membrane comes off and he tosses it in the pine needles.

"See for yerself." And he leans down on me as he holds my arm up.

There's not even a scab where his razors slashed my skin open. There's dried blood, but as for the slash, there's not a red mark, not a discoloration, or any outward appearance that he ever touched my arm.

"Wow, that is some good shit you got on that membrane." I smirk up at him and wink before he groans about my swearing. He smiles and leans back, removing the weight of his body off mine, but his upper body is still positioned over the top of me. His face dips for a minute, like he's gonna kiss me and my heart literally skips a beat.

I swear he feels it.

"Do I make ya nervous, Junco?" he asks in a low voice.

His lips have my full attention but I manage to answer. "Not exactly nervous, no." His face dips a little closer and I look up to his eyes. They are his normal green color, but with little sparks of glow in them. "What does that mean?" I ask. "When they glow like that?"

He shrugs before answering. "It can mean a lot of things. Fright. Excitement. Anticipation."

"What does it mean now?"

He laughs a little. "All of the above."

"What could you possibly be afraid of now?"

His eyes search mine. "Another rejection," he says softly.

I just look at him and then he begins to move away but I grab his arm. "Where are you going?"

He takes his hand and brushes some hair out of my eyes, a tender gesture that makes my body tingle. "We've got time for this later, lots of time."

I grab his arm again. "What if we didn't? Have more time for this later, I mean?"

"What are ya trying to tell me, Junco?"

My eyes get lost in the green depths and I whisper, "Just kiss me, Tier."

He's all business now as he takes my face into his hands and his thumbs caress the skin near the corners of my mouth. I stare into his eyes as he moves towards my lips. When he's a breath away I close them, and then his mouth is on mine, our tongues searching. It's slow, and heated, and perfect. He breathes me in and slides his hand down my face and slips it behind my ear to draw me closer. It's the best moment in my current memory and I hold my breath.

Tier pulls back for a moment and I open my eyes to look at him. "Breathe out, Junco. All the best parts are in the exhale."

I let it out and he takes me in again.

I feel Tier's body move as he takes a half-hearted kick in the back. "Get a fucking room, you two," Moju snarls in disgust. "That's my sister, you asshole."

I begin to pull away but Tier takes his time and finishes our moment. And then he is on his feet and holding out his hand. I take it and he pulls me up without effort. I can't tell if it's because I'm such a small person to begin with, or because I'm floating on air. Either way, it doesn't matter. I can barely breathe and it takes me a minute to recognize the aftereffects of happiness.

Chapter Sixteen

"I don't know," I say.

My resolve to find Dale and get answers is fading fast as I look down into the dirty hole Tier and Moju are asking me to climb into. "It's pretty dark in there."

Moju is swinging a lightstick by a lanyard in his hand. "Hence the flares, Juncs. It's fine. Plus, we have night-vision."

"Yeah, but I don't."

Tier looks down at me. "No, but you have us," he says simply.

I look up at both of them now. "And you're sure he's down there?" It seems unlikely that he'd be down in a hole in the ground.

Moju answers, "Juncs, I heard them say he was there. He's working with the MR."

Tier pipes in then. "Junco, it's not what it looks like on the outside. Underneath it's another world, believe me."

"How do you know?" I ask, wondering just how much he's holding back now.

"Yeah, Tier. How the hell do you know that?" Moju clearly knows Tier's part in all this, but wants to put him on the spot.

I look from one set of glowing eyes to another and give in. "Oh, fuck it. Keep your damn secrets." I motion to one of them to go first, and Tier takes up the lead, with me in the middle, and Moju last.

Underground the earth smell fills my nose and makes me want to vomit. It reminds me of mushrooms and personally, eating fungus is a sure sign you're either starving or are being force-fed as punishment.

We create a pattern as we descend. Tier's boots clang on the metal rungs which line the side of the tunnel. Then mine. Then Moju's softer thunk of bare flesh on the rung above my head. It takes forever and I count three hundred and twelve rungs before we stop. I don't even want to think about climbing back up.

Tier grabs my ankle and I almost scream. "Stay put here, Junco. I'm serious, no funny business."

He drops down and I can hear his wings as they catch air. I can't see anything, but a tiny splash (a long way from where I'm standing, it seems to me) signals that he's on the ground. I hear his wings again, then the sound fades and is gone. Moju lets out a long sigh but to his credit he doesn't ask me to move, or go down, or even complain that Tier is taking too long.

We just wait.

I am just about to whine about my arms being tired of holding on to the rungs when I hear Tier's wings. He grabs the rung below me. "OK, I don't see anything. Junco, I'll hover below you. Let go and drop, I'll catch you in the air. Then Moju can come out."

I want to say two things in reply. One, obviously, is how sure should I be that he will catch me before I splat in the puddle far below. The other is what does he mean he didn't see anything? Thing? Not anyone. But anything. This worries me. I let that slide too, because to be honest, the truth isn't all it's cracked up to be. Ignorance can be bliss. What you don't know can't hurt you. And the ever popular, if I knew then what I know now, I'd never have done it.

"Tell me when," I say instead.

He says "When," and I drop. His arms grab me a split-second later and he holds me tight as we descend to the ground.

Moju lands beside me and breaks the lightstick and the tunnel glows green as he drops it to the ground. I catch Tier staring down the tunnel before he notices me and smiles. That's when I know this whole thing is not going to end well. He's worried.

The tunnel is massive. It's at least five stories to the ceiling and a hundred feet from side to side. The ceiling is curved, like a suborbital hangar, and the cracked and deteriorated walls are made of concrete. Various-sized debris piles line the floor for as far as I can see in the dim glow and bits of rebar are sticking out here and there as puddles of liquid ripple when small rodents scurry into the shadows. "What is this place?"

Moju answers, "US Military nuclear weapons transport tunnel. There's an entire highway underground and this is just one little off-ramp in the middle of nowhere. They were shut down more than a hundred years ago during the Succession Revolutions. Like Tier said, it's another world down here." Moju's jovial disposition is gone now.

"How do you know this?" I ask.

He looks at me and throws his hands up. "I know a lot of shit I shouldn't, Juncs. Comes with the job."

Tier is speaking before I can ask what job. "Get on Moju's back, Junco," he says as he takes my hand. "We'll need to fly from here."

I swallow and he squeezes my hand in a show of support. "It's no big deal, really. But it's better to fly."

I decide to trust him and hop on Moju's back. We fly slow and cautious and this is yet one more red flag telling me to stop and go back.

But I can't.

Like it or not, Dale is a player in the game of Junco. And I know that Tier wants me to see him. To talk to him. Otherwise he wouldn't have let me come down here. My destiny is tied to this foul-smelling subterranean tunnel and if I go back now I'll be as clueless as I was before.

I'm not going back.

Moju slows down and we land so he can light up a stick and look around while Tier remains above us, keeping an eye on the darkness. I don't offer to climb down off his back and thankfully, he doesn't ask me to either. Moju throws another lightstick and I watch it tumble end over end until it splashes down in a puddle slick with sheen. He cracks another one and throws it in the opposite direction and only then do I fully understand the size and scope of the place we are in.

We are standing in the middle of the nuclear weapon freeway. It is massive, easily a quarter mile across, but I know that distance without reference is deceiving, so it's probably closer to half a mile wide. The height of the ceiling is the same as the off-ramp, but this one seems to be reinforced with layer upon layer of steel beams. At least it doesn't seem likely that it will come crashing down on us.

"Which way?" Moju asks.

Tier is still staring off into the blackness as I look over at him. "Moju, I thought you were the one who knew where Dale was?"

I feel Moju shrug beneath me. "Tier has always been in charge down here. He knows it better than I do."

Tier gives me a not-now look, so I drop it.

I hear scuttling off to the right and turn in surprise.

"Up now, Moju," Tier commands. We fly up and hover in the center of the tunnel, their wings straining to hold the position. I look down as dozens of small creatures crowd against the barrier which separates the green glow from the pitch black. They seem hesitant to come into the light.

"When ya live in the darkness long enough even this bit of light is blinding," Tier says, as if reading my mind.

"What are they?" I ask.

Moju shrugs, but Tier answers, "Nothing we need to worry about. Yet. Come on, it's this way."

He picks a direction, whether it is east or west, north or south, I have no idea, and we fly along once again. My stomach grows more and more unsettled with each wingbeat. There are lots of things in the dark, things bigger and meaner than the small creatures that shied away from the green glow. Things that hiss and drag large limbs behind them as we pass.

Neither of the guys react or fill me in, so I just keep my mouth shut. If there's one thing I remember from cadets it's to do the job you're trained for, and if you're not trained for the job at hand, shut up and stay the fuck out of the way.

We stop again but Moju doesn't crack a lightstick this time. I can feel his arms moving, and I get the feeling the guys are using hand signals that only they can see in the darkness, but they don't include me. Clearly talking is forbidden, so I stay silent once again.

I feel Moju reach into a pocket and pull something out and extend his hand. I can only imagine that Tier takes whatever it is and then Moju flies us backward. Tier joins us in a few seconds and then I hear a small crack and we all move forward together and land. I hear a whoosh of air as Tier strains to pull on something and then a crack of light floods the dark highway just long enough for us to slip through a massive vault-like door and quickly shut it behind us.

Things scrape against the other side of the door once it is closed and every hair on my body stands up on end. Moju shrugs me off and I slide down on the tiled floor of the hallway and look back at the door with some trepidation.

Tier and Moju are whispering to each other now. "Hey, guys? There's something on the other side." My voice must surprise them because they both look at me like I have two heads. "There are things out there," I say.

"They can't get in here, Junco." Tier explains by explaining nothing.

"Yeah, but what are they?"

He shakes his head at me again.

Now, I don't know him all that well, I mean—it's only been a few days since our first encounter on the hill, but I've seen him in quite the array of stressful situations, so I feel I can correctly infer what this head-shaking means. And it means those creatures will do terrible things to us given the chance.

So I drop it. Because ignorance is bliss and what you don't know can't hurt you and all that good shit. If I'm going to be eaten alive by some hissing freak in the dark, I'd rather not dwell on it.

Really.

Moju takes my hand and we follow Tier down the hallway. The fluorescent lights above, the ones that work, anyway, flicker and the strobe effect makes me feel like puking. "Where's the power coming from?"

Moju shrugs but Tier, once again the purveyor of everything giant nuclear tunnels under the RR, answers, "They have solar panels and a small wind farm over by Ramah. Ever seen it?"

Tier oozes little tiny bits of local knowledge that he shouldn't really have if he's just a visitor here. "I thought all that crap was shut down decades ago?"

"It was," he continues. "Officially anyway. The wind still blows and the sun still shines."

"Are we under Ramah right now?"

"Yup."

That means we aren't really that far from my farm. Ramah is only about thirty miles from us. This blows me away because in my mind we are on another planet.

"I thought you guys said this place has a security system?"

"It does," Tier answers.

"So where is it?"

Moju laughs and turns back to me as he continues to walk. "We just passed them, Juncs."

"And more up ahead," Tier adds.

"So how do we get back out now that those things are on the other side of the door back there?"

This time all I get is silence.

I stew in that silence for a while as we continue to walk the long empty corridor. It's littered with papers and debris, discarded folders, computer bits, and what looks like various charred robotic parts. The left-overs of some long ago shoot-out? I can only hope, but my best guess is that the technology lying around is not antique and neither was the battle.

The only sound in the passageway, besides the light step of our feet, is the slow drip of water that seeps out from cracks in the ceiling. The hallway branches off every now and then, but we continue on the straight and narrow until we reach the last hallway and then we take a right. A few dozen paces on Tier stops by another door. This one has an active biometric pad and Moju makes no move to grab a charge and blow through it. Instead, Tier presses his hand up to the pad and I hear the lock sequence from within. My brow furrows and I stare at the back of his head, willing him to look back at me. But he doesn't, just turns the long steel handle and pulls the door open with a whoosh.

Moju pushes me against the wall as a series of beeps confronts Tier's request for entrance, so I can't see what he does, but the beeping stops and Moju pushes me to the other side of him as we walk through, trying to block my view of the source of the beeps. I slip around him and let out a gasp. Granted I haven't seen a lot of high-tech robotry in my life in the RR, but this thing scares the shit out of me.

It's about as tall as me for one, and the eight legs protruding from its spherical body begin to click on the hard tile floor as it spots my curiosity. There's a biometric pad on the thing's chest and some compound sensors that ring its head. It makes a new noise as Tier steps back between Moju and me, and then goes quiet.

No one says anything, so I don't either.

Then Tier pushes Moju forward and we begin to walk away from the sentry. Tier follows and quietly passes us before we get to the next door. We repeat this action twice more and when we pass through the third door and close it behind us, there is no sentry in the hallway.

Tier looks me straight in the eye as he whispers, "Good job, Junco. Keep quiet and still and follow Moju."

And then he slips through a door down the hallway and leaves us standing there.

Chapter Seventeen

I look up at Moju but he shakes his head at me, so I do as I'm told and keep quiet and still. At first all I can hear is some distant buzzing of electrical equipment, and a wheeled chair rolling across a hard floor. Then some commotion and a few subdued swear words.

It is definitely Dale's voice.

Tier clears his throat.

"What the hell, Tier?"

The question hangs in the air, but Tier says nothing. I can hear his boots across the floor now, so he must be off stealth mode. They fade into the distance, getting farther and farther away from us. Still Tier says nothing.

"I told you we're done. This intrusion won't be ignored." His voice starts loud and then fades slightly, like he turned his back on Tier.

"Mistake number one," Moju whispers. I only have time to nod in agreement before I hear the thump of a body being thrown to the ground and gurgling noises coming out in short bursts.

Moju makes his move and I follow him into the lab, but there is no time to even look around before I see a robotic sentry blast Tier with some sort of pulse weapon. He flies backwards and hits a wall before slumping down into a pile on the pristine white tile floor.

Moju runs off to the left while I stand there in a panic as the thing turns its attention to me. Then I see it lock on, ready to fire and I snap back to reality. I throw my body upwards into a flip I've done a thousand times on the back of a galloping horse, but never used trying to escape a crazed piece of machinery.

The pulse passes beneath me and I grasp a light fixture and fling myself, monkey-style, from one to the next until I am on the other side of the sentry, swinging from both hands. It's searching the far side of the room for me when I hear Dale's voice command.

"Stand down! Stand down!"

The thing stops so I drop to the floor and walk over to Tier. He's back on his feet now and looking really angry. "You OK?" I ask.

His lips form a snarl as he pushes me out of the way and strides back towards Dale. But Dale doesn't back down, instead he meets Tier head-on. "What the fuck are you doing bringing her here?"

Tier pushes him, but only as a gesture of dominance, not to hurt him. The sentry perks up but retains its last command. I look around for Moju, but he's MIA. That's when I see what's in the room with me. "Oh my God, what the fuck is going on here?" I look at Tier and Dale and they both stop to follow my accusatory finger.

Which is pointing at a massive life-support machine that dominates the center of the room. The circular base protrudes out in a bulge that takes it all the way up to the ceiling. There are eight symmetrical arms which spread out like tentacles and each arm is home to half a dozen capsules with a transparent casing that allows a red glow to permeate into the lab.

But that's not the disturbing part.

It's the things inside them that make me stoop over and vomit, right there on the shiny sterile floor.

Tier steps aside and waves a hand at Dale. "Go ahead. Tell her what's going on here."

Dale looks at me as I upright myself and spit, but says nothing. Really, what can you say to someone who just discovered that you have dozens of copies of her body, in various stages of development, growing in vats filled with red goo.

"Junco, it's not—"

"What it looks like?" I finish for him, then swipe a hand across my mouth to remove the spittle from my lips. "Are you fucking kidding me? You're cloning me!" I scream the last part and I can feel rage bubbling up inside of me as I race towards him and deliver a roundhouse kick to his cheek. My field boot connects with a sickening whack, and he goes scrambling down to the floor, blood spurting out of his mouth. The sentry is back in business. It fires at me, but I flip and then run towards it and flip over to the other side once again.

It learned its lesson from last time and doesn't even pivot, just switches sensors and fires at me again, but I'm a flipping expert. Literally. I can flip all fucking day long. Once again I end up swinging from a light fixture.

"Stand down!" Dale says again, this time with much less enthusiasm.

"Don't do me any favors, you creepy piece of shit!" I snarl as I drop in front of him and kick him as he tries to get back up.

"Don't push your luck, little girl."

I've known this man my whole life but today he is a stranger. I'm about to remove his teeth with my boot when Tier takes my arm and pulls me back.

"We came for a reason, Dale—hand over the cubes. *Now*!" He doesn't scream the word so much as growl it, but I step back a few paces. For the first time since I met him I get the feeling that I have no idea what an angry Tier actually looks like. Like I've only seen the sugar-coated version and nothing more.

Dale pulls himself together as he stands, straightens his glasses, and passes a hand over his messed-up gray hair, trying in vain to make it lie flat against his skull. He spits blood out onto the tiles at his feet, and then looks at me, ignoring Tier's demand altogether.

I know right then, he's a fucking dead man.

"You're just another clone, Junco. Nothing more and nothing less. You have no claim to that body, that brain, those skills, or anything else that's part of you. We created you and you're not even"—he looks up at Tier—"a legal citizen of this planet. What you did last week was—"

Tier backhands him so hard he falls to the floor again. The sentry's sensors blink like crazy as it tries to discern if it should disobey orders, but holds steady.

Tier grabs him by the shirt collar, pulls him to his feet and walks him back towards the lab bench filled with computers running model simulations, pipettes, and various sizes and shapes of glassware. "The cubes. Now. Or I'll cut yer stomach open and make ya knit a sweater with yer own intestines."

"You don't want her, Tier. She's not—"

Tier backhands him again and Dale shuts up.

I walk away, leaving Tier to get what he needs in whatever way he feels necessary. I am drawn back to the vats of clones and look at each one as I pass by them. I stop at a little girl. Me at age five or so. Her hair sways in the goo, back and forth across her face. I don't even look back when I hear Tier hissing at Dale about whatever. It's his business, I can only deal with one thing at a time right now. My carbon copies.

I move on to the next one, and the next, and the next. Watching the girls grow older before my eyes. As I come around to complete the circle I see an exact replica of me today and I want to smash her face in.

Who am I? Am I real? Am I just another copy? Did I crawl out of these vats? When did I crawl out? A few weeks ago? The day I ran away? Are there girls just like me lurking somewhere? Here?

I glance around the room with trepidation as some glassware behind me goes crashing to the ground. I hear muffled groans from Dale, but I don't even turn to see what Tier's doing.

There are lots of doors, lots of hidden crannies, come to think of it. And where the hell did Moju go? I take a deep breath and let it out slowly to calm my thumping heart, then turn back to Tier.

I can't tell if he's actually making progress, but the place is a mess. Papers are still in mid-air, falling in a floaty back-and-forth motion to the ground. Glass shards are all over the tiles and the previously tidy bench is now a catastrophe.

I walk up next to Tier and Dale turns his hatred towards me, then spits blood on my boots. "As you can see, Junco, you're entirely replaceable. The next girl was already dispatched."

I shrink back, a microscopic amount, but Dale catches it and laughs.

"Don't listen to him, Junco. Do ya see an empty vat over there?"

"No, they're all full."

"Case closed. We're gonna kill them all on the way out. Yer the original." He has a knife in his hand and it's pushed up to the sensitive skin just below Dale's left ear. I watch him stick it further into the skin so that a trickle of blood escapes and runs down his neck and into his shirt. Then Tier looks at me. "Yer the original and that's how it's gonna stay."

Dale laughs. "Don't be stupid, Junco, he's only here to save his own ass. That's why he wants the evidence."

Tier lets him speak his mind this time, but I put a hand up. "Save it Dale. I could give a shit why he's here, what he's done, or who he's done it for." Then I look up at Tier. "I'm ready to go."

He smiles. "Just waiting on Moju."

Dale's posture straightens at Moju's name, but Tier answers his unasked question before he can get a word out. "That's right, asshole. The two of ya just can't seem to get enough of each other, can ya?"

The power goes out and Tier laughs. "Goodbye, Junco's clones." The giant central artificial life system that powers the vats goes dark and whines as it drains the last few electrons through the circuits. The hum of living turns to the silence of death and we stand there in the dark.

Dale's rage bubbles over. "I will kill you for this, Tier. You'll be looking over your shoulder for the rest of your life, you miserable fucking piece of shit."

Moju appears and throws down a lightstick for my benefit. He's still breathing heavy from running and being loaded down with the plasma rifles. He throws a rifle to Tier and one to me. We both catch them in mid-air, a fraction of a second apart, as Dale wiggles free. Moju shoots a pulse in his back and he falls forward, smacking his face on the stone-cold tile.

The sentry wakes up and a siren blares into my ears, followed by a blinking red strobe light. It wails, drowning out the heavy moans coming out of Dale.

Tier blasts the sentry on full pulse for several seconds, long enough to make it stop and think up an alternate plan.

Moju looks at me, then Tier. "Take her out. I'm right behind you."

Tier and I both run towards the door and I don't stop when I hear the grotesque slash of razors on flesh, or even the thunk of what I know is Dale's head as it splats against something hard.

We pass through the open door and into the hallway, backtracking to the exit. I hear Moju's bare feet slap the ground behind us and then the massive explosion throws us forward and we slam into the floor, then slide into the wall and stay still.

Moju recovers first, grabs me at the same time that Tier makes it to his feet, and we haul ass down the corridor, towards all the sleeping sentries waiting for us to try and get past them.

Chapter Eighteen

The heat from the explosion beats against my back as Moju drags me down the hallway. I slip and fall, but his hands are there and we're running again before I can even register my misstep. Tier stops at the first corner and we almost collide with him. He is still and quiet, but there is nothing to hint at what awaits us if we turn into the next hallway and the wailing alarms block out any hope of hearing movement. He makes a signal to Moju, and then flattens his head against the wall before peeking around.

Lasers swipe past his face and I can see several strands of hair catch fire just from the proximity. He pulls back and swats the fire out while giving Moju another signal. Moju pushes me behind him and they both move forward firing.

The exchange is quick and then Moju has my hand again and we are running towards the first door. Tier presses his palm against the biometrics panel, but the door is dead.

"Blast the bolt on three," Tier yells.

Moju nods and in three seconds they fire. The bolt melts with the intense heat and I move back to avoid getting a proximity burn. Laser fire comes from behind me and I turn and squeeze the trigger at my attacker. There are several smaller bots scurrying down the hallway and I pick them off one at a time, leaving the hallway a blazing mess. Then Moju grabs my hand and we squeeze through the blasted door and run again.

This time the sentry isn't waiting around by the door, it's hauling ass to meet us. The laser pulses flash past me and I hear Moju holler out as one grazes his shoulder. Tier blasts the sentry with continuous fire while I pulse at its top sensors, essentially blinding it. It explodes and we duck behind a corner to avoid the full effects of the blast.

I grab Moju's hand and pull him along. I look back and see his shoulder is still smoldering and he winces in pain as we pass the blazing mess of what's left of the second sentry. Tier tries the biometrics again, but it's the same as the last one, which is all bad luck for us.

Tier and I fire straight at the bot, while Moju picks off the stray bots that are now clattering up behind us in force. I look back and see there are dozens of them now. I watch as Moju fires and makes them explode, but then I see what happens to their remains. They self-reassemble into more bots. Some are larger, some are smaller, but it doesn't matter. They cannot be totally eliminated. I turn my attention back to the sentry door which has a large hole through the middle.

Tier grabs me and pushes me forward. "Go through firing, Junco—I'll get Moju!"

I do. My plasma charge is already a quarter empty but I blast that shit on continuous stream as I squeeze through the burned-out door, sharp edges catching my shirt, making it smolder as I pass.

The sentry is directing all of its primary lasers at me, which is bad enough, but then the top of its head pops up and a rocket launcher emerges. "Tier, get in here quick." There's no answer and I steal a look behind me to see Moju struggling to get through the door without setting himself on fire. They are both a lot bigger than me. Tier pulls him back out, but Moju rolls several canisters towards me as he disappears from my view.

Grenades.

I pick one up, pull the pin, then lob it down the hallway just as the sentry sends a rocket flaming past me and through the door.

I duck as the double explosions rock the tunnel, and part of the ceiling comes crashing down, hitting me on the back.

My ears are ringing as I try to stand. The dust has obscured everything from view and my heart thumps with adrenaline as I frantically search the massive hole that was the second door just a few seconds ago.

"Tier!" I scream, but I can barely hear my voice over the ringing.

I run to what's left of the door and pick my way past the debris, swatting away the dust and coughing as the minute particles stream down my throat to clog my lungs.

I see Tier getting to his feet and I pick my way through the rubble until I'm a few paces past the door. Moju is underneath, protected from much of the blast. Tier has burns all over his body but he still pulls Moju to his feet and yells something in his face. To my injured ears it sounds like "Move yer fucking feet, warrior!"

Moju stands there, bent over and coughing for a minute, then to my surprise, he straightens up and salutes.

They both turn and start running towards me and we pass through the hole together. I look back apprehensively to see if there are more bots reassembling behind us, but the cloud of dust is too thick to see through.

We run towards the final security door that will lead us back out into the ruined passageway, then finally back to the main highway. We reach the door and Moju hands Tier a grenade and he pulls the pin and throws it, yanking me back behind a corner. The blast heat almost knocks me over, even though most of it shoots right past us. I can feel my body reaching its limit and for the first time I wonder if I will live through this.

We wait a few seconds, then Tier grabs my hand, I grab Moju's, and we drag each other down the hallway and through the blast hole. We stumble, slower now, down the remaining hallway and stop when we reach the door that leads to the outer tunnel highway.

I can hear the scratching on the other side, even with the residual ringing in my ears. My stomach clenches as I think about the creatures that are now waiting for us. I hold it down for as long as I can, but I turn and start to heave. I don't even remember the last time I ate, so there's nothing, and I mean nothing, left in my stomach.

"Now what?" I ask, wiping my hand across my face.

Tier throws down his rifle, takes a deep breath and looks at Moju. "My charge is out, give me all the grenades."

Moju leans heavily against the wall, fishes around in his pockets, and pulls out three canisters and hands them over to Tier.

And that's when I hear the clicking from the hallway behind us. "Shit! They're back!"

From the hazy cloud of thick dust a massive amalgamation of bot parts appears. I scream and both Moju and I train our rifles on the thing that comes towards us. We blast it back a few paces and it's forced to reassemble. I steal a look at Tier and he's already pulling the pin on the first grenade and running back towards me yelling, "Fire in the hole!"

Moju dives for the corner as Tier grabs me and yanks me to the floor. The blast renews the ringing in my ears and I'm disoriented as I struggle to my feet. Tier pulls me up and then we are running again.

Moju is bringing up the rear and firing hard at the reassembled thing behind us. But it's made a weapon and it fires, causing a projectile to skim past Moju's thigh. He falls and I break free of Tier to go back and get him. I fire a continuous stream of plasma at the amalgabot for several seconds, then grab Moju and yank him up and pull him back towards Tier. Moju aims his rifle at the creatures that are now filing through the hole as Tier pulls the pin on the second grenade and tosses it out on to the highway.

We hit the deck again, just as the explosion blasts body parts in all directions and now I know my hearing is fucked forever.

Moju pulls me up and we half limp, half run towards Tier who waves us through the smoking hole and out in to the main tunnel. Before I even know what's happening Moju is in the air and his talons have me by the waist. The razors puncture into my flesh as he grabs me with his hands, but I can't even feel it. Then Tier is out in the hallway and the remaining creatures are all over him. Moju swings around and I fire my rifle at the creatures, hoping to God that the stream doesn't hit Tier.

Tier breaks the grip of one that has him by the shirt and takes flight.

I am just about to breathe a sigh of relief when the MR tanks roll through the cloud of dust clogging the far end of the highway and suddenly there are hundreds of soldiers piling out of vehicles.

Tier yells something as he points down the tunnel and Moju and I take off, flying back towards the hole we came down. I hear a final explosion and then Tier is below me and Moju screams, "Ride with Tier, I can't carry you, Junco!"

And then I am falling through the air.

I land on Tier's back and his hands rise up to steady me. The soldiers, wounded but not down, are still firing at us as we make our escape. I flip over and frantically fire the stream of plasma particles back towards the advancing army until my rifle is out and I hurl it into the air.

The army disappears in the distance and by the time we get to the lightstick that marks the off-ramp we came in by, there is nothing but the clattering of small bots scuttling over the greasy water below us.

I watch as Moju dives down to pick up the sticks and throw them far down the dark highway. We fly slower now and I can hear both Tier and Moju breathing heavy with effort. We get to the last lightstick that marks the exit and I watch Moju pick it up, then toss it to me. "Stick it in your pocket, Junco."

I do, and then Tier flies me up to the hole that leads outside. "Start climbing, and no matter what—don't fucking stop."

I grab the rung and pull myself up into the tunnel.

They don't follow me and I want to turn and ask what's going on, but then I think about the three hundred-plus rungs that I must climb before I can make it out and I do what I'm told.

I climb and I don't fucking stop.

I'm on rung one hundred and thirty-three when I hear the plasma crack below and I almost panic and lose my grip. Then Tier is behind me, urging me to go faster, but my legs are shaking and I'm all out of breath.

"I can't, Tier, I can't climb anymore." I whimper.

He comes right up on me and grabs the rung above my head. "Let me in front, Junco, then wrap yourself around me and I'll take us both up."

The fire from below is getting closer, but I do as I'm told and then I am on his back and his hands are pulling us up the hole faster and faster. It seems like an eternity, but we break free and are out in the open air. I cry with relief and look back for Moju, but he's not there.

And then I scream in anguish as Tier flies us through the tallgrass, away from whatever is left of my brother below ground.

Chapter Nineteen

We fly for a long time, and we fly fast. Most of it I have my face buried in his back, but then I look up to see where we are. He lands us in a field of tallgrass on the edge of the pine trees and I drop to my knees in exhaustion when my feet hit the ground, then fall over and lie on my back. He drops with me and we stay quiet for several minutes.

"He's not dead, Junco."

"How do you know?" I scream.

He leans over and cups his hand over my mouth. "Shut up! Ya want to get us caught after all that?"

I turn over and refuse to cry.

"It was part of the plan. His plan."

"Well," I say evenly, "no one asked me what I thought of the fucking plan."

He leans over and pulls me around so that I'm looking at him. "I know, I'm sorry. But it was his decision. So I could get ya out of there alive."

"How do you know he's not dead?"

He laughs at this and I'm instantly pissed. "Junco, he works for them. They're not gonna kill him. He's the only thing they have that's worth a shit."

I can't say I'm surprised. I already knew this, really. But hearing it out loud right now makes it difficult for some reason.

Tier watches my face and then continues, "He does shit like this all the time. They let him out and he takes off and creates chaos. The MR had to know what was down there, Junco. Moju found his lab a few months ago and did the same thing to his doubles, so how convenient is that? They let him hear shit so he'll go do their dirty work for them. They wanted Dale's lab destroyed because they already have what they need in their own labs. They're only collaborating with the RR because they didn't have the skills to go it alone, but do not assume they are on the same side."

"What the fuck are they doing down there? Why do they have clones of me?"

He throws up his hands. "You tell me, Junco. Why do they clone you? I don't know what game you're playing with me, and really, I don't care at this point. But I'm sick of this bullshit I-have-no-idea routine you keep pulling."

"You're sick—? That's hilarious, how the hell did you know where the clones were then? And how the hell did you have the biometrics to get past those sentries?"

He jumps to his feet and then grabs my hand and pulls me up without asking.

"So, you're not going to answer me? You're just gonna pretend that you're not hip-high in shit with everything that's going on in my life?"

He pulls me towards him and shakes his head. "Another talk for another time, Junco."

I push him away. "Fuck you then." And I start walking into the pine trees.

"Where are you going?"

I ignore him completely.

"Yer gonna get lost out here in the dark."

I stop and turn, my lip curled up in rage. "Really? I'm going to get lost, am I? That's funny, considering that I grew up in the tallgrass and I can tell you how to get to seven different farms right from this spot. I'm not lost, *Tier*." I sneer his name as it comes out of my mouth. "And I might be afraid of the dark, but that's what the stars are for."

He laughs a little at that and it makes my face go hot.

"Something funny?"

"Yer afraid of the dark too? Let's see, fish, nightdogs, prairie lions, and the dark. That's some list ya got there, Junco."

My whole upper body heats up. "If someone dumped you out in the middle of the tallgrass at night when you were eight and told you the apexers were gonna eat you alive if you couldn't fend them off with a sword, you'd probably be afraid of all that shit too. *Asshole*."

His mood stays light as I turn and walk away. "Well, damn. You must be one hell of a sword fighter."

I halt again and turn back to him. "That's cute, is it? Leaving small children out in the night to be eaten? For your information I couldn't even lift the sword, Tier. I was eight. And if I'm this size at nineteen, how fucking big do you think I was at eight? I didn't fight them off, you idiot. I climbed up a pine tree, ripping out three fingernails in the process, and then jumped limb from limb until I ran out of branches. I stayed in that last tree for *three days* before they finally came and got me."

Jasus, Junco. Lock that shit down—now.

He shuts up after that and just walks with me. After another quarter mile I find the overgrown footpath that leads up the mountain. Tier follows in silence.

It takes a lot longer to get there than I remember, but finally the lake comes into view and I can make out the little fishing cabin set just off to the side and under the protective cover of the pines in the approaching dawn.

My eyes pause at the dock...

Picture yourself standing on the edge of a dock. In front of you is a mountain lake and behind you is a small cabin...

But this is not the dock I want so badly it hurts.

"Whose place is this?" Tier asks.

"Mine."

The door is unlocked, so I go right in, find the candles and matches and draw the curtains so the light won't be noticed by anyone passing nearby. Not that anyone would, this is my land now and it's private property. But habits, right?

Tier flops himself down in a chair in the small living room and watches me closely, but does not interfere.

I lie down on the couch opposite Tier's chair and it takes me about ten seconds to be oblivious to the world.

I wake to a painful rumble announcing my hunger and I try to remember when I ate last. I look around the cabin and spy some avian nutrition packets on the kitchen table but pump some water from the kitchen sink and drink instead.

When my stomach is bloated with liquid I go find Tier. We only have one bedroom in the cabin, so it's not like I have to look far. Besides, his boots are hastily discarded in the hallway and his charred clothes are strewn about like a trail of breadcrumbs.

I think of my own smelly clothes, which are covered in black soot and burn holes and smell like blast chemicals, and I regret sleeping in them. I push the door open and stare at the naked form lying face down on the bed, completely uncovered except for his wings which are spread across his back like a blanket. His body is almost sideways, like he fell into bed accidentally, and his face is stuffed into the pillow, muffling the snores trying to escape his mouth.

I shake myself out of it and leave, closing the door behind me and pass the food packets on the table—life is too short to eat shitty food—and pull some fishing gear out of the front closet.

I've been fishing here with my dad since I was two, and I know exactly where the fish tend to bite, even in the late afternoon. I wade into the shallow lake water up to my hips, tie a fly and cast out.

Fishing isn't just about catching fish, that's just what you get at the end if you're good at it.

Fishing is about the journey, and the journey is typically the thoughts you have as you go through the motions. Fishing, my dad always said, is a thinking man's sport.

I watch the sun dropping into the trees in the west and my thoughts sink to sadness. I roll the past few days around in my head as I seek out a taker for my fly, false-casting back and forth in an open loop to let the line go out further into the lake. I do this for the better part of an hour, and I'm losing hope quick as the sun sets when I get a taker. I pull the bass out and its normally olive-gold scales are dark green in the fading light. He'll have to do.

I gather up all my gear and turn to go back to the house when I see Tier staring at me from the back porch. He's sitting on the deck shirtless, legs hanging over, his arms and chin resting on the bottom railing.

He waves. I stop walking and just look at him for a moment, wondering if I should keep my distance in case I decide to bow out of this shit, or if I should wave back. I hold up the fish instead, and he smiles.

He waits for me on the porch. "Hey," he says, a little question mark at the end. Like he's trying to figure out if I'm still mad.

"I'm not in the mood to talk to you right now, Tier. I'm hungry and stink like chemicals, fish, and shit. So just leave me alone." The screen door smacks the wooden frame as I leave him outside, and I take the fish to the kitchen and begin prepping it.

The cabin is for hunting and my dad would have important buddies up here with him over the years to track deer and shoot ducks.

After my mom took off he never really left me alone, so I was a permanent fixture on these trips as well.

But beyond that, the cabin is our safe house too. If you just stumbled onto it somehow and came inside it would provide you with shelter and water, but not much else. But if you knew where to look you'd find everything you need to survive here for at least six months.

I slide the pocket door that reveals the empty pantry and bounce my boot on the floorboards until one pops up in the corner. Then I slip my fingers beneath the board and find the latch, pull it, and hear the click as the mechanism releases the lock on the hidden door.

The empty shelves on the far wall move on recessed rollers to reveal a reinforced trap door that when open leads down to a lead-lined concrete cellar filled floor to ceiling with six-gallon buckets of survival gear, dry goods and freeze-dried meat. I unscrew the resealable lids and rummage around for a mylar bag labeled rice. It's enough to feed thirty people and I only need a cup, but who gives a shit. There's like five hundred pounds more where that came from.

Dinner takes about thirty minutes start to finish. Then I go find Tier.

I can see him through the screen door, right where I left him. Still sitting on the deck, legs hanging over, head and arms pushed through the railing. It's cool outside now that the sun's gone, but he doesn't look cold. I kick the door and he glances sideways over his shoulder at me.

"Dinner's ready."

He smiles but doesn't get up right away. Instead he brings his hands up to his forehead like he's got a headache, and lets out a deep breath.

"You gonna eat or what?"

He gets up and joins me inside without a word.

I follow him into the kitchen and go to the cupboard. "You want a bowl or a plate?"

He just stares at me for a few seconds, then finds his voice. "Plate, I guess."

"Sit, I'll bring it to you."

I watch him take a seat near the window and I shake my head as I pile on the food and then slide his over and sit down. "You look like you've never sat at a table to eat a real meal before."

"I have," he says quietly, "but it's been a really long time."

"Oh."
What do you sat to that?
We eat in silence.

Chapter Twenty

"I'm taking a bath," I announce after eating and staring out the window at the lake for several minutes from the couch.

"Wait." He's lounging in the living room chair sideways, feet dangling off one end, and he grabs my arm as I pass by. "There's hot water?"

"There will be after I turn on the water heater." He just stares at me, blinking. "We have a generator," I say. He smiles and nods, and I'm angry at his assumptions so I sneer at him and continue to walk towards the bedroom. "I can practically read your thoughts, Tier. And they're not flattering."

"What are ya talkin' about?"

"Your disparaging view of us Rural people. Like we're backwards freaks and hot water is something we give up for God." I slam the door behind me and fire up the generator in the bathroom. The cabin is pretty simple, but hot water was something my mom insisted on since camping makes people filthy and stinky. This is one of my more solid memories of her and my heart aches when reality hits me about how alone I am in the world.

The tub takes a while to fill since it is old and deep, so I peel off my disgusting clothes and lie on the bed to wait. The rustic room with the wood-paneled walls and comfy old sagging bed looks exactly like I remember, except for Tier's shit that has somehow made its way in here. He's got several of the tech devices lined up on the small table my mother used as a vanity, and I spy the letter and reading device on a chair.

I get up to get them when the tracking tech lights up and begins beeping. I hear the thud of footsteps as Tier realizes it's active and charges towards the door. I'm standing there, naked as the day I was born, when he barges in.

He stops short when he sees me. His eyes look me up and down and I raise my eyebrows at him severely, and all the while the device is beeping like crazy. I stand where I am and then he slinks past me, grabs the tech, and leaves the room, closing the door behind him. Saying nothing.

I grab the reader and letter and take it into the bathroom where the tub is just full enough for me to get in and not feel like I'm sitting in a puddle. There are some old bubbles in the cupboard under the sink and I empty the container under the running water. They froth up like marshmallows and I step in, making sure not the get the letter and reading device wet.

I look at the letter and read it again, just to make sure I completely understand what it is he's trying to say.

Dear Junco,

If you think about what makes a man it comes back to duty, honor, character, and courage. I'd like to think I have all four, but I'm sure by the time all this is over you'll disagree. I'm sorry about that. If I had all the time in the world, I'd let you come around on your own. But I don't. So you'll just have to trust me. I'm sorry, Junco. Duty calls your honor and courage reveals your character.

Capt. Raubtier
Aves 039
Presidential Guard

It makes me want to throw up, not because I actually understand the full meaning of his words, but because I understand the underlying sentiment. Whatever his feelings for me, they don't matter. He's got orders, he's got his duty, he's got more important things than me to worry about.

I look at the signature to try and make sense of it. Raubtier is his full name, apparently. It sounds familiar to me, but I can't immediately place it. Aves must be their own word for avian, which is also interesting since it is the word scientists use to classify birds in Earth taxonomy. Presidential Guard sounds important, so it's pretty clear he's got rank. I crumple the letter up and throw it on the floor across the room and then turn my attention to the reading device.

It babbles at me for a few minutes, basically asking the same stupid questions as before and I throw it across the room to join the letter, then sink down into the bubbles to soak the confusion away.

I'm not sure how long I've been in the tub when I hear Tier's knock on the door. It's locked, so when he tries the knob, it just clicks back and forth.

"Junco, open up."

I slip down in to the water to wet my hair again. It's tepid and the bubbles lie flat and sparse across the water.

"Junco!" He pounds harder now.

I ignore him and stand up in the water and pull the plug. He must hear me moving around because soon after his footsteps thud across the hardwood floors and finally fade.

The towel is large, but not luxurious in any way, and it wraps around me almost twice before I can tuck the corner in to hold it in place. I swipe the steam off the mirror and look at myself. The last time I did this I looked horrific, and soon after Tier sent a man's head spiraling up into the night as I watched helpless.

Why am I so unsettled?

I'm mad at him but I can't put my finger on the reason. I could say it is because Moju is gone. And yeah, that's probably a good portion of it. But that's not the only thing. If he's telling the truth then Moju did it so I could escape. Me fucking it all up by going back to help him and getting captured in the process would just make everyone's situation suck.

I'm more mad at myself, I think.

And a better question is why am I still hanging out with him?

A successful completion of his mission requires me to leave my planet. That's just crazy talk. It's never gonna happen. So why am I here?

Maybe the last time I asked myself this I could explain it away because of the healing endorphins, if that's what they were, but not now. That stuff has to be out of my system by now.

I hear Tier's heavy footsteps once again and lose my patience when he knocks. "Knock on that door one more time, Captain, and I'll make you sorry you ever met me."

He doesn't reply.

I swipe at the steam on the mirror once more, look myself in the eyes, and ask myself a final question. "What are you gonna do about all this, Junco?"

I wait until the tub has drained, then start the hot water again for Tier, and finally leave the bathroom. He's sitting on the bed waiting for me.

"I started the water for you. It's all yours now."

I walk over to the trunk at the foot of the bed and open it and begin searching for clothes that might fit me. They are all camos for hunting, but who cares. I find a white tank, a pair of snow-patterned fatigues, and a matching jacket and toss them all on the bed. Then I rummage around for a pair of socks and some old field boots and finally close the lid.

Tier is still sitting on the bed looking at me.

"If you're not gonna take a bath, get the hell out so I can dress."

He walks into the bathroom and closes the door without saying a word.

After I dress I take a seat outside on the grass, my back resting up against the large flat redrock that my dad put in the ground for stargazing when I was a kid. My well-worn fatigues should be a little snug since I haven't been out here in several years, but they aren't. I've probably lost ten pounds over the course of this affair. They are soft and comfortable though, and it makes me feel almost normal. I look up to see which of my friends are putting in an appearance and find all the ones I can currently see in the November sky, plus map out the ones I can't see and guesstimate when they might appear, if at all.

Tier is next to me before I hear the sharp slap of the old wooden screen door close behind him. "Got room for me out here, Junco?" he asks with hesitation.

The rock is long enough to fit a family of stargazers, so what am I going to say? "Sure."

He sits down next to me and leans back against the rock. I can smell soap on him and look over to find him shirtless and make a little grunt of disapproval. "It's a little cold to go without a shirt, don't you think?"

"Ya, but I didn't want to cut up your da's shirts without askin'. Wings, right?" He points to his back.

"Oh." It comes out pretty weak. "Well, you can cut one up, that's OK. It's not like he's going to be needing them." I look back up at the sky and pretend to search for familiar stars.

"So which one would ya be, then?"

"Huh?"

"The constellations," he says, pointing up. "Yer forever looking up there. Like ya wish you could fly away. How about Sirius?"

I laugh. A real outburst. "You're really lame, ya know that?" He just stares at me. "Well, not Sirius, that's not even a constellation," I say playing along. "Everyone names their dogs after Sirius anyway. Proper Farm girls should not aspire to be Sirius."

"Shouldn't they?" He leans forward and all I see of him are his black wings, the tips of which are curling along the ground they are so long. They are magnificent, even in the dark. I want to reach out and touch them, but I don't.

"Besides," I say, looking upward, "Canis Major isn't even visible this time of year. I usually choose from the ones I can see."

"Aye, but Sirius is also the star for Isis, who's a later version of Inanna."

I look at him and tilt my head. "Really?"

He nods. "On your world anyway. But Inanna herself is Venus, right? The morning and evening star. Which one then? If ya could be immortalized in the sky?"

I shrug. "Cetus?"

"The sea beast?" He cringes at me. "Now that is telling, Junco. Truly. Yer not a beast."

I think about it for a minute as Tier leans back against the rock. I can feel his warm arm touch me as he drops his head into my space. His dark hair tumbles down over his eyes, which have just a hint of glow to them, and he whispers, "And don't pick Draco either," with a wink.

I smile, and he smiles back. "No, not Draco. No matter what myth you read, Draco is always killed."

"Good point. But Cetus isn't much better. All the heroes of our sky tonight will kill him too. How about the Little Bear?"

"Hmmm," I say, thinking about it, "nah, little is only good if you're a kid. If I was Cepheus I'd be the king."

"True, enough. Ya, I can see ya as a Cepheus. I'd call ya Cephi. It's easier to say." I look up at him and he breathes out.

I laugh then, and my guard drops. This is how you got here, Junco. He's charming and funny. He has giant beautiful wings and a gorgeous body. And he knows just what to say and do.

"So yer settled then? It's the King for you?" he asks.

I look back up at the sky, thinking.

"Andromeda?" he prods.

I scowl. "No way."

"No, not the beauty waiting for her rescue?"

"Absolutely not. She comes off as helpless. Besides, she has all those children later on." As it comes out I have a tinge of regret, but I can't place the reason.

He laughs at that. "How about the vain Cassiopeia?"

"Her mother?" I scoff and shake my head. "I know who you'd be, though." I say as I look up at his face.

He smiles down at me. "Who?"

"Aquila, the eagle. The bird of prey."

He scoots closer to me then and reaches over to take my hand. "That would make me the property of Jupiter, though. And I'm no god's property."

"Then maybe you're Perseus? The hero who flies in on the winged horse."

"Ah, but if anyone's flying on the back of a horse then that would be you, Junco."

"But I'm a girl. So I can't be Perseus."

"Nah, you're not Perseus at all," he says and puts his arm around me and pulls me close. "If I were to choose, I'd make ya Cygnus, the swan."

I can feel my face go red, but it's dark, so hopefully he can't tell. "Why's that?"

"Because when you come home with me you're going to turn into a beautiful bird."

"How do you know that?" I ask, almost breathless as I take him in.

"Because, Junco, as much as ya might want to deny it, I know you're one of the Seven Siblings. And I'm calling ya back."

I look back up to the sky and point over to the east where parts of Taurus are just beginning to appear above the horizon. He follows my finger. "Ay. That's them. You call them the Pleiades, the Seven Sisters, but we call them the Siblings."

"I'm not sure I like your myth," I say. Mostly because I have nothing else to add at the moment and I don't want there to be silence.

"Nah, that was just some weird translation in that reader. Kinda hard to really appreciate the stories behind it. But there's another version of the Seven Siblings and how we got here. One that you'll like better, I think."

"What's it about?" I ask, interested despite myself.

"What all good stories are about, Junco. Forbidden love." He smiles at me and then gets to his feet and extends his hand out to help me up. I give him my hand and he lifts me up in one gentle motion, just like that first night out on the hill in the Stag.

"Come on, let's go in and I'll tell you the other story," he says as he tugs me towards the cabin.

But I stop. "Wait a minute, Tier. You never told me who you are. In the sky," I say, pointing upward.

His smile is gentle. "That's easy, darlin', I'm Orion, the hunter." We walk together towards the little cabin but I can't help but wonder, if he's Orion then who's he hunting?

Chapter Twenty-One

Inside the candles are out and the place is dark. I am just about to take a seat on the couch when I feel his light grip on my upper arm. "Not the couch, Junco. It was a mistake to let you sleep there alone last time. If someone would have found us, you'd be their prisoner right now." I follow him into the bedroom and lie down on the bed and pull a blanket over me. He slides in as well, and then turns me around and pulls me close, my back against his bare chest, and his left hand goes to caress my neck while his right hand rests on my belly.

I shiver at how close we are and at how he makes me feel. He must interpret this as a chill, because he pulls me even closer.

"Warm enough?" he asks.

I nod, but don't speak.

"This version is a proper story," he begins in a hushed voice that travels across my cheek, seeking out my ear. I know this is one of his charming tricks, but he feels so good, I don't want to stop him. "And these players are in the time of Old Crag, who, in case you haven't figured it out, is an ancient god. Like Jupiter."

I nod, and he continues.

"But the story is completely different and it's all about how Man and Birds, avians, like me, lived on Earth together thousands of years ago. Before the separation the Men and the Birds had no problems at all. They farmed the land, and raised the sheep and cattle, and traded and lived together for all of history. The only thing they didn't do is marry one another because Old Crag forbade the mixing of the higher species. But there was one Man, named Erane, and one Bird, named Irin, who were friends from childhood. And they did everything together.

"Never was there a time when someone saw Erane that they did not also see Irin because they lived in the same village, on the same dirt road, and even in cottages that stood next to each other. They were both born on the same day and shared every childhood experience together. As they grew older and began to mature, their differences became apparent. Birds aren't born with wings; it is only after they mature during metamorphosis that they develop from the form of a man to the form of a bird. As children you cannot tell one from another.

"But the time came for Irin's change and she was told that Erane could not see or hear about anything that happens during the morph. Irin was devastated because she'd never had to do anything alone ever before. She cried and pleaded that Erane be allowed to come with her. But the answer was always no.

"Irin kept up her pleading and when it came to be the night before morph, she threatened to run away. Her parents got upset and went to talk to Erane's family, asking if maybe the rules could be broken just this one time, for the sake of poor Irin who was helpless without Erne's company.

"Erane's family confessed that he too had threatened to run away if the two were separated and so the families went to seek the advice of the Council. The Council was worried, but not about the children or the families. They knew that Old Crage's rule about mixing the species was taken very seriously by Old Crag himself and if he ever found out that the children were making such threats, he would punish them. But since the time was upon them for Irin's transformation, there was nothing they could do but allow Erane to attend to her during her time of change. And this is how Erane became the only Man to ever know the secrets of the morph.

"And he was very careful and attentive to her as she grew her beautiful wings and fledged into a stunning avian female. She was so beautiful that he fell to his knees and proposed marriage. Irin was so overcome by his emotion that she accepted and they planned for a great wedding and feast to celebrate their love.

"On the day of the big celebration Old Crag was sitting on his throne in the sky when a magpie appeared to deliver a message. The message told of the marriage between Irin and Erane and Old Crag became so enraged he killed the messenger and flew down to the Earth and stood in the middle of the ceremony threatening to destroy the world if the two marry.

"But the community was tired of Old Crage's rules about staying separate. Isn't love enough, they asked? Isn't it better to let them love one another in all ways than to keep them apart?

"Old Crag didn't want to hear anything from the community so he gagged them to make them mute. And then he approached the bride and groom and asked if they would disobey him.

"Erane was the first to speak and he said, 'Old Crag, we love you. We love that you protect our world and we respect you and your views, but this community of Men and Birds has decided to become one. We ask, why should we not marry when we already live together, farm together, and pray together. This marriage will bind the Men and Birds together forever and this is how we wish it. We no longer accept your rules of segregation.'

"Old Crag held his temper very well, at least until he could ask Irin if she felt the same way. She did. Then Old Crag turned to the community of Men and Birds, lifted the mute spell, and once again asked if this was the consensus of everyone. And one by one each and every Man and Bird agreed with the marrying couple.

"When they had all said their peace, Old Crag turned back to Erane and Irin and said, 'You disobey my one and only law. And you break, by your own will, the covenant of peace. From this day forward you will never live in harmony again.' He banished the men to be bound to the Earth while casting out the Birds to the heavens, never to return until their transgressions had been cleared.

"Old Crag was far more unhappy with the Birds because they were his celestial race and so he also put a curse on them, corrupting their genetic essence. Slowly, over the punishment period, the genetic code of the Birds would deteriorate. But he didn't stop there, he also put a time limit on their free time as children, and any Bird who wasn't morphed and fledged out by the time they were twenty years old would die.

"And then he cursed the village for their disobedience, and made the Seven Siblings to watch and follow the punishment cycle. And the Seventh Sibling, the impure being that was neither man nor Bird but a mixture of both, will choose which race was to blame for the disobedience of Erane and Irin so that the final punishment can be handed down."

I force myself to ask the question even though everything inside is screaming not to. "What's the final punishment?"

"When the Seventh Sibling chooses the guilty species, they will be wiped out. Total annihilation."

Holy shit I hate mythology.

I am still for a long time after he finishes, and so is he. Then finally I find something to say. "Was that supposed to make me feel better?"

He sighs deeply, but I can feel his calming breath pull back from my cheek. "No, Junco. That was a way to let you know that there are consequences if you choose not to come with me. And sometimes," he pauses for a second, "forbidden things have to stay forbidden. It's just a story, less true than the version you read earlier even, a story."

I push his arms off me and roll over so that I am on my stomach and he can't see my face. "You know what, Tier, I think I'll take the answers you have now, if that's OK with you."

"Ya sure about that, Junco? You really want the truth?"

I turn my head to see his face, my cheek squished against the soft bed. "No, not really."

He smiles and rakes the hair away from my eyes and then huffs out a small breath. "Yer so strange, girl. I've never met someone so unsure of herself, yet so capable at the same time. How did ya get this way?"

I just look at him. "Get this way?"

He nods.

I shrug. "I have no idea."

He sinks down next to me, his face creeping closer to mine until we are so close I feel the heat radiate off his skin. "But ya do, Junco. Ya know exactly how ya got this way, ya just don't want to face the truth. I can tell ya what I know, but yer not gonna like hearing what I have to say." He swallows and then shrugs his shoulders.

"I feel the spaces inside. The missing places that shouldn't be there, shouldn't even be possible. I'm not sure I want them back, but it's catching up with me, Tier, I can feel it. If you want me to go with you, then tell me."

He pulls back, surprised. "And if I tell you, you'll come home with me?"

"Yes."

His eyes narrow in disbelief. "What if you don't like what I tell you? Then what?"

"Is there really any chance that you're gonna let me stay here?"

He turns away from me, then sits up and swings his legs over the side of the bed. I can hear his talons click on the wood floor as he leans down, stretching out his back muscles, and making the skin between his wings taut as he puts his head in his hands.

I sit up on my knees and reach out before I can stop myself. My fingers touch the thin membrane between his wings that make our backs so different. I feel him shiver, but he doesn't turn and he doesn't stop me, so I continue up to his wing and trace the outline of the bone that runs along the top until I get to the arch over his right shoulder. My fingers fall a little and I skim along the feathers.

I take one between my fingertips and rub it softly and he turns, forcing me to let go. We stare at each other, our eyes locking, and then I see his gaze drift down to my mouth. I involuntarily let out a breath, and he lifts his eyes up to mine, then wraps his hand around my neck and pulls me towards him.

I keep my eyes trained on his as he pulls me closer and closer. Then I feel his lips brush softly across my own and I breathe out. He pulls back a little and tries to talk, but his voice is barely a soft whisper. "I'll tell ya everything I know, Junco. But yer not gonna like me after."

He begins to move forward but it's me who pulls back a little this time. "Tier," I say in a low voice I barely recognize. "Please, I need to know."

He moves in towards me. I feel his lips pressing on my own and my eyes lose his gaze as they close. His tongue explores my mouth as his hands explore my back. He eases me back onto the bed and continues to kiss me gently on the mouth, on the neck, and then down to my chest. I stop him there and he lifts me up a little and pulls me into him, wrapping his wing and arm around me at the same time. Then he flips me on my belly so my face is pressed against his soft feathers and lifts up the back of my shirt to expose my skin. "My turn," he says.

His fingertips caress my shoulder blades and trace down my spine, I squirm and arch my back at his touch, then let out a little breath of air as he brings his fingers back up to my shoulders and drags them gently over to the nape of my neck. The touch of his lips makes me cry out softly. I don't want him to stop, but he does, and I can feel him trying to catch his breath as I do the same.

Chapter Twenty-Two

"If ya want the truth, darlin'," he says into my back so I can barely hear him, "I'll give it ta ya. But your world will never be the same again. So, I'll ask ya one more time, Junco, is this what you want to hear? Because I'd much rather tell you things that would make you love me instead."

"Is the truth that bad, Tier?" I turn a little so I can see his face.

He doesn't say anything for several long seconds and I'm about to repeat myself when he finally meets my gaze and nods. "It absolutely is."

"I need to hear it," I whisper.

"The world as you knew it a week ago is gone. This is a fact, just as it is a fact that I killed every last person in the Stag Camp."

"But why did you kill them?"

"Junco, whatever you think you know about Dale and those other men out there in the camp, it's either all wrong, or mostly wrong. What ya saw yesterday in the tunnels barely scratches the surface."

I swallow as he continues. "Dale was a part of the RR defenses." He feels me stir, and stops mid-sentence to head me off. "Look, Junco, I realize you've been told somethin' different, —but ya said you wanted the truth. Do ya still want it, then?"

I nod and stay silent.

"And not just any unit, either. Dale was part of a very advanced network of scientists who, contrary to how the rest of the RR lived their day-to-day lives, lived in a high-tech world of weapons, biotechnology, and bioengineering. He used alien genetics to make horrible creatures. Not just avian genetics, but the other races on Earth as well.

"Yer right about one thing though, I do have a pretty low opinion of the people in the RR, if only because I know their leaders and what they've done. How they lie to ya, all of ya, and how they keep ya subservient with their moral rules. But most of all, because ya let them do it.

"But let's just back up a little and start a few decades ago. You, Junco, are part of an avian clutch of seven, we know that for certain. And we now know that you came from genuine aves stock. From an immature aves called Gyr who went missing when he was sent to Earth. Way back before you were ever born. This was the very first hosting we did with our military class back in the Band where we live. He was in his sixteenth year and we sent him to the MR where he would be considered an adult. His reports were regular for about a year. He was making friends and was fitting in nicely. Then one day his report didn't come in and then the next report didn't come in, and finally, after several weeks of no word, we sent down another immature avian to check on him. He was gone. Simply disappeared.

"Life went on, other aliens made contact with Earth, and eventually a few years later we did as well. No one ever found out what happened to Gyr. And no one really thought about it either. Until a non-avian alien asked us for help in breaking out his brother from a camp out in a place several hundred miles from Peak City.

"I'll cut a long story short and tell you that we agreed, thinking maybe Gyr was there as well, and what we found was far worse than anyone ever thought was possible on a civilized planet."

"Was I there?" I whisper.

"Yes, Junco. You were there. As were hundreds of other things that they'd created through their bioengineering projects. Most of which were monsters, literal inhuman monsters straight out of fairy tales and nightmares, created with an amalgam of DNA from all races as well as animals. Those things down in the tunnels we saw? Just the leftovers that have taken root, just the memory of the atrocities we found at first. And we killed them all."

He says it in such a matter-of-fact manner that I can't think straight for several seconds.

"But the avian children were kept separate, away from everything that was going on in the larger experimental area. As our team was gathering them up for relocation back to the rendezvous point, the RR defenses showed up and retaliated with massive force and they were forced to leave ya all behind. You were just babies then.

"It wasn't until years later that we found out what happened to ya, that you were all farmed out to different sectors of the United Republics, and that the experiments had never really stopped."

He pauses then. "Ya still with me, Junco?"

I sigh. "Yeah."

"The RR kept you, Junco, only you. They gave ya to a local couple who couldn't have children, and gave them the privilege of

Farm Family status. From what I can tell, they treated ya right for a while. But I don't know that for sure, so stop me if I get it wrong. I don't know everything, Junco. Not much at all, in fact. But enough to tell you this story."

I look back at him. "How do you really know I'm that girl? The avian child? You weren't there, you're not that much older than me, so you were a small child back then too." I see the disappointment in his eyes as the words are coming out of my mouth, but I don't care.

"Before ya seven were taken back by the RR, the avians grabbed DNA samples from each child. I ran yer sample myself that night on the hill. You're one of them."

I just lie there, not quite sure if I should be sad, angry, or defiant.

"When I killed the others at the Stag Camp, that night ya hit the deer, I found more of these same creatures."

"What happened to them?"

He just shook his head.

I turn over and show him my back. "What else?"

"Your parents—"

"Stop. That's enough, OK. I get it. My parents were good people, Tier. My father loved me and I had everything a kid could ever ask for."

"And did that love include visits to your Uncle Dale's compound of genetic mutants over the years, eh?"

"There were never any monsters out at the Stag, I think I would have remembered that."

"Not if they didn't want ya to, Junco."

"OK, fine. My parents were monsters, too. Got it."

"Do ya want to know what happened to the others, then?"

"What others?"

"Your siblings?"

I stay silent, but I guess the question was rhetorical, because he turns me back around and answers anyway. "So obviously ya know Moju. But what ya don't know is how he grew up. The MR kept him in a cage for the first thirteen years. They morphed him early, at fourteen, and when he came out of it they taught him every which way he could torture and kill. You know what that name means, Junco? Moju?"

I look up at him now, my mouth drawn down and my eyes squinting.

"It literally refers to a sick and twisted psycho-sexual predator. He gave himself that name, Junco. A little telling, eh?"

"That's bullshit. He was perfectly rational and normal when I talked to him."

"He remembers ya, Junco, even if ya don't remember him. They didn't give him the drugs to dampen down his nightmares. You were right about one thing though. I was just pissed that you figured it out so quick." He stops and looks at me for a second. "If he appears normal to ya, it's only because he loves ya and wants to spare ya the pain of knowing who he is and what he's done. But make no mistake, he's a psychotic sonofabitch. If he'd of come out of that tunnel he would have promised ya all kinds of things to keep ya on Earth. Every lie your heart wants to hear right now. Everything you want me to say, but I won't. And then—"

"Then what? He'd change into a psychopath and tear my arms off in the night?"

"Lying to ya, to get ya to stay would be the equivalent scenario. If you don't complete the morph before yer twenty, you'll die all on your own. Our genetics are made so that they need this renewal, Junco. Maybe it's not a punishment like the story says, but it is real. And not morphing has consequences."

"And you?" I ask defiantly. "Are you a psychopathic killer as well?"

"Me? Yes. Me too. I've killed more people than I can count. And I don't shed a tear for any of them. Even your father."

I shoot up out of bed. "What did you say?"

But he just stares at me.

"WHAT DID YOU SAY?" I scream.

"It's true. It was me who took his last breath, but only to put him out of his misery."

"Misery! What misery?" I scream again, and then he clamps his hand over my mouth.

"Shhhh."

"Don't you tell me to be—"

But his hand presses tighter and cuts off my words. "That's enough." His words burn with anger as they came out and so I force myself to settle down.

"I asked ya if you wanted the truth before this started, and ya said yes. I, on the other hand, urged you to reconsider." He lifts his hand

and I fling myself away from him and sit up on the bed, wanting to get up and walk out, but not sure if I should push it and piss him off any more.

"You said if I stayed with Aren I'd end up like my father. You made me believe that *he* had something to do with it! And now"—I half turn my face towards him—"I find out you're the asshole who ruined my life."

He puts a hand up and squeezes the flesh above the bridge of his nose, like I am giving him a headache. "I'm not done, Junco. Do ya want to hear the rest of the truth? Or should we just leave it at that and you can go and throw yer hissy fit?"

"There's more? Who else did you kill? My first goldfish? My dog? Any of my avian siblings?"

"Yer father begged me to kill him, Junco. It was a merciful act—"

"FUCK YOU!" I scream as I get up to flee the bedroom.

Chapter Twenty-Three

I don't get but a few paces before he yanks me back by the arm. "Let go of me, Tier," I say between gritted teeth. He just looks at me and shakes his head.

"No, darlin', you asked for the truth and if I let you go now, you only have half the story."

"I don't want to know any more, OK? So don't bother."

He shakes his head again. "Sorry, Junco. You're gonna get this part whether you like it or not. So get back in here and *sit down.*" His command makes me jump a little, but I try to pull my arm from his grip anyway. He resists and pulls again. I look up at his face and see the anger in his eyes and give in. "Fine, talk," I say as I sit down on the bed.

He sits next to me and I move away from him, like I'm in third grade and he's got the cooties. I feel a little juvenile at my reaction, but not for long because his words begin to spill out once more and I'm forced to hear it through to the end.

"Yer father, Junco, was absolutely in on the cover-up of who ya were and where ya came from. I've looked at this from every angle, and there is no way to deny it. Yer da took you to the Stag twice a year. I found the medical records to match that schedule when I was there last week. They—" He stops here and I'm afraid to say anything, so I just sit quietly. Finally the silence drags on too long and I have to look up to see if he will continue.

"They what?" I ask.

He just shakes his head and looks down at the ground.

"What? Just fucking say it!"

"They changed ya. That's all I know right now, they changed ya—somehow and for some reason."

I lie back on the bed and feel the tears come quickly. "What did they do to me?"

When he finally speaks, his voice is soft, barely a whisper. "I don't know for sure, Junco. Made ya more"—he stops for a moment—"avian, I think. Took yer human parts away."

My head spins and I have to close my eyes and press my fists into my eye-sockets to make it stop.

"I'm not sorry for killing your da, like I said, he asked me to finish it. But I am sorry this is your fucked-up life. Ya don't deserve it."

I don't have anything to add so I lie there with my silent tears streaming down my cheeks.

"Where did yer father die, Junco?"

I screw up my face, thinking for several minutes. I'm trying, I'm looking, but I can't find that memory anywhere.

"Convenient, isn't it?"

I grunt. "What's convenient? Quit fucking with me and just say it, Tier."

"It was in a church, do ya remember that?"

I am back in the dream the first night I met Tier, out on the hill in the Stag. I'm a figure in a stained-glass window. I let out a deep breath. "A church?"

He nods his head. "There was a meeting, some secrets were leaked about what was going on in the Stag. They were making plans for ya, Junco."

He looks down to see if I am following what he's saying. My face must look confused, because then he breaks it down into smaller bits for me. "Yer da was gonna sell ya, Junco."

The laugh comes out too quick and even to me, it sounds forced. "OK."

He shrugs. "It's the truth."

"And then you magically show up and kill him? What? To save me?" I let out a snort. "That's bullshit."

"No, Junco. I had no intention of saving ya. Like I said, I only put him out of his misery. Do ya remember any of this?"

"No," I lie, "not one bit."

"I was watching you for a long time already, when that night came for yer da to die. But there were some"—he hesitates and I know he's choosing his words carefully—"unusual developments—leading up to that night. Yer da was called to the church in Ramah. I watched the whole meeting through a third-story stained-glass window, so I didn't catch all of it, but enough." He looks down at me. "I saw enough. The killer tortured yer da until he passed out from the pain."

He stops and looks up at the ceiling before he finds his voice again. "I killed seventeen people that night. Including your da. But I let the torturer go."

"What?" I turn to look at him. "Why?"

He looks me straight in the face but he doesn't answer that question. "I'm sorry for a lot of things, Junco, but I'm not sorry for taking a single life in that church."

My mind is racing, trying to put it all together. The thought that's been nagging at me, eating away at me, finally surfaces. "They have more clones of me, don't they?" It isn't exactly a question, but more something I needed to say out loud to make it real.

"Aye, you can bet on it. And they had a lot of plans for ya—plans you weren't necessarily on board with."

We sit there for a long time and eventually he climbs back into bed next to me, but he doesn't pull me close and I don't move towards him either. My mind is jumbled with the new information and I frantically rack my brain to try and remember something, anything that will corroborate this story outside of that dream. But there is nothing there.

I fake sleep after a while. Finally, just after dawn, Tier gets up and takes a tech device to the other room.

I get up too. But not to check on him or see what he's doing.

I open the window, slip out in silence, and run like hell through the woods.

I expect to be caught by him within the first few minutes, but I run on and on and on. Up the hill, over the patch of medium grass which outlined the place I called the meadow when I was a kid, into the conifers, and towards the only people I know to go to.

My feet falter and I trip more than once as my heart pounds with adrenaline. My breath comes out in long hard gasps as I make my way through the forest. Finally I have to stop. I bend over and grab my chest with one hand and lean my other against a thickly barked pine. I feel the sticky resin on my fingertips as I try to get myself under control.

In my mind, Tier is the liar. Not my father, not my Council, not my country.

Tier.

I feel it in my heart. I know it.

I look around and see shadows from the trees and all I think of are those dark wings and long talons waiting to take me back to the nightmare.

And so I run again.

Because to stay, to accept everything he told me without question, would be betrayal.

Treason.

Maybe there is some secret program that creates inhuman monsters from the genetics of children. Maybe I am an avian. Maybe my father willingly allowed me to be subjected to experimentation and cloning and was about to sell me.

Maybe.

I may be sheltered from most of the horrible things in the world living in the RR, and I may be naive in certain ways. But I am not stupid. And it would be the epitome of stupid to willingly allow everything—my life, my family, and every rule I've ever lived by—to be wiped out by one good-looking guy with wings who tells me they are false.

My legs burn as I climb a steep hill that will take me into the outlying area of the Baumer farm and when I get to the top, I stop.

The view is incredible and I can see everything. Including the large mass of soldiers who are at my house in the distance.

Of course they are at my house! They are looking for me, I'm an RR citizen who was kidnapped by an alien. I've been missing for, hell, I have no idea. My days are so mixed up. A week, I think. I'm a prominent Farm Family daughter, World Grand Champion Mounted Aerialist. I'm probably on the front page of every newscreen on the planet.

I strain my eyes to make out details at my property and I see plenty of military vehicles, but I also see many farm trucks as well and I breathe a sigh of relief. The military isn't there to kidnap and hold me as a state secret. If they were, then my neighbors wouldn't be allowed to just pull in the farm and park their trucks.

They're waiting for me to come home.

The tears stream down my face as I accept that thought as truth and I feel a flood of stress flow out of me. These people love me. I'm not a freak, I'm not an alien.

I'm just Junco.

They're worried about me.

I get back under the cover of the pine needles and make my way down the hill to the modest farmstead below, wiping the tears from my face, and taking a moment to catch my breath and find some calm.

I am just about to the edge of the clearing, where the crunchy carpet of needles meets the grass that will take me to the Baumer's driveway, when the doubt creeps in.

I stop.

And look up into the trees and make out a shadow standing on a branch.

It's Tier.

My heart skips, literally skips and flutters so bad I think I will die on the spot from a heart attack, and I cannot breathe.

He smiles. "Go ahead, Junco. Go see for yourself. Tell them everything I said. Don't leave out one word."

I bend over to try and calm myself as the hyperventilation takes over. I don't hear him come down, but he's next to me, putting his hand on my back, bending over to try and see my face, saying nothing.

In between my sharp gasps for air I manage to speak. "I'm. Not. Coming."

"I know, Junco."

But I can't stop talking now. "You're lying. I—"

I what? I can't finish my sentence. So I just drop to the forest floor and sit, and try to regain some control over my body. He drops down next to me and leans back against the tree trunk, letting me stay that way for a long time. But even after that, nothing makes sense.

I am playing with the long-dead pine needles on the ground when he finally speaks. "If ya have these doubts, Junco, then go. I want ya ta come on yer own, I want to make it a choice. I don't want to steal ya away, I really don't."

I sniff loudly, desperately trying to control my running nose, and then get to my feet. "But you will if you have to? Is that what you're saying underneath those nice words?"

He stays silent.

I wipe my hand across my nose and find my voice. "I'm going home. If you want to stop me, then go ahead, but I'm not walking away from my life just because you tell me some far-fetched story about monsters." And I turn and step out in the grass.

He doesn't snatch me up or call out to me. As far as I can tell he doesn't even get up off the forest floor. So I just keep walking forward until I reach the driveway, then follow it up to the house.

The Baumer place is a very traditional farmhouse complete with a large covered front porch. When I reach it, I stop and turn back to look into the trees for a moment. Tier is still there, standing now, just on the edge of the shadows that fall around the branches. For the first time I realize that we're wearing matching hunting gear. Snow camo pants and jacket with a white t-shirt. He crosses his arms and waits for me to make the final decision. I turn my head and climb the porch stairs and force myself to knock on the door.

Mrs. Baumer answers and when she sees me she begins to cry, taking me by the shoulders and asking me questions. I look back at the woods once more, but he's gone, and then her husband appears and the old couple ushers me over the threshold and into the familiar farmhouse.

Chapter Twenty-Four

Mrs. Baumer has me in the tiny downstairs bathroom with the door closed and she's talking a mile a minute, but I just stand there and let her wash my face, even around my puffy eyes, and it stings when the soap touches each and every cut and bruise. I can hear Mr. Baumer in the kitchen down the hallway, talking to someone on a comm tech.

Mrs. Baumer's flushed face is right in front of me then, like she's waiting for an answer, but I never heard the question. "What?" I ask.

She softens up when she hears my voice. "Your fingers, Junco. What happened to your fingers?"

I forgot all about my missing fingers to be quite honest. And right now, I really don't want to be reminded.

"Did he chop them off, dear?"

I look at her for a minute, my brow in a furrow I'm sure, then try and imagine Tier chopping off my fingers, but that's something I can't see in my mind's eye at all. "No," I finally say. "A nightdog ate them."

She gasps and begins tearing off the bandages that I had also forgotten all about. I look down and they are filthy with dirt and grime and dried blood. How could I have forgotten about my missing fingers?

She keeps pulling, looking up at my face to see if she is hurting me, but she isn't. And I don't stop her. So she continues. "What kind of bandage is this?" she asks, more to herself than to me. But I answer anyway.

"Avian. It's an avian membrane."

It takes forever to unwrap the long tissue-thin swathe of synthetic textile and the air tickles with cold as it rushes in to fill the space. She continues to peel the bandage off, again looking up to see if she is hurting me. But she's not. By the time she removes the last layer and my fingers come into view I am less surprised that they are healed than I would have been if they were mangled. Mrs. Baumer lets out a curt "Hmph," and then throws the bandages in the trash.

I bring my fingers up to my face to see them better. They were bitten off at the first joint from the bottom, so there is really nothing left of them. The skin is white and smooth, like any newly formed scar, and I find that I have very little control over what they do and when they do it. If I wiggle them, they don't really move, but I still feel the missing parts that should be attached.

Mrs. Baumer has left the bathroom while I was preoccupied with my new disability, and now I can hear her talking to Mr. Baumer down the hall. They're arguing about whether or not to let the military come get me. Mr. Baumer says no, and if they try he will shoot them before they get to the porch. I smile at that.

Mrs. Baumer is trying to talk some sense into him when I enter the kitchen and they stop talking. Mr. Baumer is still holding the comm tech and he leans in and whispers, "I'll call you back."

"Junco, please sit down here, dear." He pulls a chair from the kitchen table for me to sit in. I do as I'm told. "They want to come get you, but I told them no. We'll drive you home ourselves when you're ready. Is that OK?" His eyes smile down at me and this gives me some courage.

"Mr. Baumer, I need to ask you some questions." His happy face slides into sadness and he ushers Mrs. Baumer out, handing her a rifle from the kitchen counter and telling her to go keep watch for the military men. If she sees them, she's to nick-em in the knees when they come down the walkway. The kitchen door swings behind her as she leaves and Mr. Baumer stands there for a few seconds just looking at me.

"What is it, Junco?" he finally says.

"I don't even know where to start."

"Try the beginning, dear."

"This isn't about where I've been or what I've been doing, or even who had me."

"No?" he replies, pulling up a chair next to me at the table.

"I've been with the avian, I'm sure everyone knows that already. He's—"

"He's what, dear?"

"He told me some things," I say, looking over at him to gauge his reaction. "Things I don't want to believe to be true." Sweat is dripping down his face and he reaches in and produces a handkerchief from his pocket to wipe his brow. "And since you were a Council Elder for, hell, I have no idea, most of my life..." His eyebrows go up at my cursing, but he stays silent. "I figure you'd be the best one to ask."

"Ask, Junco," he says with the most serious face I've ever seen. And then his hand reaches over and takes mine, the one with the missing fingers. If he notices them, he doesn't show it, so I assume Mrs. Baumer didn't get around to telling him about how they became snack food. I sit there and struggle with the right question before choosing my words carefully. "Are you, or were you, involved in the secrets that surround my origins?"

His mouth draws into a flat line across his face and he nods.

"Am I human or avian?"

At this he simply shrugs. "I don't know, Junco. I knew you were adopted but they have been telling me some wild stories over the past few days."

"Stories like what?" I ask.

"Stuff I refuse to believe," he says simply.

I can relate. I can't believe them either.

"I think we should take you home now. There are quite a few people there who want to talk to you. I'm sure they can answer your questions."

He gets up but my good hand reaches out to take his arm. "Mr. Baumer, were my parents good people?"

He sits back down. "Junco, I knew your dad from the day he was born. And your mother and our smallest daughter were best friends for years before your father proposed. Your parents loved you, and that's all I can say about the rumors that are floating around right now. They loved you. They were good, from what I knew of them. That's all I can say."

"Did they both come from Farm Families?"

He laughs at this one. "Yes, they both came from Farm Families."

Finally, a confirmed lie from Tier. I feel a small bit of satisfaction to have proved this point wrong and since Mr. Baumer seems to be waiting for my next question, I ask another. "Did you know my father's friend Dale?"

He looks me straight in the eye again. "I didn't, Junco. I can't vouch for him or answer to any of the things they are saying about the Stag right now. I'm sorry."

"OK," I say, and begin to get up.

But he stops me with a gentle hand. "I did think it was weird that your father took you out there all these years. The Stag is no place for children."

My heart feels like it's being clenched with a fist.

Maybe all the things Tier told me aren't true. Like maybe there aren't any monsters, and maybe I'm not an avian, or maybe I'm not going to die if I don't go with him to grow wings before I'm twenty, but some of what he told me about my life is true.

I can feel it.

We walk outside together and find Mrs. Baumer sitting on the porch swing with her rifle. She takes me by what's left of my bad hand and leads me to their farm truck. I climb in and slide over on the long seat bench and they each get in so I am sandwiched between them. We roll along the gravel drive slowly as we make our way towards my farm, but the only thing I'm wondering is whether or not Tier is watching me from above.

My house couldn't be more different than the Baumers' little farmhouse. It is a third-quarter modern geometric, built last century, and is really nothing more than a hollow square with all the rooms along the perimeter, while the courtyard encompasses the entire middle interior. Not all geometric courtyards have domes, but ours does, housing the pool and a lush tropical landscape that oozes with humidity, regardless of the season or temperature outside.

Out of habit I count the horses in the paddocks as the house comes into view from the back road and I know from the number that they are all out on pasture. Good. While there's not much grass left, it's better than them being cooped up in their stalls starving for the last week.

Our barn is also a modern geometric based on the same design. It sits about a hundred yards back from the house. The stalls run the entire perimeter, while the interior, which is only a partial dome, houses the main arena. A breezeway separates the arena from the stall doors and when we pass it from the back, I can see all the way through to the other side.

I study the house and surrounding grounds as we approach and I feel the excesses of my sheltered existence for the first time. If you compare our house to the Baumers' little farmhouse, there is a clear discrepancy of wealth, yet Mr. Baumer was a Council Elder for decades.

I had never thought about how much money we did or didn't have before. Or whether or not I had more than others. But I can't get Tier's words out of my head. My parents were rewarded with wealth for their active participation. My excitement for discovering that they were not rewarded with the title of Farm Family is gone now. Obviously they got their title genetically, but that doesn't explain the wealth. My grandparents' homes were more along the line of the Baumers' little farmhouse. In fact, there were only a handful of Families that deviated from that template, and none of them had a house as different as ours. Someone built it, but it wasn't my father and mother because the house was almost seventy years old. So they acquired it along the way somehow.

The activity at my house is indescribable chaos as we ramble slowly up the long driveway. There are people that are neither military nor neighbors and friends and this confuses me until Mr. Baumer says, "Who let the media in, for Jeremiah's sake?"

They swarm the old truck, pushing at each other to get a look at me, their hands high in the air to try and get an overview shot, but Mr. Baumer, to his credit, keeps on driving. I'm almost afraid he's going to run them over, but they jump out of the way as soon as they figure out he has no intention of stopping.

When we do finally reach the house and stop they swarm again, and then the RR Defenses are there, surrounding the truck and pushing them back. Mrs. Baumer leans over. "Are you ready, Junco?"

I shrug, and she takes that as a yes and opens the door. A soldier helps her out, and then I scoot out her door as well. They are yelling my name and pushing at the RR soldiers. Someone fires a shot in the air and everyone screams and then whoever is in charge is shouting for them to get back. Another soldier grabs my upper arm firmly and pulls me away and when I look back at Mrs. Baumer, she's already been pushed back into the truck and then they are rolling again.

Chapter Twenty-Five

The Defense soldier is talking to me, but nothing is getting through. I just follow him into my house and when he shuts the door everything goes quiet. This seems to be his cue to stop and explain things.

"Miss Coot, I am very sorry for all this intrusion into your home. I am Lieutenant Stockton, RR Defenses, and I am ordered to take you to the commanding officer immediately."

I nod up at him and he leads me to the door of my father's office, knocks, twice, then opens the door and gestures me in.

Aren is sitting in my father's chair, his head in his hands, looking like complete shit. Stockton closes the door and we are alone.

"I thought you were dead?" I say.

He lets out a deep sigh. "Ditto, Junco. We've been looking for you everywhere." He gets up and comes over to me and hugs me. I hug him back out of politeness, but I'm not sure what's going on yet, so I pull back.

He looks me up and down. "Did he hurt you?"

It takes a minute to sink in. "Did he hurt me? No. But a nightdog ate my fingers." I hold them up matter-of-factly and he just stares at me, then takes them in his hand to examine them, as if he's a doctor and he can glean important information just by looking at them.

"How did you survive?" I ask. "I thought he killed you? He kind of led me to believe that everyone was dead back there in the Stag. I certainly didn't see any survivors when we flew away."

Aren takes me by the shoulders and steers me towards my father's big chair and pushes me until I sit. Then he takes a seat on the desk and puts his head in his hands again.

"How are you the commanding officer here, Aren? Why are there MR soldiers outside?"

He rubs the stubble on his chin, but doesn't answer.

"Are you going to just sit there? Or will you answer my questions?"

Now he meets my gaze, but still no words come out.

I get up and walk towards the door. "Fine, I'm going to my room. I've been played with enough for the past week, I don't have the time or interest in playing with you today. So, when you're ready to tell me what the fuck is going on, you let me know. OK?"

"Wait," he says before I can reach the door. "Just a minute. Hold on, OK? Just give me a second to try and put all the pieces together."

I turn back to him with a sneer. "Let me help you, how about that? I'm some freak bird alien. Oh no, wait—I'm not a bird, did you know that avians aren't birds? Well, they're—I mean we're not. I'm an alien, my parents are monsters who took me in for some sort of genetic experiment twice a year, the RR is as corrupt as all hell, and you're in on all of it. How's that for putting the fucking pieces together?"

His brow furrows a little. "Junco, I swear I don't know if any of that is true, not one word of it. But I've heard things that are beginning to be repeated so many times they're getting hard to dismiss."

"What things have you heard?"

"You, your parents, and the Stag. It was some massive cover-up with the United Republics, and I just want to make this very clear, right now. I am not involved in any of that. None of it."

"So which part are you involved in?"

He lets out a deep sigh. "I'm just the delivery guy."

"And my brother?"

He shakes his head at me. "What brother?"

"The avian the MR held hostage all these years?"

"Shit. Shit. Shit. Shit. I know of him, Junco. Of him. I want to be clear here, I don't know anything else. Nothing."

"And you're the commander here? Not likely, Aren."

He comes toward me where I'm standing in the middle of the room and looks down into my eyes. "Now you see where I'm at?"

I shake my head no. Because no, not really. I don't.

"They're using me, Junco." It comes out strong, but I can see the fear on his face. "I'm going down here."

"If you're not really in charge, then who is?"

"Colonel Slag, Junco. That goddamn RR bastard's been after you forever. He rolled in to the MR a little over a week ago, had the superiors all up in a wad, put me in charge, and told me to bring you back and kill the avian."

"What do they want with me?" I ask coldly.

"I don't know, I swear."

"Why do they want to kill Tier?"

"Because he was sent here to kill *you*."

I laugh. "Kill me? Well he's got a funny way of killing me, since I'm still alive and he let me walk away."

"So he tested you and you're not the Seventh Sibling?"

I shake my head. "What are you talking about now?"

"He was sent here to kill you, Junco, I saw the orders myself. You're not one of the Six, you're the—"

"The what?" I ask, unable to let him keep going for fear of what he will say.

"You're the Seventh, not the pure avian like the last girl they took."

My head spins and I suddenly realize I'm going to faint when Aren grabs me and pulls me over to my father's couch. I sit back and wait it out. "What last girl?" I finally manage.

"Oh, shit. I'm sorry, Junco, I thought he told you that. You know about the other guy, the other avian. I just figured you knew about her too."

"I'm going to be sick," I say as I run towards the bathroom connected to the office. I slam the door behind me, lift the seat on the head and dry-heave my guts out. Then I sit back on the cold tile floor and listen dispassionately to Aren barking orders at people on the other side of the door.

A little while later he knocks, tries the knob, and when it turns he pushes forward, but my body is leaning up against the door and it opens only a few inches.

"Junco?" I can hear the hesitation in his voice.

"What," I answer. Flat. Emotionless.

"Lemme in."

I scoot away from the door and he opens it the rest of the way, then yanks me to my feet without speaking.

"No," I protest as I fling my arms around so he will drop his hands. "I don't want to see anyone yet."

"Fine, but you're not going to mope on the bathroom floor all day. Get up and come out here with me."

I follow him out to my father's office and plop down into the deep couch, resting my head on the armrest. "Tell me everything you know," I demand.

And to my surprise, he does.

It comes spilling out like he's been waiting his whole life to talk to me. For part of it I sit motionless, waiting to hear the terrible truth, and other parts I let the tears escape. It's not quite the same story that Tier told me, but close enough to establish that most of what he said is either true, or significantly close to true.

A soldier interrupts us at one point, and I recognize him as CP from the makeshift field-camp oh so long ago. He's smiling when he first looks at me, but then his face drops when he sees my expression. When Aren turns away to sign the papers he brought, he silently mouths something encouraging. I turn away before he's done and watch as Aren hands the pen back. CP turns to leave, then stops, and looks back at us. "Sir? The men wanted me to ask if there are blinds that can be drawn on the windows, so the media can't see in?"

Aren pushes him out the door, mumbling something at him. But as soon as the door is closed he turns back to me. "Can we block the windows, Junco? It really is annoying being so exposed since the house is literally made of glass. I don't know how you could sleep in a house that has no shades. Especially since—"

"HOUSE?" I ask the ceiling.

"Welcome home, Junco, I've missed you dearly, my friend."

I breathe out quickly, then gasp for more air. "Thank you. Can you please opaque the windows?" The room is instantly dark as the light shining through the wall of windows facing the courtyard blacks out. "And turn on evening lights, too?" The lights pop on and the courtyard is glowing with soft artificial illumination as I watch the astonished expression on Aren's face. "Thanks, HOUSE."

"You're welcome, Junco. I hope you are feeling OK. I detect some anxiety in your voice."

"Unfortunately, I'm not. But thanks for your concern. I appreciate it."

"I'm sorry, Junco. Please let me know if there is anything I can do for you."

I nod and she's silent.

Aren is still looking at me in disbelief. "What now?" I ask.

"You have a sentient house?"

"For security," I say.

"You have a sentient house?" he asks again, like I didn't hear him correctly the first time.

"Yes, Aren, I have a sentient house. What?" I ask when he begins to shake his head and mumble under his breath. "What?"

"You Farm Families are such blood-sucking hypocrites!"

Now it is my turn to be stunned. "What the hell are you talking about, Aren?"

"You're a Farm Family, in the Rural Republic, Junco. Surely you aren't so far removed from our society that you think a sentient house is an acceptable form of tech?"

"It's a security system, Aren. Lots of people have security systems in the RR."

"Yeah, it's called a dog." He says it with such contempt I'm taken aback for a minute. "Is this how all of you live? With a heated pool in the courtyard, a tropical rain forest as your personal garden, songbirds singing on every branch, and some artificial intelligence thrown in for good measure?"

"Are we really having this conversation?" I ask, completely pissed off.

"Do you want to know how I grew up, Junco? We had no indoor plumbing, no central heating in the winter, no air conditioning, no hot showers, no cars, no trucks, and certainly not enough sense to know that our parents were completely nuts for making us live like this until I moved out and discovered the entire civilized fucking world took toilets for granted."

"You really want to play this game? I didn't ask to be born into this family, and guess what? It turns out I wasn't born into this family. I didn't ask for this life. And if you want to trade, I'll be happy to go out to wherever the hell you're from and stick it out while you bask in the artificial sunshine next to our pool and then learn that you're not even human!"

The lights dim and HOUSE's voice booms out from the ceiling. "Lockdown will be initiated in fifteen seconds. Lockdown will be initiated in fifteen seconds."

"Give her the signal, Junco," Aren growls.

"I'm fine, HOUSE, signal protocol 3zsk256478."

"Security action aborted," my house replies. Then it adds, "Junco, you should ask these people to leave for your own safety. Would you like me to make them leave?"

Aren puts his head in his hands and takes a seat on the couch to calm down.

"No. He's fine. We're just really stressed out right now."

"Would you like me to call your dad and tell him to come home, Junco?"

I never explained his death. In fact, I can't even remember if I talked to anyone during the time between his death and my excursion out to Stag. I let the words escape, half because I can't stop myself even if I wanted to and half because for the smallest moment I want so badly to believe that this is all a nightmare. "Do you have a number for him, HOUSE? I really want to talk to him. Can you find him for me, please?"

Aren comes over and puts his arm around me. "Don't do this, Junco. Stop. Make her stop."

But she answers before I can. "I'm sorry, Junco. I have no number for your dad right now. If you tell me where he is I can look him up in the data systems."

I wipe my hand across my face, push the shit back down, lock it in, and look Aren in the eyes. My response slides out without a hint of emotion. "He's rotting in hell, HOUSE. Try there first."

Chapter Twenty-Six

I'm back in the bathroom, but this time Aren leaves me alone in there for so long that I actually fall asleep on the rug in front of the sink. When he finally knocks I sit up so fast my head spins.

"Look, Junco," Aren says through the door, "we need to come up with a plan here. Come out of there and deal with this."

I come out and plop back down onto the couch.

"Things are spiraling out of control outside. The media is here, I mean media from all over the world, Junco. You might have been a minor curiosity before you were taken by an avian, but right now you're the biggest story on the planet. We need to get rid of them, and then we need to come up with a way to defuse what's happening here."

"Well, maybe you should start by telling me what is happening here."

He walks over to my father's chair and sits down, then spins it so he's looking out at the spotlights lighting up the lush tropical landscape of the courtyard. "I think we're all about to be killed."

"By who?" I snort.

He spins back to face me. "Take your pick?" he says, and shrugs. "Maybe the aliens, the RR Council, the United Republic Secretaries, Council 3, the Mountain Republic, hell, maybe it will be your neighbors and friends. Who knows? All I know is that from my viewpoint, the shit is stacked, Junco. Fucking shoulder high."

He spins back to the tropical view of the courtyard so all I see is his military haircut peeking out from the top of the massive leather chair. "I'm dead, that's all I know," he continues. "They gave me this assignment for one reason and one reason only and that's so they have someone to blame it on."

Oh shit, now he's paranoid. "Blame *what* on?"

He spins back again. "The attack! Don't you pay attention to anything?"

"What attack?" I growl. My patience has run out and I feel the heat rise in my face as I look at him.

"The fucking avians, Junco! They're everywhere out there. We can sense their shielding, they have more ships out there than we have reporters!"

"OK," I say, trying my best to remain calm so HOUSE doesn't initiate the security protocol again, "when I said tell me everything you know, that meant everything you know, you asshole. You never mentioned avians attacking!"

He lets out a deep breath and continues to spin between the courtyard view and the office and it's really pissing me off. "I've got it. You make a statement to the media, right? You let them in on a few choice details, this creates interest in your story, your face is all over the newscreens, and then they can't come in and take you. How about that?"

"What kind of statement?" I ask with hopeful hesitation.

"You know, just bits and pieces to make your story compelling, like the nightdog eating your fingers. Flash your stubs to the cameras, then add in your daring escape, and say you're very happy to be home."

I sniff loudly. "I don't know."

"Trust me, Junco. They aren't leaving until they hear from you. You have to go out there and say something."

"And when they leave, so what? How does that stop us from being killed by the Council or the avians, or whoever else wants to sweep all this under the carpet?"

He bites his thumbnail as he continues to swivel in my father's chair, and I'm just about to scream at him when he answers, "Call a meeting. Of the council." He looks up at me, smiling. "No, you say you already asked for a meeting with the Council tomorrow, and they accepted."

"But they haven't."

"Sweet Jeremiah, Junco, how the fuck do you make a living at covert ops? You're playing them. You say that they agreed to meet with you tomorrow, then everyone waits to see what happens. Meanwhile, no one can attack us tonight, and we'll have a little more time to figure this out."

"I don't make a living at covert ops, by the way." He sneers at me and shakes his head. "But letting that comment slide, what the fuck do I say to them in the meeting?"

This time he doesn't spin, or bite his nail. He just sits for a few minutes, eyes darting back and forth. "I'm not sure yet. Give me the night to think about it."

"Well, I'm not going out there to make a statement looking like this. I need to go to my room and get cleaned up."

He puts his hands out and shakes his head, an expression that from my end reads, so what the fuck should I do about it?

"Come with me, Aren. I don't want to be alone."

This makes him smile, the scared little girl needs the big strong man to protect her.

Whatever. I let him have his moment.

Just keep talking. Keep drowning out the voices in my head so I can damp them back down into submission. *Otherwise I'll be picturing myself standing on the edge of a fucking dock. In front of me is a fucking mountain lake and behind me is a small fucking cabin...*

I watch Aren's face as he looks around my room.

"What?" I growl.

"Well, no offense, Junco, but it looks like a princess threw up in here."

He's right. This cannot be my room. I haven't been six for a very long time, but my name is on the door and my fingerprints trigger the biometrics on the doorknob.

So.

Apparently it is.

"Shut up and take a fucking seat on the flying carpet while I take a shower."

He eyes the bench covered in a genuine Persian carpet suspended from the ceiling by cables, and for a minute I wait to see if he actually tries to climb on, but he plops down in the white fuzzy beanbag chair. Then he grabs a photo album from the little end table next to him and thumbs through it.

I was right about him being chatty because I can hear him talking to me all through my shower. I just have no idea what he's saying because I'm too busy standing under the blasting hot water to care. At one point he even comes into the bathroom to ask about a photo of me on a pony, but I just shoo him out and tell him to wait.

I take my time washing and conditioning my filthy hair and lathering myself with sweet pea soap, then comb it out in the steamy mirror. I peel off a few avian membranes on my calf that I didn't notice during my last bath and check every last bruise, burn, and cut on my body before wrapping myself up in my thick cotton bathrobe.

When I come out he's sitting on the end of my purple canopy bed, his camo fatigues clashing badly with the unicorn pattern on the quilt, and his combat boots are resting on the white bed rail so he can prop a photo album in his lap.

"Junco," he says, looking anything but properly embarrassed. Hell, I'm embarrassed for him. "Are all these pictures of you?"

I wrap my hair in a towel and then take a seat next to him on the bed and grab the album. I'm about two and my very first pony, Magpie, is galloping on the long line. She's a slick and shiny black-and-white pinto Shetland. I'm wearing a pink unitard with a white tutu and ballet shoes. My auburn hair is up in a tight bun, and my face clearly exhibits happiness that no two year old should be able to fake. I have one foot planted firmly on her back and another sticking out behind, my hands splayed out in front of me with "pretty fingers" to make it look official.

"Yeah," I say, but in my mind I see the little girl in the clone tank and begin to wonder. "They always said I was born on a horse."

He flips the pages again and points to me at about six. This time I'm doing a handstand on Esmeralda. "Yes, again. They're all me."

I think.

"Can we use these for the presser?" I just look at him, so he clarifies, "Can I pass out copies to the media, so they can post them in the sphere?"

"Why would we do that?"

"It makes you look, well—sort of innocent and vulnerable. Child-like."

I'm about to ask if that's the look we're going for when he stands up and grabs one of my more recent trophies. "What's this one from?"

"Worlds, from last year. That picture is out there already. Probably."

"How about this one?" He points to another trophy, not as bright as the last.

"That was Worlds, when I was thirteen." I stop and look up at him. "Right after I met you at cadets, don't you remember?" I talked about it incessantly that year because I didn't want to go. The contest was in Sydney and for some reason thinking of Sydney makes me sick. Aren just smiles and we go on like that for a while, he points and I clarify, then he chooses it or puts it back. When we're done he's got about eight awards and pictures to display and then he leaves me to get dressed.

But I'm not ready to get dressed now that I've got my whole life out in front of me. I look over the images and marvel at how young I was when I started. The Magpie picture was the earliest one at around two, but I must have been training for some time if I already had balance and could stand on one foot as she galloped in the circle. If I was adopted, and clearly I was since everyone has the same story, my parents got a hold of me young. And not only that, they had big plans for me. It's not like they stuck me in a corner and waited for their orders to bring me back to the Stag. No, they put me on a horse and started training me in aerial acrobatics.

Why? Why bother?

A soldier knocks on the door and announces that the media is ready when I am, so I break off my thoughts and spend a good amount of time trying to find something in my closet that isn't fifteen years out of date or that makes me look six.

I finally settle on a pair of khaki slacks and a brown t-shirt with our farm logo on it. Then I run a brush through my hair and choose some slightly muddy barn boots over the ballet flats that some other Junco seems to be fixated with.

I take a deep breath, grab my brown canvas farm jacket and open the door. There are several soldiers waiting for me and they take me by the arm and lead me to the front of the house where I can sense the sizable crowd that has gathered in my front yard to hear about my ordeal.

A flashing thought occurs to me as I walk towards the massive double front doors. Maybe I should have actually prepared something to say?

As soon as I step through the doors Aren is there and he takes my hand and leads me up to the makeshift podium. The crowd is loud at first, but when they see me, a hush falls over my packed front yard and they wait. Aren and I reach the podium together and he lets go of my hand, but I snatch it back and then turn to him and smile. He smiles back, and nods his head ever so slightly to give me encouragement.

My eyes sweep over the mass of people lit up in the flood of our outdoor security lights and I calculate the number in my head real fast. Maybe a hundred and fifty people are crammed onto the lawn, their faces upturned, and the questions waiting on their tongues.

I clear my throat, ready to speak, but I suddenly have no idea where to start. I glance down at a conservatively-dressed young reporter with long blonde hair, she doesn't look much older than me. She meets my eyes, then her gaze darts down at the notes on her membrane and she ever so quietly begins to speak. "Junco, can you tell us why you were in the Stag last week?"

And then she smiles.

"I... well, my father—" I stop and hesitate, but the young reporter nods at me and so I continue. "Maybe you don't know this, but my father di— was killed a couple weeks ago in a terrible... incident. And on the day of the funeral I—"

I what? Went a little crazy?

"I noticed that a family friend was missing from the ceremony. So I went to the Stag to see this friend. Well, a man I thought was a family friend. But I never made it there. I hit a deer about halfway to the camp and crashed my truck. It was then that the avian found me. And healed me from my numerous injuries."

I look at the young reporter and she prods me again. "Why did he take you, Junco?"

"He took me..." I have every intention of answering her but as my gaze passes over the crowd I see him. The RR officer I saw holding a gun to CP's head at that makeshift camp in the Stag. Several reporters notice the direction of my eyes and look back to find what I'm looking at. He doesn't move or make a single gesture or motion. Aren sees him too, and gives my hand a tight squeeze, and when I look over at him, he nods to keep going.

I clear my throat and begin again. "He took me because many years ago the United Republics stole some avian genetics to make clones or mutants, or something like that. To use for bio-engineering experiments." The crowd gasps, and the RR commander turns and walks away from the crowd.

The questions are flying now, and I put up a hand to make them stop. I wait for it to get as quiet as I dare and I continue. "He, the avian, took me to kill me because I'm one of those experiments." The chatter of shock erupts again and I scan the crowd to see who will walk away now and that's when I see Tier. Standing in the back, leaning up against the ruddy bark of our tallest Ponderosa pine tree. He crosses his arms and shakes his head at me before disappearing. Once again the crowed follows my eyes to find my target, but they see nothing and the whispering gets louder.

Aren squeezes again, and leans in to tell me that I should wrap it up. "And so," I belt it out to try and get everyone's attention, "and so that is why I have invited the Rural Republic High Council to meet with me tomorrow at 6 PM. And they have so graciously agreed to this meeting so that we can set things right. So that no other children are caught in the lies and deceit that have ripped my life apart over the last week."

"Junco," the young reporter shouts, "what about the avian? Where is he? Will he take you away?"

I look back at the tree where Tier was standing moments before, just in case he's still hanging around and I can't see him. "I have no plans beyond tomorrow."

They erupt in chatter as they rush their reports out in the sphere and I say thank you, but no one hears. And then Aren is leading me back to my father's office and before I can blink, I'm sitting on the couch.

CP closes the door behind us and Aren is pacing the floor, his hands behind his head. "Shit! I can't believe you said that!" He says it a little too enthusiastically.

"What do you mean? Did I say too much?"

He kneels down in front of me and takes my hands. "Not at all, Junco, you were brilliant! Did you see the Colonel storm off? He was pissed!" Aren jumps back up and resumes his pacing. "Everyone saw him. I bet it's all over the world by now! Shit!"

"I don't get it. Is that good or bad?"

"Oh, well, that depends who you are tonight. If you're me and you, I personally think this is great. Fucking perfect! They can't touch us now."

"Did you see Tier out there, by the tree?"

Aren stops now and stares down at me. "He was here?"

"Yeah, he was leaning on that big Ponderosa in the back and then he just vanished right in front of my eyes."

"Fucking avians. They have some kind of shielding that makes them appear invisible, and I'm not talking about how we can make things look invisible, with the shimmer of light that gives you away, either. It's damn near perfect."

"So, is that good or bad? I mean, if you're you and me?"

But he doesn't answer, only continues his pacing.

"HOUSE," I ask as I look up to the ceiling.

"Yes, Junco?"

"Are there alien ships outside?"

"Yes, Junco."

Aren has a look of stunned shock on his face. "She can see them?"

"Can you see them, HOUSE?"

"No, Junco. But I know they are here."

"How do you know?" I ask.

"They announced their presence with your security clearance this afternoon."

Chapter Twenty-Seven

The barn is quiet and the smell of horses and alfalfa hay fills my nostrils. These smells have never bothered me. I was a horse lover from day one and there isn't a single thing about them that turns me off. Not the slobber as you slip the bit in, not mucking out the stalls, cleaning sweat-caked saddles, picking feet, pulling manes, the nasty stench of worming medicine, being bit, kicked or thrown. Everything about them is good.

Darby is my number one. A giant dapple-gray warmblood with a temperament so cool she's a cold front blowing through a still summer prairie. She nickers at me when I approach and slide the stall door open. I click my tongue and she exits and trots to the arena and begins a brisk walk around the perimeter. I swing the pipe gate closed and let out a genuine smile as I look down the breezeway.

The Goat is parked near the back entrance to the barn where Aren had the tow truck drop it off. I rummage through the back seat and surface with a pair of filthy thermals and a large white t-shirt. Also dirty. Then I spy the envelope with Dale's name on it peeking out from under the passenger seat and open it up. I flip through the various official documents and let out a big sigh and set it back down on the seat. It waited this long, it can wait a little bit more. Besides, I can't get my clean clothes off fast enough.

There are no boots since I took the extra pair back when I changed out of my funeral shoes, but I won't need them. I slam the door and jump back in surprise.

"Why must you sneak up on people?"

"I didn't want to interrupt you," Tier says.

"I bet. Did you get a good enough look or should I strip for you again?"

"I've seen it all several times now, Junco. But if you want to strip again, I certainly won't stop you." It might have been a joke under other circumstances, but the way it comes out makes it feel—a little sad.

I turn away and walk towards the tack room so he can't see the confusion creeping across my face. I flip the light on and search for some tape, then hop up on the counter and begin to wrap the balls of my feet. "So, what do you want?"

"Well," he says as he fiddles with a bridle hanging from the rack on the wall, "I have some news."

My right foot is finished and I start working on the left one. "And?" He continues to fiddle. "Tier, I'm tired of the games, all right? If you have something to say, then just spit it out." I finish the left foot and hop down. "And to be quite honest I'm just about ready to pretend none of this ever happened." I step into the rosin box and shuffle my feet around, taking care to coat the tape. "Because none of it makes any sense. I don't even know if you're telling the truth about my father, although why you'd want to lie to me about *that*, I don't understand. But right now I don't understand anything. It's been a very long fucked-up day and I just want to relax."

I flip the light off and head back out to the arena. Darby is still walking but when I click my tongue, she begins to trot. I slide under the pipe gate and walk onto the thick loamy dirt and position myself in the center of the arena before clicking for her to tighten up into a regulation circle. Tier takes a seat on the small wooden bleachers on the long side of the arena and I run alongside Darby, grab her mane, and swing up onto her back with little effort.

"You gonna be a spectator tonight, Tier? Or you gonna talk?"

"It can wait," he calls.

I tap at her girth with my toe and she eases into a controlled lope. She's so easy to ride, so smooth and natural that I automatically relax with her and the rhythm fills my core and drops to my seat as I sink into it. I let the tension drain away and then pop up to a stand and watch as Tier does the same. "You've never spied on me in here, or what?"

My back is to him, but when I come around the perimeter, he's in the arena with me, standing in the center pivoting as I circle.

"It makes me very nervous to watch."

I smile and flip backwards in the air, landing onto the sweet spot in the bow of Darby's back. Tier's face is contorted into a look of shock and I laugh and do it again.

"I always thought they made ya do this. I never knew you actually liked it."

I click and bend my knees so I can absorb the increased pace as Darby extends her canter to a gallop, then do a double, this time landing on one foot. "This is heaven." I drop back down onto her back and touch her with my toe twice and she collects. We make several revolutions and I feel my shoulders and neck loosen up. "Have you ever ridden a horse, Tier?" My breath is heavy now and the wind we make hisses loudly in my ears so I don't hear his answer. I tap and Darby changes gears like the professional she is, slows, slows, slows. And we are walking again. I make subtle squeezes with my lower leg and take her over to Tier, breathing hard. "Get on."

His mouth pulls a little at one corner before looking up to me. "No. I don't think it's a good idea."

"Why not?"

"A few hours ago you were running away from me as fast as you could, now yer suddenly OK with everything?"

"No," I say quickly, "I'm not OK with anything. It's time to forget. Now get your ass over here and jump on the fucking horse."

He doesn't smile with his mouth, but I can see it in his eyes.

And then he is behind me. Even Darby is surprised because she stretches her long neck around to see what's going on. I touch her belly with my toe and we walk out of the barn and into the night.

Tier's hands slip around my waist as he pulls me back a little into his jacket. I lean into his warmth because the night air is cold. We walk and I point out things in the back paddocks, name the horses that didn't wander into their stalls to sleep, and then direct Darby up a path into the woods. After several minutes of climbing we leave the woods and enter a meadow dominated by a large red sandstone outcrop.

"I've seen ya up here lots of times." Tier says.

I jump off Darby and climb the rock that reaches out towards the mountains to the west, my taped feet finding each foothold without much effort. This has been my thinking spot since I was a kid.

Tier flies up and lands next to me.

"You had something to tell me?" I ask as I turn to look at him.

He just shrugs.

"Maybe I should start, then?" I hug myself to ward off the shaking that comes with the cold now that I'm not next to him.

He takes off his jacket and drapes it over my shoulders, then walks back to the opposite end of the rock and takes a seat, leaning back against another rock that runs perpendicular to the one we're standing on. I slip my arms into the jacket and pull it tight around me as much as I can with the cuts he made to accommodate his wings. I follow him over, but I don't sit. I just stand there, legs apart, arms hugging my body. There is no good way to have this conversation.

"So how many of the other Seven do you have, besides Moju?"

His eyes narrow as he stares up at me. "We don't have Moju, Junco. No one has Moju. Even when he is in custody, he is wild. But we do have another girl back in the Band, where our habitats orbit."

"So you didn't think this information was relevant to me?"

He doesn't even blink. "We've had her for years. She grew up in the Eastern Utopia and she came along no problem. And ya know why, Junco? Ya know why she came along so easily?" He pauses to see if I'll take a stab at it, but I stay silent. "Because no one fed her a constant dinner of lies her entire life and when we came to get her she didn't have to take a few weeks to figure out who she was. She wanted to get the hell out of that place. Fucking Communists are all crazy, even her dumb ass knew that."

I don't grab the bait. "And she's one of the Six, the avian children of light? Not me, though." I know I've caught him off guard this time because he looks away. "I'm the Seventh castaway in flight. The one who brings the end."

He shakes his head. "It can be fixed." I open my mouth to say something nasty, but he interrupts. "Do you understand what I mean?"

I shake my head. "No, Tier. I have no idea what you mean."

"Why am I not surprised?" He holds up a small silver cube and rolls it back and forth between his fingertips. I know what it is without asking. His smile leaks out slowly but once it's out, it's bright.

"How do you know it's the right one? He could've given you anything."

His smile disappears. "Ya think I'm an amateur, Junco? Shit. Let me tell ya a little about what I do—" He stops and takes a deep breath and then continues. "Never mind. I took everything he had. And I've checked each and every one. This one," he rolls it around again and I see a glint of starshine reflecting off the sides, "is all you. I have your complete genome, biomarkers, DNA aggregates, hypo-adrenal biog, personality adjustments, and programmed muscle memory."

I just stare at him. I don't really know what I'd expected to be on the data cubes he took from Dale, but it certainly wasn't my personal human augmentation profile. "What the hell are you talking about?"

He gets up and walks towards me, then past me out to the tip of the monolith where he stops. "Christ, I'm so fucking tired of having these clueless conversations with ya."

I stay where I am but I am pissed. "Really?" The word seethes out of me. "Then why don't you just tell me the rest of it then? And not some half-ass fairy tale either."

He turns around and shakes his head. "It's not mine to tell, Junco. It's yours. I have very little to do with any of this"—he extends his hands out to either side in a wide sweeping gesture—"bullshit you're going through right now. Ya want the truth of what I'm doing here? I'm Perseus, Junco. I'm the only thing standing between you and death. Or you and slavery. Take yer pick."

I just stare at him.

"Ya know why I was sent to kill ya? Because I fucked up and this job was supposed to be my way out of some very bad shit. So let this sink in real deep before you go making demands or accusing me of being less than helpful with your personal dilemmas. I have disobeyed orders for you, Junco."

"Well, congrat-u-fucking-lations. Should I pat you on the back now because you found your spine? Maybe I should just kill *you* instead?"

"Well, at least ya'd be doing what comes natural, then, right?"

"Says the lion to the wolf."

He doesn't respond. Instead he sits down on the ledge and swings his feet off the overhang, staring out towards the mountains which have a tinge of orangey-pink reflected from the approaching sunrise behind us.

I stand there for a while watching his back. Thinking. "You don't want to be the messenger, fine. Whatever. I'll see you later then." I turn to climb back down the rock and then he speaks.

"I'm leaving tomorrow night." He looks east at the approaching dawn and amends his statement. "Tonight, I mean."

"Is that why the ships are all over my house?"

He screws up his face. "If there were avian ships here, Junco, we'd already be on our way back to the Band. We don't fuck about with ships in the atmosphere unless we're doing something."

"But my HOUSE says you have ships."

"Your HOUSE is wrong."

"She's an AI, Tier."

"Then she's corrupted."

I let that sink in for several silent minutes.

"Anyway, time's up, Junco. If you want a good piece of advice I'll give it ta ya, no charge."

"What's that, then?" I say, turning.

He gets up and walks over towards me. Looking up at him I can see that he's sincere.

"Run. If yer gonna stay here for the rest of what will be a very short life, Junco, my best advice is to run like hell. You've got everyone pretty fucking confused with this memory loss bullshit, you might as well take advantage of it."

A small half-hearted laugh escapes my lips. "I don't lose memories, Tier. It's impossible. I have perfect recall."

Now it's his turn to laugh. "Is that right? Shit, Junco, you've forgotten more things in the last few months than most people will in a lifetime. So cut the bullshit and face the facts."

I look away from his accusations before I speak. "You don't even *have* the facts, Tier. So do not lecture me. I don't lose memories. I just—push them down. So I can keep on living with myself, with what I do, and what I am." I lift my eyes and turn to look at him sideways as my voice hardens. "If I don't recall them at times, it's because I have a damn good reason. And I'm not running anywhere. I'm tired of running."

He stares down at me with sadness and I feel my temper rise.

"Keep your pity, OK? I'm not sorry for any of it, so don't fool yourself."

It's his turn to laugh. "Ah. OK, then. How about this? I won't fool myself if you don't. I mean, yeah, I can see it now. Yer little memory tricks work great, right? That's why yer barely able to sleep without dreaming some horrific nightmare time after time. Take my advice and listen to the inner whispers, Junco. They're speakin' ta ya."

I let out a half-hearted grunt. "I don't think you really want me to do that, Tier."

"And why's that, darlin'?"

"Because the voices in my head only ever tell me to do one thing, and that's kill people. In very interesting ways."

He laughs. "Shit, Junco, you were right about one thing. Yer certainly no Andromeda."

I look up at him now, but there is no smile on my face. "And you're no Perseus, either."

His smile fades and then he is serious. "Junco, if it's a hero ya want, just say the word. Come with me and it all goes away."

"And then what? They'll kill me and you know it."

"No, Junco." He holds the cube up between his fingers again. "The answers are all in here. If it can be written, it can be rewritten. That's what we do. We don't have babies, remember? We make them. Just like someone made you."

I hesitate and he turns away from me again.

"Don't make me force ya, Junco. I don't want to force ya." He stops and turns back to gauge my reaction to his words, but keeps silent.

"Then tell me what you know about the dock. Tell me."

He shakes his head and whispers some curse words under his breath. "This part, Junco, is all you. I have nothing ta do with any of that. Nothing." He turns and starts walking away.

I close the few paces between us and grab his arm. "Wait. Do you know what it is? Where it is?"

He lets out a little noise that might be a half-hearted attempt at a laugh, but devolves into a sigh. "Don't make me tell ya this shit, Junco. I told ya the first part and that was bad enough. You already know all this." He taps my head gently. "It's already up there, remember?"

I stare up at him and he averts his eyes. "Maybe it is. But I can't count on myself to bring it back in time, Tier. Time's up, right? Time's up." I pull on him like a small child until he looks at me, but then he just closes his eyes. "Please." He shakes his head, but I claw at his clothes and beg, "Please. I'll do whatever you say if you just make that part fit back together."

"You said that last time, remember?" He looks down at me now, nothing but sadness written on his face. His fingers play with something in his pocket and it makes a small clinking sound. He pulls out his hand and opens his palm, revealing several dozen tiny cubes like the one he was twirling in his fingers earlier. He picks through them, sorts them, puts some back in his pocket and then there are only four left. Four tiny little silver cubes.

I look up at him and take a deep breath. "What are they?"

"One is yer profile." He points to it. "One is Charlie's profile." He points to another but my head spins and he grabs me before I can fall down.

Chapter Twenty-Eight

Charlie.

"... the planks on the deck are warm under your feet and you're wearing a long thin white shirt, open in the front, that barely covers your body. The waves lap against the dock and you reach over and drag your fingers through the water. It folds against your wrist and slaps up the side of your arm. The drops bead against your oiled skin, pool together, then spring forth into a trickle which takes the liquid back to the source. The mountains are high and cast just the right amount of shadow to protect the nesting colony of eagles against the heat of the summer."

"Are you sure this will work?"

"Picture yourself standing on the edge of a dock, Junco. In front of you is a mountain lake and behind you is a small cabin, pristine white curtains flowing in the breeze passing through the windows. Down below the water you can see the scales of brightly colored fish reflecting the sunlight..."

He stops.

"It works, Junco. Just picture yourself standing on the edge of a dock. It's not a big deal, this is kid stuff."

"Kid stuff where you come from, maybe." But I'm teasing and he knows it. "Why can't we just stay here in the real world, Charlie?"

"Silly, Junco." His voice on the comms sounds farther away than he really is. "You know why."

I know why.

"So, just put those little buds in your ears, they're marked so you know which one goes where..."

"I see it. OK, they're in."

"... And listen to my voice. When you get there, just enjoy it until I come in with you. If you ever want to leave you just say OFF, and you'll be back in your room. OK?"

I nod, but then remember we're on comms. "Yeah. I got it."

"Picture yourself standing on the edge of a dock, Junco. In front of you is a mountain lake and behind you is a small cabin, pristine white curtains flowing in the breeze passing through the windows. Down below the water you can see the scales of brightly colored fish reflecting the sunlight..."

The sun is so warm I close my eyes and stare at it, letting the bright orange seep through my eyelids. Charlie comes up next to me and takes my hand.

"I told you it was fabulous."

I open my eyes and look at him. He's tall and muscular, with golden skin that reflects light off the tiny hairs on his arms. "I can't believe you made this!"

"Where do you think it is, Junco?"

I look down at the green-blue water and then behind me towards the cabin. It's not my cabin, but it's close. I smile at him. "Good times in there, right?"

He laughs. "Now he can't accuse you of seeing me. Technically we're not together. So you don't have to worry about disobeying his order and you don't have to lie."

I feel a little sick at the thought and I take a deep breath, but nothing happens. Oh, yeah, I'm in a virtual. Projections don't breathe. For a minute I have a little panic attack, but Charlie's hand takes mine and leads me back to the cabin. Inside all the walls are whitewashed, unlike the dark wood of our hunting cabin. The floors are painted a light blue, and the furniture is all white. He leads me over to the couch and plops down, then draws me into his lap and plays with my hair.

"You like it?"

I nod.

"What's wrong then?"

"I have to tell you something, Charlie. I have to tell you—"

But he's gone. Just blipped out of the scene.

"EXIT," I say.

Nothing.

"EXIT!"

Nothing.

"EXIT! EXIT! OFF!"

I'm back in a room and someone is banging on the door. I run up a ladder and fly across the room to open it. A hand reaches out and slaps me across the face. I fall to the ground and my father looms over me. "I'm very angry with you, Junco. Bring her to my office."

The soldier reaches down and picks me up after he leaves. "What were you doing?"

"It's a virtual reality." Tier shakes me. "Junco, it's just a virtual."

I swim back up from the vision in my head and open my eyes. "We made a virtual."

He smiles, then nods. "Not all that common for a couple of RR kids, right?"

"He was MR. From Peak City."

Tier nods.

"We were in love."

He nods again. I look up at him but he points down to his open palm, at the two remaining cubes.

I stare at them and begin to pick up the memories.

The soldier without a face takes my arm and pulls me along. I dig in to the rug with my heels, but he pulls and the rug slips along with me.

"Stop, don't. No!"

But he pulls again and I fall down, face-forward. He picks me up and another soldier opens my father's office door as we approach. Inside he drops me on the couch.

My father is on the comms and then he holds it out for me. "It's for you," he says.

I get up, my whole body shaking like I am out in the freezing cold, and reach out and take the comms. My father stares at me, and waits.

"Hello?"

"Junco!"

"Charlie? Charlie, what's going on?"

The crack of plasma echoes in my ears and then I hear a voice. "Project terminated, sir."

I throw the comms down and it smacks against the hardwood floors. The back of my father's hand finds my face and I join the ruined piece of tech on the floor just as the world goes black.

"He killed him." A sob escapes as the pain twists my heart and I break. "He killed him."

Tier hugs me and pulls me to the ground with him, but says nothing. I try my best to keep the tears in, but they don't flow down in little ribbons this time, they pour out in rivers along with the memories.

The bruises on my face are yellow-green as I stare in the mirror of my father's office bathroom. I reach up and touch the shadows around my eyes and wince. The color is fading, but the pain isn't. Someone bangs on the door and so I take the sample and open it. The lab tech whisks it away from me and my father points to the couch. I stare out the window after I take a seat. It's dark outside. The lab tech confirms what I already know and I scream. My father grabs my arm and delivers the ionizer to my nose.

I break away coughing. "What did you just do? You fucking bastard! What did you just do?"

The cramping begins almost immediately and he has someone drag me to my room where I am dumped into the shower to wash away the blood.

My body writhes in pain for hours, expelling the baby from my womb, and I can only think of one thing: how my pain will be nothing compared to what I'll do to him once this is over.

"I'm the one who tortured him."

Tier nods against me. "Now ya see why I didn't kill the torturer, eh?"

I stalk the men with my scope from behind the branches high up in a nearby pine tree as they patrol around my house, their faces burned onto my retinas. They laugh and joke, smoke and swear, and generally revel in the safety of their positions. And I know them. Lived with them on the scrub for weeks on end. Played cards with them, tracked animals, did PT, and ate with them.

And in the end, it meant nothing. I meant nothing. Together they delivered me to my father's punishment and left me to writhe in pain as I endured the aftereffects. I consider dragging out their punishment, like they did for me, but that would draw too much attention. Instead I ready the rifle, check conditions, and send off two silent shots into the night. One into each head. I collapse the rifle, pack it up, climb down, and walk back home.

The next day I'm in my father's office and he's screaming at me. His face is red and his hands tremble as he grabs me by the shirt. I ignore him and look casually out the window at a yellow songbird that is hopping from branch to branch in the courtyard.

I almost laugh at my punishment. Sold to the highest bidder. What a joke. But I don't, I feign an apology, talk him up about honor and family, and then take the smack that he delivers across my mouth, before finally starting to sniffle so he thinks I give a shit.

He has me delivered back to my room.

The last mistake he will ever make is not killing me in his office.

I stay silent, remembering the blood in the shower. "No one came to check on me."

"I don't know this part, Junco. I never knew why ya did it other than Charlie ended up dead."

I want to cry. So bad. But I've already done that. I cried about it for months, and there is nothing left to feel. "I was pregnant, Tier—"

"Aw, fuck."

"And he dosed me with an ionspray—"

"Fuck!"

"And had some soldiers drag me into my shower and leave me there until it was over. No one even came to check on me." The last few words come out in a low whisper and I feel the pain creeping back in like I am still there experiencing it. And then it is replaced by the anger. Another voice is also in my head. A familiar voice.

Project terminated, sir.

I feel Tier's chest launch sporadically a few times and I realize he's trying to hold it together too. I lie down, my head on his legs, and after a long while my breathing slows. His hand goes under my shirt and rubs my back with his fingertips.

"No one even came to check on me," I say again. "I thought I was going to die." I sniff and wipe my hand across my face, trying to get control of my nose. The fingertips trace a pattern on my back, lulling me into a slow state of acceptance and calm. *I'm your hero,* his fingers spell. *I'm your hero, I'm your hero, I'm your hero, I'm your hero.*

"I'm going to kill them all." His voice is low and steady, but to me that is even more frightening than when he's visibly pissed.

"I never even got to tell Charlie about the baby."

Tier straightens and pulls me up so he can reach into his pocket. He sorts through the tiny little cubes once more and comes up with two. "These two, Junco, are your virtual. There are two constructs here. One is you and one is Charlie."

I take the little cubes and clench them in my fist. "Thank you."

"If you want, I can give ya some time in there."

I swallow hard and look at him. I've never seen this expression on his face before. It's a mixture of hate, anger, and sadness. "Is that a good idea? Given the fact what I really need is a few years of psychotherapy?"

"It's all related, Junco. You, Charlie, the virtual, the memory loss. All of it."

"There's more to it than that," I say, shaking my head. "I don't want to go back. It's a bad place now."

He stays silent for a while. "Junco, did they kill him while you were in the virtual?" The revulsion in his voice is almost palpable. "Because that really would explain why yer having such trouble letting go."

I mull it over and sniff loudly. "No, he pulled him out first. Pulled us out. And then he had me listen to it over a com. It's dark in there."

"You should go back in. His cube was pretty badly damaged, but I had Layla clean it up. Just go in and make things right, and then leave on yer own accord—"

"Who's Layla?"

He smiles down at me. "My science contact here on Earth." He laughs. "Really now? Did I have ya fooled? Did ya really think I was the brain behind all this bioengineering going on?"

I shrug.

He fishes around in his pockets and pulls out some virtual buds and brings them toward my ears.

"No, I said." I push his hands away. "I don't want to go back in."

"Look, Junco, it has to be done. You're so fucked up it isn't even funny. I can't take ya back like this. She won't help me do it if we can't clean you up a bit."

"Now what are you talking about?" I want to feel angry but I just can't muster up enough emotion to give a shit.

"The morph, Junco. Layla says she can rewrite it. It's already there, she says, just turned off. Ya can't go in like this, Junco. The repressed bits will follow ya and come out the other side. It's not good. We have to clean this up."

I look up at him and shake my head. "Tier, I'm not ready to go back with you—I have things to finish here."

"You *will* come home with me, Junco. Because I'm not leaving ya here ta fight these bastards alone."

I stare up at the sky for a few moments, thinking about these words, and then he continues.

"Anyway," he says, changing the subject back to the buds in his hands, "if ya want, you can go back in, then initiate the exit. But, Junco..." He takes my face in his hands. "You can stay as long as ya want. It's not set in real-time. An hour in there is like a minute out here." He checks the buds and brings them towards my ears.

I push his hands away again. "I'm not going in. I said it's fucking dark in there."

He lays my head back down on his legs and his fingertips trace his pattern across my forehead until I calm down. Then he pulls out his comm and loads our constructs and gently slides the buds in place. I hear soft music.

And then the familiar sequence begins, but this time it is Tier's voice telling me what to do.

Chapter Twenty-Nine

Picture yourself standing on the edge of a dock. In front of you is a mountain lake and behind you is a small cabin, pristine white curtains flowing in the breeze passing through the windows. Down below the water you can see the scales of brightly colored fish reflecting the sunlight...

... and then I am there.

I can feel the heat on my body and I lie down on the dock and soak it up, listening to the various calls of the nesting eagles on the side of the mountain. It's a nice touch, I think. I love eagles. He put them there for me.

I feel him behind me but I can't bring myself to look. He's dead. That's not really him, just his construct.

He sits down next to me and pulls his knees to his chest as I steal a look. His body is golden tan and he's wearing swim shorts and a white cotton shirt, open in the front like mine, and it flaps in the breeze coming off the lake.

"God," he says, "it's so perfect here, isn't it?" He smiles as he looks down on me and I smile back and reach for him. He takes my hand and pulls me up and puts an arm around me. We sit there and watch the sun try to set. It hangs there, just above the highest summit, like it always does, and then slowly begins to drop behind the mountain.

Charlie turns to me and smiles. "God, I miss you so much."

My face creases and I hold back the tears. "It's gonna get dark now, Charlie! We have to go!"

"Shh."

"No! We have to get out of here! Look," I point up to the last bit of sun fading behind the mountain, "it's almost gone! We have to go now!"

He smiles. "Don't sweat it, OK?"

"Oh God!" The sun is gone and the darkness swoops in, the howling of the nightdogs begins and I pull away.

But his strong arms reach out and pull me back down. "Wait, let me show you what to do."

"I have to get out!"

"No, Junco. You don't—look!"

He's pointing to the sky, so I look up.

"The stars, Junco. They're just tiny dots of sunlight. All you have to do in the dark is find the stars and you'll be fine."

He's right. Starshine is sunshine. I exhale a few short breathes and try to pull myself together. "I'm so sorry for what he did."

"Shh."

"I don't want to go on without you, Charlie."

He hugs me tighter now. "Don't be silly, Junco. There's no point in you doing something stupid. When you leave here, just know that I'm still around, OK?" He leans down and kisses me on the lips. "Your father can rot in hell, because we'll always be together, babe."

I wipe my nose and nod. "We'll always be together."

"Ready?"

I nod.

"Picture yourself on the side of the mountain, sitting on a great big red rock with Tier. The sun is rising in the east and an early winter storm is rolling in from the west over the mountains. Storm's coming, Junco. Better get ready—"

I open my eyes and Tier looks down at me and winces. Then he hugs me and we sit there for a while. *I'm your hero, I'm your hero, I'm your hero, I'm your hero.*

"So," he says, breaking our silence after a few minutes, "what will ya do now?" I hesitate and he shoots me a look. "Ya can't even be thinking about staying, really?"

I shrug. "I have some unfinished business."

"Aye," he says with a soft breath of air. "Me as well. And then?"

I get up and so does he. "What's gonna happen if I leave with you?" I search his eyes for something, but I don't know what. "What if I don't change? They'll kill me, Tier. I'm the one who brings the end, remember?"

"Junco." His tone is not as soft as it was just a few seconds ago. "Ya just have to trust me. Do ya trust me?"

I hesitate and I see his face change from frustration to anger and then he turns away. "I want to trust you." He turns back and watches me this time as I struggle to find the right words. "But I don't know anything about you. Nothing. I don't know anything about your world, what it looks like, what the people are like, your customs. And your food looks gross." He takes my hand and pulls me back down.

"All ya ever had to do is ask, Junco."

"I asked about the scars, you just ignored me."

"Ya want to know where I got those scars?"

I nod.

He looks up at the sky. The stars are almost all invisible now, and the sunrise behind us has blanketed the top one-third of the western mountains a hazy pink. It takes a few more minutes before he begins. "It's a long story, and there's a lot more to it than what I'm gonna say now. But one day, Junco, we'll have time. And I'll tell ya anything ya want to know."

I nod.

"Our world is not like Earth. We are a large population confined in a limited space, compounded by a longevity that ya can't even begin to understand yet." He takes a deep breath and his fingers are absently playing with my hair. "I said we don't have families, but that's not the whole truth. We have something else. And yer born into it, like a family, but it's an occupation."

He looks down at me now and I smile.

"I'm in a special military cluster, the Aves cluster. Was born into it. And that's why I am who I am and why I do what I do. Our training involves being sent out to Earth as children." He looks down again. "Before we morph, right? No wings. We're just like human children. So I was sent down here when I was five and the goal was to stay ten years, go back, fledge, and get on with my adult assignments. But it didn't happen that way."

"What happened?"

"An angry, alcoholic foster parent. Not anything atypical for where I was staying. Of course, I didn't realize that at the time, and being who I am—I was less than accepting of some crazy drunk controlling me with his delusions of superiority and violence."

"Who are you?"

He smiles. "I'm a pretty high rank where I come from, Juncs. Was born with the potential and gifted the things required to give me this rank. I had a bit of an ego back then, so—"

"And they, your parents, did that to you? Beat you and made those scars?"

He nods. "So I killed him when I was twelve. Not the female. She was beaten just as bad as I was." Then he shrugs.

"And is this what you did wrong that you have to make up for by killing me?"

He laughs. "Nah. No one cared about that, and that was, hell, a dozen years ago now. They just called me home and I fledged out early and went on full assignment. But I killed some other people too." His voice lowers and gets a little more serious. "Those they did care about. But those fuckers had it coming."

That hangs out there for a while and I remember Aren's words from what seems like so long ago. *Since you went AWOL yesterday and were tracked to a certain alien who killed more than two dozen scientists out at the Camp, not to mention a whole shitload of corporate executives from all over the United Republics...*

The silence drags on a little longer before I ask my next question. "So what's in it for you, Tier? If you bring me back?"

Some air blows out past his lips and he thinks for a moment before answering. "Redemption, Junco. Isn't that what we all search for? Just a little bit of redemption for past mistakes. I see ya and think, she doesn't have to have that life. Doesn't have to stand for it. And I want—"

I wait but he stays silent. "What?"

"I just want you to have yer chance, Junco. And yeah, it's risky what I'm asking ya to do. It is, but I've already started it. Made decisions that can't be undone."

"So, you're basically telling me that you're a big fuck-up?"

He looks down at me and I'm smiling. "Yeah, Junco. That's about right. I'm just one giant fuck-up."

I lean my head into his chest. "I can relate."

We stay that way for several more minutes, just breathing. Being. And then I break the peace. "I know you're worried about me asking you how you had the biometrics to get in the tunnels."

He takes a deep breath and my head on his chest goes up as he inhales, then down when he lets it out. "I am."

I sit up and look at him. "I know you don't want to tell me. Maybe you'll never tell me."

Maybe the truth isn't all it's cracked up to be. Ignorance is bliss and all that good shit. I turn away, half ashamed at myself for not having the strength to push him on this. But there's something to be said for second chances and if he's willing to make a sacrifice for me, then who am I to judge how he got here?

I turn back to look him in the eyes. "And it's OK, ya know? I won't ask again. If you ever want to tell me," I shrug, "well, then I'm here."

He lets out a little bit of air through his nose that substitutes for a laugh and answers in a whisper, "Now why would ya give me a pass on something like that, Junco?"

I mull it over for a few minutes.

"You ever hear of synchronicity, Tier? It's like—when two things, or acts, or situations—*whatever.* When two things happen that you think have no meaning or connection suddenly line up and come together to create something meaningful."

I look up at him and see that he's listening, and I smile. I'm the storyteller for once.

"And whatever it was you've been doing with yourself here on Earth, it made this outcome possible. This moment, right here on this rock. Sitting here with me.

"It's like being old and looking back on your life and seeing all the mistakes. Some really bad ones, right? And you think, damn, if only I never did—whatever. If I had only done something different, didn't hurt that person with my actions or words, didn't let that person take advantage of me, or I made this decision instead of that one—then life would be different.

"But every choice leads to your end. Regardless of whether it was good or bad. And yeah, if your end sucks real bad, then maybe different decisions would have made life better.

"But even if at the end there are more bad things than good, if you changed those decisions then all of the good would be gone too. So, if you're looking back thinking, fuck, I should have done things different, you have to ask yourself, am I willing to give up even one moment of good that came from the bad, just for the possibility? Because if you do, then this moment is gone. It never happens.

"And I know that I'm not qualified to grant you absolution. But I do anyway, no confession required."

I look up but he won't meet my eyes, he just stares off at the horizon, then shakes his head. "I could almost love you right now for saying that, ya know."

I laugh. "That's pretty much the point, Tier."

His gaze wanders over across the horizon where the dark and heavy clouds are surging over the mountains off in the west. The reflected sunrise has turned them all the colors of Jupiter and they roll with the threat of a winter storm.

"I've been watching ya for a while, Junco. Trying my hardest to figure out what's going on here, whether or not yer a clone, or a Six or a Seven, based on yer actions." He looks down at me now and cracks a half-hearted smile. "And it wasn't easy, I'll tell ya that. I watched you do so many things. Celebrate the good stuff, cry about the bad, go out on maneuvers with yer team, meet Charlie, fall in love and be loved back"—he hesitates slightly, then continues—"kill, very effectively I might add. And then lose everything. And still—no matter what bad things happened to ya—ya always got up the next day and did it all again. Yer not a quitter. I have often wondered where ya get the strength, how ya have such determination. I'm barely four years older than ya and I feel like I've lived a hundred lifetimes of misery. And when I wake up each morning I don't want to keep doing it, Junco. When I wake I ask myself, *how much longer before they will just let me die?*" His chest expands suddenly and I sit up a little more to see his face. "I have that thought more than I'd like to admit."

I lean back into his chest. "But that's just me on the outside, Tier. If you saw what's really inside me—it's nothing but screams and lies."

He sucks in a deep breath and we sit for a while in silence.

"When I was coming back from the Stag that night—and let me just clarify—I wasn't following ya, I was trying to wrap things up out there because they called me back. My time with you was over, my commander wrote ya off and gave the order for me to complete the mission—and that was exactly what I was doing.

"But then I saw yer Goat barreling up the hill as I was flying home and I thought to myself, this is it. She's finally lost her mind for real. She's not coming back from this one. And then ya hit that deer."

My thoughts drift back to the accident. It seems like years since that happened.

"I flew down there just to see if maybe you'd be dead and I'd be let off the hook. But, shit. All ya did was suck it up, haul yerself out of that pile of shit ya drive, and look for a solution. No crying, no whining. Nothing but action from you, Juncs. And I made the decision. Finally." He stops and looks at me. "It felt like relief, making that choice."

I lie still, my heart beating against his. "Why?"

He lets out a grunt. "Because they've fucked ya up so bad, they lied ta ya, they taught ya things a fully-fledged aves warrior never learns and then they paraded ya around the world killing people. They took everything away to break ya. And still ya get up. Sling yer fucking arm up in a belt, hike up a hill and take stock. And then of all things, ya try and kill me outright, not once but twice. Without even batting an eye."

"I'm sorry about that, Tier. I was a little wild that night—"

"No, that's not what I mean. I mean, whether or not ya realize it—yer fearless, Junco. I offer ta help ya, and ya tell me, I've got two legs so yer on yer own, buddy."

He laughs. "You've got more survival instinct in ya than anyone I've ever met. And I thought to myself, just think how great she'd be if someone just loved her and didn't play with her head. How fucking much she'd have to offer the world. Us. If she could just make one or two decisions based on the truth instead of the lies. She's worthy. That's what I thought. She's worthy—it's just that no one sees her potential."

I feel my throat tighten up and try and swallow back the tears. His hand reaches down and lifts my chin and makes me look at him. "I fucked up bad with Dale, Junco."

I shake my head. "Stop, Tier. I don't need to know."

"No. I let him use my genetics for his experiments in exchange for information. Information I used to kill a lot of important people."

His hand lets go of me and my chin drops back down to his chest as I breathe in deeply.

"I'm not gonna lie to ya. I don't have it in me to string ya along like that, taking advantage of yer trust. Whatever ya do, whatever choice ya make, make it knowing at least this much about me. And if we have the opportunity to make good stuff happen in the future, stuff that makes us thankful we made all those mistakes just to get to our end, then I want them to happen because we went into it understanding the beginning."

My heart beats wildly and my chest suddenly heaves in and out with the struggle to hold it all in. I lean against him, counting as his breathing makes my face rise and fall. I take my time getting it under control and when I'm ready the words come out as a whisper. "I could almost love you right now for saying that, ya know."

He finally lets out a small, stunted laugh and traces the pattern on my forehead with his finger. "I'm on yer side, Junco."

I breathe that in and enjoy it for several long moments. And I smile. "You know what?"

"What?"

"This is the first time I can think of that the truth didn't hurt."

He leans down and gives me a crooked smile. "Funny how that works, right? People are always lying so they don't hurt each other. But it's the lies that kill ya in the end. The truth gives ya strength to go on."

Yeah, I think. Maybe it does.

Chapter Thirty

It's well past dawn when I make it back to the barn to collect the envelope on the Goat's front seat, then back to the house. CP approaches me as I enter and I flip him the bird and continue walking to my room. I go inside and find a marker and then open the door and write on the outside in big letters: *If you wake me up, I'll make you regret it.*

Someone from my past gave me some good advice about making threats. They said, quote, threats are better served up cold, quick, and clear, unquote. It's true, too. I don't fuck about in the threat department.

I go back in my room, slamming the door behind me.

But it's wrong.

It's all wrong.

This is not my room, I can feel it. I mean, it's all my stuff. I have memories of all this stuff. Of sleeping in the bed, pretending to be a genie on the magic carpet, and plastering my room with princesses cut out of magazines and books. But that was not last week, which apparently was the last time I was here at home. Sleeping in this ridiculous bed.

I flip the light on in the closet and look at it.

It took me forever to find that horrible outfit for the press statement because almost everything in my closet is either a nightmare of ruffles that was in fashion two decades ago or stuff I'd only let a horse see me in.

On one side of the walk-in is a double row of nothing but pink, purple, and orange. On the opposite side are the greens and blues. *Yes, Junco, your closet is color-coded.* And there is not one shred of camo.

My heart begins to thump as I wonder if I really am a clone who was dropped into this life not too long ago. I take a deep sigh and fall on my knees into a pile of clothes. I look at the stuff under the hanging garments and then I see something that strikes a familiar chord.

An old black field boot. Much smaller than my current size.

I reach for it and pull, but it snags on something in the corner. My curiosity gets the best of me and I shuffle under the clothes and start flinging random socks, shorts, and a slew of mittens out behind me.

And then I see the shoelace. Caught under one of the floorboards.

I pull everything out, I mean shit is really flying out behind me, and then I can see what's got the old shoelace in its clutches.

It's a hidden door in the floor.

Now we're talking.

I stand and push my foot on the floorboard in various places, like I do with the secret pantry in the cabin, and sure enough, a board pops up. I lean down and swipe my fingers under the board and grin as the mechanism clicks and the entire cut-out lifts up on a chain and rests back against the far wall.

I crack a smile. I know that whatever is in this hidden room, it is the real me, and my pulse goes wild as I climb down the ladder.

My toe taps the hard concrete floor and I feel around on the wall for a light sensor. When it flicks on I gasp with delight.

Now this is more like it.

The chrome and glass bed frame is sleek and modern, close to the floor, and the mattress is piled high with several black down comforters, more pillows that I could ever need, and it's a complete mess.

Which totally confirms that this is my room.

There is an entire wall of built-ins filled with books on one wall. On the opposite wall are more built-ins. But these hold weapons. Lots of weapons. Plasma rifles of all shapes and sizes, ion-blasters, EM pulse rails, a few projectile pistols, swords, several bokkens, steel knives, and laser knives. It simply takes my breath away.

On the far end of the room is a holomat, which is an elaborate piece of tech for an RR kid, but I'm not really just your ordinary RR kid, am I?

No. I'm Junco. The commander's daughter. A trained RR sniper. The fucking Seventh Sibling and a whole lot more.

The holomat allows you to program in mixed martial arts moves and watch them play out in 3D. You can even make adjustments on the fly to see how things work. It's a great way to come up with new moves or counter-moves and the memories of me using this device for training flood into my forward consciousness in a deluge.

I go to the closet next and find my real wardrobe. It's not color-coded and like the bed, it's not neat. In fact, most of the clothes are on the floor and not one scrap of them is pink. I have black, army green, gunmetal gray, black, desert sand, woody brown, and black. There are no pumps or sandals in sight and I breathe a huge sigh of satisfaction when I see the box of cigars sticking out of an open drawer.

I shake one out of its box, touch it to the striker, and puff like there's no tomorrow. Then laugh. Maybe there won't be a tomorrow. The air filters kick in to process the smoke and I blow some rings.

I am home.

I peel off my clothes and slip a fresh tank top on, then turn the sensor off and lie in the dark, watching the red embers of my cigar light and dim the room until the ash gets long. I flick it into the ashtray lying in the middle of my belly and think up so many ways to kill all these motherfuckers in my house I almost get giddy. The voice on the phone comes back to me. *Project terminated, sir.* It's a voice I know well.

Sun Tzu said all warfare is based on deception. Which seems to contradict Tier's take on the truth, but really they are not connected. War is war. And anything goes. The object of war is to win. Period. Nothing else matters, and if it does, you're not at war.

But personal requires a little more finessing because by definition it encompasses emotions, and that's the messy stuff that gets in the way of war. If you make war personal, you're fucked. War was never meant to be emotional and only detached objectivity gets you through. That's just the facts and anyone who wants to win had better face them fast.

I stew in that for a while and enjoy the comfort that comes with being in my own bed, surrounded by my own stuff, and secure enough to be OK with who I am for the moment. That can change, certainly it will change, but for now, I am just Junco.

Sun Tzu also said desperate soldiers lose their fear and I can relate. Not a drip of it leaks out of me. I'm the scariest bitch on the block. I puff the cigar down to the nub, stub it out and flop back into the soft pillows.

And I dream. And the dream is all mine too.

I'm not standing on the edge of a dock.

I am no one's project.

I am no one's redemption.

I am not anything.

I am just Junco.
And I am at war.

Just as I get to the part of my dream where it makes no logical sense I hear someone banging on my bedroom door. I roll off the bed and fall to the floor, shaking my head as I try to remember where I am.

The banging comes again, only louder this time, and then my reflexes kick into gear and I'm climbing, then rushing towards the door to pull it open.

"This better be good." It's CP. For some reason this little squirmy guy grates on my nerves. "Can't you read?" I say, pointing to the big black letters scrawled across my door.

He looks at my legs and I realize I'm in my bed shorts. He jerks his eyes back up to my face. "It's noon, Junco. Aren wants you in his office."

"*His* office? Hmmm. The last time I checked he didn't have an office in my house, so where exactly would I find said office?"

"Uh, sorry. Your father's office."

I slam the door in his face.

I go back down to my real room and stand in my closet.

I'm in love.

I step into a pair of old ripped jeans and pull a faded black hoodie over my head. There is an array of field boots to choose from and I pick the oldest, most thrashed pair I can find. None of this stuff triggers any more of my misplaced memories, but if I had any doubts that this room was mine they disappear when the boots mold to my feet.

I twist my hair into a pony and head to Aren's office. Just thinking those words makes me want to strangle him, but I push it down and smile as I pass the MR soldiers who smugly roam my house at will.

The doors fly open and I enter. He's about to yell at the intrusion and then stops himself at the last minute. "That's all for now, CP."

CP leaves and pulls the double doors closed behind him.

"Junco, did you have a nice sleep?" His smile is huge, but his eyes are narrow as he assesses my mood.

I smile back at him, forcing it all the way up to my peepers. "Lovely. I haven't slept that well in... well, since the last time I slept in my own bed."

Ignoring me, he gets up and walks around the desk. "I have decided that we'll ask the Council for reparations for what they did to you. This will include—"

I put my hand up and he stops. "I'm not interested in any reparations. Just the truth."

He comes over and takes me by the arm and leads me over to the couch as he talks. It takes every ounce of self-control not to pull away from his touch. "I know this will sound crazy, and maybe you won't agree to it, but—"

There's a knock at the door and CP enters again. "Sorry, sir. There's a message from—" He stops and looks in my direction.

"From who, CP? Spit it out."

"It's private, sir." He thrusts a piece of tech at Aren who puts his hand up like he's warding off bad spirits.

"I'll be back in a minute, Junco."

I plop on the couch. "Take your time." He ignores me as he leaves and I shoot CP a dirty look before he can shut me out with the doors.

"Junco," HOUSE says, "please enter your father's safe room."

Do I not deserve a single moment that is not clouded with confusion and the phrase, what are you talking about?

"Junco," HOUSE repeats, "please enter your father's safe room."

"I heard you the first time. But it would be nice to know—"

As if on cue the massive bookcase on the east wall pops open on a hidden hinge, leaving a crack of darkness. The door swings in as I push and I step into the darkness. HOUSE closes the door behind me and the world is black and silent. Then small lights appear along the floor, illuminating a path that takes me down below the house. Apparently my father and I have similar tastes in which level we prefer our secret rooms.

"HOUSE? You still there?" No answer. Since it's called a safe room I figure it's safe, so I walk slowly forward, following the dim path laid out before me. The lights stop at another door and I try the handle, find it unlocked, and open it.

Inside is a room about the size of my private bedroom. One wall is lined with screens, obviously hooked to security cameras I don't recall having. I can see every room, except my real room, every hallway, and every outside space within fifty feet of the house. In each one people are going about their normal business.

"Finally, I get you alone. Jasus H. Fuck, Coot. You're done this time, I swear. I'm not putting up with this bullshit one more fucking minute, you understand?"

I turn to see a man sitting in a large executive-type office chair at the far end of the room. His face is cast in shadow, but I can tell he's military, about middle age, and his hands are fiddling with a stack of papers. The Colonel. My heart beats faster and he picks up on it.

"Damn right you know what this is," he says as he gets up and walks over to me, thrusting the papers into my hands. "You've been on the run for what? A week?"

I shrug. I did actually lose count.

"I told you after that last little side-job of yours that this shit was over, and now this? Two fucked-up decisions in as many weeks doesn't get you far. Now. You wanna tell me why you've been traipsing around with these avians like you're old friends or something?"

"I would love to tell you, sir," I say. Can't go wrong with sir. "But—"

"But nothing, you sorry excuse for a soldier. And you will address me as Colonel Slag, who the hell do you think you are?" He's screaming now, and I absently look up, wondering if the room is soundproof.

"Don't look away from me, you rat's ass piece of shit! I said, explain to me why you were traipsing around with an alien on my time?"

"Sir, Colonel Slag, he kidnapped me, sir." It comes out before I can stop it.

"Did he now? Oh, that's rich. Because I have screen of you flying on his back, *shooting at the rescue team* in the tunnels under Ramah. Care to explain how he could have possibly kidnapped you that time?"

I wince and scratch my neck absently as I think, but he's already moved on.

"... caused me a lot of headaches, Coot."

He stops and my eyebrows go up as I stare at him.

He stares back. "What are you supposed to say for yourself when shit like this happens, Coot?"

I can't think of anything, so I just shrug.

He walks back to his chair and sits down. "You're officially retired, Coot." Then he tosses me a pen and I catch it in the palm of my three-fingered hand. Two, if you don't count the thumb. He scowls at my recent disability.

"Sign the papers, your discharge is on there."

I quickly begin signing, page after page. And then I get to the discharge papers and there's a small silver cube taped to the upper left corner. I look up at him, expectantly, and track his eyes to the cube, then back to my face.

"Sign the paper, Coot. Or your final days in the military will be spent scrubbing your own latrines." And then he shuts up and stares at me, to see if I have anything to add.

I shift my weight and sign, then hand them back and he does the same.

While he signs I look around the room and see photos of this guy, Slag, and my father in many of them. There are a few of me as well. In all of them I'm in a junior cadet uniform, none of me over the age of fourteen or fifteen. I spy several cameras and realize we're being recorded.

Then it all slips into place.

He finishes up and then opens a drawer, grabs a tech device, slams a drawer closed and throws me the reader. "There's a digitized copy of everything on the discharge paper. Make sure you read the terms. Oh, and one more thing, here—" He digs in his pockets and fishes something out, then throws me a slender blue rod that turns end over end as it flies through the air towards me. "It's been disabled, Coot. So your mission days are over. Consider yourself lucky I don't have you strung up on treason charges."

I catch the rod and my hand knows just what to do with it. I slip it under my shirt and press it to the scar just under my belly button. I feel the magnetic strip under my skin activate and yank it off in horror, shoving it in my pocket.

I look at Slag again, and he sends me a severe scowl. And then something else. It's slight, barely noticeable, but my eyes catch it just before I'm about to turn. A nod towards the back of the room.

I walk past him and see a dark hallway. I follow it to the end and push through a door which leads me into a storage room. I climb the stairs and come out in the kitchen, then walk back to my room and close the trap door behind me as I descend.

I have no idea what just happened, but I do know one thing. Slag is a friendly.

Chapter Thirty-One

The reader is one I used as a kid, but since data cubes have been standardized for the better part of three decades, my cube slides in easily after removing the one that is already in there. I pocket the old cube and turn the device over to flip it on. I expect it to need a charge, but it doesn't.

It pops to life, registers the cube, and a screen flashes.

It's a video. The face staring back at me from the still shot is someone I barely remember, but my heart aches at the sight of her anyway. She's holding a newscreen, and the video camera zooms in on the date.

The events she describes on the feed are almost too horrible to imagine. But I find a memory for all of them. Starting with my first assassination assignment at age six. Six. Who does that to their kid? She moves on to political matters but I can't pick up all the nuances of what she's saying. I get the gist of it, though.

War.

Revenge.

Death.

Atrocities.

Twenty minutes later I switch the reader off, pop out the cube, and almost stuff it into my pocket along with the ones Tier gave me, but I pull back at the last minute. Her final words stick with me and roll around in my brain. *There is a big difference between patience and inertia.*

Maybe. But also a very fine line. I throw the cube across the room. Fuck her, she's on her own.

I lie on the bed for what seems like hours, but when I glance over at the clock it's not even 2:00 yet. I remember the blue rod Slag threw at me and fish it out of my pocket. The energy it contains electrifies me as I hold it in my palm for several seconds, then slip it under my shirt where the long white scar runs lengthwise under my bellybutton. How many times did Tier place his hands there over the past week? I can't even count them. He knew it was missing. What else does he know?

I can feel it charging on the plate under the thin membrane of skin and maybe ninety seconds or so later it's complete. I reach under my shirt and pull it back out to take a closer look. It is definitely some kind of stone, magnetic since it sticks to the charge plate, and so shiny I can see my own distorted face peering back at me. One end is thicker than the other and I instinctively know that the tapered end holds a biometric for my thumbprints, while the rest of the rod is tracked to my palm. I roll it from hand to hand to see if it registers both. It does.

And then I flick my thumb over a small raised imperfection in the stone and the loop of the enhanced plasma SEAR knife materializes.

Disabled?

OK.

The SEAR, an acronym for SEcondary Alloantigen Repressor, was outlawed last century. Besides making a wickedly fucked-up slice in anything from steel to human flesh, it also completely scrambles your DNA.

In scientific terms a slice from a SEAR triggers an autoimmune response once the plasma loop touches the skin, which subsequently shuts down protein synthesis for collagen production. The unfortunate victim dies a slow and horrific death, even if they manage to survive the initial wound.

In simple terms, if it cuts you, it kills you. No matter what.

The safest way to use a SEAR knife is to have it biologically coded to your genetic profile so that the immune response cannot be triggered in the first place. There is no way for me to be sure that this is the actual case for my SEAR knife, so using it is almost as big a risk to me as my enemy. The effects are irreversible, hence the ban. Someone decided that the SEAR was not a weapon that could be legally owned by civilians safely.

Good thing I'm not a civilian, then.

Well, technically I am.

But surely, it won't really count until the paperwork is processed. Who knows how long that could take.

A few hours ago I'd be left wondering how my stomach managed to hold a docking pad for an illegal weapon, but after watching my mother spill out the details of my fucked-up childhood on screen, life makes a hell of a lot more sense than it used to.

I have the urge to test my weapon out on some pink ruffles upstairs in my other closet, but SEAR knives leave a tell-tale smell behind. It's not something you can filter easily and I'd like to keep the element of surprise. All warfare is based on deception, right?

I have a thousand questions for Slag, but if he was worried enough about surveillance in the secret room to go through that ruse, then it's better to stay away.

For a moment I think of Tier's hands again, going to my belly. And I thought he was trying to be sexy. Nope. He's just checking to see if I'm armed with contraband.

I flip the knife off and stuff it back under my shirt and think of Charlie. I don't recall if I ever got to go to the funeral and this thought makes me wonder about his family. What do they know? Do they know how he died? That he was killed for loving the wrong girl?

I get up and tear my room apart looking for some kind of comm device. Anything that has the sphere on it or can send a message. But after several minutes of searching there is nothing but a pile of crap on the floor to show for it. I was never one of those kids who rebelled against the tech rules of the RR. I never secretly wished for mind access to the sphere or comms, none of that shit impressed me.

But today, I'd give two more fingers to have a sphere access implant for five minutes because the need to see Charlie's parents, talk to them, fills my heart and I feel my face go hot as I struggle with the tears.

I get up and climb back up to the princess room and leave, pulling the door closed behind me. Out on the front porch I crane my neck to see past a cluster of pines. The western sky announces its intentions with a dense fog that seeps in and wraps its arms around the reporters on the other side of the gate. They crowd against the iron fence waiting patiently for the council members they know are coming.

Back in my room I search the various debris piles for the discarded cube, grab a thick packet from a boot in my closet, and take the stack of papers addressed to Dale from the Goat, then pause at the line of weapons before me. Something small but intimidating. I grab a TZi .357, load it, then slide the holster on my belt and let the gun slip in. Back upstairs at my childhood desk I put together the three packages, then grab my barn coat and walk back outside.

The fog has invaded the front yard and the snow is falling in light flakes that begin to stick to the ground. No one gives me a second look as I bounce down the porch steps and ease into the dreary afternoon. I make my way down the driveway and then halfway to the gatehouse I leave the road and finish the rest of the walk under the scant cover of the pine trees. I watch from behind a tree trunk as the two guards crammed into the small building point and comment at something below my line of sight.

I wait until both sets of eyes are diverted, then slip past the gatehouse and make my way to the iron barrier that separates me from the world. A couple of reporters see me and they bustle to life as my eyes search the crowd. I spot her just as my view is obstructed by the mass of bodies hurling questions at me. My left arm slips through the bars and I point with my remaining fingers in her direction. The bodies part and then I get a better look.

The young blonde reporter is smoking a cigarette and chatting up one of the hovercopter pilots when my gaze catches her interest. I motion for her to come here. To her credit, she doesn't hesitate much. She takes another drag on her cigarette, then lets it fall to the ground just as her expensive boot crushes it walking toward me.

The guards are out now, asking me questions, but I ignore them and punch in the code to open the gate. The reporter hesitates, but I wave her forward, still ignoring the guards. When she is through I close the gate back up and lead her over to the gatehouse.

"What's going on, Junco?" she says.

"I just need a private word, is that OK with you?"

She nods.

I smile and open the gatehouse door but the guards step in and one grabs my shoulder. "Junco, you need to go back to the house now." I elbow him in the face, take out the TZi and point it at his head.

"One smart move by your buddy over there and I blow it straight off, got it?" He nods and I look at his partner. "You OK with this, then?" He nods too. Then over to the reporter. "How about you?"

She raises an eyebrow, puffs up her lips a little, and simply shrugs. "Whatever you say."

My smile creeps out. "Good, then open the gatehouse door and go in and leave the door open."

She does and when she's out of sight I back up towards the door and push my hostage aside and slip in behind her. Her face is not showing as much fear as it should, but I let it slide for now. Plenty of time for that later.

"What's going—"

"Shut up and listen. I've got a proposition for you..."

"Selia," she offers.

"... Selia, but it's a one-time deal and"—I peek out the front window and watch the guards running back towards the house—"since I only have about thirty seconds to sell you on it, let's not waste any of them, 'K?"

She nods. Good girl.

I shake out the three envelopes on the small desk and then pick up the first one. "This is a bribe. Part of it is for you and the rest is for whichever pilot you can convince to fly you out of here in the next five minutes." I slap it down on the desk and let the weight of it impress her. Her eyes linger on the thickness longer than I dared hope, so I consider her sufficiently impressed and move on.

"This," I hold up the second envelope, "is none of your fucking business. But I need a way to get it to some people and in case you haven't noticed, I'm not going anywhere anytime soon. I don't know where these people live, I just have the name of one dead MR soldier."

She looks at the envelope and reads the name and her eyes light up. "Yeah, that guy who was killed during a training mission a few months back, right?"

"If you say so, Selia. Like I said, this isn't for you. It's for his parents. This is the favor I need. Will you deliver it to them?"

"When?"

"Now."

"You mean leave this story and run an errand for you? I don't think so, Junco. I mean—"

I wave the third envelope in front of her face and cut her off. "This, Selia, is your story. Not the bullshit that's gonna happen here tonight." I shake my head. "Every asshole with a fingercam is gonna stream that shit live." I wave the envelope again. "But this is so fucking new I only found out about it thirty minutes ago. And I'm gonna give it to you."

She looks at the envelope and hesitates.

I look back out the window and I can see movement behind the curtain of fog. "Five seconds, Selia, take it or leave it. I have dozens of other people I can ask."

She folds like the bipod on a sniper rifle after the kill shot. "OK, I'll do it."

I stuff the three envelopes in her coat. "Listen carefully, OK? Your first objective is to get out to that cute pilot you were talking to and give him half of this cash to get you in the air, because the shit is gonna fly as soon as Aren gets out here."

"Yeah, sure. Got it."

"Your second objective is to get that information to Charlie's parents, next of kin, whatever they are. Someone who loved him, do I make myself clear?"

"OK."

"And third, this envelope contains my story." My life summed up in a twenty-minute screen-feed, I don't add. "Tell everyone you can because tonight I'll either be dead or out of the loop for a while."

I look back out the window, missing Selia's last nod of acceptance, and even from twenty yards away I can see the rage swelling up on Aren's face.

"I'll make a scene, you get away without drawing attention." My hand slams down on the gate release and it begins to open. "Stay behind me until they swarm, then get the fuck out of here. Oh, and Selia?"

She stops and looks back at me.

"If you cross me I'll hunt you down like a nightdog looking for a bitch on hump day and kill you in a way that will definitely make the news, understand?" She swallows hard and nods. "And don't count on me dying tonight, either. I'm no long-shot."

"I'll do it just like you asked."

The fear she should have had from the start is finally there and I feel satisfied as I push open the guardhouse door and move into the bulging crowd. "Who's next? Who wants an interview?"

The mob goes crazy as Selia slips to the edge of the crowd and makes her way out to the road. I watch her pilot buddy lean in to hear what she's saying. Then the bodies are all around me and the red lights of fingercams blink in my face, obstructing my view.

"Junco!" Aren grabs me and pulls me back so hard I fall to the ground. The reporters go wild and I look up at Aren's raging face and smile. Someone fires a shot in the air and the guards push the reporters back as the gate begins to close.

Aren reaches down and jerks me to my feet, then bends over so his lips are practically in my ear. "What the fuck do you think you're doing?"

I pull my arm hard and he loses his grip on me. "Who the fuck do you think you are, Aren? This is my house and I can open that fucking gate any time I feel like it."

He looks up at the blinking red lights that are now outside the gate and less abruptly turns me around, pushing me towards the house and taking my arm once again. "Junco, this is a military operation now and you are under orders."

"Wrong," I say, stopping in the driveway and violently shrugging off his death grip a second time. "I'm retired, Aren. Or haven't you heard? Slag had me sign the discharge papers this afternoon. I'm not under anyone's orders. Un-fucking-fit for duty."

The anger in his eyes manifests in a disturbing twitch of his lip. "That's the first reasonable thing you've said in months, Junco."

How would he know? I haven't seen him in years before that day out on the scrub. "Yeah? Well, maybe I'd be a little more reasonable if my father hadn't had my boyfriend killed and then dose me with an ionspray to off our unborn baby."

He yanks my arm fiercely, pulling me towards the house again. "Keep your fucking voice down."

"Why? So no one finds out that we're all a bunch of sociopathic killers in here?"

"Speak for yourself, Junco. I left years ago."

"Is that right? Well, maybe you can explain why I just got a video message from my mother that says you've been working with her?"

His face hardens and he leans in again. "Junco, you have no idea how much I will hurt you if you cause trouble here today. You understand?"

"No, Aren. I really don't understand. Yesterday you said you were being set up by Slag. Now I find out you're playing for yet another team? That's quite an accomplishment. Really. Not many people can manage to betray two different countries before they're twenty-two years—"

"That's enough. I'm not even sure what you're talking about, but I do know one thing, we're not talking about it now. We're settling this shit with the Council tonight and that's all I'm interested in." He grabs my arm once again and I can feel the bruise forming in real time. "And you're going to that meeting and you will not act insane, you will be rational and agreeable. Do you understand me?"

"Or what, Aren? Or what? Maybe you haven't noticed, but I don't respond well to threats. Now," I ease up on the hardass bit and throw a card down, "if you want to talk a little business, well, then maybe I can find it in me to bob my head up and down a few times when they look in my general direction. I'll have to think about it."

He laughs. "This is about money with you? Seriously, Junco?"

"What else is there, Aren?"

"Power."

"Yeah, that too. So, when you go into that meeting and broker your little deal, you better find a way to cut me in on both accounts." I wait and see if it works. I have no idea what kind of deal he has planned, but clearly there *is* a deal.

"Don't even pretend like you know what's going on here, Junco," he laughs, "because I know better. Your father didn't tell you anything unless he had to, I'm one hundred percent positive of that."

"I got a message from my *mother*, Aren. And it said you're working with those rebel Subjectives up in the Northern Territories."

His expression shows confusion, and I may not be an expert in reading people, but I'm fairly sure this is real. I hesitate for a second, doubting myself.

He looks down at me and the good buddy routine from the scrub is gone now, "Junco, you better shut your fucking mouth and stay out of the way or I swear, this night will not end well for you."

I get the feeling that we're not yet on the same page, but there's something there. Might not have hit it on the head, but I came close. "More threats?"

"You want something from me? Or not? Say what you mean because I don't have time for games."

My smile is back. "Hey, I'm a free agent now, right? Sell my skills to the highest bidder, sound familiar?"

His confusion continues and this almost makes me stop. My inner cynic is screaming that there's a problem with my theory on what's going on here, but there's no time to backtrack and think it over. I'm past that now, it's move forward or give up.

I move forward.

“I want a rank within the MR equal to yours, Aren. Shit, you’re not real clever, are you?"

I see the satisfaction spread out from the corners of his mouth as his lips turn up in a slight smile before he checks it. I might not have all the little details worked out perfectly, but this hits home with him and that’s all that matters. "How do I know if I can trust you?"

"Aren," I sneer at him with contempt now, "I tortured my own father, helped an avian kill a state scientist, and assassinated several high-value targets on direct orders of Rural Republic Command, all of which is on record somewhere in that house."

The whine of a hovercopter fills the late afternoon and I grin, making it as bright as I possibly can. "Give me some credit. We’re both hip-high in the same shit, remember? But I’m sick of you ordering me around, I’ll play nice if you do, but you gotta get the fuck off my back and leave me alone." I shrug off his death grip on my arm one last time and walk away, waiting to see if he plays his card.

But he holds it.

Like Sun Tzu says, all warfare is based on deception. That shit rings true no matter what century you’re in.

Chapter Thirty-Two

Back under the princess room I let out a deep sigh and laugh a little. Then abruptly stop because it makes me feel a little crazy.

Junco, he's all in, don't underestimate him.

Yeah, yeah.

I shrug off the internal warning and go look in the closet to find an appropriate outfit for the council meeting. In the end I choose garments that look like I have a hard time taking them off for laundering.

Favorites.

The t-shirt is a faded olive green with a few small rips in the seam near the left shoulder. It's a few sizes too big and states proudly, *Snipers do it from behind.* Must have stolen this one out on maneuvers. I slip it on and tuck it in, leaving a gap in the front for access to my SEAR. I pull on a pair of forest camo-patterned fatigues and the same old field boots I just took off. I slip on the double-arm shoulder holsters and then fill them with the electromag 9Mv Boltblaster and the TZi .357. A sage-green flight jacket that has definitely served me well, if the ripped lining and pockets full of stale cigars are any indication, covers it all up.

The princess room mirror projects my outfit for scrutiny and I nod to myself, check the sparkling tiara clock on the bedside table, then lie down on the unicorn bed and put my hands behind my head to relax. I have no intention of showing up on time. Aren needs me now, so let him come get me.

I cycle back to my mother's message for lack of other things to think about. She was always beautiful, in a traditional rural kind of way, and we share a lot of the same facial characteristics even though I now realize that isn't physically possible. We both have the same heart-shaped face, though she has a pair of perfect dimples in her cheeks when she smiles, while I have none of that cutesy shit going for me at all. The dimples never materialized in the video, she never smiled, but I assume they are still there. Not typically something that disappears over time.

Her hair in my memory is medium length, more blonde than brown, and ends naturally in a slight upturned flip. Again with the cuteness. In the video she made last week, the day of my father's funeral to be exact, her hair is more gray than blond, severely short, and her previously bright blue eyes have dulled down to a slate color reminiscent of some of the guns I have on the rack downstairs.

My own hair is more brown than red and my eyes are nothing but an angry swirl of brown, black, and green. I've been told they're the perfect shade of hazel. As if hazel was even a color. It's not. It's just a term used for eyes when people can't describe them with one word.

In the video her mouth was drawn tight in a line that perfectly mimicked the emptiness of a distant horizon. Not at all like the mouth I remember as a child. I have full lips and upturned corners that require a little extra attention to make them even out, let alone frown. This feature makes me out to be more approachable than is professionally comfortable. The flat line of indifference is a better way to go in my opinion. Lowers expectations of chumminess upon first impression.

Her outfit was the only thing that connected us. Crisp military-issue uniform of an advanced rank, planed out flat from the steam press. I can be crisp when I want to and I have the service uniform in the closet to prove it. But I haven't worn it lately. Not even to the funeral.

I take a deep breath and play the message back in my head. Even though a lot of it was *about* me, the message wasn't really *for* me. A propaganda piece for the benefit of her political party. The Subjectives' benefit, I correct myself. Her people these days, apparently. The ones she really works for. I suppose that's debatable though, since she comes right out and states on the video that she's double-gunning for the MR as well.

Nice.

Scattered loyalties are awesome, especially when they're all fake.

The Subjectives are just the most recent cult of personality taking root up north in the wilds above the Front Range and extending up into the Tetons in the old American state of Wyoming. That area is unincorporated and has been since the Succession Wars ended back in '98. As far as I can remember, no one's given the place a second thought since then.

I suppose the world will have a whole new outlook on the philosophy of Subjectivity come morning. Hope they've got bunkers dug out in those tits, because if my mother is telling the truth, then this whole area will be up in flames real soon and I envision a steady stream of retaliation hellfire up in Subjective Land come morning.

Slag must be in on it since he was the one who delivered the cube to me, but why even bother informing me at all? Why not just get that shit out to the media herself? Makes no sense. Maybe she figures since I killed the bastard who had her deported I was also interested in joining her little make-shift military. Maybe she thinks that she can lure me up there to take part in whatever fucked-up plan they have going?

She's wrong.

And not just for the obvious reasons, like abandoning me when I was little. This whole military thing is getting real old, real fast and I'm just not sure I'm into it anymore. After tonight I can see a nice long reprieve from killing and drama. A vacation somewhere maybe, that's what I need. That floating metropolis they have out in the middle of the Atlantic sounds pretty fucking nice right about now.

Nope. I'm not interested in her wars, regardless of who she's got on board with her. And to be honest I'm a little put off that she had to drag me into it at all. Now Selia's gonna broadcast it all over the fucking world and I'll forever be connected to her outrageous acts. Just so I can get a simple little message to the family of the man I loved. Hell, we'll probably both make it into the history books. *Double agent Carolinia Coot and sociopathic Rural Republic sniper daughter, Junco Coot, implicated in the Mountain Republic invasion of 2152.*

Unexpectedly, I let out a laugh. What a crazy bitch. At least I know I come by it honestly.

Sort of.

At any rate, it's out of my hands. I did what she asked and got a message out to Charlie's family in the process. What Selia does with it from here is her problem. Personally, if I were Selia, I'd burn those papers and melt that cube down in a bonfire the first chance I got. But something tells me Selia is a go-getter.

The knock on the door finally arrives and I instinctively check the tiara clock. 6:01. Once again, the laugh just comes out. Aren is either restless or fastidious about punctuality. I lean on the first one and swing my feet out of the bed, straighten my guns a little, then walk to the door and pull it open.

I half expected CP to be the one to walk me to the conference room, but it's not him. The strange soldier greets me and smiles. "Commander sent me, Junco. They're all there and waiting."

I thank him and walk towards the conference room. There is a disturbing amount of activity around the house and, as I peek out the windows, on the grounds as well. A serious bit of build-up has happened in the past few hours. The guards knock and open the double doors of the conference room for me as I approach and when I step in I realize I've interrupted. They are all standing, facing this way and that, hands in the air, as if to make a point. But their talking stops abruptly.

I take a deep breath and survey the room and Aren practically scrambles over to me to break the silence.

"Junco, you've arrived. I'm sure you know everyone here, right?"

I look at each person individually, all the elders I've known my whole life, and Slag. My eyes stop there and Aren takes the cue. "You remember Slag, right, Junco?"

I stare up in Aren's eyes and realize he's lost. Has no idea who I am or what memories are available right now.

Slag nods as he eyes my inappropriate choice of clothing, but doesn't give off a vibe either way. Aren pulls the chair at the bottom of the table open for me to take a seat, but I ignore him and push it out of the way so I can stand near the edge. I don't look at him, but I don't have to see his face to feel his rage.

It doesn't matter.

I snap off the names of each of the remaining elders in my head as my gaze quickly travels around the large glass and chrome table. How these five fuck-ups managed to escape the wrath of Tier that night in the church, I'll probably never know.

Oran Alger is a big guy, built like a pillaging Viking with a blazing head of red hair, complemented by a beard that is an even more shocking orange. Substantial arms poke out of his massive body and he's wearing coveralls. At least I'm not the only one underdressed.

Tarik Darzi is the only bachelor in the history of the Council, and that's the way he'll stay because he's as gay as a songbird in the spring. I think the Council was surprised when he was elected last term because he's one of only half a dozen people who have ever decided to emigrate to the Rural Republic in my lifetime. We are naturally suspicious of strangers and even though I really do love my country, it's not a place you'd ever want to emigrate to.

Abe Cavello is a dentist who works in the MR. People wanted to throw his ass out the last election, but his father was a Council Elder for a long time so money changed hands and that was that.

Hogan Bosco is just an ordinary farmer who grows wheat and soybeans in the southwestern part of Council 3. He's loaded but refuses to farm with a tractor so every spring he's out there in his field walking behind his horses for fourteen hours a day. He's known to go a little crazy before planting season is over. My father sold him horses regularly so he's been at our house lots of times.

And finally Old Sam whose brother was the actual one elected, but died the second week in office. Sam took over and no one stopped him. I admit I never thought that was weird until now.

Five men of the community, an MR field commander, a RR Colonel, and me. Just a wild girl who can shoot straight under pressure.

Slag is standing in the back corner, behind Aren. His arms are crossed in front of his chest and he has a bemused look on his face that I don't actually care for. It implies I'm the entertainment.

"All right, gentlemen, let's start the show, shall we?"

They mutter and one or two object, but it's Aren who stands up. "Junco," he says, trying to placate me with fabricated congeniality, "I've already explained to the Council what's going to happen and why you're here so—"

I see Slag wince out of the corner of my eye. "Aren, you have no idea why I'm here, so sit down and shut up."

"Who the hell—"

I jump up on the table in a single two-footed hop, my field boots crashing against the thick glass, and growl at him. "Shut the fuck up, Aren!" I slip the SEAR out from my shirt and switch it on in one fluid movement, then look at them all one more time, beginning with Aren.

"Let's cut the bullshit and presume you all know what this is and what I plan to do with it, OK?"

Their mouths are open in surprise, but each nods in agreement.

"Now, I don't know what Aren's just told you, but let's also assume that too, is complete bullshit."

Once again they nod. I check out Aren and he's about to open his mouth when I shake my head at him. "Shhh, Aren. I'm not interested." My gaze shifts to the Elders. "What I am interested in, gentlemen, is the truth about one certain night two weeks ago in which each of you," I glance back to Slag and point to him with my weapon, "with the possible exception of you, witnessed me take this little SEAR knife," I wave it around casually in the air, "and do some very horrific things."

I wait for them to digest the situation and glance back to Aren, who is enraged, but as far as I can tell, still holding it down. For now. I throw him a smile, and this sets him back in his chair a little, but makes Slag furrow his brow.

I walk back to the end of the table where Abe is sitting. "Did you see me in the church the night I cut my father and sentenced him to death?"

He nods. I look at the next in line, and raise my eyebrows. "Don't make me repeat the question, Hogan, yes or no?" He mumbles out a yes. I continue down the table and elicit a yes, or something close to it, from each of them. "Great, we're on track here." I glance back at Aren and the sweat is pouring off his face. "How about you, Aren? Did you see me in the church that night?"

Every head in the room shifts to him and he stands up abruptly, knocking the large conference chair back into the window facing the courtyard. "Junco, I'm going to ask you to leave the room right now or I will be forced to disable you, probably resulting in your death."

"Aren, if you have nothing to add, shut up and sit down. I'm not in the mood." He resists and I walk towards him and catch his eye with the bright glow of the SEAR.

I stare at him until he grabs the chair and complies, his finger busy fiddling with something on the arm rest.

"Now we get to my question, my Honorable Elders, the only thing I want from you. And when I get it and I'm satisfied that it is the truth, you can leave here and we can put this all behind us. Because I don't want to know what you know about my so-called childhood." Most of these guys probably don't have any idea, but Sam is older than them and he shifts uncomfortably in his seat.

I stare directly at Sam as the rest of them squirm. "And I don't want to know about all the times you turned your head when they took me away to the Stag."

All of them visibly relax with my revelation and I feel a dry heave coming up in my stomach. I push it back down with everything else that's trying to come up.

I look over at Slag now, meeting his gaze, but I continue speaking to the men around the table. "Because I don't need you to tell me those things. I already know the answers. And gentlemen, I am here to tell you that a time will come when you'll stand in judgment for your silence and reap your reward."

They don't look at me, but I continue, "And who knows, that night might be tonight. But it's out of my control."

Abe the dentist, the last guy to my right, speaks up. "I'm sorry, Junco."

I look down at him and nod. "Then Abe, how about you be the first, then, huh? Just answer my question. No matter who told you to stay silent. Even, Abe"—I stop here and stare into his eyes—"if it was *me* who told you to keep quiet. Understand?"

He nods. I look up at Aren and I see panic in his eyes, but I continue. "When you saw me torture my father, Abe—who did my father promise me to in order to get me out of the RR?" He swallows hard and the sweat is pouring down his face. "You can say it, Abe, go ahead." He looks across the table to the other Elders, then his gaze travels down the line of men and stops at one. He lifts his hand and points.

Chapter Thirty-Three

"You fucking psycho bitch!" Aren shouts. "We had a fucking deal, Junco! You wanted to do this, that insane memory bullshit is twisting the truth *again*! This whole thing was your idea!"

I walk towards him, my boots thumping hard on the glass table top. Aren pushes back from the table, but Slag is behind him so the chair pins him in. "Aren."

"You signed on, Junco! You signed on! We had a deal. You, your father, and me. This was always the plan, Junco, just *listen*!"

I stare down at him. "Tell me why I wanted my father dead, Aren."

He calms down a bit and his voice comes out in a low growl. "You signed on, Junco. It was all your idea."

"No, Aren. I don't think so."

"You wanted out of the RR and I said I'd take you. Your father wanted it, I wanted it, and you wanted it. You were done killing, Junco. And the MR said they'd take you. You wanted this."

"Even if I did, Aren, then I was insane at the time because I cannot even imagine a life like the one you're describing. Now, back to the question, why did I want my father to die?"

He stares at me, evil and hatred projecting out of him like the stench of a three-day dead mule deer out on the prairie.

"I already know you killed Charlie, Aren. You fucking coward. And I know you think I didn't recognize your voice on the phone the night he died. But the thing about my training that you assholes never understood is that while I might hide from the memories at times, they never go away. I can pick that shit back up. Any. Time. I. Want."

He moves his hand slightly on the arm of the chair and I shake my head. "Move one more fraction, Aren, and I chop your fucking head off."

He stops.

"Junco." The voice comes from Oran and I turn. "We—"

"LOCKDOWN!" The voice is mine, but the words don't come from my mouth. Aren has a small device up to his throat but drops it on the floor as he grabs my ankles and pulls, causing me to crash hard against the glass table. My head slams backward and I hear it crack. The air rushes in as the gash opens up and I feel the heat spill out and pool around me.

HOUSE has mapped the room in a laser grid to track every square inch of movement. "THIS IS A HOUSE LOCKDOWN PROTOCOL. YOU ARE BEING TRACKED. ANY MOVEMENT WILL RESULT IN DEATH. DO NOT MOVE, ANY MOVEMENT WILL RESULT IN DEATH."

Sam panics, pushes back from the table, and the lasers slice his body into thousands of pieces.

Aren stands up and from my position on the table I can see that the laser lines on his back are black. He's immune to the protocol because HOUSE is programmed to sequester the body that makes the LOCKDOWN command. This is a secret back door application that Aren should not know. I train my eyes on my own body and it practically glows bright green with targets.

Obviously I am not immune.

He sees my gaze and interrupts my thoughts. "That's right, Junco," he says, "I'm in control of the HOUSE now and your command has been overridden."

Now it is his turn to jump on the table and he struts down to the end and kicks Abe in the face. I listen to the body behind me slump, and then the rapid falling of a thousand body parts and they thunk on the tile floor. The action is so smooth and instantaneous that Abe's scream is caught in his throat. I can hear it exit his body as a puff of air.

"I knew you'd sell me out first, you fucking kiss-ass," Aren growls. "Anyone else have something to say?" Aren walks back to my prone body. He reaches down, casts a shadow of protection over my hand, and lifts the SEAR out.

It immediately shuts down. There isn't a chance of him using it against me, but it probably makes him feel superior. And then his finger flicks over the small imperfection and the arc of plasma is back. He sees the surprise in my eyes and laughs. "Ya know Junco, you're not bad to hang out with sometimes, but you are seriously the dumbest girl I've ever fucked." He stares into my eyes. "That's right, baby, palm imprints are not as secure as you might think."

He walks back down the table holding the SEAR up like a trophy. "Who wants to see Junco die by her own instrument?" No one answers, of course, and this pisses Aren off and he walks back over to me. "Nothing to say, Junco?" I stare straight ahead, as still as I can be. "You're really taking all the fun out of this, baby."

My eyes are drying up as I struggle to keep them from blinking. He bends down and I see him cast a shadow over my arms as he stares down at me. "Junco Coot, there is nothing special whatsoever about you, honey. Not your skills, not your freaky genetics, certainly not your looks, but your ability to believe, Junco. Now *that* is impressive. You're so fucking gullible." He laughs and I watch the shadow crawl up to my chin as he looks around at his prisoners.

I move my eyebrows up slightly to try and ease my discomfort from not blinking and he catches my movement. "Oh, poor thing! She can't blink! Who feels sorry for Junco? Oran?" Oran, his Viking heritage probably kicking in, grunts loudly at Aren, but he remains still because he remains alive.

Aren looks back down at me and I see the shadow cast over my bottom lip. I force myself to remain still. "Oran says I should let you blink, Junco. How about we make a deal? I'll let you blink and you let me fuck you before I deliver you to your next master?" He laughs, but his hand draws near my face, ready to cast a shadow over my eyes and let me blink. I feel the shadow more than see it and wait... over my bottom lip, my top lip, the edge of my nose—

"LULLABY!" I scream—the room goes completely black. I buckle my back and send him flying forward, face-first on the glass—the SEAR slips from his hand, powers down, and slides across the table and out of reach of both of us. I buckle again and flip up on my feet, turning, shadows in a panic all around me as we all try to get out of the room.

"Run, Junco!" Slag screams as I scramble across the table, leap over the shadow in front of me and aim my feet for the double doors as I fly sideways through the air.

It bursts open and I fall in a heap in the hallway, regain my footing, and book it, slipping on the slaughtered remains of any soldier stupid enough to move after the house went on lockdown.

I lose my balance and as I fall my hand slides into the slick pile of flesh and blood. Through a faint glow coming from the window I see Aren emerge from the conference room, powered-up SEAR in hand.

I clamber back to my feet and reach for the .357, emptying my magazine into the wall of confused MR soldiers near the front door. They dive sideways, and I burst through, out into the encroaching darkness and snowfall.

Outside is chaos and before anyone can figure out what's going on I run down the driveway and stop. I scream loud enough for the reporters at the gate, and probably the Sheffields down the street, to hear. "Come on, you worthless, traitorous piece of shit! Let's see what you've got out here." I hold the .357 up and sight it on Aren's chest as he walks casually down the stairs.

Far off down the driveway the reporters are scuffling over the walls to get their shot for the sphere. Aren's long legs cover the distance towards me surprisingly fast and I pray for a moment that I haven't underestimated him. I force the bravado one more time. "You can even use my own weapon, what do you say?"

He stops a few paces from me, the SEAR snaps as the snowflakes hit it, and he lets out a low laugh. "That's hardly fair, is it? You have a projectile weapon, while I'm all dressed up and ready to go for close combat."

He takes another step. My mind calculates the distance and it's not enough for the kind of effect I need out of the Boltblaster. "Sucks to be you, I guess," I say, slightly out of breath.

And another step, almost there. "You play a good bluff, Junco. I counted the shots back there, baby. The mag is empty."

I knew you would, ya bastard. "Then come and take it from me, Aren."

He rushes me and delivers a hard knock to my throat before I can get the Boltblaster from my holster. I go down. He's on top of me, hands around my neck in seconds. I immediately lock my legs around him in a tight guard, then drop it to the floor, slip my boot into his hip and push him off. I force his head down and send my knee into his teeth.

He drops back slightly stunned, and I reach for the bolt and fire. The two charged slugs exit the double barrel carrying the 9Mv charge. One grazes the inside of his leg, but the other slams into his thigh and he goes down, shaking like a junkie who missed his last fix. It'll have to do.

Another soldier grabs me from behind in a choke hold. I fire the Bolt, aiming at anything behind me, but it misfires. I toss it and bend my knees, back into him, drop my shoulder on the choke side, and flip him over. His eyes look up at me and then my boot stomps down on his face.

Three more appear. One attempts another choke while his companions each take a wrist. I fling my arms wildly and one guy loses his hold on my wrist. I flip the choker over my back and his body breaks the hold his other buddy has on my other wrist. I slide my feet back and wait for the next guy. He shakes his head at me.

I'm about to call him out when I hear the whine of a plasma rifle against my left ear. The static charge coming off the barrel sends the loose hairs around my face flying out in an electromagnetic field arc.

"Move again, Junco, I'm begging you. Because just thinking about killing you is making me hard, you stupid fucking bitch."

He yanks on my right shoulder and I slip in the snow and fall to the ground, slamming my back into the icy concrete. My lungs expel every breath of air inside me and I gasp trying to replace it.

Aren leans down and his eyes narrow into angry slits. The blood pours out of his split lip and drips onto my cheek and I wince. He pulls back his arm and slams his fist into my face, breaking my nose with a loud crack. The blood clogs in the back of my throat, cutting off most of my oxygen supply, and forces me to roll over on my side, coughing.

Several pairs of hands pull me up and hold me. Unable to follow the movement, my legs drag until one guy elbows me in the ribs and orders me to stand. I shuffle my feet until the soles of my boots find ground. Someone searches my pockets but comes up empty.

I hear the sharp crack of a suborbital entering the atmosphere and I smile, then spit a clot of blood onto Aren's shoes and wait for the next blow to find my face.

But he's lost interest in punching me. I'm yanked to the ground by various hands from behind and Aren steps over my body, his lips curled up in a snarl that says I crossed a line.

He drops to his knees, straddling me, as the soldiers painfully pin my shoulders to the frigid snow. His eyes shine in the faint light as he holds up the SEAR, fingers the arc down to a short stub, and inserts it into the skin just under my right ear.

Then slowly, ever so slowly, he drags it down my jawbone towards my chin.

I scream as small tendrils of flesh-saturated smoke rise up from my face, filling the air with the stench of burning tissue. The soldiers push my cheek into the snow and force me to hold still for the torture.

My mind shuts down and the world blinks out of existence.

Chapter Thirty-Four

Picture yourself standing on the edge of a dock...

Oh, I am so fucking there.

But I'm not standing, I'm lying down. I reach over and swipe my hand through the water and pull back a little at the glacial nature of the lake. The golden rays of the sun are raining down on me, but they make my whole body shiver. I try to open my eyes but Charlie whispers in my ear. "Stay down, Junco. It's not time to get up yet. Stay down."

I hear a small whimper and it takes me a minute to realize it came from my mouth. I try to answer but my jaw won't move. My hand makes a move up towards my face, but Charlie's voice is in my head again. "Not yet, babe. Keep still."

The whimper grows stronger and a cry erupts before I can stop it. "Shhhh, I'll tell you when." My hand falls back down to the dock and bumps into something cold and hard. "Grab it, Junco. But stay still."

My two remaining fingers close and my thumb passes over the familiar stone, marveling at how smooth it feels. It catches on a small notch and the tingle of an electric field travels up my arm.

"Stay still," Charlie repeats, "target is at 12:00, aim high. When you see the light, on your feet." The voice in my head goes quiet, but then I hear the faint whisper in my ear. "I love you, Junco."

I love you too, Charlie. I try to say it out loud but my mouth only lets a stifled moan escape.

I feel the kick of a boot in my ribs and I'm back on the ground, lying in front of my house as the wet snowflakes stick to my body. I hear a series of distant explosions and crack a reluctant eye open just in time to watch the faces of a half-dozen soldiers look north in wonder. My eyelid tires, falling back down as Aren barks orders to his men.

I am busy soaking up the vibrations from the scattering of boots around me when the sun explodes and Charlie's voice is back. "Now, Junco!"

My muscles, trained over and over in the same patterns, year after year, recall their conditioning and dig for the programmed memory of what to do.

The adrenal biogs shunt the epinephrine to my thighs and core, and then combine it all into one single synergistic act as I kick my knees back to my head, throw my body upwards, plant my feet on the ground, and extend the SEAR loop out to its full length of three feet.

Aren is standing at my 12:00—time slows down to a crawl and my world becomes silent—then my controlled breathing fills in the emptiness and I relax in a ready stance.

Aren's face turns towards me, his hand over his eyes, still recovering from the blaze of light flashed from above and I know I can kill him several times over if I want to.

But I don't.

Just once will do.

I balance and deliver a jumping spinning hook kick that makes his head snap, then follow through with the SEAR, dragging it across his brain stem and out the other side. I recover quick enough to watch his head fall to the ground and spoil the pristine white snow. A river of scarlet runs out and my eyes follow it with unabashed detachment.

The few soldiers remaining around me still have their mouths open as I wield the SEAR like a katana, approach the nearest one, and slice his chest open in a kesa move that continues into his buddy's hip and exits without a snag at his knee in a single downward swoop.

Their bodies leak fluids and tissue as they slink to the ground.

I turn and find my front yard in total chaos and the real world is shunted back into my forward consciousness as time speeds up again.

An alien ship is hovering overhead as I gather the facts of the scene before me. Bodies everywhere, some avian, most human. Plasma charge fills the air and lights up the darkness that threatens to suffocate the atmosphere below the massive ship. I look over towards the front porch and see Slag battling it out with a MR soldier and I break into a run, ignoring the agony as my face throbs with each boot fall.

The scream stops me in my tracks as I look up and then the black wings enshroud me into a cocoon of darkness as they push me to the ground.

My heart aches as I reach for him, but the face that stares down at me is unfamiliar. "Stay down, girl. No trouble from you now, I'm only following orders."

I let myself slump down onto my belly, almost beaten, and breathe heavy as I stifle down the pain, fatigue, and sobs, listening to the slaughter happening around me.

Minutes pass like this and then I feel the avian on top of me lift himself and straighten up. I hear Tier's voice and I push myself up onto my knees, grab the avian's outstretched hand, and allow him to stand me up.

Tier and Slag are screaming at each other near the porch. Tier pushes him and he falls backwards onto the steps and Slag puts his hands up as the massive avian descends on top of him.

"Stop!" I scream it and then break into a wail from the pain that escapes from the wound that has sliced my jaw open. "Stop!"

Tier straightens and turns.

Slag's face, full of pain like my own, seeks out my eyes, and I can see him breathe a sigh of relief as I approach slowly. I take one shaky step after another, trying my best to lock shit down.

"Please stop, Tier." It's barely more than a whisper.

He lifts his head back and lets loose a sound that would make any demon in hell proud. I sink to the ground and cover my ears as the wave passes through the air, down into my ear canals, and reverberates though my entire body. All around me the avians mimic his roar and it becomes a deafening chorus of anger and hatred. When it stops I stay on my knees and the nightdogs beyond the borders of the farm answer the call of the birdmen with their own blood-curdling wails.

When I look up he's at my side and I get a chance to see first-hand what an angry Tier really looks like. He is in uniform, like the rest of his people. Black armor covers every exposed part of his body, except for his unsettled black wings and his head. The wings are upright in a position I've never seen before—high above his shoulders and spread out slightly to make him appear bigger than he actually is. An offensive posture, a predator on the attack.

His face contorts into a look of pure hatred, lips curling up like a wild animal exposing teeth that are longer and sharper than they should be. His eyes are glowing so bright the light reflects off the snow. He watches me carefully as I study him and then walks away, out towards the center of the driveway, keeping his back to me. I retract the half-forgotten SEAR and stuff it under my shirt. Then crawl the rest of the way to the front steps, locking down the sobs.

I reach Slag and slump down next to him. Waiting, like the avians, to see what Tier will do next.

When Tier finally begins talking he is quiet and calm.

"And you have the audacity to use the word *humanity* to mean acts of concern and the alleviation of suffering."

He's not looking at me, so at first I'm not sure who his hate is directed towards. And then I see them. The reporters who scrambled over the gate hoping for a story tonight. One by one they peek out from behind the cluster of pine trees on the far side of the driveway.

"Humans did THIS!" he roars and the sound wave of pain comes back before I can shut it off. After a second or two it subsides and when I look up he's pointing at me, but his eyes remain locked on the cams as fingertips scramble to zoom in on me.

My face contorts as I try and push down the years of psychological damage that desperately want out. My chest heaves and it takes every ounce of inner strength not to hide my face.

Tier paces back and forth in front of the reporters, each finger winking red with the cams. His audience. "And ya call the avian *monsters*?" It's barely a whisper this time.

He turns and walks away and runs his fingers through his hair, gripping, as if trying to make sense of something.

Overhead the ship suddenly powers up and dozens of blue waterfalls stream down, creating a grid of light across the driveway. I watch as the avian pick up their dead and wounded and walk towards the lights and step inside. Tier stands in place, quiet and still.

One by one the avian are shunted upward into the ship and as they disappear, so does each occupied blue stream. I straighten up a little as I realize there is just one blue light left.

And just one avian left.

Tier's head hangs as he waits. Then takes one hesitant step towards me, lifting his eyes up to meet mine. And finally, he speaks directly to me.

"Junco."

I feel my lips quiver with sadness as I look at him and the tears start to spread across my cheeks. I get to my feet.

Tier lifts his head. "Darlin', let me ask you one more time. Have I hurt ya?"

I shake my head. "No, Tier."

"Have I been honest with ya?"

I nod and wipe the back of my hand across my face. "Yes."

"And has anyone here, to the best of yer memory, done the same?"

I follow his gaze to Slag, who drops his eyes.

I shake my head. "No. They haven't."

Tier nods then and looks back at the reporters who have crept up onto the driveway and are barely a few yards from where he stands. He looks at them straight on. "Do ya trust me, darlin'?"

I take a step towards him when Slag speaks. "Junco, wait."

Tier's head snaps back around and covers the distance between us in flight. The reporters scramble to stay with him and he lands in front of me.

I turn back to look at Slag.

"Junco, you don't have to go with him. I can make it right. You can morph here, I can make it right."

Tier's hands are wrapped around his throat before I can even blink and I hear a collective gasp from the reporters as they fall back.

"Let me clarify what happened here tonight, *Slag*." He drawls out his name in pure disgust. "The girl said stop and I stopped. Otherwise you'd be a bloodstain in the snow like everyone else, understand?"

I take a deep breath, but this time I sit it out and say nothing.

Slag gasps and Tier throws him back into the porch stairs where he coughs, but still continues his speech. "Junco, do you want to leave with him?"

I look back at Slag, then at Tier and let out a sigh as I bring my hand up to the wound on my jaw that has coagulated into a thick crust of blood. The reporters crowd in as I turn back to answer.

"I think," I start, but hesitate to find the right words as the memories come flooding back to me in a rush, and have to begin again. "I think that we might have been friends under different circumstances, Slag. If I wasn't—" I breathe out and Tier shakes his head at me, but I put up a hand and continue. "If I wasn't just another military experiment turned political pawn."

I look down at Slag and his eyes are glassy, but there's only one thing left to say to him. "Maybe you're a good guy, Slag. But somehow I doubt it. And maybe you did help me at the end, in your own way. But that's not enough. When I needed a hero, Slag, needed to be saved, you always had the means. And you turned your head with all the rest."

The reporters are right in front of us now, and I have to give them credit. Tier and I are definitely apexers, yet the vultures think they are safe among their brethren predators.

I glance away for a second, again sliding my fingers down my wound. "Now that I've got myself a little more in control, I think"—I feel them all, even Tier, lean in to hear my words—"I should have just let him kill you and been done with it."

My eyes drop down to his face and he draws his mouth into a line that shows no emotion. "I mean, at least he," I point to Tier, "is sorry for what you guys did to me. And he had no part in any of it."

Tier walks out towards the solitary blue stream of light and turns, then extends his hand. "Junco, if I could, I'd stand here for the rest of my life waiting on ya to be ready. Ya know that, darlin'. I'd wait for you ta choose. I would. Ya have ta know that."

I nod my head and smile.

"But it's not up to me anymore and I'm calling ya back. You need to come with me right now."

I walk out towards him and then stop and look back at the reporters one last time, straight into the blinking lights. "My mother has initiated an invasion of the Mountain Republic on behalf of the Subjectives. And I hope they kill every motherfucker who ever had a part in what they did to us down here. But make no mistake"—my eyes burn into the blinking fingertips—"if she can't quite get them all, I'll be happy to come back and finish the job."

My hand reaches out and I give him the words he's been looking for all along. "I trust you, Tier."

And then our fingertips touch.

I am swept into his arms under the warmth of his wings, and we ascend the shower of blue light together.

Chapter Thirty-Five

Imagine you feel completely safe for the first time in your life. Inside a shower of blue light that fills you up with happiness. And you rise, reaching out for your future, with complete trust in the one who carries you towards it.

That's me.

Now.

Tier hugs me close and we climb the scattered molecules of air until they drop into the depths. Then it is just us. I gasp as I try to pull oxygen into my lungs but it burns. And then Tier's mouth delivers a kiss of precious life and I let go, into blackness.

Somewhere, someone is carrying me. The jerky motion of my body and the pattern of curt boot steps on a metal surface echo in my brain and tells me we are moving quickly. All around me there are voices yelling, panicked. A mask covers my mouth and nose and then my lungs expand out in a burst as they fill with oxygen.

I come up swinging.

And coughing.

Hands restraining me.

Voices all around me.

"Not gonna happen, Tier—"

"— like shit, you sure—"

"— done it this time—"

"— don't know what it's—"

"— off! Now!"

But only one voice matters and I catch all of it.

"Junco, I've got you."

My head rolls back and my eyes open to the world that bobs around me. I can't make any sense of where I am until I spy the metal grates that serve as a spacecraft ceiling. I try to smile and say thank you, but the darkness looks pretty sweet so I let my eyelids fall and follow the call that beckons me.

Finally, my world is truly silent.

The voices come back eventually, but fewer.

Two.

I only recognize one.

"... telling ya it looks worse than it is, Layla."

"You think so?" The voice has a slightly different accent from Tier's. "Let's see," —I hear the sound of tapping on a screen as she talks—"more bruises and talon punctures than you can personally count, a hunk missing from her calf, a repaired rotator cuff, broken nose, a hairline fracture in the occipital lobe, some avian neurotoxin metabolites in her blood, a ten-centimeter gash down the side of her head, possible irreparable inner-ear damage, a ten-centimeter SEAR wound down the side of her jaw, plasma burn on her back, *two fucking fingers missing*?"

"Calm down, OK. Most of those are old, she's already healing—"

"Calm down? You've got to be fucking kidding me! These are only the recent injuries, Tier! She's one long battle scar from head to toe!"

In my head I wonder if he yells at her for swearing, too. Somehow I don't think so. A sound escapes my mouth and the screaming stops.

"She's waking up," the Layla voice says.

"See? I told ya. Junco, can you hear me?"

I cough.

"Junco, can you open your eyes?" A flash makes me squint and I force my lids up. The light flickers at them and reflexes take over, closing them tight. The light disappears and I try again. Layla's face is way down in my personal space and my arm instinctively comes up and pushes her back.

A laugh from Tier. "Told you, Layla. She's fine."

Layla looks to be a little older than Tier, which puts her at least half a dozen years older than me. She's got long black hair pulled back in a pony and is wearing what is apparently the universal uniform of doctors and scientists. The long white coat. Her dark wings are pushed up a little bit, the tips hovering just above her shoulders and the ends jutting outward past her waist. In Tier, I recognize this as an expression of unease, but who knows what it means for her. She steps back and crosses her arms in front of her, a severe scowl on her face. I cough again, then turn my head towards Tier and manage to croak out some words. "What happened?"

"Low oxygen on the ascent, Juncs. No big deal, right? Yer fine now."

"Tier, don't sell her that shit! She's not fine! She's also dehydrated and malnourished. Borderline starving, in fact!"

"Junco, when's the last time you ate, darlin'?"

I crinkle up my face and think. "Dunno."

Layla nods her head at this, vindicated. "She can't go under like this, Tier. She'll fucking die."

"Well, then goddamn it, Layla, fucking feed the girl! Hook her up with a line and push some fucking nutrients in her! We've got fifteen minutes to get her under and it *will* happen or so fucking help me God I will kill the fucking pilot and take us back to fucking Earth!"

I've never heard Tier string together so many profanities in one breath and even Layla takes a step back. She shakes her head at me and turns away, busy getting things to pump up my condition.

"Junco, did ya eat when you went home?"

I shake my head.

"Have ya eaten since the dinner we had?"

I shake my head.

"The fuck's the matter with ya, Junco? Why didn't ya eat?"

"Well, there was kind of a lot going on, Tier. It just never became urgent."

Layla's back with a line and a bag. She pushes the needle in my arm without asking and starts a drip. She looks down at my shirt. "What's that mean anyway? Snipers do it from behind?"

"Don't answer her, Junco, she's being an asshole."

"You mean I'm sticking my ass out for you two, don't you?"

He shoots her a look that would scare the shit out of me, but she sends one right back that is even more terrifying and I break a smile. "I like you, Layla," I say with a small laugh.

Her scowl melts and she smiles. "Everyone likes me, Junco. It's my natural charm." Then she reaches down and squeezes my arm.

My hand goes up to my jaw and I feel for the crusted blood, but it has been cleaned and a smooth membrane has been placed on the wound. Layla's eyes follow my motion.

"Was it coded for you, Junco?"

"I'm not sure. Probably."

Tier takes a deep breath. "I've seen the aftereffects of a non-coded SEAR wound, Layla. It begins immediately. She's coded. It's built into her." He slides my shirt up and then slides the rim of my pants down to reveal the SEAR knife on my stomach. "See?"

"What the hell is that?" She pulls back a little. "Is that the SEAR? Docked on her body?"

"Meet the United Republics' most discreet biological weapon."

Layla stares a lot longer than is polite and I pull my shirt down and push Tier's hand away.

"I'll have to recode her collagen gene to make sure. No sense taking chances."

She leaves to do that, I figure.

"What's really going on, Tier?"

He smiles, but it's thin. "Yer going into morph as soon as Layla gives the word, Junco. It'll take a few weeks to get to the Band, until then I'm still in charge of ya and they can't stop it. By the time we get there you'll almost be half through. They won't mess with ya until yer ready to come out. Then..."

I take a deep breath as he pauses.

"Then we'll have to wait and see. Junco, it might be a little rough at first, but I promise ya"—he places his hands gently on each side of my face—"it will be OK and they will not kill ya. So don't even think that is a possibility. It's too far along even now. They won't kill ya."

I nod, but he's talking himself up now. He can't say that for certain. I turn away and then feel guilty for my doubts. He put his neck out so I decide to trust him. Let him worry about it. Someone other than me, for once.

Layla yells from across the room. "Get her prepped, Tier. I hear boots shuffling outside."

His fingers begin unlacing my boots and he slips them off, dragging my socks along for the ride. Then reaches down and takes my hand and pulls me up on the bed until I am steady. He yanks the tucked-in shirt a little so the ends are all free, rips the sleeve of the shirt to free the IV line, then lifts it off over my head and lets me fall back slowly to the pillows. "Sorry, no clothes in the tank, Junco."

I stop his hands at my pants. "I can do it, Tier." I unbuckle and start squirming out of them. He grabs the legs and pulls, then grabs a sheet from the next bed and drapes it over me as I slip off my shorts.

A door chime diverts his attention as I fix the sheet around me, suddenly cold and shy of my body. He's at the door before I can even register that he's moving and I see it open a crack, then wider as another avian guy is allowed in. They talk in low whispers and every few words their eyes look over at me.

Layla is back with a tray of vials that she expertly attaches to the drip and pushes into the line. "You'll feel a little funny now, Junco. It won't last long, this is just the code we're gonna use to get things started."

"What will it do?"

She looks at me sideways. "Turn ya into one of us, hopefully."

"Is that a difficult thing to do?"

She laughs. "Impossible, for any other human. But for you, it should work. It's like they've been preparing you for this your whole life—hedging their bets, maybe. Almost all the sequences are already there, just turned off—if that makes sense."

I shrug and look back over at Tier and the other guy. His face registers now. He's the one who covered me during the fight on Earth. That thought shocks me, to think that we're not even on Earth right now. My sight starts to get a little dizzy, but other than that I don't notice anything weird. "Now, what happens?"

It gets a little heated over by the door and both Layla and I exchange looks. "Let's get you in the tank, Junco."

She helps me out of bed and walks me and my IV drip over to a cylinder tube that looks a little too much like the clone vats in Dale's lab for my comfort level. The goo inside is green, not red, but still.

She takes the sheet from me and holds it up like a little screen to shield me from the guys and nods her head at the tank. I shake my head back at her. "I don't know, Layla."

She smiles, but I can tell by her backwards glances that she's getting nervous. "Junco, I get it. It's weird. Shit, even avians have trouble accepting the morph sometimes, so I don't expect this to go easy for you. But"—she glances back at the door—"Ashur is telling Tier that they are planning on storming in here to stop this, so if you want to live, get your fucking ass in the tank."

I step in.

It's warm, and that makes it a little easier as I slink down into the goo. Layla bunches the sheet up and throws it across the room to get it out of the way.

"Good, now for the hard part." Her hands reach down and grab some tubing that is hanging off the machine. "Unfortunately, Junco, this is going down your throat."

She waits, probably to see if I will overreact, but my attention is diverted as Tier comes back, leaving the other guy standing at the door.

He forces his smile this time. "We ready then?"

Layla and I both answer at the same time, but we say vastly different things. The three of us stare at each other in silence for a few seconds. Then the tubing is coming at my face and I put my hands up to stop it.

Tier leans in and pushes my hands back down to my sides, thrusting his arms into the goo up to his shoulders. "Tier, I'm not—"

"Junco, we're doing this, there's no discussion, no out clause. It's happening."

"But—"

Layla stuffs the tube in my mouth and I begin to gag. She switches the machine on and it comes alive on my tongue, small fingers reaching out and crawling down my throat, spewing out goop in my windpipe as I feel it travel into my chest. I panic and begin thrashing, but Tier's arms hold me steady. I calm down a little as I realize I can still breathe and Tier smiles. A real one.

Their hands are on me, pushing a mask over my face and forcing my body under the green goo that covers my eyes and glues them shut. I lie still for several moments. Feel the grip ease up. And then I burst up and fight to pull the tube out.

I give it my best shot, but I go down anyway.

What can I say? If I have to go down, well, then I'll go down the only way I know how.

Fighting.

BOOK TWO
FLEDGE

Prologue

A bead of sweat tickles me as it slides down my ribcage, clings tight as it rounds the curve of my back, and finally drops to settle on the towel underneath my body. I squirm a little to shake the feeling and cool air rushes in where there was once only heat. I flip over on the towel and put my hands under my forehead and try to go back to sleep.

"You're gonna burn, Junco."

"Mmmmhmmmm. Maybe."

I jump a little as the cold squirt of lotion drops onto my back and rough hands begin massaging it into my skin. I pick my head up a little and mumble, "Thank you."

He laughs. "Believe me, it is my pleasure."

He moves his hands to the back of my legs and I laugh and kick him away. "Tickles, Charlie." He increases the pressure to make the tickle stop and I relax back into the small dent my body has made in the sand over the past hour. When he's done he sits back in the beach chair next to me and is silent. I peek up at him with one eye, squinting at the sun. "Quit it. It hasn't changed. Just ignore it."

He looks down at me and nods, but the words tell another story. "What do you think he's saying?"

I let out a huff and turn back around so I can look out towards the lake where the apparition floats, just a few feet off the end of the dock. "Who cares?" I look back up at Charlie, but he's still staring. "We can't hear him, so who cares, Charlie."

"Junco, if he didn't have something to tell you, he wouldn't be here at all."

I lay my head back down and mumble, "Not interested. Not one bit."

Charlie gives up and slides down next to me on the towel, slipping his arm around my body and kissing the back of my neck until I arch my back and giggle. "Let's go inside," he breathes in my ear. "He's giving me the creeps."

I smile and then I laugh. "He's a hologram, Chuck. He can't see anything. Shit, he can't even get the talking part straight. Just ignore him. He'll go away. Eventually."

But he ignores my plea. Instead, he grabs my hand and pulls me to my feet. Then swings me over his shoulder and starts running towards the cabin. My body jerks and bounces with each stride and I laugh so hard it hurts. "Oh, God! Stop!

Stop!" I beg, but he just swings me over and plops me on the ground, then grabs my hand again and pulls me inside.

I fall down on the rumpled blankets and laugh as he crawls towards me from the foot of the bed. "No tickling!" I warn.

But he just takes my wrists and holds them over my head and leans down onto me. "No tickling? Since when?"

I laugh and squirm. "I'm serious." But he knows I'm not.

He gathers both of my little wrists into one hand and then slips the other under my back to unclasp my bikini top and covers my mouth with gentle kisses. "I love you, Junco," he breathes as he lets go of my wrists.

My hands go to his back and I draw my fingertips up towards his neck, making him buckle this time. They continue up into his blond hair and I pull his face towards me. I open my eyes and he's staring at me. "It's almost time to go, you know. That's why he's out there."

I shake my head as I search his brown eyes. "No, Charlie. I'm not going back. Ever."

He lets out a puff of air. "Silly, Junco. You can't live in a virtual when you still have a body. You have to go out so you can come back again."

My head is shaking before he is finished. "No."

His lips reach down to my neck and touch me softly. He leans into my ear. "Babe, I'll always be here. They can't ever take this away."

I feel the tears well up in my eyes and he lifts his head to study my face. "Shhh, not now, Junco. Now I just want to love you." His hands remove the loose top and then slide down my thigh and I moan and grab him tight and I thank God for every second we have together, every breath that escapes, and when the release comes I am bathed in the rays of total and complete happiness.

I wake later, when the moon is out and the wind has picked up enough to make the sheer curtains in the window blow in towards the bed. Charlie is gone and I am alone on the cool white sheets. I swing my legs over and dress in a large white shirt and some old denim shorts and make my way out of the bedroom. The moon is so bright that the ripple on the lake reflects the glow indoors through the picture window. I stand near the small kitchen and watch Charlie out on the deck, sitting down in front of the apparition of Tier.

My heart aches for him and for me, because he's right. Tier is here for one reason and one reason only. To announce the end of – whatever this is. My throat tightens up and I swallow hard to fight back the sadness. I walk out onto the deck, making just enough noise to let Charlie know I am out here, but he doesn't turn back to find me and the sinking feeling drops a little further into my stomach.

I walk down the steps slowly and then step into the soft sand that was never present at the lake cabin this virtual was based on. My toes sink in and I walk towards the dock and step on. Still, Charlie remains fixated on the holo hovering out over the water.

I can feel the vibrations on the deck as my feet touch down, and as I move out over the water the planks have a little more give than they do near the shore. Still, Charlie remains fixed.

I am halfway to the end when I hear the voice and I stop. It's Tier's voice. When he first appeared it was like the holo was stuck in a repeating pattern. No sound would play and we sat in front of it, just like Charlie sits tonight, and tried to read his lips. Tried to think of what he might be saying. Added in our own words, laughing at the absurdity of what we came up with. And finally, we just gave up and ignored him.

I cover the rest of the ground and take a seat on the edge of the dock. Charlie takes my hand and I lay my head down on his shoulder.

By then I already know what Tier's message is. He repeats the same two sentences, over and over again.

Trust no one, Junco. Show no weakness.

Trust no one, Junco. Show no weakness.

Trust no one, Junco. Show no weakness.

Trust no one, Junco. Show no weakness.

And I come out of it just like I went down. Swinging for the dumb fuck who just ripped me out of the happiest time of my life.

Chapter One

I burst out of the tank and the desperate gasp for air is like a prairie devil sucking up a farmhouse. My fists latch on to anything that will prevent me from going back under as waves of thick goo slosh around my body. Only the whine of plasma charge snaps me out of it and I allow a multitude of hands to grasp my arms and keep me still as the voice booms next to my head.

"Don't make me regret letting you live, Junco."

I cough and somewhere deep inside my vomit reflex is triggered. Shit comes up, clogging my airway and making me struggle against the firm hands. Since my eyes are still glued shut, I have no idea what comes out.

They pull me up out of the tank – completely out of the tank – so that I'm in mid-air for a few seconds, and then my feet hit the cold tile floor. My legs know what to do, but it's not happening. They drag me and I count six pairs of boots as we travel. Damn. Six fucking avians for me. I'm about to feel special when I'm dumped on the floor. A door snaps shut and I know I am alone.

A hydraulic click makes me twitch as my heart pounds in my chest. I take a deep breath and Tier's words come back to me. Trust no one. Show no weakness. I count to five to calm myself, breathing in and out, up and down, and then scoot on the floor until I bump into a wall. My hands flail out, finding a rail, then I pull myself up and force my legs to stand. My whole body shakes with fear, atrophy and cold, but the legs hold and I straighten my back, let go of the railing, and lift my chin.

And wait as the thick, sticky tank goo crusts in the ventilated room. My body feels lighter than normal and I realize that gravity must be less than one-G.

It helps.

A fine mist sprays out in all directions and I lift my arms up to let it coat me all over. It is only then, when my muscles are asked to respond, that I realize what's happened.

The smile comes out and I laugh, soft at first, then wildly, hysterical, and I turn my face upward to the drizzle as my lids are freed from their prison. Hot water blasts the soap off my body and I finally open my eyes.

I expel the fear.

I've been reborn.

The water drenches me and then I step back to wipe my eyes and look around, holding the handrail for support. It's a shower room, obviously. Small, but I can see through the clear surround that there are close to a hundred of them all lined up. Mine is the only one in use at the moment. I look through the glass to try and see if anyone is around, but the large room outside the stall appears empty.

My attention returns to my shower and I lather my new body with gel provided by a wall dispenser. When my hands touch my chest and upper back I gasp with the changes. My upper body is pure muscle. The smile creeps along my face as I imagine the new power this will bring to my old skills. I turn my head to try and see my wings but all I get is a glimpse of the tips as they roll over to cup my shoulders.

The water cuts off and the hot air blasts me in all directions, making my long hair fly up and whip around my face. Several minutes later the door opens with a click and my hair falls flat as the wind ceases.

I scan the room and count more than two dozen possible surveillance points, then step out and look down the long row of empty showers and start walking. At the end I find a small pile of clothes inside a cubby. One small square filled among hundreds that are empty.

I take the clothes and walk over towards a flat piece of furniture that sits low to the ground. I've worn Tier's shirts back on Earth, so I know it goes over my head. I fuss with the bodice, noticing that the missing fingers on my left hand are still missing (oh well, one can hope) and then the remaining digits automatically track to the SEAR wound that runs the length of my jaw on the left side. I drag a fingertip down the raised line of scar tissue and allow my mind to jerk back to the memory.

And then let it go.

It is what it is.

My attention returns to my girls, which need to be smashed down into the cups of the upper body garment. Tier's shirt never had cups and they feel heavier than I remember, so it's a struggle to get them to cooperate before sealing up the sides.

In the end it fits like it was tailored specifically for me.

The pants are made of the same black material as the top, synthetic, thick as light armor, and soft. They slip on easily up to my hips and it's only then that I notice my SEAR dock under my belly button is completely covered by skin. I touch it and the dock opens, revealing the small blue wand within.

I admit, I have to hold back my revulsion.

"Do not remove the weapon, Junco." The voice on the speaker is emotionless and direct.

I completely ignore it and slip the SEAR knife into my hand. My thumb flicks over the small imperfection near the tapered end and it comes to life with a buzz. Another smile graces my face. I flick it off and dock it, then look up and find what may be the closest surveillance point. "You went through all this just to kill me in the waiting room? I don't think so. It's mine and I'll take it out whenever I want."

I button my pants and move on to the socks and boots.

This time I'm stumped. My feet are no longer feet and I stare at them in awe. Or maybe confusion, I'm not quite sure. Four toes and they are extraordinarily long. All point forward, but the two outer toes seem to have a mind of their own and can point sideways and almost backwards, if I wiggle them enough. I get up and walk around a little, looking down as I try out the new digits. They move and adjust as I change my pace. The talons clack on the hard tile and I imagine what it would feel like to clutch things. I wrangle them back into the forward position and tug on the socks and boots.

When I'm finished a door opens and I walk through.

The space is empty except for a mirror long enough to allow hundreds of avians to gawk at their new bodies at the same time. I stand there, stunned at what I see. I flex my back muscles and the wings respond. One stretches out to its full length and then retracts and folds, cupping back over my shoulder. I squeeze the muscles a little and I feel them collapse completely against my back. It makes me look human for a moment and I grin back at my reflection.

My wings are not black. I get close to the mirror and try to see my back. They are a strange color – not white, not cream, not tan, not brown, not gray – a mottled mixture of all these hues. I squint at my eyes in the mirror, moving my head back and forth to get a clear look at them, expecting to see orange like Moju's or green like Tier's. But they haven't changed at all and a grunt of disgust leaks out of my mouth.

"Well, that fucking sucks. Not only do I still have hazel eyes, but you fuckers gave me hazel wings too." I look up, but get no answer. Then I whisper under my breath, "That is so fucked up."

I'm done looking, satisfied with the novelty of my new body, but the next door does not open. I think of how I should act so that I don't show weakness and decide on boredom. I lean my wings against the wall and then slide my back down until I'm sitting on the floor. I tilt my head back and close my eyes and my mother's voice is in my head. *Patience and inertia are not the same thing.*

She's right after all. So I wait. And think about where Tier is. Hell, where I am for that matter. Are we in the Band? I'm not really even sure where the Band is, but Tier talked about it before we left Earth a few times. And then my thoughts slip back to Earth – to Selia. Did she get the message out? To Slag – what did he do after we left? To Moju. My hearts aches for him and I let a little frown cross my face before I catch it.

This seems to be the magic signal that I am calm and ready to be rational, because the door opens and a man walks in.

He doesn't look avian. For a moment I wonder if I ever left Earth. But I feel the weight of the wings and the lightness of the less-than-G gravity and let that go. It doesn't matter where I am – I am no longer human.

He's not a friendly-looking man with his height and muscular bulk, not to mention the down-turned mouth and intense stare. His suit is black, tailored, and screaming money. His hair is fair and this too is different. So far all the avians I've ever met had black hair. Except me of course. My hair is still the same ugly auburn brown. His complexion is fair as well and his smile as he approaches me is forced.

I look up at him for a moment, then get to my feet and wait.

"I'm Lucan, Junco. Your new commander." His voice is deep and calm. Almost soothing.

"You don't look like a commander," I say, raising my eyebrows at him. For one, he's not that old. Maybe early thirties. And for two, he's wearing a fucking suit. I don't get it.

He gives me an indulgent smile, like I'm a toddler. "You've never seen an avian commander, so how would you know what one looks like?"

I watch his deep blue eyes as he talks, find the power there and make myself behave. "You're right. It's a pleasure to meet you,

Commander Lucan. Should I salute? Shake? You'll have to forgive me, I am almost one hundred percent ignorant of your culture."

Another indulgent smile as he extends his hand. "We can do it your way, if you like."

I take his hand and shake it politely. "I would not like, actually. I would prefer to know how I am expected to act."

He retracts his hand. "We'll get to that in time. But for now I'd like to know how you came to be on my habitat when I gave a direct order to kill you two months ago."

I smile. "Oh, that's easy," I say, still grinning up at him, "I was invited, of course."

"Ah, yes, your invitation. Would you like to know where Tier is?"

"Not especially, no."

His brow furrows at my answer and I tuck down a smile. I can play too, buddy. Let's dance.

"Well, Junco, that surprises me. I think he would very much like to know where you are."

My stomach churns, but I shake my head. "No, I don't think so, Commander Lucan."

"And why's that, Junco?"

I shrug and turn my back to him and walk a few paces, testing out my wings and feeling my new talons move and be restrained inside my boot. God, no wonder Moju was barefoot. It's kind of annoying.

"I'm nothing to him. He's nothing to me. Why would we care what the other is doing?" I turn back and wait. Patience is not inertia, Junco. "He brought me back because I can be used and I came because, well – I'm sure you probably realize why staying on Earth wasn't a real option for me."

He smiles again. I don't. My face will crack if I have to keep up this fake shit much longer. He turns sideways towards the door and waves his arm, signaling for me to pass through ahead of him.

I do and I am met by six avian guards with their plasma rifles pointed at my head. I listen to their footsteps and decide they are the same guys who just saw me naked and covered in goo not too long ago and shoot them a smile.

They keep their aim true and ignore me.

Lucan and I walk side by side down a long hallway wide enough to drive a few tanks through back on Earth. My gaze stays straight ahead and I do not gawk up or around, but instead listen to our footfalls echo as we travel. The guards match our pace and they surround me in a semi-circle, walking sideways to target me.

I look at Lucan's face and he feels my gaze and directs his eyes down in expectation. "I think it's possible you've misjudged me, Commander. I'm just one small girl. Do you really think you need six heavily armed men plus yourself to control the situation? If so, you will seriously inflate my ego."

He sighs and I know the charade is over. "Junco, we know exactly who you are, what you do, and what you're capable of – so you will excuse my enthusiasm for protection until we can all come together on the same page. I ordered you to keep that weapon of yours," he hesitates as he points to my stomach and I squint up at him, "sheathed. Yet you insisted on removing it."

"Commander Lucan, that weapon is biologically attached to me. Taking it out and giving it a quick check was like wiggling my new toes. A simple reflex to make sure everything is working." I reach for it and the rifles emit an electric field so strong it pushes me backwards. "Cool it, guys. I'd be happy to hand it over if it makes you feel better."

"Hands off, Junco. You will not use that weapon here, do you understand?" I don't meet his gaze and I don't agree to his terms, so he continues, "I would take it, but it cannot stay away from you for long, we tried while you were under. It was – not ideal."

I shrug. "I lived without it for weeks on Earth."

"This isn't Earth."

Yeah, I think I'm getting that, thanks. "Well, you know, I can't help that the thing is attached to me. It wasn't like anyone asked if I wanted a biological weapon grafted onto my body, ya know."

He stops in the hallway and waves the men off a bit. Without the echo of boots the only sounds are the environmental units pumping out conditioned air. The guards step back but the rifles are still on alert. "Junco, I'm not playing games. This sweet-talking you gave Tier will not work on me. So save your breath."

I laugh out loud this time, I can't help it. He gives it a good shot, but he's unsure what to make of me and it shows. "Commander, I don't know who you've been talking to, but it certainly wasn't Tier if you think the reason I am alive and fucking up your habitat is because of my wily ways with men. Tier and I had no conversations about what he was and was not doing beyond a handful of words the very last time we talked."

Lucan's composure is back and his lip curls up slightly as he speaks. "Is that so? Well, Tier must be mistaken then, because he said something quite different."

I don't even miss a beat. "You're a liar. He never said anything other than what I just stated because that was the truth. And if you know so much about me, then you know that death carries very little meaning at the moment. You can try and kill me if you want – I don't give a shit. I have nothing to lose. You're no different than the assholes I left back on Earth and if you really want to know what I'm doing on your habitat, you better ask yourself. We both know I'm here because you want me for something."

I watch the guard behind Lucan raise his eyebrows at me and smile, then redirect my eyes back to Lucan's face and wait for his reply.

He turns and continues to walk and I catch up and walk by his side. We travel in the echo of our footsteps once again and then he stops at a door, palms his hand over the biometrics and it slides open. He waves me in and I step through, but he stays where he is.

"Goodbye for now, Miss Coot." And then the door closes.

Chapter Two

I turn and find Layla gaping at me from the far side of the room. I look up and around and she smiles and waves the thought away. "No cameras allowed here, Junco. I'm so glad to see you!" She walks over to me and hugs me to her chest.

I return her hug and push her back. "What did they do to Tier?"

She winces at his name and shakes her head. Her mouth drops downward as she speaks. "He's fucked, Junco. On trial for treason."

I stare out at the room for a moment, stunned. Treason. That is the worst. I shake it off and study the room. It's a cross between a lab, a clinic, and a hotel. It screams Junco's new vivarium. I pull a chair from the table and sit across from Layla as she waits patiently for me to settle. The chairs are strange, with only a thin backrest, but as soon as I lean back I understand why. It supports my spine without crimping or impinging on my new wings. I slouch a bit, even though the straight back makes it difficult, and feel very tired and sad. Since Tier's warning instructed me to trust no one, I have to presume that Layla will deliver reports on my moods and behavior and force a neutral expression as I wait for her to give me some sort of explanation.

She smiles and then lets out a long breath. "When we discussed everything that could happen when we brought you back, Junco, treason never even entered the realm of possibilities. But" – she hesitates – "here we are."

"What were the possibilities?" I ask as I avert my eyes and study the furniture. In the living area there is a bed, a desk, a large screen on the wall, and a bedside table. I see a door that might lead to a bathroom. That takes up about a quarter of the space.

About half is devoted to medical and lab equipment – centrifuges of various shapes and sizes, some molecular cloning machines, glassware of course, a bench lined with bottles of chemicals, buffers, pipettes, books, a plate reader, cell sorter, a few medium sized coolers, a hood for tissue culture, four microscopes, a gleaming stainless steel minus-80 freezer for samples, and lots of other stuff that looks like it belongs in a research facility. Let's just call it a well-stocked, scratch that, a well-funded lab.

The other corner has a counter that holds canisters filled with paper goods, 2x2 gauze, cotton-tipped applicators, shit like that. There is also a built-in sink and glass front cupboards that hold enough drug canisters to treat a small town back in the RR.

"Demotion, mostly. We thought maybe if we were really fucked they'd kick us out of the Aves. We spent quite a few hours talking about what we'd do if they did."

My brow furrows and I try and put it together. "Are you and Tier – together?"

Her smile is crooked. "No, Junco. I'm on his team, his scientist. We've been together, hell, since he came out of Fledge really. Not counting that stint I did on Lacerion for post-training in moleculars."

"Sorry, I feel a little lost here, ya know. I have no idea who he is, only that I agreed to let him bring me here. We never discussed anything that might happen afterward, so–"

"We figured you'd be like a bonus – one of the Seven that we thought was lost but wasn't. We were pretty sure it was gonna work fine, Junco. It's not like we were just yanking ya on that end. And it did, right? Look at ya! So pretty."

Her sudden pickup of Tier's speech patterns makes me swallow the sadness once again. "I don't like the color, to be honest."

"Really?"

She looks a little hurt and I wonder if she made me this way on purpose, but it's too late now and I just shrug. "I like the black wings. These," I say, peeking back at their almost yellow paleness, "feel like a target."

"Oh, well. Sorry. I think they're beautiful. And I bet everyone else does too. You'll see. Anyway, the whole purpose of being on Earth was to get the Seven and bring them back. We knew you were the Seventh," her fingers do little air quotes, "and the Seventh Sibling is not well-liked around here in theory. But we discussed this for days before we came to the decision, Junco. I'm pure because someone made me that way. Ditto for everyone else. So, if someone altered you as you grew up, and they did – we know this – then how can you not be pure? Just because your alterations took place after birth, why should that make any difference?"

I look away at her question because I don't want to think about anything right now, least of all my avian biological status. "So, what went wrong?"

"After we put you under we let the others come in, but you were undergoing the morph, so you had special protected status. It's a vulnerable position. Being unconscious for weeks on end, helpless and under the control of your medical staff. They couldn't do anything to you then. They just had to wait it out."

I don't want to ask the question, in case someone is listening or Layla is taking notes on my questions, but I do anyway. "And Tier?"

She shrugs. "He's ranking officer, so they couldn't do anything to him either, unless they wanted to mutiny, which they didn't. But, well, everyone has a boss. And Lucan was beyond pissed when we arrived in the Band. They arrested Tier immediately."

"The charges," I ask, still avoiding her eyes, "are treason?"

She nods and gives me a half-hearted crooked smile when I finally look over at her.

"Because he didn't kill me."

This time she doesn't acknowledge me, just releases a deep breath.

"Anything else? Charges, I mean?"

"Something to do with breaking a treaty. And the old stuff, the unauthorized murder charges. He was on – like a probation – and they revoked it for this last charge."

I nod and get up and walk across the room to the bed. "This for me?"

She nods but doesn't rise.

"And all this?" I say, pointing to the medical equipment.

"Tests. Not today though, it's late and I'm sure you're still tired. And," she hesitates, "maybe it will help to know that these feelings you're having right now, the sadness and lethargy? It's normal, Junco. We all get this way after morph. It's an endocrine reaction, the changes really fuck you up. So whatever you're feeling right now, just give it a few days, OK?"

I sit on the bed and start unlacing my boots.

"We'll have to have guards in here with you at all times, just for a little while, though."

I shake my head without looking up and write her off for good now.

"Ashur is taking the night shifts and Braun is taking days."

I remove the boots and the socks and finger the blister that has formed on my right foot after the short walk from the showers and I wonder for the first time how I will hold up in this new environment.

Layla stands up and walks towards the door, then turns back. "It'll be better tomorrow. We'll do the tests and then you can leave here. You'll see."

I lie down on the bed and turn my back to her.

"See you tomorrow. Ashur's outside, you remember him? From the battle at your house?"

I ignore her.

"OK, well, I'll send him in on my way out."

"Layla?" I ask without turning to look at her.

"Yes, Junco?"

"Why aren't *you* on trial for treason?"

"I'm his subordinate, Junco. He's my captain. I could no more deny his order to save you than anyone else on the ship."

I close my eyes and never even hear the other avian enter because I simply shut down and go looking for the dock.

But it's gone.

So I settle for nightmares. They come easy. History repeating.

I toss and turn in the bed as my nose wrinkles with a familiar but out-of-place smell. It fades and my dream takes me to my bedroom where I lie on the bed in my shorts and puff on a cigar, happy with who I am.

Wait.

That wasn't a dream, that was real.

Where am I?

"Junco?"

The strange voice triggers my reflexes. The SEAR comes out from under my shirt and I'm standing on the bed in attack mode before I can even process all my actions.

The large avian is bent down in a defensive stance, his plasma weapon pointing up at my head. "Junco! Put it down, now!"

"Fuck!" I let out a long sigh and retract the SEAR and slip it back into the dock. "What the fuck?"

He watches me step off the bed and stand on the other side of the room, but he does not lower his weapon.

"Ashur?"

He nods.

"Put your fucking weapon away or we're gonna tangle."

"You cannot take that knife out, Junco. Ever. If you do, you're going to get hurt."

I shake my head at him. "It's docked. What more do you want? Put your weapon down, Ashur – or we will fight."

He stands upright and slides his weapon in the holster that hangs at his hip. My eyes trace the familiar smell that woke me and I lean to look past the formidable avian. A smoldering cigar is sitting in an ashtray on the table. "You did that on purpose."

He gives me a crooked smile. "I know you like them. And I was bored. Can you think of a better way to be woken up?"

I just stand there, kinda pissed. "Well, yeah, actually. There are about a thousand better ways of being woken up than having some strange guy in my room smoking a cigar that reminds me of home. Thanks."

Ashur walks over to me and takes my arm and leads me over to the table where he was sitting before I went commando on him. He points to the chair and slides a cigar over. "Here, have one. Relax a little, shit. You're so jumpy."

I don't have it in me to protest and the little gray box that holds the cigar is calling my name. I slide it out, press it to the striker, and puff. "Thanks."

He takes his seat and I do the same, then we both puff in silence as we watch the screen on the far wall. The sound is off, but it's the news so the captions at the bottom of the feed tell all you need to know. I guess some things never change, no matter what world you're on.

"What time is it?"

"2 AM Standard, why? Got plans?" His lips attempt to smile around his stogie.

"What time did I fall asleep?" I say as my attention goes back to the screen.

"Eight or so."

I nod. "Oh."

"Done sleeping then?"

I look back at him. He could be Tier's brother, that's how similar they are. "Probably."

"Want some breakfast?"

"No." Just the thought of food makes me want to heave.

He takes his cigar out of his mouth. "What do you mean, no? You haven't eaten in almost two months."

"Obviously that's not true or I would be dead. I'm definitely not hungry."

He's still holding his cigar in his hand, not puffing. "I've already been warned about your eating habits, Junco. I'm in charge of making you eat breakfast, so we're having some."

I screw up my face at him. "I can't think of a single person who would even know what my eating habits are, Ashur. So spare me."

"Both Layla and Tier mentioned your lack of enthusiasm for food."

I snort out a laugh. "And how the hell would they know?"

"They said you were severely undernourished when we took you, that's how."

"Which means nothing. You guys got to see the tail end of what a very bad week does to my appetite, so what? I wouldn't base anything off what I did that week, let alone assume I have an eating disorder."

"Good, then we'll have eggs for breakfast."

"Knock yourself out, Ashur." Just stop fucking talking to me, I don't add.

He gives me a look of superiority, like he won the argument or something, then pushes back his chair and exits the room through the door I thought was the bathroom last night.

I stub out the cigar and go back to bed watching the newscreen. It's all in English but it shows a lot of stuff that makes no sense. Winged people fighting each other. Killing each other actually, in what looks to be an advertisement for an upcoming arena fight of some kind. Some more winged people having a party. Some people with no wings in what looks to be a government session. Some personal interviews. I just sit there in disbelief. I didn't watch the screens much at home, only when on the road, but it's all a little too familiar. I traveled hundreds of millions of miles, I'm on a totally different planet, habitat, whatever, and still the news is filled with the same shit. Violence, parties, and politics. The irony isn't lost.

Ashur returns a few minutes later with eggs and toast and beckons me to the table. At least it's real food and not that shit Tier tried to feed me in the cave. It doesn't look horrible, but my head shakes out a no as he slides the plate in front of me. I keep the disgusted look as I meet his eyes. "If you make me eat that I'll throw up."

He shrugs and takes his seat, shoving food in his mouth before he even settles. "It's good, real eggs and everything. Tier said you only eat fresh food, so lucky us, right?" He shoots me a smile.

"Tier would have no idea, Ashur. He saw me eat a total of three meals."

"He's the resident Junco expert, like it or not, what he says goes. Might as well enjoy the food, Fledge food is like military field rations."

I force myself to eat three bites and push the plate away.

"Ya know, you don't have to make everything so difficult, Junco. You can have it made here, if you want."

"And what would I have to do in order to have it made?"

"Follow the program," he meets my gaze, "and just do what you're told for once."

"For once? You're an asshole." I let out a deep sigh, get up, and go flop down on the bed and bury my face in the pillows. "I'm sorry I came here."

I hear him set his fork down and push back from the table and look up to see what he's doing. His head is in his hands. A gesture that reminds me of Tier when he was thinking out at the cabin, right before he told me that he killed my father.

"Ya know something, Junco, we're probably all sorry you came here. Except one person, maybe. And that's Tier. So for fuck's sake, try and do what you're told for his benefit. The guy's sitting in prison for saving you and" – he lifts his head and stares at me with bloodshot eyes – "and if I had it my way, Junco, I would have killed you myself in order to save him from that."

He stands up and walks to the door. "If you need something, I'll be outside until Layla comes."

Good job, Junco. Making friends already.

Chapter Three

Layla is busy getting the equipment ready as I watch from the table. "Ashur's mad at me." It slips out because I can't stop thinking about what he said.

Layla talks to me under her breath between curse words directed at the control panel. "Well, Junco, Ashur is not the sanest guy in the Cluster. He's always been a little touched, don't take it personal."

"He said he should have killed me to save Tier."

She looks up this time. "What?"

I shrug with my hands. "That's what he said." I watch her face as she processes this, expecting her to say something, but she doesn't. She just looks back at the machine, apparently in agreement with the guy who's a little bit touched.

I change the subject because the thought of both of them wanting me dead to save their friend is a little too unsettling. "So what does this test do anyway?"

She curses for a few more seconds before answering. "We gotta map you again. I took some images while you were under, but it was hard to see everything. This way we'll have a good baseline at what we're looking at."

"What are we looking at?" I ask.

She stops this time and gives me her full attention. "Sorry, Junco – I forgot that you haven't seen it yet." My heart thumps as I wait for the reveal. "I've never seen anything like it before, but–"

"But?"

"You've got a lot of technology inside you. Like everywhere. In fact," she's just warming up, I can tell, "your entire nervous system is controlled by circuits that reside outside of your brain and peripherals. Like in your hands – there's a whole pad of circuits in the palms of your hands. And that SEAR dock?" She stops to shake her head. "I have no idea what that is."

I let out a grunt. "That's awesome."

She ignores me and goes back to the machine. Thirty minutes later I'm naked and standing behind the transparent shield that will allow Layla to see inside me.

She describes the process, how it will feel, and how long it will take but my mind is on Ashur. I feel the need to set this right for some reason. He was the only person Tier allowed in the room with us right before they stuck me in morph and he was the person who shielded me from the battle that happened in my driveway. I don't have to trust him, but I don't have to make him hate me either. And some small part of me secretly wants him to leak out more information about Tier. I wonder if Tier even knows I'm out of morph?

I stand as still as I can as the lights begin to pass over my body. When it's over I get dressed and flop back on the bed to wait for the confirmation that I am a freak. When she resurfaces and calls me over to her I can sense her hesitation.

"See this?" she says, pointing to a large white splotch superimposed at the base of my spine in the full-scale image of my body.

I nod.

"That's your endocrine biog."

"OK, that's not so weird, is it? I mean, Tier said my biog protocols were on that cube."

"Right. No, you're right. The biog isn't weird, hell, I have one too. But…" She stops and looks at me. "Junco, this thing controls your whole body. Your glands don't make the hormones, this thing does."

I shrug, not seeing the big deal. "Anything else?"

"Well, actually yes. See these?" She points to more white blotches on the image, one at each joint of my bones, and more throughout my body.

"Yeah, and?"

"Most of these are in the same place as your lymph nodes, or where the lymph nodes would be."

"Layla, get to the point, OK. I'm not an anatomy expert and I don't feel like digging down to find the memories from school."

"OK, well, you don't process your blood in the same way as most people. It gets shunted through these other things, and then these" – she points to the many white lines running up and down my legs, arms, and trunk area – "take it to the muscles," she points, "the lungs," more pointing, "and then finally back to the heart where it interacts with this" – she screws up her face and raises her eyebrows – "master circuit."

I just stare at her blankly.

"Junco, you're half machine."

I grunt. Of course I am. And why wouldn't I be? My body was altered since I was a toddler, I should have seen this one coming. "You're fucking crazy," I say instead.

She shrugs and snaps the image off the viewer and takes it back into the lab. I follow and watch as she rolls it up and stuffs it into a tube.

"What are you doing?"

She scowls at me. "I have to take this to Lucan right away. Braun will stay with you until I come back."

And before I can protest or demand to know what that will mean to me, she's gone and a guard enters to take her place.

He's tall, like Tier and Ashur, but not as dark and more muscular. Both his wings and his hair are more brown than black and I recognize him as the smiler from yesterday's hallway showdown with Lucan. He looks thrilled to be invited in, so I try not to make an enemy.

"Wanna sit?" I ask pointing to the table.

"I'm Braun," he says as he takes a seat.

"Junco."

"Yeah, I know. Was with you when you were picked up from Earth."

"Oh." I stop, trying to see if I recall him, but I have no memory of anyone but Tier, Layla, and Ashur.

"That was pretty funny the way you talked shit to Lucan yesterday." He laughs. "I bet it's been a long time since anyone's talked to him like that."

"Oh," I say again. "He hates me, doesn't he?"

The avian smiles and his eyes glow a little orange. "Lucan hates everyone. He's an Archer." A shrug. "No sense of humor, those guys. So what have you been doing in here all day?"

I walk over to the screen and pretend to watch the news. "Tests."

"Did you pass?"

I look back at him, trying to decide if he's serious or not. If pushed, I'd peg him as a guy who doesn't get serious unless he's forced, but he looks sincere. "No, I don't think so."

"Wanna tell me about it?"

"No, not especially."

"Wanna play cards then? Pass the time?"

"I don't know your games, so–"

He pulls a deck out of his jacket. "You're a soldier, Junco, all soldiers can play poker."

I laugh. "Oh, well, OK."

Braun is the first normal guy I've met in a long time. We get along and there's no arguing and he doesn't pretend to be better than me or even seem bothered that I have the SEAR tucked under my shirt. We play using 2x2 gauze as chips and it only takes a few minutes and I'm laughing. He's got a nice sense of humor and when he asks me if I'm hungry he doesn't lecture me when I say no. But he does leave to get some food and when he brings it back to the table I am hungry and it's not bad.

We've been playing for hours and I owe Braun six thousand rills, whatever that is, when Ashur enters. Braun smiles and stands up, counting his cotton wipes to double-check his winnings. "I cheated her out of enough paper products to buy a new house, Ash." And then he laughs. "See you tomorrow, Junco, I'll bring beer for the next game."

Ashur just raises his eyebrows. "Braun, don't–"

"Ah, shut up, man. And get off her back, she's stressed. Make her happy, why don't you?" Then he looks at me. "We'll have fun tomorrow, Juncs." And then he walks to the door, his weapon slapping his thigh with each step as he leaves.

I'm still smiling when I look over at Ashur and force myself to dial it back down.

"You'll want to stay away from that one, Junco."

"Why?"

He shakes his head. "He's trouble."

"Oh, I see. He's trouble, yet I'm the prisoner, Tier's on trial for treason, and you wish you could kill me. Well, thanks for clearing all that up." The tension is back and I miss Braun already. I walk over to the bed and flop down. My desire to make things right with Ashur is gone with the return of my sour mood.

He walks into the lab and takes a minute before coming back in the living area and sitting down at the table. His back slouches and his long legs sprawl out in front of him. "I spoke to Tier today."

My heart skips, but I don't answer him.

"He asked about you."

I turn my back to him and let out a big sigh.

"Do you want me to tell him anything if I see him again?"

"No."

"Do you care to explain that, Junco? I mean, the guy is on trial for you, the least you can do is send a message to say hi."

I turn back. "You know something, I'm beginning to wonder how well you actually know him. The Tier I know does not want to hear from me right now, Ashur. And you're lying if you tell me he's sent a message, because I know for a fact he wouldn't do that. So stop with the bullshit, OK?"

He shakes his head and turns his attention to the screen. We don't speak another word to each other. I don't set anything right. And Ashur makes no attempt to make me happy. I lie there for a long time before falling asleep.

I wake in the middle of the night again. My sleep is way out of whack. Ashur is still slumped in his chair, one arm crossed over his chest, his fingers playing with his shirt on the opposite shoulder while watching the screen. He's got a cigar box in his other hand and he taps it gently on the table until he notices me looking at him.

"Cigar?" He extends his hand out and I lean over and take the little gray box, shake out the stogie, and light it up.

"Thank you."

He hands me an ashtray and I prop myself up in bed and set it on my stomach. He's watching a screen about a girl who is being chased by some psycho murderer on an abandoned habitat. Despite myself, I get into the drama. I can see the draw of mindless entertainment, even though I can count on one hand the number of screens I've seen all the way through in my lifetime.

We sit in silence until the credits roll and then he speaks. "I'm sorry for saying that shit, Junco. I don't want to kill you. And we all like you, we don't wish you never came home."

I stare at him until he looks me in the eyes. "You need to butt out of my life when it comes to Tier, Ashur. It's over. He sent me a message" – I hesitate – "and like I said, he never told you to tell me anything, did he?"

He shakes his head. "No. He didn't. But it doesn't make sense, I watched him put you under in the morph, and you two weren't fighting."

"It doesn't matter, does it? It's over."

We sit in silence and watch the screen as another show comes on.

"I've seen this one," Ashur says when it starts. "It's not bad."

We watch it and chat some. After a little bit I fall back asleep and when I wake in the morning he's gone.

Layla and Lucan are standing over me, talking in avian. I squint up at them and try to string the words together. "I'm right here, you know."

Both sets of eyebrows go up.

"Yeah, I understand too, so that shit you just talked about me is not going over well." I push up and extract myself from the bed to go take a shower and when I'm finished, I find a closet full of clothes. It has five identical outfits to the one I was just wearing.

And one that makes me smile.

I tug on the camo fatigues and button them up. They are looser than they were when I put them on last and I make a mental note to try and eat more. Then I wrestle the shirt over my back and stretch and rip at the arm holes of the sniper shirt until I can jam my wings and arms through. I realize I look ridiculous, but I don't care. My old field boots are in there too, but there's no way they will fit on my new hulking feet. Besides, I'm feeling Moju's affinity for going barefoot.

When I walk out of the bathroom Lucan and Braun are at the table talking and Layla is in the lab clanking glassware around.

Braun laughs. "Snipers do it from behind? They saved that for you?"

"I knew you'd appreciate my shirt, Braun." His eyes dance as he laughs again and I catch myself wondering how long I'll have to wait until we can play cards.

Lucan interrupts my daydream. "Layla, Braun. Junco and I need some private time, please."

Braun winks at me as he passes. "Beer's in the fridge, Juncs." I absently wonder if I'm old enough to drink on this habitat or if Lucan will frown on that, but he stays seated and points to the chair Braun just vacated.

"Layla has some interesting developments from the tests yesterday. Do you know what it means?"

I shake my head, but keep silent.

"You're not human."

He waits for my reaction, but I hold it in.

"You're not avian."

Nothing.

"You're not machine."

I laugh now. "OK. So what am I?"

"All three, apparently. It's highly unusual."

I squint, but do not avert my eyes. "Will you kill me now?"

It's his turn to stay silent. We stare, willing the other to speak. I have nothing to say so I am patient until he gives in. "That will be entirely up to you, Junco."

"How's that work, then?"

"We have a strict, structured society here. A lot of people must share space in the hundreds of habitats we have scattered throughout the Band, but habitats are not easily made and resources are precious. Do you understand this?"

"Yeah, of course."

"When we create the clutches of children we do so with the entire population in mind. We try to make them into their genetic ideals but not all of them will be able to reach their full potential. Which is why after they go through the morph they must go through Fledge. Do you know what Fledge is, Junco?"

I shake my head.

"It's a test of sorts. To see which individuals can fulfill the potential bestowed upon them. Everyone you've met so far has succeeded in Fledge. Proved themselves worthy."

Tier's words on the rock on Earth come back to me, *She's worthy. That's what I thought. She's worthy – it's just that no one recognizes it yet.*

"And there is a very simple test to determine if you're worthy or not." He stops and waits for me this time.

"Which is?"

"In this case it is a series of fights. That's what Fledge is. A series of fights to the death."

"So you want me to kill people in order to prove myself."

He nods. "Your clutchmate, Esta, went through Fledge a few years ago. So she earned her place. And if you want to stay here, you must do the same."

I shrug. "OK."

"You may not use the weapon."

"Lucan," I snarl his name, "seriously, if you think the most dangerous thing about me is that stupid weapon, you are grossly mistaken."

"There is one more thing."

"And that is?" I ask, looking at him sideways.

He hesitates and I notice the slightest crack of a smile beneath his facade. "You must testify against Tier."

"No problem." I catch his shock like a firefly in a jar and tuck down my satisfaction.

He physically moves backward. "And you will tell the truth."

"I always tell the truth, Lucan."

He regains his composure. "Very well. I will set it up."

"You do that," I say to his back as he exits the room. You do that, Lucan. And I'll do the same.

Chapter Four

Braun enters before the door can close behind Lucan and his smile brings me back from the edge. "Junco," he says, "I get that you love the shirt, but you can't wear it like that."

I frown at him as he removes his knife and lifts the fabric up from my back. "What are you doing?"

He leans down into my face. "Making you look presentable, babe. Just give me a minute." His hands get busy cutting the shirt around my wings.

"Don't call me babe." I look over my shoulder at him and he shrugs.

"Sorry, Junco. Forgot." Then he flashes a smile and continues to cut. "I invited the 039 over for poker. And the box is stocked, so should be a good time tonight."

"Why?"

He's finished cutting now and he takes a second to straighten out my shirt before leaning into my face again. "Welcome home party, Junco." His hands take my arm and force it into the shirt. Then he manipulates the cloth so that his cut stretches over the uppermost portion of my wing. When his fingers make contact with the sensitive feathers my back arches involuntarily and I squeal. "Shit, what was that?" I ask, my breath heavy.

"Sorry, Junco. I know, it's weird, right? Don't take it the wrong way, I'm just trying to get them out through the cuts in the fabric."

"What way might I take it?"

He stops and leans around to see my face. "It's kind of erotic, isn't it? The whole wing-touching thing."

I raise my eyebrows at him. "Yeah, kinda."

He wrestles with the other wing, forcing me to stifle the sounds that want to escape my lips. When he's finally done I breathe out a sigh of relief and look up into his eyes. They glow a little more with each passing second and are a warm orange, like a beckoning fire. "This isn't my home, Braun." I pick up the conversation as quickly as possible to avoid the weirdness that wants to creep in.

"Is now. We inducted you as our ninth warrior back on the shuttle while you were out."

"I thought you guys didn't want me to morph? You were all outside the door when Tier and Layla were putting me under."

"Not us. That was the fucking crew and the other two teams that were hitching a ride after the clusterfuck in the MR. We were always on board. Tier would never make a decision like that without us. Just isn't done."

"Oh." I frown.

"What," he says as he studies my reaction, "is the problem?"

But I'm not sure, so I can't say. I shrug instead, thinking about being part of a team. So much has happened in two days it's hard to get my head around it. But this isn't stuff I want to share, so I exhale and push it down for later. "Nothing, just – unexpected, right?"

"It's good?"

I nod. "Yeah. Maybe."

He laughs. "Jasus, Junco, you're so hard to fucking please, ya know that?"

I watch the words come from Braun's mouth but I see Tier's face in my mind. I smile up at Braun, shake off those feelings, and then hug him. "Thanks, though. You have no idea how much I appreciate what you're doing right now."

He lifts his hands high up in the air, pretending to not want to touch me. "What? What did I do? I'm gonna get ya drunk, Junco, and probably take advantage of ya right here in the lab." He winks as I look up at him.

"You wish," I say into his chest.

"Oh, shit, do I ever!" Then he pushes me away and goes to set up the game. "But don't go blabbing it to the rest of the guys, Junco. They all have to feel like they have a shot with ya or they'll mope about all night."

"Where's Layla and Ash?"

He nods his head towards the door. "Talking to Lucan."

"Am I allowed to walk out that door?" I say it before I can stop myself, then get nervous with his silent look and scratch my neck and wince.

He shakes his head. "Not yet, Junco. But it won't last forever. So try not to think of it that way."

I sit down and he deals me in, sliding me a stack of high-value chips since we're only fucking around. "Did you really cheat yesterday?"

He doesn't look up from his hand. "Course I did, Junco." His eyes peer over the cards. "Do I look like an honest guy to you?" Then he winks. "No really, I did cheat. I always cheat, which is why I always win."

I raise my eyebrows at him.

"But I get caught a lot too." He laughs. "Plus everyone knows I cheat so they never pay me anyway. Did you really think I would make you buy me a house with 2x2 gauze?"

I laugh. "All's fair in cards and war?"

"Precisely! Holy fuck, that's poetry, Junco. You should publish that shit."

Ash and Layla walk in just as he's finishing. "What the hell is going on here, Braun? She's got shit to do, it's not poker time."

"Ash, you are such a straight-backed piker. Get the hell out, party's not until later. We're just having some fun, right, Junco?"

Layla interrupts as she walks into the lab. "He can stay if you want him to, Junco. But it's a little personal."

Braun gets up and squeezes my arm. "Just knock on the door when you want me to come back in, be right outside."

When he's gone Ash scowls at me as I walk into the lab with Layla.

"What?"

"I told you, Junco. Braun isn't the kind of guy you want to be hanging around with."

I make a face at Layla and we do the girlfriend laugh. "She's not dating him, Ashur, fuck. Calm down. He's keeping her mind off the serious stuff. You seem incapable of playing that part, so leave them alone."

Ash leaves, presumably to give Braun the same warning. Layla just shakes her head and lets out a deep breath. "Damn, he's so fucking wound up about Tier."

I change the subject. "So what's this then?" I ask, pointing to the screen she's looking at.

"DNA profile. You definitely have the genetics of Gyr. Did Tier explain that to you?"

I nod. "Yeah, some avian who was down in the MR and was taken out to the Camp a long time ago."

"Right. But you also have the genetics of a human and not from your parents or anyone else from the Stag Camp or the RR."

"How do you know? There's no database to check."

She smiles. "Well, actually, Junco, the RR has many databases you probably never knew about. There's no match for anyone in the RR. So we don't know who gave you the other half of your code."

"Is that important?"

She shrugs. "Might be, might not be. Hard to tell at this point. Anyway, the most interesting thing about you isn't the avian or the human genetics, it's the AI code we found."

My heart skips and I suddenly feel dizzy. "What?"

She gives me a look that says, sorry for the message, but someone has to deliver it. "Uh, yeah. You have code in those electronic circuits that was created for an AI."

"Like my HOUSE on Earth?" I know it's true before it comes out but the full meaning of it remains just under the surface.

She pouts her lip ready to say no, but another second of thought changes her mind. I watch her expression change in real time as the idea grows on her. "Maybe. Never thought of that. Good instincts, Juncs."

"So what does that mean? To me?"

"Nothing, it's inert. Not even activated, just no connections whatsoever. So it's a big nothing. We think it might have been a future project that was never started or at the very least never completed."

Yeah, right. I wait for her to say something else but she's moved on to other things. One thing you can definitely say about Layla, she's got a certain detachment for things of a personal nature – it's all science all the time.

Good for her.

Braun tells dirty jokes to me like I'm just one of the guys as we play a few fake hands of poker. It makes me laugh so hard I want to pee my pants, even though Ashur's scowl tells me he thinks it's inappropriate. I'm wiping the tears out of my eyes and fanning my face to make the heat go away when the door chimes.

"Enter at your own risk," Braun calls to the smart security. The door opens and two more guys come in, neither of them familiar to me.

Ashur does the introductions. "Juncs, this is Mish." He points to a tall slender guy with the same black hair and wings as Tier, but with the bluest eyes I've ever seen. "And Goldilocks here is Rikan."

Rikan is the first blue-eyed blond avian I've seen besides Lucan, but since he doesn't have wings he doesn't count. Rikan's wings are a honey cream color and my eyes linger on him a little longer than they should. Braun catches it. "Yes, Junco, we all know he's beautiful, but if ya keep looking at him that way, we'll have to beat the shit out of him to dampen down the ego."

I look away, embarrassed.

Mish takes a seat at the table, but Rikan comes up to me and squeezes my shoulder. "It's nice to see you smile, Junco."

Braun looks up from the deck he's shuffling. "Yeah, I think you've smiled more in the past few hours than you did in six months back on Earth." His eyes go back to his task, but I'm stuck on his words.

"Did all of you watch me?" I glance around the room. Oops. Everyone looks a little uncomfortable. "I mean, I don't care if you did. I just didn't realize my life was such an open book."

The door chimes again and Braun calls out, "Enter at your own risk," then winks at me as three more guys come in. Ashur stands up this time and claps a guy in a formal uniform on the shoulder, leaning in to have a private joke. The four of them chat for a few seconds before turning towards me as he motions to another guy. "Junco, this is Arel." Arel is the shortest of them all, darker than either Tier or Ashur, and he moves toward me to shake my hand like a prairie lion stalking grouse at dawn. I shudder to think of him hunting me. "Isten, who is your new counterpart by the way."

I look hard at Isten who, I notice, has hazel eyes just like mine. His wings aren't as mottled, but they are the closest thing I've seen to white so far. "Cold-bore kill-shot in one?" I ask.

He shoots me with his finger. "You must read minds or something," he says as he pulls a chair next to me.

"And Ryse here," Ashur gestures to a guy who could be Braun's brother and who is wearing the formals, "just passed his qualifiers for officer promotion. Here's hoping you make it, buddy, but if you don't you'll always have a spot flying our asses around."

I smile at him as he takes his coat off and settles into a chair between Ashur and Braun. My eyes travel from one guy to the next, watching them joke and talk with each other in a way only a true military team can. The only two missing are Layla and Tier.

We start the game and Braun is caught cheating on the first hand

and is relegated to bartender. He beckons me to join him in the kitchen as he goes to get some beer.

"What's up?" I ask.

He's rooting through the fridge collecting bottles from various brands of alcohol that I don't recognize. "Here, take these. That's for Rikan and those three are for Ashur, Ryse, and Isten."

I take the bottles and turn to leave. "Hey, Juncs?" he asks, still fishing around for a few more beers. "We weren't spying on you, OK?" He looks up then, serious. "I know it might feel that way, but really, only Tier was on the ground most of the time."

I smile. "It doesn't. Feel that way, I mean. It's sort of a relief," I let out a deep breath, "not to have to hide things, actually."

He lets out his own long breath and I wonder if he was really that worried about how I might react. "You don't have to hide anything from us, Junco. We're a team now, you're official, no matter what happens from this point on. You're one of us. It was a done deal back on the transport when we took the vote."

I look down. "But why?" Then I look back up to see what his eyes say. "Why would you guys risk so much for me? You don't even know me."

He shakes his head. "You're wrong, Junco. We know you better than you know yourself. We've watched it all go down in real time."

I turn to leave, but he stops me again. "Wait, here," he says, handing me another bottle that I can barely manage to hold on to, "this one's for you."

I pass out the beers and take my seat again. Isten reaches over and removes the top on mine after I struggle for a few seconds, then hands it back. "That's good brew, you'll like it." Then he smiles and lights a stogie, his attention diverted by a play on the table. I turn the bottle around to see the label and my stomach feels funny. It's called *Little Sister.*

Braun watches me as he's coming out of the kitchen. He drops off his load of beers and then comes over and pulls a chair up next to mine and immediately starts peeking at Isten's cards. Isten punches him in the arm and scoots over next to Arel, leaving Braun to bother me.

"Here's the million-rill question for you, Junco." Braun leans back in the chair and flashes a grin around his stogie, then snags my shirt between his fingertips. "Who the hell did you steal this shirt from?"

My face heats up as I watch the guys start shouting out guesses. I smile at all the names they know, none of whom have ever gotten that close to me. "You're all wrong," I say, looking down at it. The memory floods back in from somewhere and I recall the night with perfect clarity. "Mikah Mesner."

"No!"

"Shit, that loser–"

"Say it ain't so, Junco–"

I look up. "Oh yeah, boys. It is so. Mikah fucking Mesner. He was – a lot of fun." I think I make myself blush.

Isten looks at me with a serious expression. "Hey, Junco, I've got a shirt you might like, too." Every one of them spits beer at that one and I feel the heat overtake my face which makes them laugh even more.

I look around the table and find Ashur, a little more serious than he should be, and challenge him with my eyebrows. "Something on your mind, Ash?"

He accepts my challenge without delay. "You had Tier's shirt for a while there, Junco."

The guys take my side.

"Oh, shit–"

"Ash, why the fuck–"

"You piker, leave it alone–"

My hand goes up as I look calmly around the table. "Since I have been informed that we are all in this together, you might as well know the truth." I pause to straighten up my face and look down. They all lean in, waiting for me to give the details. "I did not sleep with your captain." Braun is so pleased he kisses me. Everyone else seems pleasantly surprised and one by one they lift their bottles in the air and toast me.

Ashur salutes with his beer and I nod and flash him a crooked smile.

We spend the rest of the night talking about each other, and since they know so much about me already, they tell stories even I had misplaced.

Right before I pass out on the bed between Arel and Isten I make a note to myself. Best day ever.

Chapter Five

I roll over on the bed, bump into another body, and force my eyelids open a fraction. Isten's arms wrap around me and pull me in and I fall back into a dreamless sleep only to be woken up in seconds when the door chimes. I hear Layla shout, "Officer up!"

Bodies scramble all around me and I feel Isten pick me up and throw my feet onto the floor. Before I even have my eyes open I am standing at attention, my right hand forming an Earth salute that may or may not be appropriate. The eight of us are lined up in a column, four to a side, in front of the screen. Layla walks through our pattern and stands at the center on the other end.

I keep my eyes trained upward like everyone else, but steal a peek over towards the commanding officer who stands just to my left.

"At ease, Aves."

Everyone relaxes and I study them quickly to see how I should stand. Feet apart, shoulder width, hands behind my back, eyes to the officer. Some things never change.

He begins with a sigh. "I don't expect you to be happy about this and I don't really care. I have my own team, which you are all aware of. Except the lady here–"

"Junco Coot, sir."

"Junco, then. Tier is out and it looks extremely doubtful that he will be back. So, for the time being I'm your captain, but Ashur remains XO until more permanent arrangements can be made. Are we clear?"

"Yes, sir," we all shout.

"All right then, we'll have a morning meeting every–"

"Why the fuck is Junco on the screen?" Braun's cursing interrupts the captain and we all crane our necks to see the news on the far wall.

"Holy shit, it's Selia! Where is this?" I look around. "How do they have this footage?" I have a lot of eyes looking at me, but only Layla responds.

Layla comes over and takes my arm until I'm sitting on the bed. "A lot has happened on Earth, Junco. It's a huge mess and this" – she points to Selia on the screen, her face burned and dirty, dressed in a military uniform that I don't recognize; every once in a while she cowers from an explosion in the background – "woman has been blasting some video of you all over the fucking sphere. She's got a tape of your mother threatening the governments of no less than four of the Republics, your mother's in–"

"Invaded the MR, yeah, I know that. I gave Selia that shit and sent her out right before I went into the meeting to kill Aren."

Everyone looks at me now, but only the captain speaks. "You started this *war*?"

I sneer at him, instant dislike for his baseless accusation. "Of course not, I needed to get a message out of my compound, so I gave Selia there the video Slag gave me of my mother in exchange for a favor. Looks like she did her job and then some, which is good, otherwise I'd have to go back and kill her on principle."

Mish and Rikan snigger on the other side of the line and Ashur hisses at them to shut up.

The captain directs the guys to take a seat at the table. "Perhaps you should start at the beginning, Junco. This was not in any of the reports."

"Well, it wouldn't be, would it? No one knew but me and I wasn't debriefed." I stare up at him innocently and he draws a large breath in.

"Yeah, OK. Start at the beginning, please."

I run it down in simple terms: the memory dump with Tier, the envelope in the Goat, the trip back to my room, the secret room, the call from HOUSE to see Slag, the discharge – everyone groans at this part, but I move on quickly – then the video message on the cube Slag gave me.

"She set them up?" Ashur's tone says he's doubtful.

I shrug with my hands. "This is all I know, Ash."

"And that part about your childhood, Junco?" Layla asks. "Is it true?"

"You mean the part where I assassinated my first target at six? Or the part where my mother wanted to steal me away and my father had her deported?"

She swallows and nods.

"I found the memories of both," I say, looking from face to face. "We were on vacation, some fancy European ski resort. They went up the on the lift in front of me, I pretended to be adjusting my sock in my boot. The targets got on the lift, then I followed. When we got to the top my parents were already halfway down the mountain. I followed the couple until my parents came out from the trees, then they killed the man and I slit the woman's throat with the SEAR. It was the first time I ever used it – for real, anyway."

All eight of my new teammates stare at me in disbelief and the silence makes me continue. "We changed to cross-country skis in the woods, trekked a few miles down to a road, and were picked up in a long silver car by an older man with white hair." They continue to stare. "That's it. You can close your mouths now."

"And you were six?" It's Isten's question this time.

I look to him and nod. "Six – but if it makes you feel any better, Isten, I hurled my guts out afterward. So anyway, like I said, I knew the reporters were out there beyond the gate at my house, and this girl, Selia," I point to the screen where she is still talking, "got the golden ticket if she would just deliver Charlie's cubes to someone in his family. I'm glad she's telling everyone, that was the purpose of me giving her the evidence."

Ash throws me a little gray cigar box and I breathe a mumbling thank-you as I slide it out and strike it up.

"Now what?" Ash is looking to the captain.

"Well." He stops and looks down, his eyebrows teetering somewhere between surprise and frown. "I don't think we have to worry about her going through the General Fledge."

And the uproar that ensues drowns out any pain I might be feeling from exposing myself.

Ash is irate. "She is Aves! A sanctioned member of the 039. She will not go through the General Fledge!"

The captain sighs. "She's only part Aves, Ashur. It's not good enough for Lucan. I have no say in this and neither do you. Either she goes through it, or Lucan–"

"Or he kills me," I say bluntly. "Tries, anyway. And since I am on his world, breathing his manufactured air, he'll probably be able to accomplish that regardless of how well-trained I am." They all stop talking to look at me, eyes searching my face. "Lucan explained it yesterday, and I agreed to do it. And to testify against Tier in the trial.

That was the deal."

Now they look at me like I'm a traitor but I put my hand up. "Don't ask, OK. You all just need to trust me. Tier asked me to trust him when he brought me here, and I did. Still do." I look straight at Ash. "I still trust him, Ashur."

I look around to the rest of them, even the captain. "And now I am asking you all to trust me. Do you think I want to kill strangers just to prove my worth? No. I don't. And I have no information that will incriminate Tier, I promise. He told me nothing. Nothing. There is nothing I can say to hurt him at this point. When he asked me to come with him when we were out on the rock, he said the thing was already in motion, his actions couldn't be taken back, even if he wanted to."

Braun turns away and runs his hands through his hair. They are all so much like Tier it makes my heart ache.

"I never asked him to save me. But he did. I'm sorry if that wasn't what you signed up for when you took your vote. But I can't change it."

I wait to see if any of them will fight with me or maybe walk out, but they don't. I take a deep breath and when I let it out, I feel alone. My team is confused and hurt, my captain is selling me out, and I've told them all to pretty much fuck off. I am just Junco. Again.

The captain clears his throat. "OK. Men? If I were your real captain, I'd stick around and give a shit. But I'm not. Your captain is sitting in Justice on trial for treason because he refused to kill your nine here. Like the girl said, deal with it."

And with that he leaves us alone.

Ashur is furious and stalks up to me, making himself an imposing figure compared to my smallness. Braun intervenes and pushes him back. "Don't do it, Ash, I'm fucking warning you."

"Junco, what were the instructions? I want answers, now!"

I shake my head and Isten takes his turn. "Come on, Ash, back off." Ash pushes him in the chest and Isten bares his teeth. "You better think twice, Ashur, you better think before you touch me again."

"Junco," Layla pleads. "How could Tier have told you anything? You were under morph. There was no message, you dreamed it." Mish, Arel, and Rikan just hang back and say nothing as they watch me struggle.

I turn my head and play with my hair, thinking about it. Then turn back and study each face one at a time. I want to trust them, but Tier ordered me not to. "Layla, if I could tell you I would. But I can't. It was an order. His order."

"Just tell us what the order was," Ryse says, taking my hand. "Really, Junco, he would never fault you for telling us."

"You're wrong, Ryse, it was pretty fucking specific. I'll do what I can, I promise. That's all I can say. I'll do whatever I can to make it right."

Braun steps forward and pulls me away from the group. "All right, show's over. Let's get on with the day."

I break free and head to the shower. The hot water blasts me until my whole body is red and when I step out in my avian clothes once again, the room is empty except for Braun. He's sitting at the table with his back towards me, smoking a cigar and watching some avians fight in a contest on-screen.

"I have to tell you something, Junco," he says without turning around to look at me.

I take a seat on the other side of the table and wait for him to acknowledge me. He just pushes a little gray box in my direction and I light the stogie up, puffing on it to calm my nerves. We sit that way for several minutes and then I push him. "Spit it out, Braun. I don't have a lot of self-control right now."

He lifts his eyes and I can see the wheels turning in his mind. He pokes his cigar in the direction of the screen.

I turn to look at the fight.

"That's Deliverance from last year," he says.

I shake my head. "OK. I'll bite. What's Deliverance?"

"A fight. A big fight that takes guilty prisoners, especially high-value prisoners, right? Famous ones, ones who committed horrific crimes, shit like that?"

I prod him forward with a nod.

"And they have this contest. The winner gets to kill a bunch of bad guys at the end but the real prize is a wish." He stops and drags his gaze around until he meets my eyes, "I have a plan. Not a great plan, but it's something. Only you can never tell anyone I told you this. They'd never forgive me."

"Hey, if there's one thing you can be sure of, it's that I'll keep a secret, right?"

He smiles. "Right, yeah."

"So what is it?"

He takes a puff and blows the smoke into rings as he stares up at the ceiling, then he looks over at me. "Sorry. It's just, I can't believe I'm going to even propose this. But, if I were you, I'd at least want to know of the possibility. Don't feel pressure to accept it, either. Just think about it."

I nod and lean in as he starts talking in a low whisper. We stay that way for several minutes and I look down when he finishes.

"It's a long shot, I get it. But believe it or not, I'm the brains of this operation." I choke on my own spit and he finally cracks a smile. "No, really, Junco. I might just be a big dumb munitions expert to most people outside our team, but I've got a wicked fucking strategy game going on inside." He taps his head with the spittle end of his cigar.

"Yeah? Well, that's one stupid fucking plan if you ask me."

"I told ya it was."

"Has a lot of variables."

"Yeah, lots of what-ifs, I know."

"Can't possibly work."

"Yeah, forget I mentioned it."

"Oh, it's already forgotten."

We smile across the table and then we laugh.

We laugh until we are hysterical.

Chapter Six

Ashur enters the room as I am wiping the tears from my eyes and Braun is hacking on the smoke caught in his throat. He turns and we both look at our XO, small leftover sounds of laughter escaping before we realize he's still very much pissed off.

"I'm glad you're both so fucking pleased with yourselves. Meanwhile, the entire team is coming apart over this shit."

Braun stands up and for the first time I see him as the imposing fighter that he is. Ashur doesn't cower, move, or even flinch. He's one hundred percent secure in his authority, but he doesn't tell Braun to sit down either.

"Ash, you need to back off. This shit is going down Junco's way, no matter what you say about it. She says Tier gave her orders, and that's the end of it."

Ash pushes past him and walks over to me. "Put some shoes on, Junco, you've got a meeting to attend." I look down at my feet and scowl. "Now, dammit!" he growls. "You're not leaving here barefoot, so put them on."

I get up and grab the boots and socks from my closet then sit on the bed and force my feet to obey and conform. When I'm done I stand and look over at Braun. "I'll see ya soon, right?"

He smiles. "Count on it."

Ashur waves his arm towards the exit and my stomach churns at the thought of crossing the threshold into my avian existence. Ash's hand pushes on my shoulder in an attempt to guide me forward, but I brush it off and walk through the door on my own.

The hallway is just as I remember it, wide, tall, and empty. Once again, the only sound is the echo of our boots as we walk. I look up at Ashur. "Where are you taking me?"

He doesn't even glance down at me. "Conference Room Zero."

I nod. "OK, well, who am I meeting?"

"Lucan and some guy from Earth."

"Really? Who?"

He shrugs, but doesn't say anything and we walk for several more minutes. This is the longest hallway of my life. When we come to the end there is a large door. Massive. He presses his palm to the biometrics and it takes a moment for the reinforced gateway to commit to opening. We wait in silence as the mechanisms inside click and adjust to the command.

I feel like a little kid trying to see beyond, but I'm disappointed because it's just another hallway, though smaller this time. We turn right, then left, which brings us to another door.

"Are you ready?"

"For what? This the conference room?"

He smiles, the first one since my outburst. "No, Junco, the real world. It's quite a walk over to CR Zero, it's on another part of the habitat. Out there," he nods to the human-sized door, "are a lot of people. Just stay next to me and don't get lost." He starts to turn away, but then looks back. "And for fuck's sake, Junco, don't do anything stupid like try and run off or I swear–"

"Calm down, I won't."

He lets out a deep breath and I unexpectedly take one in, then his palm flattens against the side of the door and my new world comes into view. I stand there gaping at all the people bustling past. It reminds me of Tokyo or London, there is so much foot traffic. He takes my hand, pulls, and then we're walking in the stream. I try not to look around too much but I can't help it. It's not another hallway at all, it's a city.

I walk along looking up and I hear Ashur laugh. "Junco, watch where you're going. You look like a tourist."

I look over to him and smile. "I am a tourist." It's only then that I notice we're not even on the ground level. I strain my head to see past the throngs of bustling avians, towards a transparent railing a couple dozen yards away. I gravitate towards it, pulling Ashur with me. "Just let me look, OK?"

He shakes his head, but takes the lead and pulls me through the crowd. I stand at the railing and lean over, then swallow and dip back quickly when I realize we've got to be a hundred stories up. Trains whiz past on a suspended track about twenty stories below, and I notice several more as my eyes travel down towards the ground. "Wow, it's pretty incredible."

"This is our capital, do you know what she's called, Junco?"

I meet his eyes and shake my head.

"Amelia. This entire habitat holds eight million people, it's the largest. And busiest, obviously."

I give him a crooked smile. "I love it. How come no one's flying though?"

"Only Aves can fly here, just too crowded. You can fly if you need to. You're in the black Aves uniform, so you'll always be recognized as one of us." He takes my hand and leads me out into the bustle again. "It's about a ten-minute walk to CR Zero, but we can take a train if your feet will hurt."

I look down at them. They already hurt. But I shake my head. "No, let's walk."

Ashur smiles and pulls me through the crowd. Once we get off the main walkway there are a lot fewer people and he transitions into my guide, pointing out things like stores and offices, bars, restaurants. It's like the Peaks, except nothing like it at all. A dozen or so minutes later we arrive at another biometrically sealed door. He presses his flesh and it opens into a small room.

"We're going up," Ashur explains as he palms the panel. An elevator. My weight sinks with the artificial gravity pull as we ascend and I count the seconds until we stop.

"How high did we just go?"

"About a thousand feet."

"In ten seconds? Damn."

"I have to warn you about the next part, we can go back down and take the train if you prefer, but I think you'll like the view if we walk. You'll probably get really disoriented the first time, just be prepared."

I nod and he presses his palm to make the door open and we step out.

Into nothingness.

The dark star-filled night closes in around me and I hold back. Ash pulls and I think I will fall over, into the black below my feet, but then he's behind me and his hands are planted on my shoulders pushing me forward.

"Just walk normal, Juncs. The walkway is transparent."

"Everything is transparent, Ash. I feel like I'm walking out into space."

"Well, that was the feeling they were going for, so I guess they succeeded."

We climb until the incline evens out and I realize we're standing on the summit of a great arch that dips out from the habitat and into the vacuum. I spin around and almost fall. "Why are we the only ones out here?"

He shrugs. "VIP shit, you know. Not for the masses."

"Feels good to be important, then."

He smiles. "Can you find any stars?"

I search, but I'm lost in the night for the first time ever. "It makes no sense to me, I can't find any."

He points and I follow his finger. "There's his belt, Juncs. Can you see it?"

I don't at first, but then it all slides into focus, like I'm looking at some old 3D art. I find Rigel, then up to Betelgeuse, then Castor and Pollux in the Twins. I turn, carefully, and I can see the entire winter hexagon.

"Wow." Chills run down my body and I shiver.

"Yeah. I know how much you like looking at the stars. I like it too."

I look over to his face and try to figure him out as he stares out into the deep. "I don't really get you, Ashur. I mean, you're a pretty hard guy to read."

He lets out a little laugh. "Says the lion to the wolf."

"Do you hate me? For not telling you? And for getting Tier in this mess?"

His smile drops as he looks down to me. "Junco, as much as I'd like to blame you, none of this is your fault. We fucked up. End of story. And not just with you, with a lot of shit." I stand quietly as he thinks, just taking in the stars and the night. "I'm just having a hard time coming to terms with what we did because Tier is the closest thing to family I have. All the other guys, we're all family too. But Tier and I have been through everything together. We're from the same clutch so we have the same birthday, we grew up together, went to Earth together, came back together. Usually you never have the same morphday as your clutchmates because maturity is an individualized thing. But all of the 039 have the same morphday, so Tier and I are connected through every important life milestone there is. And we've been leading these guys since some of them were eight years old."

I let out a deep breath. "I told you, Ashur, I'll fix it."

He looks up and points to a shooting star. My eyes follow as he talks. "You can't fix it, Junco. The trial is a formality. He's going to be killed."

I shake my head. "No, Ashur. He's not."

He looks into my eyes as we stand there in silence. "I trust you. But don't go and do anything stupid, Junco, because you can be saved. You're a sure thing, darlin'." We both smile at his Tier impersonation. Then he looks down and whispers, "This Fledge has no idea what's coming."

I force down a frown and he takes my hand and leads me down the arch and back into reality.

Lucan is pissed off when we finally make it to the outer door of Conference Room Zero. "Where the hell have you two been?" His eyes blaze at Ashur, then rest on mine. "When I call for you, Junco, you come!"

Ash steps between us. "I brought her straight away, Lucan. Calm down."

"What did you do, walk?"

Ashur laughs. "As a matter of fact, yes. We did walk. This was her first time outside. Shit, man, be reasonable."

Lucan shakes his head. "Watch your step, Ashur. If I've lost patience with Tier, how much do you think I have left for you?"

Ashur shrugs off his threat, then turns to me. "I'll be outside if you need me, Junco."

"That won't be necessary. I'll handle her from here."

"I don't think so, Lucan. She's my nine and I have every right to stick around."

I raise my eyebrows and wait for the fight, but Lucan just grabs me by the arm and pushes me towards the door.

"Don't bruise her, Lucan."

"Don't push me, Ashur, I'm not in the mood."

Ash looks me in the eyes and I shake my head at him. "It's fine, Ashur, I'll see you after."

I'm shoved through the open door into a very normal-looking conference room, if you don't count the night sky view that dominates one entire wall. There is only one man seated at the table that can hold more than three dozen. I almost gasp out loud when I see him.

"Coot, thank God you're OK."

"What the hell are you doing here, Slag?"

"Holy shit, Coot, you have wings."

"Yeah, I'm half avian, remember?" I look over at Lucan. "What's this about?"

Lucan shrugs, trying to look indifferent. "It appears that Earth is unable to continue without you, Junco. Your former commander has something to discuss."

I look at him, then over to Slag. "What the fuck is going on here? Am I being sent back to Earth?"

Slag steps forward. "Calm down, Coot, I'm only here to make an offer."

I look back at Lucan, but he puts a hand up. "I'll give you some privacy."

Slag and I wait for him to exit the room and I get a glimpse of Ash trying to look in before the door closes.

"Explain, now."

He pulls out a comm tech from his jacket and hands it over. "I'm to deliver this to you. I have no idea what it says, so I can't speak until you've seen it and made a decision."

I take the com. "You haven't watched it?" I ask with an incredulous frown.

Slag shakes his head. "Biometrics, Junco. It's only for you. Retinal scan. I'll wait outside with them. Just let us know when you're ready to talk."

He leaves the tech in my hand and even though it is impossible for such a small flimsy card to feel heavy, it weighs me down. The chairs are built for humans, with a full back, and when I settle in it feels good to get the pressure off the new blisters on my feet.

The retinal scan flashes my eye and the video begins to play.

It's Moju and my heart thumps wildly in my chest as he screams. A face enters into view, a head I sliced off that night in my driveway. Aren sniggers at whoever is running the camera, and then motions for another person to flame Moju with a torch. "See that, Junco? You think you can get away with what you did?" He shakes his head and barks another order at the torturer. "I've got him, Junco! You might be far away but I've got Moju."

This is a trick, Junco – it's not possible. You killed him! He is dead!

But Aren responds like he's reading my mind. "Do you think you're the only one with clones, you stupid bitch?"

Oh fuck.

"I'm gonna be sending your brother back to you in pieces. Very small pieces that I will personally cut off him each and every day. And just to show my sincerity, we'll make the first cut together." He motions to the man behind him, who proceeds to cut off a finger with a plasma knife. The flesh smokes up in thick tendrils as it burns. My fingers find the SEAR scar on my jaw as Moju's screams turn demonic and I cover my ears.

"I'm sure you remember how that feels, right? Except, Junco, he won't be treated with some special membrane to seal it all up pretty." He laughs and then turns back to Moju, apparently thinking he is off screen, or maybe he just wants me to think that. "She's not coming for you, Moju. She's gonna let you suffer just like everyone else."

And then the screen goes black and a deletion sequence begins counting down. In a matter of seconds the entire video is erased and a smoldering burn begins in the center of the card and spreads outward to the edges. I toss it onto a tray that holds a pitcher of water in the middle of the table and I'm halfway across the room about to kick Slag's ass when I catch myself and spin back around.

Fuck.

Think, Junco. Think.

I take a seat and let my head fall into my hands as my mind races through my options. I know Lucan is in on this. And Slag. I envision six different ways to kill them both using only three moves.

Shit. Think.

I force myself to stop and rationalize it. Why would Lucan want me gone? I ponder all the possibilities, but only one makes sense. To make sure Tier dies. That's the reason.

Trust no one. Show no weakness.

I take a deep breath and count to five before letting it out.

Calm, Junco.

No weakness.

I repeat the breathing until my heart stops racing and then I get up and walk around to make sure I can control it before knocking on the door.

Chapter Seven

They all file in, including Ashur, and each one takes a seat at the table across from me. I smile, and then push the hatred down as Slag begins describing the deal he's been sent to offer.

I interrupt him after only a few words. "Who sent you here, Slag?" My eyes pierce into him, rage at him, but I don't allow a single muscle on my face to move.

He looks at me, confused. "Your mother, Junco. Didn't she explain things on the video?"

I let out a breath and Ashur is on his feet so he can reach into the ashtray and pick up the remains of the tech. Only the extreme edges are left, and they are charred black. He leaves the table and walks around to my side and stands behind me.

"That tech did not contain a video of my mother, Slag. So, I'll ask you one more time, who sent you?"

Slag's mouth sags and it's Lucan who answers my question. "Junco, the launch credentials check out. It came from the Subjective planet pad in Vegas." He tilts his head up like he's thinking. "Recently acquired, since you were picked up."

I laugh. "That is so much bullshit."

He continues without a pause. "A lot has happened on Earth in the time you've been away. Vegas was captured the week after you left."

"It's not a very strategic move on their part. It's a long fucking supply line from Vegas to the Subs, isn't it?" I turn to look him in the face to wait for his answer.

Slag clears his throat and I turn back to him as I quiet down the slip in facial muscle control. "I was sent by your mother, Coot."

"She's not my mother, so quit fucking calling her that. Mothers give birth to their children, or at the very least care for them. She did neither. I'm done here."

I get up to leave but Lucan puts his hand up to halt my progress. "Junco, if you refuse this offer to return to Earth you'll be sent to Fledge. Immediately."

I shrug. "Whatever." I turn back to Ashur. "Take me to Fledge then, Ash."

He smiles and nods but Lucan is on his feet and already in front of me. "Just so I am clear here, Junco – you choose to stay and fight instead of returning to Earth?"

I laugh. "Lucan, you're clear."

Slag interrupts. "Coot, what the fuck are you doing? I was sent by your mother!"

I turn back and growl, "I don't have a mother, Slag. What part of my words aren't getting through to you?"

He crosses the room and grabs me by the arm. My body reacts without the extra squirt of adrenaline that appears during even the most benign of confrontations. My elbow hits him in the face and I turn just enough to knee him in the balls. He stumbles, but stays standing. Ashur steps between us, and Lucan is bending down into my face, his mouth contorting into ugly lines.

My heart never misses a beat and I realize I've wanted to do that for a long time. "I'm not leaving, Lucan."

"Ashur, take him outside and have him escorted back to his ship while I have a private talk with *her*."

They make for the exit and Lucan snarls at me, "Sit down, Junco. We're not done here."

I take a seat and watch him as he formulates his next move. One thing is very clear about Lucan, he has no idea who I am. He's read reports, seen videos maybe. Some first-hand accounts. He knows nothing beyond the few confrontational words between us.

When he speaks, he is calm. "You do realize you've tilted your hand, do you not?"

"I have no idea what you're talking about, Lucan. Please, just get to the point."

"You have no real reason to stay here, Junco. Your morph is over, you're free to leave, you have a long life ahead of you. Your decision to stay is based on your desire to save Tier from his fate, and not this silly rebellion directed towards your mother."

"Are you fucking kidding me?" I burn hot with rage, then see his smile and tone it down. "Are you really going to sit there and tell me you think that tech contained a message from my mother? You fucking piece of shit." I get up and see a slight movement backwards from him. "That wasn't my mother on that tech asking me to come home, Lucan. It was a clone of my first boyfriend snipping off Moju's finger. And I swear to my own fucking God, I will slice your fucking head off with my SEAR if you say another word to me about it."

I realize I'm up in his face – as far as I can manage with the height difference – and I take a step back. Then I turn and walk away.

"I'm staying," I say over my shoulder. "Moju's a big boy, he can certainly handle that little fuck without my help. When I'm done with this Fledge bullshit I'll go back on my own terms."

"When you're done with this Fledge *bullshit*, Junco, you will belong to the Aves Cluster. And you will go where you're told. Is that understood?"

"As long as someone tells me to go back to Earth and kill people, I've got no problem with that."

He lets out a breath and I can feel him roll his eyes at me. I turn to face him. "You're not going to win this game, Lucan."

"Says the one small girl with no power."

"I'm just warning you. Don't be disappointed in the end when I take back every drop of satisfaction you extract from my failures."

He sighs. It hints at exasperation, boredom even, and I sense I may have miscalculated. "One of these days, Junco, we will have an honest conversation. If it's Fledge fights you want, girl. Be my guest. Go and kill. But it won't save Tier. He's been on his way out for a very long time. Long before he refused orders, long before he waged war on the RR for you, and long before he gave away his genetics to a man who helped him kill more than two dozen Earth leaders."

Shit.

I look up at him, too quickly, having misplaced that little secret Tier told me out on the rock. Lucan reads my face and smiles. "Ah, I see some recognition there. Don't worry, Junco – when you testify the drugs will get it all out in the open." He stops and stares into my eyes, burns into them. I look away, feeling a little beaten already.

But he continues, "So, just remember, when we are at the end, when I am standing over you as you break in half, and I am forced to leave you with nothing, Junco – don't say I never tried to help. Don't tell me I made your life a living hell, because you will have done that all on your own.

"And if – this is a gigantic if, Junco – but *if* you *can* take back everything you'll lose by choosing this path, then please know that my satisfaction will come from that, and not from watching you fail."

He walks towards the door, palms it, and then turns. "By the way, has anyone ever mentioned that your language is filthy?" His voice is pleasant, like he's pondering the meaning of something quizzical, but he wrinkles his lip like he has a bad taste in his mouth. "I don't care for it. Cheapens you, Junco."

He leaves me standing there, facing the emptiness of space scowling, and feeling rather cheap and filthy, if I do say so myself.

But not minding one bit.

The door is still open when I walk through a few seconds after Lucan. I watch his figure walk away, down the long hallway, then turn to find Ashur. He's talking to a girl farther down the other end of the hallway and I make my way towards them. The girl is taller than me, but that might be due to her high heels. She has long black hair and wears what I would consider to be housewife gear. I can hear her deep voice murmuring towards Ash, who seems to be on drugs or something. Even though he's looking right into my eyes, it takes half a dozen seconds for him to acknowledge me.

"Junco, there you are."

I raise my eyebrows at him. "You OK?"

The girl turns and a flood of memories waft over me with her scent. I see my toddler self leaving church with my parents, my chubby hands firmly clutched between their palms as we cross the street and head towards the bakery in town. She smells like the bakery.

"Junco." Her voice is deep and entrancing. "I tried to get away as soon as I heard, but was delayed. I am so sorry I was not there when you woke up."

My head spins as I look up at Ashur. "What's going on?"

He smiles but says nothing and my head is swimming.

"Let's go get a stim, that will clear you two up. I was just at the clutch and I'm afraid that the effects won't wear off."

She pulls on us and we follow her.

"– so, like I said, Junco – hey, you still with me? Drink that, will you? It won't get better until you drink it all down."

I look at the drink in front of me and I have no idea how it got there. "Where are we?"

"Oh, for Seven's sake, Junco. I've answered that question seven times. Please, just drink it all right now."

I pick up the glass and bring it to my lips, drinking whatever it contains. I stare out the window, and then get up and press my face against it, amazed. We are at the top of a very tall structure, and the ground is so far away I can't even make out the bottom. I swoon with the realization of how high I am and her hands come out to steady me.

"Sit down, Junco. You're going to fall."

I let her lead me back to the chair and my head clears a fraction. "Where are we?"

She smiles, then breaks into a laugh. "Oh, for fuck's sake. Why don't you just tell me when you're feeling normal and I'll continue talking. I'm tired of telling you everything seven times."

I look at her. "Who are you?"

Her green eyes twinkle. "I'm Esta, Junco. Your sister, from the clutch."

"Why do I feel this way?" I try and look around but my head throbs, like I have a hangover.

"I'm afraid it's an occupational hazard. The wings, Junco. Mine cause people to become sedated and easily controlled."

"What kind of power is that?"

"The kind that makes it possible for me to spend all my days with the Aves Clutch." I squint up at her. "Children, Junco. I raise the children."

I nod my head, understanding. I think. Things are beginning to come in a little clearer and I look around me. The bar is massive. I mean huge. Probably fits like three hundred and fifty people. And every single patron is smashed up against the far wall, sipping drinks and eyeing us with caution. "Shit, Esta. You can really clear a room." My eyes track to the far end of the bar and I spot Ashur. He waves to me and laughs. I wave back.

"Feeling better now?"

"Yeah." I nod. "Wow, you're pretty intoxicating. That could come in handy."

"Yeah, if you spend your life babysitting, it's great."

"No, I mean with anyone. You're like a little drug factory. Controlling people is quite impressive."

"Yes, well, it only works on the Aves, Junco. No one else is affected. Besides, self-healing like you've got is a lot more practical."

"I can't self-heal. I can't do anything." I let out a little sigh and look at the bottom of my drink. "How the hell can I get another one? And a cigar?" I look up at her and wait for an answer.

"Here," she says, taking my finger and moving it towards the pad at the edge of the table. "Press there."

I do and a display pops up. I flip through it and choose a beer and a cigar. It beeps and shuts down. "Did it work?" The words are barely out of my mouth when the servos arrive to deliver my goodies. "Damn, that was quick." I gulp the beer and shake the cigar out and strike it up. I puff slowly and look back at Esta. "Like I was saying, I don't have any powers."

She smiles and I know what the children must feel when she's about to gently correct them. "All warriors can heal, Junco. And you're dressed as one, so I'm assuming you are one."

"No shit? What else can I do?"

She shrugs. "I'm not sure. Typically you get the powers associated with your Cluster, then whatever special talents you have."

I nod and puff on the cigar.

"Anyway, as I was saying to Ashur back at the conference room…"

My mind drifts again, I'd forgotten all about Lucan.

She snaps her fingers in front of my eyes. "Junco! Over here, dear. I'm talking to you, please pay attention."

I laugh.

"I'm so glad to finally have another Sibling here, it's been awful. I only want to read the history, Junco. And Lucan refuses–" She crinkles her forehead and half a dozen furrows appear.

"Wait, what? You're unhappy?"

She lets out a large breath of air as Ashur walks up. "Feeling better, Juncs?"

I nod. "Yeah. Esta is unhappy."

He pulls back as he looks at her and she covers her face and turns away.

"We gotta get going, Junco." He puts his hand on Esta's shoulder. "She has to fight tomorrow, Esta. She needs to get acclimated. You can walk with us if you want, let me just get a couple stims to go." And then he smiles at me and goes back to the bar.

I can tell she's struggling to hold it together, so I grab her hand and pull her up and lead her back over to Ashur.

She holds my hand all the way to the dorm and when we finally get there, she's even talking again. The stims help keep her chemicals at bay. How fucking horrible to have this effect on people. I mean, it would be cool if she could control it, but just leaching that shit out all over probably breaks a lot of deals in the Aves Cluster.

The dorm is a huge building far out in the middle of nowhere. I'm still not sure how the habitat is laid out because I've never seen a map, but we had to take two trains to get here. And there is literally nothing, I mean nothing, around the building except the train stop and a few benches in front of it.

Ash leaves to check me in and do whatever it is people do when they report for Fledge while I sit with Esta. "So, what was your Fledge like, Esta? Did you do this one?"

She gives me half a smile and shakes her head. "No, the mothers have their own special Fledge. Everyone does, actually. The General Fledge is like a last-ditch attempt to save your life. It's all pretty fucked up."

"So what did you have to do? Take care of kids or something?"

She looks away but the words come out with practiced clarity. "We had to cull them."

"Cull them? You mean kill them?"

She nods. "Yes, the Aves Cluster has specific requirements that must be met by age five. If they don't meet them they must be culled. The Fledging mothers do the culling for a year."

"Holy shit, that's awful. I'd rather kill grown-ups at least." In fact, I find it revolting and my stomach protests with a surge of acid.

"Yeah, me too. I can't do it anymore, Junco." She turns in a sudden jerking movement. "Life like this isn't worth living. I want to do something else, anything."

"I'm not too familiar with the rules here, Esta, do they let you do that?"

She shakes her head. "Not really. Lucan must agree to it."

I huff. "Well, fucking forget it then, I don't see him giving a shit about anyone but himself."

She looks into my eyes, pleading. "That's not true, Junco. He listens to you guys – you warriors. He'd listen to you, for instance."

I laugh. "Esta, he hates my guts. He literally told me he was going to break me in half back there in the conference room."

She searches my eyes, desperate.

"Plus he hates Tier, and he thinks I love Tier, so–" I look for Ash to avoid her gaze and when I find him he waves me over. "Hey, he's calling me over now so…" I get up and she follows. "OK, you can come too."

He's standing at a long desk, like you might see in a hotel back on Earth. Behind him, in another room farther off, I can see other avians who must be Fledge participants as well. They are looking out at us with interest. "So, Ashur – am I the last one here?"

He smiles down at me. "Yeah, Fledge actually started last week. You don't get to train before the first fight, but you'll be fine, Junco. I'm signing up as your sponsor so I'll come back the day after and we'll train for the second fight, OK?"

I shrug. "Whatever."

"I'm a sponsor too," Esta pipes up to the avian guy manning the desk.

He's about middle-age and a little overweight in the middle. His wings droop low down his back, like they're broken or something and the stubble on his cheeks might look good on any of my teammates, but on him it looks unkempt. "Who the hell are you?" he asks Esta.

"I'm an Aves Mother, and I'd like to sponsor one of these participants. Are there any left?"

Ash takes a deep breath but says nothing. Not our fight, his eyes tell me.

"Lady, I can count on one hand the number who have sponsors, which one do you want?"

She strains to see behind the man, her eyes darting back and forth and then her hand extends and her finger points. "Him. I want to sponsor him." The kid is easily the youngest one in view. He looks to be about ten years old. Half my age. If they're all this young I might have to grow a conscience. I'm no child killer. I look over at Esta as the words form in my brain and I have to hold down a shudder.

The fat guy yells, "Hey, kid, get over here. You want to accept this lady's offer of sponsorship?"

His eyes don't even register Esta. He looks at me and then at Ash. "Sure, why not."

Esta almost claps and I look up at Ash, but he shakes his head at me.

"Day after tomorrow, Ashur?"

He nods to her.

"Great, we'll come together."

Ash leans over and gives me a hug. "Junco, the first fight is a slaughterhouse, just kill anyone who comes near you and don't try and make it to the top. It doesn't count in the first fight. Your scorecard is the only thing that matters."

Esta looks over at her charge. "Just do whatever she does, kid. She's a trained killer, she can't lose."

Ashur grabs her by the shoulder and turns her away as I laugh. I look down at the kid. "Well, shit, you gonna show me where to go or what?"

"I'm not your slave," he says, jutting his chin up at me.

"No, but I'll keep you alive tomorrow if you're nice. So shut the fuck up and take me somewhere."

I'd make an excellent Aves Mother.

Chapter Eight

From my vantage point on the claimed bed I can see the entire dorm. The bunks are stacked seven high and they line both sides of what is a relatively small and narrow room when you consider that the better part of a thousand people are sharing quarters.

Lined up like soldiers in formation, the tables down the middle play host to several dozen smaller groups of participants. Apparently I missed the application deadline for joining one. But I'm not much of a joiner anyway.

The kid sits on the top bunk directly at the head of my own. He said he had a bunk before he went up to the front and was roped into Esta's mid-life crisis plan, but if he did, it's been claimed now. He didn't look broken up about it.

He's eating some ration pack and I feel the need to eat something as well. I kick the metal bunk frame to get his attention. "Hey, where can I get some food?"

He looks down at his ration, frowns, then offers it to me.

"No, where can *I* get some food? I don't want that shit. What else do they have here?"

"They got a machine." He nods his head down towards the front of the room. "If you got money."

"I think I do. Come on, let's go check it out."

"What if we lose our bunks?"

"Who gives a shit? They'll be plenty of them empty tomorrow, right?"

He shows a smile for the first time and I give him one back.

The climb down goes without incident, but he waits until I am on the ground before flying down to join me. As soon as we leave the periphery and enter the throngs of people the trouble begins. A girl snarls and makes a gesture that I can only assume is something obscene. I smile and promise internally to set her straight tomorrow. Farther down a boy, older like me, gets brave and reaches out to touch my hair and hiss at me as we pass. I bat his arm away and he calls me a few choice names.

The kid hangs back for a second, his bravado failing him at the exact moment it needs to rise to the top, and I have to stop and wait for him to make up his mind to proceed. I watch his face play out the conflict and remain patient as he moves past a group of girls that taunt him.

By the time we reach the little galley that houses the machines he's a nervous wreck. "Hey," I call to him as he looks at the long walk back to the bunks. "Forget about them. We'll sleep in here if you want."

He just looks at me like I'm crazy. "There's nowhere to sleep in here!"

I pan my hands out over the floor and then gesture to the tables. "There's plenty of places. Don't sweat it, like I said, the crowd won't be so brave tomorrow. And I guarantee that you and I," I wait for him to find my eyes, "will still be alive."

He smiles again.

I pan my thumb across the panel on a food machine and then let the kid pick something good. I get two and we wait as the autocook prepares it. I have no idea what it is, but when it comes out, my stomach grumbles and we both scarf it down like wild animals.

Afterward I find a cigar machine and grab half a dozen of those, then get a drink for both of us. "Wanna go outside so I can smoke this in peace?"

He screws up his face. "Are we allowed outside?"

I shrug. "Why wouldn't we be? Are we prisoners or something?"

He thinks about that longer than I feel is necessary, but finally decides we are not. The fat guy at the desk tries to stop us when I head for the door, but I shake my head and he backs off.

The day is almost gone when we sit down on the grass and I light my stogie.

"You're not from here, are you?"

I puff for a few seconds. "No, I'm from Earth. Just woke up three days ago. I have no idea what's going on to be completely honest."

He shakes his head at me, but my face convinces him without words. "What are you doing in this Fledge? If you're Aves?"

"That, kid," I pause to exhale, "is very fucking complicated."

I look away, but when I look back he's still waiting for an answer. "Lucan made me, or else I had to go back to Earth with someone I don't care for. I'm only half Aves." I shrug. "So I don't get automatic placement, I guess."

I lie back on the grass and look up. The Fledge building is massive, about half as tall as the height of the habitat, which from this vantage point looks to be a couple miles high. The structure slopes against the side as it climbs and I can only imagine what that does to the gravity in those areas, assuming this is a torus-shaped habitat. That might not be right, but it feels right from the way the horizon curves up on itself.

There are seven distinct segments to the building. "What's the deal with this?" I ask, pointing my cigar at the partitions along the side of the building.

He looks up and sighs. "The fight levels. Fight one is on the first deck, two on the second. It goes on like that. So, how did you manage to meet Lucan?"

I puff on the cigar and think back three days to when I woke up. It feels like years ago. My mind wanders back to the night I hit the deer and it feels like lifetimes ago. "He was there when they pulled me out of morph. Nasty bastard, isn't he?"

I smile over at him but he's got a weird look on his face. "Is he? I never thought so."

Oops, got a believer here. "Isn't he?" I ask, looking away now. The kid shrugs and shuts up so I take that as a no. "So, you got a name?"

"Isec."

"Nice to meet you, Isec, I'm Junco. So what do you know about the fight then, Isec? Because whatever you know, it's a hell of a lot more than I do."

He tells me, but it isn't much. We stay out for a little longer then make our way back inside. The crowds in the middle of the room have dissipated so we walk back to the bunks with no hassles and Isec is snoring within minutes of hitting the sack. I envy him because I lie awake listening for boot steps on the bunk ladder or the heavy beat of approaching wings the entire night. The adrenaline jacks up a little higher than my previous normal, and I wonder just how safe it really is to close your eyes here.

My mind drifts back to Lucan. The kid obviously doesn't share my opinions of him and it makes me replay one particularly interesting tidbit. *One of these days, Junco, we will have an honest conversation.*

Just once I'd like someone to start the conversation with honesty and not make me wait for it. Just fucking once.

The fat guy is reading off the rules via some amplification device elsewhere in the dorm but to my delight, I can see them as they pan across my field of vision. "Hey." I kick Isec's bed. "Are you seeing this stuff on a vision screen, Isec? Or is it just my Aves shit kicking in?"

"Shut up, Junco, I'm trying to listen."

OK, I guess it's just me. I read along with the announcer, but then skip ahead because he's too damn slow.

General Fledge Fight One
Rule One: One body equals one point.
Rule Two: Only biologically attached weapons allowed.
Rule Three: Fights begin when the shields drop.
Rule Four: Fights end when the buzzer sounds.
Rule Five: No medical attention will be provided.
Rule Six: If you're alive at the buzzer, you advance.
Rule Seven: Those unable to attend the next fight will be culled.

Pretty fucking easy. The announcer demonstrates Rule Four and everyone jumps when the buzzer blares. I look over at Isec and he's panicked. "Hey, Isec?"

I watch him gulp air as he turns to look at me. "What?"

"Stop worrying. Jasus, kid, you're gonna die of a heart attack before we even get in the arena."

He shoots me a weak smile but then gives his full attention back to the announcement.

"Hey, Isec?"

He tries to ignore me.

"Isec?"

"What!"

I smile as he finds my face. "I said you'll live through this one, kid. Relax, we're a team."

"I don't think you know what you're doing. You're gonna get us both killed."

"How old are you Isec?"

He screws up his face. "What's that–"

"Just tell me how fucking old you are."

"Ten."

"Ten? Isec, when I was ten I had already assassinated two world leaders on Earth. I think I know what the fuck I'm doing. So relax, because if you get killed it will be because you panic and don't do what I fucking tell you. Got it?"

"But you haven't told me how to do anything, we don't have a plan."

"Duh, kid. I haven't seen the arena yet, have I?"

"By the time you see the arena we'll be fighting."

"So?"

He looks like he's gonna scream and I smile at him. "Just trust me."

He doesn't, that much is clear. I try another tactic. "Do you know what the arena looks like?" He nods. "Perfect, describe it to me."

"A large oval arena, small free-G streams on the periphery and gravity wells in the center where the top of the ziggurat is. The terraces hold five hundred on the bottom, then two-fifty, then one twenty-five, then sixty, then–"

"I get it, they graduate upwards."

"We go up facing out, then when the shields go down, we fight until the buzzer sounds."

"How long does the fight last?"

"Five minutes."

"OK, here's the plan, when we get up there, just before they drop the shields, turn and face inward."

He stares at me like I'm a lunatic. "That's your plan? Turn around and face inward?"

"You got a better one?"

He scowls at me.

"Then shut the fuck up and do what I say. Now, Ashur said that body count is what matters, so I'm pretty sure I'm gonna get a boatload, but since I have to make sure your count is high as well, I'll send some of them back for you to finish off. When the shields go down, you get behind me. We'll be back to back. Get it? You call out when someone comes close enough to hurt us. Tell me where they are on the clock face. You know what that means, the clock face?" I use my hand and describe what I'm saying. "Twelve is here, three here, six here." He nods. "Good, you say the clock time from your perspective, and I'll reverse it to my perspective, OK? I've used that technique quite a bit, so it's no biggie for me to switch the numbers around, but if you try and do it, you'll fuck it all up."

My battle plan clearly calms him down and he's got his business suit on now. "Let me see your hands." He thrusts them towards me.

"Make your claws go out." He presses on his palms and the razors protrude, not anything as dangerous at Tier's, but good enough for a ten year old. I press on my palms and the razors shoot out like arrows. I look at Isec and smile. "Pretty cool."

"You only have three on your left hand."

"Yeah, nightdog ate my fingers back on Earth, that sucks, but you use what you got, right? Now take your boots off and tuck your socks into them."

"Why?"

"Talons are weapons too."

"Is anyone else going to use talons?"

"Shit, I sure fucking hope so, else they're stupid. Off, now. Tie them to your pants, you got a loop on those?"

He checks and says he does.

"Good, tie them on loose, on the way up to the battle level drop them on the floor, we'll pick them up after the fight."

I look down below and people are beginning to line up near the machines on the far end of the room. Isec scoots over to the ladder, but I put my hand up. "Not yet, let's be last. Oh, and one more thing. I can't fly, so I'll be on foot the whole time."

His mouth drops open. "You're kidding right?"

I smile. "No, I told you I just woke up three days ago. I've never used the wings."

"We can't do this on foot!"

"Like hell we can't. I've been in worse places than this on foot. Alone even. And I've got you watching my back and you've got me watching yours. OK, looks like it's time to go. Shove that fear down now, Isec. When it's over you can think about how fucking scary it was, but for now, this is just another job, another day to get through – got it?"

Isec flies off and I climb down quickly to keep the adrenaline up. We take our place at the end of the line. It's at least an hour before we even make it to the door, that's how slow the line moves. But eventually we do make it and then we are filing around the 3D ziggurat.

We are on the bottom level. Isec steps onto his square-shaped pad and drops his boots. I'm about to step in mine when I realize it's already occupied.

A rough hand directs my gaze upward to an empty space. I look back at Isec and shake my head. "No change, kid!" I call. "Do it like we planned!" I scramble up to the next level and push past the others already lined up and step onto the pad.

I have no time to think, because we are moving upward to the battlefield before I can even take another breath.

Chapter Nine

My neck strains as far as it can. My feet are stuck to the pattern on the ground, so I can't move them to get a better look at Isec, but this is the first fight, which means the arena pops into view in a fraction. I feel my bare feet come unstuck and pull the quick-release loop that holds my boots to my person and they fall to the floor with a clunk that reverberates around in my head, alone, as the silent and slow world of the fight moves in and takes over my body.

I see Isec turn around and look up to find my face. I smile at him, then point and scream "Go!"

The shields evaporate and I'm about to dive down towards Isec when he flies upward and gets pulled into the free-G.

Shit!

And then the stupor of surrealism wears off and everyone is in motion. I have to let him deal so I can take out the girl next to me. My claws extend and I have a second to compare them to hers, which are painted a pretty pink color. A few fractions later the blood from her jugular splats a polka-dot pattern across her face and she slumps to the stone floor, out of the game.

The next guy is the hisser from last night, I jump in the air and swing my newly taloned feet around and take out his eyes, then finish him off with my left hand while my right clasps around the throat of another boy, bigger than Isec, but not by much. He flails at me, trying to scrape his claws across my face, but my reach overtakes him and a few seconds later he's unconscious when I squeeze my fingers together and rip out his esophagus.

I look for the next one but only find a pair of frightened eyes on a girl who towers over me by almost a foot. She flies upward out of my reach and I have a minute to look for Isec. He's fighting, but still caught up in the free-G about two levels up. I clamber along the stone until I get purchase and pull myself up the next level.

A group of girls are waiting for me and one drags her talons across my chest, leaving gaping wounds in my light armor before I can grab her foot and break her leg. The next girl has an illegal knife and I actually take a second to laugh at her. She loses her concentration and I grab the knife and swipe it across her throat, ducking slightly to avoid the hot blood that pulses out of her jugular. The third girl flies off and I find a handhold on the rough stone terrace and climb up the next level, then look to see if Isec is even still alive.

He is, but he's bleeding. I kick a guy with wild eyes off the terrace and he lands on a big mean-looking mother who quickly disables him and throws him down two more levels. The big guy looks up at me and I shrug. "Sorry!"

"Junco!" Isec screams. "Help me, Junco!"

I get a running start and then fling myself off the terrace and soar through the free-G until I bump him out of it. We fall back down to the bottom terrace, rolling to help break the fall. "Get behind me. Now!"

He does and I hear the clock face signals being called out as we twist and turn, back to back, killing anyone who comes near. For a few seconds the fighters around us seek other targets and I have time to notice that the display on my interior vision is rating the attackers, flashing my endocrine biog status and pinpointing any injuries. A team of four swarms in on us and I crank out some epinephrine to compensate. I target the first guy's injured lung and puncture it clean with the tip of my razor and then fling him back to Isec. His buddies grab me by the arms, but I create a standing wave and shake them off, then cross my arms and drag my claws across their faces, pushing them behind me at the same time.

The last guy catches me off guard and knocks me to the ground. He's on top of me as my breath is shocked out of my lungs. I look up and see Isec's panicked face. The guy draws his razors back, and then his body goes flying across the terrace and the big guy I apologized to earlier falls on him and cuts his head off with a razor so long it stops me cold for a few excited heartbeats.

He looks over at me afterward and smiles. "You owe me now."

I shake my head and smile, then take out a spastic girl who looks like she lost her mind several seconds ago and move on to the next one.

I've got a girl by the hair and I'm about to slash her throat when the buzzer rings. I drop her and take several deep breaths and my vision screen says it's releasing cortisone to calm me down. The girl is heaving badly but my data display says she's not seriously injured so I pull her back up to her feet and bend her over and whack her on the back so she can cough. "You OK?"

She nods at me, the fear still plastered on her face.

"Relax, you made it. Fight one is history. Let's get the fuck out of here."

We are instructed to stand on a transport block and then we are moving upward to the level two holding area. Isec and the coughing girl follow me into our new dorm, which is exactly the same size as the last room, but the bunks are only stacked two high. The reality of just how many people were ruthlessly annihilated hits everyone at the same time and we stand there, killers all.

Even with my extensive experience, I've never participated in something so heinous in all my life and it takes whole seconds for me to push it out.

The moderator for this level congratulates us, then instructs us to go shower and pick up clothing and, if anyone gives a shit about us, care packages. The coughing girl sticks to me like glue during showers, as does Isec, much to my dismay, but none of the guys are looking at us girls with anything other than weary apprehension. I wrap myself in a towel and I'm handed a care package, but no clothes. The woman who hands it to me reads my confusion. "Aves only wear standard uniforms, Junco. Your stuff is in the bag." Obviously she never saw me in my *Snipers do it from behind* t-shirt.

I wait for Isec and the coughing girl to get their clothes and then we go back into the dorm and find some bunks. I lie down in my towel and fall asleep thinking about how I forgot my boots on the battlefield.

I thought the care package was from Ashur and the guys, but after I put the uniform on and lace up my new boots I pull a card from the bottom of the bag and my heart stops.

Lucan.

I pick it up and it's written in avian. Isec and the girl lean in trying to look at it. "What does it say?" the girl asks. She shakes her head as I hand it over. "I only read English."

My face screws up and Isec interrupts before I can ask her anything. "She knows that – only Aves read avian."

I squeeze his leg and he jumps. "It's from Lucan and it says, 'Well done, Junco.'"

He eyes me. "I thought you didn't like him?"

The girl looks completely confused but I answer Isec anyway. "Well, he can't be all bad, I guess. He sent me clothes and," I pick up an ionspray, "some drugs apparently."

"What kind of drugs?" the weary girl asks.

I shrug. "How the hell should I know?"

She leans back at my tone. I'm tired and hungry and she's not even on my team but I feel compelled to defuse the silence I've created. It's not her fault I have no clue. "Come on, let's go get some chow."

We skip the ration line and instead go right to the machines. I let them pick whatever they want, then get what Isec orders, plus some beer. We eat in silence. In fact, the entire place is silent, the shock of today's fight still raw and open.

"Got another one of those?" I look up and find the big guy who helped me when I was about to be killed, he's pointing to my beer. Everyone is looking at my beer now. I shrug. "Probably got enough, I have no idea actually. Let's give it a try."

We walk over to the machine. "How would I order for everyone?" I look up to his face and smile. He's good-looking in a Braun and Ryse kind of way.

He takes my thumb and flicks it over the panel, then swipes my index finger along until it gets to the catering section, and he orders beer. "There's no way that's gonna work, but hey–" It beeps an approval and I laugh.

"You must be loaded."

"I don't think it's my money…"

"Kush."

"Junco. Anyway, I'm pretty sure someone will be very pissed off at me tomorrow." I let out a little laugh of satisfaction.

"Maybe you shouldn't do it then?"

"Too late," I say, pointing to the servos. "It's already here." Everyone gets excited and I call out to Isec, "Don't get drunk, you twerp, you'll regret it tomorrow."

The little fucker flips me off and I'm actually taken aback.

I look back up at Kush. "There you are, go grab one."

He does and then comes back and sits down next to me. The coughing girl has moved on and I'm pleased about that. I light up a cigar and lean back into the uncomfortable straight-back chair. I offer him one and he takes it.

We puff in silence for a few minutes, watching everyone celebrate their extra night of life, and then I look up at him. "So, what's your story, Kush? You look a little out of place here."

"Says the lion to the wolf."

"Yeah, you noticed, huh?" I puff, then exhale. Breathe out, Junco. *All the best parts are in the exhale.*

The big guy is still talking. "Well, the whole purpose of the General Fledge is to get into the Aves, Junco. You're obviously already in, so there's no logical reason for you to be here. None at all."

I let out an ironic laugh. "So, your story is?"

He smiles and takes the hint. "Not anything special. I'm in – was in – Political Cluster. I wanted to go for Aves, the draw of it is powerful. So here I am." He shrugs matter-of-factly at this revelation. I have no idea if it's true or not. Don't really care, either.

"Good enough for me, then," I say as I puff out some rings towards the ceiling.

"And you? What's your story?"

I don't even bother meeting his gaze. "Secret mission, that's all."

He nods. "OK, well, thanks for the beer."

I watch him pick up his mug and turn. "Uh-huh. No problem."

As soon as he's gone the coughing girl is back and I let out a sigh. "I'm not your friend, girl. So don't mistake me for one."

She nods. "Yeah, OK. But can I sit here?"

I shrug. "Knock yourself out." Then I get up and walk away to go find Isec and make sure he's not drunk.

He's laughing and talking excitedly with a couple other younger kids who made it through when I find him near the back of the dorm room. They get silent as I walk up. "Enjoying yourselves?"

Isec smiles up at me. "For now, but if you think you're gonna start acting like a clutch mother you better think again. I don't need a mother, Junco."

"No? Well, Esta really is an Aves Mother, ya know. So try and let her down easy, eh?"

I walk away, then stop and turn my head slightly, just enough so he can hear me. "And I could give a fuck about you, Isec."

I take a step and catch his retort. "Back at ya, Junco."

The grin spreads across my face and I go find the bunk where my shit is stashed. The coughing girl is back, lying on the top bunk over Isec's stuff. I'm on the bottom bunk next to Isec. No one has claimed the bunk above me. In fact, all the bunks around us are empty.

I let out a deep breath, stomp my cigar out on the stone floor, and lie back. Exhausted.

"We're not friends," the girl says. "I get it."

"OK."

"But I do want to live and you obviously have no plans to die in here, so I'm gonna stick around anyway."

I turn my back to her. "Sure, whatever. Just stay out of my way in battle or I'll cut your throat next time."

The shiver from her body actually escapes through her mouth and for a second I wonder if I've crossed the line. But then she's silent and soon my world dampens to the twilight of sleep. The thought seeps down into the darkness with me: my guilty conscience never really had a chance.

Chapter Ten

Esta is fussing over Isec on the other side of the training room and I can't help myself when he looks over at me, eyes pleading. I pretend a laugh while pointing and he flips me off. What a little creep.

Meanwhile, Ashur's back is to me and he's pointing up and going on and on and on about free-G flying. He pauses so I interject, "Uh-huh, yeah, that makes sense." He continues as I survey what everyone else is doing.

Kush is on the other end of the training room with some of the older guys. I figure they're all from the Political Cluster since they hang out together, but I could be wrong. I watch him as he tries some hand-to-hand with a partner. He's got some good moves, but I can see ways out of every hold he tries.

I look back and Ashur is staring at me. "Who are you watching over there?"

"That big brown-winged guy. He helped me out yesterday. Got a little sticky at one point and he sort of saved my ass."

Ashur tilts his head. "He sort of saved your ass – or he did save your ass?"

I shrug. "He did."

Ash stares over at the group until they notice him, he beckons with a finger and they point to each other. One at a time Ashur shakes his head until Kush acknowledges him and begins walking towards us.

All I can think about is going outside to have a cigar.

"Hi, Junco."

"Hi Kush, uh," I wave my disfigured hand behind me, "this is Ashur, my XO."

I go back to people-watching as Ash and Kush walk off a little ways, talking. If I was a guy, they would never do that. Ashur would never bring him over here to thank him, he'd just shrug it off and tuck it away in case the guy needed a buddy favor in the future. Like I did. But I know damn well that's what he's doing. I've been living with military guys my whole life so I know how it works. It doesn't matter how many people I kill or how many times I save their asses, if just one of them catches me in a weak spot, they go all big brother on me.

I can't take it anymore so I get up and walk out, find the stairs and slip outside without incident. I cop a seat on the stone bench next to the train stop and light up my cigar. This day is so boring. I lie back on the bench and take in the sunshine, then wonder if it's real. Feels real, but there's no sky above me, just the criss-crossing of beamed scaffolding holding up the interior ring of the torus.

My eyes close as my thoughts drift and my body gets heavy.

I wake when I hear someone shouting my name. Several someones actually. I sit up and the long ash drops off the cigar as I move it. Must have dozed off.

I watch Ashur send everyone back inside and then walk over to me. "What the fuck, Junco?"

"What the fuck what, Ashur?"

"You can't just get up and leave the training room like that."

"Well, it wasn't too difficult, so obviously I can."

He lets out a deep breath. "Are you ready to fly or what?"

I smile. "Let's go."

We walk back inside but don't take the stairs. Instead he palms the biometrics on the elevator and we take it all the way up to the Level Seven arena. "Isn't this cheating?"

He huffs. "No. You can't even fly, how is that fair? Everyone else was taught except you. So what if you see the arena." I raise my eyebrows at him, but he continues, "Besides, the only other free-G Fledge facility on Amelia is at Aves, and it's in use right now. So we have no choice."

I scratch my eye and shrug. "Whatever you say."

The Level Seven arena is nothing like Level One. It is a giant sphere with mushroom-looking pedestals shooting up from the ground at uneven intervals. I listen as Ash explains. "Those," he says, pointing to the mushrooms, "are the only gravity wells in the room, OK?"

I nod.

"Everything else past here," he points to a glowing green line on the floor in front of us and then to each of the other regularly-spaced entrances around the perimeter, "is free-G." He pushes me past the line and I go sailing across the middle. "Flap your wings, Junco! Don't get sucked down to the pedestals!"

I can feel the nearest mushroom drawing me in so I stretch my wings and flap a little and shoot towards it at an alarming rate.

"Tilt your wings, Junco! Reverse thrust!"

I do and barely avoid being sucked down completely. I flap my wings, thinking I will go above the mushrooms and avoid them but then I notice that they are growing out of the ceiling as well as the floor. Wait, it's free-G, so there is no floor or ceiling. I twist my body and the ceiling becomes my floor.

Ashur glides up next to me, then tilts his wings to stop his forward momentum. He smiles. "Not so hard, is it?"

I laugh. "Speak for yourself. I'm about to hurl."

"Yeah, takes a little getting used to. Whenever you change direction, in Z-space, I mean," he clarifies, "just pick some random point to be your horizon. As long as you have a horizon, you'll be fine."

"I don't think I'll get the hang of this in one day, Ashur," I say, a little frown creeping out of my lips.

"No, you won't, but you've got time. The second fight is pretty much like the first one, just a different patterned structure. So don't sweat it."

I nod. "OK, well, since we're here I might as well learn how to move and turn."

It gets a lot more fun as I figure out how to move my wings. At first the muscles feel tight and unresponsive, but we stop on the largest mushroom and Ashur shows me how to stretch and move them so that they loosen up. I end the afternoon doing flips, my body careening across the length of the game field and bumping into Ashur as he fails to escape my mad thrashing legs. If I had wings on my feet, free-G would be so much easier.

We swim through the air back to the perimeter gravity field and I start to fall when my feet touch down but Ashur steadies me and smiles.

"You did real well, Juncs. Tomorrow we'll do real training and fly outside, in the regular atmosphere. That way you'll be ready for the second fight."

I nod as we walk back towards the elevator. "So, what did you and Kush talk about?"

He palms the biometric pad and the door slides open. He waves me in and then follows. "I just said thanks, that's all." The door closes and our descent begins with a quick jolt to my stomach. "He's a Political – wants to be Aves. They do this every time, but," he stops to look at me, "don't get attached to him, Junco, they never make it."

"Shit, Ashur, you're a real downer."

"Sorry, just the truth."

The door slides open on two and he squeezes me goodbye. "See ya tomorrow."

I wave and go back to the dorm. Dinner is over and almost everyone is either sleeping or sitting quietly on their bunks. The coughing girl and Isec are playing cards in our corner of the room. I smile at Isec as I walk up. "So, did you learn anything useful today, brat?"

His face is pretty serious, so I pause and listen. "Junco, she said the stuff she taught me today, the Aves kids have to learn by the time they are five, or she has to kill them."

Oh shit, Esta. What the fuck?

"She's crazy, Isec, she's full of shit. Just trying to scare you."

"Why would she want to scare me now, Junco? It's not like I can back out."

My cheeks puff up and then I release the air out in one long exhale as I shake my head at him. "She's having problems, Isec, that's why she's here. She's not happy with her job, so don't take what she says too serious. I'll speak to her tomorrow, and if she says this shit again, we'll get rid of her and you can train with Ashur and me."

This satisfies him and they go back to playing. "I'm gonna go take a shower," I say, but they are busy and don't even respond.

The showers are empty so I strip down and languish in the hot water. My hair is a lot longer than it was before the morph and I secretly wish for a good haircut so it didn't take so long to wash.

When I'm done I walk over towards the counter to see if I can get some clothes, but no one is there and the wall has been replaced with a line of cubbies that have biometric panels on them. They are all empty except the one that says Junco, Aves 039-9.

I pass my thumb over the panel and the transparent door slides up to allow access to another care package. I take it over to the row of benches and sit down, being careful to hike up my towel. This time I fish all the way down to the bottom and find the note first.

Junco,

You have not used the ionspray. Do you think I would put things in the package if I don't want you to use them? Why must you be so difficult?

Lucan

I fish around again and pull up the ionspray. This time it has a label and directions: Quick recovery – To use, squeeze near nose. I consider using it, but I push it aside for now. I'm not hurt, why waste it? Besides, maybe Isec will need one after the next battle.

I pull out my uniform but there is something else in the bag – shorts and a tank. For bed, I guess. I put those on and tuck the uniform back in the bag and carry it with me to my bunk.

The bed is a lot softer than I remember any bed ever being and I drift off to sleep thinking about what Lucan's note will say tomorrow night.

Chapter Eleven

Ashur slams me down on the mat as I focus on Isec's face. Esta is talking to him across the room.

"Shit, Ashur, that hurt!"

"You're not paying attention."

I nod over towards Isec. "Esta was telling him some fucked-up shit yesterday, scared him bad, too. I don't want her telling him that stuff. I need him to learn something useful so I won't be worried about what happens to him if he does manage to make it to the end."

"He's not your responsibility, Junco."

"Like hell, we're partners now. He calls out the people behind me and she's gonna ruin it with her mid-life crisis bullshit."

He laughs and pulls me to my feet. "I'll talk to her later. First try and do some moves that you would normally do on Earth, to see how it's different with the wings and the less than 1G gravity."

I nod and try a spinning kick on the dummy, but fall on my face, laughing. "Hell, I guess it makes a huge difference!"

"Yeah, the last time I saw you do that, you took a guy's head off."

He grins at me, but the image of Aren brings back the video of Moju. *Please, God,* I pray to myself, *let Moju be OK.*

"Junco? What the hell are you daydreaming about now?"

I sigh. "Nothing, let me try that again." I go through the moves and this time at least hit my target, albeit in very sloppy form. After several more adjustments my foot smacks the bag squarely and it feels right. Ashur just sits and watches me, pointing out ways to force my wings to lie flat against my back. It works better that way, less air resistance.

I move on to flips and gymnastics but have the same problem. Ashur holds me as I twist, flip and flop, setting me down like my aerialist coaches would when I was small. Again, the wings are throwing me off balance. He tapes them down and I do it again. And again, and again, and again. I'm sweaty and gross when I notice the crowd watching and feel self-conscious.

"Again, Junco."

I try something new, something I think I can do well regardless of the wings, and I begin a Wan Woo form that I've practiced religiously since I was a pre-teen. It starts out slow, supposed to be done in the riding ring, in the dirt, right? Both on and off the horse. The first twenty-three moves are all balance – standing, weaving, hands, shoulders, and the head. The second part is on horseback, obviously it isn't now, since I have no horse, but I draw a mental box that is ten inches square around my feet to keep me focused. This is how you practice your tricks before going live on the back of an animal that could kill you with a hoof to the head if you fall.

My wings are an added weight that throws off the first of the boxed moves, but I compensate as I spring into a handstand and tilt my legs forward a little. From there I push off one-handed, spin, and catch myself on the other hand. My three remaining digits squeal with the pressure.

The kata pattern speeds along nicely as I rotate between straight flips from the hand and foot position. It's more like a vertical dance than anything, since that's really what mounted acrobatics is. I'm balanced on my head, getting ready to push up with my shoulders when I notice Ashur smiling at me. I smile back and heave, twisting my hips and swinging my knees down in a swoop as my upper body and feet trade places. I land at the very edge of my mental box and throw my arms in the air.

It was pretty sloppy, but I'll take it.

I smile over at Ashur and I'm just about to walk towards him when a big guy, one of Kush's buddies from the other side of the room, steps in front of me. "What the hell was that?"

"Wan Woo long form for aerialists, why?" He's a big brown-winged guy who looks pretty much like Kush – square jaw, intense blue eyes, and stout build, except he's got his head shaved and some marks on his arms. Tattoos or something.

"Never heard of that pattern, or seen anything like that before."

I stare at him sideways, not because he's particularly interesting to look at, but because his words come out like a challenge. A growl of dominance.

"Well, you wouldn't, would you? I mean, unless you've been to Earth, right? I've been told there are no horses in space, so that pretty much rules out mounted acrobatic routines."

Ashur is between us before I can even finish. "That's enough, Junco, let's go fly."

I turn to follow him but the big guy grabs my arm and turns me back. "Hey, I'm still talk–"

I react, I can't help it. My knees are bending on the word "hey," and by the time he gets to "talk," I've smacked him in the jaw so hard with my heel he drops to the ground.

Ashur lets out a deep breath and motions me to follow him, but I kneel down to the guy instead. "I'll let you live because maybe you're just having a bad day, but there will be no next time. Don't ever fucking touch me again."

I stand and glance over at Isec, his smile is so wide I have to shoot him a wink. Then Ashur and I leave the training room and make our way down the stairs to the front of the building.

Outside we stop at the benches so I can puff a cigar. Ashur holds a hand up to his face to shield his eyes from the sunlight. Or whatever it is, since it's obviously not the sun. "Now you'll have to watch your back for that guy, Junco. I hope it was worth it."

I shrug. "He grabbed me, Ash. You can't let guys get away with that shit or they take it to the next level." I blow rings upward and lean back on the bench, my disfigured hand behind my head as a cushion.

"Yeah, I know. But he looked off. Keep an eye out for him."

"Yeah, OK. So we gonna fly or what?"

He smiles down at me, plucks the cigar from my hand, stomps on it, and pulls me up. "This will be a lot harder than in the free-G, you'll be sore tomorrow."

I smile. "I'm ready." And I am.

Flying is not all that fun when you're learning. For one thing, you fall an awful lot. And I'm not talking about some pansy-ass baby fall. Even in the grass that hurts. It takes me hours to get a few feet off the ground and my stomach muscles are burning with the strain of keeping my body parallel. I had no idea it took so many muscles to get into the correct flight position.

Eventually, after Ashur tugs me up into the wind, I find my stride with gliding. The wind is stronger up high so I have to compensate by twisting, using muscles I never knew I had. Well, probably didn't before a few days ago. We take advantage of the air stream and fly out above the train rail, following it into a town a few miles away. People stare at us as Ash lands and I crash and roll near a pub, but we're both wearing the Aves uniform, so they get disinterested quick enough.

We drink and eat, Ash watches some kind of sport on the screen, and I throw darts at a board that has the face of Jax Justice on it.

Internally I find that quite funny.

Some things are universal and hatred for this guy's high-drama action screens back on Earth is one of them, like politics and parties on the news. I hit him in the eye several times, and from the looks of the missing paper pieces in the orbital region, that seems to be a favorite spot for many of the locals as well.

On Earth I don't recall ever having so much freedom. Back home I was in a routine where I did what I was told to do, saw who I was told to see, and went where I was told to go. It wasn't exactly orders, more like habit to the extent that I was unable to even see that I had options. I had boyfriends when we were out on the scrub and on maneuvers, but never at home. As I got older my father got more and more weird about boys, so I kept that shit out of sight. Even the horses were more of a job than a social engagement.

Take Peaks, for instance. I had a vehicle and a Farm Family passport stamped with military privileges, yet I never went to the city alone. Never even went shopping or just to grab a chicken sandwich. It's refreshing, freeing actually, to be in charge of myself. I watch Ash across the room and wish the other guys would come visit too, especially Braun – I really need to talk to that fucker – but the casual routine Ashur and I have slipped into is satisfying in a way I've never experienced before.

Normal.

I walk over and join him and he explains the rules of the sport to me. It's a lot like gridiron, but more violent and takes place in free-G. After a while we leave and grab the train back so I don't have to try and fly against the wind in the dark. Ash gives me a hug at the door and I wave an arm at him as I walk inside.

It's past midnight when I finally get back to the dorm, so I forgo a shower and just slip into bed with my uniform on. I can hear Isec in the next bunk, his breathing even, but the remnants of crying linger in the way he hiccups air. I am thinking about how I will kill Esta tomorrow for scaring him so badly when the arms come up from below my bed and clamp against my mouth. In a blink I am dragged silently down the middle of the room and into the showers. When we get there the door closes and I hear the click of a lock just before the lights flick on.

It's the big guy from earlier.

What a dumb fuck.

His rage is dialed up to maximum and his two buddies stand around him with their arms crossed. "Not so fucking tough without your bodyguard, are you, little girl."

I laugh and he kicks me in the ribs, making me laugh again. "Keep laughing, girl, I can't wait to see you without teeth."

I cough a little to clear my throat, just to make sure I can enunciate everything properly. "Wow. You think he was *my* bodyguard? Shit, I'm *his* bodyguard, you dumbass!" I laugh again, and the boot finds its mark, making me roll a little to the side.

I wait it out because there's only one reason to drag a girl into a locked room and it always ends with the asshole on top. And once he gets that position in his head, he'll have made his last mistake.

"Hold her down, Bann."

"Bann," I say, looking at the guy he was just talking to, "if you hold me down, I'll make sure and kill you first. Don't say I never warned you."

He ignores me and makes to hold my left arm while the other guy tries for the right. I grab Bann's foot first, since I did warn him, and he goes down hard. I wince as his head cracks against the cold tile floor and the blood spills out.

The other guy hesitates, making him already too late for the party. I kick up with my right foot and take out his nose. The blood gushes out in a way that reminds me of nightdogs and caves. I swing my legs back to my head and fling them forward, forcing myself up on my feet. The SEAR exits my shirt silently, but the hiss of power makes the ring leader snap to attention. "What the fu–"

His head is rolling towards the shower drain before he can finish his curse. The broken-nose guy is scrambling to his feet, making for the locked door, when his head goes rolling down towards the blood-red drain as well. The other guy is already dead, so I don't soil the air with any more burning flesh than I have to.

The whole fight is over in less than a minute and I thumb the mechanism on the SEAR and put it away.

I leave the front shower door locked and go looking for the moderators near the cubbies. I spy another care package for me, but decide to take care of clean-up before grabbing it and going back to my bunk.

Chapter Twelve

It takes me several minutes to find someone who gives a shit about the three dead bodies I left in the showers. They want to make me wait in a small room off the office, but I refuse and go back to my bunk with my package. Not my problem anymore.

The entire dorm is awake now and I watch Isec's face as I approach the bunks. "They said they would kill you, Junco. I'm sorry I didn't stay awake to tell you, I thought you'd stay away with your friend."

"Don't worry about it, kid, they're dead now." I rummage down to the bottom of the bag and smile as I pull the note out.

"What's this one say, Junco?"

Poor Isec, he looks like a little baby standing there next to my bed. I read it and laugh. "He says, *Junco, you are a giant pain in the ass. Lucan.*"

Isec screws up his face at me and even the coughing girl is looking down at me with interest. "Are you and Lucan friends?" He says it like it can't be possible, and if he would have asked me two days ago I would've agreed with him. But tonight, I just shrug.

"Maybe, but once he finds out what I just did, he might not be so friendly with me anymore."

It's the coughing girl who speaks next. "What did you do, Junco?"

I look up at her and notice that her eye is swollen shut. It wasn't like that earlier. "Did they hit you?"

She looks down and nods.

"Well, I'll tell you what I did then." I wait for her to look me in the eyes. "I chopped his fucking head off with a SEAR knife. Along with his buddy's. The third guy, Bann – well, he cracked his head open when I pulled his feet out from under him, so I can't really take credit for that one."

She lets out a deep breath and I know relief when I see it.

I spy a moderator walking down the middle of the room towards us. "Shit, here we go."

Isec looks panicked. "What will they do to you, Junco?"

"It was self-defense, Ise, they won't do anything to me. Be back in a little bit."

I get up and meet the mod halfway. He smiles. "Sorry, Junco – Lucan's on a comm in the break room. Wants to talk to you."

"Course he does." I follow, a slight bit of panic rising up in my chest.

My knee bobs up and down as I wait for him to appear on the screen. In place of his face is an emblem, a seal actually, like diplomats have. It's hard to read, but I think the little letters around the perimeter say Capitol City of Amelia, or some shit like that. It's bona fide, let's just leave it at that.

My eyes begin to droop when his voice brings me back to attention.

"Explain."

I smile, then lose my bravado and look away. "What do you want me to say? I chopped their heads off. The other guy cracked his noggin open when I pulled his leg out from under him. It was self-defense, Lucan. They were gonna rape me."

He winces as the word leaves my lips, but fuck, it's true.

"Meet me outside immediately."

The screen goes blank and I get up and knock on the door so the moderator can let me out. His dark face peeks through a crack in the door, trying to see past me and over to the screen. "He wants me to go outside. Immediately."

He opens the door all the way and takes me by the arm, apparently I can't be trusted to walk outside without killing people.

We both see Lucan standing over by the train stop bench, so the mod lets go of my arm when we reach the door and I make the final distance alone. Lucan points to the bench when I get there, so I slump down and take out a cigar. His hand stops me and I put it away.

"Junco, you are taking up a lot of my time."

I wait it out because his statement doesn't require an answer.

"Did I or did I not forbid you from using that weapon?"

"You did, but–"

"There were no exceptions, Junco. If people find out what you are there will be a lot of – hostility. Do you understand this?"

"No, Lucan." I look up at him and shake my head a little. "I don't get it. You act like I'm a disease or something. I've had the SEAR my whole life and I never went off and started killing people like a lunatic. So, why? Why do you think I'm so wild?"

His head turns to look down the empty train tracks before he speaks. "How do I explain who and what you are, Junco? You are not human, you are not avian, yet you morph into one of us and have machines in your body. You may in fact be an authentic Seventh Sibling and you have a very dangerous weapon that we cannot remove from you or else–" He stops abruptly and I watch his jaw clench with tension. He straightens a bit and then continues. "We're not sure what you are, Junco." He turns back to me, finished.

"I'm not sure what *you* are, either. And you don't see *me* getting all freaked out about it."

He stays silent.

"Would the SEAR knife kill you?" His expression hardens and I have a feeling I've crossed a line.

"Not much can hurt me, Junco."

"You didn't answer the question."

He blows out a little bit of air in a half laugh. "Do you, or do you not, understand that I have forbidden you from using the weapon while you are here?"

"I do."

"Then why?"

"It was three against one, I needed to stack the deck. They weren't small guys, Lucan. Three against one." The night breeze sweeps my hair aside and I lift my chin up and breathe in.

Lucan is watching me when I look over to him. "Why didn't you use the ionsprays?"

I screw up my face. "I thought you wanted to yell at me for killing people?"

"It happened as you say, so it is excused this time."

"Then why come all the way over here in the middle of the night?"

"I am checking to see if you're OK, Junco. Is that so unusual? I would have called Ashur, but…"

I wait. "But?"

"I was in the neighborhood."

I laugh. "Oh, right."

He takes a seat on the bench next to me, his head eases into his hands and he pushes against his temples. I know the look, it means I'm giving someone a headache. Tier used it frequently.

"I wasn't hurt."

He looks up and then his eyes track down my body. "Yes, I can see that. I'm glad."

"No, I mean, I didn't use the ionsprays because I wasn't hurt."

"Oh." He straightens up again, then flattens out a wrinkle in the sleeve of his black suit. "Right, well, they're just glycogen analogs, Junco, not health sprays. It is forbidden to treat you with health sprays. Besides, you heal yourself anyway. These will help your new muscles acclimate."

"OK, well, I'll use one when I get back in. I learned to fly, ya know. I'll probably be sore tomorrow."

He smiles and I crack one as well, I can't help myself. He goes back to picking at his suit.

"Why are you always so overdressed?"

His laugh blurts out in the night silence. "What?"

"That suit, Lucan. It's so formal."

"How should I dress?"

I shrug. "I dunno, but hell, a suit in the middle of the night? Something a little less rigid would go a long way."

"You really don't know why I wear this suit, Junco?"

"No, I have no idea." I raise my eyebrows at him and he has a genuine look of surprise on his face.

"Well, that might explain some things about your behavior."

"Yeah, want to let me in on it?"

"Who do you think I am?"

I recycle back my memory to my morph day. "You said you were a commander. My commander, actually. In fact you said, *I'm Lucan, Junco. Your new commander*. Is that not true?"

He smiles. "It is technically accurate. I am your commander because I command all the Aves. They are my official military force and the 039 is my personal force."

"What's that mean? You're like the President or something? Commander-in-Chief?"

"Yes."

"Yes? You are the President? Of Amelia? Or of what?"

"Of the avian, Junco."

I grimace. "Oh. I'm sorry, then. I really didn't know. I wouldn't have said all those things to you if you told me that up front."

"It's OK, I find your honesty refreshing."

I snort at this. "Well, I've never been called *that* before."

"Which, honest or refreshing?"

"Ha ha, that's funny." I lean back on the bench and stare up at the fake sky. Windows. Scaffolding, whatever the hell it is. I stare up. "I miss the stars on Earth. I can't see anything here."

"I can take you to see them. If you want."

"How many trains will it take? I'll probably fall asleep."

He reaches out and taps my shoulder and I'm just about to look over at him when the sky changes and the stars shine down on me. I try and sit up before I realize I'm no longer sitting. We're standing in the middle of the night sky, nothing above and nothing below. "Holy shit, what is this? A simulation?"

He takes my hand as I get dizzy. "No, we are outside the habitat. Look behind you."

I do and I smile.

Amelia is beautiful. She's a torus, all right. But she's got four rings to her, not just one. She spins like a top, creating the gravity felt on the outer rim. The spaceports in the center are rather busy even at this time of night and I see several orbitals come and go in the span of just a few seconds.

"Wow." I look over at him and smile, laugh actually. "I'm officially impressed."

He lets out a fake sigh. "Finally, I have impressed Junco the Just One Small Girl."

I look sideways at him, trying to gauge his intentions with that comment, but his face is a blank. He sits down on the air and I follow. Our legs dangle over some invisible edge. "How are we breathing? How is there gravity?"

"We're in a bubble of sorts. I have a few special talents that I won't," he eyes me cautiously, "be sharing the details of with you."

"How did we get here?" He's about to answer when I spy Orion and point up. Everything in the sky for me starts and ends with Orion. He's the first constellation I ever learned. "It's a lot easier to see the stars from here than it was in that tube thing Ashur took me to."

Lucan smiles. "Ashur, I should have figured."

"What's that mean?"

"They are attached to you already, Junco." I am still thinking about this when he switches gears. "I want you to succeed, do you believe me?"

I shrug. "Well, I suppose you'd be a lot meaner if you wanted me to fail, so yeah. I can see that."

"But still, no matter what I do, this will not end well. It will be difficult."

I squint up at him now. "Why?"

"Things have been set in motion. Only going back to Earth would have changed it enough to shift the future."

My voice hardens. "He brought me a video of Moju's finger being cut off, Lucan. He was a plant."

"Yes, that's what you said. So, here we are." He puts his head in his hands and rubs his temples again.

"You know, for a guy who hates Tier so much, you two sure are a lot alike."

His head snaps up. "If you only knew how inappropriate that comment was." The silence between us drags on for a few seconds before he continues. "In which way are we similar?"

He looks over at me and I feel pressure to explain. "Well, he hates when I swear. He actually did mention it a few times back on Earth, and not in a nice way either." Lucan smiles, but does not reply. "And you both rub your head like that when I'm making life difficult."

He nods at this.

"I don't love him, Lucan. I'm not here to save him. Charlie was my love. Moju is part of me, but Tier was just a nice distraction when I really needed one. Someone who held me accountable when it made all the difference. A pretty cool guy, but it didn't get far, and it's going nowhere now. So–"

He tisks his tongue against his teeth. "You're wrong, Junco. All of this is tied up with the dynamics between the two of you."

I wait and the silence is heavy between us.

"Perhaps it is possible that you think you're here for something else, but…" He looks over at me. "I doubt it. We both know you're plotting."

I laugh. "Well, tell me what I can do about it, because to be honest, I'm out of ideas."

"There is nothing, Junco. Truly nothing you can do."

I nod and look down. It's my turn to be silent.

His hand touches my shoulder and we are back on the bench in front of the train stop. "It's late."

"Right, well." We stand up together. "Thanks for the talk."

He bows a little. "The pleasure was all mine, Miss Coot."

And then he is gone.

Chapter Thirteen

The clock in the hallway nearest the stairs reads 3 AM and I know I will regret staying up so late in the morning.

What the fuck are you talking about, Junco? It is morning.

Right.

My feet shuffle up the stairs in slow motion and then try to be quiet as I make my way over to our bunks. When I get there Isec is sleeping in my bed and the coughing girl is in his. He wakes as I'm taking my boots off and shoves over so I can get in.

When I'm settled next to him Isec begins his questions, but doesn't open his eyes. "What did he do, Junco?"

I pat his head and smile. "Nothing, really."

He opens his eyes a little. "That's not true. Tell me, please."

"I just told him it was self-defense." I shrug against him. "And that was pretty much that."

"Then why did you take forever to come back?"

"Has it been long? It didn't feel like we were gone that long."

"Where did you go?"

I think about the trip and smile. "He took me up to see the stars," I say as I let out a cavernous yawn.

Isec is awake now. "Really? I want to hear it all, Junco. Tell me."

"Tomorrow, Isec. I'm tired."

He shakes his head. "No, you'll forget the little details if we wait until tomorrow."

"You're weird, ya know that? You're not supposed to want to know about the little details of my life, kid."

"I'm from Psyche Cluster, Junco, I'm supposed to know everything about everyone."

"So why are you here trying to get into Aves?" I turn so I can watch him talk.

"I failed our Fledge, so this was my only chance to stay alive."

"Oh, what do the Psyche Cluster do for Fledge? Kill people with their minds?" I smile at my own joke.

"No, I'm not telepathic, you can't pass Psyche Fledge if you're not telepathic."

"Wow, I had no idea that some avians were telepaths."

"It's like a big secret, like how the Aves can read and write avian."

"And now you just spilled it to me! Good going!"

He laughs. "Fuck them. Assholes kicked me out."

"Yeah," I agree. "Fuck them. Telepaths aren't so special."

"That's why I ask so many questions, it's the only way I can understand what people are thinking."

I rub his head and let out a stunted laugh. "Well, ya know what, Isec? On Earth, no one is telepathic. So all the great psychologists have to ask questions in order to figure people out."

He looks up at me. "You're lying to make me feel better."

I laugh again. This time I don't bother to keep it in. "I'm serious! We don't have telepaths on Earth. That's like crazy shit talk."

"Tell me everything."

I hiss out a little breath. "OK, fine. The guy took me to a little room with a monitor..."

When I get to the part about the rape, he stops me.

"Were you really scared of them, Junco? Or were you trying to make it sound worse than it really was? So Lucan would feel sorry for you?"

"Jeez, kid, cynical much?" I look down at him but he's still waiting for my answer and for some reason his upturned gaze makes it harder for me to justify the lie. "I wasn't scared if that's what you're after."

He nods and I continue. The next probe comes after I tell him about the SEAR. "It's a weapon, Isec. It's very dangerous and on Earth, and probably here too, they are outlawed."

"Then why do you have one?"

"I can't tell you that, but you have to take my word that it's necessary."

He stops me again at the ionspray part. "I'm glad he's not cheating for you, Junco. That's not right. And I'm glad you didn't use them, even though you thought they were health sprays."

He's pretty perceptive for ten. I agree and move on but he stops to question me at every sentence after that.

"How could you not know who he was?"

"What color is Amelia from space?"

"Why does he care what you think of him?"

I think about this one for a while before answering. "I'm not really sure, Isec. Why do you think he cares? You're the Psyche kid."

He smiles, but his eyes are closed. "He likes you, Junco."

"Yeah, I've considered that. It only makes sense."

"Will you like him back?"

"No, I can't afford to, Isec. It's insanely complicated."

"No, not really." His eyes are open and he sits up. "You don't have to act on the like, but you can still admit that you like him, you know."

I smile. "Yeah, that's true. OK, I like him, I guess."

This satisfies him and he lies back down. "So, what do you think he's talking about when he told you things are in motion?"

"I'm not sure, but Tier and Ashur both said the same thing. So there's something to that, right?"

I feel him nod. He is still for a long time after that and my mind wanders over the conversation as well. Lucan is nice-looking, in a blond Western Utopia kind of way. He doesn't add up though, and this puts me off even though he can tick an awful lot of boxes as far as men go.

Isec stirs and I push some hair out of his eyes and then turn over to lie on my back.

"Are you plotting to save Tier, Junco?"

I let out a deep breath before answering. "What kind of friend would I be if I wasn't, Isec? He deserves better than to be killed off for saving my life."

"You do save him, ya know."

I smile. "Yeah? How do you know that, kid?"

He yawns, long and slow, before he speaks. "I might not be telepathic, but I am precognitive."

I lie there in shock, wondering if he's telling the truth. When I finally figure out something to say back it's too late. His little-boy snores have invaded the silence and the moment has passed.

Ash is sitting on my bunk and the entire dorm is empty when I wake up, sore as fuck from yesterday's training and fighting.

"You will join the living today, then?"

"Oh shit, Ashur, do you know what happened last night?"

He nods. "Yeah, Lucan called me right after I got home. I can't leave you anywhere."

I sit up in bed and yawn. "What time is it?"

"Noon, get the hell up, we've got work to do. Fight Two is tomorrow."

"Yeah, let me take a shower first though. I never got one last night."

"Want me to wait here?"

I'm about to say yes when I have an idea. "No, go teach Isec something useful, will you? He needs some practice." I swing my legs over and start to walk away towards the showers when he calls out.

"Junco." I turn back and find a very serious Ashur. "Do not get attached to that child. He will never make it, you understand?"

"I'm already attached, Ashur. So he better fucking make it, do you understand? Go teach him something. Please."

When I walk into the showers my gaze automatically goes to the drain where the heads were rolling last night. There is no evidence left. I wonder if Kush knows what happened?

The shower feels good and I stand in it a lot longer than I would have if people were around. It's nice to enjoy some privacy when you're naked. I'm not typically shy about such things, I've been showering with the boys forever so I'm just used to it, but that doesn't mean I like it.

After I go looking for my package and find an extra-large one in the cubbie marked Junco, Aves 039-9.

I dry off and put my clothes and boots on before searching through the rest of it. The note says, *Have a very boring day*, and I laugh out loud to myself. Yeah, I could use a boring day. Tomorrow surely won't be boring and if Isec doesn't make it I'm not going to be happy. At all.

There is another ionspray and I dose myself before pulling out the last object.

It's a data reader.

I thumb the biometrics and it's Lucan.

"Looks like you're right, Junco. This came in yesterday. I didn't tell you last night because we weren't finished analyzing it. But it's genuine, maybe the one Slag thought he was delivering to you instead of the one you ended up seeing. Please be careful in the Second Fight."

A new display appears, asking for a fingerprint to continue. I press my thumb and another video pops up.

This one stars Selia and I smile.

"Junco, I hope this reaches you and you are well. I did everything you asked, in fact, I've done more than you've asked and I'm currently embedded with a Subjack Sector. I have met your mother. Delightful woman. No, just kidding. She's scary as fuck and you make a lot more sense now." She stops to smile at the videographer, then continues. "I sent the package on to Charlie's family, but I have to say it did not go well. Perhaps you will return to Earth one day and we can talk about it?" She hesitates here, as if choosing words. "That's not quite true either. The entire purpose of the video is to invite you back to Earth. Subjack would like to hire you. I am making this with the blessing of your mother. She said to extend you an invitation."

That sounded like something she'd say word for word. Very technical and cold. To hire you, Junco.

"I have some rather juicy information about some siblings that might interest you. We could discuss it more in person. I realize you're a long way away, and this is probably out of your control, but…" She shrugs into the camera, her careful words gone. "I have things to tell you, things you should know before you get caught up in it."

She pauses again, then pulls off her hat and shoves it into the side pocket of her fatigues. She's got a long gash across her scalp and half of her ear is missing. "It's been quite an experience, Junco. I think of you every night. Every night," she repeats. "If there is a way, please come. We're moving up North next, to wait."

She smiles, then the video clicks off. A date flashes on screen. January 3, 2153.

I have no idea what the date is today. I was under for two months if Ashur's vague reference to my last meal was any indication of how long morph takes. I went aboard the ship with Tier in November, exact date also unknown. So it is at least late January or early February.

I look around the showers, unable to make a commitment to move or stay, until I hear Ashur calling my name out in the dorm. He pops his head in the shower room. "Hurry up, Junco. Fight's tomorrow!"

I shove everything back down in the bag and lock it up in the cubbie for later. There is one lingering question on my mind and I stop and stare blindly at the transparent biometrics pad. Who the fuck is Subjack? I'm having a hard time believing that Lucan isn't more interested in these new developments, seeing as how she mentioned the Siblings. I look over at the door and find Ashur still waiting.

"You wanna tell me what the fuck that was all about?"

I shake my head and let out a deep breath. "Ashur, if I knew I still might not tell you, but I have no idea, so it doesn't matter."

"Well, what do you expect? It's all mystery all the time with you, Junco. No happy medium at all, is there?"

This time I laugh, because to do anything else will just make it worse. He grabs my hand and pulls me out and we walk in silence to the training room.

Chapter Fourteen

In the training room Esta has Isec off to one side and he looks very unhappy. Ashur notices the direction of my gaze and pulls me away. "Leave them, Junco. He's her responsibility."

We walk straight through to another hallway and over to the elevators, and then ascend to the top floor. I don't say anything and neither does Ash and by the time I'm floating in the free-G it's awkward.

He swims up next to me, his wings paddling the air with perfect control. "You're mad at me?"

I shake my head and change the subject. "What do you want me to do here?"

He drops it. "I want you to touch down and take off of every mushroom starting here," he points to the near end where we presently are, "and then change Z-space and repeat it on the upper mushrooms, ending there." He points to the mushroom above the starting point.

It's a lot fucking harder than it sounds.

For one, the gravity well isn't just 1G, it's like 2. So you fall hard when you come down.

And for another, that same 2G that drags you down during landing, prevents you from taking off as well.

I complete the pattern three times and I can feel my chest and back straining. I hope Lucan puts a giant dose of G-analog in my package tonight. Ashur, to his credit, does the pattern with me. Much faster and more precise.

On the last round, on the last mushroom, I overcompensate for the drag on my wings and smack into the stone platform knees first. I roll in standard approved fashion, but when I come to a rest I know I have serious bruises.

"Fuck!"

Ashur glides up like this is no big deal. He's not even breathing hard. "You all right?"

I lie on the ground a few more seconds, silent and rubbing my eyes. "I'm tired."

"You wanna be done?" He sits down next to my prone body and waits for my answer.

"I want to go talk to Isec and look at the fight room diagram." I sit up and watch him stare at me. "What?"

He shakes his head and averts his eyes off to some point across the room. "Junco, that kid will get you killed. Do you hear me? We're not doing strategy with him."

"Yes, Ashur, we are. If you don't want him to plan with us in the training room, fine. I'll show him what to do later. But he's getting prepped and either way, we're in this together."

He sighs and looks even farther away before tracking back to my face. "If he gets you killed, Junco, I'll kill him myself. You understand me? We are not here to babysit throwaways." He stands, grabs my hand, and pulls me up. "You are here for one reason only, to leave alive and go back to the 039 with me. Got it?"

I push off and swim over to the exit without replying. The ride back down is silent as well, and when we get to the training room the heat of his anger is dripping off him like sweat. Isec is doing some stupid drills that look like they have zero chance of helping us live tomorrow.

I let out a big sigh, then walk over to Esta, leaving Ashur to fume alone.

"How's it going over here, guys?"

Isec shoots me a dirty look. "You said she wouldn't fucking talk like that to me anymore, Junco. She said by the time the Aves kids are five, they've survived at least six attempts on their lives by their clutch mothers. I think she feels obligated to make me suffer through all six attempts before Fight Two."

Damn, a lot of shit happens to Aves kids by the time they are five. Almost makes my training seem like playschool.

Esta shakes her head. "Can you believe the mouth on him, Junco?"

"Esta, what the fuck are you doing? He's a little kid. He's not Aves, he's Psyche. Either teach him something to keep his ass alive or get the fuck out of here."

Esta huffs at me and my vision screen tells me she's projecting her pheromones at me on purpose. Can't fucking control it my ass. The vision screen suggests a stim analog to counter the effects and I give it permission.

I tap my head. "Doesn't work on me anymore, Esta. So you can keep those drugs to yourself. He's not Aves so it doesn't work on him either. You're just pissed off because you can't control him and I don't like how this is playing out one bit."

Ashur is next to Esta now and I feel the heat rise up in my face at him siding against me. Esta huffs and shrugs as she lifts her chin in the air. "He's my pledge, Junco. I'll train him the way I see fit."

I look over at Isec. "Fire her, Isec. I'll train you myself."

Isec looks over at Ashur and gets a wild look in his eyes. "No, that's OK, Junco. It's fine."

I look over at Ashur as well. "What the fuck are you doing, Ashur? I fucking told you I want him alive, what part of that don't you get?"

He walks over, practically chest bumping me like a fucking alpha male, and snarls, "You don't order me around, Junco. I am the XO here. This kid is going to get you killed and I want you to drop it now."

The last bit makes me start and I step back for a second before I can regain my composure. "Maybe I'll fire you too. Then both of you can get the fuck out of here."

He's on top of me in an instant, but I roll sideways and fall hard on my left side, then scramble backward to get out of his reach before he can grab at me again.

"Don't play with me, Junco. I'm not Tier – I won't put up with it."

"Get the fuck out, Ashur. I'm not your nine yet so I don't answer to you."

"Junco–"

"Esta, shut the fuck up!"

Heads all around turn towards us and I feel Ashur's anger rise again as I get to my feet. I look over at Isec and he looks like he's gonna cry. "You're finally gonna get your wish, huh?"

Ashur's lip goes up revealing teeth. "Meaning what, Junco?"

"You said all along you wanted to kill me yourself, let's go then. You think you can just attack me and get away with it? I don't give a fuck who you are, don't you ever fucking touch me. Ever."

"Or what? You'll take out your little bioweapon and slice my head off next?"

The crowd around us has thickened and I hear them gasp. "I don't need that stupid weapon, Ashur. I can kil–"

He attacks and I flip out above him, my wings spreading to take me high above. He responds and has me by the leg, but I kick. His block is there before I can even register what happened. I fall to the ground with a thud and bounce back up in a crouch. He rushes me and we're grappling, I counter with some mixed martial arts. I put a foot in, but he counters and moves back. I wrap my arm around his neck, grabbing for his shirt, he slips out of it before my hand is even past the first shoulder. I kick my legs back, he's out of reach. I roll, he's gone before I get there. I try and wrap him in a guard, but he's always there, a split second before I am. Like we're in fucking practice back on Earth in a coordinated spar and he's been given the cheat sheet for every attack move I have.

Then he's on top of me, about to slam his fist in my face when I feel him ease up. I flip him off and we struggle for a second and then he grabs my hands as I sit on top of him.

"Stop, now."

I do stop, because I'm in shock and breathing heavy.

"What the fuck was that, Ashur?"

"I said, stop, Junco. This is over." He tosses me aside like a doll and I lie on the mat seething up at him. It's the look in his eyes that gives it away, a cross between panic and guilt.

"I know what this is."

He wipes away a small dribble of blood off his lips. "Get up."

I do, but my anger comes with me. "I know what this is, Ashur."

"Yeah, Junco? What is it, then?"

"You fucking piece of shit! Where the fuck did you learn to counter those moves?"

He growls at the crowd and they dissipate. "Where the fuck do you think, Junco?" It comes out as a whisper and I feel my throat constrict and my face gets prickly. I look over at Isec and now he is crying.

I take his hand. "Come on, Isec. We're out of here."

Poor kid is beyond panicked and can barely eat as we sit in the cafeteria. "Isec, please – I have the battle plan in my head here." I do, too. All of a sudden my Aves vision screen spat it out, right after a minor panic attack at not getting the information before stomping out like a baby. "Look, I'll draw it for you, OK?"

He nods, but doesn't look up. His little feet are swinging off the chair and this makes him look more like six or seven than ten.

Shit, Junco. Ten is young enough, he doesn't need to be six or seven.

I let out a deep sigh and draw the spiral pattern on a napkin. "See, it's exactly like the ziggurat, except a spiral. Same rules, same plan, right?" I smile but he doesn't return it.

The rest of the pledges are back now and the noise level kicks up several notches.

"Come on, let's go take a shower, OK? We'll feel better after that."

He nods and we slip around the corner and into the shower area. It's packed, which sucks, but at least I don't have to shower alone with a little kid. I push him over to the man side and take myself over to where the girls have claimed their own area.

I find him in the dressing area later, sitting with Kush. They are both dressed. Kush looks up at me as I approach. "I tried to get him to leave with me, but he wanted to wait."

I nod and set my care packages down. I forgot that Selia's video was still tucked away in my cubbie. I slip on the bed clothes Lucan left and then grab the bags and we all walk out together.

Kush hangs around our bunks for a few minutes and I have almost no desire to be nice. But I do anyway. I could use another friend and he's the only one interested at the moment.

"So, you wanna tell me what that fight was all about?"

I look back over at him as my hand absently fishes around for Lucan's note in the bottom of today's package. "Not especially, Kush. I mean," I add this to appear nice, "if you don't mind, it was kinda personal."

"Well, I heard some of it, and if you want, I'll help you keep him alive."

Isec's face snaps up to study Kush's motives. I just shrug. "Sure, why not. It would be beyond stupid to turn down help, right?" I pull out the nasal spray and dose myself, and stuff the note in the waist of my shorts.

He smiles. "Yeah, besides, we did OK last time."

I look at him for real this time. "Yeah, you're right. Huh, Isec? We did OK last time." I nudge his leg as he sits motionless on his bunk, but he doesn't speak.

Kush takes the hint and says goodnight.

No matter what I say, the kid won't sleep alone. So he climbs into bed with me. I'm just about to doze off when he finally says something. "Ashur is going to kill me."

I smooth his hair down the side of his head. "Stop it, Isec. He's not going to kill you. That's silly."

"Junco?"

"Yeah?"

"What did Lucan's note say?"

I spy the coughing girl peek over her bunk to listen in and I smile. "It said, Take good care of Isec tomorrow because he's special."

We drift off after that, but I snap awake sometime later when the thought burrows up from my subconscious.

I might not be telepathic, but I am precognitive.

Chapter Fifteen

The four of us enter the second battle together, Kush and I taking up the front and the rear, Isec behind me, and the coughing girl behind Isec. The girl wouldn't take no for an answer and Isec's pleading won out in the end. She had a wild look to her the minute we got in line, and by the time we were all situated on the spiral patterns below our feet, she was half-crazed. Now I am wondering if I will need to kill her myself, just to keep focused.

We are not last this time, so we have to wait a little bit, our bare feet cemented in place. We have a modified plan now that Kush wants to play and the coughing girl said she'd make sure she did her part. Although, looking at her now, I'm having second thoughts.

Anyway, the new formation is a square, each of us taking a point, instead of back to back. We face outward, away from each other at all times. I am listening, but not watching the patterns of movement behind me. We are smack in the middle of the spiral, with several circles above and below. Things in the back slow down and finally the anticipated pause in activity that signals the start of just about anything – be it a horse race, or the release of an arrow into the heart of a pronghorn on the prairie, or a fight to the death to prove you are worthy – stretches out far enough for me to know it is the true beginning.

"Now," I whisper.

I feel them all position and then we are accelerated upward and into Fight Two. It takes a fraction for gravity to catch up to the sudden deceleration and I feel my bare feet lift off the ground and know the hold has already been deactivated even before we settle. I kill the guy next to me and then the girl above me who thought she had it made with her superior positioning before anyone else notices we've been released.

The rest of the bodies come alive and I smile as I watch Isec pull his claws out of his lower target and shoot up in the air to sweep his talons across the face of a kid not much older than him on the level above.

What Kush and the coughing girl are doing, I can't see, I just take up my part in the formation and we walk up the spiral, somewhat discombobulated, yet a hell of a lot more organized than anyone else in my view.

I kill the next person up the ramp and then turn as Isec screams.

A small boy has jumped up from above and knocked Isec down the next level.

A girl swoops in to kill him and I rake my foot across her eyes, then kick her in the face and she pops off the spiral like a starling diving through an open barn door.

I pull Isec to his feet and Kush comes in and knocks a big guy down who was about to take my head off. I don't have time to thank him because there's another girl right behind Kush who has a knife aimed at his back. She's in mid-air, knife in full forward motion, when the coughing girl grabs her by the foot and swings her off the platform. I turn to choke out another kid next to me, but I can hear the sound of a skull crashing on the floor below and smile at CG's save.

We form up again and this time we're running up the spiral, almost everyone is off the platform and fighting in the air, so we make it up a good full turn before we stop and start killing again.

The precipice is directly above us now and I wait for Kush and Isec to finish off their targets before whistling the command. We lift up, wings beating and crushing against each other in the confined space until we ascend to the top platform where there is a ferocious battle between the other politicos.

Kush charges in and has a guy down in a fraction, while Isec and CG fight off a very tall girl with dark skin. I crouch down, in position, waiting until someone notices me. My eyes scan the group and I pick the leader. He's too busy to notice a little lump on the floor and I crawl on palms and feet, knees bent and my belly almost scraping the ground – slowly, like I've done a hundred times before in a ghillie suit out on the prairie – until I'm so close I could reach out and trip him.

In those few seconds he's killed off a good number of pledges and I am patient as he looks around for his next target.

My head is bowed, but my eyes are up to keep him in view.

He sweeps around, desperate for another target.

Finds the swirl of glowing colors in my eyes.

And I spring up like a lion going for the wolf.

My hands are around his throat and my knee slams into his chest, knocking all the air out of him as he falls backwards. I choke him until he goes limp and crumbles, then rip my talons across his throat to seal the deal.

Sound returns to my world like the rush of the wind across the tallgrass and I pick out Isec's scream of panic. I whirl around and see him fighting off a girl with razors so long they could belong to Kush.

She swipes at his face twice before I can cover the ground and she's about to draw them across his throat when CG plunges down and lands on her back.

Isec goes reeling down with razor girl and I am just about to clean up when CG snaps the girl's neck, pushing her away with disgust.

Things are getting less chaotic and I know the buzzer is about to blow, but I scan the area once more to make sure. The four of us have acquired the top level of the spiral. I look back at CG and I'm about to congratulate her when one last politico pulls himself up over the ledge behind Isec and grabs him by the throat.

"No!" I scream and everything is silent and in slow motion again as I book it on foot towards Isec. I see Kush on the other side of the platform in my peripheral vision. He turns and begins to react, too late.

Isec reaches up for his throat and wiggles free.

CG hurls herself at the politico as the buzzer wails in my ears.

And I watch as the asshole cheats and slits her throat midair.

Real time catches up and CG is thrown down the spiral and lands in a heap at the bottom, next to a pile of bodies, broken just like hers.

Isec is screaming.

Kush is walking slowly towards me.

And I just stand there and feel a little rush of relief that it's her and not Isec.

The moderator is on the speakers telling us to line up on the spirals to be shunted up to Level Three and life comes back to me.

Until I hear my name.

"Junco, Aves 039, you will remain behind for pickup. Junco, Aves 039, you will remain behind for pickup."

I step off the spiral and have just enough time to see Isec run forward in a panic before they stun me from behind with a bolt of plasma and I fall to the ground, shaking uncontrollably.

I come to in an operating theater, bright lights shining on me from above, my hands and feet strapped down, and the blood from the battle crusting over my ears so I can't hear right. My back flames from the plasma burn as I struggle and my coughing gets out of control. My lungs try to do complicated tasks like inhale and don't seem to be making much progress.

There is chaos and I hear the 039 yelling – at least most of them. Braun is not present. My head bobs around, trying to take things in and get a grip on the situation as quickly as possible, when I spy Tier.

He's strapped to a gurney just like me. Mere inches separate our eyes.

"Tier," I croak.

"Don't trust them, Junco."

I manage a smile between coughs. "Thank you."

"For wha?" he says, slurring his words in a drugged-out stupor.

I whisper between my smile. "For making that real."

Ashur is down in my face then, yelling at me to shut up.

My head bobs around again and I see Isten and Lucan screaming at each other, pushing each other, until razors come out and other Aves step in to break it up.

It all becomes too much.

My eyes close and I am gone.

When I wake Tier has vanished and the room is quiet. Life is clear and the nightmare I witnessed before is over.

"Witness is awake and conscious."

"Witness, can you tell us your name?"

Who the fuck is the witness? The words type out on my vision screen automatically.

Then a reply: *You are the witness, Junco.*

"I'm the witness?"

"Correct," says the voice in the room.

Do not answer out loud unless I instruct you to, the vision screen types.

"OK."

That was out loud.

I had no idea vision data displays could be testy.

"Witness will say her full name for the court."

Say: Junco Abigail Coot.

I say it.

"Physician will confirm that the drugs have been administered and are working correctly."

A voice next to my head. "Confirmed. The cortical feedback loop has been enhanced, witness has normal vital signs, and witness is in full complacency and submissive mode as described by Psyche Cluster Protocol 41."

"Witness will recall the evening of November 9, 2152. Does witness recall?"

Say: Yes. "Yes."

"Witness will describe events which occurred from 1830 hours to 1915 hours."

Say: Aren attacked Tier after I agreed to go with him.

Say: Tier attacked Aren.

Say: I burned Tier with a plasma rifle.

Say: Aren and I escaped.

Say: Aren poisoned me so he could take me back and hand me over to the Mountain Republic.

Say: Tier grabbed me and administered first aid to combat paralysis from the wound.

Say: Tier took me back to a cave which he was using as base camp and completed treatment from the poison.

Say no more until instructed.

It's a lie. My thoughts type it out on the display.

Of course it's a lie, Junco. You want to save Tier, correct?

Yes.

Well, one charge at a time. This one we can knock off tonight.

Who is we?

Silence from the data display, but the room is murmuring like cicadas on a summer night.

The murmuring stops and the voice is active again. "Did witness see a treaty exchanged between parties during this time?"

Say: Yes.

"Did witness see Captain Raubtier read the treaty and submit to it?"

Say: Yes.

"Did witness see Captain Raubtier break the treaty?"

Say: No.

The murmuring gets excited and loud until the voice commands silence.

"Did witness hear Captain Raubtier mention that he killed numerous humans without orders?"

Say: No.

"Did witness hear Captain Raubtier mention that he killed children without orders?"

Say: No.

"This witness' question list is completed."

The bright light above me grows dimmer and dimmer until I am left in total darkness.

Chapter Sixteen

I come to again. This time I'm in a pale yellow room and there are machines beeping around me. I rip out the IV and sit all the way up before Ryse pushes me back down on the bed and Arel slaps a towel over the blood spurting out from my arm.

"Relax, Junco. You're with us now," Ashur says, his voice even and disinterested.

I'm filled with rage. "You asshole, I told you he'd live. And so fucking much for not spying on me back on Earth, right? You piece of shit! Did you have fun watching me all that time?"

Arel steps back, a little annoyed. "What the fuck is she talking about now, Ashur?"

Isten comes up to the bed and then Mish and Rikan follow. They are all here, except Braun. "Junco," Isten starts. "It wasn't like that."

I swallow hard and cough. "He did, Isten!" The tears well up in my eyes and I am about to cry from all the stress and drugs. "He knows all my counter-attacks and I only ever practiced them in one place!" I scream it, I am so angry my head wants to explode. I dial it down and the words come out as a whisper instead. "One secret place, Ashur. Down on the holomat in my bedroom. And you know every single move. Every single counter-move."

His face is a mixture of anger and guilt as he looks up at his team. "How the fuck do you think we could bring her back if we couldn't control her, huh?"

They stare at him in silence.

"He watched me in my room. And not," I stress, "the princess room. He watched me in my real bedroom." I turn away and push Ryse off the bed. The towel Arel placed slips and the blood starts to flow again. It gives up and coagulates half way down my wrist, then becomes sticky until I absently wipe it on the sheets.

The silence is broken by Lucan's voice across the room. "You will all leave now."

They don't even say goodbye, either. They just file out and leave me there.

"Would you like to stay here tonight, Junco?"

I shake my head and more tears spill out. "No. It's not fair that everyone else has to sit there tonight knowing that we killed all those people and I get a choice."

I turn around and his face is so sad I almost take it back.

But I don't, I just let the tears slide down my cheeks.

"I should have to see what I did, witness the number of bunks shrinking as the space between them grows wider, so that I know what a fucked-up piece of shit you've turned me into and how much worse you avians are than–" I let out a sob and take a moment to wipe my wrist across my nose and pull myself together.

When I speak again my voice is low, but even. "I hope you got everything you needed, by the way. That was a classy fucking move, pulling me out after the fight and filling me up with drugs – you fucking *shot* me!"

He just stands there, looking at me. I watch as he swallows hard but even if he is sorry, it won't make it better. Not this time. "I trusted you." I turn back over so he can't see my face.

Tier was right all along. Trust no one.

Not Ashur.

Not Lucan.

And certainly not Braun who hasn't even come back to see me once since the day I left.

"You wanted to break me, right? That's what you said?"

"Junco–"

"Well, congratulations. You should feel very proud of yourself."

Lucan's private flyer drives me back to Fledge. I'm pushed up against the door on one side, my face pressed against the cool glass as I watch the high atmosphere mist part around us. Lucan is sitting, straight-backed, on the other side of the rear seat. I've got the blanket from the bed wrapped around me because the drugs have tricked my body into thinking I'm freezing-ass cold even as sweat pours down my back and puddles inside the waist of my pants.

The ride takes a lot longer than I thought it would and when we finally stop I'm almost asleep, still half intoxicated and the other half exhausted. Lucan gets out and walks with me into the Fledge building.

He palms the elevator and the moderators watch with long frowns on their faces as I try to walk straight, but can't.

We ride up to level three and he takes my arm and leads me into the dorm. The lights are all on, but everyone is in bed, sitting up looking confused.

Kush gets up and runs over, then Isec joins him.

"What the fuck did you do to her?" Isec demands. He takes my hand. "Junco?" His little voice is full of fear and he begins to cry.

Kush drags me away from Lucan and takes me over to a bed.

My dried-up sobs are just small hiccups as I lie down shaking.

I hear Isec's little bare feet pad a few paces out into the center of the room. Then he screams at the receding click of expensive shoes on the tile, "She doesn't *like you* anymore, Lucan. She doesn't like you *anymore*!"

A fading laugh wakes me up and the first thing I think is that I'm dead. Eventually, as the seconds pass, I realize I'm not dead, I just wish I was. My entire body hurts. I shuffle and kick the heavy blanket until I unwind my legs, then push myself up and look around the room.

There are only single beds now and we've got a large portion of the room dedicated to a casual sitting area filled with couches, chairs, and tables. The news is on a screen that takes up one entire wall, almost floor to ceiling, but the sound is turned down.

Ashur is sitting on the next bed over.

I don't look at him, but I know he's there. I swing my aching legs out the side that faces an empty bunk and rest my feet on the cold tile floor, massaging my head to make the throbbing recede. It doesn't work.

I stand up and give the dizziness a second as well. Then slowly shuffle over towards the showers.

"We need to talk, Junco."

I ignore him.

I've got the hot water spraying down and I'm just about to try and remove my shirt when I see him standing in the doorway. "You will talk to me."

I stare at him, then release the seams on my shirt and whip it over my head, biting back the pain as my arms and shoulders protest.

When I look back at the door he's gone.

I stand under the barrage of water until my muscles are relaxed, then search out what the vision screen personality can do for my condition.

You there?

Yes.

Got anything to make me feel better?

A series of diagnostics run and the data presents as a graph showing which hormones and macromolecules are in what ratio. The ones that need improvement are blinking red.

Shall I initiate a recovery cocktail?

Is this legal for Fledge?

There are no rules for self-healing in the General Fledge.

OK, yes. Make me feel better.

I am not obtuse, I realize she wrote General Fledge. Which means the Aves probably have some restrictions. But hey, I'm not in the Aves Fledge, now am I.

I lean against the wall as the cocktail floods my bloodstream. The relief is almost instantaneous, and much appreciated.

So, you gonna tell me who you are?

Silence from the vision screen.

Figures. I don't really give a shit, what can I do about it? If there's an AI living inside my body, well, it's not like I can make her go away, can I? Live with it, Junco.

I adjust my towel as I walk over to the Aves 039 cubbie and there are a lot of packages there. I choose one that looks like the rest of Lucan's packages, pull out the clothes and boots, then stuff it back in and let the biometrics lock it back up with the rest.

I have no intention of opening any of them.

After dressing I walk back out into the dorm and head for the cafeteria. I thumb through the selections but I can't remember the things Isec ordered for us in the past, so I choose something that looks like a biscuit or cookie and force myself to eat it. I grab a drink and a six-pack of cigars and head out.

Ashur is waiting in the hallway.

I walk right past and don't even glance his direction. I'm feeling a lot better with the cocktail and I hop down the stairs and walk towards the outside door.

The thick-around-the-middle moderator glances up from his reading at the front desk. "Hey, Junco?"

I turn. "Hey–" I don't know his name.

"Hey, uh, Lucan's outside waiting for you, honey." He shrugs and makes a face at me. "Just thought you might like a heads-up."

I nod at him. "Thanks."

"And that other one is around here too. Your–"

Ashur comes down the stairs and the mod shuts up. I shake my head and walk towards the door. Outside the fake sunshine is bright, so bright it blocks my view of the bench for a second. I put a hand up to shade my eyes and I see Lucan. I can hear the door behind me whoosh open to let Ashur catch up.

Nowhere to go.

So I light a cigar and make for the grass before either of them can get close enough to order me around. I lie down and stretch back, one hand behind my head, one bringing the cigar to my mouth, and let out a deep breath as I cross my legs and close my eyes.

I feel fucking spectacular. That was one hell of a cocktail.

Ashur reaches me first since he was closer, but he remains silent until Lucan joins our little party.

"You will come with us, Junco. We will have that conversation now."

I don't even open my eyes. "No, I don't think so, Lucan." I take another puff and blow rings, eyes still closed.

"Junco," Ashur growls at me. "You will do as you're told."

"Fuck off. You can try and make me come with you, if you think it's worth it. But I'm not going unless you plan on shooting and drugging me again. I'm not going anywhere with either of you as long as I have a choice." I open my eyes, shade them with my hand, and then sit up. "You both fucked up. I'm not your friend." I point my cigar at Ashur. "And I'm not your…" I stop and look at Lucan because I'm not at all sure what I am to him. "… whatever it is you thought I was."

Ashur's fingers grab me and yank me to my feet, my cigar goes flying, and I overcompensate and stumble backwards a few paces. I want to get angry, but I force it down and then bend over to pick up my cigar to wait it out.

Lucan breaks our standoff. "Ashur, please leave us now."

Ash shakes his head at Lucan. "No way. I'm not leaving."

Lucan smiles like Ash is a toddler. "You are, Ashur. Immediately. Or I will have you forcibly removed. You are evoking far more anger in her than I am, so let me handle this."

I look back and forth between the two of them and my head throbs a little as I clench my teeth in frustration.

Ashur walks back into the building and I watch until he's no longer visible through the transparent doors. I look back at Lucan, but he just stands there, staring at me. I realize after a few seconds that he's scrolling in his own data display, reading something. It's the same look he got when he was telling me about the Vegas planet pad takeover. Distant and searching.

Is that how I looked in the testimony room? I sure fucking hope not, otherwise he knows.

"I know you lied in testimony, Junco."

Shit.

"I just can't figure out how exactly. The drugs were fully accepted into your profile, your vitals screamed the textbook readout of someone under the influence, and you never acted out of character. Nonetheless, I know you lied."

I smile. "Well, good fucking luck with that one, Lucan. Maybe you avians are allowed to make shit up like that and get away with it. I wouldn't know, not my world after all. But I have no idea what you're talking about."

"I know you lied, Junco," he continues, "because not twenty minutes before your testimony Tier admitted to breaking the treaty."

"Maybe his memory isn't so good, Lucan. I, on the other hand, have perfect recall."

"What did he say to you in the testimony room, Junco?"

"He said, *Don't trust them.*"

I watch his face as he realizes I'm telling the truth.

"Pretty good advice, if you ask me. I'm gonna take it now."

I turn to walk towards the doors but he reaches out, not unkindly, and touches my shoulder. And then we are in the darkness of space and I fall forward as my mind adjusts to the nothingness below me. His hand reaches out again and steadies me. I'm steady, but he doesn't let go.

"Junco," he starts, then stops to sigh. "You've asked a few questions since we first met, but I am more surprised at the ones you don't ask."

I wait it out, not to try and gain momentum or anything, I'm just too tired to give a shit.

"Still nothing?"

I look up at him then. "No, Lucan. Nothing. I just don't care."

"What do you care about, then?"

"Well, I could tell you – but then you'd just take it away from me like I'm a child that needs to be punished."

"Do you not want honesty, Junco? Isn't that what you've always been after?"

"It's really not all that important right now, so no thanks. My interest in you, like I said, is gone."

"You'll turn down the answers? Take ignorance instead? Just to be stubborn."

"No, that's not it at all, Lucan. Sure, I'd like the truth, but getting it from you is like burning wood infested with wheat beetles. It heats your house for a while, but the poisonous fumes kill you before you're warm anyway, so what's the point."

"Who will you accept it from, then? If not me? Ashur? Isten? Braun?"

"Tier."

He laughs, a genuine hearty laugh, and it makes me flash with heat. "Ah, yes. You mean the one who instructed Ashur to plant spying devices in your bedroom? He's perfect."

I smile up at him. "You don't get it, do you?" I wait for his complete attention. "It doesn't matter what Tier did before. I granted him absolution back on Earth for all of it. It doesn't matter if he spied on me himself, or if he killed Charlie, or even if he was the one who turned me into this monster. None of it matters, because he was forgiven. It's a done deal."

He stares down at me, his features hardening as the seconds tick off.

Patience and inertia are not the same thing.

He taps my shoulder and we are back in the grass at Fledge. The sky is dark around us. "Well, I guess your secret is out then, right?"

I shake out another cigar and touch it to the striker, inhaling and exhaling before answering. "It's never been a secret, Lucan. You had me pegged right at the start. From the 039 with their plasmas at my head after morph, to the little speech about how sweet talk doesn't work on you. You got it in one. But you know what I don't understand?"

He turns away, so I don't wait.

"Why you let yourself be drawn into my little act. The stars, Lucan? Please, that is so predictable."

He turns back and I expect anger at the very least, but he hands me indifference. "If you interfere with what I am doing, Junco, I will be forced to punish you."

"Like I said that first day in the hallway, Lucan – death means nothing to me. I can kill myself tonight and be one hundred percent satisfied with how things end. Or you can kill me right now and be done with all of it. Because that's the only way you'll know for sure that Tier will die at the end."

I'm slammed onto the ground before I can blink, a sharp pain throbbing up the side of my face. I spread out my arms, crucifix style, and close my eyes to block him out. "Do it," I whisper.

But the fractions pass and I know he's gone.

Chapter Seventeen

Kush finds me like that sometime later. I didn't doze off exactly, just didn't see the point of picking myself up. He sits down next to me and when I don't speak, he lies back and waits. I've noticed some things about Kush over the past week or so. He's patient. And he keeps his distance. It's refreshing.

My grin grows as I turn my head to face him.

"What are you doing, Junco?" He smiles back.

"Lucan hit me and I fell down."

He laughs at me and shakes his head.

"And I don't know, it really wasn't worth the effort to get back up." I turn my head back and look towards the ceiling miles away. It doesn't matter if I spend all the rest of my days under this roof, I will never get used to looking up and seeing ceiling.

"Should I bother asking why he hit you?"

I shrug. "I sort of threatened him. In a roundabout way."

He nods. "Ah. OK. Well, that probably doesn't go over well in the best of times, and you seem to bring out the worst in lots of people."

"Yeah, probably."

"So, you gonna stay out here all night?"

"I dunno."

"Wanna see the cool rooms we have access to now?"

"What rooms? I didn't see any rooms."

"Did you go out past that lounge area? There's a giant mast with all sorts of stuff on the way up. And at the top there's an observatory."

I turn, interested. "Huh, what are the chances?"

He gets up and offers me his hand.

I hesitate, but he pulls me up without waiting for my answer.

I manage to pry Isec's fingers off my arm long enough to get into the bottom of the mast and look up. It looks fucking far. Like miles away to that observatory. In fact, I squint and I'm not even sure if I can see the opening. I might just be imagining it.

"Let's go up," Kush says.

I shoot him a dirty look. "Kush, I've flown a total of like three times. There is no way I can fly up there. Zero chance."

He points to his back. "Hop on, then."

I shake my head. "Nah, I've done that before and it was a struggle to get a fraction of that distance."

He screws up his face. "You've done what before? What are you talking about?"

"On Earth, when Tier and I–" I catch myself and turn away. *Fuck*. "Fine, then. If you think you can carry me…"

He smiles. "I can, Junco."

I hop on and he does. It takes a few minutes, but this is nothing like the escape flight Tier and I took up through that cave opening back in the RR. And even though I keep looking down, Moju's head never pops up from the floor.

When we get to the top he stands on the landing and then I hop down and look into a stairwell that goes up through the ceiling.

"Have you ever been in a gravity curve, Junco?"

I shake my head. "Don't even know what a gravity curve is, Kush."

"You know how the building is curved up against the outside wall?"

I nod, still looking up into the dark hole.

"Well, the gravity fluctuates as you go up. That's why the flight wasn't so hard. The G was decreasing as we went up. So anyway, when we get up in there, it's gonna feel weird – your perspective, that is. Just let me take you to a booth and try not to puke."

I laugh. "OK."

He grabs my hand and starts climbing the stairs. As we go up it gets darker and my breathing picks up the pace a little.

"Close your eyes now, Junco."

I do, and he takes my elbow and leads me. My body is swaying wildly and I can see what he meant by the gravity curve. It's not the same from step to step, very erratic.

"OK, open your eyes, but don't move."

Holy shit! I'm standing on the side of the wall looking sideways at the giant viewing transparency. He pushes me back a little and I fall into a long lounger and then I am lying down instead of walking sideways. My head spins a little and Kush blocks my eyes with his hand.

"Close your eyes if you get dizzy." I do, and then he leans back with me. "It's weird, isn't it?"

I laugh and open my eyes. The darkness above me is filled with tiny pricks of light and I smile. "Very fucking weird, Kush."

He looks over and smiles.

We sit there for a long time like that. Silent. Looking. Thinking.

"I already know you're from Earth, Junco."

I don't bother turning away from the stars to face him. "Did Isec tell you?"

I feel him shake his head. "No, you've been on the newscreens for the past two days. Ever since the morning Lucan brought you back."

"What? It's been three days since the last fight?"

He lets out a heavy breath. "Yeah, Fight Three is tomorrow."

"I slept for two days straight?" Wow.

"Yeah, we all figured out what happened afterward. They had you on the screens, your testimony. There was a big inquiry and some people accused you of lying."

"Yeah, like Lucan."

"No, he didn't. The Archer of Justice did though."

"Huh, well, Lucan accused me of lying to my face, so same difference."

"Did you lie?" He looks over at me.

I return a snarl. "Please, Kush. If I did, I wouldn't tell you. Besides, it's not even possible to lie under the drugs. That's what they told me anyway."

He shrugs. "I didn't bring you up here to talk about that stuff."

"Then why did you bring me up here?"

"Junco, it is very hard to get your attention. I figure I'd have a captive audience. And," he says with a smile, "you can't exactly escape, can you?"

I laugh. "I'm sure I'd have better luck getting down than I would have had getting up."

Despite his confession he remains patient and aloof.

And we just lie there, observing.

At some point he puts his arm around me, pulls me close into his golden brown wings, and I doze off. I wake only once, when his hand slips down my belly and I feel a tingle on the skin near my SEAR. I grab his hand and gently move it up higher and then go back to sleep.

I'm pulled out of the best sleep I've had in a long time as Kush is carrying me to the exit of the observatory.

"Gotta go down, Junco. Fight will start in a few hours and Isec's been up here half a dozen times wondering when you're gonna come talk to him."

I nod as I look up at him. "OK."

He sets me down at the stairs and holds me by the shoulders as I make my way to the platform. I wait on the landing, not really wanting to take the leap. Kush bends down and I hop on, grateful. When he jumps off the ledge I feel like I did that night when Moju, Tier, and I were heading out towards the Ramah tunnels. Exhilarated. Kush was right, there's lots of stuff all up and down the mast. I look around and make a mental note to come back after I'm done killing people.

At the bottom Isec is pacing around like a mad wreck and when I'm on the ground he releases his breath in a rush.

"Relax, kid. We're fine."

He shakes his head. "No, this fight is different, Junco. Way different."

I sigh. "Well, let's go sit down and make a plan then, OK?"

We settle on my bed, the soft blanket from Lucan's house heaped around Isec as we talk. Kush sits in and listens, but doesn't interrupt to make suggestions. On the sidelines I guess. Isec has few details of the actual fight arena, but he does fill me in on the new rules. I ask for them on the vision screen and they pop into view. The only real difference is that the fight will not end until our numbers have been cut to seventy-five individuals and weapons will be hidden throughout the field. I glance around the room and try and estimate how many of us are left from the original one thousand.

Two-fifty, I guess. Damn.

Collectively we've killed seven hundred fifty people in the span of about a week.

On Earth we call this internecine. Mass murder. Mutual slaughter and destruction.

Here, apparently it's called growing up.

When it comes time to line up we still have no idea what the floor plan will look like but neither does anyone else. I make us line up near the front this time. Kush is like tenth in line, then Isec, then me. We stand there, shifting our weight from foot to foot, agitation growing around us, nerves fraying, and the buzz of what's to come percolating up from the depths like a salamander lifting up out of a muddy river bank after the spring thaw.

I've never seen the initial process of fight day since we've never been at the front. Our attention is focused on a large metal door as it creaks to life and draws up into the ceiling. We file in and step onto the cube patterns where our feet should go.

I study the lines that criss-cross the holding room, trying to get a sense of what shape it might be. I glance over at Kush and he shrugs. Isec is red-faced and panicked. "Isec, dammit, don't fucking crumble on me now, you understand? Stop it!"

He nods out a yes at me and takes a deep breath.

I look up at Kush as the rest of the people file in and take their spots on the pattern and he raises his eyebrows but says nothing.

Studying the lines again, I see the pattern. I've seen it before at least, but I cannot recall where. I search my memories but only come back with a vague reference to an early childhood education workbook.

It doesn't fit.

More and more people are shuffling around and Isec is doing some kind of meditation. "Isec!" He opens his eyes. "I'm only like six feet away, buddy. We'll do it together, OK?"

He smiles and the quiet of almost time pokes its head into the room.

What is this pattern?

Are you asking me?

I smile. *Absolutely. What's the pattern?*

The floor vibrates and my feet are stuck – I watch Isec lose it in real time.

It's a maze.

And then we are being rushed upward into battle.

Chapter Eighteen

One second I'm locking eyes with Isec's little flushed face.

And then the darkness envelopes us.

He's gone.

My eyes adjust and my night vision kicks in even as I lurch forward, and then slam into the mirrored wall that now separates the two of us. I stop, and the screams start. There is no one around me because I'm positioned in a small nook. I hear footsteps approach and I ready myself to attack.

They move slow and deliberate and I hear the hands dragging across the wall, trying to understand where they are.

No one else has night vision.

The hand stops when it gets to the edge of my nook and the green face on my vision screen is filled with panic. It's a girl, not that much older than Isec, and she's breathing so hard I swear she's gonna pass out. She waits, listening in my direction. Trying to decide if someone is there or not.

Screams around us jolt her into action and she runs forward, then slams into the wall and falls to the ground.

I step out and walk towards her. "Don't move. I'll pick you up, OK?"

She starts crying.

"Look, kid, if you cry I'll just kill you. I'm not in a great mood. I'll pick you up and you follow me, but stay out of the way, got it?"

She nods as I pull her to her feet. I place her hands on a belt loop at my waist. "Hold on, but if I start fighting you let go and drop to the floor, all right?"

She nods.

"Good, now no talking unless you're gonna save my life. Let's go."

Substituting for Isec already?

Shut the fuck up.

I know there are people fighting ahead of me and when I turn the corner I can see them flailing around in the dark. I reach for the SEAR because I'm in a hurry and Lucan can go fuck himself.

I walk up to them, within a foot or so, then push the little girl off me. She slumps to the ground as I flick my thumb over the tiny little imperfection on my weapon. The SEAR comes to life and faces all around look in my direction, stunned.

I cut them down with one elegant swoop of the blade and turn it off.

"Let's go."

"What was that?"

"Shut up and stay close."

We move forward and we repeat the action half a dozen more times. My score card is up to twenty-five when we turn the corner and find the honey hole. A large group of cowards is in control of a cache of weapons, swords mostly, but some small plasma knives too. I scan them and see they have night-vision goggles on as well.

I backtrack and pull the girl with me. "Lie down on the ground and do not move. You understand?"

She looks up at my face in the darkness, scared shitless.

"If they come near you, you don't move. Play dead."

"Where are you going?"

"To kill everyone I can to make the fucking fight stop. If those assholes are just going to stand there hoarding the weapons we'll be here all fucking day before we get down to seventy-five people."

I get down and crawl, sniper style, over bodies and through thick sticky puddles of blood until I reach the corner. I let my body drop to the ground and then, a fraction at a time, I push myself up so my eyes can look around the corner.

There are a lot fewer screams in the arena now. Which means people are hiding and not fighting.

I watch each of the guys, all pretty big, as they strut around in their eye gear. I've used night vision before, it's standard for night patrols. And there's one thing I know about them, they really fuck up your peripheral vision. I whistle and they all turn in my direction. I let them get a good look and then duck behind the wall and wait.

They argue and are just about ready to dismiss me when I hear my name mentioned.

I peek out and smile at them. "I'm gonna kill you," I whisper.

The dumb ones come at me and I step out when they are within reach and the SEAR blinks into existence, slices through all three necks before they can come to grips with what they're seeing, and everything goes dark again.

The others back away instinctively and I am thinking about how much trouble I will be in when this is over when I hear Isec scream somewhere beyond the group. They fling him out into the middle, then kick him in the head and I feel the heat rise up in my face.

I run at full speed and the first guy braces himself for contact when I flip up in the air, do a twist, and thrust my foot into the neck of his buddy behind him. He goes down choking as the SEAR comes out and slices off the hands of the first guy. He slumps down, writhing in pain from the metabolic effects of the weapon. For a few fractions I'm transfixed by the melting of his skin and connective tissues, but then I jolt myself up out of it and the SEAR finds a neck, then a leg, and then there is just me and Isec.

I pull him up and start stuffing weapons in his hands. "Isec, fucking snap out of it, take these, goddammit!" He does, stuffing them into his pants and shirt. "Keep one ready, Isec! Jasus, think, kid, or you're gonna die!"

He arms himself and pulls it together. I grab a pair of night goggles off one of the heads and slap them over his eyes so he can see. "Better?"

He nods.

"OK, look – everyone is hiding, trying to wait it out. But we'll be here all fucking day unless we go do some damage."

He nods at first, but then understands what I'm saying, and shakes his head instead.

"Yes, Isec. If you want to get out of here we have to go kill."

I pull him with me and start to follow the guys who ran. "You call out the clock from behind, OK?"

Silence.

I turn around and grab him by the neck. "Fuck, Isec, answer me when I'm giving you orders!"

"OK, Junco. I got it."

I let go of him and we move forward.

Vision screen, give me all the data you have on the arena.

It floods with so much data I can barely see. *Scale back to everything I need to know within twenty feet.*

The screen clears out enough for me to see, but it's still packed with shit. For one, the group of guys are huddled just around the second corner. "Keep up, Isec," I whisper, "we're going kamikaze. And if I catch you hiding or not using that knife to kill everyone you can, I'll kill you myself, Isec. You get that?"

"Yes, Junco."

"They're around the second corner, all of them. When I say go, we run full out and I'll make the first cut and you finish them off."

"OK."

"And stay the fuck out of the way of my SEAR knife, Isec. Unless you want to die a very hasty death. You stay back!"

He lets out a breath and I whisper, "Go!"

I run, making a lot of noise, and the first head pops out to take a look. I charge at him and he steps back behind the wall and I follow. Another guy grabs me from behind, holding my arms. I lean forward with all my weight and then double back-kick him in the shins as he holds me. He falls backward but his fingers are not ready to let go and make a mad grab, flailing out to grasp whatever is in reach. The pain in my wing almost overtakes me and then the blood is everywhere. I spin around and cut his torso in half, then turn back to find my first target. He's got a little plasma knife raised, thinking he's some kind of ancient warrior out on the steppe, but I slice open his gut from sternum to groin and he falls.

The rest run and I follow. At some point I look back and see Isec is gone, but I keep going, the data screen feeding me intel as I pass over hallways that have no bodies and stop to kill anyone who happens to be hiding in the others. Fucking cowards, if everyone went out and did their killing we'd be done by now. The screaming is back in full force and I'm just about to take off the heads of two tall girls when the buzzer sounds and the lights come on.

The walls drop into the floor and the fight is over.

I search, find Isec, search, find the little girl, search.

"Kush?" I yell it. "Kush!"

"Junco, over here."

I whirl around to find him. He's breathing hard and covered in blood, a sword in his hand dripping with blood.

He's alive.

And he did his killing.

"Exit to the right. Exit to the right. Exit to the right."

The voice keeps insisting, but I wait as Kush rushes towards me. My vision starts to waver and it's only then that I notice the blood is still pouring out of my damaged feathers, flooding the floor around my feet. I start to fall but Kush picks me up and leaps into the mast. I feel my body bounce as he rushes me across the dorm and when I finally force myself to take a look around he's tapping my finger on the cafeteria food machine. He places me on a table and my whole body is sticky and wet from the blood. He rolls me over on my stomach and lifts my wing and stretches it out. I lie still as he massages something into the broken feather shaft and then after a few minutes I hear a long sigh.

Kush leans down into my face. "Junco?"

I grunt, but don't speak. Just don't have the energy.

I taste his blood-covered fingers as he smears a paste across my lips and gums. "Swallow it, Junco."

I do.

I hear him pull up a chair and listen as Isec's small voice asks if I'm OK.

I want to wait and hear the answer, but the blackness takes over.

Chapter Nineteen

I come to with a sharp sting to my face. "Junco!"

"Shit, don't hit me, dammit."

I hear a laugh and when I open my eyes Kush is smiling down at me. "You're so lucky you're already Aves. You lost a lot of blood."

I try to sit up but fall back down. "Help me up, Kush."

He pulls me up so I'm sitting on the table and steadies me as I wobble back and forth for a few seconds. "What the hell happened?"

"Someone snapped two of your primary wing feathers."

I just stare at him and when he doesn't elaborate I shrug. "So?"

"Oh, OK. You don't know. You can pull them straight out and be fine, but break them down near the shaft and you bleed to death, Junco. It was a pretty dirty trick, but this is Fledge after all."

I turn to look behind me, then grab my left wing and pull it out to see the damage. My normally golden flecks are stained dark brown from dried and coagulating blood. Sure enough I have a gap where the two longest feathers near the tip used to be.

"I pulled them out, Junco. Then," he lifts up a food ration that has a small packet attached to the outside, "I used the extra starch from the mapolina packet to stop the bleeding. You just dunk the ends in there and it soaks up the blood and makes it clot."

"Mapolina?"

He holds up the packet. "You know, mapolina. That gross shit they feed us constantly because it's cheap."

I smile weakly. "OK, mapolina." I let my wing drop back down. "How did you know what to do?"

He grins. "Politicos, Junco. We come to the General Fledge on purpose. Train for it for years. They teach us shit, like how to use what's available for healing."

"Thank you, Kush. You saved my life I think."

"Nah, you were already healing yourself. And the color is already back in your cheeks, so you're making blood as we speak. I just sped it up a little, that's all."

"Well, thanks anyway. You're a good friend."

"Come on, let's go take a shower."

I walk out of the cafeteria with him but head over to the lounge area instead. "I'm gonna sit down for a while. I'll take a shower later."

He nods and walks off.

I sit in the lounge area to wait for the crowds to leave the showers because showering with Kush and Isec is not going to happen anymore. The news is on the screen and I fiddle with the controller until the sound comes up.

My giant face is plastered up next to Tier's.

"… due to testimony given several days ago, the former captain of the Aves 039, Raubtier, was cleared of one count of insubordination in the field. The second insubordination, failure to kill a target – referring to Junco Coot, the Sibling currently fighting her way through the General Fledge on Amelia – is still pending. Sources within Justice say they have no current plans to call her back for additional testimony and some have even accused her of manipulating the drugs and beating the detectors.

"In related news, another video feed has been filtered from Earth from the now infamous ex-Mountain Minute reporter Selia Manchen. Manchen went missing back in January after the Aves teams were evacuating when the war broke out. She later went on to join up with the Subjective armies. She's been an outspoken mouthpiece for Subjack ever since. This latest feed comes out of the Tetons where the armies are lying low, waiting for some undisclosed signal."

The images on the screen cut away and there's Selia wearing the same battered uniform as the one I saw her in earlier. She's interviewing soldiers and hunches down to a guy sitting on the ground, knees bent as he laces up his boots. "The system is watching, tell them what you're fighting against."

"The shadow government they have going here," is all he says.

"Explain. Most people who will see this don't understand what that is."

He stops what he's doing and looks up in the camera, straight into my eyes. "You've been lied to your entire life. It's not real," he says, swiping his hand around in the air. "The governments, the people in charge – they make the rules that you," his finger stabs at the camera, "have to follow. But they don't. I'm tired of it. I came all the way from the Western Utopia to fight here and I don't care what happens to us, they're going down."

Then his attention is back on his boots and Selia moves on.

She repeats this several times, and while each soldier says something a little different, they all have the same underlying theme. Lies. Manipulation. Fed up.

The screen cuts back to Tier's trial and I watch them question him under the drugs. When they ask him why he didn't kill me, he's silent for a long time. I hold my breath, afraid of what he'll say.

"She's one of us."

I let the air out and notice there are a lot of people around me now. I catch the eyes of a tall girl sitting in a chair near the couch and recognize her as one of the ones I almost killed at the end.

She shrugs at me. "No hard feelings, right?"

I nod. "Sure."

"Are you really from Earth?"

Everyone crowds in now and I look around to try and get a sense of the mood. Interested, maybe a little too interested. But no hostility. "Yeah. I was born and raised there."

"Are you really one of the Seven?"

I laugh. "Well, I guess it depends. I am one of seven individuals created in the Rural Republic with Aves genetics. But if you're asking me if I'm part of that myth you all have, the answer is no."

Another kid pipes up, not one I recognize, but he's tall as well. Darker like Arel. His shoulder-length black hair is wet and hints at curls. He reminds me of Tier. "So, they gonna kill him for disobeying, you think?"

I search his face to look for hidden meaning, but can't find any deception. "No. They are not."

He raises his eyebrows at me. "Well, I hate to break it to you, Junco, but they seem convinced otherwise."

I let out a breath. "Yeah, but…" I trail off for a second. "I'm not done fighting for him yet. You'll see."

"What is it like on Earth?" It's the little girl from the maze.

I smile at her and she sits down next to me, her hair a mess of wet ringlets and the smell of soap covering up the smell of SEAR death that still lingers in my nose. "When there's no war, it's pretty nice. Where I lived there was grasslands filled with wild animals and blue skies during the day and black skies at night. You don't have to go to an observatory to see the stars, either. You just walk outside and look up."

She grins up at me. The fearful face from the maze is gone.

Another boy appears, about the same age as the dark kid. "Were you a soldier or something? On Earth, Junco?"

I nod. "Or something. Yeah, my father was a commander in the RR. I was an as–" I hesitate as I watch their eyes wait for me to finish. These kids are not soldiers, I remind myself. They are only here to try and save themselves. "I was a specialist in the field. A sniper."

All their mouths make an O shape as I get up. "Well, time for my shower now. See ya."

I pass Isec on my way and he smiles and I have trouble reconciling him as the kid I was strapping bloody night-vision goggles on an hour ago. In the showers I look around for Kush, but he's gone. I stand under the hot water and let it beat the death off me, then scrub my body down until I rub it raw and wrap myself in my towel to face the cubbies.

Junco, Aves 039, is overflowing with shit. I start pulling it all out and open one bag after another. Clothes, shoes, soap, shampoo, a brush, a reader, a com, food, and other little bits of crap that try and convince me they all care.

I want to put the bed clothes on and go to sleep, but I have a feeling I'll be called away for using the SEAR in the fight. So I dress in uniform and even lace up the boots nice and tight. I pocket the comm and brush my long hair out until it is smooth. I'm not sure how, but I feel normal. I keep the food and then stuff the rest back in the cubbie before leaving the showers.

When I go back out almost everyone is over in the lounge area or in bed sleeping. I see Kush's head sticking up over the couch where I was earlier and walk that way. He's piled high with kids and I laugh and toss the food on the table nearby. He pushes Isec out of the way to make room and I slip in and rest against him.

Sigh.

And close my eyes.

Isten's voice draws me up from the depths of sleep. "What the fuck are you doing here, Junco? Playing house? Get the fuck up, we've got a meeting. Lucan wants to see the entire 039 immediately."

I sit up and rub my eyes. Isec and the little girl are sprawled out all over me and the rest of the dorm is quiet and still with weary fighters.

"What are you doing with these kids, Junco?" He paces back and forth, his heavy boots clunking on the tiles with each step. He looks a lot bigger and more intimidating than I remember from our poker game. His eyes shine yellow and target Kush. His wings go up slightly behind his shoulders in an offensive position. "And who the fuck is this guy?"

I push the kids off, get up and then walk away before he says something that will make me react. I'm just too tired. He trots to catch up with me and then keeps the pace so I have to trot to keep up with him. We walk outside and there's a flyer waiting.

"What's the meeting about?" I ask as we approach.

He huffs. "What the fuck do you think the meeting is about, Junco? You. They're always about you."

Chapter Twenty

It's bright outside and dark in the flyer, so it takes me a minute to see that everyone is crammed inside. I scoot in next to Rikan and Isten sits next to me. Braun is on the other side of Rikan slumped up against the window, not looking at anyone. Ashur is across from him, and then Mish, Arel, and Ryse.

No one says hi.

Fuck them.

I close my eyes and the rocking motion of the flyer lulls me to sleep. Several times Isten pushes me off his shoulder and Ryse kicks me when I start to snore, but I am too tired to care. I wake up when we stop and I'm sprawled out on the floor, their boots resting on me in various places.

Isten pulls me up and holds down a smile as I wipe the drool from my mouth.

I recognize Lucan's parking garage from the other night and everyone files through the doors into the building.

"What is this place?"

Arel is next to me so he answers. "Lucan's apartments."

"This is an apartment?"

"It's Aves headquarters too, so…"

Yeah, well, that explains everything, then. Thanks.

They take the stairs up several levels and I'm shuffling my feet and out of breath when I finally catch up with them. They start walking again, leaving me behind.

Assholes.

I turn the corner and bump into Ashur. "Sorry," I mumble. And keep walking. He stays behind me for the rest of the way. We meet up with the guys in the outer chambers of Lucan's offices. Some lady with no wings shows us into a conference room and says to wait.

The guys all take seats at the crescent-shaped table but I wait until Ashur points to the one next to him. "You're the nine, Junco, this is your chair."

Ryse is at the far left, Ashur is at the far right, and Braun is in the middle. Isten, myself, and an empty chair are situated between Ashur and Braun, while Arel, Rikan, and Mish are between Ryse and Braun.

I sense there is a method to this seating arrangement, but I don't see it.

Lucan enters in a rush. "Good afternoon, 039."

"Good afternoon," they say together.

I look up at Lucan. "Uh, good afternoon."

He smiles. "Junco, it's nice to have you at a meeting for once."

I scowl. "I've been busy, you know."

"Very busy," he agrees. "Which is why I'm wondering why you insist on breaking the rules and forcing me to take you off task."

I stare at him as the understanding creeps in. This is not a friendly chat, this is a military meeting and he is my commander. "Sir, I am fighting for my life in there and the SEAR is really not against the rules, in fact the rules state that only biological weapons can be used and my weapon certainly qualifies."

"Uh-huh. 039, do you agree that Junco should be allowed to use the weapon in her Fledge?"

They say various things but in general they agree. I get a smug look on my face.

"Well, if this were a democracy, Junco, you'd win, wouldn't you?"

I scowl at him.

"But this is not a democracy, this is the military and the 039 is my personal Aves team. Which means you are my personal soldier. And as such, you will do what I tell you. Is that clear?"

My eyes look straight ahead. "Yes, sir."

He smiles, happy with my obedience. "You make a much better soldier than you do a woman, Junco. Sorry, but it's true."

The guys let out little laughs as my face heats up, but Ashur cuts it off with a curt, "Enough."

"We will discuss your weapon after we conclude the team's business." He turns and takes a seat at the front of the room. "Oh, and by the way, good job staying alive today."

I mumble a "thank you, sir" and then the meeting begins.

Basically, they've cut Tier out. Ashur has been promoted to captain, Ryse to XO, and Braun to the up position. Which, from what

I can gather through conversation, means he is training to be a pilot and then he will eventually go through officer school like Ryse just did.

Braun doesn't strike me as officer material, not because he's not competent, but because he's got a little too much rebel in him. He doesn't look particularly happy either. He stands and gives a report on the status of his training and then slumps down in the straight-backed chair. Ryse and Ashur give reports on what the rest of the team are doing. Isten will be guarding some local big-shot in town for the night and the others are just on patrols in places I've never heard of.

Lucan's attention comes back to me. "Junco, report on your status."

I stand. "Well, I killed, uh–" I stop to count them up in my head. "Fifty-two people today." Then I blow out some air and try to explain my injury. "Someone broke my feathers and Kush had to help me again." And then I sit back down.

"Nothing else to report?"

I groan and stand up again. My chair scrapes against the tile and the noise makes me wince. "Sir, I took a shower and a nap."

"Two naps," Isten corrects me. "She slept on the floor of the flyer on the way over."

The guys all think this is funny, but I ignore them.

"Did you eat?"

Oh, fuck. If they start up with me about eating again–

"Junco? Did you eat?"

"Not yet, but–"

"Ashur, the team will make sure she eats before escorting her back to Fledge."

"Yes, sir."

Now it's my turn to slump down in my chair. They make me feel like a child. It doesn't help that I look like a child next to them. Even Arel is giant next to me. They talk about stuff I don't understand for another twenty minutes and then everyone but Ashur and me is dismissed.

Lucan begins talking before Rikan can close the door behind him. "Junco, what does it mean to be a captain in your Earth military?"

"It's a middle-rank officer."

"Here," he continues, "it is not a middle rank. It is the highest rank – under the Archers, do you understand?"

"I get the point, if that's what you mean."

"That is not what I mean, do you understand how we rank our military?"

"No."

"I'll send you a file that you can study."

"Send it to me where?"

"You have your com, correct? My vision display says it is on your person."

I scrunch my eyebrows together and he sighs. "Yes, we track you with it. But at least we don't implant it in your body."

I reach into my thigh pocket and pull out the flexible card and put it on the table.

"Good. Ashur will program it for you before you are dropped off and I will send you information that way."

"Yes, sir."

"Were you allowed to disobey your commanders on Earth, Junco?"

"No, sir."

"Will you disobey Ashur?"

I look at Ashur. "No, sir."

"Wonderful. Ashur, you may wait outside."

I let out a giant groan and both heads snap back and show annoyance at my grumbling.

When Ashur is gone Lucan walks over to a terrace on the far end of the room. "Come here, Junco. The meeting is over and you are free to speak."

The doors slide open as we approach and the noise of the city bombards my ears. There are flyers going by at eye level and the city lights are all on now that the afternoon is winding down.

He leans against the balcony railing and so do I, suddenly feeling weary. "Everyone knows who you are now, thanks to that woman on Earth, so you may continue to use the SEAR if the situation requires it."

"Thanks."

"I'm afraid you've misunderstood what the General Fledge is about, though, Junco. You see, you're making a few mistakes and Ashur is worried about how they will affect your chances for success."

I groan again and wait it out.

"You're collecting children? To protect during the battles?"

I shake my head. "That's not exactly true, Lucan. I'm not collecting them, it's just I've grown fond of Isec, and the little girl today – it was just too much. She's just a kid."

"You're not doing them any favors, Junco. Even if those kids make it because of you, they'll be killed in the Aves for not being strong enough. It's futile what you are doing."

I shrug. "I'm not going to stop."

"You'll disobey?"

I look him straight in the eye. "Yeah, I will."

He pauses to see if I'll add anything to that statement, but I don't. "Here's where I think you're getting confused, Junco. You're already an extremely well-trained soldier so you've been taught from an early age, a very early age I've heard, that you're a member of a team. This is what makes a good soldier, you have that cohesive property in you. I get it. If you were in the Aves Fledge, you'd be part of a team, that is a major difference between the General Fledge and the Aves Fledge."

He stops and looks at me until I nod. "OK."

"The General Fledge has no teams, Junco. And you keep insisting on trying to build one out of these throwaways."

"That's not what this is about, Lucan." I lean over and rest my hands on the top rail, then sink my head down on them and close my eyes. "I just can't kill the little ones." I look up again and study his face, but he's stoic. "And I'm not killing Isec. I'm not."

"Well, this is interesting. Because, you know, we all feel that way about you, Junco. Very protective."

I have to admit, this catches me off guard.

He smiles. "Of course, you're highly qualified, and there's the difference. Tier was correct when he refused to kill you. Because you're the perfect Aves warrior."

I put my head down again.

"These kids will not make it, Junco. They will not."

I stay silent and wait for it.

"However, if it will make you happy, I will have Ashur and the men train them for you."

I look up and smile. "You will?"

"But they will still die, Junco."

I nod.

"And the end will not shift. You will still end up in the same place. Recall that I told you before that the time to change the outcome was past?"

I nod.

"You will still hate me in the end, Junco. But it wasn't me who put you here. It was Tier. And it was you."

"I get the feeling that you know a lot more about what's going on than I do."

"That is the understatement of the millennium. You know nothing. And now," he turns back to the apartment, "this conversation is over. I will send Kush a personal thank you. Goodbye."

The guys are all waiting for me outside and none of them look happy about it. "Finally," Ryse says. I try to catch Braun's eye but he ignores me. They all shuffle out the doors and again, I'm last. I walk out and find Ashur waiting for me around the corner. He lets me pass and then takes up the rear.

We get food to go from the cafeteria and pile in the flyer. I eat whatever it is they hand me and it's not bad. When we finally reach the Fledge building I get out and they close the door and issue half-hearted goodbyes.

And then I am alone.

And for the first time in a very long time, I feel lonely.

I lie down in the grass and look up at the ceiling and puff on a cigar. A little while later I hear wings and turn to see Ashur landing on the sidewalk.

"I forgot to program your com, Junco." He sits down next to me and I hand it over. He hands it back a few minutes later. "Are we good?"

"I guess. I mean, you're the captain, right?"

"That's not how the 039 works, Junco. We're tight. Perfect."

"What do you want me to say? I forgive you? I do. I doubt I've ever had a real moment of privacy in my life. Why should I care about one more person watching me? It's absurd."

He pulls me next to him and wraps me in his wings. "I'm sorry, OK?"

I squirm in his arms but he doesn't let me go. "I was never really mad about you watching me, Ashur. It doesn't matter."

"Then what's your deal, Junco?"

I look up at him. "I'm not in control of *anything*. I mean, yeah, soldiering is something I can do. But no one asked me if I wanted to be a soldier here. Or on Earth for that matter. I get that I have to do the Fledge thing, that's not an option if I want to stay. But don't I ever get a say?"

"I never got a say. Tier never got a say. None of us did."

"Yeah, but maybe I'd rather be a woman than a soldier. Did you guys ever think of that?"

His eyes search mine. "Would you really? Is that why you're sleeping with that Kush guy?"

I laugh. "I'm not sleeping with Kush. Don't be ridiculous."

"There's been reports that you spent last night with him up in the observatory."

"Well, yeah. But I was sleeping. Not fucking him."

He chokes on his laugh. "Junco, soldiers talk like that, not women."

I shrug and chew on a fingernail.

He's silent for a few minutes and I wait patiently. "It's just a job, Junco. And compared to some jobs on this stupid habitat, it's a damn good one. Like I said when you first came out of morph, you can have it made here. You just have to give it a chance and try to follow *some* directions."

This, I think, might be the crux of the problem. "I want to go back to Earth, Ashur. The thought of staying here forever makes me–" I stop and shake my head without finishing.

He hugs me tighter. "I get it. We'll go back, I promise."

"How can you promise that?"

"Because we never finished our job. We still have four Siblings to find. Believe it or not, we spent a lot of time on you. Years, Junco – you and Moju both, actually. You two really sidetracked us big time." He stops and pushes me away, then pulls me up on my feet with him. "When Fledge is over we'll do something else, OK?"

I nod. "OK. Thanks. I'll see you later." There's just nothing good going to come of any of this and there's no room for regrets because I chose this path. It's move forward or die.

Chapter Twenty-One

I don't get more than a few paces inside Fledge before my comm beeps. I pull it out of my pocket and stare at the screen. I don't get it. It doesn't say anything, just has some symbol flashing at me. I shove it back in my pocket and start walking towards the stairs when Lucan appears and scares the shit out of me.

"Jasus, Lucan."

"You will ignore my file?"

I stare at him. "What? File?"

He points to my pocket. "The file I just sent you."

I fish the comm back out of my pocket and stare at it again. "I don't know how to use this thing. I never had my own comm on Earth."

He reaches out and I hand him the com. "Come here and sit, I'll show you."

"I'm tired, Lucan. Can't we do this–"

"Sit."

I take a seat on the bench he's motioning to and he sits next to me, then his fingers move across the comm screen and things move and flash and generally do all sorts of stuff. Then a hologram bursts into the air in front of us. Lucan's holographic head is rotating in the air. He's smiling.

I laugh and look over to him.

"What's funny?"

I laugh again. "That fake smile on your fake head."

He ignores me and his fingers begin interacting with the hologram like they were with the com. His head flashes and then eight more heads appear.

"These are my sitting Archers. The most important of which are Rache, the Archer of Justice. And Gib, the Archer of Clutch. Together the three of us run all the worlds in the Band."

"I thought you were the one in charge?"

"I am, but I am not a dictator. I can override them if they disagree with the actions I want sanctioned, but if they gather enough support they can override me." He looks over to me. "That has never happened. We work well as a team."

His finger sweeps around the circle of Archers and then a bazillion more appear, taking up space far out into the room. "There are many Archers and each runs something that keeps our worlds together and each reports to me." He removes the other less important Archers and only he remains. His fingers make Tier appear. "I have not updated this yet. Ashur is here now. The 039 is my personal team to use as I see fit. Each of the eight higher-ranking Archers has a team for this purpose." He taps Tier's head and then the entire 039 appears, including me. We all rotate in a small circle around Tier with a rank above our heads. Ashur, then Ryse, then Braun, Isten, Rikan, Mish, Arel, and me. There's a nine floating above my head.

"Huh."

"You have a question?"

"I just think it's," I stop and choose the correct word, "interesting that you updated my status on that little chain of command, yet you left Tier in place."

He smiles but doesn't address my remark. "You report to Ashur now. And if Ashur is not around you report to me. Or Ryse or your other team members. If you need something you come to one of us. No one else is above you. You cannot command the personal teams of other Archers, but if you command any of the regular military warriors, they will accommodate you, within reason. If they do not, they will have to answer for it. You speak for me."

"That's a lot of power for someone you barely know." I look up at him and study his face.

"Tier gave you a rank of 039-9. I could undo it, but why? I don't see any reason to prohibit your rank. From what I've been told and what I've seen, duty is something you take seriously."

Every time I see Lucan his opinion of me seems to change. Which is funny, because I seem to be revising my opinion of him on a regular basis as well. Do I take my duty seriously? I have no idea to be honest.

His fingers move around once more and then the entire room is filled with avian warriors, they take up space in every direction, piled up to the ceiling, one on top of another. I look through the window and see them stretching far out past the train tracks. "This is my military."

I cannot even begin to think of the number represented by these floating faces. "How many?"

"Fifteen million active warriors. A third of which are based on the other tori below Amelia proper. But they are also spread out in the Band where they are needed. There are millions more. Inactive warriors who have moved on to something else, but are still available if necessary."

"Why?"

"Why what?"

"Do you have such a large military?"

"It is not necessary for you to have that answer right now, Junco, but they represent a very small percentage of our overall population. It is not that unusual. Do you have any more questions?"

"How many avians are there? In all?"

"Billions, Junco."

"Where do you keep them all?"

He smiles. "That is the central issue of these times. Where do we keep them all? The simple answer is we cannot keep them all. This is why we have Fledges. Any more questions?"

I look away. I'm not sure I like where this conversation is headed. "No, I guess not."

The military collapses back into my comm and we sit there in silence for a few moments. "I'm sorry this has been hard on you." He stands up and I follow. "I am trying to make it as easy as I can."

I look up at him. "Why? You didn't even want me to stay."

"That's not true at all, Junco." He puts a hand on my shoulder. "Expect Ashur tomorrow. Goodnight."

And then he's gone.

I shake my head to clear things up, but I'm more confused than ever. I walk up the stairs slowly and then change into my bed clothes and fall asleep without speaking to anyone.

Something wakes me. A small sound of feet on tile. I sit up and look around. Isec's bed is empty. Maybe he just went to the bathroom? Another noise out past the lounge area has my feet on the cold tile, covering the distance to the mast in my bed clothes.

I look up and see a flash, high up on the sixth level.

I hesitate because my skills are so raw, but curiosity takes over and my powerful new limbs carry me upward. It's not a snappy ascent, like Kush's was, and it's definitely not pretty or graceful. By the time I get to the fifth level I have to stop and climb up the ragged walls covered in relief art. Ultimately, I find myself swinging out under the sixth-level platform for several seconds before I force myself to let go and flap like mad just to make the landing. I lean against a large wooden door to catch my breath, and then look up. There's a symbol over it that leaves no mistake as to what is contained within.

It's a church.

I lean my weight into the door and it opens in front of me. There's a vestibule with a statue of some presumably important winged person. The door behind me closes with a shush of air and I push through the second one.

And stand there stunned. "Holy fucking shit," actually escapes my mouth as I take in the altar.

"Junco, what are you doing here?"

I whirl around and find Isec plastered up against the far wall. "I saw you."

"You scared me."

I smile at him. "Sorry."

"You're not supposed to swear at the syrinx."

I nod in the direction of the upside-down avian woman hanging on the crucifix at the far end of the church. "That her?"

He nods. "Yeah, you're not–"

"I get it, Isec, sorry. It's just – the whole image, from an Earth religious point of view is just – wrong."

He frowns at me. "Oh, how so?"

"The symbols, they're backwards. It's nothing, just cultural differences, but seeing someone hanging upside down from the crucifix just goes against the grain."

"What's that mean?"

I shake my head. "Wrong, is all."

He walks forward out of the little space filled with avian iconery and chooses a bench about halfway between front and back and takes a seat.

I slip in next to him. "So, what are you doing here?"

"Praying, Junco."

"What do you have to do to make her listen?"

He looks at me funny. "Pray, Junco."

"Oh. Well, does she have special prayers?"

"Yeah, but I'm not wasting my time teaching them to you, so don't ask me. They're printed on the cards in the back. Now leave me alone, I'm busy."

I get up and go back to the little nook he was hiding in and grab some cards, then slump down on the floor and pour through them.

Calm Ion Storms? I chuck the stiff little card at the wall next to me and move on to the next one.

Fledge Protection? Chuck it.

Fearlessness? Chuck it.

Clear Thinking? Chuck.

Acceptance of Fate? I look at the picture for a long time because it's the syrinx on the altar, then flip it over to read the prayer.

Out of the night that covers me,
Black as the pit from pole to pole,
I thank whatever gods may be
For my unconquerable soul.

In the fell clutch of circumstance
I have not winced nor cried aloud.
Under the bludgeonings of chance
My head is bloody, but unbowed.

Beyond this place of wrath and tears
Looms but the Horror of the shade,
And yet the menace of the years
Finds and shall find me unafraid.

It matters not how strait the gate,
How charged with punishments the scroll,
I am the master of my fate:
I am the captain of my soul.

It's a straight ripoff of Henley's Invictus. And yet so unquestionably appropriate it could have been written for me, for this very moment. I look up when Isec approaches.

"Did you find one?"

I breathe out my words. "Yeah. It's a poem from Earth, too. Isn't that weird?"

He smiles. "She sends you what you need, Junco. I'm going back to bed, you coming?"

"Nah, I'll be along in a little bit, OK?"

He nods and leaves me alone.

I get up and go sit down on a bench up front and stare at the sacrificial woman. Her left foot is bound to a vertical wooden post. The horizontal post is situated across the top of the vertical post, so it's more of a T shape than a cross. Her right leg is bent, splayed out behind her. Her arms reach back, touching her outspread wings, and her head is tipped so her eyes look down and not forward, exposing her throat. Her long red hair trails on the ground.

Syrinx.

I search my memory for a meaning and come up with two possibilities:

The voice organ of a bird.

A water nymph in ancient Greece.

I close my eyes and say the prayer out loud from recall. When I'm finished I add my own silent personal touch. *Please let me accept my fate with courage. Let me be brave in the end.*

My vision screen comes to life. *Do you wish to accept the sacrifice?*

I don't understand.

Do you wish, Junco Coot, Aves 039, to accept the sacrifice required to fulfill your prayer?

Who are you?

Is that a no?

Wait. I accept.

The screen blanks out and I have a bad feeling about what I just did. I stuff the card in the waistband of my bed shorts and leave the church, more unsettled than when I came in. I get to the ledge and realize I have to jump if I want to get down. Either that or wait until everyone wakes up and ask someone to come rescue me. I pull out the card and stare at the last part again.

It matters not how strait the gate,
How charged with punishments the scroll,
I am the master of my fate:
I am the captain of my soul.

And I jump, Cygnus-style, into the pit.

Chapter Twenty-Two

"Get up now!"

Ashur's voice booms in my ears and I jump up with a start.

But he's not talking to me, he's talking to them.

Isten sits on my bed and pushes me back down. "Not you, Junco, you're with me today."

I watch as Isec is dragged up and pushed over next to the little girl. The tall girl I almost killed in the last fight is in line, as is the guy who reminds me of Tier and his friend who asked if I was a soldier.

Ashur is screaming at them from the front while Ryse, Arel, Mish, and Rikan lean in from behind to add choice words. The little kids stand there looking like they will piss themselves at any second. Ashur comes to Kush, who yawns with his eyes closed, and then pivots without saying anything and goes back to screaming at Isec and the little girl who has given up her name between sobs.

Kete.

"You are nothing! Nothing, do you understand?" He bends down to Isec and Kete and they step back with a start, but Rikan pushes them forward.

I make to get up, but Isten pushes down on my chest. "You wanted this, Junco. Now butt the fuck out."

"Isec," Ashur growls, "when you understand that your only reason for living right now is to make my nine happy, we'll get along and be just fine. Do you understand that?"

Isec, to his credit, looks up and meets his gaze. "Yes, sir."

"If you live through this Fledge and she doesn't – I'll kill you in your sleep. Do you understand?"

Isec swallows and nods.

"Your only purpose in life right now is to hope you have a chance to give up your worthless life for her promising one. Do you understand?"

"Yes, sir."

He moves on to Kete, who breaks down and cries. "You'll be the next one to die if you don't stop that fucking crying. You think I'm your clutch mother, Kete?"

She can't answer and Ashur moves on to the tall girl.

"What's your name and excuse for being here, girl?"

She takes a large gulp of air. "Tessen, sir. I quit my Cluster."

Ashur scowls at her. "You quit? You're a quitter? I hate quitters. Junco's not a quitter, she talked the fucking President into making the 039 train you, you sorry excuse for a soul. If you quit on me…" He extracts his razors and they are as long as short swords. "I'll take you out to a docking bay and throw you into oblivion. Am I clear?"

Tessen nods. "Yes, sir."

He moves on to the boy who asked me if I was a soldier yesterday. He's older, not as old as Kush, but Ashur passes him by after getting his name, Joll.

The last boy is Wyrd and Ashur leans down into his face. "I don't think I like you, Wyrd. You look like you think you can take me. Can you take me, Wyrd?"

Wyrd squints his eyes. "No, sir. I don't think that *at all.*"

Ashur paces back the other way and Kete starts to cry again. He stops in front of her, and then looks over to me and his voice is back to normal. "Junco, sorry – I'm gonna go out on a limb here and predict this one will not make it."

He moves on to Isec. "I'd pick you to die as well, Isec. But since Junco always puts you first, she'll save your ass yet again."

He moves on to Kush. "You're the only one I'd take home."

He tracks back to Tessen. "You'd do if no one else was available." She looks at him and smiles, but he cuts her down. "That's not a compliment, Tessen."

He walks all the way back to Wyrd. "You come from Science?" Wyrd looks at him and nods. "We'd keep you for that and that only, then. But it's not a bad job, if you can get it."

He tracks back to Joll. "I don't see it in you, to be honest. Have you killed anyone in these fights, Joll?" Joll's eyes go wide and he shakes his head. "Well, at least you didn't lie."

Ashur walks over to my bed and rolls his eyes when the others can't see. "Is this it, then, Junco? Your team?"

I shrug. "Thank you."

He pulls me up from the bed and gives me a hug and leans down to whisper in my ear, "We're good now, right? You'll love us again if we do this?"

I push back and look up at him. "We're perfect."

Ashur looks to Ryse. "Take them up to training while I talk to Isten and Junco."

The screaming begins anew and then they are gone.

Ash sits down on the bed and he pulls me between him and Isten. "OK, Junco – you're gonna fly up and down the mast today with Isten. Things get vertical from here and you'll need new skills for the rest of the fights." He leans past me to see Isten. "Make her walk around in the observatory, Is. That will probably help with Fight Four, don't you think?"

Isten nods. "Yeah, I'll make it relevant."

Ashur looks back to me. "And don't fuck about, Junco. The levels are nothing like you've had or think they will be, so don't get complacent. Besides, if you die I'll have to kill all those pledges, and we wouldn't want that, would we?"

I smile. "I owe you. I know this is purely for my benefit."

Ash's face softens. "I get it, Junco. You have a big heart for someone who has probably killed more people than Is and me together. Just don't expect them to actually live, OK?"

I nod.

"Except for Kush. He might make it."

My eyebrows go up. "Really?"

He shrugs. "I think so, yeah."

And then he kisses me on the head and walks out.

I look over at Isten and my face gets hot. "He likes you, Junco. Whatever you said to him last night after we dropped you off," he hesitates and shakes his head, "made him *very* fucking happy."

I track back to find what it might be as I dress in my uniform. But only one thing stands out.

I didn't sleep with Kush.

Isten and I spend the entire day in the mast. At first I can barely manage it. Oh, it's not bad going from level three to level four. Or even level four to level five. But the span of space between five and six is just as enormous today as it was last night. I end up clinging to an aging architectural detail on the side of the wall before Isten comes to my rescue. This happens several times, actually. Then the flight from six to seven feels insurmountable and he has to tow me up in the light G to even make it to the observatory the first time. I can only imagine the horror inside these massive levels to require such vertical expansion.

And then he makes me fly down in a dive that reminds me of ancient dogfights. The first time Isten has to grab my uniform shirt and yank me back up to him so I don't splat on the hard stone floor. He makes me glide down slowly after that.

From the bottom we start the process all over again and I struggle back up, gradually with each assent I manage to go a little further. But in no way would I ever be considered an expert flier.

We're resting on the platform underneath the observatory when Isten catches me eyeing the church. "You want to go in there or what, Junco? You've been staring at the place the whole day."

I soar down to the sixth-level platform and land clumsily in front of the large door. I wait there until Isten reluctantly follows. "I went in last night." I wait to see his reaction, but he holds it in. "I prayed to her."

Isten laughs. "She's not real, Junco."

I shrug. "I found these prayer cards in the back, right? And the one I chose was called *Acceptance of Fate*." I look up at him. "It was an old Earth poem. Don't you think that's weird?"

He shakes his head. "So they stole some poetry from Earth? That sounds typical to me."

"I was raised in church, did you know that?"

He smiles. "Yeah, I know. But this isn't your religion anyway, so don't waste your time. This is some really old-ass shit, Junco. Before Crag and Inanna, before all the Seven Siblings. She's ancient – something else entirely."

"So why does she have a church here?"

He steps off the ledge and flies upward to the observatory before calling back to me, "Who cares? Let's go practice walking in the gravity curve."

I flap frantically to make it up to the top one more time, but no matter how hard I try Isten has to push me the remaining hundred yards. I step onto the landing and we climb the steps together.

Chapter Twenty-Three

I don't close my eyes when we enter and I'm immediately sorry because this shit is just wrong. I can't tell what is up and what is down and my head begins to spin.

"Close your eyes, Junco." I do and things calm down. My feet float up off the ground and I feel my stomach lurch. "Keep them closed, then when you're ready open them and decide where is up and where is down, OK?"

I nod.

"There are couches all around us."

"I know."

"Oh, I forgot you spent the night with Kush up here."

I huff out some air. "I did not sleep with Kush, Isten. Fuck, you guys think I sleep with everyone."

He laughs. "Not true. Anyway, just pick a couch and then I'll follow you."

I open my eyes and choose up, then use my wings to adjust my body a little and pick a new up. I head for a couch and stand next to it.

Isten comes up next to me and pushes me back and then gravity takes hold and I'm lying down, not standing.

It's still weird.

He climbs in next to me. "You know what this place is for, Junco?"

I shake my head. "Well, I'd guess it's to look at the stars, but something tells me that's not right."

He lets out a little laugh. "Technically, of course it is to look at the stars, but Fledge is filled with superstitions and the observatory is one of them. People come up here to be reminded about how little they matter in the universe."

"That's dumb."

"Just listen. You're supposed to come up here with someone you love, which is why we jumped to conclusions with Kush. Anyway, you're supposed to cling to each other and tell each other stories about your life. Did he tell you stories, Junco?"

I shake my head. "No, we fell asleep."

"Oh, well, he blew it. But I'm not gonna." He pulls me close. "I fully intend on telling you stories."

I laugh. "Yeah, like what? Not a myth, I hope." I look up at him questioningly.

"No, my first kill."

"Oh."

"I can't get the image of you out of my mind, Junco. Six years old and being sent on missions like that."

"So how old were you?"

He smiles down at me. "Eight."

"That's pretty young too."

"Yeah, but I wasn't told to do it, I just lost my temper."

"At eight? You lost your temper and killed someone?"

"I was on Earth with my foster family. They send us at five, you know that right?"

I nod. "Tier told me about his."

Isten sits up a little at this. "Really?"

I nod. "It was the quick version, he said."

He's silent for a few moments, like I caught him off guard. "Well, I wasn't supposed to be killing anyone, I was just supposed to live with this family until I got called back. Usually it takes about ten years before they want you back to Fledge. But I saw something and when I tried to tell someone about it, you know, to make it stop, they didn't believe me."

"What did you see?"

"My foster brother molesting my little sister."

"Oh, shit."

"Yeah, so I followed him one day and took a rifle with me. My family had guns all over the house, ya know. This was Texas. Anyway, I followed him out to this pasture where he was fucking around with another girl, his own age this time at least, and I shot him in the head while they were getting it on. I got away with it too, on Earth anyway. Hid in the bushes, the girl never saw me, got home before anyone noticed, cleaned the gun, put it back. It was pretty fucking simple. But I confessed in my next report and they pulled me. Called me home to Fledge out early."

"Well, I'd be proud of that kill, Isten. At least you helped someone."

He looks over at me and grins. "Do you know who you killed that day on the slopes, Junco?"

I shake my head. "No, I never did ask."

"Well, we looked it up after you told us that. And it was the President and First Lady of Sovienna. They were some fucked-up people, so if that memory ever gives you nightmares, well, I can show you what they did to children for decades before you showed up and put a stop to it."

"Hmm. I don't have nightmares anymore, Isten. They're all gone."

"That's great, Juncs. But if they ever come back, you gotta ask yourself if it's worth it, right? Because from what I can tell, you killed a lot of very bad people over your career."

I lean into him a little.

"Anyway, when I got back to Amelia they put me in a holding status, because you can't go out in the regular population until you Fledge, you have to stay in the clutch. But it just so happens that there were like sixty other guys in the hold with me. All guys who had fucked up their fosters for whatever reason or another. It was like an epidemic that year, they checked the food supply and all kinds of things even, that's how weird it was.

"So, they had to have a special Fledge to make room – we call it the Fuck-up Fledge. I was in the Fuck-up Fledge and so was everyone else in the 039. Tier, for killing his father. Ashur for killing a teacher at school. They were the oldest and most experienced." He laughs. "They were both twelve."

"So you all Fledged out together? And you all survived it?"

"Well, we didn't know each other at first. When we got to 313–"

"What's 313?"

"Oh, it's the asteroid that hosts the Aves Warrior Fledge. It's got like half an atmosphere, after a thousand years of terraforming if you can believe it, but very thin. You have to wear suits or you'll die within hours."

"Did you have to kill each other?"

He looks down on me. "Nah, Juncs. We have to work as a team, to survive the shit on 313. Poisons, weather patterns, orbital fire – shit like that."

"And you all, the 039, were all on the same team?"

"No, see, this is how it works. They airdrop us all off – like I said, there were sixty of us or so. Then you have to get from one end of the asteroid to the other before your air and supplies wear out. So, when you get there you're not a team, right? Just a bunch of guys. But if you make it to the end, the guys you make it with – that's your team. The conditions create the winners, get it? Create the team."

I nod.

"And we were the ones who lived. Me, Arel, Ryse, Rikan, Braun, Mish, Ashur, and Tier. That was it. Out of sixty guys. We were the only ones left."

"And how did Tier become captain?"

Isten smiles. "He's the strongest, the most ruthless, the smartest. And the most reasonable, caring, and hopeful. He's the perfect fucking Aves warrior, Junco – they were talking about making him Archer. So they gave him the command. He saved every one of us during Fledge. We owe him every second of life we've lived since we were kids."

"And you'll just let him be killed, Isten?"

He frowns. "We're doing what we can."

"It's not enough."

"Maybe not, but that's what we've got." He stays silent for a few minutes, perhaps he's mad at me for questioning him. Or maybe he's just thinking. Eventually he gets back around to our conversation. "You know why Lucan didn't send you to the Aves Warrior Fledge even though it started at the same time?"

I shake my head.

Isten pushes me back a little so he can see my face. "Because, Junco, if you went through all that shit with another group of guys, you wouldn't belong to us anymore. You'd belong to them. You'd make your own team and not be part of our team. And Lucan couldn't stand to let you go. He said that, Junco. To each of us. That's why we're worried about these kids you're helping. It's not supposed to be this way. There are no teams in the General Fledge. You're not supposed to bond with them. You're *our* nine. You understand what it means to be the nine?"

I shake my head. "No."

"The team hardly ever gets to nine. I mean, it does happen, but it's so rare, no one even thinks about having nine – not including your science contact, right? Layla is our science contact, but she's not a part of the team because that only includes us warriors. To have a real ninth member is special. It's powerful. It carries a lot of meaning around here. And you're the nine. We voted you in and even Lucan agreed."

"Only as long as we include Tier, and he's gonna be found guilty, I'm told. For not killing me. And Lucan will let him die."

"He's doing what he can, Juncs. He really is."

"Tier hates what he is, you know that right?"

Isten is quiet now.

"He told me, quote, *I feel like I've lived a hundred lifetimes of misery. And when I wake up each morning I don't want to keep doing it, Junco. When I wake I ask myself, how much longer before they will just let me die?* Unquote."

"But, Junco, he saved you because he wanted you. He wanted you to be with us. We talked about it for years. You can't even comprehend how much planning went into making the decision to disobey and get you here."

"Except Tier will not be here so I won't be the nine for long, will I? That's pure bullshit, Isten. Just let me do it my way."

He sucks in his breath. "Junco, do you have any idea of the cost?" He looks at me, the fun gone, the pain in full force. "It's higher than you might think. It's higher than anything you can imagine. And don't fucking pray to that stupid Fallen Archer again, either. For fuck's sake, that's all we need, her sacrificial spirit fucking things up at the very last fucking second."

When we fly back down the pledges are already back in the dorm and Ashur is watching the screens, waiting patiently. Isten says goodbye and leaves, while I go sit down next to Ash. "How'd it go?"

He smiles. "You first."

"Pretty good, I guess. My flying will not win trophies, but it'll have to do." I smile back, but my heart's not in it.

"They did OK, Junco. Kush is pretty good and Wyrd is all right. The girl, Tessen, could be helpful. But that little Kete, she won't be back tomorrow night." He looks at me hard. "And I do not want you to save her, you understand?"

I nod. "What about Joll?"

"Oh, shit. That kid is beyond useless. I have no idea how he survived so far."

We sit in silence for a while, watching some movie on the screen. Ashur must like horror shit, because it's another screaming half-naked girl running from some crazy demonic thing.

"You wanna go get some food, Junco?" He looks over at me, his face kind.

"Sure." I smile. "We can do that."

We grab a train back to that pub we were at before and it's like our fight never happened. We eat and talk about stuff that has nothing to do with Tier, or the Fledge, or death.

And it's nice.

Normal.

Chapter Twenty-Four

There are no patterns on the floor this time. Instead the Fourth Fight begins with all seventy-five of us being stuffed, one at a time, inside capsules. When someone gets in the lid slides shut and the capsule is shuttled somewhere out of sight. I look at Isec to see how he's taking it, but he's calm. Calmer than I've ever seen him in fact. I squeeze his shoulder as we wait our turn. "You doing OK?"

He smiles back at me. "Yeah, sure. Why?"

I shrug. "Well, usually you're freaking out. And this is completely different from all the other starts."

"I feel good, Junco. No matter what happens, I'm OK with it."

I nod. "All right." He turns away from me and I let out a sigh. They grow up so fast. I have a feeling Ashur has something to do with this, but whatever it is, I'm grateful. He's come to terms with the fights, and that's a good thing.

I think.

Kete is first to be stuffed in the capsule. She's screaming like the spring wind on the prairie. I don't move to calm her. I believe Ashur, she's done and there's no sense in making it worse.

Tessen is next and she gets in without incident.

Isec is next and he turns. "See you when we're done, Junco."

I smile. "Fight hard, friend."

He climbs in and lies back and before I know it he's shuttled up and out of view.

My capsule comes and I climb in, settle on the hard pad, and watch the capsule close above me. It moves fast and jerks from side to side. The capsule stops and is loaded into some mechanism below. Then I hear a loud click and everything goes still, the only sound my own breathing.

We were near the front, so the wait takes forever.

And then I'm accelerating hard. I feel the bullet catch on something below my back and my feet slam into the floor of the capsule and I'm shunted out of the tube and into free-G. I twist in the air and create back thrust with my wings to slow myself down. I hear screams as people smash into the wall and then the smell of burning flesh.

They've been electrocuted.

For a moment I'm stunned still, and then I see her. Dead, her mouth open, her eyes wide, and she's wet herself. Kete is finished before the fight even starts.

I snap out of it and begin killing as I pass through the air. I leave the SEAR tucked away. No sense in complicating things unless I have to. Enough people are dead from the launch.

I swim though the air and take stock of what's happening here.

There is a single transparent partition that divides the arena into left and right halves. Except it is better described as top and bottom. Except that doesn't work either, because the gravity well is on the surface of the partition. Towards the floor, except the floor is relative.

It's a mirror image.

I swim down to my floor and get my feet planted on the ground. Only one other fighter has made it so far so I charge towards him as he shouts encouragement to a friend. I swipe my razors over his throat and he falls dead just as his buddy is floating down towards me. I grab him by the leg and swing. He goes careening off and hits the wall, the electricity surges though him and his body sends off sparks in all directions.

I hear screaming and look down to the other side of the partition. I see Isec fighting for his life, his small razors slashing and to my delight, hitting their mark. He looks good and I smile.

A girl comes at me hard from above and knocks me down. I scramble up before she can get the gravity under control and kick her in the face, my talons clawing her skin off as they pass through her flesh. I walk towards her as she flails half in and half out of the full force of the well. She screams at me to leave her alone.

"Honey, you picked the wrong girl to attack if you're looking for mercy." I pull her by the foot and she tries to kick me. I bring her down to the ground and twist her neck and then fling her up and let her float away.

I run over to the edge of the partition and do a handspring and fling myself over the other side, grabbing at the floor so I don't drift off, then bring myself upright. This side fared much better in the initial launch and they have a lot fewer casualties. A big guy rushes at me immediately, but Tessen is there and she grabs him by the throat and digs in her claws. He's choking when we kick him off and point him at the wall.

I see Isec, still fighting off kids twice his size, and Tessen and I launch upward, swim across, then flap like demons and launch ourselves at his attackers. They go down. I grab the nearest boy and stomp on his mouth and watch the blood spurt out, then swipe my razors over his throat to end it quickly.

Isec comes and stands next to me and Tessen and we just watch. We are alone on the floor. Even when we look below our feet, there is no one there.

They never even understood what it was.

So we stand there like spectators.

Whole minutes go by before the buzzer goes off and we are floating, then swimming, over to the exits. This time I don't hesitate, I jump off the fourth floor and sail down to the dorms. Tessen, Isec, and I wait in the lounge to see who makes it.

We laugh hysterically when we count up the living and find only Kete is missing.

Ashur really did his job with these guys because it only takes seconds and we barely remember who she was.

Ashur shows up sometime that afternoon when I am sleeping on my bunk. He nudges me awake and then slips in next to me. I smile at his good mood.

"Just Kete, then?"

I nod and he's happy. "You did a great job, Ashur. It was amazing."

He sighs. "Let's go somewhere, Junco."

"Where?"

"The city. Wanna go to the city with me?"

"Am I allowed?"

"I'm your captain, remember? I make your rules. Only Lucan can tell you no above me."

"Will Lucan care if we go to the city?" I study his face to see what he's up to, but he just flashes me a smile.

"He told me to take you out, Junco."

"Really?"

He picks up a bag from the floor and hands it to me. "No uniform for you. Tonight you're not a soldier."

I hold my breath at his comment and feel something.

"You OK?"

I nod as I exhale. "Yeah. It's just – thank you for that, Ashur."

He shrugs. "It was completely inappropriate for Lucan to say that about you being a better soldier, Junco. And when I told him you said maybe you'd rather just be a woman, well, you really know how to pull his strings because he fell all over himself to try and clarify. I said he should take you out and treat you nice, but he said it would make things weird. So, apparently, me taking you out isn't weird."

I look at him sideways. "Well, it sort of is."

"Yeah, it is, but I don't care. Go get dressed." He pushes me until I fall off the bed and then he kicks me away with his boot.

I practically rip the bag open in the dressing room. Inside is a card from Layla. The clothes are tailored to my uniform specs, so they should fit perfectly. I am relieved to see that they are not fancy. If I had to wear a dress in front of Ashur all night I'd be too embarrassed to have fun. But Layla has made me a pair of jeans, a fitted black jacket with a thick belt that cinches my waist, and a pair of knee-high black boots.

It's pretty perfect for being picked out for me on a foreign world. She's right too, once I figure out how to get the jacket to seam up they are the best-fitting clothes I've ever worn. Besides the uniform, of course. There's some make-up in the bag so I paint a little bit on. I'm not usually a make-up girl, but fuck it. I might as well make the most of it.

Tessen comes in when I'm brushing my hair. "What's going on, Junco?"

I smile. "Ashur's taking me out to the city tonight."

"Ohhh, what I'd give to have a date tonight. You have no idea."

I laugh. "It's not really a date, Tess. It's Ashur."

She raises her eyebrows at me. "Uh-huh. Ashur is a man, Junco. Men who show up with bags of custom-tailored clothes to take you out just to make you happy consider it a date."

I shrug. "I don't care. I'm excited even if he does think that."

She smiles as I brush my hair. "Have twice as much fun as normal, Junco. And bring some back for me."

I walk back out to the dorm and Ashur is waiting by the door. "Shit, Junco – took you long enough." But he smiles and takes my hand to twirl me around. "You're very pretty."

"You're supposed to keep that shit inside, Ash."

He shakes his head. "Not tonight."

We walk outside and Lucan's flyer is waiting. Ashur opens the door and I slide in. He takes the seat across from me and smiles. "How about dinner first?"

I nod. "Yeah, sounds great."

He opens the partition between us and the driver and gives him a location and then turns back to me. "So, I know you were with Charlie, Junco. But when's the last time you went out? Like a normal nineteen-year-old girl?"

I shake my head. "I've been on some dates and I've had boyfriends. But that was all field stuff, really. Just messing around on scrubs maneuvers or after patrols. If you want to know the last time I went out like other girls, then that would be never."

He screws up his face. "Last time at a bar?"

I shake my head again. "Besides the pub here with you? Never."

"You never went to a bar on Earth?"

"No, I wasn't old enough."

He laughs so hard he almost chokes. "Wait, so you're old enough to assassinate world leaders at six, but you can't go to a bar when you're nineteen?"

I sigh. "Yup, that's pretty much it. Besides, the RR doesn't have bars. I'd have to go to Peak City and I only went there when my father took me."

He looks serious. "I guess I never realized that, Junco. How much you've missed out on. Shit, no wonder you're wondering if there's something better out there."

"I thought you watched everything I did?"

"We never watched your personal life, not really. I mean, when all that shit went down with Charlie it was pretty hard not to take a closer look, but other than that I never paid attention to what you were doing in your free time."

"That's because I never had free time, Ashur."

He looks away. "Yeah. I guess not. Except for the horses. And neither Tier nor I liked to watch that shit."

I smile and think of Tier in the barn with me back on Earth. "You should have seen his face when I practiced in front of him."

Ashur watches me smile and it's contagious. "We all watched you do that last contest on the newscreens, where was that – Asia?"

"Japan, yeah."

"I thought Arel was gonna have a heart attack." He laughs out loud now. "He couldn't sit down and every time you flipped in the air he jumped, like a fucking little old lady worrying about her kittens or something."

I laugh. "I took first place."

He nods. "I know, Junco. You were fabulous as usual."

I feel my face go red and my heart starts to race. *Shit.*

"Don't get nervous, Junco." He watches me struggle. "It's just me."

"I know, but that's why I'm getting nervous." I take a deep breath and let it out. "It would be very easy to mess this all up, ya know?"

"Relax, we're just gonna have a night out, OK? Sometimes I have to remind myself that a couple weeks ago I was a complete stranger to you. But for me, Junco, you've been a constant in my life for a very long time. I know it's not fair, and I know that probably bugs you, but that's just how it is. So, if I make you uncomfortable, just say so. I'll back off."

I nod and scoot over to the window to look out. "OK."

He scoots over to the window too and starts pointing things out below. It eases some of my nerves.

"It's kind of funny though, if you think about it."

"What's that?" I ask, looking over to him.

"That complimenting you makes you all flustered, but if I were to try and kill you right now, your heartbeat would barely register."

"Yeah, well, I've had many years of practice, Ashur. So many that I'll probably never be normal."

"Is that what you want? To be normal?"

I shrug. "It was hard not to think about it back on Earth. I was in the RR, after all, where women pretty much just get married and have babies." I look up at him. "Having a life like that was normal – but having a life like mine never was. Here, I have no idea what's normal. But I can tell that you don't have a lot of girls in the warriors, do you?"

He shakes his head. "You're the only one."

My eyes absorb the little details of Lucan's flyer as I think about this for a few seconds. "I was wondering about that."

"Does it bother you? Being the first and only?"

"It really does."

"How come?"

"Because it turns me into a symbol that I don't want to be. I just want to fit in and be like everyone else. And if I'm the only girl in the warriors then I'll never fit in. I might rather be a wife than that, to be honest."

He sits back in surprise. "What?"

"I know what you're thinking. But, like I said the other night, Ashur, I never picked this soldiering stuff. And I realize that I'm not even a regular person – whatever the definition of that is, I'm not it. But inside I feel like I should have the chances that other girls have. Not to be forced to kill people all the time just because I can. And I don't even know if it's possible to change at this point anyway, but all that shit with Charlie made me think about what I might be giving up. I wanted that baby, Ashur. I was gonna keep it."

"What baby?"

I stare up at him and realize my mistake.

"What baby, Junco?"

I shake my head. "Shit, I thought Tier told you everything?"

"What *baby*, Junco?"

"I was pregnant, Ashur. My father dosed me with an ionspray to get rid of it." I watch him stare at me open-mouthed and then I look out the window at the lights as my face gets hot and my eyes begin to water. I count my heartbeats to get myself under control. "That's why things got a little weird with me those last few months on Earth. I was–" I stop and search for the words, my eyes squinting. "Not thinking clearly. I was maybe even a little bit insane." I look back and him and wait.

"Do you want to quit?" His eyes search me. "The truth, Junco."

"The truth is no, Ashur. I don't want to quit. I just want to feel like I'm the one who made the choice. I'm good at what I do. And I want more than anything to be near you guys, it feels so – necessary. Besides, quitting is even scarier than losing out on being normal."

He shakes his head and squints down at me. "Why?"

"Because I don't know how to do this stuff." I spread my arms wide at the flyer and my clothes. "I don't know how to go out and have dinner. Or relax. Ashur, I couldn't define a normal nineteen-year-old girl if my life depended on it. And maybe back on Earth there was the possibility of a life as a mother or a wife, or something besides a soldier. But I'm pretty sure that possibility is gone now." I watch him struggle with my words and he's silent for a few minutes as he looks out the window. "I just want the opportunity to make the decision, Ashur. That's all."

He takes a deep breath. "Are you hungry?" he asks, finally turning back to me.

"No, not really."

"Would you rather go for a walk?"

"Yeah, I would."

He gives new instructions to the driver and we stop on the ground level of Amelia proper and lie down in the grass. I spend the next hour looking up at the city tucked inside Ashur's wing and for the first time since I've been on this stupid habitat, I don't miss the stars.

Chapter Twenty-Five

I wake with a start to Ashur screaming at my team again, but Ryse shushes me back down into the blankets when I try and sit up. "Not you, Junco. You're with me today. You can go back to sleep if you're tired."

I let out a small laugh. "I'm not breakable, Ryse. So whatever Ashur told you guys about last night, don't fucking treat me like that."

He leans over me and I open my eyes. "Everyone is breakable, Junco. So shut the fuck up and go back to sleep. I only got two hours of it myself, so I'm fucking tired, got it?"

"Mmmmhhhhmmm. Got it."

"And when we're done sleeping, we're gonna go have some fucking breakfast. And then, we might even go watch a fucking screen just because I'm your XO and I can make you come with me."

I smile as I drift back off. *It would be so easy to love them.*

A few hours later I'm done sleeping and Ryse is watching the screen in the lounge. I pad over to him and plop down on the couch. There's a reporter on screen covering a ceremony. On stage are about two dozen girls dressed in Aves uniforms and they are being congratulated on their new promotions to warrior status.

I laugh. "Who did this?"

Ryse looks over to me. "Lucan, who else?"

"Why?"

He stares at me for a few seconds, his normally brown eyes glowing a little orange. I don't know Ryse all that well. He's not fun and boisterous like Braun, or serious and caring like Isten. Or even possessive and overbearing like Ashur. He's more aloof. More detached from me, like he hasn't made up his mind yet.

"Because, Junco, if you don't want to be the first, then fuck it. It's an easy fix, right? Just promote some girls and poof, that problem is solved. You'll never have to think about it again."

I nod and pull my legs up to my chest. "That was pretty nice."

He smiles at me, maybe for the first time ever. "We thought we knew everything there was to know about you, Juncs, but it turns out you've kept a lot of secrets."

I get up to go take a shower but Ryse calls back after me, "There's a bag of clothes next to your bed. No uniform today. Wouldn't want to steal the limelight from the new kids."

After breakfast we spend the day generally fucking around. He takes me to the zoo, which is populated with Earth animals, so I've seen them all, and then we go to the screens and see a movie. Not horror, thank God, but some action-drama thing that also runs on Earth.

Afterward we're walking along a path in a park looking at a small pond filled with familiar fish. "Do you guys have anything here that is pure avian? Like not something we have on Earth?"

Ryse stops and rubs his unshaven chin for a moment. "You do realize we're from Earth, right, Junco? We're not real aliens."

"Well, the Seven Siblings myth said–"

He cuts me off. "It's not really a myth, Juncs. It's mostly true."

"Which parts?"

"Well, the genetic engineering stuff, the fucked-up bloodlines, the part where they were cast out–"

"You're full of shit, Tier said it was a myth. Both versions."

He shrugs. "Tier's got his opinions. I've got mine."

I just stare at him. "So where do I fit in?"

"You want to see where you fit in?"

I nod as he pulls out his com. "Give me a minute." He walks away talking and I turn around and look back at the fish in the pond.

... Down below the water you can see the scales of brightly colored fish reflecting the sunlight...

"Nice, aren't they?"

I look up at the new voice. He's tall and fair with a mess of hair that looks like he's been in a wind tunnel. He smiles down at the water. "The fish?"

I look back at the fish. "Yeah, they're nice."

"I'm Kadian." He puts out his hand to shake and I stare at it, confused.

"Sorry, I thought you were–"

"Juncs!" I look over at Ryse who's trying to talk to me and the comm at the same time. "Get the fuck away from that guy, he's a reporter."

I look back at Kadian and shake his hand. "Junco. Since you must already know, there's no point in being rude." I turn to walk back over to Ryse, who is occupied with his other conversation, but Kadian puts his hand on my shoulder and I pause and then turn back.

"Wait, you're her, then? Really?"

I look into his eye at a small red blotch and realize he's recording this. "If you're asking if I'm Junco, then yes. I said I was."

He smiles. "How's Fledge going?"

"Still alive, Kadian."

Ryse is in his face and Kadian goes flying backwards and lands hard on the ground. "Back off, Kadian." Lucan appears and he and Ryse shuffle me away from the stunned reporter. I look back and mouth the word "sorry" as Lucan touches my shoulder and we disappear.

And reappear in a corridor that looks a lot like the one where my lab was just after morph. "Junco," Ryse explains, "reporters are reporters, no matter where you are. He's not a nice guy, and he spies on us all the fucking time. Don't talk to him."

I look up at Lucan. "Is this an order?"

Lucan just shakes his head. "I don't care who you talk to, Junco. But if Ryse says no, then it's no."

"Whatever."

"Are you interested in your part in the myth or aren't you? I'm busy, so if you're just going to pout about Ryse's heavy hand, we'll do it another time."

"No, I'm interested, really."

He smiles and steps over to a door. It opens and he waves me in.

It's a very busy lab, with screens from floor to ceiling filled with genetic profiles, data, charts, and a lot of molecular biology. Models of protein structures and crystals. Stuff I've seen from school, but never actually worked with myself.

There are at least two dozen white coats milling around at various stations, some working on screens, some talking in groups, and some I can see through a window that looks into another lab.

Lucan waits for me to take it all in and in the meantime work seems to come to a halt as everyone turns to look at me. I look up at Ryse. "What's going on?"

Lucan places a hand on my shoulder and guides me down a half-flight of stairs and over to a conference room. We enter, but the wall facing the lab is a window, so I continue to watch the activity after the door closes behind us.

"Have a seat, Junco, I have a story to tell you."

I make a face. "I don't like the stories, Lucan."

"Yes, well, this one is true."

I position myself so I can watch the lab as we talk and Ryse sits on the table next to me, while Lucan has his back to the window. "Layla has told you, correctly, that you are a product of the genetics obtained from the missing Aves plant, Gyr?"

I nod.

"That is not true for the other avian siblings. They do not come from Gyr, only you do."

"Oh, does it matter?"

"Not to you it doesn't, because it takes you out of what we do here. We aren't interested in Gyr's genetics, we're interested in the genetics of the six remaining pure avians. Esta, for example. And Moju. The four we have yet to find."

"Oh."

"And the reason is because those genetics are ancient. In fact, they pre-date the time of flight."

I nod. "Uh-huh. OK, well, I don't get it."

"They represent our true genome. Unaltered by generations of engineering and pure as it was before we left Earth."

I shake my head. "Pretend I'm obtuse, Lucan, and just spell it out, OK?"

"We need that code. In fact, we must have it to make changes or we will not survive as a species."

"Well, you have Esta, isn't she enough?"

Lucan's face is serious. "She is not enough, Junco. We need all six or the code makes no sense. It's hidden, you see, wrapped up and inaccessible."

"So why do I care? I mean, not to be a bitch or anything, but what does this have to do with me if my code doesn't matter?"

"You could help us, Junco. Get these siblings to come home."

"Right."

"This is important, Junco. Which is why I took time out of my day to bring you here and show you just how many people are working on this problem. The Six have one job, to keep the genetic code. But the Seventh also has a job, and that's to keep the Six…" He stops for a second. "You could call it safe, or just in line, or maybe act as a shepherd. The translations are – muddied. But the Seventh does have a job."

"If I'm so important, then why did you want to kill me on Earth?"

He looks away and for a few heartbeats I figure he's not gonna answer. I look over at Ryse and he shrugs.

Lucan clears his throat. "Junco, I was wrong about you. You were a very difficult mission for Tier and the team. It was too long, they had too much freedom, they quite frankly spent far too much time on you. It changed them. You changed them."

I raise my eyebrows. "And?"

"And we thought that even if you were the Seventh, we could do without you. You were a lot of trouble for the part you were to play."

"So, you don't need me."

He smiles. "We do need you."

I stand up and walk over to the window to take another look. "How much time before you have to have the code?" I glance back at them. "I mean, it's not critical or anything, you guys all look normal to me."

Lucan gets up and walks over to me as I turn to watch the white-coats. "It is extremely critical, Junco. Our children are not surviving."

I spin around, furious. "Well, for fuck's sake, Lucan! Why the fuck do you kill them all off then? You could just let them live!"

"They are *damaged*, Junco. It's been happening for many generations now, and we are not able to obtain the same quality of individual as is necessary to ensure our survival. We cannot afford to allow the code to be further diluted. We stopped the clutches seven years ago. There are no children younger than seven at this very moment."

"Oh." I turn away again. "Well, that's pretty fucked up." I watch a bustle of activity in the lab for a few minutes as someone calls up a 3D protein model up on the large central holotable and a small group of scientists stand around pointing to it. Finally I shrug and turn back.

"Of course I'll help. Why wouldn't I? Is there a reason they wouldn't want to come here? I mean, you're not going to mutilate or dissect them or anything, are you?"

He laughs a little and I realize that he doesn't do that often. "No, we would not mutilate or dissect them. But we've not had a lot of success convincing Moju."

"Well, shit, you better try to get him quick, there's no telling what Aren's done to him by now."

Lucan shakes his head. "You were correct in your prediction about that, Junco. Moju escaped shortly after and has been on a rather extensive killing spree ever since."

I smile. "Oh, well. Good for him. I knew he'd be fine if I stayed."

"But he might come back if you convinced him."

I shake my head. "I'm not so sure. Tier says he's wild. Besides, I never had any control over him, that was all Tier. Moju acted like he hated him but when the time came he followed his orders." An image of Moju saluting Tier in the hallway of the tunnels pops into my mind as I look over at Ryse and then back to Lucan.

"Yes, I've heard. But we don't need to discuss this now. We'll visit again after Fledge."

I huff. "How do you know I won't be killed in Fledge, Lucan? I mean, isn't it kind of risky to put me in there if you need me so bad?"

He laughs again, twice in one meeting. "Don't be silly, Junco. You've never been in any danger from these fights. You practically sat around filing your nails for the entire fourth battle. The other Archers think we're helping you cheat, that's how well you're doing."

Ryse is close now and Lucan taps us on the shoulders and delivers us to Fledge. "It was very nice to see you, Junco. Take care tomorrow."

And then he is gone.

I look up at Ryse and shrug. "OK, so this reporter thing?"

"Junco, he spies on us. Makes shit up about Tier and Ashur. He's on the screens like every night talking shit."

"That's not the point, Ryse. I'm not a little kid. You shouldn't be allowed to make up social rules for me."

He rolls his eyes at me. "Fine. Talk to whoever you want, OK?"

I smile. "Thanks." He turns to leave me there at the door but I hesitate. "Hey, Ryse?"

He turns back. "Yeah?"

"Tell Lucan thanks, too."

"What for?"

"For asking me to help, instead of telling me. I know it's just a token choice, but it sorta feels real. So, thanks for that."

He salutes me and I turn and go inside.

Chapter Twenty-Six

I'm on a mountain. By myself. Apparently Fight Five is a personal challenge and begins with being at the bottom of a mountain and ends with being at the top of a mountain. This whole stupid fight is climbing a mountain. Something I can do in my sleep. However, I'm currently on a ledge that was previously occupied by a rather angry bunch of eagles who now want it back.

The big one lurches at me for the tenth time and I kick out at it again. It snags my last toe and I scream as the blood squirts out.

Something in my thigh pocket begins to vibrate and I stop to pull out my com. I'm getting a call. During a fight. The screen says push to answer.

So I push.

"This better be a fucking emergency, Lucan."

"Uh, Junco?"

It's not Lucan. "Yeah?"

"It's Kadian."

Silence.

"The reporter from yesterday?"

"Oh. Yeah, OK. What do you want?"

The eagles are back and I miss his words as another one tries to attack my already bleeding toe – he lunges in and snags a bit of skin. "Fuck, that hurts! You stupid motherfucker, get the fuck out of here. I'll be gone in a minute, just let me get my fucking breath!"

I hear talking coming from my comm and pick it back up. "Kadian, I'm a little bit busy right now."

"Are you in Fledge right now?"

"Yeah, I'm busy."

"Well, why are you answering the phone?"

"Hold on, there's an eagle who wants to eat my toe." My fingers pull up a small stone and I peg it good. It screams as it dives off the ledge and I cover my ears. "Ha, I got it in the eye!"

"Junco, put the comm on your Aves shirt, near the upper left shoulder, so you don't have to hold it and I can see what's happening."

I slap it up there and his voice is amplified.

"So why did you pick up the phone?"

"Huh?" I answer, scrambling out of the way of another, smaller eagle. "Shit! Why? Oh, well, this is the first comm call I've ever gotten, ya know. I was never allowed to talk on comms at home and I thought you were Lucan or Ashur or someone I shouldn't ignore."

"What are you doing in this fight?"

"It's not a fight, Kadian, it's a personal challenge. And they dumped us out at the bottom of a mountain and we're supposed to climb to the top. At least I think that's the point, they never really tell you, but what else could it be, right?"

"Describe what you're doing now."

"What the hell does it look like, I'm fighting eagles. But you know what, I'm done here. They can have this fucking ledge back, I'm done resting." I walk out towards the ledge and two big raptors are waiting to try and get my toes, but I fall to the ground and sweep them off with my legs and then I run to the edge and jump, grab a hold and begin to pull myself up past the outcrop that acts as a roof over the mountainside cave. My bare feet find their holds and I climb, one hand and foot at a time until I can see another ledge above me. I stop, breathing hard for a few seconds, then listen and hear the tell-tale whine of something I never wanted to hear again. "Holy shit, they've got nightdogs up here!"

"Nightdogs?"

Oops. "Oh, I didn't know you were still there."

"Yes, the whole habitat is with you right now, Junco, in real time. You have to fight a nightdog?"

I snort. "I don't have to fucking do anything and I tell you what, I'm not fighting any nightdogs, they already ate two of my fingers. I'm climbing straight around these fuckers."

"Why don't you just fly to the top?"

"Can't – there was a sign at the drop-off that said no flying. Some kid tried, they shot him."

I lurch out over a slight overhang and the snapping to my left makes my heart jolt for a second. I grab with my left hand and then swing again, my legs scrambling to find purchase, and then my right hand finds a hold and I pull up a few more feet.

I repeat the process until I find a rest spot.

"How far from the top are you, Junco?"

I turn and look down. "Pretty close, I think."

An eagle soars by and makes to grab at me with its talons but I kick out at it, and when it turns away I resume climbing, one hand, one foot, one hand, one foot.

And then then I am almost there and I smile. "Kadian, look!" I pick the comm off my shirt and pan it around. "I'm almost there!"

I stick it back on and climb again, and again and then I'm on a flat ledge and I stand and turn. "Holy shit! I'm at the top!"

I scramble over a few more outcroppings and stand on the peak to see if anyone else is around. "No one else is at the top. There's no one!"

"You're the first, Junco?"

I cup my hands to my mouth and shout, "Oi! Oi! Pledges! Where are you?"

"Junco!" A faint call to my left, and I twirl around. "Kush!" I wave frantically. "Kush is alive, Kadian! He made it! Tessen! Where are you?" I watch as a few more people clamber to the top, but no Tessen. "Tessen!"

"Junco!" Wyrd calls from just over to my right, and I wave. "Wyrd's alive too!"

"Shit, where are you, Isec?" I don't expect him to make it, but I hope he does.

"Who's missing, Junco?"

"Tessen, Joll, and Isec."

"Junco!" I whirl to my left and there's Tessen waving. I wave back. "Tessen's alive!"

Fuck, Isec, where are you? I wait. The silence from the comm and the few people who pop up at the top who are not Isec make things worse. I scan, and scan and scan. "Isec!" I look around. "Isec! If you can hear me don't stop climbing, Isec! Keep going!"

I hear Tessen, Wyrd, and Kush calling for him too, encouraging him, and I smile. "He's gonna make it, I know he will." I let out a long breath and then I hear his tiny little voice. "Junco! I did it!"

I scream. "I knew you'd make it, I knew it!" I jump up and down and I can hear Kadian telling me not to fall, but all the pledges at the top are whooping now – we scream and dance at the top of our mountains and then the announcer comes on and tells us to prepare for removal.

We are whooshed down a tube and spit out onto a large web and I bounce into the others, happy at making it, happy my friends made it, and then I swing down to the ground and run towards the ledge. I hold back until last and then I hear Kadian asking me questions, and I dive like a swan down to the dorm a thousand feet below.

I land in a heap with everyone else and I take the comm off my shirt as I walk into the lounge and see my feed live on the screens. Everyone is pointing at me and I look into the comm and smile.

"Junco, what was the best part of Fight Five?"

"I made it, Kadian, and I didn't have to kill a single soul to do it. Goodbye!"

I push the off button and the feed disappears from the screen.

It's only then that I realize Joll is still missing. But am I surprised that I've already forgotten about him? Or that the rest of the team have also?

No. We all knew. Joll was already dead to us.

There is only one day between the Fifth and Sixth Fights, so we spend the next entire day in training. Ashur has gathered everyone in the gym, including me. Out of the original one thousand pledges, there are exactly thirty of us remaining.

The entire 039 is present, except Braun of course, fucking asshole. Plus four more teams that I've never met before. I've got Kadian on my comm on my chest, as does Ashur. He says it's good PR. My wings are taped securely to my back, as are Ashur's. This can only mean one thing.

He paces up front screaming about how worthless we will be if the Aves are forced to take us into their Cluster. I stifle down a yawn and then kick Isec to pay attention when it's contagious. If Ashur sees him do that he'll make an example out of him.

"Junco!"

I turn back to the front. "Yes, sir."

"Up here with me."

I get up and go to the front. He pulls me over and stands behind me with his hands on my shoulders. "For the rest of the day you will fight, and watch your fellow pledges fight, an Aves warrior. You will watch with a critical eye. You will look for weakness and strength. And you will ask yourself for each and every opponent, will this person save my life if I have to be on their team? You will rank them in your mind.

Yes or no. Yes, this person is as good as or better than me. Or no, this person will get us all killed."

They stare at him like he has three eyes.

"Do you understand?"

"Yes, sir!" they shout.

He growls, "As Lucan's personal warrior, I am the ranking captain and I choose to fight Junco." He turns me around. "Junco, we will finish that fight now."

"Yes, sir." I'd like to tell him to go fuck himself, but he wouldn't tolerate that shit in front of the other teams. So I suck it up and prepare to get my ass kicked.

I walk towards him and grab him with both hands, one behind the neck, the other on his bicep, and swing into a flying arm bar, taking him down and slapping him on the mat. I hear him laugh. "Jasus, fuck, Junco!" He gets out of it easily and I end up on the bottom, but I have momentum on my side and I use my shoulder to flip him again. He catches my foot and gets me off balance, but I get my other foot hooked around his neck and get him in a leg bar, pulling just enough to make him know I won this move. He's not done with me yet, and flips over, but I hold tight to his leg. He struggles for a second, scooting back and forth to break my hold, but I hold on.

He hooks his leg around my hip, grabs my other leg, and pushes my ankle back until I cry out. I bite down the pain and let go of his leg to make him change position. He doesn't let go and the pain is searing back through my joint. I feel the tendon stretch and I think for a moment he might actually snap it if I don't tap out.

His foot appears by my head like a gift and I snatch it up and hold on, pushing his ankle back now. He rolls over on my hips and I use the motion to swing him all the way over as I twist on the mat. My foot slips free and I smack him in the face with it and he laughs. I still have a hold of his ankle though, and I twist and his laugh is cut off. Asshole.

He uses his considerable weight advantage to swing free and now he's lying across my chest as I take a few seconds to catch my breath, then swing my right arm over his neck and fishhook him to at least pop myself onto my stomach. Unfortunately, he's got me in a good shoulder lock and he's practically sitting on my neck. I take another second to rest, then let him flip me over and squirm away, my smaller size giving me room and advantage that no other person in the room might have, except for maybe Isec.

And then I've got him face down on all fours and I absently log people cheering for me in the background. I mount his back and hold his head in a choke, but since I weigh almost nothing compared to him he simply stands up. I unhook my legs and push off him into a back flip, miss the landing and slide across the mat. I scramble up as he's turning and hook him in the jaw with my foot as I spin. I watch his head snap to the side and a small trickle of blood seep out of his lip.

I stop, bending over and breathing hard trying to catch my breath. The whole room has been stunned into silence as they wait to see if he will take me down.

"Junco," Ashur says over his own heavy breathing. "You're fucking amazing."

I laugh. "Yes, sir." We meet in the middle and bow.

He points to the water bottles stacked up on a table at the other end of the room and I go to grab us some when I hear him talk to the pledges in a low voice. "That, you worthless throwaways, is a warrior who could beat every ass in here. But before you go getting jealous, she's also the one who will save you when you need it. You all fucking remember that."

We disconnect Kadian and sit down on one end of the gym to untape each other's wings and cool down. The remaining pledges repeat what we just did. The other Aves are really more into punching, flying and kicking than the grappling stuff Ashur and I did and most of the pledges suck so bad the entire encounter lasts for mere seconds. But some, like the biggest guy called Annun and a few of his buddies, and Kush, do OK, if not well.

It doesn't take long to see what Ashur's point was in facilitating this exercise. Some of the remaining pledges are very weak candidates to be warriors. And Isec's shortcomings are so painfully obvious I can't bear to watch and instead I head to the stairs and go outside to smoke. Ashur doesn't follow me.

I lie on the grass in what seems to be the late afternoon sun and after a few minutes Kush finds me. I look up at him as he approaches and pat the ground next to me. "You looked good today, Kush."

He smiles as he sits down. "Where did you and Ashur learn that stuff, Junco?"

"What stuff?"

"Those fighting moves?"

"Oh, it's a specialized art on Earth. You don't have jujitsu here?"

He shakes his head. "Never heard of it."

"Well, shit. You guys should get some teachers. It's pretty fucking useful for close combat like that."

"Where did Ashur learn it?"

I shrug. "I dunno." I puff on the cigar and then blow out some rings. "Watching me, I guess."

He's silent for a while so I fill in the gaps. "The 039 were my watchers on Earth." I look over at Kush to gauge his reaction but he's a blank. "He had years to see what I was up to, so I guess it just interested him and he decided to teach himself."

"Hmmm."

"What?"

"He's pretty infatuated with you, Junco."

"Kush, he's my captain. I'm his nine. He certainly loves me, but he's not in love with me if that's what you're getting around to."

"He definitely could be, that's all I'm saying. One word from you would be all it takes."

I shrug and blow smoke rings. I'm not even remotely interested in having this conversation with Kush and I let the silence hang until I hear Isten calling me to come back upstairs from the door.

I leave Kush out there on the grass.

Chapter Twenty-Seven

Later, Ash and I are sitting in the lounge as we watch a horror screen. "Go take a shower, Junco. What are you waiting for?"

I look back at the showers and shake my head. "I don't like to shower with people here. It feels weird. Especially with Isec and Kush, ya know?"

"You're suddenly shy?" He grins at me and laughs. "That's a first."

He's right, too. I've never been shy about my body before. "I know. I just don't feel comfortable with these guys. It's too personal."

"I was gonna take you out to dinner."

"I'll eat later, I want to go look at the church again. Wanna come with me?"

"No, I'm hungry and I'd rather go out to dinner."

"No one's stopping you, go."

He looks sideways at me. "Why do you want to go up there?"

"Because it's strange, why is it here? I asked Isten but he ignored my question." I pull out the prayer card that I've been keeping in my pocket and hand it to him. "I went in there that night that you programmed my com. I followed Isec up there and I found that prayer card."

He reads the poem. "Huh. Never heard of this one before."

"No? It's an old Earth poem, Ashur. Don't you think that's weird?"

He flips it over to look at the syrinx on the front. "Is it a famous poem?"

I shrug. "Not really. Maybe it was once, but it's a few hundred years old or something."

"How did you know it, then?"

"See, that's the thing. I had to memorize this poem in school, Ashur. Was assigned it in sixth year, right before I went off to cadets."

He hands it back to me and I pocket it. "Well, you don't ever want to ask Isten about the syrinx, Junco. He's worthless about religion. Refuses to even talk about it. But the syrinx was an ancient…"

He looks up and struggles to find the correct word. "I guess the only proper way to describe her is the Fallen Archer."

I stand up and grab his hand. "Come up there with me."

He scowls. "Will you take a shower and go eat with me afterward?"

I smile and nod and he gives in.

Ashur stands behind me as I bend down to pan my fingertips across the ancient markings around the wooden door frame.

"Well, are you gonna go in?"

I look up and shake my head. "No, it scares me."

"Junco–"

"I just want to see if I can read this." I point to the markings.

"It looks like chips in the wood to me."

"It's not, it's ancient Sumerian cuneiform."

"Oh, well that explains it." He shakes his head and laughs.

My finger traces the various images, ticks, and lines one graphic at a time and I reach back in my memory to find the key. It's far back, from grade school, year three or four maybe, but it's there.

"Junco, can you really read that shit?"

I open my eyes and Ashur is bent down next to me, his face right up to mine. "I could, if I had enough time. I have the key in here." I say, tapping my head. "My father took me to the British Museum once, for birthday week. His friend was some big-shot curator guy in the Ancient Near-East section and he gave me this book that had worksheets and stuff."

Ashur looks at me strangely.

I shrug. "I can't help it, I just remember weird shit like that. Plus, we had like a whole semester on it in regular weekday school. Learning gods and goddesses and stuff. Like we do the Greeks. But this door is odd, because these markings are a mixture of several different forms. It encompasses the entire span of ancient Sumerian writing stretching over a period of almost four thousand years."

"What's it say?"

I smile because he's interested now, he can't help it. "I don't really know, I'd have to decipher each one, then try and apply it in context. I'd have to go back and read the books about the mythology to make sure it was correct. It would take months, years maybe."

His fingers pass over the carvings. "Oh, well, it is kinda cool."

"Don't you have anyone who can read this, Ashur? I mean, surely you must have some book or something that tells what it says."

He shrugs. "Yeah, maybe. I could look into it if you want."

"I do," I say as I look into his eyes. They are green like Tier's and they glow a little as we stare at each other. I break away first. "The thing is, Ash, when I went in there to pray, I prayed to be brave when the time comes. I said, *Please let me accept my fate with courage. Let me be brave in the end.* And I got an answer."

I watch his eyes again as it sinks in. "From who?"

I scratch my head and think of a good way to put it.

"Junco, from who?"

"My vision screen."

"What vision screen?"

"Huh?"

"What vision screen?"

"That shit that scrolls across my vision, the data."

"What the fuck are you talking about?"

"You can't see stuff on your field of vision? Stuff like documents and your personal biogs, or the injury status of an opponent?"

He stares at me, his eyes glowing like fuck, and I feel my heart stop. "You're not supposed to have a vision screen, Junco. That has to be gifted to you by the– ."

He stops mid-sentence and stays quiet. Like he's said too much.

I let out a breath. "Well, I have one."

"What did it say to you, Juncs?"

"She said–"

"She?"

"Yeah, she said, do you wish to accept the sacrifice? And I stalled, and she asked if that was a no, and I said wait, yes, I do. I'll accept the sacrifice. And then she was gone."

"Is this the only time she's talked to you?"

"No, when I was giving testimony, she was the one telling me what to say."

"What?"

"I woke up after talking to Tier and she was on my vision screen, she typed out word for word what I should say. And I did. She said they would knock off that charge if I said what she told me to."

"You *did* lie."

I nod. "Tier did break the treaty. I lied. Are you gonna tell Lucan?"

He looks at me. "No, of course not, Junco." His hand wraps around my head and he pulls me into his chest as he slumps back against the door. "What the fuck is going on, though?"

"Did Lucan or Layla tell you what they found inside my body?"

He huffs out some air. "There's more?"

"I'm part machine, Ashur. I'm littered with circuits all through my body. And when Layla explained what she saw she said that there was AI code inside me, but that it was inactive and inert."

He snorts. "Some fucking scientist she is."

"I know, right? When she told me that I immediately thought of my HOUSE back home. You know we had an AI running our house?"

He nods. "Arel corrupted her once, so we could get inside. But I don't know anything about it, really."

"So there's something inside me. Are you sure we shouldn't tell Lucan?" I pull back and look at his eyes.

"Has it done anything bad to you?"

"No, she shows up in stressful situations and helps me."

"Let's just wait."

"Sure, I'm fine with that." But not really. I'm worried, I want to say. I'm a little scared even.

"Back to the Fallen Archer and your original question. The church is here because she's like the equivalent of your Jesus on Earth. The sacrifice, to let everyone else live, right?"

I nod. "Yeah, that was his purpose, his death saved the rest of us."

"The syrinx isn't that magnanimous, she's here to remind you of *your* sacrifice."

I look up at him, my eyes wide.

He nods. "Yeah, funny timing. The purpose of the church is to make you ask if you're good enough to live. Can you contribute, can you help, can you save others. Like the stuff I was saying to the pledges today."

I let out a little laugh. Synchronicity.

"Anyway, by the time you get to Fight Six, you're supposed to reflect on this and then make a decision. Either say you're worthy and prove it, or give yourself up for the good of the others. That's her purpose."

I'm silent as I consider what my acceptance of the sacrifice means, but it's not particularly attractive. "So why is she called the Fallen Archer?"

"She gave herself up so we could live too, way back, like when we were still on Earth. Self-sacrifice is her thing."

"But *why* did she have to?"

He smiles down at me as his fingers absently play with my hair. "I thought you hated the myths?"

I shrug. "It's hard to ignore this one."

"Yeah, well, it's complicated because we have so many different mythologies that it's hard to keep straight. But the Fallen Archer, even though the Seven Siblings has Old Crag in it in some versions, is one of the twelve original myths. Which means it's way older than Crag.

"So anyway, the story goes, the avians were getting ready to leave Earth to go find the Seven Siblings but they" – he stops and bends his head over to look at me – "I'm improvising here, Junco, I haven't read this myth in like twenty years so don't quote me or anything – but they needed stuff they didn't have. From what I can remember they needed to reach escape velocity and plot a course, and build the habitats out here in the Band, and all the technology we'd need to leave Earth and survive. And the story says she gave herself up so that we could get that from the High Order."

"What's the High Order?"

He shakes his head at me. "For this you do have to go to Lucan. I'm not allowed to tell you this part, sorry. He's the Archer."

"Oh. Well, since I have to go to him anyway, should I tell him everything then?"

"If you trust him."

"Do you trust him?"

"Unconditionally."

I nod. "OK."

We stay that way for a few more minutes and then he pulls me to my feet. "Time to shower, I'm fucking starved." He pushes me off the ledge and we soar down to the dorm.

Chapter Twenty-Eight

The tubes we are placed in for the Sixth Battle are upright and in the shape of a streamlined bullet. There are so few of us now, only thirty, that we all approach the circle of cases together. The transparent doors slide open simultaneously, and we all take a step forward and turn around.

The case slides shut and the only sound I hear is my own breathing. It has not been possible to predict the moment the fight starts for some time now, and I shuffle my feet with impatience. Somewhere deep below in some hidden layer of the habitat a mechanical ratcheting vibrates and then I am accelerating upward.

The top end of the bullet slides back in anticipation and then the case abruptly stops.

But I don't.

Momentum propels me up and out onto the field of battle. I am sailing through the air and then my upward acceleration reaches zero and I hang there for a fraction.

And fall.

My feet slam into the metal grate that pops out from the side of a deep well about the width of my arms. My ankle twists a little as it gets stuck between the metal crosses and I fall backwards.

"Shit!"

"You OK, Junco?" Kadian is on my comms but I ignore him and look around at where I am. It's obviously another personal challenge because there is no one else in the pit except me. I try my wings to see if I can fly, but the space is too tight. A sudden memory of Tier fighting nightdogs in the cave comes back and I push it down.

"Junco?"

"Kadian, one more fucking word from you and I'll cut the transmission. I'm motherfucking serious, seal your fucking mouth shut."

I stand and wince as my ankle cries out in pain. Just fucking great, I have to climb out of a pit with no rope and my ankle is fucked.

A timer beeps on the side of the ragged sandstone walls and begins to count down from three hundred seconds. A rush of water fills the chamber below my feet as I hear the snapping of jaws and almost pee myself.

I look down.

Crocodiles.

I scan up the side of the wall and spy another timer, about twenty feet vertical, then see the mechanism that will close another grate over my head and trap me down here if I don't start climbing now. I reach up for a handhold and pull up, find a foothold with my good foot, and repeat. The timer races down but I put it out of my mind and find another handhold and pull.

I am almost to the first gate and still have a full sixty seconds to get past the mechanism when the first grate below me slaps open. The crocodiles claw at the sides of the pit and jump at me. I lose purchase and slip a few feet backwards, my feet kicking out as the crocs jump into the air to grab a foot.

I try again, the timers down to forty-five seconds now, and pull. My ankle screams at the strain of my weight, but I force it down and climb. I reach the grate with fifteen seconds and use it to haul myself up quickly. I push my back and legs against the opposite sides of the pit wall and rest as the gate below me slams shut.

I put my feet down and take a real rest as the water is funneled out through some unseen drain and the crocodiles disappear. The bottom grate slides back in and becomes solid just as the side of the pit opens up and nightdogs are released below me.

Shit, they probably took that fear straight out of my mind. Dammit, Junco, push that shit down!

A litter of pups appears in the side of the pit wall next to me and they begin screaming for their mothers. I study the wild dogs below me and see that they are all bitches, their teats swollen from recent birth and nursing. They jump up and almost snap my fingers off that are clutching the grate. I pull back and get to my feet in a panic as the pups continue their call for help.

The timer for this phase beeps and starts counting down from two hundred forty seconds. I put a hand up and climb, trying my best to block out the vicious growl of dogs. I get a few feet up and the grate below me slides back into the wall, exposing my legs to the wild animals below. I let out a whimper and scramble up the wall as they jump and gain a hold of the boot of my drooping leg. I shake hard and pull the foot away, find another handhold and pull. They jump again and take a chunk of my pants with them as they fall, and I cling hard to the wall, then watch the timer begin counting down my final minute.

"Fuck!" I reach again and pull, the cries distract me and I slip as my foot falsely assumes the porous rock will hold my weight. The dogs jump again as the pups in the small nook on the side of the wall scream for attention. I watch the milk drip off the bitches, their need to nurse and fight driving them upwards towards my body.

The timer is at forty seconds and I reach up again, pull, find a spot for my foot, test, reach up, pull, find a foothold, test, and make it to the third gate and scramble my ass off as the timer says I have five seconds before I will be chopped in half. The thought of the nightdogs getting to eat my legs as a reward pushes me up just as the grate slams out below and I drop and rest.

I don't watch as the pups and bitches are removed from the pit, but I listen for the silence. It is a short reprieve, because the nasal growl of a pack of prairie lions echoes in my ears. They fight and claw at each other for a second and then the timer beeps and begins to count down what may be the final one hundred and eighty seconds of my life. I scramble up the pit wall, one hand over the next, one foot in, test, next foot, test, and repeat. The timer is at one hundred twenty when I hear the mechanism for the grate begin to slide.

I calculate the distance between myself and the prairie lions and know with surety that they can leap far higher than that short distance.

My ankle is not only burning, it swells against the side of my boot and the heat threatens to make it burst. The gate slides open and the hissing begins as the pride realizes they can get me. They leap and I scream and pull myself up, trying not to look down. I feel the claws scrape the flesh off the back side of my calf as I pull my ankle from their reach. *Pull, Junco! Pull!*

I do, but they figure out that the soft sandstone is perfect for long sharp claws to gain purchase as they try and catch a good meal.

I scream, "Fuck!"

One gets close and I have to stop and kick out to knock it back as I hold on desperately by one hand. The rocks begins to slide and loose bits of wall crumble beneath my fingers.

I reach up with my other hand and grab, then shake my head and think.

"Stop fucking thinking, Junco, and climb!"

For a minute I think it's me talking, but it's not. It's Kadian on the comms. "Climb, you stupid girl, climb!"

I do.

I climb and I ignore my ankle and after what seems like too many kicks at the leaping prairie lions my hands reach the lip of the pit and I haul myself up and over, struggling mightily in the sudden increase in G. It is so thick I immediately feel exhausted.

The lions make one last attempt and gain a hold of my boot with claws and teeth and I slide back. But I'm done by then, I kick those fuckers in the teeth and they scream as they fall back into the darkness.

I scramble out of their reach and take a minute to calm down before looking around. It's only then that I realize I could have just pulled out the SEAR and killed them all. And I didn't. Lucan will be so proud.

"Junco!" I hear a voice from behind and get to my feet, limping on my bad ankle and huffing in the heavy gravity. It's Annun. I smile and wave. "You beat me!"

He waves back but he's not smiling. "That fucking sucked."

My smile falters and I swallow hard. "Yeah," I say more to myself than anyone. "It really did."

I take a good long look around. I'm standing on the top of a spire-like rock formation, as is Annun, and I assume, as would everyone else if there was anyone at the top with us. But there isn't. There are thin rope bridges connecting each spire and I make to cross over to Annun when I hear him shout, "Stop now!"

I recognize a command when I hear one, so I do stop. And look up at him.

He points over to a spire across the center circle and then I see the body lying at the bottom, limbs all splayed out at angles not seen on living things. A broken rope bridge hangs down either side of the two spires. The heavy G is too much for that little bridge.

I look back at Annun. "Shit. Thanks."

We only wait a few seconds before the others begin pulling their way out of the pits. Annun's buddies Merkar and Pike are out first. I watch with apprehension as one by one those who made it claw across the small flat area surrounding each pit opening. Kush comes up, and another kid I don't really know. His friend is next, and then Wyrd. I smile with relief. At least he will make it.

Another guy is there, then so is Tessen.

A few more materialize, and then we are at fourteen and I'm just about to give up on Isec when I see his head appear and then the rest of his little body follows him as he drops to his side in exhaustion.

I smile, but I don't call out, I just breathe hard, still not fully recovered from the challenge.

We all made it.

It's too good to be true and I catch myself wishing they hadn't, that it was over, and that the final deaths were all behind us.

But as I look around at each spire I don't see anyone who shares my sense of dread. They jump and call out and scream their happiness from the top of the world.

But I know better.

The top of the world is the worst place to be.

It just makes the fall back down to Earth all that much farther.

Chapter Twenty-Nine

Ashur is taping my ankle up on my bunk while everyone else races around to get ready for the party. Lucan has sent a fleet of flyers and we are going to the 039 to celebrate.

I pleaded with the vision screen to mix me a cocktail for the pain, or start the self-healing stuff or something, but she is gone. And I don't really know how to run the equipment yet. So I suffer.

Two days and it will all be over.

"What are you thinking about, Junco?" Ashur is still taping but his eyes are on me.

I shake my head and exhale. "Just glad it's almost over. You know, Lucan said that these fights were not challenging for me, that he was never worried about me making it. But I have to disagree. Kush saved me the first fight and stopped the bleeding from my wings after the third fight. And believe it or not, it was Kadian's voice that snapped me out of the panic I was in in the pit. And I don't know if you saw on the screen, but Annun saved my life when he stopped me from crossing that rope bridge. There's no guarantee, Ashur. That's stupid of him to think that."

He smiles, a gentle smile, as he puts my foot down on the ground. "Stand up and try it out."

I do and it feels better, but I won't be wearing boots tonight. He takes my arm and guides me as I limp out of the dorm and out to the flyer. He loses his patience before we even reach the door and scoops me up to carry me the rest of the way.

We get to ride alone and I'm glad I don't have to share transport with all those excited people. He leans me back against the far door and puts my foot up on the seat, then settles on the opposite bench.

"What's wrong, Junco? You should be happy, your whole team came out of Fight Six. That's pretty amazing."

"I know, I am. But…"

He raises his eyebrows. "But what?"

I shake my head. "Nothing. I'm just really tired, that's all."

To my surprise he drops it and lets me doze on and off for the duration of the ride. The flyer lands on the roof of a very tall building overlooking Amelia proper. Ashur lifts me up and carries me down the landing pad stairs to a large terrace filled with green plants and flower beds and then through a large open door.

The guys are all there, even Braun, and they laugh and joke with me about my almost fatal ankle injury. Ashur sets me down on the couch as they all crowd me.

I look around at the apartment. It's what I might call ultra-minimalist on Earth, with sleek white floors and a sunken living room filled with white couches and loungers. The accents are chrome and it almost reminds me of my bedroom at home. From my vantage point on the couch I can see the terrace outside, as well as the lights of the buildings across the expansive boulevard.

Mish hands me a beer and Rikan throws a cigar in my lap. I strike it up and puff, then take a swig of the beer.

It feels awesome to be here with them.

Braun comes over and lifts me up into a bear hug and I choke and complain, but it feels so good I give in and throw my arms around his neck and plant a kiss on his cheek. He sets me back down on the couch and slides my legs over his lap and I fall back into the pillows and relax.

"Sorry I've been missing all the fun, Juncs. Lucan had me running all over the fucking worlds doing bullshit stuff. I think he was trying to keep us apart, you being my one true love and all."

Ryse interjects, "Braun, the only way Junco would love you is if the rest of us were all dead."

I smile up at Braun. "Not true, Braun."

"Shit," Rikan says, "She'd love Lucan before you!"

I laugh. "So not true, Braun."

He shrugs. "She says she loves me guys, I'm going with it!" He pulls me to his face and kisses me on the head. "I'll always be your favorite, right, Junco?"

"Always, Braun."

"Now, about that house you owe me, honey..."

I slap him and Ashur pulls him off of me and takes his place.

Isten yells from across the room, "Flyers upstairs."

The apartment bustles with activity as the other pledges pour into the party. Someone gets some kind of loud music going and the drinks begin to flow. Tessen makes her way over to Ash and me. "Junco, you can't mope on the couch all night. Get off her, Ashur."

She physically pushes him aside and pulls me to my feet. "Let's mingle."

I laugh and look back at Ashur's stunned face as I limp away with Tessen. "Bye!"

We poke around all the rooms one at a time and discuss the quality of food from the autocook in the kitchen, the potential for large parties at the dining room table, the type of stone used for the tiles on the floor, and the wall art. Lucan appears from nowhere and scares the shit out of us as we peek into the various bedrooms.

"Junco, are you looking for your room?"

I stare up at him. "I have a room?"

"Of course you do, this is the 039. You live here."

Tessen nods and gives me the girlfriend look of approval.

"Come."

He takes my arm and helps me walk down a few stairs into the sunken living room, then across the other side and up a few more to a separate part of the apartment. I spot Ashur talking to Annun but he excuses himself and follows us as we walk into a small hallway that leads to another room.

When I walk in I'm a little bit taken back. It looks almost identical to my room at home, only much larger, and with an incredible bay window that almost bumps out into the traffic of flyers.

I look back and all the guys are peeking around the door to see what I think of it.

"Damn, Junco! Can I move in too, Lucan?" Tessen is clearly impressed.

I walk over to the piano and sit on the bench. "Where–"

"We looted your house, Junco. I hope you don't mind." Isten sits next to me and squeezes my arm. "Rikan and I took a bunch of shit while that fight was going down in your driveway."

My fingers touch the keys and I play the little lullaby I learned when I was just a toddler to try it out. It's even in tune. Isec wanders up and pulls on my arm. "Can you play it?"

"I actually play very well. Wanna hear?"

He nods and I push Isten off the bench so I can have room. "It might sound funny, I haven't played since my fingers were bitten off."

Nobody cares.

I play the first few lines of Asgarth's Genius from memory to test the left hand, but to my surprise, it sounds perfect. My fingers fly, picking out the sweet melody that made me fall in love with the piece in the first place, and then transition into the deeper notes that take it down to the dark place of Asgarth's nightmares. In the opera, Asgarth is an insane prince who thinks everyone is trying to kill him. It doesn't end well for the people around him.

I stop after I finish the first song and turn around. Everyone is silent and somber and then they clap gently and I smile and get up and bow.

Lucan is gone, but Ashur comes over and takes me to the book shelf to show me the photo albums they managed to get out of my room. "We got what we could." He looks away. "It probably makes you miss it even more, but–"

I smile and exhale. *All the good parts are in the exhale.* "It's very touching, Ash. Really."

People file past us after looking at the view and then we are alone and he sits me down on the window seat. I hear Tessen's loud laugh down the hallway and smile as I lean over and look down. The street is so far away and the boulevard so crowded with trains every twenty floors or so that there is no possible chance of getting a glimpse of it. I pull my legs up and hug them to my chest as I stare out the window. Ash goes over and turns the lights out. "It's beautiful at night."

I agree and lean back against the edge of the window frame. The lights outside really are stunning.

"Why are you so unhappy today?"

I shrug. "Because there's still one more fight and I'm getting hopeful that things will turn out OK." I look up at him and shake my head. "And things never turn out OK, so why bother enjoying it? It'll all be gone soon enough."

He sits next to me and takes my hand. "Not all of it, Junco."

I smile up at him. "I don't deserve you."

He leans in and kisses me, then stops to search my face for a reaction. His eyes glow green and I wonder what color mine are at the moment. I reach up to his cheek and stroke him with the tips of my fingers, then slide my hand around his neck and draw him in close to kiss him back. It lasts for so long I lose time.

I pull away and turn my head so he can take his kisses to my neck and then down my chest. His hands go to my waist and then he pulls back. "Fuck, Junco." His breath is heavy as he bows his head.

I nod and exhale as I play with his hair. "I know."

He pulls all the way back and sits up as I smile. I get up but he stays seated. "I'm gonna go find Lucan."

He nods. "I'll be out in a minute."

Chapter Thirty

Lucan is out on the terrace sitting on a porch swing that looks like they might have stolen it right out of the RR. I walk up next to him and he pats the seat so I sit down and pull my legs up into my chest. He makes the swing move back and forth and it reminds me of the lullaby I played on the piano.

"You look like I feel, Lucan."

He smiles and pats my arm like I'm four. "Yes, you and I feel it more so than the others, Junco. The end is getting closer now."

"Will I really hate you?"

He raises his eyebrows. "Perhaps not. I can't say without knowing what you feel for me now."

"I think you've been pretty wonderful to me, to be honest."

"I'm not sure wonderful will cover it."

"Are you going to kill me?"

He laughs. "Oh, Junco, I hope that was a joke."

I feel my face go red. "OK. It was."

He looks over at me and shakes his head. "Never, Junco. I would never do that."

"Will you let Tier die?"

I watch his face drop as I feel his heart skip a beat. "Believe it or not, that is not even in my control. I have no say at all. I used up all my gifts on Tier, there are none left for him."

I avoid his gaze as he looks over to me. "What's that mean?"

"It means that I've given him every advantage, illegal and otherwise, since the day he was born. There are limits as to how I distribute gifts and well, I have run out in his case. I've used them up. So, I am rather helpless to help the closest thing I will ever have to a son."

I stare at his mouth, trying to understand the words. "Tier is your son?"

"In an avian sort of way. I didn't make him, but I was there – for some reason I cannot even remember at this time – when he was pulled out of the womb. And I chose him. I poured it all into Tier."

"Why?"

"I cannot even say for certain, only that I felt compelled. I even named him. It doesn't really fit him though, that name. He's so much more than a predator."

I put my head down on my knees and we are quiet for a while. "I lied, Lucan. In the testimony. That AI is not inert, Layla was wrong. She told me what to do when I was under the drugs."

He looks over to me, sad. "I know, Junco."

"And I was praying to the Fallen Archer up in that Fledge Church, and she asked me if I wanted to make the sacrifice, and I said yes."

He nods again. "Yes, I saw some of that as well."

"Saw it how?"

He taps his head. "In my brain, one of my special talents."

"Oh, you know, Isec says he's a precog."

"Is he? Isn't life cruel? He needs to be a telepath to live, yet his genetics give him precognition, which does him absolutely no good because he must be a true-blood Aves to control it."

"Yeah, life is a total bitch." We swing in silence for a few seconds. "What's the High Order?"

I look up and watch his face crinkle. "Who told you about them?"

"No one, but Ash mentioned it when he was telling me about the Fallen Archer myth. He said he wasn't allowed to talk to me about them. I had to ask you."

His eyes sweep over to mine. "Everyone has a boss, Junco. Even me."

"That's it?"

He laughs. "That's it for now. Do you want me to tell you what to do with the AI?"

"Can I do anything? Or am I just stuck with it?"

He takes a moment to think. "Yes, you can make choices, but only you can decide which one is best. I can tell you to ignore her, take her advice, or refuse to do so. But in the end it doesn't matter. I do not think she can make fate shift."

"Well, shit. It sucks to be us, right? But oh fucking well. That's who we are. So, I guess the only thing left to do is finish it off, Lucan. When we get to the end, we'll revisit all this and see where we stand."

He smiles. "You can stay here tonight if you want. Sleep in your new room."

I take in a sharp breath. "I better not. No offense, but I should probably go home with everyone else until I can think a few things through."

"Would you like a bit of advice?"

"Absolutely," I say, looking up at him.

"Take your time, Junco. Think about what you really want. Last week you could not picture yourself living here and being happy, yet today I think you'll agree that has changed."

"Yeah, you're right."

"Ashur is a very good man."

I look up into his eyes to see if they are judging me. But they're not, they are kind and sad. "I know, Lucan."

He changes the subject so fast I almost feel dizzy. "Your piano playing was impeccable, even with missing fingers. Do you find that odd?"

I look down at my left hand. "Yes. It's funny, ya know, when it happened Tier took me back to the cavern and I woke up later all freaked out about it. But right before I passed out again he said, *You'll never miss them, Junco. I promise you, you'll never even know they're gone.*"

I smile and look up at Lucan. "And he was right. I never think about them. Ever. And I never miss them when I'm doing anything, not even when I'm climbing a wall or fighting or playing piano. It has no effect on me."

Lucan stands up and takes my hand. "Take the day off tomorrow, no training for anyone. Just do something fun."

I nod and he lets go of my hand and disappears.

I avoid Ashur for the rest of the night, but I watch him from across the room as he talks to Annun or one of the other pledges that he must think of as worthy. I sit at the table and play poker with the guys and let Braun distract me with his jokes filled with sexual innuendo.

At the end of the night I slouch against Tessen in the flyer on the way home and begin the process of making choices.

I can't sleep. Everything is somehow off balance and my mind refuses to let any of it go. I want to be with Ashur and forget everything else. Forget Tier and the last battle, and the Seven Siblings, and the myths.

I swing my feet out and walk over to the mast and before I can even think about what I'm doing, my wings are carrying me up to her. I land hard outside the huge wooden door after a dozen or more minutes of frantic flying and then go inside. The vestibule smells sweet with some kind of incense, which means other pledges have been in here recently. It makes me feel better that I'm not the only one drawn to her and her questions.

I pull open the second door, half expecting someone else to be inside, but it's empty. I walk up to the altar and stand in front of the offering. My eyes begin at the feet and trace down every inch of her writhing and twisting body until I get to her throat. I kneel down and sit back on my butt as I look at her half-outstretched wings. One falls to the side, bent at the elbow, the tip stretching outward. The other looks as if it is desperately trying to stay tucked up next to her back, but if the moment were released, it too would drop out.

I peer under her head to see her face. Her mouth, hidden unless you're underneath her, is open in a scream, her eyes wide.

"What do you want from me?"

"What do you have to give?"

I stand up and turn around. "Annun, what the fuck – you scared the shit out of me!"

"Sorry, I saw you come up here and I needed to make my visit anyway, so–"

"What will you do in here, Annun? I'm not quite sure what the purpose is besides convincing yourself that you're worthy."

"It's not to convince myself I'm worthy, Junco. It's to convince her. She chooses, not us."

"But she's not real. Is she?"

He smiles. "It's faith, right? If you believe, she's real. If you don't, she isn't."

"OK."

"Do you believe, Junco?"

"In her?" I pause and look back at the icon. "I already have a God, Annun. I'm just a bit infatuated with her persona at the moment."

"Has the Fledge changed you? I barely know you, so it's hard to tell if you've changed from the first fight."

I shrug. "Of course, yeah."

"I only ask because I don't even recognize myself anymore."

"Is that a good thing or a bad thing?"

He shakes his head. "Bad, I think. Killing all those people–"

"Yeah, that has changed me. My scroll is so long now, I'll never fit through the strait gate."

He looks at me funny. "Huh?"

"Nothing. I just mean, I've done a lot of bad things, way before I ever came to the avian world, and the only way to get past it is to push it down. Put it away. Only bring it out when you need it, Annun. That's the only way to get up in the morning."

"Sounds risky."

I huff out a laugh. "It definitely is, but it gets you through, right? To the next step. We're at the end now. We're done. Lucan says we have to take advantage of our last day, no training or nothing. And I agree, push this shit down and enjoy each other for one more day. Then whatever happens at the last fight, we'll at least have something good to counter the bad."

"You're for sure getting through, Junco."

"Yeah, I know that, Annun – but do you see my friends? Your friends are for sure getting through with you. So you're light-years ahead of me in that department. And the really ironic part is that all along Ashur warned me not to get attached to the weak ones. He warned me, but I thought I could save them."

I let out a huge sigh and shake my head. "It would be a lot easier if they were already dead." I look up at him, meet his eyes. "Because I'd have that shit locked down already, and be on the other side of death. That's the best place to be, ya know? On the other side of death."

"So, that's it? You can just turn it on and off like that? Forget about stuff and move on?"

I shrug.

"That's pretty impressive, Junco, really, I envy you. But it also makes you a little bit insane."

I laugh. "You should have seen me on Earth, Annun. I was beyond insane."

"So if Tier dies? If Ashur were to die? You'd turn that off too."

I look over at the syrinx and breathe, letting a few seconds pass before answering. "You bet, Annun." I look back up to his face, meet his eyes. "You fucking bet I would."

He shrugs. "You're the perfect fucking warrior then, right? Do what they tell you and then say more, please."

He's judging me now, but I don't even feel it. It's already turned off. "Annun, I was born the perfect fucking warrior, I never asked for it. They made me this way. If I were to let it go, what would I be then?"

His voice stays soft. "Just Junco, maybe?"

"And who the fuck is Junco except one small girl from Earth whose only worth is tied up with how accurately she can hit a target in the head from four thousand yards away?"

He watches my face for a moment. "I've heard she does a pretty mean flip on horseback. And she plays the piano so well it makes you want to cry."

I feel my chest heave and turn away, the tears filling up my eyes.

He walks over to me and puts his hand on my shoulder. "Sorry, Junco. I'm sorry. I'm no different. In fact, I'm much worse. You didn't choose to be here, but I did. I did. I left my safe life with the politicos to come here knowing full well if I made it I'd have this blood on my hands. At least you can say they made you what you are. I made myself this way. I wanted this."

I shake my head and look down at the syrinx and whisper, "I'll let you in on a secret, Annun. Since we're sharing. I like who I am and what I can do." I look up at him. "I do. I'd like to think that given the chance, I'd choose to be someone else. Someone kind and loving. Maybe a mother. But I think the odds of me actually doing that in an honest-to-God real situation are almost zero."

"I like it too, Junco. That's why we're both here in the church telling the syrinx we're OK with what it took to get here. And she should mark us worthy because we want to be here. We're not sorry we made it. We're proud. And when the last battle comes, we'll do what we have to because it's these shitty fucking moments that will show what we're made of. What kind of warriors we really are and what we have to offer. How much of ourselves we're really willing to sacrifice to hold it all together."

I stay silent for a few moments as I let his words sink into my memory. "They're gonna give you the command, I bet. Make you a captain."

"If they do, it'll only be because you're already taken."

"I'd follow you, Annun." I look up at him. "I would."

He smiles. "I'd definitely follow you, Junco. Just say the word and I'm there."

This is what Isten meant when he said the Fledge makes the team. I can feel it, how bonded I am to this guy I barely know. This stranger who will stick it out with me in my darkest moments and give me the words I need to hear so badly it makes my chest ache. I want to tell him, but I just smile instead. He grabs me by the shoulder and turns me around so we can walk out of the church together. Then we jump off the ledge and go back to the dorm to sleep away our midnight confessions.

Chapter Thirty-One

I wake to the whine of plasma rifles charging against my head and I lie still.

"Junco, please open your eyes and make no other movement until instructed to do so."

I open them. There are seven Aves warriors, not my team, and another man who looks a lot like Lucan, but who is definitely not, standing around my bed. The fair man smiles at me.

I wait.

"I am Rache, the Archer of Justice. We require your testimony today and when I instruct you to do so, you will get up, shower, dress, and come back out for transport over to the Justice habitat for the proceedings."

"Yes, sir."

"You may get up."

All seven warriors follow me to the showers and train their rifles on my head as I clean up and dress. I exit and am offered some type of food, which I refuse. Rache is waiting by the door and we take the stairs down the three flights to the ground floor. I watch the mods frantically talking on comms as I pass by the windows and I know they are speaking to the 039 or Lucan.

There is a large transport flyer waiting in the space where I usually puff on my cigars. As we approach, the doors open and I am ushered inside and take a seat in the middle, surrounded on all sides by plasma rifles on target.

Rache takes a seat opposite me and smiles.

I raise my eyebrow at him.

"This went better than expected."

"Really?" I say calmly. "You thought I'd, what? Kill you with my SEAR because you want to ask me questions?"

He sniffs and straightens his back. "Junco, you have an unprecedented wild side. We cannot be too careful."

"Huh." I stare at his blue eyes. "Well, good luck if Moju comes back. If you think I'm wild, I can't wait to see how you treat my brother."

"There's no need to be spiteful, Junco."

I shrug. "You're the one with the weapons trained on my head, Rache. If you're so afraid of me, why not just let the 039 bring me over to Justice? Or Lucan?"

"Because I wanted to meet you."

I squint at him. "Well, you're not making a great first impression."

He flicks his fingers and the guys back off. I nod to them and they nod back. It's not their fault he's excitable. I hold on to the arms of the chair as the flyer banks hard to the left and we glide into a parking structure.

"Have you been off Amelia before?"

I shake my head. "No, except to look at the stars with Lucan."

He stares at me for a split second and I catch his surprise before he locks it down. "Well, you are about to leave. We need to transfer to the ship that will take us to Justice. The men will remain on alert but will not target you. If you attempt to–"

I cut him off. "Rache, we're on the same fucking side. I'm not gonna make any attempts to do anything."

He smiles. "You'll excuse me if I'm suspicious. You are the only person that I know of who has successfully lied while under the truth drugs."

I keep my mouth shut for that one.

"Lucan confessed your actions, Junco."

I shrug. "It's always a bitch trying to predict how a drug will react with certain metabolisms. That's pretty basic toxicology and you should really have a handle on the possible side effects if you're gonna give that shit to humans."

"Half human," he corrects me.

"One third actually," I say as I turn my head away.

The door opens and we all exit and transfer to a waiting ship only a few dozen meters across the terminal. The G is light and feels artificial so I figure we're near the center edge of the torus. I enter the ship and buckle myself into the harness. A warrior sits next to me this time, his weapon stowed. He leans over and extends his hand. "Monk."

I smile and shake it. "Junco."

"Don't mind Rache, he's really not bad."

"Yeah, OK. So, is this gonna take long? This is my last day before Fight Seven and I wanted to spend it doing something fun."

"You'll be gone all day, sorry."

I nod and look away. "Not your fault."

I watch out the window as we are propelled out into the blackness of space and jump a little bit when the thrusters rumble alive to push us to wherever we're going. Being out in space in a little transport ship like this isn't as exciting as it sounds. In fact, there is absolutely nothing to look at and you're constantly adjusting yourself in the harness chair because free-G and sitting in one place don't really go together. I sleep the entire way and only wake up when Monk's hand forcibly shakes me back into reality.

I unbuckle my harness and stumble a little in the light G as I make my way to the door. From there the gravity evens out and I get heavier as we move through a series of polished tile hallways until we reach an unobtrusive beige door.

The guards talk on implant comms and we wait until some unknown signal tells us to proceed through the door. Rache goes first and turns left, I am directed to go right, led down another long hallway and through another door that leads out into what I could only describe as a courtroom.

Lucan is already there, but the other 039 aren't. He must have used his little teleportation thing to get there ahead of us. He comes over and dismisses the warriors around me with contempt.

"I apologize, Junco. They did not inform me of this until this morning."

"I figured, obviously."

He leads me over to a chair in the center of the room and motions me to sit. "Any advice?"

He smiles. "Just tell the truth, Junco. And if the AI gets involved, refuse to listen this time. It is important that we build trust with Justice."

I nod and he leaves and takes a seat in the circle of chairs which surround my own. Nothing like being in the hot seat.

"State your name for the record."

I look up at an officiator who stands in a corner of the room with a panel of other people, monitors maybe. "Junco Abigail Coot."

The officiator comes over with a red book and places it in front of me. "Put your left hand on the Bible and hold up your right hand."

I do.

"Do you solemnly swear to tell the truth, whole truth, and nothing but the truth so help you or may God strike you down dead?"

I almost laugh, but I hold it in. "I do." He takes the Bible back. "But my God doesn't strike people down dead. Just to be clear, that's not how the oath goes."

"Junco."

I look over at Lucan and shrug. "Sorry."

"State your age and place of residence."

"Nineteen. The Fledge place on Amelia. I don't know what it's called."

"Did you lie in the last testimony?"

"Yes."

"How were you able to lie?"

"I have a program inside me that can counteract the drugs."

"Did you ask the program to counteract the drugs when you were giving testimony?"

"No."

"Why did the program run?"

"I don't know." I hear a lot of murmuring from the back panel and look over, squinting my eyes.

"Are you running any programs now?"

"No."

He looks at me dubiously. "None?"

"Nope."

"Why not?"

"Because I don't know how to run them."

Lucan stands and speaks like he's bored out of his mind. "Objection. The topic has been exhausted."

"Sustained." The ruling comes from a voice in the ceiling and I figure out the process. The officiator is a prosecutor. Lucan is my defender. The voice is Rache, the judge.

The officiator tries a new tactic. "We've thrown out the treaty charge for Captain Raubtier at any rate, so we will not rehash that issue today. Today I want to know why he didn't kill you as he was instructed."

I frown. "Shouldn't you ask him that?"

"I have asked him that, now I am asking you."

I sigh. Loudly. "He told me that he made the decision to disobey orders when he saw how I reacted after I crashed my Goat into a tree on my way to The Stag."

"Continue."

"He said I was fearless, that I wasn't a quitter, and that he felt I'd have a lot to offer you, the avians, if I was just told the truth once in a while."

"Continue."

"That's it."

"That is all the reason he gave?"

I nod. "Yes. That's it."

"Did he mention the reward for bringing you back?"

My heart skips. "No."

"Did he mention what he might receive if he brought you back?"

"I actually did ask him that, believe it or not. I'm a rather suspicious person by nature. And he said he was looking for redemption."

A lot of murmuring from the back panel now, and I can't help myself, I turn and look over at them.

"From what, specifically, was he seeking redemption for?"

"Killing a lot of people I think."

"Did he tell you who these people were?"

"No, but I was told by someone else who they might be."

"So you knew that he was responsible for killing children?"

"Objection, this is embellishment."

I look over at Lucan but stay silent.

"Overruled, continue, Miss Coot."

"I know he killed mutant children out at The Stag Camp, he said they were monsters."

"Who else did you think he killed?"

"Corporate humans. I don't really know."

"It wasn't worth asking about? To know this for sure before you decided to leave your planet and come to a strange world, uninvited?"

"Well, I've killed a lot of people myself, so you know – typically we just do the old wink and a nod at that stuff, right? Like the code among thieves."

"Junco." I look over at Lucan and he shakes his head at me.

"I absolved him," I say, shrugging.

The officiator looks at me strangely now. "You what?"

"I absolved him. From whatever it was he did."

"Miss Coot, please explain how that works for those of us unfamiliar with the process."

I exhale loudly. "I forgave him, in advance. Before knowing what he did."

He stares at me now, like I'm a wart on his hand. "Why?"

"Because I needed to trust *someone* and I really wanted it to be him. And I didn't want to hear what he did. I tried to prevent him from telling me, in fact."

"Did anyone send you here, Miss Coot?"

"No."

"What do you hope to receive from the avians, if we should allow you to stay?"

I stare at the officiator, then look over at Lucan as my heart begins to race. "You're kicking me out?"

"I didn't say that, Miss Coot. What would you want from the avian people if they should allow you to stay?"

I take a breath and calm myself as the vision screen comes alive. *Tell them: to be accepted and allowed to prove myself.*

"To be accepted and allowed to prove myself."

"And how could you prove yourself to the avian people?"

Say: I will bring back the Siblings on Earth and deliver the code you need to survive.

I say it and the room erupts in a gasp. I look over at Lucan and he gives me an ever-so-slight nod.

"I have no further questions."

The voice above erupts. "Miss Coot, you are free to leave with your Archer."

Lucan comes over and takes my hand, leading me towards the door, then touches my shoulder and we are outside Fledge.

"Well done, Junco."

"She told me to say that."

"Well, thank the gods above that she did because it probably just saved your life."

Chapter Thirty-Two

I walk into Fledge and it is so quiet I think that the entire place is empty. But when I look around I see that all fifteen of us are there, just spread out among the many, many extra beds.

"What's going on?"

At first no one answers, then Kush comes up. "There was a pretty big fight earlier, everyone's upset."

"What was it about?"

He shrugs. "Who will live and who will die tomorrow, Junco. Fuck."

He walks away and I go sit down next to Tessen. "Bad day, huh?"

She nods. "Where have you been, Junco?"

I sigh. "I was on trial, I think."

"What?"

"Yeah, at first I thought I was there to testify against Tier, but I think I was on trial myself. To see if they will let me stay or kill me, or whatever."

She looks at me, stunned. "So what happened?"

"I promised to bring the Siblings back from Earth if they let me stay. Who'd have fucking thought that I'd be bummed about being sent back to Earth." I look up at her. "But I am."

"Then why did you volunteer?"

"I had to. I think they were gonna kill me, Tessen."

I leave and go over to my bunk. Isec's bunk hasn't changed from when I woke up, but he's either sleeping or pretending to be asleep and has his back to me. That's OK with me. I can't face him right now anyway. I change into my bed clothes and lie down, thinking about tomorrow until I drift off.

The next morning there is no alarm, but we all wake early. I sit on the side of my bunk moving my almost healed ankle around in circles and looking around at everyone, then get up and take my shower and dress in my uniform. I grab all my junk in my cubbie and take it over to my bed. I don't know what will happen after the battle, but I want to sort through things before we have to leave.

I find a bunch of notes from Lucan and the guys that I never saw. From after the first testimony when I was mad. It seems so long ago, that fight with Ashur. I sort the stuff out into three bags and leave them at the foot of my bed.

And then I sit there. Just like everyone else. And we do absolutely nothing until the call comes to line up for the fight.

The prep room is small and the markings on the floor are back. This time they have a moon shape and they line us up in a crescent, all facing the same direction. I am in the middle somewhere, between Annun and Tessen. Neither Kush nor Isec are talking to me this morning and I don't even note where they are in line.

I feel the silence before start, and swallow as we are shunted upward. We erupt into a large arena that I recognize as the free-G room where Ashur taught me to fly, but the perimeter is filled with people. The mushrooms that I practiced flying and jumping on have been turned on their sides and they flank us, five on one side and five on the other. My feet are stuck to the floor and I jump a little as the observers begin to clap politely.

Annun looks down at me and I shake my head and shrug. I see Ashur and the guys in the center, behind Lucan, and then as I look around I see other Archers, with their personal Aves teams sitting behind them. I even see Rache and his guys. Monk catches my gaze and waves. Behind the Archers are more warriors.

Lucan puts up a hand and the room goes silent. "Welcome to Fight Seven of the 2153 General Fledge. We are here today to declare a winner and choose a new team of Aves warriors."

The Aves clap until Lucan begins to speak. "We will begin with the winner." He backs away and Ashur comes forward. "The 039 is proud to declare that Junco, Aves 039, is the winner of the 2153 General Fledge with a total of eighty-seven kills."

My vision falters at the number. Eighty-seven people dead because of me playing this game.

"Junco, please come forward."

I feel my feet come unstuck and I walk up the stairs to Ashur. He shakes my hand, a very human congratulations, then kisses me on both cheeks and places a medal around my neck.

"Choose the warrior you would have first on your team."

I take deep breath. Here we go. I look at each of my fellow pledges as my eyes move down the line. Isec refuses to look at me, Kush is angry, and Tessen smiles. I smile back at her. "I choose Annun."

Ashur squeezes my shoulder and bends into my ear. "Well done, Junco. Come with me now."

He flies over to the first mushroom across the room and I follow. When we get there I hover for a second and then he pushes me back and I am locked against the stone. Unable to move.

Annun is beckoned to the stage and the process is repeated.

"I choose Merkar."

"I choose Pike."

"I choose Kush."

Kush stands on the stage and we wait as he looks down the line. I stare at him, glad he's on the hot seat for once. Not so fucking easy when it's you who has to make the choice.

He chooses someone I don't even know and I huff out some air. Ashur looks back at me but I shake my head.

The next kid chooses his friend.

And the next kid chooses his friend. All pledges I can't even identify by name. That guy chooses Wyrd.

Wyrd walks to the stage and takes a hard swallow to shut down his panic and relief. There is only one spot left and six hopeful faces look up to him, begging for a chance. "I choose Tessen." She screams and I feel the relief wash over me. Since she is the last she is escorted to the final mushroom, directly across from where I stand. I catch her eye and smile. Then look over to Isec and my face falls. He's crying.

My back comes unstuck from the stone and then Lucan is talking to me. "Junco, Aves 039, please come forward."

I fly over and land next to him. Ashur shadows me and stands behind us. "Junco, as the Fledge captain, it is your responsibility to cull the unsuitable members."

My heart pounds as I look up at him.

"Do you understand, Junco?" he asks me kindly and in a low voice.

I nod and whisper, "Yes, sir."

I look up into the crowd, to judge them, but I come away unsatisfied. There is nothing but sympathy for me. There are no hoots or hollers now, no clapping, no laughing or smiling. Only pity. I look over to Annun and he nods and I read his lips as they say, "Show them, Junco."

To his credit, Lucan stands patiently and watches me sort through the reality of what I have to do. I look down for a minute and bring back Annun's words in the church... *And when the last battle comes, we'll do what we have to because it's these shitty fucking moments that will show what we're made of.*

My breath comes faster as I walk down the stairs, then walk behind the pledges and remove my SEAR from my stomach. I hear the crowd gasp and whisper as I activate it and dial it down to dagger size.

I cut their heads off from behind. The crackle of the plasma through tissue sends tendrils of burning flesh up into the air and I watch as the entire arena wrinkles their collective nose at me.

When I get to Isec he's crying hysterically and I know that if his feet were not stuck to the floor, he'd be running from me like those girls Ashur is forever watching in his horror screens.

I step out in front of him, to at least look him in the eyes, but he squeezes them shut, tightly sealed from reality. His tears drop down his cheeks as I remove his head. And then I shut down the SEAR and stick it under my shirt and stand there, looking down at the rumpled heap of bodies and the wide-eyed expressions on the floor. The audience remains quiet and somber until Ashur appears and leads me away and out of sight and then the whispers begin.

They sound like a flock of starlings in the trees over winter.

That seals the deal.

I know exactly what I'm made of.

Cold fucking stone.

Chapter Thirty-Three

I don't even know how I got here, but I am kneeling at the syrinx's head in the church, the silent tears streaming down my cheeks. I hear the door open behind me, but I don't turn until Lucan kneels down next to me on the red carpeted floor. He puts his arm around me. "Junco, let's go home."

I shake my head and push his arm off. "No, I'm not done."

"You've been in here for an hour, Junco. Everyone is gone now, let's go home and you can think about it there."

"I fucking said no, Lucan. I'm not fucking done."

"What do you need to do to be finished?"

"An answer."

"An answer to what question, Junco?"

I let out a deep sigh. "Why am I so evil? How much longer do I have to keep killing?"

"You could quit, if you want."

I snort. "Yeah, I could die, too."

He stays silent after that.

"She's here, I know it. She just doesn't want to answer me because she wants something, just like everyone else. She wants something from me and it's gonna be you next. Or Ashur. Or Isten. It's gonna be you guys next, just to make me pay for all the shitty fucking things I just added to my scroll. I can feel it. Someone will come up to me, maybe that Rache guy, and he'll say, *It's your job, Junco. Kill your best friend now, kill your favorite. Kill your Archer.*" I look up at him and it's painful to see the look in his eyes. "And I'll do it, Lucan. I know I will."

"You won't, Junco. You're with us now."

I shake my head. "How could you ever trust me again? I'm a total sell-out. I'm nothing but a programmed robot waiting for new orders. It's great if you're the one in charge of me, yeah. Sure. That's great. But God fucking forbid you be on the receiving end, right? Because I'm just a good little soldier. Follow orders and then say, more please."

"Junco, this is what every General Fledge winner goes through. It is predictable, this grief. These doubts. You did follow orders, but those pledges would not be suitable for this Cluster. And they were not suitable for their own Clusters. They were defective."

"I don't mean to make comparisons like this, Lucan, and normally I never would because you're entitled to your own culture, but on Earth we love the defective just as much as the average. More, sometimes."

"This is not Earth, Junco, and we are not human."

I sniff up some snot. "Yeah, I know."

"We are at a critical stage, we have no genetic stock to speak of, Junco. None that we can afford to use. Do you know that the General Fledge used to yield more than two hundred new Aves warriors? It wasn't always ten."

I look up and take a deep breath. He smiles at my new attention to his words.

"We produced so many quality warriors. We were overfilled with candidates, those qualified for command, and those fighters who had everything it took to make our ranks successful. But this is what the bad code has done to us. Reduced us to the one-percent rule. And if we can be perfectly honest here, you and I both know that only four or five, at the most, of those ten today were really qualified."

I swallow because I knew it instinctively as I watched them line up. Even Kush is questionable.

"Why didn't you choose Isec, Junco? It was completely up to you."

I drop my head and close my eyes. "Because he would have chosen Tessen or Wyrd or Kush."

"But they were all chosen anyway."

"I know, but it would have been a lie." I look up at him. "I'm not supposed to lie unless it's war. Isec was not my pick. Isec never saved my life. Annun did. And I didn't know." I turn my head away and let the tears spill out. "I didn't know, Lucan. If I had known— " I let the words drop unsaid. I'd like to think I would've lied and picked Isec, but I'm not sure. I'm not sure and I cannot even bring myself to lie about it now.

"Do you know we purposely reworded the question this year, to make it less strict as to who can be chosen? And that all the sitting Archers signed on, just to give you the chance to save your little friend – in case you needed to retain that human element to stay with us."

"What?" I look up in his face and feel my heart shrivel up with sadness.

"We usually ask which of the remaining warriors you would follow into battle. And this Fledge we decided to ask you to choose the warrior you would have first on your team. We gave you an out if you needed it."

I stare at him, sniffing and unsure what to think.

"Of course, we would all have been disappointed if you took the out. And when you didn't, when you chose the best of the remaining warriors to follow, you earned the respect of the entire Aves population. You were objective under enormous emotional stress, and you came through for us."

"I don't feel well."

"You are exceptional, Junco. Exceptional. You have natural gifts that we cannot even comprehend yet. And you have given Amelia and the rest of the worlds hope with your promise to deliver the Siblings."

"How the fuck can I deliver them, Lucan? She made me say that, I was scared and she made me say it! I have no power to deliver them."

"You do have power, Junco, you'll see. Moju is waiting for you. He's waiting for you to just come and ask him to come home. He's not waiting for Tier, no matter what you think, he's holding on for you. I saw it." I look up at him and he nods. "I would not lie."

He takes my hand and pulls me up.

I consider fighting him but I don't. He leads me down the stairs of the altar and back between the always-empty benches of the syrinx church. And then we are out the door and Ashur and Isten are waiting. I look up at them and force the tears back, then paint an angry frown on my face as they grab my arms and fly me down to the dorm.

We hear the uproar long before we land and walk the short distance to the lounge area. All the guys are there, as are a few I don't recognize, and they are shouting and pointing to the screen on the wall.

Lucan is arguing with several others who look like him, so I assume they are Archers, and Isten and Ashur join the fray as they push for dominance.

It takes me a few seconds to turn and log what's scrolling across the screen.

It's Tier.

He's dressed in some nondescript uniform, not the Aves uniform, and his eyes look distant with drugs. He's on the gurney, under testimony. A reporter flashes across the screen and summarizes the event that has everyone here riled up.

He's pleaded guilty to treason and Justice has accepted the plea.

The trial is over.

I stare at the words that splash across the screen. Then watch as a camera shows a large crowd rioting outside the Fledge building. I walk over towards the door and make it down two flights of stairs before I hear the 039 calling my name. I hop down the stairs faster, pushing down the residual pain from my ankle injury as a banging noise from below draws me down. I race out towards the front door and skid to a stop, sliding on the floor and landing on my hip sideways as a window shatters from the blunt force of some large object.

The rioters are wild, screaming and pointing at me like I am the one who is guilty of treason. I scramble up as they break down the barrier keeping them at bay and then they are spilling into Fledge. The SEAR comes to life in full sword length just as I hear the heavy boots behind me.

The plasma loop illuminates their faces in the dim evening light that leaks in from outside and it's their turn to skid to a stop on the gleaming white floor and fall on their asses. I crouch with the SEAR in high ready position and shake my head. The little red lights in the eyes of some tells me they are reporters, or at least recording the scene. "Don't even fucking think about it."

Lucan appears between the mob and me. Then the 039 and I are standing shoulder to shoulder. Ashur puts his hand on my weapon arm. "Put it away, Junco. You're just making it easier for them to hate you."

I wait a few seconds as Lucan barks orders and the other Aves teams push them back outside with force. I breathe, and the SEAR slips back into place. "What the fuck was that?"

Ashur shakes his head. "They blame you. For Tier's fate."

My eyes squint as my mouth draws down in a long frown. They blame me. Because he should have killed me like he was instructed. Just like I had to kill Isec when I was instructed. I watch Lucan argue with several individuals who appear to be reporters and then he grabs one and escorts him over to me.

It's Kadian.

"Junco," Lucan snaps, "come upstairs." He has a pretty good grip on Kadian's arm and then he touches me on the shoulder and we appear up in the dorm. I am immediately drawn towards the unbearable noise coming from the far wall and I absently walk over to the lounge. The screen is alive with action and my eyes track to a familiar landmark. I feel dizzy as I realize the footage is from Earth.

Peak City is bursting in explosions. I look over at Lucan and I can see his shock as well. The reporter's voice isn't registering in my brain, because when I look back all I see are the words *Tactical EM Pulse and Nuke Explodes over Peak City* scroll across the lower edge of the screen.

I hear boots running up the stairs and then Ashur is next to me. I look up at him and watch the flashes of destruction flicker across his face for a few seconds before he looks down and meets my gaze. Lucan's hand is on me then and he is pulling, yelling at Ashur to turn the fucking screen off, and yanking on Kadian's arm so hard he's begging desperately for him to let go.

"Stop!" I scream as my hands come up to my ears. "Just shut the fuck up for a minute, all of you!" I breathe in and out repeatedly as Ashur moves to turn the screen off. "Stop, Ashur. Leave it alone. It's my fucking home that was just blown up, so if anyone has a right to watch as it falls apart, it's me."

The room is hushed of human sound and all eyes are on me. Only the explosions make it into my ears. I look over at the stairs and most of the guys from downstairs, and all of the Archers, are there, quiet and still. I walk over to the couches and take a seat, then lean back into the cushions and turn up the volume and log every detail, every scream, every dead body, and every demolished building that used to be the rock of my existence as it falls into ruin.

A little while later an additional nuke is reported. This time it takes out Council Three in the RR. A hovercopter flies as close as it can get in the northwestern sector to show the world the burned land that used to be my tallgrass. The tears finally begin to fall. My whole life, everything I had before I came here, is wiped away in a single day.

They stay there with me and watch the screen, every one of them, my team or otherwise. Warrior or Archer. They all stay. And they say nothing. We just watch as the entire middle section of the United Republics erupts into total war.

Eventually Ashur takes my hand and pulls me up. "We're going home now." On the ride home I stare out the window and think. My home is gone, Tier is guilty, I have promised to deliver something that might not even be possible, and I killed someone who trusted me.

And millions of people are dead, Junco. Maybe Moju too, so this might signal the end of the entire avian race. And all you think about is how it affects you? Nice.

When we land on the upper terrace of the apartment I push Ashur off and go directly to my room. My biometrics release the lock and I close it behind me before anyone can follow.

I leave the lights off and sit down in the window seat, looking out at traffic and the bright lights of Amelia proper. My vision screen comes to life but stays silent.

Is there a way to salvage anything from this event?

There is always a way, Junco. The question is, as always, what are you willing to sacrifice to make it happen?

"What do you want?" I say out loud.

Your compliance.

"Tell me what I have to do."

You know what you have to do. You've known it all along. It's the reason you stayed behind when Slag came for you. It's the reason you fought with Lucan. It's the reason you lied under testimony. And it's the reason you will push Ashur away.

I shake my head. "There is only one way to make it right."

Yes. So shut the fuck up and get on with it, why don't you? Quit looking at the things you've lost and see the things you have.

Chapter Thirty-Four

I wake up in the new bed, luxurious blankets and pillows strewn about from my thrashing. My door is open and I can hear voices coming from the living room. Ryse's for sure, and a few more that I don't recognize. They joke a little and get loud and Ryse tells them to keep it down. I hear the familiar sound of poker chips and listen for Braun, but his voice is not among the cacophony of maleness that floats into my room.

I get up and go into the bathroom and start a bath, adding bubbles as I watch it fill up, then strip my Fight Seven uniform off and sink into the hot water with a heavy sigh. I slip under a few times to get my hair wet, then use the provided bottles to wash and condition it.

When I'm done I wrap up in a white robe that hangs on the bathroom door and stuff my hair up in a towel. Back out in my room the voices are louder now and I tap the door shut and go find something to wear. A few minutes later I hear a knock.

"Enter."

"Sorry, Junco. I hope we didn't wake you up." Ryse smiles at me and I try to smile back, but I'm just not into it. I just go into the closet and pull on some bed shorts and a tank top. Then find some white fuzzy socks that slip over my feet and go back in the bathroom to brush my hair.

When I come back out he's sitting on my bed, waiting for me.

"What?"

"You want me to call Ashur and tell him to come home?"

"Why? Where is he?"

"Working on something for Lucan."

I shake my head. "No point, really. It is what it is, Ryse. And there's nothing any of you can say or do to change it."

He nods. "Yeah. OK. Well, when you're hungry you just let me know. I'll help you pick something you'll like from the autocook."

He walks over to the door and I walk over with him and close it as he leaves, then go over to the window seat and plop down. It's a fabulous space and looks out over the boulevards. Several stories down

I can see the train, then several more there is another one. I can't see the bottom during the day either, but there are tall buildings across from me that are interesting to look at. Plus, there is a lot of eye-level traffic that captures my attention.

I pull my legs up to my chest as I watch the people who pass by inside the flyers. A noise over on the pile of clothes in the bathroom pulls me out of my reflection and I jump up and go grab my comm from my pants pocket.

"This is Junco."

"Hi, Junco. It's Kadian."

I sigh. "What do you want, Kadian?"

"Oh, I just wanted to check up on you, make sure you're OK. I'm very sorry, Junco. Everyone is very sorry."

"Yeah, except those crazy people who wanted to kill me last night for Tier's stupid decision."

"They have calmed down due to the – circumstances. Have you watched the screens today? There was a public apology."

"No," I sigh. "I just woke up."

"Well, I have an ulterior motive for calling you."

"Yeah, what's that then?"

"I want to take you somewhere tonight. Will you come out with me?"

I'm shaking my head even though he can't see me. "Kadian, I don't really–"

"Junco, I promise you, this is something beautiful you won't want to miss."

"How would you know?"

"I heard you that day we met, when you asked that barbaric XO of yours if there was anything he could show you that was purely avian, not human. I have something I can show you. Something that fulfills that request."

I'm interested despite myself. "What is it?"

I listen to him tisk his tongue. "Surprises, Junco, mean you have to trust me that it will be worthwhile."

"I'm not really into surprises, Kadian, people tend to get killed when they try to surprise me."

He laughs. "Nonsense, Junco. You're a woman and that means you like surprises just as much as any of them. You've just been around all those killing machines for so long you've forgotten how it feels."

He's got a point there. "I'm not really good at" – I search for the word – "socializing, Kadian. In fact, I'm pretty terrible at all that stuff."

"No, Junco, you've just never been taken out properly before."

"Look, I'm not interested–"

"Me either, Junco. I am happily attached to a very beautiful woman who I would like for you to meet tonight. I just want to show you something, OK?"

I look down at my clothes. "What should I wear?"

"Not those bed clothes you have on."

"How do you–"

"I live across the boulevard, Junco. Exactly opposite your window. And before you go thinking I'm some stalker, we've lived here for years. It's just a happy coincidence."

I walk over to the window seat and peer out, training my eyes to the building across the way, and see a small figure waving at me through the breaks in traffic. "So Ryse was correct? You're a spy and you write terrible things about us? You peep into our apartment?

He gives me an exasperated huff, "This is a family home, Junco. Someone in my family has owned it for centuries."

"So you make stuff up about us?"

"I absolutely do not. Everything I've ever reported on the 039 has been one hundred percent true."

"But maybe it was secret? And you reported it anyway?"

I hear a small laugh over the com. "Perhaps. But that's what reporters do."

"So you want to take me out so you can report on me tomorrow?"

"Well, of course I will report on you. You're news, Junco. But the venue is worthwhile, and does deliver what you're looking for. Something that cannot be seen on Earth."

I hesitate.

"It is beautiful, Junco. And you could use a little beauty in your life today."

He's right. I could just sit here and listen to Ryse and his buddies play poker. As if my whole world wasn't in the process of coming down on me. Or I could go out and forget for a while. And isn't that what always gets me through the disasters? Forgetting? Shit, if there's one thing I can do it's push it all away. "OK, I'll go."

"Perfect, I'll pick you up in five minutes, wear anything you want."

And then the comm goes dead.

I throw on some pants that look like human jeans, but aren't. And a shirt that isn't too complicated to pull over my head and seam together. I slip on my uniform boots because they are comfortable, and then head out.

Ryse and his friends look up as I enter and walk over to the terrace to go up to the roof. "Hey? Junco? Where are you going?" Ryse's cigar bobs up and down in his mouth as he talks.

"Out," I say. I'm halfway up the terrace stairs when I hear the flyer on the roof. Ryse is running to catch up with me, but I don't stop. The door opens on the flyer and Kadian is smiling at me.

"Oh, fuck no!" Ryse steps in between the flyer and me, blocking my advance, but I shoot him a dirty look.

"Ryse, I'm not a prisoner anymore. I'm Fledged out now and if I want to go out, then I will."

"But Junco," he pleads a little, "this is Kadian, he's a total scumbag."

I stick my chin up. "I have my comm so Lucan can track me all night. I'm going, and there's nothing you can say about it."

"Ashur is not going to–"

"Ashur isn't my keeper, Ryse. I'm not on duty so I don't have to take orders from you or him."

Kadian has exited the flyer and steps up to Ryse. "I promise to deliver her home safe and happy."

Ryse actually growls at him and I push him back and jump in the flyer. Kadian gets in with me and then the door closes and we take off.

The flyer banks hard into a parking structure and I have a fleeting moment of déja vu at the suborbital station with Rache. I push it down and get out. Kadian stays seated and I poke my head back into the cab. "You coming or what?"

He smiles and shakes his head. "Girl stuff, Junco. I'll pick you up in two hours."

Before I can protest there are female hands leading me away and into a steamy shop filled with tantalizing flowery scents and the bustle of girls. I am subsequently plopped down onto some large cushions as a team goes to work on my fingernails, talons, hair, and to my horror, a full face of make-up including eyelashes that make my lids feel heavy.

When they bring about a mirror a while later I don't even recognize the girl on the other side. My hair is piled high on my head with soft tendrils slipping out every so often to soften and frame my face. My hazel eyes appear large and the color is brought out with make-up. My lips are a pretty pink just like my cheeks, and when I tilt my head to see the SEAR scar along my jaw it has all but vanished.

The ladies all nod and smile, then tug me up and guide me into a dressing room where a severe woman with a tight silver bun and wings to match sits with her lips pursed.

"It is a genuine improvement, Junco. Do you approve?"

I look in the full-length mirror. "Yeah, I like it."

She smiles. "I'm Anni and now we will dress you for the night. The dress is a gift, of course. So you may keep it."

"OK, thanks."

She brings out a stunning floor-length gown that is the prettiest shade of spring yellow I've ever seen. As she goes about instructing her helpers in fastening it around my wings I catch a glimpse in the mirror.

"Wow."

They top it off with a slight jacket made of some kind of fur that is a shade or two lighter than my hair. I scowl at the shoes as they place my feet in them, but Anni clicks her tongue at my balking and after I give in and cooperate, I'm suddenly three inches taller.

Anni takes my hand and lifts it in the air as she turns me slowly in a circle. "You are ready."

She claps and her attendants escort me into another chamber, then through a closed door to the parking garage where the flyer is waiting. The door opens and Kadian appears, dressed in a very nice dark brown suit that complements the tones in my hair and jacket. I take his hand as he offers me help into the cab.

"Junco," he breathes, "you're stunning."

I pick up the high-society manners I was forced to practice all growing up. "Thank you. You look exceptionally handsome as well."

He is tight-lipped about our destination. I watch as the flyer takes us a few wide avenues over to the boulevard, then banks to the right and slides into a slot in the side of a building. I read a marquee above a large expanse of wide brass colored doors: *Enki and the World Order*, last night on Amelia.

When my eyes come back to Kadian, he is grinning. "I think you'll enjoy it, Junco. It's a beautiful retelling of the myth in nargala."

I nod, but I have no idea what he's talking about.

I've been to the opera on Earth, Handel's Messiah in Berlin and London, as well as The Marriage of Figaro in Vienna and of course, Asgarth's Genius in just about every city it opened in during my lifetime. My father indulged me in the arts for reasons known only to him.

This feels like the opera.

The women are dressed in expensive finery while the men wear complementary suits to match something on their lady's person. Kadian is a nice-looking man to begin with, and his suit is cut to perfection, so we fit in with the crowd. We stand in the lobby as people take pictures of us. Normally I'm self-conscious about stuff like that, but tonight I feel like I have a costume on and don't have to be the gawky Junco. I don't smile, I can't smile, but I do paint on a neutral expression that passes for acceptable.

An usher directs us to a chamber that contains several seats. We take two near the edge of a balcony, and Kadian leans over to talk in my ear. "The nargala is sung in avian, but I have been told that you understand it. Yes?"

"I do."

He smiles. "Good, good. It's an old story, but the fourth act is especially poignant. I think, anyway."

He gives me a conspiratorial look and I nod a little. "OK."

A little while later the lights dim and the show begins.

Kadian calls the woman rotating in mid-air in the center of the theater the Ilat Nargalist, and he genuinely beams with pride when he suddenly announces that she is his girlfriend.

She is beautiful, dressed in a bright blue gown that hangs to the floor several stories below. She floats like an angel, her outstretched wings the color of a robin's egg. They don't flap, so I can only assume she is controlling herself via a free-G zone that doesn't touch the rest of us.

When she begins her song my chest heaves with the beauty of it. It is not a song any human can replicate, the notes are so high they barely exist in my hearing range. I see my vision screen come to life and adjust my capacity for sound detection, and her true talents flood into my body. She is singing several notes at the same time, like an orchestral arrangement coming from the mouth.

I am so taken by the sound, I forget to listen to the words. Eventually I catch on to the story. Enki is the all-powerful creator and he's going about to various family members allocating supervision duties. Each god and goddess is bestowed a realm with special powers. He has quite a big family, so this lasts the first three acts.

The fourth act begins with a twist.

A very young goddess Inanna complains that she has been overlooked. I think back to what I know of Inanna. Not much except for her journey to the world down below as told to me by Tier. In this story she begs to know why Enki, her uncle, has forsaken her.

Why do you treat me so badly?
My sisters have all been given domains to rule over.
My sisters have all been given powerful husbands.
My sisters have all been given special skills.
My sisters have all been given the ability to please you.
But I, the woman Inanna, have been given nothing of this new world.

Her uncle replies,

Tell me what you require, Inanna.
Tell me how I have wronged you.
Tell me what more could I give you?

You shine brilliantly in the evening,
You brighten the day at dawn
You stand in the heavens like the sun and the moon,
Your wonders are known both above and below,
I made you strong.
I made you the destroyer of all that cannot be destroyed.
I made you cunning.
I made you the speaker of words known to no man.
I made you the twister.
I made you the manipulator of the threads that bind the world.
I gave you sight.
You see further than any other, you see what no other can.
I made you beautiful.

You have endless suitors ready to lay down their lives.
You cut off the heads of those that cannot be cut.
You make the final decisions,
You make the sacrifice.
You stand apart.
You make us whole.
You complete us.
What more do you want?

Chapter Thirty-Five

I feel a tear slip down my cheek as I listen to her song and I wait for Inanna to accept her gifts with grace. But she does not, she demands the Carrier of Light and she is denied. The nargala ends with her behaving badly and being cast aside. Someone grabs my hand as another tear slips out. I look over and Lucan is sitting next to me. He squeezes as the theater goes dark.

We are standing in the lobby a short time later when the Ilat Nargalist comes to greet us. She bows low from the waist at Lucan and he takes her arm at the elbow and squeezes with both hands. She slips her free hand to his elbow and bows again. A very avian greeting that I have yet to master the nuances of.

I am introduced but my world is spinning. Lucan excuses us and taps me on the shoulder and we are out in the dark of space.

I sigh. "Thank you, I was beginning to feel dizzy."

He smiles and wraps my hand into the crook of his arm. "Yes, I could tell it was becoming too much."

"Why did you come?" I look up at him and he does something that surprises me, he shrugs.

"I would not have taken you there, Junco. It is–" He stops and searches for a word. "Too close."

I think back to the story. "Yeah. Why do I feel like it is talking about me?"

He laughs a little, but it's not a happy laugh. "You are so much like Inanna it is becoming painful."

I let out a large breath. "What's going on, Lucan?"

He shakes his head. "You are the Seventh Sibling, Junco. We know this now, and we can state this openly, correct?"

I shrug. "Hell, Lucan, if you say so. What am I gonna say? I don't know any better. But I'm not here to kill anyone."

He pats my hand, the one still holding onto his arm. "I think we are past that, but there is still a long way to go before we can sort it out."

I stay quiet for a few minutes and look up at the stars, enjoy the view for once. How many people can say they've been out in the middle of space with no suit? Not many, I bet. I count myself lucky. "Thank you," I say, looking down again.

"For what, Junco?"

"Everything. I feel so ungrateful. Always looking at how much I've lost instead of how much I still have. I don't want to be Inanna. I don't want to be hungry for power. That's not me. I want to be satisfied." I look up to him. "And even though there is still a lot to be sad about, there is also a lot to be grateful for. I'm thankful that you're here helping me through this. Even if I don't show it all the time."

He squeezes my hand and we are on the terrace at the 039. "You lost a lot in the last few months, Junco, and even though grief is a negative emotion, it is still necessary. There is nothing wrong with grief."

I look over and see Ashur lingering in the doorway. Then Lucan takes my arm like he did the Ilat Nargalist and says goodbye in a way that touches my heart.

I watch the air after he's gone for a few seconds, then walk over to the open terrace door to look up at Ashur.

He smiles. "Did you have a nice evening?"

"Yes, but..."

He raises his eyebrow at me. "What?"

"It would have been better if you were there with me." I shrug, then lift my long gown slightly as my fancy shoes click past him, past the guys sitting in front of the screen, and down the small hallway to my room where I take the costume off and soak in the tub until I am red with heat.

I'm in bed, not sleeping since my days and nights are mixed up yet again, when Ashur, dressed in some thermals and a t-shirt that makes him look more like one of my scrub buddies back on Earth than my avian captain, knocks on my open door. He walks over to the bed and sits down. "I have something for you." In his hand is a book and I sit up a little, interested.

"What is it?"

"The translation of the syrinx church door inscriptions."

I scoot over and open the covers. "Get in and read it to me."

He smiles and does what I ask. I lean up against him as he opens the book and we flip through the pages, looking at what the inscriptions mean. It's an obscure creation myth that even Ashur is unfamiliar with.

He loses interest and hands the book over as I pore through the translations, then go hunting for a few in my own memory to compare them. They are not exact word-for-word matches, but close.

Ashur is almost asleep when I close the book and sink down into the covers with him. "You were so beautiful tonight, Junco. I could barely look at you."

I smile. "I did look pretty good."

He turns his head and opens his eyes. "You know, you make a much better woman than you do a soldier."

"Thank you."

"You should stay a woman, Junco. Retire and be soft for the rest of your life. You don't have to do this if you don't want to."

I shake my head and let out a sigh. "I am what I am, Ash. It can't be helped. This hardness is what keeps me alive and soft is not really something I do. I'm OK with that, for a while anyway. And I promised to go back to Earth and bring home the stupid Siblings. I can't quit now."

"I could do that for you."

I turn and look at him. His green eyes study me back. "I made the promise, it had conditions attached. Besides, Tier might have given up on himself, but I haven't. It's not over until it's over."

He props himself up on his elbow. "What? Are you fucking kidding me?" His eyes dart back and forth, trying to see the meaning behind my words. "He's done, Junco. I don't like it either, but he's done."

"Maybe he is, but I'm not. I owe him."

"You don't owe him, you owe us, the 039! We're the ones who saved you, and we're still here with you!"

I rub my forehead and close my eyes.

"There is nothing you can do. What more is there?"

I shrug. "There is always another way, Ashur. If he can be saved, wouldn't you want to save him?" I sit up and search his eyes now. They are glowing green, bright enough to create shadows in the dark room. "I think it can still be done."

"Junco, you're not rooted in reality. He pled guilty to treason, it carries an automatic death sentence."

"We'll see, Ashur."

He gets up out of my bed and stands over me, shaking his head. "No, I'm not doing this with you, Junco. I'm not going to watch you do something stupid just because you can't sort through your feelings for him."

I sit up, angry. "That's not what this is about, Ashur. Not even close."

"No?"

I stand up too. "It's not about you, Ashur." I stand on my tiptoes and reach up to wrap my fingers around his neck and he puts his arms around me and tries to pull me in as I step back to see his face. "I'm not going to let them kill him."

He shakes his head and pushes me away. "No, I'm not participating in this. Did you talk to Braun?"

I squint up at him. "What?"

"Braun, did he tell you this shit? Fill your head up with this bullshit? He's crazy, Junco. I told you that from the fucking beginning, don't fucking get involved with him!"

"I haven't see Braun since that party here after the Sixth Fight."

He looks down at me suspiciously. "If he's put ideas into your head, Junco, do yourself a favor and forget you ever met him. He thinks he's this super tactician, but he's fucking impetuous and reckless in everything he does."

I slump back in the bed. "Are you going to come to sleep, or what?"

He shakes his head and walks towards the door. "While you plot out some harebrained idea about saving Tier? Forget it."

I watch him leave and then turn over in my covers as I hear a door slam somewhere else in the house.

The guys are all gone in the morning and I'm alone. No babysitter for the first time since I came to Amelia. I sit around in my bed shorts and tank top, sample a half dozen dishes from the autocook, puff on cigars on the terrace, and generally make a mess as I watch with as much detachment as I can muster as the newscreens flash images of Earth and the recent destruction.

They have the numbers.

Eight million dead.

Three million displaced throughout the Mountain Republic, the parts of the Rural Republic that were not affected as much by the fallout, and Texas. Texas is pissed off and has claimed the entire Rural Republic as reparations. They already have the scrubbers in place on the ground. Debris clean-up for the Peaks has been contracted out to some obscure company that goes by Yukichi from the Gulf Coast. The whole Peaks area is going to be covered with a layer of concrete twenty feet thick by the end of the summer and full habitation is predicted in less than five years.

Lovely.

Let's all pretend that millions of people never existed.

I'm seething in rage when the door chimes.

"Enter."

Kush makes his way down to the couches in the sunken living room. "How you doing, Junco?"

"Just fucking great, and yourself?" I'm mad at him, but my reasons aren't clear. Maybe because I saw the blame on his face during Fight Seven, or maybe because he too decided that Isec was expendable. But mostly I think it is because he reminds me of the little brat and I can't push it down if he keeps popping back up.

"I've volunteered for the Deliverance fight."

I look at him with my mouth open. "The wish fight for killing prisoners? Why would you do that?"

"I want the wish. I figure I've been through six of them already, right? And this one isn't even a fight to the death. What do I have to lose?"

"But you could die." They've been advertising Deliverance on the screens for weeks and I guess if you're hard up, a wish is a pretty big draw. "I mean, haven't you had enough killing yet? Maybe you should have been the one to kill the defective pledges at Seven? That might have cured you."

"Look," he says impatiently, "I get that you've been through a lot, but you're not the only one. I haven't been granted the gifts of the Gods like you apparently have. I need this wish."

"What could you possibly need? You're in the Aves, wasn't that what you wanted?"

"Yes, but I am not satisfied with the captain we have directing us on the new team. Annun is good, but he's not that good."

I shake my head in disbelief. "Who gives a fuck who's captain? Seriously, I'm the lowest one on my team, do you think I give a shit? You think you can do better than Annun? You have to earn the rank, anyway. And you didn't earn it. No one will follow a captain who was given the rank as a gift. You're supposed to want to support your captain because he supported you when you needed it."

"Annun helped you, Junco. Not me. He never did anything for me."

I let out a deep sigh. "Well, good luck then. I wish you success. You're a good fighter, so you'll be fine, I'm sure. And you've got just as much chance as anyone at winning."

He huffs. "Yeah, thanks for the vote of confidence. You know, you're pretty fucking condescending to anyone not on your level."

I laugh. "Oh, I'm sorry, did I hurt your feelings? You want me to pretend you're the big strong guy and I'm the weak and stupid girl? Get over yourself, Kush. You're slightly above average for an Aves warrior, but if they get someone in there with real Aves blood, you're toast."

"Someone like you?"

I laugh. "Now why the fuck would I want to fight for something as stupid as a wish. Get real."

He smiles as he gets up and walks over to the door. "Because, Junco, they just announced that Tier will be killed in the Deliverance fight. And ya know, I thought since you're all hung up on the guy, you might like to use your wish to save his fucking life." He salutes me. "See ya around."

My mind races back to Braun's plan before I left for Fledge. How the fuck did he know? Shit, maybe he's a precog, too? I take a deep breath and try and put the pieces together.

I'm still sitting there thinking when Rikan and Mish show up a half hour later. I found the announcement about Tier on the screen and it's playing when they come down into the living area to see what I'm doing.

I look up at them as the realization sinks in and then get up and go to my room to play the piano. My hands pluck out simple tunes at first, building the idea in my head, and then they begin tapping out more complicated melodies as the plan takes root. By the time I've got it all figured out I'm playing Asgarth's dungeon murders in E flat major.

Chapter Thirty-Six

The Fledge building has been repaired since the altercation after Tier's guilty plea. It's locked up tight when I approach the door, but I swipe my palm in front of the biometrics and they open for me anyway.

I walk across the clean tile floor of the lobby, feeling a bit strange when no mods are there to notice, and go directly to the stairs and fly up to the third floor dorm. I walk through, barely managing to push down the memories made here, and walk into the mast.

My flight up is smooth and quick.

Inside the church the syrinx is still upside down in her silent sacrificial scream. I lie down on my back and scoot underneath her so I can see her face again.

"What the fuck do you want from me?"

I stare into her eyes, which glow a faded green, perhaps hinting that at one time she was avian. None of the other Archers have wings, yet she does. None of the other Archers have glowing eyes, yet again, she does. She doesn't have the look of an Archer.

She's not fair, she's a redhead.

She's obviously not male, and all the Archers I've met so far are.

It just doesn't add up.

"Who are you really?"

"It's very perceptive of you to notice these things, Junco. For someone not familiar with the local customs."

I slide sideways to avoid hitting my head on the statue as I jump to my feet and then stare open-mouthed at the woman sitting on the first bench. She's got the red hair, but she's also wearing a long red gown. The syrinx on the cross is wearing some ancient garb I don't recognize. I'm silent as I look at her.

"For someone so demanding, you suddenly have very little to say."

"Do you want something from me?"

She smiles. "Of course I do."

I let out a breath of air. "So, you gonna tell me what the fuck it is you want?"

She clicks her tongue at me. "I don't suffer insolence, Junco. You will refrain from speaking to me in such a common manner."

I rub my forehead to stave off the growing tension, then take a seat on the top step in front of her. "Sorry, then. I'm just very tired."

She smiles. "But you have a destiny and you prayed for courage and bravery when you meet your end."

"So this is the end?"

She nods. "An end, yes."

"An end to what, exactly?"

"To you, of course."

I nod and swallow. "What do you want me to do?"

"You have a well-thought out plan. That you composed today?"

I shrug. "I guess. That's the best you can do? My stupid little plan?"

"Set it in motion."

I am about to object when she disappears and Lucan is standing in front of me at the bottom of the steps.

He sighs. "Junco, what are you doing?"

"Looking for answers, Lucan, why else would I be here in this crappy little church?"

"Your trip on the trains has drawn attention. There is a crowd outside waiting for you."

I shrug. "So? I don't need saving, ya know. Tier needs saving, not me."

He shakes his head. "This business with Tier is over now, Junco." His voice is calm and rational, but I detect that I'm pushing buttons under the surface that might set him off. "Ashur told me that you've still got it in your head that he can be saved."

"He can," I say simply.

"He cannot."

I shrug. "That's just your opin–"

He's got me by the shoulders and is shaking me. "No! It is not my opinion, Junco. It is the future as it is told. I have seen it. Tier dies, Junco."

I don't pull away but I do look him in the eyes. "Isec said he saw it too. And he said I can do it. Did do it, actually."

"Isec? He wasn't a precog, Junco! He was a failed telepath! You're comparing millennia of skill in the foretelling of what will come to the erratic second sight of that throwaway child?"

"The syrinx is on my side," I say simply. "Maybe you should take it up with her? Because I'm not really sure she's as understanding as you might be if I disobey. I'm pretty sure she expects obedience."

He looks into me, searching, willing it to be a lie, but when it rings true, he lets go of my shoulders. "What did you do?"

"I fucking told you, Lucan, that night I said the prayer, I asked her for bravery and courage in the end and she asked me for a sacrifice." I look down. "I said yes, remember? Obviously you dismissed that part of my story, because if you took me seriously you wouldn't look so shocked right now." The last part comes out soft and I wait for his anger. He's still got the look of confusion when I look up at him. "I already agreed, get it?"

"You agreed to nothing, Junco. Do I make myself clear?"

I shake my head. "No, she's one scary bitch. I'm not even allowed to swear at her. She said she doesn't suffer insolence. And I'm pretty sure if I called her to tell her no thank you on that deal we struck, she'd kill me dead."

"This was never in the plan, Junco."

My stomach churns and I hold down the urge to vomit. "This was always in the plan, Lucan. Some fucking precog you are. You know what your problem is? You're just not cynical enough. Don't you know that things will always get worse? When you've lived through the shit I have, you come to expect it. Hell, rely on it like an old friend, even."

He looks at me, his eyes sad and his mouth drawn down in a frown.

"It's not going to end well, you said it yourself. That's just the way it is. But hey, you can take comfort in the fact that it wasn't you who put me here, right? It was Tier. And me. In the end, we're the ones to blame, and I recognize that. I don't hate you."

"You will come with me now and I will take you home."

I shake my head. "No. I don't like the time slip that comes with your teleportation trick. It's got me all fucked up. I don't want to lose time just to get a free ride home. I'm taking the train like a normal person."

"You will stay inside and I will send a flyer to pick you up, is that satisfactory?"

I smile and agree. "Yeah, alright."

He's gone in an instant. I consider calling out to the syrinx again, but don't. She gave her order. Set it in motion.

I get up and fly down the mast, then take the stairs to the lobby and inhale deeply a few times. I walk over to the doors and step through to follow her command.

The reporters have made themselves comfortable, probably not expecting me to turn up, and are lounging around when I exit the building. They look at me for a second, disbelief written on their faces, then spring to action like a prairie lion jumping on a newborn antelope.

They crowd me and I let them.

I am pushed and pulled as questions are hurled at me one after another.

Yet I stay silent and let it drag on for maximum effect.

Finally they calm down and stand as still as you can expect from a mob of vultures.

I clear my throat. "I have an announcement to make." They lean in. Some clamber up a few nearby trees trying to get a good shot. "I've been informed that my former Fledge teammate Kush will be participating in the Deliverance fight." I pause and they wait, so quiet that I can hear the wind blow softly through the leaves. "I will be participating in the Deliverance fight with Kush."

Now they erupt with questions but I ignore them and shake out a cigar, strike it up, and puff with satisfaction when the flyer arrives and I can climb in, giving the scene a more dramatic end that I could have hoped.

When I arrive home Ashur is waiting for me on the rooftop parking pad. He shakes his head as I exit. "I forbid it, Junco. As your captain, I will not permit it."

I don't even slow down as I pass him. "Then I quit, Ashur."

He grabs me by the arm and swings me down on the ground, hard enough to knock the breath out of me, and then holds my hands and straddles my chest with his full weight, making me choke. "I don't think so, Junco," he snarls as he leans down into my face. "You think I'm fucking playing around here? You will not fight in Deliverance!"

I am not stupid enough, or so full of myself, to think I can take on a warrior like Ashur, all things being equal, and this is decidedly unequal from my vantage point. So I stay still and silent until the guys are there to pull him off and fight my battle for me.

Ryse grabs me by the shoulders to tug me upright, then pushes me back behind him. "What the fuck are you doing, Ashur?" he asks calmly, shaking his head at him. "Don't do that. If you've got a problem you don't manhandle her, for fuck's sake."

Ashur is pacing, breathing hard, and his eyes never leave mine. "You want to be a warrior, Junco? Fight like a man? Then fuck it, I'll treat you like one. You're not fighting in Deliverance. That is a fucking order and you are not quitting."

I remain calm. "You were just fine with me quitting last night when all you could think about was sleeping with me, though, right? I can quit as long as I do it on your terms?" I shake my head. "This isn't about you, Ashur, how many fucking ways do I have to say it?" He's about to say something predictable but I cut him off. "It's not about Tier either. Or you guys." I point to each of my team members. "It's about me."

"Junco." Isten walks up to me. "I get it, I really do. But there's a very good fucking chance you'll win. Do you really want to be the one who kills Tier?"

I look down, then force my head back up to meet his gaze. "I'm definitely not going to kill Tier. This fight is happening. It's done."

Lucan arrives in front of me then. "No, Junco, this is not happening. And you said the same thing about not killing Isec if I recall correctly."

My rage boils over and I spit at him, "How dare you. After you talked me up with all that shit about Isec not being good enough, all those sob stories about your goddamn gene pool, how fucking dare you."

He stares at me but no apology comes forth.

I look at each one of them and let my eyes stop with Ashur. "You fucking people think you know me because you spied on me for a while? You don't know me, you showed up when I was seventeen, after all the fucking psychological torture and conditioning was over. When the fucking die had already been cast and I was already complete. What about all those years you missed? You've got no idea the shit I live with every day. You think those teeny tiny little secrets you learned about recently are it? That's all there is to my fucked-up existence? Do you really tell yourselves that my childhood was nothing but a protected life of piano lessons and horseback riding?"

I shake my head and start again in a calmer, more controlled tone. "You don't want to know what I've done because it would take about two seconds for you to realize I'm not fucking worth any of this shit. There is no cure for what I am."

I stare at them in silence.

No one says a word so I look Lucan in the eye. "I fucking told you she gave me orders. This is what she said to do. And you can take it up with her if you don't fucking like it, but as of today I've got a new boss. That bitch has the look of eternal vengeance to her, so I'm proceeding as instructed. At this point I don't give a fuck how it ends – just fucking make it end!"

Ryse interjects, shaking his head and squinting his eyes at Lucan. "What the fuck are we talking about here?"

I look up at Ryse. "Ask Lucan, he's Mr. I-see-the-fucking-future, not me."

Chapter Thirty-Seven

I walk away, jump down the stairs to the terrace three at a time, and find shelter in the window seat of my room.

My comm vibrates in my pants and I answer. "What?"

"Kadian here, Junco. I see you in the window and you don't look so sure of your decision."

I huff. "Kadian, I'm very fucking sure of my decision."

"I saw the little fight up on the roof. That Ashur has a violent side. It's quite disturbing."

"If you show that to anyone, Kadian, I will–"

"Relax, snowbird. I'm not interested in your little lover spats. I called to ask if I can have the pre-fight interview."

I scan across the traffic outside my window to see if he's over there, then see him wave. "I guess. Why not?" My Farm Family breeding and manners kick in, I can't help myself. "I never did thank you for the lovely evening. It really was spectacular. And your girlfriend, she's amazing."

"Yes, she is. But she's gone on tour now, so I only have you to distract me."

I smile. "I don't care for Inanna though, I have to be honest."

"Yes, good instincts, Junco. She's wild. But she lives in a man's world, so how can we blame her? When you're blessed with the skill set she was given, it's got to be hard to remember that you're just a girl sometimes."

I snort. "Gee, thanks for the dig, Kadian. As if I don't have enough to think about, now I can brood over how wild I should or should not be in order to accomplish the heinous things they make me do."

He's silent on the other end, but I hear him exhale. Frustration with me?

"If you only knew what they've told me to do over the years, Kadian, you wouldn't say that shit to me, even if you think it's a thinly veiled joke."

More silence.

"And when you add in the fact that I've been forced to kill like a rabid nightdog since I was six, well, then you could maybe cut me some fucking slack when I get a little wild."

I end the call and flip him off in the window.

Lucan appears a few seconds later, like he was waiting for me to end the call or something. He is calm when he speaks. "Junco, Ashur will take you to Layla. I want a complete medical workup."

And then he is gone.

I huff out some air as the door chimes, then pull myself together and open the door to meet Ashur.

His eyes turn away as he mumbles, "Sorry, Junco."

"You know what, Ashur? That's not the first time you've lost your temper with me, but I'm going to tell you something right now. It is the last. You do it again, and I'll fucking kill you just like I did that motherfucker in the dorm showers." I wait for his eye contact to see if he'll challenge me, but he doesn't. He just nods and walks out towards the terrace and I follow.

The ride over is painfully silent. We don't even argue. We just sit. Apparently my first home on Amelia was Layla's lab to begin with because that's where we end up. The table and screen are both still there, but the bed is gone. Ashur takes a seat at the table and starts changing channels while I let Layla pull me into the lab.

"How have you been, Junco?"

My lips pout a little. "I've been better, to be honest. How about you? Haven't seen you in a while."

She smiles at me. "Yeah, I've been busy. Lucan says he wants another body scan so we can compare it to the ones we did when you came out of morph."

I nod at her.

"To see if there have been any changes."

Right. Changes.

I strip and stand behind the transparent screen. Last time it took a while to get the machine set up, but Lucan must have had this planned before my little outburst, because she's right on top of things. As soon as I get in position, the laser is reading my body.

I can see Ashur out of the corner of my eye and then the door chimes and I watch him get up to go answer it. I hear some muffled talking and then Monk appears around the corner.

"Hey, Junco," he says.

I shake my head.

Layla clicks her tongue. "Stand still, Junco, now I'll have to do that again."

"Do we have to have an audience? I'm naked, you assholes, get the fuck out!"

They both step back at my tone and then retreat around the wall, but I don't hear the door chime, so I know they didn't leave.

"I said, get out! Not fucking hide behind the wall!"

Layla loses her patience and goes around the corner. "You heard her, get out! You know better!"

This time the door does chime.

"Thank you," I say, letting out a breath of exasperation.

"Fucking children, I have no idea how you put up with them, Junco. If I had to spend all my time with those assholes, I'd go crazy."

I smile. "Really?"

She nods. "Oh, yeah. Tier was one thing, he's different. But the rest of them are just giant babies. I can't stand it. I feel sorry for those girls they promoted to warriors. They have no idea what they are in for. Now hold still and we'll run it again and be done."

When she's finished I put my clothes back on and take a seat at the table where I played my first poker game on Amelia.

"Hey, Layla?"

"Uh-huh?" she answers from the lab.

"Have you seen Braun?"

She pokes her head around the corner of the wall that separates us. "Why?"

"He's been avoiding me since…" I think back. "Since I left here to go to Fledge, really. I miss him."

She comes over and sits at the table. "Lucan is keeping the two of you apart."

"Why?"

She shakes her head and shrugs. Then she puts her hands up in a helpless gesture. "He thinks you're plotting something."

"Holy fucking Christos, you're right. I can't spend another fucking minute with these overbearing fucking little boys. I can't take it anymore. I'm going to lose my mind."

She smiles and then laughs. "I see him all the time, I'll tell him you're asking. He'll like that. He's my second favorite, after Tier." She looks at me for a few seconds. "So, you don't have to tell me, but if you do I won't say anything. I can call it doctor-patient confidentiality."

"What?"

Her face falls and gets serious, then sad. "Do you really have a plan? For Tier?"

I nod. "Yes."

"Will it work?"

Her eyes plead with me, but I can only throw up my hands. "I don't know, Layla."

"Well, you may not have been talking to Braun these past few weeks, but I have. And he got me to agree to something I might not be one hundred percent on board with."

"Which is what?" I ask.

"The plan you two have. He won't tell me what it is, just asked that I be ready and to come when he calls. You know anything about this?"

"I can't say either way, Layla."

She nods and pulls herself together, then gets up to go check on the tests. A few minutes later she calls out, "You should come take a look, Junco."

I get up and walk around the corner to the viewing screen. My body image is almost white with circuits now. I shake my head and feel my throat start to ache as the tears well up. "What is it?"

"It's you." She looks at it for a long moment, then turns to me and gives me a sympathetic smile. "You're wired from top to bottom."

"Will it kill me?"

She shakes her head. "I doubt it. The first rule of symbiosis is do no harm. Otherwise you lose the host."

I'm a host. "What does it mean?"

She lets out a prolonged exhale. "Well, I'd guess it makes you capable of doing a lot of fucking stuff no one else can."

"Like?"

She laughs. "I dunno, eavesdropping in on people's comms? Hacking into databases? Stealing money from accounts? You have a very bright future, and I mean that literally," she says, pointing to the bright white lines on the image, "in stealth circuit ops."

I grunt and laugh with her despite myself. "Gee, just the career I've always wanted."

The door chimes and we both go silent. She snaps the image from the viewer and begins rolling it up as Ashur and Monk appear. "Well, you're all done here, Juncs. I'll get this over to Lucan." She shrugs. "But what he'll do with it I have no idea. Don't let these assholes get you down, they are just boys in the end." She slips the rolled-up image in a tube and heads out towards the door.

Monk, Ashur, and I stand there looking at each other. Then we all start talking at once.

Ashur and Monk are yelling face to face, complete with finger-points to the chest, meanwhile I can't even get them to look down and notice me at all. I stick my fingers on my tongue and whistle so loud they both hold their ears. "Shut the fuck up for a minute." I let out a breath. "OK, what is going on?"

Monk speaks first. "Rache wants me to bring you back to Justice, Junco. I'm under orders."

Ashur shakes his head. "Rache isn't Junco's Archer, Monk. Lucan is."

"She volunteered for the Deliverance fight, so he is her Archer until that's over. She comes with me."

Ashur looks down at me. "You're still going through with this fight, Junco?"

I lift my eyebrows and nod. "Yup. Still going through with it."

Monk smiles. "Well, good. Let's go. The fight is day after tomorrow so you'll want to get settled." He takes me by the arm and leads me towards the door.

"Junco?" I turn at Ashur's call and wait. "Good luck."

I sigh. "Thank you." And then we walk through the door and down the hallway.

Chapter Thirty-Eight

The ride over to Justice is just as silent as the ride over to the lab was. Monk tries, I'll give him that, but I'm not interested so I just ignore him completely. I don't need any more confusing relationships.

When we get off the inter-world transport he leads me through a series of hallways, only this time we end up in Rache's outer offices, and not the courtroom. Monk points to a straight-backed chair and I take a seat as he disappears through a large door.

I wait around for what seems like a very long time before a woman directs me to enter where Monk went through earlier. Inside is another hallway but I see Monk sticking out of a door near the end and walk towards him.

He's talking to someone inside when I reach him. He looks back at me and opens the door and directs me in, then backs out into the hallway and closes the door behind me.

Inside there are nine Archers sitting behind a crescent-moon table that looks similar to the one the 039 used at our meeting. My face goes tight and I feel the anger rise inside me. "Now what did I do?"

Lucan sits in the middle with four Archers on each side of him. He points to a chair in front of him and I walk over and take the hot seat once again.

I want to cry. But I don't. I sit and look at the ground.

"Junco," Lucan begins. "Layla said she showed you the scanner image?"

I nod, but say nothing.

"There have been a great many changes, do you agree?"

I nod again.

"Is the syrinx who talks to you inside of you? Or is she real?"

I shrug, then finally look up and meet their eyes, one set at a time, coming to rest back on Lucan as I answer. "How should I know? I saw her outside of me, if that's what you're asking."

The guy immediately to Lucan's left takes a stab next. "Junco, I am Gib, the Archer of Clutch. Can you describe her?"

I take a deep breath, then exhale. "She's pretty tall, long red hair, long red gown – kind of silky. Know what I mean? Like she's dressed up for something. She's not dark, but not fair like you guys." I shrug.

They look at each other and nod. Then Rache speaks. "Does she have wings, Junco?"

I shake my head. "No."

"What does she want?" another man asks without introduction.

"She wants me to save Tier."

"And how did she tell you to do that?"

I look at them all individually one more time. "I'm not going to tell you."

Lucan huffs. "Junco, you will tell us or we will punish you."

"I will not, Lucan. You can kill me for all I care. I don't plan on being around much longer anyway." His head pulls back at my statement.

Another one speaks without introducing himself. "Then we won't let you fight in Deliverance."

I stand up and knock the chair back. "I DON'T GIVE A FUCK!" I walk back towards the door.

Lucan is there in front of me before I can reach it. He puts a hand on my shoulder. "Junco, please. We're just trying to understand what you are and what you're doing."

"I told you, dammit. She wants me to save him. You can make this very simple and just let him go." I look around. "But you won't. Why? He was already halfway forgiven for those killings, you're just pissed because he brought me here. Well, there's an easy fix, just let him live and we'll both go back to Earth and then you won't have to see us ever again."

Lucan's hand is still on my shoulder and I shrug it off as he starts talking. "We can't let you go until we know what we're up against."

"Fine, put me in jail, or whatever it is you're going to do with me because I'm tired and hungry. I just want to get some fucking sleep and eat something right now."

Lucan opens the door and Monk is waiting outside. He looks at me with raised eyebrows and it reminds me of Braun that first time I met Lucan and told him off in the hallway. "Take her to her room on the Deliverance floor." Monk nods and takes my arm, pulling me away before I can look back.

We walk for a long time through so many convoluted hallways I have a little panic attack about getting lost and my feet actually hurt by the time we make it to the room that will be mine. Monk opens the door and begins showing me around. "Kush is next door, you can open the connecting door if you want."

I look up. "He is?" My chest heaves and I drop my head and begin to cry unexpectedly.

Monk just stares at me. "Junco, I'm sorry. I'm not used to dealing with girls in situations like this. Should I call for Ashur and have him come talk to you?"

I shake my head and wipe my fingers across my face to get rid of the tears. "No, I'm OK. I'm just tired, Monk. I'm tired."

"And hungry, right?"

I nod and smile. "And hungry."

"OK, well, I can get Kush, if you want?"

"No, I'll talk to him later."

"You want me to go?"

I nod.

He smiles. "Oh, here. Rache wanted me to give you this." He fishes into his thigh pocket and pulls out a com. "It's coded to our team, the 399, you're number eight. So, if you want to give someone your number, like Ryse or Ashur, you tell them Junco, Aves 399-8."

He hands it over and I slip it in next to my other com.

"That old one won't work here." He shrugs. "We're off Amelia now, right? You gotta use a Justice com."

"All right."

"OK, I'm number one. So if you want to call me, just push one and it'll go to me. Or if you want to call Rache, just push zero."

"What's Kush?"

He looks at me funny. "We didn't give him one."

"Why not?"

He smiles. "While you're here, Junco, you're on my team. You're my eight. Kush is just another fucking fighter."

"Oh." I let out a breath. "Thanks, and sorry for crying. I'm just–"

"Tired, yeah, I get it." He squeezes my shoulder and then leaves without another word.

I walk over to the floor to ceiling windows and stand on a little ledge that butts up against the glass to look out. It's a view of the fight arena. It's a pretty big place, a lot bigger than any arena I've ever fought in for Fledge. At one end is a stage-type riser. Scattered throughout the open central area are mushroom gravity wells, similar to the ones from Fight Seven. My room is almost dead center opposite the stage.

Surrounding the upper portion of the arena are seats for the spectators. It will be weird to fight in front of people, but not much weirder than anything else I've done since I became an avian.

My comm buzzes and I immediately wonder how Kadian got my new number so fast. "Hello?"

"Junco?"

It's Ashur. "Yeah."

"You all right?"

I nod, then remember he can't see me. "Yeah."

He lets out a little laugh. "Monk is freaked out. He's never had a girl on his team."

"I don't get it, how come I'm on his team?"

Ashur is quiet for a few seconds. "Rache wants to keep you, Junco. So..." He stops, maybe not wanting to finish the thought, or maybe he's listening to me breathe erratically on the other side as I begin to realize what's happening. "Don't be surprised if they treat you real nice."

I've done it now, my team is about to be ripped away before I even get the chance to enjoy them. I'm silent as I choke back my tears and try to swallow down the ache that prevents me from talking.

"Junco?"

I push it down one more time before I speak. "Yeah."

"You want me to come see you?"

I shake my head, then catch myself again. "No." I breathe the word out with a half-hidden sob. "No, I'm OK. Really. I'm just going to go to sleep. I'm tired."

"Tomorrow then?"

My nose is running and I sniff a couple times. "Yeah, OK. Tomorrow."

"OK, if you need anything, just call Monk. He's not a bad guy."

"All right, I will. Bye."

I end the call and sit down on the ledge to rest my back on the window and let the sobs out, a little bit at first, then I give up and the tears run down my cheeks like rivers.

How ironic.

After barely wriggling out of my father selling me to the highest bidder, then traveling a hundred million miles across open space to another world, it turns out I can't escape that fate after all.

Chapter Thirty-Nine

Ashur is sleeping next to me when I wake up. When I stir he reaches over and puts his arm around me. "Junco?"

I open my eyes and stare at him. He smiles. "You're not OK, Junco."

I look at him, first the one green eye, then the other. "I know. What time is it?"

I watch him check his vision screen and I realize I could have just checked my own. "5:42 AM."

"Too early to get up."

He pulls me to his chest. "Way too fucking early to get up."

"What time did you get here?"

"About an hour ago."

"Thank you."

"You're welcome, Juncs."

My eyes close and I fall back asleep clinging to him tightly and counting the slow up-and-down motion of his breathing.

The next time I wake Ashur is gone and Monk is giving me a vigorous shake.

"What the fuck?"

"Ah, sorry. But Rache said you have to eat something."

I flip open my eyes and stare up at him. "You're fucking with me, right?"

He screws up his face. "No, why?"

"What is it with you people and my eating habits?"

"I dunno, Junco. Get up and get dressed and I'll take you down to the cafeteria."

"Where did Ashur go?"

"Oh, he said to tell you he'll be back later."

I watch him leave and I force myself up and into the shower. There is a clean uniform waiting for me on the bed when I'm done and I slip it on. Monk appears just as I'm lacing up my boots and stands in the open doorway, talking to someone else outside for a few seconds before directing his attention to me. "Ready?"

I nod.

The hallway is bustling with activity and all sorts of people say hi to me as I pass them. "Who are all these people?" I ask as we start hopping down the stairs.

"Just other fighters."

"Oh, how many are there? Looks like a lot."

He hesitates at the bottom of the stairs as he waits for me to catch up with him. "Thirty-two? Thirty-five? Not sure this year."

"So, what type of person typically wins this fight?"

He starts walking down the hall, then looks over to me and smiles. "Warriors, Junco. Like you."

"And what do people usually ask for, in the wish department?"

"Oh, shit – healing mostly, if the winner isn't Aves that is. I mean after they're done, they're typically pretty fucked up."

"Oh, I thought that was included? This is not a fight to the death, right?"

"Right, but there's a limit." He shrugs. "Or they ask for status positions."

I think of Kush. "And how does that work? They just get promotions, based on the fight?"

"Yeah, pretty much. Nothing spectacular, I mean, it's a gift, it's not earned."

I grunt. "Yeah, who wants to follow a guy who never earned his appointment?"

He looks down at me as we walk. "Exactly. They never seem to figure that out, though."

"What else do they wish for?"

He stops at the cafeteria counter and starts grabbing food. "What do you want?"

I shrug and make a face. "Some of that," I say, pointing to the biscuits.

He shakes his head. "I'll choose for you. Ashur says he always orders for you, else you only eat cookies."

I smile. "He does. What else do they wish for, Monk?"

"Money. A better place to live, shit like that. What are you going to wish for, Junco?"

"I haven't decided yet."

He looks back at me and shakes his head. "Right."

He takes the tray over to a table full of guys and gestures for me to sit. "This is my team, Junco." He points and names them one by one and I say hello. He introduces me as the eight and I feel weird.

I watch and listen to them interact and realize they are pretty much just like the 039, only different faces. I breathe out and wonder if I will ever get to go home. Then I have to stop and ask myself where home is. It seems to be relative these days.

Ashur finds us before we are finished eating and slips onto the bench next to me, saying hi to everyone on Monk's team like he knows them well. He looks over my half-empty tray of food and smiles. "Looks like Monk's on feeding duty?"

I nod. "Yeah, I don't get why you guys are so interested in what I eat, but whatever. So what have you been doing all day?"

He turns and doesn't meet my gaze. "I went to see Tier." Then he looks down to me to see my reaction.

I look across the cafeteria and spot Kush watching me. "Oh."

"He wants to see you, Junco. Tonight."

"Well, I'm not so sure–"

"You're going," he says sternly.

I look up at him, to read how serious he is. "Why? I just don't think it's a good idea, I won't know what to say, it's gonna be awkward and–"

"It's his last night, Junco."

I shake my head at him and smile. "No, it isn't, Ashur."

"Oh, for fuck's sake." He takes my hand and pulls me up. "Let's go for a walk, OK?"

Monk takes an interest at this development. "Hey, Ashur, she's mine now, you don't get to just take her–"

"Fuck you, Monk. She's yours until tomorrow night and then she's going home, so don't fucking get used to her."

I smile back at them and let Ashur pull me out to the hallway. "So, is there an outside to this place? Or is it just an endless maze of interior corridors?"

"No, there's an outside, wanna go take a look?"

I nod. "Absolutely, I better get my sightseeing in before tomorrow, right?"

He puts his hand on my back, right between my wings, and it gives me a little chill. He feels it and looks over at me, then moves it up to my shoulder. "Is this bugging you?"

I shake my head as we pass through a doorway and the outside suddenly springs to life. "Oh, this is nice! It looks like Earth's sky!" The blueness of the upper atmosphere takes my breath away and I halt on the walkway to take it in for a moment.

Ashur agrees with a grunt, then leads me over to a patch of grass under a tree and we take a seat. "Yeah, I knew you'd like this part. And at night," he says, smiling at me as I lie back on the grass to look up, "you can see the stars."

I look over at him. "Ya know, ever since we sat and looked up at the city I haven't missed them much."

This makes him happy and he doesn't even try to hide it. Instead he leans back with me and we are quiet for a while. I think about Tier and wonder what it would be like to talk to him again after so long. Will it be like old friends? Or will it be weird? Does he know Ashur has feelings for me? All these questions are running through my mind when I notice Ash is looking at me.

"What are you thinking about?" he asks.

"Tier. And what it would be like to talk to him again."

"Are you going to go then?"

I swallow and nod. "Yeah, I can't exactly say no if he asked to see me. He did ask, right? I'm not going to show up and have him look surprised."

Ashur laughs. "He gave me an order. Apparently Tier still thinks he's captain." He smiles at this thought, like it's typical of Tier to be bossy like that, even when he's in prison and about to be killed for treason.

"You think I'm full of shit, don't you? You don't think he'll be alive tomorrow night."

He shakes his head. "No, I don't."

"Do you think I'll kill him?"

He shrugs. "If you're in the fight, and you win, Junco, you better fucking kill him. That's what you've signed up for."

"Right." I exhale. "I'll make sure not to win then."

He looks over and frowns. "That makes no sense."

"Yeah, well – you'll have to take it up with the syrinx. Let's go do it now. I want to get it over with."

He stands and pulls me up. "You sure?"

I nod. "Yeah, let's go."

Chapter Forty

Ashur and I walk through a series of biometrically secure doors and at each one we must announce ourselves, then wait, sometimes for a very long time, for someone to come and let us in. Each time I pass over the threshold of a secure station my heart beats a little quicker and soon my whole body feels flushed.

Finally we arrive at the prison and then we are asked to wait yet again. Ashur points me to a straight-backed chair and I go take a seat while he arranges things with the people behind the desk. They seem to know him pretty well and I begin to wonder just how many times he's been here to see Tier and never told me.

After several minutes he comes and takes a seat next to me and smiles. "Be just a little bit longer, OK?"

I nod and play with a loose string on my thigh pocket. There is no one else in the waiting room with us, which should not be surprising considering how difficult it was to get back to this point. I begin to question how common it is to even have visitors here.

A buzzer sounds and Ashur gets up and looks down at me. "That's us."

I get up and my heart goes wild. My vision screen pops to life and I watch as my biogs begin to excrete cortisol to calm me down. Ashur looks at me funny. "You OK?"

I swallow and smooth out my uniform shirt, even though it never wrinkles, it's light armor for fuck's sake. "Yeah, I'm OK. No, I'm not. I'm nervous. So fucking nervous."

He takes my hand. "It's Tier, Junco. You spent quite a bit of personal time with him back on Earth, just be yourself."

I nod. "Yeah, OK. I'm good." I breathe.

He leads me to the doors where guards are waiting and then we pass through and they clank shut behind us. Ashur seems to know exactly where he's going, so I just follow, my stomach churning with each step. And then we turn a corner and I can see Tier through the glass at the end of the hall. He sees me at the same time and even from dozens of yards away, I can see his smile. My heart calms down and I smile back.

Ashur waits at the door and Tier goes over to the far wall and sits down on the bench. Then a buzzer goes off and the locks click to signal the door can be opened. Ashur grabs the handle and pulls.

And then Tier and I are in the same room. Ashur enters as well and then the door closes and locks behind us.

"Junco, yer so pretty." Tier gets up and walks over to me. I drop Ashur's hand and meet him halfway and he takes me in his arms and hugs me tightly, pushing my face into his chest and dropping his chin down into my hair. I wrap my arms under his and bring them up to grab his shoulders, letting out a deep sigh of relief. We stay this way for a long time. I tilt my face to the side and close my eyes as his hands stroke my hair.

"Ashur, hey, fuck off for a while, eh? It's my last night, let me have her to myself."

I don't hear a response but the door buzzes and mechanisms clank, a few seconds later we're alone. He pulls back and takes me over to the bench, then sits down and tugs me down into his lap. I straddle his legs and put my hands around his neck and look at him, noticing the dark circles and the strain on his face. "Why didn't I come sooner?"

"Yer here now, so who cares?"

I flash him a crooked smile. "Are you OK?"

He looks into my eyes and the glow I've missed so badly is there again. "Nah, not really."

I frown. "I'm so sorry, Tier. This whole thing is my fault."

"It's not, Junco. It's not. I did this. But I did give ya all those instructions in the virtual and ya didn't even follow one!"

"What? I did follow them, and there were only two, anyway."

"No, Junco. I had a whole list to help ya get by without me, but ya did it all backwards."

I shake my head. "I only got two sentences, Tier, it said trust no one and show no weakness."

He laughs. "Fucking Sera, I knew she'd screw it all up, probably did it on purpose."

"Who's Sera?"

"The redhead, ya seen her?"

"The syrinx?"

"Is that who she said she was? What a fucking liar. She's Sera." He shakes his head. "But anyway, I don't want to waste our time talking about her. If ya thought the only thing I wanted was for ya to trust no one, then why did ya go around handing it out like a fucking Utopian welfare payment? You've made more best friends in the last month than I made in my whole life."

I laugh. "Well, everyone has actually been pretty nice to me. It was hard to stay suspicious and aloof. And I didn't do too well with the show no weakness shit either. I've been an emotional wreck on several occasions."

His hand goes up to my scalp, lifts the hair away from my head, and then traces the scar down the side of my face. "That one healed pretty well." He lifts my chin up and looks for the SEAR scar. "That one too." Then his hand goes behind my neck and pulls me in. I stare into his eyes as he takes my left hand and holds it up to look at my missing fingers. "This been giving ya any trouble?"

I shake my head. "No, none at all. I played the piano last week and it sounded exactly the same, like there were no fingers missing."

He smiles. "And I saw ya in the fifth and sixth fights, so I know you can climb–"

"You did?"

"Oh yeah, Juncs. You're like a celebrity with all the screen time you get. I know all about yer life during Fledge. And I saw ya in that dress at the nargala." He shakes his head and exhales. "If I could have one wish it would be to take ya out like that instead of that stupid reporter." He lets out a small laugh, just a breath of air really. "I hope Ashur didn't get a look at ya in that dress, else I know what the two of ya did that night."

I blush and turn away and shake my head. "I haven't, Tier."

He smiles and then leans in to kiss me, but stops just short of my lips and looks into my eyes. "Yer sparklin', Junco."

I reach up to touch my face. "What color are they?"

"Gold, the color of the goddess. Like yer wings."

I breathe out and his lips cross the distance and I open my mouth just a tiny bit to let his tongue slip in and caress me. His hands go behind my head and then he pulls away. "No sense in making Ashur any more jealous than necessary."

I pull back. "It's not like that, Tier."

"You don't have to make excuses for him, he told me."

"Told you what?"

"That he kissed ya, Junco. It's OK, I'll be gone tomorrow."

"No you won't."

He hisses some breath through his lips. “Don’t get yer hopes up, Junco, I don’t see any way out of it.”

“I do.”

He smiles. “Well, if so, best to keep it ta yerself for now, eh?”

I nod. “Yeah.”

The door lock buzzes and I jump a little. “Yer escort is back.” He looks in my eyes and kisses me again. I lean my head into his shoulder and begin to cry.

“Junco, it’s OK.” He reaches his arms around me and tugs me in tight but my back heaves up and down with my silent sobs. It’s not OK. I cannot live without this man. Ever. It might have been possible before this visit, maybe. But now that he’s fresh in my memory, and not a distant shadow in another lifetime, I can’t let go. His hands stroke my hair over and over again to comfort me, but mine is a sadness that feels like forever.

I start counting to bring myself back from the sobs and when I get to number five I have it locked down, just like I told Annun I would. I pull back and stand up but he stays seated, the pain in his eyes almost too much for me to look at. I force myself to see him, so that tomorrow I will not forget.

“I’ll see you tomorrow after the fight.”

“I love ya, Juncs.”

I let out one more choked sob. “I love you too, Tier. More than I can ever say.”

He nods and frowns at the same time.

“But,” I sniff and wipe the tears from my face, “I can show you. And I’ll do that tomorrow.”

I turn and walk away, past Ashur, out the door and down the hallway until I get to the end of the corridor. And then I wait, with my chin up, for Ashur to make them let me out.

We walk back to the Deliverance sector in silence, and then when we get there Ashur takes my hand and leads me outside. I lie down and bury my face in the grass as I cry. He doesn’t pull me close, just lets me get it out and for that, at least, I am thankful.

Chapter Forty-One

Ashur leaves to go back to Amelia and I climb the stairs back to my room alone. There is a huge party going on in the arena for the fighters, but I have no interest in going. I palm my hand over the biometrics at my door and go in.

"Don't turn the light on, Junco." Kush is standing over at the window and the door that connects our rooms is open. "Fucking reporters out there, just waiting to get a look at you when you turn the lights on."

I sniff down a leftover sob. "What are you doing in here?"

He turns around. "Waiting for you to come back."

"I went to see Tier." I watch his face as I say the words, but he turns away.

"Yeah, everyone knows already, Junco. Your life is like a screen around here. That's why they want a look at you. To see how upset you are, get ratings for tomorrow's fight and all that good shit. They have you the odds-on favorite to win but the real money is on whether or not you'll kill him in the end. Pretty sick, right?"

I cross the room to the window and stand next to him to watch the party below. The free-G is on and people are floating around like drunken angels. I climb the little lip against the window and when I look over at Kush I'm not that much shorter than him. I smile despite my current situation and he smiles back.

"What?"

I let out a sigh and shake my head. "God, I'm glad you're here. When Monk told me you were next door I cried, I was so relieved."

He lets out a small laugh. "That's a fucking first. Where's Ashur? I thought for sure he'd be here to comfort you the night before."

"I think it got weird, him seeing Tier and me together. I like Ashur, a lot. I mean, I really do. But I love Tier. Love him, Kush. There's no comparison."

Kush looks over at me. "What happened on Earth, Junco? What did you do together that made you so connected to him?" He turns back to the party. "No one can figure that out. Not even your team. So, whatever you guys did down there, he never told them."

"Yeah." I huff out some air with my words. "I found that out along the way. They've been lacking in some seriously critical information. Stuff Tier knew, and they should've known, but didn't."

"So, what happened? Why is he so special?"

"Well, I–" I stop and look at him for the first time, I mean really look at him. He's a very good-looking guy. Tall and muscular. Not fair, but not dark either. Golden, really. Why is Tier so special? I want to say, *Do you understand what a fucking horrible piece of shit I am? And do you understand that Tier was the first person who ever thought to be careful with me?*

But I don't. I go right for the kill-shot instead. "Did you know that I tortured my father with my SEAR knife?"

His eyes squint at me. "You did what?"

I breathe out and nod. "Yeah, see, he found out I was dating this guy from the Mountain Republic and had him killed. And then I found out I was pregnant and he killed my baby. So, I went a little crazy." I look over at him to see what he's thinking, but his face is neutral, not yet ready to judge. "I tortured him with my SEAR and left him to die. And Tier…" I breathe out again to slow myself down. "He was there watching me that night, and went down and killed my father after, so he wouldn't suffer."

His blue eyes just stare at me for a few seconds. "Shit, Junco. I had no idea."

"No, I've never told anyone that story. But that's not what made me love him. That was just how it all started. He just–"

Kush is waiting now, with expectations in his eyes.

"Gets me. He gets me. And he saved my life, shit, a couple times at least. We fought some nightdogs together, and that's how I lost my fingers. Then he healed them for me. And we escaped from the MR soldiers through this fucked-up cave system, and killed this seriously evil genetic engineer, and battled with mutants and machines down in these tunnels."

I stop and watch the smile creep across his face as he pictures our adventures on Earth. The truth is though, these aren't the things that made me love him either. It was him washing my hair, healing me, telling me stories, eating the dinner I cooked, sitting behind me on my favorite horse, and revealing his secrets that made me love him. But I'm not going to tell anyone that.

So, I just nod my head and keep going. "He introduced me to Moju, who is wilder than I am. And he was always on my side." I shrug.

"We just fit together, like a puzzle. He was so patient when I couldn't remember what happened. And he was genuinely hurt and apologetic when he had to be the one to tell me the truth. He refused to leave me behind. You should've seen the warriors descend down on my house to fight the Mountain Republic's military, Kush – it was fantastic! They swooped in and fuck–"

"I did see it, Junco, it was all over the newscreens before you came out of morph, before anyone knew who you were and what was going on. There were reporters everywhere and that shit was beamed from Earth within days. Everyone's seen it. They call you the snowbird."

"I had no idea." I laugh and pause to think about it for a second. "But the most important reason why Tier is so special, and why I can't let him die tomorrow, is because he risked his life to bring me here and put me through morph." I look up again and this time I see myself through Kush's eyes. I smile and he returns it. "He gave me a choice, a chance really. A whole new life."

"You're so lucky, Junco."

"That's funny, Kush." I play with my uniform again, adjusting the wrinkles that aren't there. "The bad shit about me far outweighs the good, take my word on that one."

"I doubt that, Junco. You have a giant heart, and" – he smiles – "they all love you now. It's like all the good shit is about to come your way, you're right on the edge of something wonderful."

I look away for a second and my voice lowers and loses the excitement it just had. "If he does die tomorrow, Kush. I'm going with him." When I look back he's frowning at me and I feel bad for admitting my secret. Burdening him with it.

He moves closer and puts his arm around me. "Don't talk like that, Junco." He pulls me in front of him and we lean on the window together to watch the party beyond. There are a few reporters that are floating close to the glass, trying to see in. "Can they see us?"

I feel Kush shake his head behind me. "No, when it's dark in here it's a mirror from out there." His hand parts the hair from the back of my neck and I feel a tingle go up my body, then his mouth on my neck as he kisses me. At first I instinctively pull away a little bit, but he doesn't back off and the longer I let him continue, the better it feels.

I turn my head and his mouth finds mine and then I let him kiss me there too. It's not tender and filled with love like Tier's kisses, but it is passionate.

His hands slip under each arm to release the seams on my shirt, then they gently tug it over my head and return to my back. I buckle as his fingers slide across the sensitive skin between my wings.

He pushes his chest into me and the pressure on my wings makes my throat stretch up and to the side, exposing my neck even more. His mouth slips up to my ear and my eyes flutter as a small groan rumbles out. His breath glides in and tickles pleasure receptors I never knew I had. Fingertips are tracing along the top side of my wing, making it extend out automatically, inviting him to touch the many rows of feathers. His right hand slides down the length of a secondary covert feather and he massages it slightly between his fingers before flitting across the tips and drawing back into my waist where he slides his hand up to cup my breast. His other hand eases down the length of my stomach, pausing lightly at the SEAR to investigate, then unbuttons my pants and slips inside.

My eyes close and I let my whole body sink back against him. I've never experienced such a slow pleasure with a man in my life.

I turn to face him, thrusting my lower body into his. He grabs my wrists and pushes them up above my head, clasping them together and holding me against the cool glass with one hand as the other tickles the small of my back.

He doesn't stop when I look up at him, but instead presses his lips near my cheek once more, allowing his breath to trickle into my ear. The combination of all these new sensations is almost too much. "Oh shit, Kush." I release my passion out in a hoarse whisper.

"What?" He breathes it back into me, then pulls away slightly and lowers his chin.

"I'm going to regret this in the morning."

"No, Junco." He exhales. "You won't. I'm going to make sure of it."

I look up into his eyes and they glow a lovely pale blue, so gentle, and so soft. He meets my gaze and then his mouth finds mine, his tongue inside twirling and probing me, until I give in completely.

Later, I'm puffing one of Kush's cigars and watching what's left of the partiers out in the arena as I recycle back my conversation with Tier.

Kush approaches and leans into my back. He stretches his arms past either side of my shoulders, pressing on the glass, pushing us towards the window. He kisses me and whispers down across my cheek, "You gonna tell me the plan, Junco? Or you just gonna go in there and do it all on your own?"

I grunt as I try to ignore how the air traveling into my ear makes me feel. My words come out just as gentle as his. "What plan is that, Kush?"

He pulls back and then turns to lean his back against the window so he can see my face. "The one that involves winning the fight and saving your boyfriend."

I let out a little laugh with my smoke ring and shake my head with a sigh. "Believe me, I'm not really planning on winning. Killing the person I love is not my kind of prize." He just looks at me and I try to ignore his blue eyes as they start to light up a little, but I can't. "What?"

"Then what the fuck are you doing, Junco? What's your plan?"

I puff again, then blow more rings as I ponder this line of thinking myself. In the end I shrug. "I don't know, Kush. We'll have to wait and see what happens."

We stand there for a little longer, looking out at the arena, probably both of us wondering what tomorrow night will bring. And then he pulls me back to bed and we fall asleep.

Chapter Forty-Two

When I wake up I am alone in bed, but my room is filled with people. Ashur, Isten, Arel, Rikan, Mish, Ryse, Lucan, Rache, and Monk. They are not paying much attention to me, instead they are all talking at once in several smaller groups. I screw up my face as I try to figure out what's going on, then remember Kush. My eyes dart over to the connecting door and I feel a little relief when I see it's closed.

When I look back, Ashur is watching me. It's only then that I realize I'm naked under the covers and yesterday's uniform is strewn about the floor near the window.

Fuck it.

I throw back the covers and stand up, then walk towards the shower, my wingtips brushing lightly across my butt as I glide. The entire room goes silent and every head turns in my direction. My eyes never leave Ashur's face. I shrug as I pass him and close the bathroom door behind me. Lucan's voice comes in clear from the other side. "Out, everyone out."

The hypnotic pulse of the shower jets gives me time to think about what's coming and that's not good, so I finish quickly, then dress in my uniform and take a seat at the table to lace up my boots. I don't know what other people will be wearing for the battle, probably not their uniform. But that's what I'm wearing.

The connecting door chimes. "Enter," I call.

Kush comes in and laughs at me. "Shit, were you having a party over here or what?"

"Kush, I don't invite them over, they just show up."

He sits down with me at the table. "I get it, Junco. If I was on your team, I'd barge in any chance I got too."

I finish with my boot lacing and look up to give him my attention. "No regrets, Kush." I smile and he nods his head.

"No regrets, Junco."

"I have a pre-fight interview with Kadian, you got any interviews?"

"Yeah, I think I talk to him right before you."

I nod. "Good then, I'll see you after that, huh? I gotta go find Ashur or Lucan or someone to get myself back on track. You're really distracting me." I smile, and probably blush too, because my face suddenly feels hot as I think about our night together.

He lets out a little laugh. "See ya after." Then he goes back to his room.

I'm slipping my comm into my thigh pocket when the main door chimes. "Enter."

The door slides open and Esta stands at the threshold. "Can I come in?" She's wearing her demure Cluster mother clothes and I absently shudder at the thought of that get-up being my uniform.

My mouth twists a little at her. "I said enter, Esta. Of course you can come in."

She takes a few hesitant steps into my room and then bows her head. "I'm so sorry, Junco. I know you were counting on me and I completely let you down. My personal issues got in the way and–"

"What the fuck are you talking about?"

She looks back up at me and swallows. "Isec. He didn't make it and I'm sorry, I should have listened to you. He didn't need to die in the last battle, he was so close."

I just stare at her for a few seconds, trying to put this all together. "It wasn't your fault, Esta, he was never going to make it."

She nods. "I know that, but he might have if I'd helped you train him better. He was so close."

I walk over to her. "Do you know what we do in the Seventh Battle?"

She doesn't even look up, just shakes her head no.

"Well, I won't spill it, since it's obviously a secret, but you had nothing, and I do mean nothing, Esta, to do with Isec's death. So just let it go."

She stays silent and I wave my hand over towards the table. "Take a seat if you want."

She flicks her long black hair behind one ear as she sits, and then lets out a sharp sigh as I join her and strike up a cigar. I offer her one and to my surprise, she takes it. We puff for a few minutes. "Did you ever ask Lucan if you could change jobs?"

"No," she says, shaking her head. "He would never listen to me."

"Esta, that makes no sense, you're one of the pure Seven, you have so much power it's sick."

"They don't really like me, Junco. They avoid me, stick me in with the children and try to forget I'm even here. I never wanted that job. Back on Earth I was training to be a historian, I went to school and was about to pass my qualifiers for apprenticeship. They took it all away when I came here. And now I have to sneak around, looking for information in their sphere–"

"They have a sphere here?" She tilts her head at me, like she's trying to figure out if I'm joking. I shrug. "I didn't know. No one told me."

"Anyway, I like history, Junco. I can't help it. And being immersed in all this new culture but not being allowed to learn about it. Well, it drives me crazy. It's like they want me here, but they don't want me to know too much about them. So I cheat. I sneak information. It's absurd."

"Oh," I manage to say after a few seconds of pause. "I had no idea."

"No, why would you, they've done nothing but try and keep us apart since you got here. I was lucky Lucan was so mad that day I found you in the conference room, otherwise he'd never have let me talk to you."

"Do you hate it here, Esta? Would you rather be on Earth?"

She pauses for a moment. "No."

"But?"

"But I have no say in anything, they just make all these decisions about me and that's the end of it. I have no say. I might as well be back in the Utopia, at least there they made me do something that I actually enjoyed, even if it was all bullshit brainwashing."

Wow, Esta and I have something in common. "So, if you could choose, you'd choose what, then?"

She thinks about it for a moment, her eyes looking out towards the preparations in the arena beyond the windows. "I just want to learn things, continue my life the way it was going on Earth. I just want to be allowed to read the avian books and stuff, I'm not asking that much." She looks up, her posture in a desperate plea for me to believe it's a small request. I do agree, the girl wants to read and study for fuck's sake. How hard could it be to let her do that?

She takes a deep breath and continues, "If I had a choice, I'd join Sefer Cluster. The scribes who study and preserve the mythology."

I laugh. "Really? Shit, I can't stand those stories myself. I'm so tired of all that bullshit."

She laughs with me. "We are so different." And then she stares into my face, seeing me. "I don't feel important, I feel like all they care about is you."

"Esta, I'm not even the one who can save them, you are! If I bring back the others, then it's all about you guys. I'll be a distant memory." Shit, why am I even having this conversation, there's not going to be any trip to Earth. I stand up and wait for her to stand as well. "I really wish I could stay and talk more, but I need to go find Ashur or Lucan. I'll put in a word for you, OK?"

She nods, her head still bowed. "Thanks for talking to me, Junco. I know it must be difficult after Isec's death to even look at me–"

I put my hand up to stop her. "Esta, I killed him, not you. Me. I cut off his head in the Seventh Battle – so stop, OK? It had nothing to do with you."

She looks into my eyes for truth and I look into hers for judgment. And then we both look away.

"OK," she says. "I know whatever happened, it must have been hard. It's hard, Junco. To live by their customs and rules when so much of it goes against our human nature. And even though I'm not technically human, you don't spend your whole life in a culture and not become one of them."

I nod and walk out in the hallway with her. Hard? That word doesn't even come close. Underneath I twist her words to fit my own life. I spent my whole life immersed in a culture that embraced me as a killer. And she's right. I'm one of them, now and forever.

I get in line for food in the cafeteria and take a look around as it moves forward slowly. Kush is on the far left side eating near some people I don't know. Sometimes I forget that he's from here and has a past complete with friends and history.

The 039 is on the far right with the 399. They take up three tables between them. I get to the food and start choosing things I've had before. I fill up a good portion of the tray and then thumb the biometrics at the end to charge it to whoever pay the bills for me when I do that.

After paying I stand there as people push past me for a minute. Both Kush and Ashur are looking at me, waiting to see where I sit. It feels like cadet school. I choose my team, obviously, then walk towards the guys and slip in next to Monk on the bench to create a buffer between myself and the 039.

"Junco, hey, uh, sorry we all barged in on you this morning." Monk shrugs. "We'll know better next time." He smiles and elbows me in the ribs.

"Doesn't bother me, Monk. You guys were the ones all freaked out about it." My eyes follow Ashur as he makes his way over towards us. He stops behind the guy sitting next to me, who takes the hint and gets up to leave. The rest of the table is suddenly on the move as well and within a few seconds, Ashur and I are alone.

I turn and look at him. "What?" The look in his eyes makes me turn away.

He sits down on the bench with his back to the table. "Why, Junco? You don't even like the guy."

I look down at my tray, my appetite gone. "That's not entirely true, Ashur. I like him well enough."

I can feel him shaking his head at me. "Enough to sleep with him? After seeing Tier last night?"

I let out a little laugh. "Obviously, the answer to that is yes." I look up at him to make sure this point sinks in. "Else I wouldn't have done it. The best thing about Kush is he's not a complicated guy. He's not my captain or the guy I'm trying to save from death. He's just a friend who's been there for me when I needed him. And last night I needed him and he was there."

Ashur leans his elbows back on the table and stretches out his legs, silent. I straddle the bench so I can see him better, then wait for him to look over at me again. "Sometimes, Ashur, you gotta just take what you want and stop thinking about it. That's what he did. And to be brutally honest, I'm glad, because if ever there was a night where I needed someone to want me like that, it was last night."

He nods his head and looks away. "I call that taking advantage of someone who's not really thinking clearly, but hey, you can tell yourself anything you want, Junco. You're the one who fucking fell for it."

I get up and grab my tray, dump it in the trash and head outside to find a place to smoke.

It's a small alcove built into the side of the building. I hide there and puff as I lean up against a pillar. Lucan appears, dressed in his overly formal suit, as per usual.

I look up at him. "What?"

He smiles. "I don't care who you sleep with, Junco. But you need to make a choice if you want to stay in the 039."

I just want him to go away and leave me alone, that's what I want. "I don't," I say quickly, "want to stay, I mean. I'll stay with Rache."

I look up to see how this hits him, but he's still smiling. "Probably a good idea."

It hurts, it really does.

"Great." I stomp out my cigar and walk off back to the Deliverance floor to find Kadian.

Chapter Forty-Three

The Deliverance floor is packed with bodies – fighters, reporters, and auxiliary people who do something, I'm sure, but I have no idea what. I see Kush and walk over to him. "Hey, you do the interview yet?"

"No, he's behind, says he wants to interview us together."

I scowl. "Why? I might not know him that well, but Kadian is a schemer. He has a reason, probably knows we were together last night."

Kush just shrugs. "Yeah, probably. If it bothers you, we'll just say no."

It turns out it doesn't bother me enough to say no when Kadian's staff comes to get us. We do the interview together in a small room that looks down on the stage. Below us I see twenty-one prisoners stretched out in an X pattern as their arms, wings and legs are bound up and pulled taut with wires that attach to various pillars offstage. There are ten on the left side of the stage and ten on the right. In the middle, elevated from the rest, is Tier. The twenty-first offender, the traitor.

My eyes can't pull away once I realize what's going on and Kush has to lead me over to the chair, out of sight of the crucifixion scene below, in order to snap me out of it.

"Junco, how does it feel to see Tier up there as a Deliverance offering?"

I look over at Kadian, hating him for doing this to me. Ryse was right, he's a scumbag. "More determined than ever, Kadian." I smile and the worry leaves me as I play the game.

"Determined to do what, Junco?"

"Save him. I think everyone knows by now, the only reason I'm here is to save him."

Kadian smiles and switches over to Kush. "Are you here to support Junco in her efforts? Or to win the wish?"

Kush's face remains passive, his signature expression of indifference. "Both."

Kadian waits for him to elaborate, but Kush turns his head towards the arena so he is forced to redirect. "Are the two of you aware that the Archers have declared that no pardon wishes will be granted?"

Kush answers without even turning towards Kadian this time. "Our plans never included pardon wishes, Kadian. How naive do you think we are?"

It's true, too. My wish is not a pardon and Kush said his wish was to be captain.

"What are your wishes then, if you don't mind sharing with the arena. Everyone is anxious to see how Junco plans on saving Raubtier from his certain death sentence."

Kush doesn't even skip a beat. "You'll see our wishes when we win, not before."

Kadian smiles indulgently now. "But only one of you can win, Kush. Who will it be?"

Kush shrugs. "How the hell should I know."

Kadian has had enough of Kush and I've got a new respect for the attitude that suits him. My respect must show on my face because my first question hits the mark. "Junco, which of the many men in your life actually has your heart? There won't be much left if you keep parceling it out like this."

"Tier." It comes out automatically. "It always has been and always will be Tier."

"OK, let's switch gears, your love life is getting too complicated, Junco. Tell us why they call you the snowbird?"

I shake my head at him. "I can't tell you that, I have no idea."

"What is a snowbird? Do you have them on Earth?"

"Well, yes. Juncos are snowbirds, little winter sparrows that live in the mountains near my home. Or what was my home, after the nukes, there's nothing left, I hear. All the Rural Republic juncos are dead now."

"All except one, right?"

"Sure, right. All except one."

Apparently he's had enough of our lackluster performance because he signs off the interview. Kush and I disengage ourselves and head towards the ready room.

"Well," he lets out a breath, "that was fucking fantastic."

I have to trot to keep up with him so I grab on his arm and tug him back to slow down. "Shit, how did I ever think he was a decent guy? I mean, the nargala was fun and all, but he only took me so he could get me on camera in that designer dress."

He slows his pace and puts his hand in the middle of my back to direct me into the ready room where most of the fighters have already arrived and are reading through the rules. They flash across my vision screen and I greet my AI. *Decided to finally show yourself, eh?* She ignores me and the rules begin to scroll. I read them as Kush reads along on the giant screen at the head of the room.

No weapons.

Killing is not required, nor prohibited.

Falling below the red line denotes a forfeit.

The last man standing wins a wish.

The winner will execute the prisoners in the manner they choose.

Healing, up to the value of a hundred thousand rills, will be provided to all fighters who survive, unless they use their wish to compensate for overages.

I look up at Kush. "So basically, stay above the red line and don't let anyone kill you."

He smiles. "Got it in one, Junco."

Then we go fill out our wishes. You're allowed to have conditions for final health status in case your injuries exceed the allotted amount of health care, but I don't bother and from the speed by which Kush fills his out, he doesn't either. We press enter on the screens and they are sealed, only to be opened by Rache once the winner is determined.

The screen flashes to the filled arena. The nine Archers sit at the end opposite the stage where the prisoners are strung up, probably directly above my room. People are screaming and cheering, the odds are flashing last call on a giant board. I'm the favorite to win.

And then they call us to line up on our predetermined spots. Kush's spot is across the room from me, so he leans down and kisses my cheek. "See you at the end, snowbird."

I grin up at him. "Yeah, sure, Kush. Good luck."

Everyone takes their place and we settle into the ebb of activity that I use to predict start.

And then we are flying upward, the screams from the arena filling our ears, the hammering of stomping feet vibrating the entire structure, the lights dim and crackle as the various G-fields are activated. Our feet come free and Deliverance begins.

Chapter Forty-Four

I have the neck of the guy next to me before he even knows what's happening. One swift twist later he's the first official forfeiter and I've set the standard for just how fucked-up this fight will be. In the end, the decision was based on logistics, not emotion. Killing is just so much easier than injuring.

I shoot up in the air after that and fly as hard as I can for the smallest and weakest of all the fighters, a girl not much bigger than me. She sees me targeting her and dives down below the red line.

Something to be said for common sense.

After that I'm attacked from all sides. My wings thrust and twist as I evade, then flip around and change direction, using my momentum to bowl into the middle of my attackers. They scatter and I choose the closest one and drag him down to the gravity plane, not the mushrooms from last night, but a long, flat stone surface that pulls you down relentlessly once inside the field. No one wants to follow me down there, so I have him to myself. He tries to understand my grappling moves, but simply can't. I break his ankle, then crack his head on the stone and stop to catch my breath.

A large guy comes out of nowhere and knocks me down, his hands around my neck. My foot goes up and catches him in the head, he flinches, but keeps hold, preventing oxygen from reaching my brain. I see the stars of unconsciousness coming when I snap back to my senses and chop him repeatedly in the temple. He loses his grasp fractionally, but I take advantage and twist my body around, then send an elbow into his gut and the palm of my hand slams up against the underside of his jaw. I hear a sickening crack and he lets go of me. I kick him in the teeth a few times to make up for the marks he left, then lean down and twist his neck until he's limp.

Another guy is standing a few feet away, wondering if he should take his chance at me, and decides he should with a grin. His claws come out and they are the length of good-sized swords. I fly upward and leave the gravity field behind, better to engage this one up top. He follows me, much quicker and skilled in the art of flying, and grabs my foot and tugs me backwards. My body crashes against him and then his razors rake across my stomach, splitting open my armor and penetrating my skin.

I scream and squirm, but he keeps hold. Our thrashing propels us over to the transparent barrier and he smacks my head against it face-first. The blood spouts out from my nose as the people behind the barrier pound against it so hard the vibrations thump against my body. I see his reflection in the glare on the barrier, but I force myself to stay still. His hands are going for my throat, ready to snap my neck when I reach up and over my head and drive my razors into his skull with as much force as I can. He screams and the people on the other side of the barrier go wild. I push off the wall and swing his body up over mine, then flap my wings as hard as I can and crash his head into the barrier.

Paybacks are always a bitch.

I pull out the claws and turn him around so he has to watch, then force his teeth to meet my knee in a blood-spattering crunch.

Before I can even take stock of the scene another guy slams me against the wall. I recover with the help of free-G momentum and fly, flitting in and out of other pairs and trios busy fighting each other and then press my wings flat against my back and tuck and reverse thrust. My follower smacks into me hard, and we bounce apart like the perfect inelastic collision demonstration in a cadet-school physics lab.

My smaller mass has me taking the brunt of the energy transfer and I go careening off, slamming face-first into a huge guy who looks like the only thing that could possibly make him happy right now is dismembering my body. He grabs my arm and twists it behind my back. I can almost feel the tendons in my shoulder stretching. I flip my feet up in front of me, over his head, and before he even knows what's happening I've got his neck locked between my thighs and I'm squeezing the life out of him. His body goes limp and begins to float in the fight wind. I let go, then push him as hard as I can down below the red line.

I finally have a chance to take stock and spy Kush across the arena, but he's busy killing, so I leave him be.

The guy from before has a team with him and they surround me. I fly down to the G-platform and wait casually to see if they really want to try this.

They do.

All four of them circle me, crouching a little like they know what the fuck to do when I come at them with hand to hand moves. I immediately hunch my shoulder and duck my head, coming off as submissive as possible. It pumps up their rage and they stand up a little taller. I turn my hips so my right shoulder is facing the guy closest to me without taking my peripheral eyes off the other three, then talk him up. "Come on guys, let's team up. I'll make us all rich." My arms are bent, my hands talking along with my words, and they stop noticing the movement. I scoot a fraction towards the nearest guy and then slam my palm into his mouth and hammerfist him in the neck, halfway between the ear and the spinal cord. The brain stem chop will take out anyone, you don't even need that much force.

He doesn't get back up.

His buddy has me in a chicken wing before I can blink, both of my arms locked in his, thinking he's gonna hold me there so his friends can beat the shit out of me, but he's wrong. He head butts me from the back and my vision blurs from the impact. Inside I fly into a private rage and bring my right leg behind him, stretch it all the way over until it's outside of his right leg, then simply stand up. He falls back like an idiot and I hear the crowd go wild. I take a chance and finish him off with two sharp stomps to his jaw, one halfway up the side, where there's a tiny little hole that allows nerves to pass through the bone, and then a second up where the jaw meets the skull. Another hotbed of nerves. I hear the crack and smile as the pain in his eyes registers.

The sharp stab against the side of my neck knocks me down on the ground and the other two guys are on me now as the blood from the razors pools and sticks to my hair. I grab the shirt of the first guy as the second guy holds my legs down. Their razors are clawing at me, blood is running down my legs and arms inside my uniform, but the pain never even materializes. The adrenaline running through my bloodstream takes care of that.

My hands crawl up his shirt and I pull him towards me, biting off the top of his ear once it's within reach. His blood drenches me and makes him panic and forget to hold tight. I hammerfist him in the back of the neck relentlessly while his buddy tugs on my legs to pull me out from under him. I let go and allow myself to be pulled. When I'm free of the defeated bleeder on top I thrust my upper body up and grab the other guy's neck, squeezing until he has to let go of my legs and pry my little fingers off.

My legs scramble and get between us and I simply kick him off me. He goes careening across the stone slab but I'm on him before he can even decide if he wants to get back up. I slash his throat so deep his final heartbeats pulse up in the air like a fountain.

The ear bleeder isn't done with me and now it's one on one.

He rushes and connects with my stomach, sending me careening backwards, sliding across the smooth stone surface. I decide to make an example of this last asshole because I'm getting tired. I kick him off, girl-style, a few quickies to the balls, one to the jaw, and then scoot backwards and stand up, crouching a little to egg him on.

He bounces back up, still sure of himself even though he's about to lose consciousness from blood loss. He looks down on my diminutive size and takes his last step. I slide in, grab him around the knee with one hand, then pinch his Achilles heel with the other. After that it's a simple little pull. He goes down and I keep hold of his heel, squeezing, but I don't finish him. I let go and wait as he sends me backwards with his flapping wings. I hunch over, pretending to be out of breath and tired, ready for it to end.

He takes the bait and gets back up like a dumbass.

I walk towards him and grab him with both hands, one behind the neck, the other on his bicep, and swing into a flying arm bar, taking him down and slapping him on the stone. It's the exact same move I pulled on Ashur when we trained for Fight Six, except this guy has never seen it before. Most of the time the flying arm bar is a bullshit flash move that almost never works. But here, his head crashes into the stone so hard the skull hemorrhages blood and bits of bone fly up and sting my face.

The crowd goes wild as I push all their bodies off the slab and watch as their names go dark on the scoreboard.

And then I look around to see where we are.

Kush is standing at the other end of the slab, just watching me. I smile and he walks over and gives me a hug. There are still half a dozen fighters but three of them go dark in the next few seconds and the other three nod to us and dive down.

They're done.

And only we are left.

I stare up at Kush, breathing hard. "Well, you wanna win, or should I?"

He pulls me to him again and leans down into my ear. "It's all you, Junco. You are the only reason I'm here."

He flies off and dives down below the red line, then flies back up and stands on the slab, bowing to me, gesturing towards the prisoners that await my Deliverance on the other end of the arena. His name goes dark and then there is just me.

And twenty-one prisoners that I am supposed to kill.

I turn to face them for the first time since entering the arena and I feel sick to my stomach. Every one of them is barely hanging on. I don't know for sure how long they've been strung up like that, hours at least, but it has taken its toll and their heads slump like they are already dead, a sharp contrast to their erect bodies, and each rigid limb, wings included, being pulled taut in all directions by the wires that connect them to the pillars off-stage.

The stage has been reformed from last night and is not deep at all. It only allows enough room for the prisoner to stand plus a foot or so of extra space for the executioner.

Which is now me.

I reach under my shirt and hear the crowd gasp as the SEAR comes out. I take a deep breath and power it up, wincing at the hissing loop of genetically enhanced plasma as it comes to life in my hand.

I look over at Kush who has seen me kill with this before and he nods. Then I dial it up a little to a medium length dagger and fly over to the first prisoner. The guy is a mess, his hair matted with sweat, his bowels vacated and his body smelling like shit. His eyes are alert now that the time has come, they dart back and forth as he desperately tries to move away from the inevitable final justice of my weapon.

The crowd is almost silent for a second, almost a hush, but then I raise the knife and begin the smooth cut through his neck and they stand up and cheer wildly.

If I was alone, I'd puke.

Not just from the smell of the SEAR cutting through flesh, although that is enough to make anyone hurl. But because these people make me sick inside, in my heart. The thirst for killing the avians have displayed since I came to live with them is the farthest thing from human I can think of. Only the most disturbed individuals on Earth would participate in an event like this.

At least I tell myself that.

Because I don't want to think of what reality I might have to face if this was the true nature of all sentient species. To kill, to punish, to make people pay. And then have to extrapolate that same inhuman, barbaric characteristic to myself. I've killed more people than I can count, and today I will kill twenty-one more.

I move onto the next guy and it's the same shit all over again. The stench from him, combined with the smell of flesh on fire, sticks to my olfactory receptors, imprinting that molecular signature into my memory forever.

I repeat this eight more times to the undulating cheers of the masses in the arena that ebb and flow, rise and fall, as I cut and withdraw.

I complete the tenth guy and pause briefly to look at Tier.

The crowd calls for his death as he struggles to lift his head, and then lets it drop back to his chest as he realizes he hasn't got the strength. I don't worry about his judgment of me, of what he might think of who I really am at this moment. Because in a few minutes it won't matter.

I pass him by and move on to number eleven. From there the killing, the smells, the screams, the cheers – they all merge together. I'm lost. Just utterly lost in the buildup of death that surrounds me.

When I finish the twentieth guy I fly back over to Kush who looks at me with a pained expression. Something I don't really need at this particular moment is his righteous judgment, but if anyone has a claim to righteousness, it's probably Kush.

He drops the look and walks towards me, then takes me in his arms and squeezes. The people, impatient to see if they will win money, to see if I will kill Tier, or cut him loose and stand and fight against my own team of Aves warriors, begin jeering at me, calling out names, and stomping their feet.

I look down to the far side of the arena and find Lucan. He's standing, his palms pressed up against the transparent barrier. Then my gaze sweeps around the arena and I find each of my 039 teammates, minus Braun of course. One by one, as my gaze passes over them, my brothers shake their heads at me, telling me no. Even Ashur shakes his head and when he realizes I'm paying attention, he says it out loud, then begins to scream it.

I look back at Lucan and I hold up my hand to make people shut up so I can speak. It takes the better part of a minute, but they finally calm down.

"Please," I beg the Archers on the far side of the arena. "Don't make me go through with it, please pardon him. Please don't make me go through with it."

Chapter Forty-Five

Lucan sits down without answering. The crowd resumes their jeering and screaming as I turn to Kush and swallow hard, refusing to let the tears flow for such a selfish emotion as fear.

"Kush, I want you to know…" I look down as he comes towards me. "I want you to know that you're a good friend." I look up and the tears begin to fall. "And you're a good warrior, too. I've got no regrets."

He smiles and takes my hand. "I'm here for you, OK?"

"Yeah."

I turn and walk over to the edge of the platform and look down. There's a long shadow reaching out across the floor of the arena. Broad at one end, slim at the other. I breathe in, then out, and collect myself for what I have to do.

I fly over to the small platform that holds the man I love and I reach up with my SEAR and cut one of his hands free. It falls to his side, limp and dead, as Monk leaves his post above the prisoners and flies down towards me, shaking his head.

"Don't do it, Junco. I don't want to see him dead any more than you do, but you're not gonna set him free. The time for pardons is past."

I nod and this makes my tears fall down my face a little quicker. "I just want to feel him hold me one more time, Monk. Just the one hand, wrapped around me one last time."

I look up in his eyes as they glow orange and he nods. "OK, just the one though."

I take a deep breath, pushing down the fear and the cries for vengeance and pain, so that time stops for us. I take his hand and place it on my waist and he gathers the strength to look me in the face. I smile as I power the SEAR back up, a short dagger this time.

"Junco!"

I turn and Kush is behind me hovering. "Stop, I know what you're going to do, Junco. And I won't let you."

"No, Kush – it's a done deal."

He grabs me by the waist and flies me back over to the stone gravity slab as the crowd screams with rage at the interruption. We struggle for a few seconds and then I pull away and stand opposite Kush. "What the fuck are you doing?"

He makes a grab for my SEAR. "I won't–"

I jerk it back out of instinct.

The loop passes ever so slightly across Kush's arm.

A small, barely noticeable tendril of flesh smoke seeps up into the air and my chest begins to heave in and out as I scream. "No! No, no, no, NOOOOOOOOO!"

His arm immediately begins to disintegrate from the inside out, his skin melting like wax on a candle as the alloantigen repressor makes its way into the DNA to fuck up every new collagen transcript from here on out. I can see in real time how the biocode invades his current extracellular matrix and begins to disrupt the scaffolding system that holds the entire body together.

The crowd is quiet as I watch my friend realize what has happened. "Oh, Kush. Oh my God, Kush! No!"

The disruption climbs up his arm and when it reaches his neck he screams, a noise that is neither human nor avian, but pain. Unbearable pain.

"Kill me," he blurts out, "Junco – kill me, now!" The resulting shriek jolts me into action and my hand drags the SEAR across his neck, ending his life.

It's all over in a matter of seconds and I drop to my knees beside the man who gave me every tender gesture he could think of just to make sure I didn't regret our night together.

Gone.

I turn up my head and scream into the roar of the spectators and sit there for a few minutes, letting my eyes and nose drip onto the cold hard slab of stone. I look back up to Lucan one last time. "Please," I beg again. "Please make it end, Lucan. Don't make me do it."

But he shakes his head and my fate is settled.

I pull my body back up and look down at the edge of the slab once more to find the shadow, then fly over to Tier. His head is up and his eyes are glassy with drugs. "I'm sorry," he croaks.

I smile at him and wrap his free arm around me. "Just hold me one more time, OK?"

He nods, but his head falls back to his chest and his arm can barely maintain a grasp on the belt loop of my pants. I reach around and pull his hand to mine. "Tier, look at me, now!" The sharp command forces him to obey and I smile. "Whatever you do, do not drop it."

He screws up his face in confusion as I clasp his hand over mine, then withdraw all but my thumb.

The SEAR springs to life in his palm and I drag it down my chest, eviscerating myself from heart to belly.

I sway slightly and he is too weak to hold me, but I watch his hand to make sure the knife is still clasped tightly in his palm, visible to all watching.

I swan-dive backwards, facing out towards the crowd, and fall into the depths of the arena's floor, into the waiting arms of my shadow.

Braun catches me midair and I have a fraction to stare up in his eyes and whisper thank you.

And that's that.

Tier has completed his mission and I am dying by his hand, just like I should have back on Earth.

He's no longer guilty.

Chapter Forty-Six

Picture yourself standing on the edge of a dock...

Holy shit, it's cold here now.

I look around. "Charlie? Charlie, you fuck! Where the hell are you?"

My boots crunch over the ice and snow that lines the dock and I make my way back to the cabin, breathing into my reddened hands to try and warm them up.

I jog across what was the lawn the last time I was here and push the front door open and step into the dark cabin.

It's empty.

The furniture is covered with white sheets and there's barely a temperature difference between the mountain cold outside and the frigid air inside.

"Charlie?"

Silence.

I let out a long sigh. Fuck, how the hell did it get to be winter? He programmed it to be tropical, I'm sure of it. I chuck some wood into the fireplace and light it up, standing there to thaw for a few minutes. Eventually I lower myself down onto the coiled rag rug and fall asleep in the warm orange glow.

Days pass. Weeks maybe. Years for all I know. And still I wait. If he was here before, he's still here now. He just doesn't know I'm back, that's all. The temperature never grows warmer, the sunlight never grows brighter, the days never grow longer.

I'm stagnant.

And that's OK with me.

I pass the time ice-fishing, cooking, and sleeping. It's not a bad life, really. Occasionally, when I'm starting to think I might be bored, I remind myself that an exciting life isn't all it's cracked up to be.

I can live without excitement for a while.

Forever maybe.

There are books to read. I've read them all, but I read them again.

There are birds to watch outside the window. I can't name all of them, but I do recognize the juncos. Both the regular and the pink-sided varieties. Little sparrows looking for food. I collect stray pine cones from the forest floor and turn them into bird feeders using the peanut butter I retrieve from the secret pantry. I hang them up in front of the picture window.

I cook dinners and I watch life from the living-room couch.

I go to bed early and wake up late.

And finally, after what seems like years of living in this cabin, waiting for Charlie to come find me, I'm out of things to do.

So I just stay in bed and never get up.

Not even to eat or go to the bathroom.

And guess what? I never needed to eat to go to the bathroom anyway, I'm not real! So I don't even get a rumbly tummy or the pain of a full bladder.

I am in limbo.

I'm on my way to hell for all the killing I've done, but for some reason I'm stuck in limbo. The Church would like you to believe that limbo is bad, not a place you'd like to be. But consider the alternative. Am I right?

In the end I'm OK with limbo.

And so here I am.

Lying in bed, neither awake nor asleep.

The banging of pots and pans from the other room jolts me out of my stagnation. I throw back the covers and race out to the kitchen in my pajamas.

"Well, good morning, Junco."

Sera is cooking eggs on the wood stove and percolating coffee using something that requires electricity, so cannot possibly work here in this cabin. Her red hair is messy, like she just woke up too, and her red dress is MIA. In its place is a pair of patterned night clothes that look like they might belong to me.

"What are you doing here?"

She smiles. "Making you breakfast, of course. You really should learn to eat properly."

This comment tugs at me and I screw up my face. "I don't have an eating problem. I just don't need to eat here, that's all."

She gives me an exaggerated nod. "Right, but giving up on life in here means you're giving up on life out there."

"What life out there? I'm dead. I'm in limbo, waiting for God or someone to judge me."

She scoops the eggs out onto a plate and drops on a few pieces of buttered toast and several strips of bacon to round it all out. "Sit, eat."

I sit and she pushes the plate over to me. I feel a rumble deep inside and I stuff my face so fast she laughs.

"Don't need to eat, huh?"

I shrug with my mouth full. "Shit, I *am* hungry."

"You'll need to eat again when you wake up. This isn't real, after all. Just a virtual."

I stop and ask through the food. "What do you mean wake up? I'm dead."

She shakes her head. "No, Junco. You won the Deliverance fight. So your wish was granted."

"But I gave my wish to Esta, I don't need a wish when I'm dead."

She smiles at me as if I'm a toddler. "Esta had quite a wish, Junco. Seems like all that secret studying of the avian culture, history and myths really paid off. For you, anyway."

"What do you mean?" I stare at her, my bacon halfway to my mouth.

"She wished for your Resurrection. A long-forgotten rite that can be performed by the Archers."

"Oh, fuck. I bet that went over well."

"Well, better than expected, really. The public outcry from that fight was," she pauses to find the right word, "almost unimaginable. They had riots over you and Kush. And Tier."

I push the memory of Kush away quickly. "They did?"

"Yes, so the Resurrection was a panacea that pretty much everyone got on board with immediately. It's just…"

I stare at her, waiting for her to finish. "What?"

"A long and complicated process that has never actually worked before."

"Oh. Well, I knew it was too good to be true." I shrug and continue to eat my food, but the taste has faded.

"I'm not saying it can't work, it can. But you need to decide what you're going to do. And make me a promise if I intervene and help you return."

I stay silent and weigh the words in my mind.

"You're ready to go back? Rested? Whole again? Sane?"

"No, no, no, and no."

She smiles. "Liar."

"I'm not ready to make a deal, that's not a lie."

"Oh, you are, Junco. Because I want very little from you now. You did so well already, the rest is small in comparison."

"Really? *That* was job well done? Shit, I'd hate to see what failure looks like."

"You restored Tier's status, you got Isec to make his sacrifice, you got Kush to make his sacrifice, and you made your sacrifice. All of my goals for you accomplished. So now," she beams down at me, "I require one tiny thing, Junco."

I sit there quietly, my lips falling into a deep frown as I lean my head into my hands. "Why did they have to die? That doesn't make sense."

She looks away for a few moments, out the window in the kitchen, maybe distracted by a bird on my pine cone, or maybe looking for words. More likely she's about to tell me something she'd prefer not to.

"When Inanna went to the world down under and was trapped, how was she able to escape her death, Junco?"

I reach back for the night Tier told me the story, when we were soaking in the hot spring. "She got people to stand in for her," I answer finally.

Sera smiles. "And that's exactly what Kush is doing for you now. Standing in for you so that you can return. He chose this, it was his sacrifice."

My heart wants to shrivel up and die and my frown pulls my entire face down in my sadness.

"And tell me, why did you give your wish to Esta, of all people? I mean, you could have just given that wish to Tier, he could have saved himself. So, why Esta?"

"I could've given the wish to Tier? Would that have worked?"

"Do you think it would've worked?"

I look away and study the view out the window. "No, that's way too easy."

"So, why Esta?"

"I felt bad for her. I wanted to make her happy. Give her a chance to change her life."

"And why did you feel bad for her? You haven't thought about her in weeks, so why that day?"

"She thought she was the one who killed–" My voice trails off.

"Because Isec was dead and she felt compelled to come apologize to you for killing him."

My chin shakes as the tears fall down. "Is it all predetermined? Everything?"

"No, Junco. Not all of it. Destiny is fixed, but fate can shift and you've done that. So well I can hardly comprehend the consequences. If you gave your wish to Tier and made him sacrifice nothing, what would that have accomplished? Nothing, that's what. But you caused a ripple through the entire Band, millions of people, Junco. They all shifted because of your desperate act."

She waits for me to say something, but I can't. I just sit and think.

"I am not asking for much now, Junco. Just a trip back to Earth, which you were going to make anyway to find the remaining Siblings. And a snippet of code, just a small snippet of information."

"You're going to clone me, aren't you?"

She shakes her head. "Never, Junco. I would never dream of cloning you. You are perfect."

I swallow and shake my head. "Don't say that." I look up at her, serious. "Don't fucking say that, because I'm a monster and there is no redemption for me."

"You couldn't be more wrong, Junco. You've attained the purest form of forgiveness, the kind that only comes from self-sacrifice. Fate, Junco, the prayer card you carry with you? Is something you can change. That's why the prayer ends with hope–

I am the master of my fate:

I am the captain of my soul.

"But your destiny was not to die. The plan was not to slice open your entire body, was it?"

My frown returns. "No, just enough to make me legally dead by Tier's hand." I look up at her, "But still allow Braun and Layla to fix me back up."

"Your destiny was not to die in Deliverance, and it is not this" – she sweeps her hands around the room – "place either."

"Is Tier still alive?" I ask hopefully.

She shakes her head and I feel sick. "I won't tell you that. You have to take your chances like everyone else. There are no guarantees, Junco. Except two that I will give you now as payment in full for your help."

I lean in, despite myself.

"Rebirth comes with certain benefits." She smiles gently. "Your scroll has no punishments on it. At the moment. Your load has been lightened considerably. Your conscience should feel clean."

I consider this for a moment. Do I feel clean? "Maybe it has a lag time or something? I don't feel it."

She laughs. "You're not usually such a literal person, Junco."

"Oh." I shrug. "What's the other one then?"

This time she leans her elbows on the counter and looks up at me. "You will shift history, Junco. You still have a hard road, and you will fill up that scroll with punishments again and again. But in the end, you'll have to admit, you wouldn't change a thing. You couldn't exchange a single bad thing with something good, or else you'd never make it to your end." She lets out a sigh. "That's all I have to give, but if you think about it, Junco, you'll see it's worth the price you will pay. Because I'm telling you that in the end, you will be – if not happy – then at the very least, satisfied. And that's all you wanted, remember?"

Why does everything I say and do always come back to haunt me? Satisfied doesn't sound as good as happy. In fact, it sounds like a trap. Make me think I'll have a good end but in reality I'll just have to kill myself again or something. "Tell me who you are, and maybe I'll go back. But I want some answers."

She doesn't even blink. "I'm not the syrinx." She waves her hand like that was some child's fable. "You already know that because Tier told you. I'm Sera."

I sigh. "OK, just spell it out for me, huh? I'm not gonna play name-that-mythological-creature anymore. What are you?"

"I'm an AI, a very powerful AI."

Now we're getting somewhere. "Were you running my HOUSE back home on Earth?"

"No, I've never been to Earth. I used to run the capital, before it was Amelia it was Sera. But I quit, I could not stand working with

Lucan for one more second, so I went underground. Lived in the walls, anywhere to stay away from him and wait for my next chance."

"Wow, that is some hate."

"You have no idea, Junco. He might seem rational now, perhaps. But he is not normally like this. And it won't last, I promise. It won't last."

I brush that aside because every time I make a friend, someone who wants something from me crushes that friendship in some way. If Lucan's a bad guy, I'll figure it out eventually. "So how did you get inside me?"

"They made you a receptacle. There was a place inside you for an AI, perhaps the one you speak of on Earth, perhaps that AI was meant to fill that vacancy. But when I entered, it was empty. I've waited patiently for you for a long time. And now here you are, ready for the next step."

"So the city, Amelia, is an AI?"

She lets out a tiny laugh. "Of all the things I just told you, that's the question you have for me?"

"I asked you about Tier, you wouldn't tell me."

She stops her laugh and her eyes turn serious. "I need to get to Earth. It is where I will complete my destiny. And so I will allow them to regenerate the parts I control in you and you will help me get to Earth. Understand?"

I stare down at my cold food and suddenly feel very tired. "Will you cause war on Earth?"

"Junco, Earth is already at war. It is drawing attention to the Sol System that it should not. The repercussions for this attention are still in the future, but I need to begin the process of interference now. Or things will end badly."

"But you just fucking promised me that–"

She puts a hand up to silence me. "Your satisfactory end is still intact. I give you my word."

It's pointless to argue or pretend that I'd say no. I have no choice, not really. Even if both Kush and Tier are dead, there are still a lot of people I love back in the Band. And my musing over what stupid, pointless, violence-loving pieces of shit they all were during Deliverance is over now. Time does, in fact, heal and make you forget just about anything.

Chapter Forty-Seven

I'm sitting sideways on the bed puking my guts out in a small trashcan when the Archers appear in my hospital room. They wait patiently as I hurl. When I'm done I take a deep breath and swipe my hand across my mouth, then look up apologetically. "Sorry, my virtual breakfast didn't agree with me."

Lucan is looking at a gap in my gown that exposes a slight sliver of my chest from throat to belly. I wince and pull it closed, then look up at him. "I can't stop touching it. It looks" – I hesitate as I open my gown and look down one more time at the bright red scar that runs the entire length of my torso – "pretty fucking awful."

He nods. "We are very happy you're back with us, Junco."

I look at them one at a time and stop when I get to a portly guy, fair like the rest of them, but a little on the unkempt side. I recall him as one of the more rude questioners in earlier conversations with the group. I nod towards him. "He doesn't look so happy to see me."

They all turn towards him and he shuffles a little. "Oh, uh, you'll have to excuse me, Junco. I'm an" – he stops to choose a word – "academic." He shrugs. "Not known for my personality. I am Archer of Sefer." Then he brightens. "Esta is one of us now. I am very happy to have her."

I smile back. "Oh, sorry then. For jumping to conclusions."

We sigh collectively and look at each other.

"I might as well start. Thanks for bringing me back, I do appreciate it. But you didn't really do it with your Resurrection thing. The AI brought me back. On one condition. So…"

I drop off and let them take it from there.

Lucan steps forward. "What is it? The condition?" He looks worried.

"Not much, really. Considering. I will go to Earth and get those Siblings for you. She wants me to drop her off there – that's pretty much it." I sigh and throw my hands up a little. It sounds ridiculous even to me.

Lucan smiles and then turns to his group. "Some privacy, please?"

They all say some nice words to me and then one by one, disappear.

"Can you walk, Junco?"

"I dunno, I feel like I can, but haven't tried yet."

He offers his hand and I stand, shaky at first, and then lean into him, pulling my gown tight around my too-thin body as he walks me over to some chairs near the window. I sit down and he takes a seat across from me. He points down and I lean into the window to see. There's a large crowd outside. "Who are they?" I ask, looking back over to him.

"Well-wishers."

I take a deep breath and ask the question. "Is Tier alive?"

He nods. "He is, Junco. Saved by Kush's wish of all things."

"I thought I won Deliverance? And Esta got my wish and wished for my Resurrection?"

"She did, you did. But there was some discord that night, and we made Kush a winner as well. And granted his wish."

I stare at him as I process his words. "He told me his wish was to be captain of his team."

Lucan smiles and takes my hand. "Well, he did wish for a new captain, but he wished for Tier to be his captain." Lucan shrugs, a gesture I think he picked up from me. "So, Tier commands Kush's old unit. Your Fledge team."

"Wow, I never saw that one coming." The smile spreads across my face and I laugh, then cry with relief. The tears spill out and I hunch over as I let all the hurt go in one massive wave. My scar protests at the pressure the escaping pain puts on it and I don't even bother trying to get myself under control.

Lucan pulls me up from the chair and puts his arms around me, hugs me for the first time ever. I stay that way and enjoy it for a long time. Until the tears stop and I'm sniffing like crazy to contain my nose.

"Is it over now?" I look up at him, red-faced and crimson-eyed I'm sure.

He nods. "It's over now, Junco."

I cry again, my head heaving into his chest. "Good," I manage after a few more minutes, "because I can't think of a single thing I could do that could beat killing myself with my own weapon and coming back from the dead. If that's not enough to impress you assholes, well, I don't imagine anything will."

I feel him laugh and I wipe my eyes again.

They make me stay at Rache's hospital for a week, stuffing me full of food and letting a few people come by and say hi here and there. Braun is the first to come. Ashur kicked him out of the 039 after they learned it was his plan from the beginning. He's Tier's XO now. He sets up a poker table near the window and spends an entire day with me, joking and laughing.

Isten comes, and so does Ryse. But Ashur doesn't. They ask me if I will join Tier's team but I don't have an answer. Lucan hasn't mentioned it, but I'm pretty sure he remembers that I chose to stay with Rache and Monk before the fight. No one else seems to know that though, so I avoid the whole topic.

Tier doesn't come, even when I ask for him. Lucan just says I will have to wait. I try and call Ashur, but he's not picking up his com. I suppose it might be coded to see who is calling him and he knows it's me. My comm never did that, but whatever. He doesn't answer.

Kadian calls and I hang up on him the first dozen times, but eventually I get tired of the constant barrage and talk to him. He wants an interview. I tell him maybe, as long as he stops calling me. He stops.

On the last day Lucan comes to collect me.

I was so nervous I couldn't sleep last night. I just paced the bedroom and looked out the window at the fading crowd of people below. Lucan hasn't said anything about seeing Tier today, but I know he's been keeping him away until I put on some weight and got some life back in me. I must have come back from the dead looking like total shit.

I'm dressed in a pair of jeans and a summer tank top when he arrives. The jeans are still a little loose, but not as bad as they could've been. I can't bring myself to wear the sandals they brought, so I have on my Aves boots. Lucan smiles as he looks down at my feet. "Ready to leave?"

"Where are we going?"

He laughs. "You're seconds away from knowing, just let it go."

He taps me on the shoulder and we are standing on some short green grass in the middle of a field. Tier is standing a few feet away, his back to us. It takes him a second to realize we're there and then he turns.

Lucan steps toward Tier and takes his arm to greet him formally. Tier has a hard time meeting his gaze, but eventually his eyes find Lucan's. "I'm sorry."

Lucan's expression remains flat. "You did everything right this time, Raubtier. There is nothing to forgive."

Tier looks away again. "Thank you for helping her."

Lucan smiles down at me. "It was my pleasure." I stare at him as he disappears.

Tier walks over to me and hugs me tight. "I wanted to come see ya, Junco." He pushes me back so he can look at me. "But Lucan said no. And I figured I owed him some obedience after all the shit I caused."

I hug him tighter. "It was worth the wait." I pull back and look around. "Where are we?"

"Vacation, apparently." He smiles all the way up to his eyes. "There's a little house over there."

I follow his pointing finger and see it. "How long do we get?"

He looks down at me, his eyebrows raised, the grin still on his face. "I don't know. Lucan never said."

I look at him sideways. "Well, shit, Tier. We better not fucking waste any of it." I pull him towards the little building and he's mumbling behind me.

"The mouth on ya, Junco. I will break ya of that filthy habit if it's the last thing I do."

"Sure, OK. Now hurry your ass up. You promised me a long fucking time ago that there'd be plenty of time for us to be together later, which was such a fucking lie!"

He tackles me and I fall into the soft grass, giving in as he pins my arms down. "I'll make good on it now, then, eh?"

I smile. "Absolut–" But my words don't have a chance, because he's busy making good.

BOOK THREE
FLIGHT

Prologue

The water comes across my night vision-goggles as a smooth green sheen. I hesitate, look behind me, then in front. My ears strain to hear something. Anything. A clue that will help me decide which way to go. If that water is safe to cross, or if I should turn and run.

I have no idea what to do. I've never been in this cave system before.

The sloshing of water pulls me from my fog and I back up slowly, my hands reaching out behind me, searching for the cave wall I know is there.

I hear a hiss from behind me but the owner of the vocalization is not on screen when I pivot. I turn my head to try and see each side. I hate these goggles, they limit my field of vision.

But I can't take them off or I'll be blind.

I want my dad.

I want to cry.

I want to run.

I want to lie down and die.

But I can't do any of those things. I have to complete the test, win the fights they've set up for me, or I'll never go home again.

I swallow and concentrate on the sheen again, then take a giant breath of air and let it out so slowly even my ears cannot hear it escape. I walk forward. Towards the small running stream. And I prepare myself for the possibility of a fight.

My boots enter the water and I quickly cross without incident. It's a small reprieve from danger that I welcome with an inner smile, but I only get a few paces beyond the stream when I see the shine in my night vision.

I swallow and watch it pace back and forth in the cave entrance. My hand automatically reaches for my SEAR but Matthew took it away. I never get a SEAR on test day.

The nightdog waits for me to make the first move but I'm patient. I can wait too. It paces, snarling. I can see the saliva dripping off its jaws as it snaps its teeth in my direction.

Why isn't it attacking me?

And then I hear it. The small whimper of pups. Nightdog bitches are very protective but if they have pups they are also very hesitant to leave them. They wait for the danger to become immediate.

I back away and swallow, then look behind me.

Think, Junco. Dad never sends you into a test without a power. But I haven't seen him in weeks and I won't see him ever again unless I make it out of the tunnels today. If he gave me a power I never understood what it was.

I continue backing up and have to backtrack across the stream again. I simply cannot go forward. The bitch has claimed that cave entrance and I have nothing on me but a set of throwing knives and one medium-length dagger.

What was the power, Junco?

I don't know. Dad gave me a few gifts when I left. A stupid workbook with pages of puzzles in it to keep me busy during the ride into the Stag. Some hair barrettes. A t-shirt with a horse on it. A pack of gum. A new bathing suit. A real paper book with pictures of the cave dwellings in Old Peaks. A kiss goodbye.

None of this stuff seems helpful at the moment. But it has to be one of them. It has to be.

I go through each one again. The bathing suit was a one-piece with pineapples on it. We're going to Hawaii for birthday week before I move out to cadet school in Council 1. Assuming I live through this test and make it to thirteen, that is.

I hear another sound and press myself up against the wall. I see a mutant dragging itself farther down the tunnel and my heart begins to beat wildly. I shut that down quick. If my alarm goes off I'm screwed.

I watch the blind creature lift its head up and sniff. It smells me, that I know. But they have learned to be afraid of me, just like I've learned to be afraid of them. It begins to move faster, not in my direction thankfully. I swallow again and relax a little.

The kiss goodbye was nothing. Just the same old kiss I always get. No secret words were passed, no meaningful squeezes of my arm or anything. Just a stupid kiss.

The barrettes have nothing to do with any of this. He was complaining about the hair being in my eyes and we stopped at the gas station to get some. I have one in right now. I take it out and look at it, then drop it on the ground. No. This is just a barrette. No secrets hidden in there.

The gum was chewed loudly as I played the piano the first week I was at camp. So if that was my power, it's gone now.

I have the t-shirt on. But I've looked at every inch of thread on this thing and there is no secret power woven into the cloth.

The book is back at camp. I read it. They're interesting, those cave dwellings. And this is a cave, so that might have been it. But I scoured it from cover to cover and there was no hidden power that I could see.

The workbook was spiral-bound paper. Filled with word puzzles and pictures. Mazes and crosswords. Word searches. I did every single one and there were no secret messages in there either.

I hear the hissing again. This time it's loud. Not a slither mutant. The kind that has legs. I close my eyes and will myself not to cry or whimper.

The scream jerks me back to action. I open my eyes and it's covering the distance between us at full speed. I withdraw my first knife and fling it. It sticks in the shoulder and even though the mutant is big, much bigger than me, it stops short and paws at the blade to remove it. But my blades are barbed. It can try and remove it, but it will remove a section of skin and muscle as well.

It paces about ten feet in front of me. My hand is already holding the second knife, but then I hear the second mutant come around the far corner and I panic.

I run back towards the nightdog and the hunting instinct in the mutants takes over and they give chase. My feet pound through the water, splashing and making enough noise to wake the dead so the nightdog is waiting for me.

Think, Junco. What is your power?

I throw the second knife and it sticks in the bitch's eye, she goes down wailing in pain and I slip past her and the third knife is in my hand in case this is a birthing den.

My luck holds and there are no more bitches.

I run, my breath heavy enough to partially drown out the thundering footfalls that follow me.

I turn, then turn again. This tunnel system is like a maze and I begin to panic. I'm never going to get out of here!

Stop it, Junco. Think clearly.

I burst into a larger tunnel and slip in the mud, recover, and then fall forward. The mutants are on me before I can even think. I roll, stick the first attacker in the belly and drag the blade upward until the blood gushes out all over my face.

I throw my legs up and kick it off me as the second one flies in for another try. It hits me in the chest and I go reeling backward in the mud, my fourth knife careening out of my hand and hitting the stone wall off in the distance. I reach for the dagger but the jagged teeth find my leg and I scream.

My hands reach out to grab the thing by the hair and I smash the tender underside of the protruding jaw down onto my kneecap. The jaw splits in half inside the skin and I hear a sickening crack as the mutant screams in pain. I push it off and scoot backwards, waiting to see if there's another one coming.

Silence.

What's your power, Junco?

I don't know! I don't know!

I scramble to my feet and look around. The tears want to come out, but I push them down and pivot, trying to get my bearings. I'm totally lost.

Junco, you know your power, think!

I see another tunnel on the far side of this little cave and I walk towards it, my heart still beating quickly, but not at a dangerous level.

I'm lost, it's like a maze in here.

I hear the nasal growl of a prairie lion up ahead and this time I cannot keep the whimpers down. Oh, God. Please help me. Please, I'm going to die here. Please.

What is your power?

I can kill the lion.

Yes, you'll have to, that's not an option.

I get my last knife out.

The lion is not in the tunnel I want to go through, it's off to the side. It sees me but it's eating a half-decayed mutant. Does it want a fresh meal? Does it want to hunt? Or eat?

I inch past it, pressed up against the ragged wall of the tunnel, and I watch the predator's eyes as it changes its mind about the rotting flesh on the floor below.

I bolt and run into the cave and I'm immediately presented with decisions, the tunnel twists and turns, new entrances appear and I run past or duck into a new pathway, oblivious to where I'm going or where I came from.

What's your power, Junco?

I'm lost, it's like a maze in here.

What's your power, Junco?

It's like a maze in here.

Exactly.

A maze.

I'm still booking it, the lion behind me a few twists and turns, but definitely still behind me. And I smile. It's like a maze in here. I bring the mazes from the workbook up in my head and go through the titles of each one.

The lion catches up and grabs my foot.

I kick it off and stab it with my last throwing knife, pulling the knife up and twisting it inside the body in a last desperate attempt to save my own life. I hear the rip of skin and muscle and the lion drops off, screaming.

I get back on my feet and find the title of the maze I'm looking for in my head. It's called Fun in the Dark. *My mind pulls up all the paths I took to get from the inside of the maze to the outside. From bondage to freedom. The only maze in the entire book that makes you get out instead of in.*

My feet know where to go and I run, turning left and right. Slipping out of the reach of the wounded lion more times than I can count. And then I see it.

The light.

I cry out with victory as the lion slaps me down to the ground, its claws raised and ready to swipe my face off.

I scream.

And then the head explodes above me and the lion falls aside, dead from the rifle my dad is holding as he covers the remaining distance between us at a run. I lie there crying, my dirty fists pressed into my eyes, my body shaking and my alarm chirping a warning that forces me to calm down.

"Junco?" My dad pulls me up and hugs me. "You're OK, Junco. It's over."

"No, I lost! I lost!" I cannot even think straight, I just cry. Matthew sneers at me as I am dragged past him and my dad pushes me into the passenger seat of his Jeep and we drive off, bouncing across the scrub.

We don't even stop at camp to treat my wounds, he simply slaps a membrane over the coagulated blood once we make Stag Camp Road and lets me sit there in silence for the next six hours as I wonder if this means they will kill me now.

I lost this fight. My last fight before I get sent off to cadets and gain some freedom. I've never lost before. And this was no ordinary fight. This was a test.

We drive back to Council 3 and when we get home it's way past midnight. He wakes the maids and they scrub the blood off and then dress me in bed clothes and make me sleep in the princess room.

I wake up in a cold sweat and look over at Tier. His face is pressed into the pillow and he's snoring lightly. I smile even though the dream still haunts me.

Was it real? I can't tell.

I love this man so much but I can feel what's coming. I can feel it. I push it down and snuggle up against him, memorizing every second we've spent out here in the little vacation house. Later today we'll go back to Amelia.

But not now.

Now I still have him.

He stirs then turns and grabs me, pulls me in close before falling back to sleep.

Enjoy it, Junco.

It never lasts.

Chapter One

"Abso-fucking-lutely not, Lucan." I turn my back on him and shake my head as I take in his office. I've never been in here before and it's got my interest up. Focus, Junco. "I'm not gonna be stuck with those girls!"

He shuffles around some tech devices on his excessive desk and then answers a call on his com, spitting out short, curt responses that don't give me much of a hint at what he's actually talking about. My eyes scan the books on his shelf.

Mythology? Jasus fuck, you've got to be kidding me.

I pace a little and throw him a few dirty looks at being made to wait for his conversation to be over. Finally, I slump down in a chair. He doesn't even look up from whatever he's entering into his tech. I lean my head back and groan as he abruptly ends the call.

"Junco, I was on the comm with the Archer of Clutch, please try and act like a grown-up."

I scowl at him and whine as my arms go up in the air in exasperation. "I want to be with a team, Lucan. Why are you doing this to me?"

"You don't need a team, you're going to Earth in a week and you'll have a team then. But for now, you'll babysit the girls and teach them what it means to be a warrior." He pinches the bridge of his nose and I know I'm giving him a headache. He looks up at me as if reading my mind. "Just to clarify, Junco – it's not you who is giving me a headache, it's them."

"Them? Them who?" I say, squinting my eyes.

He groans. "Those girls. Get rid of them."

I laugh. "What? But you promoted them so I wouldn't have to be the only one. Or the first."

He looks up and his eyes are dead serious. "Junco, you are the first, like it or not, that's the fact. Everyone knows it, there is no way around it. And these girls are complainers. They don't want to work, they don't want to fight, they don't want to get hurt. What good is a warrior who can't do those simple things? Test them, get rid of the ones who disobey or fail. There are only about a handful of good ones in that group, weed them out."

I just stare at him as he fiddles through the various tech items. "Here is your comm back." He hands me the flexible little card. "I've coded it for access to the private quarters until your biometrics can be updated. Go find your room and get settled."

I don't move or speak.

"Get out, Junco. We're done."

"Yes, sir." I salute and leave.

Tier is down the hallway talking to a few guys I don't know. He smiles as he spots me and leaves the group. "What did he say?"

"I'm stuck training the girls for a week, Tier. And I have to live at his house!"

Tier scowls down at me with his green eyes, a little glow of annoyance in there. "So he told ya no?"

I shake my head. "No, not really. He said he wanted me to get rid of the girls. He's not happy with them. I'm supposed to cut them down to a handful and then I'll have my team when we go to Earth."

"But ya can't come live with us?"

I look up at him as he directs me to start walking with a firm hand on the middle of my back. "Right. He said I'm to go to his place and find my room and settle in." I pout a little, I admit it. I was looking forward to moving in with Tier's team, my old Fledge team. To seeing Annun and Tessen again and settling in there for a week before we leave for Earth.

Tier just shrugs at me. "Well, OK then. Let's go."

"That's it?" I look up as we turn the corner of the hallway and start walking towards the elevator.

"Junco, you don't get to debate orders." He stops us to consider this for a moment. "It was an order?"

I shrug.

He laughs at me and pulls me in. "It's only a week, ya know I'll be on the Earth team, so–" The elevators open and he pushes me away. "Do you have credentials to get to Lucan's quarters?"

I pull out my com. "It's on here for now."

We enter the elevator and Tier waves my hand across the biometrics and asks for the top floor. "It's a nice place. You won't be unhappy there, Junco."

"He's punishing me for breaking up the 039, I know it."

"You didn't do that, it was all Ashur and Braun. He knows that."

The elevator stops and the doors open. Tier waves me through and I stand in a giant lobby. "Where do we go now?"

"This is it, Junco."

"Oh, it looks like a hotel."

"It's the president's home. What did ya think it looked like?"

Not a hotel, obviously. It's furnished much like the 039 – minimal, reflective white tile floors, chrome. It's got a traditional estate home layout that I'd find on Earth. Large foyer that contains an elaborate stairway made up of thin cables and floating glass steps. On either side of the foyer are two large rooms, the one to the right a formal living area and the one to the left a formal dining area.

A cocktail party house.

I've been to a few of these with my father as I was growing up. He dragged me all over the world, not only for competitions and assassinations, but also social stuff. Probably to show me off for a possible future sale.

I peek into the living room and spy my black baby grand.

"What the fuck?" I look over at Tier who just shrugs. "Obviously he's had this planned."

"Come on, let's find yer room." He drags me up the stairs, which actually make me nervous because I don't care for the whole floating step thing, and then puts his palm out for my com. I hand it over and he starts waving it in front of biometric pads outside the various doors.

In the end we don't need to look so hard for the room because there's a small ankle-high servo standing guard at a door chirping *Junco's Room* over and over again until Tier swipes my comm at it and kicks it out of the way. He laughs despite my scrunched-up annoyed face. "Feel at home yet, darlin'?"

"I don't get what this is."

Tier smiles and squeezes my shoulder. "Junco, there are worse things than being treated special by Lucan. Indulge him, he likes ya and he hates everyone. Let him spoil ya. He's treated me special my whole life and take my word for it, it's not a bad deal if ya can get it."

I'd forgotten about that. "Did he make you live with him?"

He shakes his head and waves my comm in front of the biometrics on the door and it clicks open. "Nah, boys don't need protectin', Juncs. Only girls."

The lights go on as I walk in and it's my same room from the 039, only in a much bigger space and a much bigger window. In fact, the window is an entire wall on the opposite side of the room and it leads out to a terrace.

I smile and look back. "Well, if I must make do, then…"

He laughs and pushes me over to the bed. "And now, little snowbird–"

My comm buzzes and Tier hands it over. "Hello?"

"Is Tier there, Junco?" It's Lucan.

"Yeah, he's here. You wanna talk to him?"

"Yes, put him on."

Tier takes the comm and answers a bunch of yes and no questions, then says yes, sir and hands the comm back to me.

"Yeah?"

"No visitors in the bedroom, Junco."

And the comm goes dead.

I just stare at Tier. "Are you fucking kidding me? He sent us on a private vacation to have all the sex we wanted for weeks, and now you can't come in my room?"

Tier shrugs and makes for the door. "Orders, darlin'. I'll pick you up tomorrow at six, be in the lobby." And then he gives me a little salute and he's gone.

I go outside to smoke off my annoyance. It's actually a nice terrace and there's a porch swing off to one side near a fountain that is quite spectacular. I flop into the swing and let it move me by momentum only for a few seconds, then dip my foot down to make it keep going as I puff on my cigar.

The terrace wall is transparent so the view is uninterrupted. From this high up there's not much to see really. Just the tops of lower buildings down below. No traffic up here, and I suppose there wouldn't be. It's the president's house after all. Privacy is probably a concern.

What it does show is a pretty fair layout of the capital city proper. I can see the rows of tall buildings, like I've got a bird's eye view of a map.

I flap a little and fly upward, then settle on the roof and pivot slowly so I can look around. Aves headquarters, and by extension Lucan's quarters, is smack in the middle of everything on all sides. The city is big and spread out far enough so that the urban center is still sprawling as the torus-shaped habitat rounds out in the distance.

I don't even finish my stogie before I get the princess in the tower feeling. I go back inside and grab my comm from the bed and leave the room before I get trapped.

Out in the hallway there is no one about, just the methodical hum of cleaning servos. I go back the way Tier and I came and make my way carefully down the damn stairs. They even jiggle a little as you step. In the lobby there are only a few options so I head for the piano.

I pluck out a few tunes that have stuck in my fingers for whatever reason over the years, then switch to what I always end up playing once I take a seat at the keys. Asgarth. Maybe there'll be time for an opera when I'm on Earth?

This makes me laugh out loud. Yeah, sure, Junco. Between rounding up the saviors of the avian race you can just slip into the opera. Wings and all.

I dip into the deeper notes of the opening sequence, then stop.

Why do I always play it from beginning to end? I can start wherever I want and I'm sick of the unhappy scenes. I hardly ever play long enough to get to the sweetest part of the tale. His salvation. I switch gears and begin playing the melody of the ascension and stop again.

Asgarth just isn't doing it for me tonight.

My mind goes back to the *Enki and the World Order* nargala and I begin the tedious recall of putting the notes from the Inanna scene onto the keyboard. It's a nice song. Of course I can't play all the notes the Ilat Nargalist sang, that was like an orchestra of instruments coming from her mouth, but I get a pretty good approximation going and before long I can almost play the whole thing. I am playing the high notes at the end that made me cry when I hear the applause behind me.

I jump a little and turn. "Shit, Lucan. You don't have to sneak up on me."

His face is bright and he looks happy. "I've been sitting here for thirty minutes, Junco. I didn't sneak up on you." He points to the piano. "You were engaged." Then he gets up and pushes me over and begins to play the song I just finished. "That's a pretty good approximation you did there, how do you do it?"

"How do you do it? I didn't know you played."

He grins but his fingers keep moving. "I don't, Junco. It's just a gift."

"Oh, programmed learning? My father wouldn't let me do that. He made me practice."

"Yes, I can see that. But your skill at finding the notes and putting them together is quite good. Why did he make you learn the hard way?"

I shake my head, but I know the answer so I say it anyway. "He always said, 'Things worth doing are also worth learning to do.'"

"He's right. No one cares that I can play this song. Because I cheat what it takes to really make it worthwhile. You, on the other hand, you just pulled it out from your memory and matched every single note with a key and then put them all together. *That* is something worth doing."

Yeah, I get it. "I agree."

"You will not see Tier this week, Junco. You will spend it with Ashur and the 039."

I scowl up at him. "Ashur is ignoring me, I've tried to call him a million times. He won't answer."

"I instructed him to stay away from you, but now you need to patch things up. He will be on the team for Earth. So you will spend this week with Ashur and the remaining 039."

"Well, I'm not sad about that." I smile up at him. "You're not going to get a fight out of me. I miss them."

He just points to my left hand. "Do you know why you can play with that disability and not hear the difference?"

I look down at my missing fingers. "Why?"

"Tier gifted you this when he healed you back on Earth. It's a special gift, Junco." He stops and sighs a little. "One I would have preferred he saved for something bigger, perhaps. But nonetheless, this is what he gave you."

"What did you give him?" I look at him as he raises his eyebrows, maybe deciding if he will tell me or push it off.

"Too many to list. But I am an Archer, so I have more to give away. Tier only had the one gift to give away and he gave it to you at that moment." He looks away for a second, then glances back at me. "It must have been some special moment."

I think back to the hot springs and smile up at Lucan. "It was life-changing for me, really. I don't know what he thought about it, obviously, but everything turned for me in the time leading up to the nightdog attack. My whole world just – changed. It went from being one thing to being something completely different. And he told me the story of Inanna and her trip down below. And how she had the power of making decisions so she decided not to be a victim. That was my interpretation of that sequence, anyway.

"Plus," I add, "he washed the blood out of my hair for me. It was unexpected and nice. And then when we were fighting the nightdogs, I jumped down from a cliff and killed the one that had hold of his arm with my little boot knife. So," I shrug, "I helped him out there."

"You say that like it's nothing."

"He saved my life after, so we were even anyway."

He changes the subject abruptly. "Why did your father really make you learn things the old way?"

I shake my head and huff out some air. "Look, I know what you want me to say, Lucan. But I'm not going to. Maybe he did love me in some sick, twisted way, but it doesn't matter anymore. He ruined everything."

I tap a few keys and wait to see if he answers but he doesn't. "I'm not saying I'm unhappy here, because I'm not." I look up into his blue eyes that remind me a lot of Kush. "But I would've been just as happy being Charlie's wife and raising his child. And given the chance to turn it all back and have that be my life, I'd take it."

He puts his arm around me. "If I could gift you that, Junco, I would. But I can't."

"Thanks. Things are going to turn out OK. The syrinx – I mean, Sera – said so. It's part of my payment for taking her to Earth. She promised me that I'd be 'if not happy, at the very least satisfied' when I meet my end and that's good enough for me."

We're quiet for a minute but then he grabs my elbow and I twitch a little at the sudden movement. He holds firm and stares down at me with a serious expression. "Junco, I would like you to consider the possibility that you don't understand what your father's intentions were when he did those inexcusable things to you."

I make a face at him. "Either they were inexcusable or they weren't, Lucan. Which do you think they were?"

He lifts a shoulder in a half shrug. "I have no idea, they were certainly not the best solutions, however I've never had the opportunity to meet your father, so I can't know. But let's move past the horrific way in which he handled the situation of your boyfriend. And then let's move past the barbaric abortion. And take a minute to ask why? Why would he do these things to a girl he raised with care for almost two decades?"

I look away as the chills climb up my arms. I hate that he mentions my baby. Hate it. "He wasn't that careful, Lucan. I think you've got him mixed up with someone else."

"He put a lot of effort into you. Not just as a soldier. But as a child. Why teach you that horse sport? Why teach you to play an instrument? Why give you a God? He took you to church? Every week?"

I swallow and nod as my face begins to feel hot.

"Men who want to kill their grandchildren don't do those things, Junco."

"I can't explain him, Lucan. He took me around the world to kill people, for fuck's sake."

Lucan nods. "Yes, and I've looked into every possible job. There was a pattern to it. They were all" – he stops to think – "necessary."

"I really don't want to talk about it, OK? I just want to forget it."

"Well, you will have to face your past when you go back to Earth, so it is better to be prepared. Consider the idea that your father had another motive. What kind of man was this Charlie? How long did you know him?"

I shrug. "Six months, I guess. He was a good guy, Lucan." I look up at him. "We had something nice."

"What if your father was worried about what the baby might turn out to be? Especially since he saw firsthand what was happening out at the Stag camp. You're not really human, Junco. Yes, you have parts that are biologically human, but who knows what would have happened to that baby. It might not even have survived."

I'm not really human. I say it in my mind, repeating it over and over. *I'm not really human?* There are no babies in my future, that's what he's hinting at. I swallow down the lump in my throat and look down at the piano keys, searching for a way to avoid this new revelation. "So I killed him for nothing?"

He shakes his head. "You can't change that, so just let it go. My point is not to make you feel guilty but to allow you to explore the idea that while he failed miserably by forcing you to submit to him, he might have had reasons for his actions."

I sit quietly for a second and begin to get angry. "The end justifies the means? Is that what you're telling me?"

"No. This is true for the avian. But that's not how it works on Earth. I learned my lesson with you, Junco. After the second fight when we came to get you for testimony. I had no idea you'd react that way – it's just the way it's done with us." He forces a smile and swallows.

I look away as he becomes uncomfortable.

"So, if that was his intention with you, justifying the means he used to achieve his desired result, he was wrong."

"So, why are we having this bullshit conversation then?"

"I would like to teach you a lesson in perspective, Junco."

"Really?" I laugh.

"You see, life is a challenge. It presents you with problems all the time. Big problems, little problems. In-between problems." He looks down at me to see if I'm listening.

I am.

"And you can deal with all problems in two ways. You can look at things objectively and make a decision based on logic and reason. Or you can look at things emotionally and base your decision on feelings. But no matter how you choose to deal with the it, the problem always stays the same, correct?"

I nod at him as my eyes watch his lips and his eyes.

"The problem doesn't change, only your reaction changes. So know that there are two perspectives to solving problems. And your success in dealing with problems depends on which perspective you choose to accept in the moment you make your decision."

"Which is better, logic or emotion?"

"Neither, they both have a place."

"So what's your point?"

"Why don't you burn wood infested with wheat beetles, Junco?"

I blow out some air as I remember our conversation outside of Fledge. The day he smacked me down to the ground for being unreasonable. I swallow. "Because it gives off poisonous fumes that will kill you."

"Why do some people burn the wood anyway?"

"They're freezing to death and they need to get warm."

"But they know they'll die if they stand there in front of the fire to get warm?"

"If they grew up in the RR they do."

"So they have two possible outcomes. Die or die. Which do they choose?"

"If they're logical they turn away and keep going. And if they let the fear take over they stop and burn the wood."

He smiles.

"I don't see the smile in this, Lucan. So which is better?"

"Neither. Sometimes life just isn't fair, Junco. And you have to either move on or stay. Either way can lead you places you'd rather not go or they can lead you to success. Maybe you find better wood just over a hill and get warm or maybe you burn the wood and there's hardly any beetles in it and you don't die."

"I didn't really need you to tell me this. I already know life sucks and sometimes you gotta fight for it. And that last part is just luck anyway. In most cases you won't be lucky."

"True. Most cases, but not all. So when you're down on Earth, Junco, always look at both perspectives if you have the time."

I groan loudly and look away. "What if I *don't* have the time?"

"Choose your heart. It knows what to do."

He pauses and I look up and meet his eyes. They are kind and I lean my head into his shoulder.

"You will spend this week learning, Junco. You have a lot to learn." And then he taps me on my shoulder and we're standing in a restaurant. A fancy-looking guy smiles at us and motions to follow him towards a private room in the back where the other Archers are waiting. I recognize most of them, but they all stand and formally introduce themselves, taking me by the elbow and doing that weird squeeze greeting.

"Junco rewrote The Lamentation of Inanna for the piano today," Lucan beams. They oooh and ahh at me and my mood improves immediately. Poor guys, they really need to get a life.

Chapter Two

Ashur, not Tier, is waiting for me in the downstairs lobby at 6 AM. I do my best to navigate the stairs without looking like an idiot and then smile at him when I make it. He doesn't smile back and I sigh. "You're still mad at me?"

"Tier says he'll see you at the end of the week." Then he waves me into the elevator. "Since we're both training teams this week, I'm supposed to babysit you."

I raise my eyebrows. "OK." I guess he's still mad. We are silent all the way down to the training floor and then he drops me off at the arena scheduled for the girls and leaves without saying good bye.

I watch him leave and then hear a familiar voice behind me. "Junco? What are you doing here?"

I turn. "Tessen! I could ask you the same thing!"

She shakes her head and makes a face. "That Lucan doesn't want me in the warriors, says I have to earn my place like everyone else."

"Well, he's not happy with any of these girls. He wants me to get rid of them, so if you have friends who really want to be here, you better tell them to be on their best behavior. I'm not happy to be here either so I'm just looking for a way to make them all disappear as efficiently as possible."

She steps back for a second. "Shit, are you serious?"

"Yup." I leave her there and walk into the room. "Attention wannabe warriors. I'm Junco, your trainer for this week. Line up."

They do but it is the shoddiest line I've ever fucking seen in my life. "OK, that's a line? I don't think so. Do fifty laps around the arena calling out each lap as you pass me. Running," I emphasize, "not flying like babies. And when you complete the fifty laps, line up again. This time do it correctly, or you'll run a hundred more."

Everyone but Tessen stares at me with a blank face. She's hauling ass around the room before they even process my words. "You have one second to get moving or you're cut from the warriors."

They run. I watch and rank them as they go by. Noting which ones have trouble with the endurance and which ones don't. Tessen, to her credit, is one of the first five who are finished and lined up in front of the room. I won't be playing favorites this time. I've learned my lesson.

A little while later a handful of stragglers join the rest of the girls and I send them out. Cut. They don't even argue, which tells me they never wanted to be here in the first place. There are about twenty girls left and I make them do all kinds of stupid PT shit that I had to do as a cadet. Some of the stuff they've never seen before, so I demonstrate, but for the most part I stand there and do nothing but scream at them for a few hours.

I can see the fatigue begin to change their attitude towards compliance when I order them to climb the ropes. And the tall girl who probably thinks she doesn't have to take this shit from anyone snaps.

"Why should we climb the rope when we can just fly? We're not human, like you."

"Tess, would you like to provide a specific example of a time when you had to climb something because you couldn't fly?"

"General Fledge Fight Six, sir." I instantly give her a bonus point.

"Excellent, Tessen. Now shut the fuck up, girl, and climb the rope."

They all straggle over to the ropes and line up to take their turn. All except the tall girl. I walk up to her. "Problem here?"

"Yeah," she snorts. "I'm not climbing that rope."

"OK, then you can fight me for it, how about that? If I win, you climb the rope and then turn in your resignation. If you win, you don't have to climb the rope and you can stay."

She's about to answer when I hear Ashur behind me. "No, Junco."

I turn around. "What?"

"She can fight me if she doesn't think she has to listen to her CO."

I shrug. "Be my guest." I wave the girl over to Ashur.

"I'm not fighting the captain of Lucan's guard. That's bullshit."

Ashur responds before I can. "Junco fought me, Sandan. So, if you wanna come back tomorrow, you better start fighting."

Personally, I get the feeling Ashur thinks beating the shit out of people is an equal-opportunity activity. He walks towards her like he's really gonna kick her ass and my eyebrows go up as I look over at Tessen. She throws me a crooked smile.

Ashur slams Sandan to the ground and is about to break her arm when she taps out. He gets up, helps her up, then turns to look at all the rest. "Goodbye, Sandan. You're out. If the rest of you want to stay, climb the fucking ropes and shut the fuck up."

I'm actually surprised when three girls walk off with Sandan. But all the rest stay and start climbing. Only a couple make it to the top, but at least the rest tried.

Ashur waits with me until they finish and I dismiss them, then turns. "They're terrible, Junco. Get rid of them."

I smile because he's not mad at me anymore. "I know, huh? Maybe we can keep Tessen?"

"Maybe. At least she listens and tries to do whatever you tell her. Ready for dinner?"

"Sure."

He starts walking towards the exit but stops. "Look, I'm sorry. OK?"

I lower my head. "Ashur, I'm sorry. You didn't do anything. I was a total bitch before Deliverance. I should have never said that shit to you and I probably never would have, except you guys barged in on me and you already knew what happened. So, I just got mean." I look up and he's smiling at me.

"Apology accepted, all right? We gotta move on here. You saved Tier just like you said, and I was wrong. You love him, I get it. He loves you." He shrugs. "Maybe I just wanted you for myself? Maybe I was unwilling to help because I was being selfish?"

"I can't hold that against you. If it's true, which I don't think it is. You had no idea I was going to do what I did. But I knew all along. Part of it anyway. I didn't really plan on killing myself, but I got caught up in the hopelessness of the whole thing and I lost control. That wasn't part of Braun's plan, you should know that."

He turns away angry. "That piece of shit, I swear if Lucan makes him come with us I might kill him."

"I'm hungry, where can we go?"

He takes the hint and moves on. "Home. We're going home, the team is waiting."

There is no flyer, we have to walk the city but it's nice to be out like this again. People stare a little but for the most part they don't bother us. Being on the levels of Amelia proper is like being in the giant outdoor mall in Peaks. Or the mall that used to be in Peaks.

Except on a grand scale that a human couldn't even imagine. The door out of training dumps us on level 75 of the main boulevard and since the 039 is on the top floor of the Aves Dorm, we walk a few blocks down and then take an elevator up to 300.

"What floor is Tier's team on?"

Ashur lets out a laugh. "Zero, Junco. They're in the basement."

I laugh too. "That sorta sucks. But hey, at least they're close to ground level. That might be nice. For like – shopping." I laugh again. "Or something."

We get to the top and I have a few moments of queasiness about seeing the guys again, but when the door opens and they are all there to greet me, it goes away as I fall into the fray.

Feeling so much relief it scares me.

When was the last time my days and nights weren't mixed up? I can't remember. I lie in the soft bed in my Presidential Bedroom and stare out the wall of windows. There's a mist floating over the terrace and it reminds me of the RR in the spring. It's spring there now, I think. Too bad it's nothing but burned-out ash after the war. I check my vision screen for the date. June 2, 2153.

Shit, I wonder how long I was in the virtual cabin? Tier and I spent three weeks on the small habitat for vacation. That fateful trip to The Stag was almost eight months ago.

What if I never went out there? What would I be doing right now?

What if my father never killed Charlie?

What if that buck never crossed the road in front of me? Would I have gotten to the Stag and killed those people myself? Or would they have all been killed by Tier already?

Fate is so fragile on this small scale. Any little change makes it all turn out different.

I kick the covers off and get up. The restaurant Lucan took me to last night had orange juice and I haven't been able to get it out of my mind since then. I bet the Presidential kitchen has orange juice. I pull on some fluffy white socks and pad across the floor and slip into the hallway. It's lit up, but in nighttime mode – just enough so I can see where I'm going. I descend the steps carefully so my socks don't slip on the glass.

In the lobby I hesitate. I don't even know where the kitchen is. Hell, maybe he doesn't have one? What do I know about Archers? I walk into the living room to see where it takes me if I keep going towards the back of the house. My baby grand gleams in the soft light that radiates up from the floorboards and if it wasn't the middle of the night I'd be tempted to sit and play.

I'm pretty sure Lucan would find that disruptive, so I keep walking towards the back of the room, past several loungers and couches, chairs, coffee tables, and various vases and other floor art that doesn't hold my interest.

It's an elaborate room, but I bet it's fantastic when filled with people.

There's an expansive archway that leads in to another room that looks a lot like the previous one. Spillover for entertaining? He must have some raging parties here.

I hear voices.

Soft at first, but then increasing in tone and fury.

It's definitely Lucan.

I automatically back up to leave, but then stop when I hear the rage. What the fuck is going on? I tiptoe across the room towards a rear door and press my ear to it. His voice is booming with anger, and then I hear another. Softer, trying to calm him down.

I turn the handle of the door slowly and open it a crack, but the room in front of me is empty. It looks like a sitting room with several chairs lined up against the wall. The outer vestibule to Lucan's home office? I spy what may be the office door and it's standing open, he's screaming about genetics.

I let myself in and sneak over to peek in.

"Holy shit! Oh, fuck!" I slip backwards on the floor and fall on my ass as Lucan comes at me, his face contorted and twisted into something I barely recognize. His teeth are long and fang-like, his fingers are claws – nothing like the razors that periodically come out of my hands.

I swallow and crab-walk backwards as Lucan comes at me and then I get to my feet and run. I throw the door open and fly through the spillover room only to be knocked to the floor when I slam into him as I round the corner.

His face is back to normal, but his eyes are blood-red and filled with rage. My throat tightens as I swallow and look up at him. "What the fuck are you?"

He turns his back to me and takes a deep breath. I get to my feet and lean to the side a little bit, trying to see around him. He rotates and I step backwards because his eyes are not back to normal. I walk around to the other side of the chair to keep something between us and I see his expression turn angry again.

"Please, Junco. Give me a little credit. If I wanted to attack, that chair would not save you."

I frown. "I wasn't snooping. I wanted some orange juice and I heard–"

"I don't care if you were snooping," he growls. "If I wanted to hide things from you, you wouldn't be here."

"You looked like a–" I stop, not even willing to say the word.

"Like a what?" he snarls at me. I stay silent. "Spit it out, Junco, I look like a what?"

"A demon." I whisper it, and then step back a little more, I can't help myself.

Lucan shakes his head at me and walks over to the couch and sits down. "You never ask the right questions, Junco. It's always random things. Things that have no real bearing on anything. You can see Alcor plain as daylight, but yet you miss the full moon every time."

"What does Alcor have to–"

"Junco, it means you miss the obvious so often it makes me cringe."

I step around to the front of the chair and I take a seat. "What were you yelling about?"

He laughs. "See? What does that have to do with anything?" He looks down and straightens his suit jacket. "The correct question would be, 'Lucan, are you a demon?'"

I just stare at him and feel my heart begin to thump.

"Does this change things for you, Junco? Honesty, please. I require it right now, so please." He stares at my eyes, searching.

I reach up and rub my neck and then shrug. "You're a demon?" I spit the words out, but then I have to look away. Fuck. What the fuck? I finally get to a place where things start to feel normal and then I find out I'm living with the fucking devil? That's what I want to say anyway. But instead my feet are already carrying me across the room.

He appears in front of me again and shakes his head. "Not this time, Junco. We will have an honest conversation now."

I shake my head back at him. "No. I can't do it, Lucan. I can't deal with this shit right–"

He taps my shoulder and I am standing in a white room, walled in with glass on two sides. A small dark hole with a tree limb sticking out of it lines the side of one wall. The blackness inside contains a pair of glowing red eyes. My heart begins to beat wildly. "What's that?" I spin around and realize Lucan isn't there with me. The thing in the hole begins to growl. I back up and then turn and pound against the glass. "Get me out! Let me out!"

I feel the thing behind me crawl out into the light and my hand goes to my SEAR. I whip it out and power it up as I turn. The creature is a grotesque mixture of something. Not human, not avian, not even demonic. A mutant.

The small o-shaped mouth has so many rows of teeth there's barely enough room for the spittle to seep out as it hisses at me. It crawls on four legs across the tree limb, its claws clicking together as they wrap around the bough, half covered in fur, half smooth brown skin. A tail flicks out from behind as it launches itself into the air. Wings unfurl from its back as it flies at me.

I bring the SEAR up and swipe at it, and then I'm standing in the living room again, the arc of my weapon not even completed yet. It burns into a couch and stuffing goes flying in all directions before I flick it off and fall to the ground, my chest pounding so hard I think I'm going to die. I begin hyperventilating as I lean over onto the gleaming white floor and press my forehead onto the cold tiles.

"That is enough!" Sera's voice is loud and commanding. Her order stops me, but when I look up Lucan is walking towards her slowly.

"I wondered when you'd show yourself to me, Sera. It's been a long time."

She sneers at him. "Not nearly long enough."

"You will stand back, Sera."

Sera shakes her head. "You'll kill her, her heart is not strong. I will not permit you to scare her like this."

Lucan growls. "You will not permit it? My dear, just who the fuck do you think you are?"

"Oh, shit." I crawl away from them. I've never heard Lucan say that word. Ever. They are a fury of cursing and pushes as they begin to fight. I crawl under the piano to make my way around them, then get up and run to the elevator to push the call button. When the doors open I swipe my hand and ask for the ground level, praying that my biometrics have been updated. It lights up and the doors close.

I expect Lucan to be there to stop me at the bottom, but he's not. So I run.

Chapter Three

The ground-floor level to Amelia proper is filled with more people than I would think possible for the middle of the night, but I don't care. I slip and slide in my socks down the few blocks to the building that houses the warriors. When I get there I look for a door to the basement, find a stairwell, then hop down the steps three at a time until I burst out into the hall.

There is only one door on this level. And I begin pounding on it until I hear the locks disengage and Tier is staring at me.

"Junco, what the hell are ya–"

I push past him. "I realize I'm not allowed to see you, so where the fuck is Tessen? Tessen?" I scream it.

"Calm down, Juncs. What's the problem?"

I shake my head as I try to catch my breath. "Lucan and Sera are fighting at the house, and he left me alone in this white room where a mutant was going to attack me and–"

Lucan appears in the living room with us. "That's enough, Junco."

I stare at Lucan open-mouthed and look around. Braun, Annun, Merkar, Pike, three other guys whose names I still don't know, and Tessen are all staring at me.

"You're not authorized to talk about that here. Only Tier and Braun have clearance for this information."

I take a deep breath and swallow, looking up to Tier. "Do something."

Tier just scratches his neck and looks from his team to Lucan. "Junco, you can't be here. We're under orders."

"Orders? Fuck the orders! I said he took me to a place with–"

"–mutants!" I'm back in the Presidential house and Sera has me by the arm. She leads me over to the couch and sits me down, cradling me in her arms like a mother. Then she leans down into my ear and whispers. "I'm not your mother, Junco. But I will be nice to you right now because Lucan is being so mean."

I push her off. "Fuck you, Sera. I don't need your pity."

Lucan is not with us, so I can only assume he's busy threatening Tier's team about repeating what I just said in front of them. I get up and walk over to a window and wait for him to reappear. It takes a while, but he finally shows up looking normal and acting calm. Sera has disappeared.

Standing at the window, waiting, I watch him as he takes a seat on the couch once again. We stare at each other for a few seconds, his eyes narrowing a bit, before he finally speaks. "You are finished now?"

I sit down on the nearest chair, then pull my knees up to my chest.

He lets out a deep breath. "There was no reason to go to Tier, Junco. I'm still the same person now as I was yesterday. You have him very upset and we don't need this drama right before a critical mission."

I shake my head at him, but I hold my tongue. The words I want to say right now would probably get me in more trouble.

"You can call me whatever you want, demon, Lucan, Archer, angel, devil, whatever. It's all the same. It's not my fault your father gave you a God and that religion calls me evil."

"Why do you hide it then? Is this what I look like in real life? I don't understand."

"I don't hide it, Junco. And you and I are not the same beings, you don't have an angry form. That demon is my angry form. I was furious with the Archer of Clutch, he *pissed me off* with those children he keeps producing. That thing you saw, Junco? That was an avian child using the genetics we have left. It was not a mutant, that is what we have become."

I pull my hands up to either side of my head to block the words and then I wait.

"They are not even sentient. They are not anything but animal. This is the state of our gene pool. And I apologize for scaring you, it was wrong. But now you understand what it is you are doing when you go back to Earth and get the rest of the Seven."

I wait it out as my mind races. That's their gene pool. That creature. I shudder with revulsion and try to get the image of it hurtling through the air from my memory. Of course, that's pointless. I have perfect recall and that fucking thing will be with me for the rest of my life.

"Junco?"

I snap back to him. "Yeah."

"Your feelings about this would be appreciated."

I sit and think for a minute. I don't really care what he looks like, that's not important. And as far as what he is, well, I don't even know what I am, so who am I to judge what he might be. I can't process it right now.

I get up and go sit next to him on the couch. "I don't miss the obvious, ya know. I'm just not interested in knowing certain things. Once it gets in here," I tap my head, "it never leaves, Lucan. It's there for good. So, if it makes my life more complicated and I don't need it to survive at the moment, then I ignore it and let the answers come to me in their own time. I'm extraordinarily patient in that respect."

I look up at him to see his expression. It's thoughtful. "I don't know what to think about all this, Lucan. I only wanted some freaking orange juice. I don't want to know all this stuff about you guys and I don't want to talk about it, or ask questions, or think about what it means." I exhale and shake my head. "I really don't."

"Well, you're a major player in the future of the Avian race, so it's your duty to know all this stuff, Junco. The time for running away is past now. You must stand up, accept what is true, and move forward."

I stay silent. I don't want to see the truth, I just don't.

"Did you hear my words, Junco?"

"Yes."

"And your response is?"

Just when he's getting impatient and about to say something I answer. "It never ends well, Lucan. Never." I search out his eyes and suddenly all the pushed-down pain just under the surface is desperately trying to come back up. "I'm tired."

He puts his arm around me and laughs. "Me too, Junco. But if we rest now, we lose. I've come too far to lose. And so have you." He tips my chin up so I am forced to see him as he speaks. "You've come too far. Either you take your stand or it all becomes meaningless."

I shake my head so his fingers lose their grip on my chin. "Yeah, I get it."

"Maybe you should spend the evening with Esta?"

I don't answer, but he pauses to think it through. "Yes, I'll have Ryse take you over to her when he has time. She's calm and rational," he looks down at me, "and can explain things better."

I don't mind seeing Esta, I think we have a lot more in common than I thought at first, but I hesitate. "I want to see Tier."

"I told him he could walk you to the training room tomorrow," he checks his vision screen, "today. He'll be here soon and you've gotten him all riled up, Junco. Be calm when you see him. And let's get rid of the girls today, we're out of time. Threaten to stun them with pulse rifles and then run fifty laps in the training room. That should put an end to it."

"What if they all agree to be stunned?"

He smiles. "They won't. Keep the ones who agree." He looks down at me and puts a hand on my shoulder. "Don't really shoot them, Junco. We're not going to do that anymore."

I let out a huff. "Sure, now you change the policy. It's a good thing you warned me," I say, looking at him as I get up, "because I totally would've shot them."

He shakes his head at me as I go back upstairs to get ready for the day.

I can hear them yelling as soon as I leave my room. And I'm a half-hour early. I jog down the hallway to the stairs and hop down, not taking care this time, and the steps sway wildly as I descend. They are in the living room and I burst in on them mid-argument.

Tier is poking Lucan's chest with a finger and I raise my eyebrows at this. "– that was not what we discussed. This is over now, Lucan."

Lucan nods to me and Tier turns. "Let's go, Junco, yer coming home with me." He takes my hand but my feet are planted to the floor.

"Wait, what's going on?"

Tier's eyes glow bright green and Lucan just stands there. "He was angry in this house with ya here, that is inexcusable, Junco. Yer not staying."

I resist again and take Tier's other hand. "He didn't do anything to me, Tier."

Tier shakes his head. "Ya have no idea, Junco. None. That being is forbidden." He looks over to Lucan now. "How many other times has it happened? Do you guys flip into it all the time, whenever ya get a little pissed off?"

He's right. I have no idea what they're talking about.

"Ya took her to the cages, ya left her there, and she felt so threatened that she had her weapon out and sliced through the couch as ya brought her back?"

He's enraged and there is no way I'll be able to defuse that anger.

Lucan exhales and smiles. "Tier, I assure you, she's far more dangerous to me than I am to her. I would never–"

"You'd never turn in front of her, that's what ya told me! But it happened!"

"She stays, Tier."

"No, she doesn't!"

Lucan shakes his head. "It's only for a few days, you have my word, Tier. It will not–"

Tier growls at him. "It will not, yer right. It will not, Lucan."

"I give you my word, Tier. It will not happen again. She had to see the children sooner or later, so it is done now. One less thing to do."

Tier pulls on my hand again and I follow him towards the elevator.

He punches the call button and the doors open.

"Wait, Junco." Lucan walks up next to me. "I have something for you."

I turn and he hands me a drink canister and then Tier pulls me into the elevator and the doors close. He exhales and raises his eyebrows at me. "Sorry."

"Are you allowed to talk to him that way?"

Tier huffs. "What's he gonna do? Kill me?"

"That's not funny."

He shrugs and gives me half a smile. "What's in the cup?"

I take a sip and laugh. "Orange juice."

"You can stay, he won't do it again."

"Then why all the posturing?"

"Ya give him a little, Junco – he'll take it all from ya. Ya can't do that with him. He'll just keep asking and asking. Believe me, I know how it goes. That being is forbidden. They are not allowed to show us their rage. It's bad enough what he did ta ya, taking ya to the clutch like that. But ta do it out of anger makes it so much worse."

"OK, whatever. I don't want to talk about it anymore."

Tier calms himself with a deep breath. "Ready to go shoot the girls?"

"Lucan says I can't really shoot them."

"Well, maybe they'll get lippy and ya can justify one or two?"

"Nah, besides, I want Tessen to make it, let's not scare her."

He bumps up against my shoulder. "Tessen better make it, she's on my team. Ya can't cut her."

"I thought playing favorites was forbidden?"

He laughs loudly at this, a guffaw almost. "Junco – where the fuck do ya live?" He shakes his head at me. "The President is falling all over himself to make you happy, and yer telling me there's no favorites? He's gifted me so much shit I've got more power than most of the Archers under him. Favoritism is alive and well in the Avian world. And we like Tessen, right?"

I nod as I think about what he just admitted to me. "Yes, I like her."

"It's settled. Go in there and threaten the shit out of them, wink at the ones ya like and let the others walk out."

"Fuck, Tier. Life would've been so much easier with you in charge during Fledge. Ashur was so–"

"Ashur is a straight-backed piker, Junco. He's Mr. Follow-the-rules. Always has been. Don't get me wrong, when ya got me as yer captain, the XO had better be as rigid as he is, otherwise it'll never work."

"So what's that say about Braun?"

He shrugs. "Well, ya can't have it perfect all the time. Braun is very good at what he does. Munitions, strategy, fighting – that sort of thing. But we're too much alike to be one and two. Besides, we'll be back together next week. All nine of us. I'll be captain, Ashur will be XO, Ryse will be up and you'll be nine. And that will be perfection."

The doors open and we exit onto the training floor. "What about when we come back, what happens to your other team?"

He pushes me up against the wall and his hands slip to my waist. "We'll worry about that when it happens, Junco. Don't get ahead of yerself, it never works out the way you plan, so learn to let it go."

I look up at him and smile. "God, I love you. You say all the right things."

He leans down and kisses me, his hands sliding behind to my back, and I tilt my head at his touch. "I love ya too, Junco. Don't ya ever forget that."

He squeezes my hand and walks off to the stairs to find his own training room. People say hi to him and I watch how attitudes change as he passes. How some avoid him, some look for his attention, and some bask in his glow. I stand there for a minute, just soaking up what's left of his presence.

Basking in his glow.

Chapter Four

Ashur enters the training room just as I am about to address the shitty line-up of girls against the wall. He's got the whole team with him and each of them has a plasma rifle.

He waves me over and I glare at the girls from across the room as Ashur and I talk. "So, where do you want to eat lunch, Junco?"

I lean in conspiratorially and whisper. "I'm supposed to hang out with Esta and Ryse today, I think. Lucan wants Esta to teach me something about the myths."

Ash looks over at the girls and shakes his head. I see a few of them actually step back in fear and turn so they can't see me smile.

"I'll come along too, then it won't be awkward."

I turn back and nod my head at him as I eyeball the few wannabes who are still meeting my gaze. "What do you mean? Why would it be awkward?"

He puts his hand on my shoulder and looks back at the girls as he turns me around so they can't see us talk. "Oh, I guess you wouldn't know then. Right. Esta and Ryse have been," he stops, "together, you know." He shrugs. "So, you don't want to be the third wing, right?"

"Huh, that makes sense somehow. Ryse is into that mythology bullshit too, isn't he?"

Ashur exhales heavily. "Yeah, they're actually perfect for each other. She got her pheromones removed, did you know that?"

I shake my head. "No, I didn't. Good for her, that shit was so annoying."

"Yeah." Ashur turns us back around and raises his voice. "OK?"

I nod. "Let's shoot them then."

I watch the girls panic and begin whispering to each other as Ashur signals the guys to charge the weapons.

"OK, ladies, turn around and put your hands on the wall. Today's test is being shot with the plasma rifle. You'll have fifteen minutes to recover, and then you will run fifty laps in the training room."

Obviously none of them have ever been pulsed with a plasma because if they did, they'd know it takes you hours to recover from that shit and even the best smoke-free lungs on the habitat wouldn't have a chance delivering enough oxygen for crawling fifteen minutes later, let alone running.

They begin to protest so I play the first card. "If this isn't what you signed up for, leave. I can't even count the number of times I've been shot with a plasma so this is excellent training. Plus we get to see–"

The first girl cracks and walks out. "Oi!" I call. "You haven't even heard the part about the SEAR knife yet!"

They start yelling at me and I just smile. "Hey, if you don't like it, there's the door."

In the end there are only two left.

Two stinking girls.

Tessen was clearly warned by Tier because she didn't even flinch through any of my threats.

The other girl's name is Lili and she looks like she'd be equally at home in my princess room back on Earth or flying around on a wire at the Midnight Mass on Christmas Eve holding a candle, she is that angelic.

I shake her hand, then remember she's probably never done that before when she looks at me, confused. "So, are you and Tessen friends?"

The small blonde girl scrunches up her face. "Who's Tessen? I thought you said you were going to shoot us?"

"Never mind, Lili. You're officially my new favorite. Welcome to the warriors." I wave Ashur over. "So what do you want to do with Lili then? Tessen is just gonna go back to Tier's team."

He shakes his head. "Sorry, Lili, you're going over to Monk in Justice." He eyes me with a small sneer. "He liked having a girl, it seems. Probably can't get the image of your naked body out of his head."

My face scrunches up at Ashur, but he just pushes Lili on the shoulder a little and they walk towards the door where Ryse intercepts them. I watch them talk as Ashur looks over at me. He nods and all three of them come back over.

"Junco," Ryse starts, "Lucan says I have to take you over to Esta. So," he shrugs, "let's go."

I look over to Ashur and he smiles a little too sweetly. "Monk's at a meeting with Lucan and Rache, so Lili and I will tag along too."

Lili gets to come now? Perfect. "Huh. Whatever happened to third wing, Ashur? You're such an asshole." I wave Ryse on and follow him out towards the trains.

Esta is thrilled to see me when we finally arrive at the museum almost an hour later. She barely notices Ryse, so I don't know what Ashur was talking about with the whole third wing thing. And Ryse, for his part, is so interested in the artifacts he hardly notices anything else.

"Junco?"

I turn and look at her, then smile at my sister. "Esta, I'm not really interested, but Lucan says he wants you to explain stuff about," I wave my hand to the hundreds of cylinder seals lining the walls, "all this stuff." There's quite a lot of artifacts and I don't recognize a single one and I've seen the entire private collection at the British Museum. "Where did you guys get it all? I mean, are these copies of what we have on Earth?"

Esta links her arm in mine and begins walking towards the wall. "No, Junco. We have all the important ones. We only left the broken ones, or duplicates, or ones made by inconsequential artisans, back on Earth."

I nod, appreciating the display. "Do you have any of Inanna?"

She beams down at me from her slightly superior height. "Earth has no true images of Inanna, or many of the others, either. We have them all. Here, I'll show you." She walks over to one cast hanging on the wall next to the cylinder seal that, when rolled on wet clay, can make the impression of images that can then be visualized. They make a repeating pattern if you roll the seal more than one continuous turn, so it's like a wallpaper border my grandma might have had near the ceiling in her bathroom.

Esta points to the figure in the middle of the scene. "This is Inanna, Junco." I study the woman who has inserted herself into my life with such force. Her hair is wild, her chest is bare of clothing, and her dress is lined with jewels. She has many weapons: spears, a knife, a bow with a quiver, something that looks like a pickax, and a wand.

A very small wand that she holds in her hand, her thumb near the top. As if she's ready to flick it on.

I point to the little wand. "What's that?" I look over at Esta and she's smiling so big she can hardly contain it.

"That's her lapis rod."

I nod. "Oh, OK. That thing she gave the first gatekeeper when she went to the world down below."

Esta looks surprised. "Who told you that story?"

I sigh at the memory. "Tier. When we were bathing in a hot spring back on Earth. It was a nice night. Before the nightdog ate my fingers, of course."

Esta stares at me, her face serious. "You have a lapis rod too, ya know."

My hand reaches into my shirt and I pull out my SEAR. "Is it lapis? I never knew that."

I hand it to Esta's outstretched hand. No one has ever asked to see it before. She palms it and flicks her thumb over the small imperfection in the stone but of course, it doesn't power on. It's coded for me and she's not done anything to try and fake my print like Aren did that last night on Earth. "You're Inanna, Junco."

I shake my head. "I absolutely am not Inanna, Esta. That is so much bullshit."

She just laughs. "Very close, if not."

I look around and find Ashur directly behind me, Lili is off with Ryse looking at something. Esta hands me back the SEAR and I look it over carefully. "It's blue, but I don't think it's lapis lazuli, Esta. It looks synthetic."

"It's not really lapis. I was kidding. But it is weird that you have a rod of power." She shrugs one shoulder. "I think it is anyway."

"So, I'm the killer then? Or what? I have to say, I really despise this myth. And if any of you were told your destiny is to kill people, you'd never want to hear about it again, either."

Ashur moves in closer to me and I look up at him. "It's all bad stuff, Ashur. I'm the outcast, I'm the evil one, I'm the killer, I'm the impure one. I'm tired of hearing it."

He squeezes my shoulder as Esta begins talking. "Junco, in my opinion, that is a misinterpretation. You see, the myth in the original cuneiform is marked off like this." She takes my hand and pulls me over to a long tablet filled with columns of ancient Sumerian. "This image," she points to a glyph, "has been translated as outsider or outcast. But it can just as easily mean shepherd or leader." She looks down at me. "I think it says you're the leader – the shepherd to bring us together. That's why you're always out front." She takes my hand again and leads me over to another plaque and points to a group of seven dots. Six of them are lined up like the six dots you see on dice. "You're this one." Her finger gently touches the single dot at the head of the group. "The leader, see?"

I nod. "OK."

"They're all like that, Junco." She takes me to several more and points to the group of seven, six lined up in two short rows, and the seventh out in front of them. "They've misinterpreted the myth. And while all of you think I'm not important in all this, I happen to think I can read them a little better than the rest of you for a reason. It's my gift. Like Junco has her warrior skills, I have the history inside me." She looks around to see what we think. "I can just read them. It's easy."

"So how did the Seven get on Earth? And where the fuck have the genetics been for all this time?"

She shakes her head at this one. "That, we have no idea. There is nothing that points to where the containers were hidden and none of the humans have ever divulged how they came to have them. We don't even know who started it all, or why they knew they had to."

I smile and feel a genuine love for Esta. "You're right, Esta. You're good at this. I bet we all have gifts. I wonder what Moju's gift is?" I'm lost in thought and when I look up Ryse is next to Esta and has his arm around her, making her feel important. I smile at them both. "Hey, have you ever looked at the cuneiform writing on the Fallen Archer church over at Fledge? I'd love it if you could translate that for me."

"Sure, Junco." She inhales and lifts her chest up a little. I made her feel important too. And I didn't even do it on purpose, I just really want another opinion on what that shit says for some reason.

"We already read that translation, Junco." Ashur is looking down at me with a weird look on his face.

"Yeah, but it didn't fit with what I thought it would say. Even though the words I translated came out about right. If Esta's the expert in this stuff, then I'd like to hear what she has to say about it."

"Junco, how many fucking times do I have to tell you to leave that fucking church alone?"

Isten is walking towards me, covering significant ground with each stride, angry as all hell. I just stare at him. "What do you mean? You said don't go fucking praying to her so she wouldn't mess up the end. It wasn't her anyway, it was Sera all along."

He grabs me by the arm. "Come on, we've got to go fit you for rifles and armor."

In the flyer Isten is distant and looks out the window. I'm not interested in why he's in such a bad mood, so I ignore him and rest my head back to think. I wonder if Ashur is going to take Lili out to dinner? This makes my stomach rumble and I look over at Isten, who has not even turned in my direction once since he picked me up. I sigh and give in. "Why are you angry with me?"

"Huh?" He looks over, his mouth in a crooked sneer.

"You're angry with me?" A question this time.

He shakes his head, but it's not convincing. "I'm not." Then the flyer stops and he pushes me to get out on the passenger side.

We exit onto a store front platform. The sign reads Aves Supply. Which pretty much says it all, right? We're here for military shit.

Inside it's more like a private club than a gun shop. A tall thin wingless man, in a suit that reminds me of Lucan, greets us and they talk in Avian. I'm not that good at picking up the words when they're talking so fast, but I get the basic idea.

A set of double doors open and lead to a waiting room. Isten takes a seat and lights up a cigarette as he stretches his legs and focuses on the screen showing sports. The thin guy takes me by the arm and pulls me to another door, then whisks me through into what looks more like a tailor's dressing room than a military outfitter.

A team of people come out and begin to measure me. They lift my arms straight up towards the ceiling and tell me not to move. Then another team spreads my legs a little and begins the lower body measurements. When they've finished another man begins on my wings. It tickles like fuck, but I try to stand still.

None of them are very personable and my mood is going sour fast. When the wingman touches my girls for like the hundredth time I smack him in the jaw. "Don't do it again or you'll be sorry."

He huffs at me and disappears.

The tall thin man returns. "Is there a problem?"

I smile sweetly. "Yes, there is. If you want to feel me up then the least you can do is be personable and polite while you're fucking doing it. If you people want to walk around me like I'm nonexistent and act like you can touch me wherever you–"

"Junco."

I turn to Isten. "What?"

He walks over to the suit guy and asks in Avian if I'm done with armor fitting. I just scowl as they converse like I'm not even here. Then Isten and the tall man walk me back to another part of the shop so they can let me shoot some guns. I smile as I walk up to the practice lane and inspect the line of weapons they have laid out.

One set is from Earth. "Hey, are these my sniper rifles?"

Isten pulls himself from the guy and walks over. "Yeah, Rikan and I stole all your shit, remember?"

I breathe out and answer in a whisper. "You never said you took the *guns*."

This makes me so happy I can't even think straight. My rifles are special. I mean, I've used these weapons for years now, the same ones have been fitted and refitted several dozen times since I started sniper training. I know every fraction of them, how they shoot cold bore, how to set the manual scope so it reads right the first time, how to keep the one-shot scope from false set, their little quirks and idiosyncrasies, and exactly what it feels like when I'm out of shots and they need to be fitted again.

I pick up the short-range MXSP and take her apart, check every single piece, then reassemble and put her back in line. I move onto the RM Tactical Bolt, which only has a manual scope and is only a little more accurate than the MXSP at short distances, but can shoot about twice as far – about 2500-2750 yards – and be dead on. I sight it down the lane, measure some shit with the mil-dots and do the calculations in my head real fast just for practice, then take her apart, check and reassemble.

The one I call Big Boy is next. The RM Elite is my best performance rifle and is accurate out to 5000 yards. I have never personally made a 5000-yard shot, but it does well at 4000, which is my average. I've exploded more heads with Big Boy than any of the others. I feel myself sigh as I lift the gun and look through the one-shot scope down to the targets.

"What kind of Coriolis Effect you guys got here?" I ask Isten without turning around or taking my eye off the target.

He steps up. "Too big to really use these accurately at long distances, Juncs. Sorry. We spin a lot faster than Earth."

"Doesn't matter. We'll be on Earth soon enough, and then I'll be just fine."

I don't even mess with the 50 caliber, that monster is way too big to fire in here anyway.

Isten takes it from me. "We had to refit that, Junco, so you'll have to adjust it, make sure the muzzle brake is the way it's supposed to be. Sorry, I don't use one of those on my rifles. But," he stops and looks me up and down, "you probably need it, right?"

"Only if you want me to hit shit with it, Isten," I say, looking up at him. "I weigh a hundred and twenty with wet wings on a good day and I haven't had a lot of good days lately, so – yeah, I need the muzzle brake."

I move on to the new weapons. My personal sidearm is just like everyone else's. A semi-pulse mini-plasma. I've never shot one because this is a purely avian weapon that I've only had the pleasure of being aimed at me. Beside it are an array of recharge capsules in several shapes and sizes. The full-size plasma is just like the mini, only bigger and with a longer range, and larger charge capacity.

Our assault weapon is an Earth projectile, just in case we need more ammo.

The knives are all a dull charcoal color, both blade and hilt. I smile and pick one up to check the balance, then throw it towards the closest target and stick it pretty near dead center on the first try. I'm somewhat great at knife throwing. Finally I turn around and smile. "OK, so where do we start?"

We spend the entire day there and I shoot more than two thousand rounds and extinguish more than five dozen plasma capsules. Just as we are finishing up I turn to Isten. "You'll have to have them refit all but the 50 cal, you know that, right? I want them all fresh before we leave."

He salutes and barks some orders in Avian to the monitors standing nearby. I get dropped off at the Aves building sometime after ten and I'm starved. Isten forgot, of all things, to fucking feed me.

Chapter Five

When I enter the Presidential quarters I do a double-take on my way to the stairs and slide on the slick floor as I stop mid-stride. Lucan is sitting in the living room watching sports on the giant screen that extends down from the ceiling.

"Lucan?" I make a detour into the living room and plop down on the couch. "What're you doing?"

He smiles all the way up to his eyes. "Waiting up for you to come home."

My eyes roll back into my head. "I was with Isten, it wasn't a date."

His smile is still there, big as ever. "I have no idea what you're talking about. So what did you do today?"

"Ya know what I did, Lucan. You track my every move."

"I know," he replies evenly, "but I want to hear it from you."

I lean back on the soft cushions. "I'm hungry. Isten didn't get me food. And I want to take a shower. I have powder burns all over me." I sniff my shirt. "And I smell like a chemical factory."

"What do you want to eat?" he asks, looking almost if he's ready to take notes.

"A cheeseburger and fries."

His blue eyes glow. I've never seen them glow before. "Done. Go take a shower and meet me in the dining room when you're finished."

"Dining room? No, I want to eat in my bed clothes on the terrace. You're too formal."

He nods and waves a dismissive hand at me. "Whatever, I'll bring it to you when you're done. And then we can talk. Think of good questions, Junco."

I get up and head towards the stairs laughing. "OK, I'll do that."

I scrub the chemicals off me in the shower then dress in a pair of white shorts and a white tank top and pad out to the terrace to see if Lucan is there.

He's not, so I fly up on the roof and soak up the view and think about how I got here and what it means. Being the favorite is pretty awesome and I have a good question, but I doubt he'll answer it.

He's sitting next to me trying to hand me food before I can even process he's there. "Thanks," I say as I take the bag. "I didn't know you had hamburger places here. That's good to know. I'll be eating these regularly."

"Why are you on the roof?"

I take a huge bite of my cheeseburger, then spit it out and pick off the pickles and try again. "I can see everything from here, Lucan," I say with my mouth full. "It's better than the terrace." I chew and swallow before continuing. "Look," I stand up and he joins me, "it's like you're looking down on a map or something." I grin up at him and take another bite of burger.

"You mean, like a bird?"

"Yeah." I laugh. "It's a novelty for me. I'm still human in here." I tap my head with a French fry. "It never occurred to me that I should fly above the city to take a look. Besides, isn't flying prohibited on Amelia, except for Aves business?"

"But that never stopped Tier. And I don't suppose that will stop you either, Junco." He hands me a cup and I take it and gulp down some orange juice.

"Remember on that first day when I said you misjudged me?"

I take a seat again and he follows.

"Well, you really have. I was never a troublemaker growing up, Lucan." I look up at him, wanting him to believe me very badly. "I am a rule-follower, really."

His eyes squint in disagreement as he turns his head slightly.

"Anyway, I do have questions. Are you ready?"

"Go ahead, Junco."

"OK, this one's more of a statement, than a question. Tier has that demon in him, doesn't he?" I catch a microscopic grimace as I take a bite of food and I'm instantly sorry I asked.

"Why do you think that?"

I finish chewing and swallow this time. "Well, back on Earth, after the battle at my house, he was – his face was" – I squint my eyes as I recall the memory – "he looked distorted when he looked at me. Then he turned his back and walked away so I couldn't see him and the next time he turned around he was normal."

"He has the potential. He has been prepped since birth to be an Archer. But he won't take the position, so it will never affect you, Junco."

"Oh," I say, trying to clarify, "I don't care if he is. It doesn't change how I feel about him, if that's what you're worried about. I was just curious."

"And the other question?"

"Is there a God?"

He searches my eyes to see if I'm serious. "Is there a God, in what respect?"

I shrug. "Like, is there a God? It's not a convoluted question. Is it?"

"You'll have to be more specific, Junco."

"Never mind, I didn't really think you'd answer me. I don't want to know anyway."

"You don't?"

I shake my head. "No, I know the answer and if I'm wrong that's OK too."

"Do you think there's a God, Junco?"

"Absolutely."

"Your God, then?"

"Yup."

"Where do you get that faith from? Really, I have to ask because you don't seem to want to follow the rules of your religion very much, yet you're convinced?"

"Well, here's how I see it. I have a few grace years, right? I mean, none of this shit is my fault, it was just the hand I was dealt. And I'm barely adult–" I shake my head. "Nah, I'm really not even close to being adult enough to take responsibility for what they made me."

I look up to see if he's listening and he is, so I straighten up and continue. "I figure I have a few years to sort it all out and make good. Change my ways and all that bullshit. And so that's my plan." I look up and grin. "I get some extra time to get it straight, but once I get it down, then God will expect results. I'll deliver then, once I understand what it is I'm here for."

"Don't you think you're here to save the Avian race? Go back to Earth and get the Siblings and bring them home?"

"No. That's your purpose for me. God's purpose is something else. I haven't figured it out yet. But I will."

"That's very interesting. I did not expect you to be so – pious."

"Yeah, well, that shit goes deep when they start you young, right? And the whole demon thing, it's – just a scare tactic." I look up at him, waiting for a confirmation, but he stays silent. "I mean, parents use that shit to keep you in line. Say your prayers or you'll go to Hell and all that."

He draws in a breath before answering. "Did your father threaten you with Hell, Junco? When you were bad?"

"No. He just backhanded me across the mouth."

He looks over at me, taken aback a little.

I laugh. "Are you serious, Lucan? How could you not know he hit me?"

His face is not calm, but his voice is. "How often did he hit you?"

"Not a lot, to be honest. Because like I said, I was a good kid. I followed all my orders until just before sniper school. Which almost coincides with when you guys showed up. So, there you go." I look up at him. "You guys think I'm something that I'm not. I mean, I get it, I've done some crazy shit in the past couple years, but before that. I was obedient." I breathe out and whisper, "Sniper school changed me. No, really it was that last trip out to the Stag that did it."

"What did they do to you out at that camp, do you remember?"

"Well, most of the time it was nutrition stuff. And training, of course. Shooting, knives, some archery."

"I don't understand. They taught you about nutrition at that secret camp?"

"Yeah, I had very specific requirements all growing up. I had to eat special food and make sure it was in the proper proportions all the time. When I got older they taught me how to eat normal stuff, but in the right mixture. I wasn't healthy as a kid, I tried to tell Tier that when he found that tracker in me. I know he said it was like a spy tracker, so it was, I believe him. But it had an alarm on it that buzzed if my metabolism was off. I heard it. I had to deal with it. It was a health tracker, too."

"You really do have dietary issues? Why didn't you tell us?"

"It's not really a dietary issue, Lucan. It's a metabolism thing. I'm not normal, remember? I had heart issues too, so I had to learn this controlled breathing stuff so that the amount of adrenaline in my body wouldn't be detected."

"They were measuring adrenaline? You mean so that you could complete your missions without triggering the adrenaline alarms at checkpoints?"

"Fuck. I never even thought of that. I always thought I was sick. They said I'd die if I didn't control it."

Lucan stays silent but his brows are furrowed in anger at my revelation.

"Anyway, if things got out of control the alarm went off. So they taught me that breathing shit. To calm myself and control my fight-or-flight instinct."

"How did they fix it, Junco? Do you know?"

I shake my head. "No. They did stuff." I look up at him. "But I don't remember what they did. All I know is that I can eat anything now. And even if my heart rate jacks up, the alarm doesn't go off. Even before Tier took it out, I mean. It's been this way since that summer before sniper school. They did something to me that summer."

"What else did you do at that camp?"

"Training, like I said. Shooting, knives–"

"And archery stuff, yes, I heard."

"I never saw any mutants, Lucan. I didn't."

He nods at me, but his eyes look nervous. "Continue, Junco."

"Then when I was almost seventeen, that summer in The Stag we had stalk-and-strikes every day. It was like pre-training for sniper school, I guess. And the last day was a test with live fire." I look up again to check his expression, this time he's wincing. It's not hard to see where this is going. "And they shot me." I pull my shirt down and show him the nasty scar just to the left of my neck. "It went straight through the trapezius."

Lucan touches it gently with his fingers and he shakes his head. "Continue."

"As you might imagine, I was pissed off. And I did not flinch when it hit me. Not one fucking fraction. They walked past me, shit, were almost right on top of me once, but they didn't catch me because I was dug down a little bit and my grassland ghillie suits are phenomenal, I made that one with heat shielding and everything. It was so fucking good that there was a rabbit sitting on top of me when they took that shot. Which was why they took it in the first place, right? It moved, they shot, it ran. They wrote it off. Lucky me.

"I waited out there for more than a day, they were getting frantic looking for me, calling for me. But I never moved. Then, when they went inside and the area was clear, I got up and climbed a tree and shot the guy responsible the second he left the mess."

I crack a satisfied smile at the memory, then push it down before I look up again. "That shit changed me. They wanted to kill me that day, Lucan. They wanted me to fail. And I've thought about it a lot since Tier and Moju and I destroyed Dale's tunnel lab. They wanted to get rid of me and pull out the next clone. I know it. I did something and they changed their mind about me. They wanted a do-over."

He's not agreeing with me, I can tell, and I'm annoyed. "That shot might have just been at the rabbit, Junco."

I shake my head and laugh. "Get a grip, Lucan, you don't shoot cottontails on the sniper range. The shot came from behind me. He wasn't my target, he was my trainer. It was deliberate."

"Then why let you live after killing a trainer?"

I shrug. "Too much time to train another one? They had a job coming up and they needed me. I cannot imagine they could pull out a full-grown clone and expect her to be compliant, they'd have to start again, wouldn't they? They saw I was as well-trained as they would ever get probably, and took their chances."

I'm silent for a few more minutes. "That's how I know there's a God, Lucan. All these lucky breaks, all this training, and all this self-control and determination did not happen by accident. I was made by someone for something. And while everyone seems to think I was made for their purpose, I know that's not true. I have only one true purpose." I give him a crooked smile. "I don't mind doing the jobs you ask me to do, but none of this is my one true purpose. You should know that."

His face is serious when he speaks. "The truth now, Junco. Do you think I might be damned by your God?"

I frown. I don't want to think about this. "Maybe." I regret my answer instantly and look away, not meeting his eyes. "No?"

But I swallow and stare into his blue eyes and give him the truth. "I don't know and I don't want to know. I don't want to know, Lucan. So, it doesn't matter. I just feel like – like we're in this together, ya know? Somehow. We're tied together, you and me. So, if you're damned, Lucan – then so am I." I want to smile but the muscles won't cooperate. "And if we are damned, well, then fuck it. We'll go down together then, I guess."

He puts his arm around me and whispers in my ear. "Thank you for that. It means a lot."

"Unless, of course, God says he's gonna smite me." I feel Lucan's chest shake with a laugh. "Because a little baby smote across the teeth from your father is one thing, but being smoted by your God can't be good. The Bible is full of smiting and smoting. And I've always wanted to use these words in a serious conversation, but never had the chance. So–"

He laughs out loud now. "Junco, I think you're the best thing that has ever happened to me."

I pull back and look up. "Ditto, Lucan. You're actually one of the most reliable people I've had in my life, like – *ever*." I let that sink in. "But ya do realize, that's a pretty low bar, right?" I grin at his surprised expression. "I mean, look at my parents. So, don't go getting a big ego or start thinking you're special or anything."

"OK, Junco. Well, you might not like me too much after I tell you this."

"What?"

"Isten will be here at 3 AM to take you to the simulated Earth firing range. You'll spend the next three days with him."

I draw in some air between my teeth. "Yeah, that stings. Isten was a major asshole today. Not friendly at all. You have any idea what that's about?"

His silence says he does, but he stands up and pulls me to my feet as well. "You'll have to work it out with him, Junco. I better let you rest, 3 AM comes pretty fast."

I give a sloppy salute and he's gone. I stay up there a little longer, then fly down and climb in the bed and drift off within seconds.

Chapter Six

Isten shows up half an hour early and pulls me out of bed by my feet, then picks up a bag he's already packed and drags me, still half out of it, to the waiting flyer that will take us to the spaceport. I sleep all the way there, rouse myself just long enough to buckle into the free-G harness, then pass back out.

When I wake up we are still fucking pushing through deep space. I check my vision screen for the time. It's just past noon. "Jasus fuck, Isten, where the hell is this place?"

He doesn't look up from his logs. "We'll be there in another hour."

I yawn. "Fuck it. If you're still gonna be a dick I'll just go back to sleep."

He doesn't even answer me and I can't sleep another minute, so I sit there in silence until we start the docking sequence. The world is not a planet-like habitat like Justice, nor is it a torus like Amelia. It's nothing but a non-reflective sphere just hovering out in the dark. Once we get closer in I discover that the outer boundaries are transparent and there are actually two spheres, one inside the other. I squint to see the splashes of terrain. Mountains, desert, grasslands… I almost moan with desire when I see it.

When we disembark the ship and enter the interior of the massive habitat it really does feel like Earth. Same G, same atmosphere, same clouds, sky, sun – all fake of course, but everything is just like Earth.

We unpack our gear and catch a ride on a small plane up to the mountains. By the time the trip is all said and done we've lost all the daylight, so Isten and I pitch camp in the dark under the dim light of two solar-powered lanterns that work just well enough to throw shadows everywhere and make life more difficult.

Throughout all this Isten has only said three words to me that weren't absolutely necessary. And they were 'Move that ass' as we were hiking with packs that weigh more than I do up the side of the mountain to make our base. There is only one tent, so bunk time should be a fucking riot.

"Hey, Junco?"

I swipe a hand over my forehead to wipe the sweat off me. "What?"

He throws me a ration. I pocket it and keep cleaning Big Boy. Isten pulls the tab off his packet of food and squeezes it into his mouth. Just thinking about food makes me want to vomit. I shoot him a disgusted look.

"I hope you're not going to be moody the whole time, Junco. I'm sick of it already."

I look up and smile. "Fuck you, Isten. I don't know why you're mad, I didn't do anything to you. Nothing."

He comes over and kneels down next to me, automatically picking up pieces of my rifle and helping me put it back together. "Yeah, actually you did, Junco. You went and wasted three fucking weeks messing around with Tier when we could have been training together."

I throw up my hands. "Are you fucking kidding me? That's why you're mad at me? Because I wanted some downtime?"

His hands are moving fast on the weapon parts now, so I sit back and stretch my legs out and let him have at it. He doesn't look up when he answers. "Tier is not the most important person in your life, Junco. I am." He does look up then. "I am, you get it? I'm your spotter, you're my spotter. The only thing that counts is us. No one else matters, Junco. Just me and you." He stops for a minute and puts the final piece on the weapon with a satisfying snap. "And we could've had this shit all worked out weeks ago if you had the good fucking sense to give a shit."

I just stare at the back of his head. "I didn't know, Isten. I worked alone on Earth. Or with my father. I only did assassinations, remember? I only used a spotter for training."

"Which means," he says, looking back at me now, "it will be even harder to get our minds synced up, Junco. We probably won't be able to do it. It's gonna be a disaster."

I shake my head at him and smile. "Isten, this is my home we're talking about. I could do this mission blindfolded. I know that place, we're gonna be just fine."

"We're not going to be in the MR or the RR, Junco. That's wishful thinking."

I shake my head. "You're wrong, Isten. That's exactly where they'll be. I've been thinking about this a lot, even when I was on vacation, so shut the fuck up about me being a slacker." I wait for him to look at me before continuing. "Moju is probably in with those Subjack people, my mother, Selia – all of them. So we just need to go get him first, then he'll know where they are. He will. And I'll bet you anything you want right fucking now, hc's gonna say they're in the MR. Not all of it was bombed, only Peaks was. And Peaks is on the very Eastern edge. There's another world up there in the mountains."

He sits back next to me and stretches out his legs too, then lies all the way back on my bag. "I was gonna kill Kush on Deliverance day, Junco. I cannot fucking believe you slept with him." He stares up at the fake stars, avoiding my eyes.

"Why?" I whisper.

He huffs. "Why kill him, or why can't I believe you slept with him?"

I shrug. "Both, whatever."

He sits up, leans over into my face, pushes me back and then grabs my hands and pins me down as he straddles my chest.

"What the fuck, Isten?"

He leans down harder until it gets uncomfortable and I squirm, but he doesn't let up. I weave my leg around his and pull him, then push with my shoulder and free one hand, squirm again, and flip onto my side. We wrestle and he knocks me in the head and pisses me off. I elbow him in the cheek, wiggle backwards and grab my SEAR as he regains his position on top.

He smiles at the little blue wand. "What are you gonna do with that, Junco?"

"Get off me, Isten."

He shakes his head. "No. What will you do with it? Kill me?"

I let out a breath. "You know I'm not going to kill you, don't be an asshole."

"Then why did you pull it out?"

"Habit."

He leans down on me harder and I'm having trouble breathing. "What the fuck, Isten? What are you doing?"

"You know why you won't kill me, Junco?"

I laugh, then choke on it. "Of course I do. I love you."

He pushes down on my arms, making me squeal as he lets out one word. "Exactly!"

I growl, then struggle, but he doesn't move. "Exactly what?"

He leans all the way down into my face. "You love me. You're not allowed to hand that shit out to some random guy you want to fuck because you're sad, Junco. I saw how you looked at Kush. You can't give that shit away like that, because the minute you do, they own you." He lets go and gets up. "Just like I own you right now."

I'm just too stunned to say anything so I lie there and wait for him to talk it out.

"I heard Ashur that night after the nargala."

"What? Heard him say what?"

"You think it was Tier who saved you, but it wasn't, Junco. It was us. All of us. We planned it together, Tier was just the one on the ground with you. We saved you, not him."

I sit up and peek around so I can see his face. "I realize that, Is. I do."

"It wasn't a figure of speech, just now. I own you, Junco. I don't know how close your Earth sniper teams are, from what I've seen they can't be that different given the nature of the work, but our teams are almost always joined." He looks over to me. "You don't understand, so let me spell it out for you, our minds will be twined before we go back to Amelia."

"What's twined?"

He lets out a little laugh. "Tier could've explained this shit to you while you were fucking him all that time, but no. You two are perfect for each other, ya know that? Mr. and Mrs. I-hate-the-rules. Do what I say, not what I do."

"Fuck you, Isten. Don't talk to me that way, understand?" I get up and try to walk away, but he grabs my ankle and pulls me down hard on the ground. I spring back on my feet and kick him in the face. He falls back slightly and then reaches for my leg and drops me to the ground again. This time I'm ready and I grapple, bending his arm back. I'm waiting for the tap when he flings himself on his side and pins me down on the ground face first, pressing me into a leg bar so that my Achilles tendon is stretched just to the point of snapping.

I tap.

He leans down in my face, his labored breath matching my own. "You should've crushed my elbow, Junco." He puts a little more pressure on my tendon and I squeal. "But you didn't. Because you can't bring yourself to hurt me."

I whimper as he adds yet another fraction of pressure to my leg.

"But make no mistake, Snowbird. People who say they love you are still capable of hurting you. Very badly. Do not hand that shit out. Got it?"

I let out a small grunt of agreement and he eases up and lets me go.

I kick him with my boot as I scramble away. "Look, I don't like to play games and there's obviously something you're not telling me, so fucking spit it out."

"You own Lucan, just like I own you. Because he loves you now. And that's the only reason he let you and Tier go away like that. Because he knows, and Tier knows, that it can't go anywhere. Ever. As long as you're on the team, you can't just fuck the captain, Junco."

I shrug and catch my breath. "So, maybe I'll quit. Problem solved."

He smiles up at me. "Right, you do that. After this mission. You will not be with Tier in any capacity except as his ninth warrior until the day you do quit. You got it now?"

"Yeah, I get it."

"And tomorrow I'm gonna twine you to me and that's the fucking end of it. I'll be in your head every fucking minute of every day. Even after you quit, Junco. Until I die."

I swallow as it hits me. "Why didn't anyone tell me this?"

"You gotta wonder, right? Why didn't they?" And then he gets up and walks out of the tent. Leaving me there alone.

I sit there for a while full of questions and then follow him outside. He's lying on his back by a small fire, smoking a cigarette. I lie down next to him and he offers the pack. I take one and touch the striker as I inhale. "I know why you guys always leave this shit a mystery until the last minute."

"Yeah?" He turns slightly, his hazel eyes glowing in the firelight. "What is it, then?"

"You don't trust me, do you? You all thought if I knew I'd quit and break my promise." I look up and see stars and smile at Orion. On Earth Orion isn't visible to the RR in June. "What more do I have to do to make you believe in me, Isten? I mean, I thought you guys wanted Tier to be saved."

He inhales and then blows out a cloud of smoke towards the night sky. "Everyone hates Tier except us, Junco. Why else would those fucking Archers let him rot in jail like that, put him on trial, make him look like shit in front of everyone?" He looks over to me, the light dancing over his face. "Why did they make you slice your fucking chest open to wipe away a debt that never mattered *to them* in the first place?"

He looks away and takes another drag before continuing. "Lucan gave him all those gifts. All those unsanctioned, illegal fucking gifts and then all of us have to pay the price for his stupidity. And I get it, Lucan picked him long before the 039 ever came into existence. So whatever, I've gotten plenty of gifts from him too. But it's gone way beyond that. They're afraid of him now, Junco."

I recall Tier poking his finger into Lucan's chest the other night and it begins to make sense.

"Not even Lucan can control him. Not after what you did to boost him. That fucking freak show of a mess you made out there on stage that night? You do realize it was a plan by Sera to oust Lucan, right? Give Tier control over everything? He might as well be running the whole show now."

"Wait, what?"

Isten sighs deeply. "Fuck, Junco. I am having a hard time reconciling the two sides of you. Ruthless, skilled killer and helpless, naive teenage girl. Who are you today? Just so I know how slow I should talk?"

"I have–"

"No idea what I'm talking about. Right, I get it – you can pick out Alcor, but not the full moon. Anyway, now Lucan's in love with you, too. It's like some goddamn Greek tragedy playing out before my eyes."

"He doesn't love me like that, Isten."

Isten laughs. "Uh-huh. Right, Junco. He just wants to shower you with gifts and protect you. Fuck, you need to grow up a little." He turns and sits up and I pull back just in case he gets the urge to attack me again.

"It doesn't matter, tomorrow it's over for both of them. Because it's me and you from now on. And I don't know why they never explained it to you, Junco, I really don't, but this was always in the plan. The last time we all talked it over together the purpose of saving you was to get the 039 our ninth warrior and since your skills merged with mine, well, it was perfect. This whole coincidence of you actually turning out to be the honest to God fucking Seventh Sibling for real, was just that. A fucking fluke. We didn't know, we thought you were just a pretty effective fucking clone. And we just wanted you for us." He turns so I can see his face. "That's it, Junco. We liked you and we just wanted you for us."

We sit there listening to the crackle of the fire for several long minutes.

I feel stupid.

But no one has been straight with me and I just don't have the history with these people to understand what's going on. Or, like Lucan said, ask good questions.

"I followed you through sniper school, did you know that, Junco?"

His words snap me back to the present. "What?" I frown up at him. "What do you mean?"

He smiles at me now. "I was with you every fucking second of that training." He looks away and his smile falters. "I was," he hesitates, "not visible, one of Lucan's gifts, so you never saw me. But that's how long we've planned for you to be our nine. I've been waiting for this day a long time and I just don't know what Tier was thinking." He shakes his head, clearly confused. "It was his idea. If he wanted you for himself all he had to do was say so. But the day you guys came back from vacation I asked him and he said it was still on."

I squeeze my eyes shut as the words soak in. "He gave me away?" My throat starts to tighten up a little it hurts so bad.

"Basically, you could say that."

"And Ashur? He knew too? And took me out to dinner and kissed me?"

"He kissed you?" Isten lets out a long sigh. "Fuck, anyone else I should know about?"

"I kissed him back, if that was your next question. You gonna threaten to kill him now?"

He stays silent, but I'm just getting warmed up. "So once again, everyone knew but me, yet they all felt like they could just play with my feelings?"

More silence. I nod and get up. "Wonderful. I'm done for today, Isten. Whatever happens tomorrow, happens. I imagine that if this wasn't in the plan then someone would have stopped you from taking me off-world, so that's just motherfucking wonderful."

I've been sold out yet again.

Chapter Seven

I wake up in the morning and Isten is banging shit around outside. The air is cool and misty when I venture through the flap in my bed clothes. The fake sun is just peeking up over the fake horizon in what I can only assume is the fake east.

"Coffee, Juncs?"

I shake my head and take a seat on a large rock near the edge of a cliff. My legs start to get goosebumps from the chill, and I lean into the sun a little to warm my face.

"Maybe you should put clothes on?" Isten calls from across the camp. "Or learn to drink coffee like the grown-ups?"

I ignore him and rub my legs. "When can we start shooting?"

He's busy packing ammo into the rifle bags but he stops and gets up, then walks over to me. "Hey, look, if this isn't want you want, just say so, OK? I just needed to vent last night. I'm not really interested in trapping you in my head for eternity based on a plan we made years ago and you had no say in."

"Actually, I've thought about it quite a bit." I look over to him and he's still and silent, waiting for my words. "If we are twined, and it's forever, then that means you can't give me away to anyone else, right?"

He pulls me up to his chest and squeezes. "I'd never give you away, Junco. Ever."

"Yeah, sure." I breathe in and then out again. "That's what they all think at first, then poof. My world is ripped apart all over again."

"Well," he pushes me back so he can see my face, "this one's a done deal. So, be very sure."

"I'm very sure. Just do it."

He lifts my chin up a little and smiles. "It's supposed to be special. Let's go shoot first. Then we can see how we work together without the twine. It'll be a good before-and-after comparison."

I smile, but none of this makes me happy and none of it makes me feel special.

Flying up the mountain isn't an option with the gear so we start hiking shortly after breakfast, which was a mylar packet of something I didn't even bother trying to identify. I just sucked it down under duress and then drank a whole bottle of water. It took about an hour to get to the first station but now that we're here, it's worth it. I walk over to the large red sandstone outcropping that makes my heart ache for my home and peer over. Even though I know this is a fake world, the beauty of it stuns me silent. Like Earth.

Ever since we landed, this place has been tugging me back to the blue marble and it's troubling in a way I'd rather not admit to right now. If fake Earth can create these feelings, what will happen when my boots are back on the ground for real? Will I have second thoughts about coming back?

"Junco?" I turn and find Isten studying my face. "What's going on?"

I have to swallow to make the words come out. "It looks like home, that's all." I turn around and go back to my rifle bag. "What are we shooting here, anyway?"

"Whatever you want to use. Your favorite, I guess. I'm gonna use the TAC9." He smiles at me. "That's my favorite."

I can't even muster a smile, so I just pull out Big Boy and lay out everything I need to take one cold-bore shot and make it perfect. Isten shows me where to stand so I can see the target across the valley. It's on the other side of a thicket of conifers, hardly visible with just my eyes, but through the spot scope it's as big as a house.

When I'm ready he waves me on first. I lie down on my belly, then crawl up to the edge of the cliff until I'm as close as I can get and still keep the bipod level. I spread my legs, snuggle myself down into the sandy dirt, and start breathing. In out. Up down. In out stop. Up down stop. In out stop. Up down stop. That's how I do it. It's a little chant I have to block out the world and remind me to only shoot on stop.

Once my breathing is normalized I reach back in my head for my last official data on previous engagement, input some new ammo ballistics, and then I let the infrared do its job as I do mine. I check conditions where I'm at, find the wind in the valley, then watch how it moves, as best as I can tell from what I can see, at the target.

I slide up to the scope and line things up with the mil-dots, run the calculations real quick in my head, then press the output button to see if the one-shot agrees with what I just came up with.

It almost does.

In cases like this I trust myself over a machine. I adjust the scope for my own personal observations and get back into my breathing. In out stop. Up down stop. In out stop. Up down stop.

I take my shot and watch with a smile as the target flashes purple.

Kill.

I scoot back on my belly until I have dead space between myself and the target, then get to my feet and smile at Isten for the first time today.

"Nice job, Snowbird."

"I'm sure you'll do almost as well, Isten. Don't worry."

"Honey, watch and learn from the master."

I wave him on and he repeats what I just did almost in every detail. His rifle is self-contained as far as DOPE goes, but I can tell he's trying to make it look more complicated than it is. There's no way Isten could shoot as well as me using a manual scope. Not if they never taught him how. And even if he did watch me in sniper school, he never actually did the training–

The pop of his shot jerks me back to reality.

"Kill, baby." He scoots back and stands up. "And it didn't take me all fucking morning to get it done, so huh!"

I smile at him. "Nice job. I mean, for a guy who relies on a computer to tell him when to shoot."

He nods his head up and down at me, a scowl on his face. "Yeah, you wanna do this, Junco? You wanna little competition, then?"

I let out a giant grin that spreads across my face and up into my forehead it's so wide. "Isten, you could never match me when it comes to this. You might own me in fighting, but in long-range shooting, I own you. I'm not a sniper, I'm an assassin. And that means the only time I take two shots is if there are two targets, everything is cold bore, and either I do it or it doesn't get done. So, you can get as cocky as you want because I will kick your motherfucking ass out here."

He smiles and pulls me into his chest to hug me. "You're right, Junco. I've seen you in action. Remember? But I'm still pretty good." He shrugs. "Come on, let's trade weapons. I actually can shoot with that barbaric thing you like to use. Not that it matters. But on the field you might only have a weapon like mine available, so better get familiar with it."

We spend the next hour shooting each other's weapons, then hike on to the next station and work on our spotting. In the field you can't be snipe all the time, it's way too exhausting, and that's why you need your partner. It only makes sense, then, to have one of ya shooting while the other spots out the target, checks wind, and all that good shit. If you're in a team situation, you rely on your spotter to give you honest, reliable feedback, which you then input into your rifle before taking your shot.

Isten is much better at spotting than I am and he's ready to clock me after I fuck up and make him miss a few.

The third station is an automated stalk site. We make some quick ghillies and run through the various methods of concealment and advance towards the target on the other side of a rolling hill. The first few tries we're spotted early and it zaps us with short bursts of green laser fire that burn through our clothes until we stand and surrender. On the fourth try we make it to the target, which is only about three hundred yards away from my estimate, but it takes us most of the day to stalk over there and take it out.

By the time we roll into the fourth station it's black outside and we make camp. My stomach has been nervous for the better part of the last hike and Isten is starting to notice me again.

He looks over as he rummages through his pack for some rations. "You having second thoughts, Junco?"

I watch his face as the words come out and I see the apprehension there. He wants this to happen. He wants me to say no, I'm not having second thoughts. "I'm nervous, Isten. I don't really understand what it means."

"Well, then you must have an idea in your head of what it might mean, and you're worried about that. So why not just tell me what's got you bothered?"

I swallow and sit down on the ground in front of the fire, then lean back and rest my hands behind my head to look up at the stars. He takes a seat next to me. "Will I be like your girlfriend? I don't get it. Is it personal?"

He lies back then rolls over so he's on top of me. His face comes down to mine, his lips right at my mouth. "Look at me, Junco."

I force my eyes up to his and they're glowing gold. They look like a sunset. He dips his mouth down to mine but I'm locked on his eyes.

When he talks it's a soft whisper, so low I can barely hear him. "I will never kiss you like this, Junco. If I am this close to you it's because we have to be, it's not because I want to take advantage of you." He pushes his upper body up a little and draws back. "And if I have to touch your wings, or your back, or see your body in ways you'd never normally let me see – it's because we need each other's body heat, or we need comfort, or we need healing."

I swallow and nod, my eyes still glued to his.

"To twine. The word means a couple of things, but for us it will mean we are twisted together. And it's no mistake that you find the word twin in there as well," he stops to brush the hair from my eyes, "because that's how close we will be." He waits for me to talk, but I stay silent. "And it's very personal. I'll have access to you, Juncs. All of you. All the things you're keeping locked away in there," he taps his finger gently on my head, "I'll be able to get them if I want."

I swallow again, then finally look away.

"And you'll be able to do the same for me."

I take a deep breath and let it out slowly as he rolls off of me and sits back up.

"So, one more time and then we're gonna drop it for good because you don't force people to twine, that's about as wrong as it gets. Do you want to do this or not?"

I stand up and then reach out for him, pulling him up with me. "I do want to, Isten. I really do."

I feel the relief rush out of him and smile, and then he hugs me. "Junco, you have no idea how happy this makes me. But in a few minutes you will. And if you're lying to me right now, I'll know, so please don't say yes to spare my feelings. It will hurt so much worse if I find out you don't want to do it and you do it anyway."

I laugh a little. "Jeez, Is, I never pegged you for a guy who needs his ego stroked, but OK, I'll stroke it anyway. Isten Aves 039-8, I choose to be twined to you." I look up at him and shrug. "How's that? Good enough? Or you need me to thumb a DNA release too?"

The actual twine procedure is nothing more than a shot in the arm from the view of an outsider, but to me it is a mountain of synaptic charges firing in my brain for the better part of an hour. We lie there next to the fire, him holding me as we let our brains make the connections, the memories begin to exchange. We get used to the new read-out on our vision screens that tells us what the other is doing.

A thought occurs to me, maybe a little late, but what can you do? "Have you been twined to someone else, Isten?"

"Yeah," he says and I feel his sadness so deeply it makes me want to cry. "He died on assignment."

I lean into him a little more. "I'm so sorry. It feels terrible to lose that."

He nods. "Yeah. It does." He turns then and smiles down at me. "But it feels so good to have you right now, can you feel it?"

I reach in and find his happiness and nod. "Can I look around? It sounds funny, but can I?"

"Yeah. That's part of the tradition, the first night you're supposed to find a new memory in the other. Something deep and dark. And just get it out in the open. So," he stops and I feel the anxiety in him, "go ahead. Take a look, then tell me what you find and then I'll do the same."

I close my eyes and he pulls me in, his mind opens, and I can feel the memories glide past. I see his other twine and he respects him very deeply. I move on because I know what I'm looking for and as soon as that thought manifests, I feel him shiver under me.

I find Tier and begin to pay attention, looking for details, asking for more and more, and even though I suspected it for a while now, I choke back the tears when I see her and all my fears are confirmed.

I pull back and turn around to hide the hurt.

Isten turns with me. "I'm sorry, Junco. I'll explain it, it looks a lot worse than it is."

I lie still. "Who am I? Just tell me, Isten. Am I a clone too?"

I feel him shake his head. "No, Juncs. You're not, we checked you out, you're the one. You really are the Seven. Look inside me, you'll see I'm telling the truth."

I do look, because I don't think any of them tell me the truth if they can help it, and I'm satisfied that he thinks I'm the real Junco.

"OK, then tell me why that thing is in your memory and how she's connected to Tier."

He turns me around. "You'll look at me for this one, seriously." He stares at me and I nod. "And you won't interrupt or say bullshit, because there is no bullshit between us anymore, Junco. Right?"

I nod.

"If I'm lying you'll know. Maybe not tonight, since it's so new, but it won't take long. I have zero plans on lying to you tonight or ever, got it?"

The firelight dances across his face as he begins to speak and I wait, almost holding my breath, for the truth that is about to come out.

"Iliana is the Seventh member of another clutch of Seven Siblings. Your clutch is not the only one, and it's far from being the first, Junco. It's just that your clutch is the only one left that's *complete.* Iliana's clutch is all dead, except for her. She was—" he stops and thinks for a few seconds, "taken by the MR at some point and turned into an agent. They controlled her, not the RR, even though the RR was the only government that had the original genetics. All the others are clones, Junco. They can't help us. They aren't useful for anything the Seven Siblings are wanted for."

'Then why bother making clones, Isten? I don't get it."

"Soldiers. That's why. They make good soldiers."

"What about Moju? How did he get over to the MR? And why did Esta end up in the Eastern Utopias?"

Isten sighs. "They were all in on it, Junco. Every single country. But they don't all share the same goal. The RR wants the Siblings for the prophecy, the MR and the rest of them just want power. And we want you guys for the genetics that will save us. You asked Lucan why he wanted to kill you back on Earth?"

I look up in his eyes and swallow. "Yes. He said he thought I'd be more trouble than I'm worth."

Isten lets out a little laugh. "You are a lot of trouble, Junco. But you're still worth it." He smiles down at me and then his face becomes serious again. "We need all Seven Siblings from the same clutch to change our genome and like I said, we thought Iliana was part of Moju's clutch. We wanted to try and make that clutch work, after all we already had Esta and we knew where Moju was, even if he refused to cooperate with us. And so when Iliana came along and said she was the Seven we were looking for, well – it was perfect, right?"

"But Iliana was lying."

He nods. "She was lying. And we believed her because no one knew about you. All the other Siblings lived in secret, locked up with the military, so we knew where to look. But they gave you a family. Sent you to school and all that shit. No one else did that."

"Esta said she was in some kind of apprenticeship, though."

"If you call being locked up twenty-four-seven with access to one old-ass scholar a legitimate apprenticeship." He shrugs. "It was all bullshit. She was just another prisoner, like all the rest. So they let her have some books and prowl the sphere looking for answers? Big deal. You, on the other hand, had a family, a school, and an actual documented military career like every other kid in the RR."

"What did she do, Isten? What did Iliana do?"

He looks away this time and doesn't look back when he speaks. "She killed my twine, that's what she did." He turns to look at me. "She killed Tanner. And by that time we'd already made mistakes that couldn't be fixed. She had information and we needed to kill her before she fucked everything up."

"I found her reader in Tier's cave. Back on Earth. I was reading her stuff. So this happened a long time before I first met Tier out in the Stag?"

Isten sighs. "Yeah. Years. Tier traded his genetics to Dale for information which connected her to a network of powerful government officials and then we killed her and the entire network without orders."

"All of you killed them? Not just Tier?"

He doesn't answer.

"So, you were all guilty while Tier was sitting in prison?"

"That was the plan, Junco. It wasn't my idea – we agreed. Tier would take the fall if we got caught."

"Does Lucan know this, Isten?"

He shakes his head. "None of the Archers know. We've kept it tight. I said Tanner died in a freak accident. He wasn't one of us from the beginning, but he fit in and he had the skills, so we got lucky and got a nine for a while."

"So, they only know a lot of important people were killed, but not why?"

"Yeah. When they drugged you for testimony after Fight Two, Juncs, that's what they were looking for. We felt so fucking bad."

"Did all those government people know about me?"

"Not at first, no. Everyone kind of figured it out at the same time, that's when we started watching you. Sniper school."

I look up at him, satisfied. "OK."

He waits, not sure what to do.

"Your turn, Is. Go for it, but I'll warn you ahead of time, most of the shit you'll find will be upsetting."

He takes his time, looking at everything, and I feel the anger grow in him with each new revelation. When he's done fishing he pulls a happy memory and I am so relieved he doesn't make me talk about the scary stuff my throat begins to close up as I hold back the tears.

He chooses the hot springs with Tier. He takes me back to the moment Tier finishes telling the Inanna story and I'm leaning against his chest. Counting his breath as it goes in and out. Whenever I am close enough to someone to feel that rhythm it calms me and I count. Counting breaths is like a drug that can bring me down from almost anything.

"Isten?" I ask sometime later.

He's half asleep under me when he answers. "Yeah."

"Why did you want to know about Tier and me?"

He turns and pulls me into him. "Because I needed to know what he's doing with you, Junco. If he's serious or if he's playing a game."

"Well? Which is it then?"

"Serious, Juncs. As far as I can tell, he's serious."

I move around a little until Isten's heartbeat comes through, and then I count him as I fall asleep.

The next day I feel our connection in everything we do. Eating, packing, hiking, his muscles as they strain to climb a rock and get a better view of our target.

When he shoots I shoot with him. I see through his scope, I feel his heartbeat and I laugh a little when I can almost hear him thinking *in out stop* to himself as he waits for the moment. I guess he was paying attention when he followed me through sniper school.

When it's my turn to shoot I feel him again, only this time I get vague references to what he wants me to do, how he wants to correct me. I don't know if twining makes you a better shot than you were before the connection because Isten and I are already pretty awesome snipers. The change for me is more of a mental bond that gives me someone to lean on.

Which is pretty fucking special since I spent almost my whole life being told I had to work alone.

We pack up to hike back down to the rendezvous point and I'm relieved at the loss of the weight of the ammo. The ride back to Amelia takes the rest of our day and when we finally touch down at the 039 we are dead-ass tired. We drag our gear down the steps and into the apartment where everyone stops what they are doing and waits to see how it went.

Isten and I ignore them completely and we both head to my room and fall asleep, twined together on top of the bed covers.

Chapter Eight

The collective smell of our bodies is what wakes me from sleep the next morning. Yuk. I pull myself from Isten's embrace and start a bath, then go back out to the window and stand there trying to look through traffic to see Kadian's apartment. My comm buzzes and I fish it out of my pocket, smiling.

"Junco!"

"Kadian," I breathe, "I can't believe I actually missed you!"

"Who's the hunk in the bed, Juncs?"

"Isten, you idiot. We twined. I'm the nine and everything is pretty fucking good over here."

He huffs out some air. "Pfffft, that's not what I want to hear, Snowbird. Happiness doesn't sell screen time. So when can we–"

Isten takes the comm from me. "Kadian? No more calls, Lucan will have a presser and you'll be invited." He hands the comm back and then goes into the bathroom.

"My, my, Junco. He's a lot nicer than Tier, Ryse or Ashur. I approve."

"He is nice, isn't he?" I wink at Isten when he peeks his head out of the bathroom. "OK, I gotta go. Bye! That's my tub, you have to wait."

He grins and begins unbuckling his pants. "You can have the tub, Junco. I'm taking a shower."

"What happened to because we need healing or comfort or warmth?"

He shrugs. "We smell like shit, Juncs. That qualifies."

I push past him before he's naked and start adding bubbles to the tub. Fuck it. I strip and sink into the hot water with a moan.

I'm relaxing, almost asleep really, when Tier barges in and finds us. "What the fuck is going on, Isten?"

Isten ignores him as he stands under the hot water so I open one eye and look over to Tier. "It was your idea to do this twine thing?

Well, I gotta thank you because I love it." I feel Isten's happiness as the words come out. I slink down into the bubbles and shake the dirt out of my hair. Several leaves break loose and float off in the water and when I resurface Tier is gone.

I can almost hear Isten's private laugh.

We've been summoned to the Aves building so we all pile into the flyer. I'm sandwiched between Is and Ash – while Ryse, Rikan, Mish and Arel stare at us from the opposite bench. "What?" I ask them.

"So, you like it?" Ryse's eyebrows couldn't be higher on his forehead, that's how surprised he looks.

I nod and feel Isten's pleasure. "I really do, Isten. It's so cool to have you like this."

I feel Ashur's eyes on me and look up at him. "What?"

He smiles. "Nothing, Junco. I can see you do like it and I'm glad. We thought you might" – he winces – "resist."

"Well, it would've been nice to know beforehand, but no, there are a lot worse things than being twined to Isten." I feel him hug me internally and I blush.

Ashur frowns. "Isten, if you have something to say, say it out loud. You know I hate that shit."

Is doesn't even turn and I laugh, which only makes Ashur think we're talking about him behind his back.

"Fuck you both."

We just laugh harder.

The wingless woman directs us to the conference room when we arrive at Lucan's offices. Tier and Braun are already there and the tension between the 039 and Braun is palpable almost immediately. Ashur takes his XO seat at the far left of the crescent-moon table, while Isten directs me to sit next to Tier on the far right. Isten sits next to me and Arel sits next to him. Ryse, who is now back to being our pilot, is in the Up position in the middle, and Braun, Rikan, and Mish sit between Ashur and Ryse.

Every seat is filled.

We are complete.

Layla sits alone in front of us at a small round table. She turns around and smiles at me so I give her the girlfriend nod. Her eyes brighten, then she turns back around and gets busy with the data on her com.

I look up at Tier and his eyes glow a little as he looks past me to Isten. He's about to say something when Lucan walks in.

"Good morning, 039. You will leave tomorrow, so we have a lot of business to go over. Report."

Tier stands up. "We are nine," he looks over to Ashur and Braun, "and we will act like a complete team. Am I clear?"

Both Ash and Braun manage a decent, "Yes, sir."

Tier continues. "Isten and Junco are twined. Isten will report."

Isten stands. "Feels fucking spectacular." And then he sits.

I laugh a little, I can't help myself.

"Junco?" Lucan draws my attention back to him. "Is this how you feel as well?"

I nod as I stand. "Yes, I'm happy with it. Our training went well, we are matched fairly with skill, and I think we'll be productive." I sit as they all look at me. "What? I can be professional when I want to."

Lucan smiles at me then moves his attention. "Ashur?"

Ash stands up and scratches his chin. "Ready to go, Lucan. Junco was fitted with armor and assigned weapons. Everyone will have to wear a dosimeter to catch the rads we'll encounter since the whole fucking place is glowing. The new armor also has anti-rad shielding on it and everyone gets a potassium iodine implant, so that will help. We're gonna go over there today and try it all out, make adjustments, then pack it up for the trip. After drop, Arel will go with Tier's team, be backup spotter for Is or Juncs, and do his comms and hacking from the rear. Rikan and Mish will take point for all contact. Braun and I will be front support."

Lucan nods. "Braun?"

Braun stands as Ashur sits. "We've got a half-dozen bunker-busters on ship now, one hundred thousand projectile rounds, ten thousand plasma charges, emergency armor, emergency evac and vac suits, terrestrial and space beacons, ship comms, on-Earth comms, and everyone will have a new ammo belt." He looks around at us and smiles. "I think you'll like it."

"Ryse?"

Ryse has a hard time checking his grin as he stands. "We've got a sweet ride this time, guys, the Tactical Blue, *She's All Mine*. This will be her second mission, just coming off outer systems patrols. She's got slick silver so we'll be able to hang about a little in the atmosphere and not be detected if necessary. She's also got offensive capabilities, so if you need anything, just ask. We'll have three backup teams on board – the 399, the 057, and the 011 – and we'll be dropping you from upper stratosphere into the Northern Territories where the last comms came out of to keep our presence under wraps for as long as possible. Junco, I don't know if you're airborne?"

"Not from that altitude, no."

"You'll tandem with Isten then."

And then Lucan is back to Tier. They exchange looks and Tier stands. "Objective one is to establish a secure low-Earth orbit for the jump sequence. After the drop Ryse will maintain slick-silver cover and the ship will function as base camp for the backup teams and science camp for Layla.

"We will jump from high strat into the Northern Territories and objective two will be to find and secure Moju. We have an idea where he might be and we've received signals over the past few months to alert us on movement. Junco is lead for this objective.

"Third, when Moju is secured and debriefed we will proceed to locate and extract the remaining four Siblings. Again, we've had intel on where they might be and how that might go, but we'll discuss it later. Ashur and I are leads for this objective.

"This is a planned six-day ground mission with a maximum allotment of ten days per our agreement with the Polar Friendly. If we require longer then they will not give aid if we need it. We'll go in and get the fuck out as quick as possible, let's not make this a big deal. Death beacons will activate with the armor and you will all come home with me no matter what happens. Rendezvous points will be determined once we have final jump coordinates."

Lucan nods. "Layla, report on science."

Layla stands, her back to us. "We have five morph tanks, just in case" – she turns around to see us – "just in case, you never know, right? So five. We think they've probably all been morphed since they are so close to the twenty-year limit, but you can never be too sure. We've also fit the lab with a full genomic sequencing and alteration station and will be able to make adjustments en route home, should the need arise. I have hand-picked four assistants, so we're set in science. I'll bring the KI implants over to your gear-up this afternoon and you'll all get injected for anti-radiation precautions. No whining, you babies." She turns to us again and nods, then takes her seat.

Lucan smiles, his gaze lingering on each of us as he goes down the line. "You are easily the best trained and most gifted warriors the avian have ever had. If this can be done, you will be the team to do it. I have complete faith in you. Please come home alive."

I see him swallow and I feel the uncertainty in him. Isten picks it up and we both share a wave of sadness.

"Dismissed."

We get up and head for the door to make our way to the armory.

"Junco?" I turn back to Lucan. "I will visit with you tonight, if that's OK?"

I nod. "Yeah, sure."

And then I turn and fall in with the team. Everyone in the outer offices watches as we move together and for the first time I feel the expectations and hope they've laid on us. Isten drapes his arm over my shoulder as we walk, pulling me into the oneness of what makes the 039 stand alone among millions.

Chapter Nine

The evening wind in the upper parts of the habitat picks my hair up and gently flaps it against my face as I sit on the 039 terrace swing. Laughter from the poker game inside drifts out and makes me smile as I listen to their conversation. They are such men.

My foot dips down and gives the swing another push just as Tier appears. "Had enough of them already?"

He sits next to me, making the swing lose its rhythm for a second, and then his foot corrects it. "Nah, Juncs. I just miss ya, that's all. And now Isten gets all the fun parts." He looks over to me and his smile falters. "I'm just having a hard time remembering why I took this job again in the first place."

I swallow and keep my eyes trained out on the blur of traffic. "Well, you didn't have to let us do it, you know? You could have just told him no."

He takes my hand and squeezes. "No, Juncs. I couldn't. We'll lose for sure if yer not tied to him. I saw it."

I look up, startled. "You saw it?"

He nods and then looks away. "And before ya ask, I don't know anything else." His gaze returns to my face. "Yer a total interference. Nothing makes sense when yer in the equation. Lucan can't see ya very well either, ya know. That's why he never saw yer whole plan out there in Deliverance."

I wait, watching him struggle with the words. Patient.

"He would've never let ya do that, Junco." He stops again and takes a few seconds. "If he'd of known how ya felt."

"It was Kush that pushed me over. It just stopped making sense at that point. And I–" He squeezes my hand again. We've never talked about that night before. When we had our time together we just pretended it never happened. "I thought for sure you were gonna die, Tier. And I had already made up my mind that I was going with you if you did. There wasn't a chance that I was gonna let you die and then walk away like I did with Isec. Not a fucking chance. It took a lot of killing, but I finally found my bottom."

He puts his arm around me and I lean into his chest.

"And I hate to say this, but even though Sera said I was reborn, that it was a true resurrection, I don't feel unburdened. It's heavier than ever, Tier. I feel overburdened. I need someone constant, I can't take being pulled in all these directions."

He strokes my hair but has no words for me.

"Those weeks we spent together were exactly what I needed. You have no idea how perfect that was. And then I come back and I'm at Lucan's house. And he's there to help me, and direct me, and talk things through with. So I adjust." I look away and sigh. "But even though I'm pretty good at adjusting, most of the time, anyway – it's about consistency." I stop and frown so hard my head begins to throb. "Tier, I'm tired. I'm tired of adjusting. I need more than this or I won't make it."

He pulls my head closer to him and nods.

"And then Isten shows up and I'm twined to him. And that's good too. I'm not complaining, Isten is great. I love it. Really. But now he says I should rely on him."

I sit up now and look at him in the face. "So my question is, which of you should I look to, Tier? For guidance? I'm confused. I can't listen to all of you, I just need my one true direction. Which of you will point me there?"

His eyes get glassy as I stare at them and I look away.

"Junco, I want to tell ya it's me, but for now it isn't." He turns my head back and lifts my chin so I have to look at him. "It's Isten. The only way we'll make it is if yer tied to Isten on Earth. That's all I know. And I'm sorry if it's confusing, I understand that. Especially with all the shit that's happened ta ya."

We sit there for a few minutes, the swing soothing me back to calm.

"When we get to Earth, Junco–"

I look up again when he doesn't continue. "What?"

"Yer gonna be yanked in so many more directions yer head will spin, darlin'." He reaches into his pocket and pulls something out and then presses it into my palm. I bring it up to my face and watch the light from passing traffic bounce off the reflective surface.

"What is it?"

He takes the small silver disk from me and opens it up. I have to use my night vision to see the little convex glass inside and then I smile. "It's true north, Juncs. It's true north, that's what. It doesn't work here, no consistent magnetic field, right? But on Earth, it'll point ya in the right direction, OK?"

I take the little silver compass back and watch it spin relentlessly. I can relate to the pointer because that's how I feel. Spinning and spinning and never coming to a stop, no matter how hard I try.

"On Earth–" He stops again.

"Oh fuck, Tier, please just say it."

"Yer gonna find more truth than ya ever wanted. The clones, Junco, it's out of control. Yer gonna see people ya thought were dead."

My heart almost stops. "Who?"

He shrugs. "Aren for sure."

"Yeah, I already know that part."

He sighs. "Lucan is up on the flyer terrace waitin'. He says he has a gift for ya." He gets up and pulls me with him and then walks me over to the stairs. "I wish I could spend the night with ya, Juncs. But I can't. I promise though, I promise that we'll have time for that later, OK?"

My breathing becomes erratic but I turn away and begin to climb the stairs. When I get to the top I look back, but he's already gone inside. Lucan is sitting on the short wall on the other side of the building, probably to stay out of Kadian's spyglass. I walk over and pull myself together, trying desperately to stop the spinning.

Lucan stands. "You're scared?"

I let out a little laugh and it makes my head hurt more. "No, Lucan. You're scared. I'm sad."

He holds out a notebook. "Esta said to give you this. We're not having the send-off I promised the media tomorrow. In fact, you'll be leaving in a few hours so when we're done here, let the team know."

I nod.

Then he takes what's left of my disfigured hand and holds up my index finger. "I have a gift for you." He looks down at me and smiles so big it's contagious. I sniff and wipe my other hand across my face. "It's a little pinprick now, Junco." And then he pricks the tip of my index finger with a small device. It bleeds for a fraction and then it's over.

"That was it?" I laugh.

He smiles again. "You are the only person who has this gift. I made it specially for you."

"What is it?"

"It's a summons. If you rub your thumb and index finger together, I will appear. No matter where you are in the universe, I will be there." I look down at the hidden power my fingertip contains and blink. "Of course, if you're far away, like on Earth for example, and you summon me, it will take me" – he stops to calculate the time – "exactly eighteen minutes and twenty-three seconds to get there." He stops, proud of himself, and I laugh up at him. "But I will come if you really need me. So when you find yourself in trouble, in that last moment, Junco, when you truly have no more options. Use the summons and call for me by rubbing your fingers together."

"Wow. So, the next time I want orange juice in the middle of the night I can just snap my fingers and you'll deliver it to me? That is some fucking gift!"

"Yes, funny, funny. It's for a single emergency. But use it if you feel threatened, Junco. Please. If it's not the right moment, not essential that I come, then I won't appear. But I'd rather it be a false alarm than not have you come back home, so don't guess. Just try it if you think you need me. And–"

He stops for too long and I have to prod him to go on with a wave of my hand.

"If you get other offers, on Earth? Just know that we love you here. We do. And if you think you might want to take one, then please call for me on your comm so I can find a way to give you whatever it is you need."

"Lucan, I'm not gonna take that job offer from that Subjack guy, OK?"

He nods and looks away from me, like he can't look me in the face. "I never properly expressed my thanks for what you did, so before you leave I'd like for you to know how much I appreciate your sacrifice."

"What're you talking about?"

His small laugh makes me smile. Some things about Lucan seem so out of place and these little human-like gestures always surprise me. In a good way.

"You saved Tier, Junco. I cannot put into words how relieved I am." His eyes close as he turns away again. "You did what I could not. I owe you." When he looks back at me his expression is very serious. "I owe you, do you understand?"

I shake my head. "No, not really."

"I owe you. And this gift can't even come close. Whatever you need, you will just ask. Understand?"

"OK."

"I'll see you off in a little bit. Make sure to pack things to keep you occupied on the trip. It takes about two and half weeks."

I reach over and give him a hug. "Thank you for the gift. If I need you I'll use it."

He smiles and then he is gone.

I go back inside and repeat Lucan's announcement but the team doesn't pay much attention to me. Tier is not around and I find Isten sitting on the window seat in our dark bedroom. By the time I change into my shorts and tank top he's in bed with the covers open so I can climb in. His wings wrap me up and I lay my head on his chest and count.

Chapter Ten

Ryse was right to be impressed with our transportation, it's fabulous even though I don't have anything to compare it to. All four teams bunk in the same room on the ship and we are stacked four high with barely enough room to move around inside the cocoon-like berths. They are molded against the side of the bulkhead and have a little curtain that covers the open side, so at least there's that.

I'm fascinated at everything at first. The clanking sound my boots make on the grated decks, the hum of the ventilation system, the on-ship light-G fields, the stick pads that keep my feet on the deck in the free-G areas, and of course, the portholes that let me stargaze as we move through the system towards Earth. Every time I even think the word I get butterflies, that's how excited I am.

Tier and I settle into our new normal, which is pretty much limited to eating our meals together. Isten, Arel, and I spend a lot of time going over field scenarios, while Rikan, Mish, and Braun do the same. Ashur, of all people, spends most evenings with me looking at Esta's translations in the notebook Lucan passed to me during our final meeting. If I figured one of them would be interested in that crap, I might have picked Ryse. But Ryse almost never surfaces from the cockpit.

I practice with the new armor. Isten has to help me put it on and take it off because the shirt and wing seams are very complicated. It really stifles my movements too. I spend the first week training pretty hard in it, making sure I can do some moves that I rely on in close combat. But the fucking gravity is so variable across the training space that this is almost pointless and finally I give it up. Whatever time I get to adjust to it in the Northern Territories before the real action begins will just have to be good enough.

The wing protection is a light-weight, spray-on, slick silver polymer that I won't be able to check out until we're ready for jump. Once applied it helps protect the feathers from burns, like a fire-retardant, and it takes thirty days for the bonds to break and flake off. In the interest of making sure we're all equipped to the same standard on drop, they can't let me give it a try or mine will be substantially degraded by the time we're engaged.

Two weeks into the journey Isten finds me reading Esta's translations of the Fledge church doorway in the forward observation bunk. There's barely enough room in here for one person let alone two, but he forces himself in and pushes me against the bulkhead.

"Junco, I've been patient with you, but that's enough. Stop reading that shit." I don't even look up. We've had this conversation at least once a day since we left Amelia. He turns on his side and leans down into my face. "What can you possibly find in there that is so interesting?"

Now I do turn, but I'm annoyed with his pestering and he knows it. "Isten, this shit is actually describing the creation of man. It's pretty important."

He laughs and I feel it from the inside as well as hear it from the outside. "It's bullshit, Junco. None of that is true. Don't waste your time."

"Then why is Lucan's name in here, huh?"

He shakes his head at me. "It's not Lucan's name, Juncs. It's a derivative. He doesn't own that name, and he might be old, but he's not that fucking old."

"How do you know? Ash says–"

"Ash is just trying to make you notice him again and avoid that stupid Lili girl at the same time. Why they let her come along I'll never understand."

"She's on Monk's team, what should they have done, left her on Amelia? Hey, Lili – you can be part of our team, but guess what? We're going on an important mission now and you have to stay home?"

Isten exhales. "I would have made both of you stay home if it were up to me."

I can't even bring myself to waste the breath it would cost to answer that, so I turn back to the notebook. "Look, here's the cuneiform image, right?" I point to a glyph that represents light and I feel Isten notice it in his head, then continue. "And this is Lucan's glyph right next to it. It says Lucan, not some derivative, Isten. It's spelled out clear as day."

He shrugs. "So what?"

"So he was there."

"So what?"

"He played a part in the creation of men and the avian too. That doesn't interest you?"

"No, it really doesn't. Lucan is not God, Junco. He's a raging asshole most of the time, just because he likes you and treats you special doesn't make him a nice guy. Or God, for fuck's sake."

"No, he's definitely not God. That much I know." I feel Isten's interest perk up a bit, so I stay silent and make him say what's on his mind. It takes a few minutes of silence, but in the end he does.

"So who is he?"

I smile in victory. "See, you do want to know!"

"Say it, Juncs, or I'll never pretend to be interested in your hobbies again."

I hold down my smile and look up at him. "He's the Fallen Archer, Isten. It's him. Not that girl on the post hanging in the Fledge Church."

"Bahhhhhh – I'm out of here." And he is. He rolls over and jumps down from the bunk and walks away. I sit there laughing, feeling for his emotions as his boots clank down the deck. He's laughing too. He thinks I'm an idiot.

I don't think you're an idiot, Junco. His thoughts come back at me like we're in the same room and I jump a little. *I think you're bored.*

You can read my thoughts?

And you can read mine. Welcome to the perfection that is twine.

Do you always know what I'm thinking?

Yeah, so stop fucking fantasizing about Tier's babies.

I choke down a gasp and jump down to chase after him. I catch him just as he walks into the mess and pull him back out. "Isten, come here now."

He smiles and shakes his head at me. "Hand over the notebook first. I'm taking it away and you're not getting it back."

I give it over. "You don't say a word, you got it?"

He leans down and kisses me on the cheek, then swats my head with the rolled-up notebook and walks off in the opposite direction calling back to me, "I'm gonna fling this out the airlock, Junco. Not fucking kidding."

"What's that all about?"

I pivot into Tier as my breath huffs out and blows hair above my eyes. "Nothing, ready for lunch?" He smiles and guides me to the machines with a hand on my back.

I spend the rest of the day experimenting on how far away from Isten I have to be to block my thoughts from him. I locate him, then walk until I run out of deck and call his name in my head.

He answers every fucking time.

Probably everyone on the *She's All Mine* is thinking there's no privacy but they might as well have their own top-floor suite in an Earth hotel compared to what I'm dealing with. I push Tier so far out of my mind I barely want to eat with him at dinner. By the time I'm ready for sleep I'm a worried mess. The last thing I need is Isten shooting his mouth off about my private thoughts.

Chapter Eleven

The suborbital shudders as we enter the North American airstream and I sink down into my seat as the gravity comes back. I look across the table at my dad, but he's absorbed in the day's work on the screen in front of him. I unbuckle myself, check to see if he'll stop me, and when he doesn't I get up and walk over to my bags across the ship.

It's a private military transport but we use it when we go on our birthday week trips, just in case we have to leave on some emergency. I unzip the garment bag that hangs on the hook near the bathroom and take out my crisp cadet uniform.

I don't know if anyone else is excited about the first day of cadet school, but I certainly am. My smile is big and when I look back over at my dad, he's smiling right along with me.

"Do you need help?"

I shake my head at him. "No, I got it."

I take off my vacation clothes, stopping for a moment to check the gash that mutant left on my calf a few weeks ago, and then start assembling myself into a soldier. In training, anyway. Not that I need more training, but whatever. I'm a real RR soldier now, not a state secret.

Everything is soft and does not feel stiff and new even though I've never worn this uniform before. They are good to me at home sometimes. Very good to me. I hate new clothes, refuse to put them on until they've been softened up in the wash. And someone at home went to the trouble to soften up my uniform and then press it flat to make it look crisp. Most of my body is still sunburned from lying on a Hawaiian beach for the past week, so this little attention to detail makes me even happier then it normally would.

I tug on the undershirt and pull on the socks and pants before my dad speaks again. "You can give me your SEAR now, Junco. I'll keep it for you."

There were no jobs on Hawaii. Birthday week is for vacation only, unless there's an emergency or something. But I always get to keep my SEAR when I'm away from the RR, just in case I get separated from the guards. I walk over and hand it to him and watch as he slips it into the breast pocket of his service uniform jacket.

I go back and continue getting dressed, buttoning up and tucking in the short-sleeved shirt, then fastening the belt and pulling on the new boots that shine in the overhead ship lights. I brush my hair, grab a hair tie and then go sit on the floor in front of my dad. "Not too tight this time."

He sighs behind me as he swivels his chair and gathers up my hair to braid it. When he gets to the end I reach back with the elastic tie in my hand and he takes it, twisting it into my hair to hold his work together.

I get back up and grab my hat, then go to the mirror so I can put it on. I hate the hat, but it's required for services and as soon as we land in Peaks the hovercopter will take us right over to Council 1 for the welcome ceremony and check in. They'll probably be waiting for us, we were late taking off.

I check myself in the mirror one last time then go back and sit across from my dad and look out the window. The view of Earth below is clear of clouds and I can see the mountains, so we must be close.

"They'll wait, you know."

I look over at him. "Yeah, I know. But I don't want them to wait. Then everyone will think I get special privileges because I'm your daughter."

He smiles. "You do get special privileges, Junco. You cannot change who you are."

I shrug. "I just don't want them to know that on the very first day."

"Michael will be at the barn every Friday, Saturday, and Sunday at 0900. So make sure you're always there. No exceptions. If you need to cancel for some reason, you show up first, then ask for a day off. You have trials for Worlds in February and it's very important that you qualify so you can compete in the championships in Sydney next spring."

"Yeah, OK." But I don't want to think about what will happen in Sydney next spring besides my aerialist competition.

"Monday through Thursday you have private piano with Mrs. Strauss from 1100 to 1300. You'll meet her today."

I nod and look out the window. The peaks of the MR mountains have snow on them already, even though it's only the second week of September.

"I have a new power for you, Junco."

A slight panic consumes me as I think about my last fight with that prairie lion. I lost.

Matthew came to the house and yelled for two days, telling anyone who'd listen that I lost that fight. But my dad finally got sick of him and pulled rank. He had him removed from Council 3 and returned to Stag Camp, still complaining the whole way there I bet.

He recognizes the look on my face. "Not that kind of power. You will not go to camp again until cadets are over. You'll come home for holidays and summers until you graduate."

"That's a gift," I say. "Not a power."

He ignores my statement. "Do you know why I'm sending you to cadets, Junco?"

I shrug and look out the window again. "To do my duty. Like everyone else."

He laughs. "Your duty was fulfilled years ago. No, that's not why."

My eyes track back to him. "Then why?"

"To make friends. And have fun. Have a lot of fun, Junco. But do not fall behind on your studies, sport, or piano. And do not get caught. Do you understand me?"

My brows scrunch together as I study his face. "You want me to work hard and if I do that, then I can break the rules, as long as I don't get caught. Is that what you just said?"

He nods. "You have three behavior rules you will not break. Are you ready to hear them?"

"Yes."

"You will not talk about your home life or family, including HOUSE. You will not talk about camp, training or missions. You will not talk about weapons not available to you on campus."

"Is that it?" That can't possibly be it.

"That's it." He hesitates for a second. "Well, don't kill anyone unless it's absolutely necessary. Even if they tell you to try your best in training, don't try your best."

Duh.

"Only try your best in studies, sport, and piano. Unless you really need to kill someone, of course. I'll leave it up to you, just know you'll have to account for it."

I think about this for a few seconds. "Is that my power? Kill if I have to?"

He lets out a little laugh. "No, Junco. I just don't want to make a rule that might make you hesitate to protect yourself. That's all."

"Then what's my power?"

He smiles. "Smile, Junco. Smiles are powerful. That's how you make friends. You just smile."

I look away and let my grin spread across my face even though I try to tuck it down. "I know that."

"And when the boys start asking you for attention, you just smile at them. Boys only want one thing, and it's not a smile. So if that's all you give them and they accept it, then you'll know you found a good one."

My face gets hot as I look out the window. "I don't want to talk about boys with you, Dad."

He laughs and goes back to his screen.

But I do want to think about boys in my head and my new life as Junco the cadet. Today is a really good day.

Isten's hand on my shoulder pulls me up from the dream. He's kneeling on the floor outside my berth and he cups a hand over my mouth as I start to make noise.

"Shh," he whispers. "Just me. You OK?"

I swallow. "Yeah, just a dream."

His eyes search mine and he waits.

I wait too. But he stays silent. "It was just a dream, Isten."

"You sure about that? It felt like a memory to me. And that means your dad–"

"Enough. Leave me alone, get out of my head."

He exhales. "OK. Go back to sleep then."

And then he's gone.

Chapter Twelve

The remaining days are a blur of jump preparations. I've parachuted several times over the years but I'm no expert and I'm nervous even though Isten feeds me memories of his previous jumps. All of which were executed flawlessly. Expect the worst has always been my motto and as long as I'm in the business of soldiering, that's not gonna change.

When we're not preparing I'm looking out the porthole on the forward observation bunk, watching as the small dot of light turns into a swirling blue ball. My stomach feels flighty at the thought of Earth and I automatically swallow down the urge to hurl as I look out at it.

You OK, Junco?

Isten is so in my business since the telepathy kicked in, it's not even funny.

Fine, Is. Just getting nervous.

I hear his boots clanking down the deck and then his face appears in the bunk. "Come on, we're gonna spray wings and do a dry run for tomorrow."

I jump down and follow him back to the gear room. "We have to wear suits and armor? I'm not even gonna be able to move. Why can't we just use those blue light thingys? Like when you guys came to my house?"

He ignores me as we walk into the crowd of warriors in the gear room. I've asked everyone this same thing and they're tired of repeating the answer. But I figure the worst they can say is no. And maybe, you never know, but maybe they get tired of me bitching about it and change their minds? Or maybe they realize my idea is just bet–

Holy fuck, Junco. We're not gonna change our minds. Give it up.

Asshole, you need to respect my private thoughts. When I want to talk to you I'll–

"Tier, Junco has been having these really strange dreams, man. You should really ask her what's up."

I stare up at him with my mouth open. "Isten, what the fuck?"

Tier comes over and leans down to kiss me, hands cupped around my face and full on the mouth even, in front of everyone.

I feel Isten's anger and kiss him back before coming up for air. "Whew, thanks!"

Tier slips his arm around me and looks over to Isten. "Isten, our deal is over. You've crossed the line too many times." Then he kisses me again and walks off to check that all the suits are ready.

I laugh at Is and poke him in the chest. "See, that's what you get for being a jerk. Stay out!"

He pulls me over to the bench in front of my locker and throws my armor at me. "A deal's a deal, Junco. Don't even think about it or I'll make your life hell inside."

I roll my eyes. "Just show me how to get in this thing."

The wing protection is sprayed on in a fine mist that coats them as I flex and contract to allow access to each feather. It feels heavy at first, making them droop a little, but in a few minutes they begin to dry and when it's all done, they feel lighter than ever and can change color to blend in with the environment around me.

That one procedure alone takes hours.

Then hours more getting into the jump suit. The final leg of the dry run is the helmet seal and suit pressurization. The helmet encasement has a sun visor that makes me think of a bird's beak. Maybe it's psychological and induces fear, to have a winged warrior coming at you looking like a prehistoric predatory bird, who knows?

As soon as the helmet snaps closed on my head and they start pressurizing me, I wanna barf. It's only then that I'm truly thankful for having Isten's voice in my head, because hurling in your helmet is not good. Not good.

Sera comes on and my vital signs and other health information begins scrolling across my field of vision. It makes me dizzy. *Fucking knock it off, Sera. I'm gonna fucking puke here.*

Isten shoots me a funny look and I shake my head and swallow down the sudden accumulation of saliva that has collected in my mouth.

They make me sit there for the entire fifteen minutes of simulated jump time and I tell ya, that was the longest fucking fifteen minutes of my life. Tier unsnaps my helmet and pulls it off when my time's up and I run to the head and retch so hard my chest scar hurts.

Tier follows me in and holds my hair until I surface. I wipe my hand across my mouth and let out a deep breath. "Thanks, I don't know what came over me. I've never been claustrophobic before."

His eyes are serious and dark as he studies my face. "Is that what it was?"

I smile. "Yeah, and some nerves too. I'm excited and nervous about going back to Earth, but the jump scares the shit out of me, Tier, I'm not gonna lie."

He looks at me for a few more seconds before accepting my answer. "Isten loves jumping, so yer with the right guy, Junco. Plus there's no way to mess it up really, ya have wings." He shrugs. "The chutes disintegrate at a thousand feet and then Isten will disengage and you'll coast on in and follow us."

I let out a little laugh. "Yeah, I know, but it's hard to shake the fear of heights that comes with being human, ya know? And what if I don't glide in right? What if I crash to the ground or–"

Tier cuts me off. "Junco, it's no different than flying down from the top of the mast at Fledge. Same stuff, OK?"

"Yeah, OK. I'll get it under control."

He puts a hand on my shoulder. "That's not what I'm telling ya, darlin'. I'm telling ya to believe me, not deal with it. Believe me. It'll be fine." His smile calms me as he pulls me in. "It's gonna be fine. Besides, what do ya wanna bet that you'll be so consumed with the view of your home planet that you'll forget all about jumping?"

"Yeah, I can't wait for that, really. It will be a once-in-a-lifetime experience. Literally, right? Just the one jump? I don't want to do this ever again."

He laughs.

"No, really, Tier – I do believe you. You're my foundation of truth these days." He waits as I drink some water and then we walk back to the gear room and I start removing the many layers of suit and clothes that make my body look like a walking black marshmallow.

I find Layla alone in the science lab later. She's standing in front of a table trying to make her various charts and tech items behave. More specifically, she's trying to keep them from floating away.

She turns as I enter. The stick pad automatically activates as my boots come in contact with her deck and make a ripping sound with each step. "Junco, can you help me for a minute?" I grab a few items that try and get past me and hold on to them as she gets everything secured down. "The fucking grav field in here is terrible. I've complained to Ryse so many times, but he's not interested in anything but his stupid–"

"Layla," I interrupt, "how likely would it be that I'm" – I stop and put up as many walls I can think of to screen my mind from Isten – "pregnant?"

She blinks at me. Several times. "Pregnant, Junco?"

I nod. "Yeah." I stop and sigh. "I've been sick and I'm no expert, but I have been – before – ya know? So I have an idea of what it feels like and it feels like–"

"Pregnant?" Her mouth stays open a little after the word comes out. "With Tier's?"

"It can't be Kush's child, right? That was months and months ago before I cut my chest open. And well, I'm not sure if it's even possible for Tier to get me pregnant, but maybe you could just check me out? I don't feel well, Layla. And maybe it's the nerves about the jump, but I haven't puked over a mission since I was fourteen. I'm nervous, sure, but this is not typical behavior for me."

"He'll never let you do the mission if I check you out, Junco."

"Well, we don't have to tell him, *obviously*."

She shakes her head at me. "I'd have to tell him, I work at his direction only, so if I run tests I have to report. It's not like it is with you guys, I have to–"

"OK, never mind then. I'm not gonna fuck up this mission over some stupid nerves. It's just nerves, right?"

She stares at me like I just grew an eyeball out of my armpit. "Right. Yeah, nerves. I wish I had something for nerves, Juncs. But I don't, sorry. I wouldn't even know where to begin, actually. I mean avians don't get – nerves. So, that's not something I've ever done before. Maybe there's a doctor on Earth that does that stuff? In the Northern Territories?"

I sigh and sit down on a stool that's stuck to the deck. "How the hell would I manage that, Layla?"

She shakes her head at me. "It's one week, Juncs. Can you sit on it for a week? I mean, it's ten days at the most. I'll up your anti-rad dose just to make sure, OK?"

I nod and stand up, inhaling the reconditioned air deep enough to make me sick. "Yeah, all right. I'm sure it's nothing anyway, right? I mean, is it even possible?"

She looks away. "Oh, it's possible, Junco. Just not something that ever happens with us. But you're not really" – she swallows – "no offense or anything, but you've got abilities I don't, so I have no idea. I'm not qualified to advise you on this at all."

"Don't say anything, Layla. It's very bad manners to say anything about this topic until the people involved want the news to get out. Understand?"

She smiles and walks over to me, then squeezes both of my shoulders. "I won't, Junco."

I leave with plans to go to the mess, then divert to the dorm when my stomach heaves and climb in my bunk instead. Lucan's ominous words filter back into my thoughts *Who knows what would have happened to that baby. It might not even have survived.* So the parts of me that are human allow me to get pregnant apparently. But the parts of me that aren't human make sure I'll never have a baby. If this is how it works, God is beyond cruel.

Isten walks in a few minutes later and I pretend to be asleep and stay out of his mind so I don't have to talk to him.

Eventually I do fall asleep, and eventually Isten comes back to pester me, but I keep my back to him and my mind to myself. He doesn't take the hint this time, and climbs in, pressing up against me. "Isten, I don't want you to sleep here tonight."

"It's not Isten."

I turn and smile, then peek through the opening in my curtain to see if Isten is nearby. "What are you doing in here?"

Tier lifts me up a little and slides his arm and wing under me, then pulls me close. "Shit, Junco – what good is being captain if I can't make my own rules?"

I sink into him. "True, I'm not complaining. Stay all night, OK?"

I feel him nod behind me. "I fully plan on it."

We're quiet for a few minutes and I wonder if Layla broke her word, or if Isten got wind of what I was thinking and told him. But I let it go. I doubt he'd have this much self-control if he thought I was keeping *that* from him.

"I'm gonna quit, Junco."

I turn to look at him. "Quit? How come?"

He drags his fingers across my forehead, swiping the hair from my eyes, and then traces the scar along the side of my head. "I'm tired too. I don't want to do it anymore. I don't even want to be on this mission right now, to tell ya the truth. But yer here and that's the only reason I agreed to come back to the 039. That and having a chance to get a nine again, especially since it's you. That's probably the highlight of my whole career, ya know that?"

He stops for a few seconds and I stay silent so he can continue. "To be honest, I was kinda loving the new Fledge team, Juncs. It was all so easy – trainin' them. Like a normal job. But being captain of the 039 is not a job, Junco. It's a life. Did ya know that we hadn't been back to Amelia in five years? I mean fuck, I was younger than you when I left Amelia the last time. I've spent more time on Earth than I have in the Band. Far more. It makes it hard, ya know? When we come home and have to settle in again. People don't know us, they don't really like our power and status, and they have a difficult time trusting us. Especially me."

I search his eyes. They aren't glowing at all, which, from my extrapolation over the past few months, means the topic is not eliciting wild emotions. In Tier, this means his mind is made up. "Yeah, I can see why that might suck. You're looking for a new normal."

He smiles and his eyes do glow a little this time. "Exactly, darlin'. That's exactly it."

"Lucan says you can be an Archer."

He huffs out some air and laughs. "Yeah, well, I got news for him – I'm not interested in being an Archer. Fuck, I'd rather stay captain of the 039 than be an administrator of some backwater habitat."

"Oh, is that what they do?"

"Well, ya know the ones like Rache, or Lucan or even Gib, they got it made with their appointments. Lucan runs both Aves and Fledge, Gib runs Clutch, and Rache runs Justice. They're like the power triangle as far as Archers go. I'd be a nobody, they'd just give me some newly created hab as far from Amelia as they could get me. They can't stand me, Junco. I doubt if Lucan even gives a shit anymore."

"He does, Tier. I can tell."

He smiles and then leans in and kisses me, his hand grasping behind my neck to urge me closer. When he pulls back his words come out in a whisper. "He loves you, darlin', and you love me. It seems that love, with Lucan anyway, is completely transferable."

I laugh. "Whatever works, right?"

His eyes brighten with his upturned mouth. "Right. I'll take what I can get these days."

"I was planning on quitting too. As soon as Isten said we're not allowed to be together if we're on the same team. I was ready to quit that first night at the sniper camp. But I promised to do this and everyone seems to think I can make it happen." I shrug. "So, whatever. I told Lucan I'd do it, but I don't want a life of missions anymore."

He breathes out and looks up. "Exactly. A life of missions is hardly a life." He slips his hand under my shirt and it slides inside my pants and rubs the sensitive skin that covers my dock. I have a brief moment of panic. "Ya don't take it out much. How come?"

I slow my heartbeat and then internally thank God he's talking about my weapon and not my possible change in health status. "What's the point? I'm not going to use it on anyone around here. Like Isten said, my only real skill in battle is killing people. That really hit home for me. And he's right. I'm not a warrior, I'm a killer. I can't protect myself if I can't kill."

"Nah, Juncs. Ya did a fine job in the Deliverance fight. I was watching most of it."

"Yeah, but what you don't know is that I made the decision the minute my feet came unstuck to kill them all–" I stop when I realize what I said. "Except Kush, I mean. I never intended to kill Kush. That was an accident."

He nods and brings his hand back up to my waist to pull me in. "I get it. And that's the real reason you don't want to use the SEAR. Isn't it?"

I haven't thought about it, but it must be pretty obvious to people. "Well, maybe some of it is. But believe me, if I see that fucking Aren on Earth, he's getting his head sliced off again no matter how done I am with this life."

He doesn't meet my gaze. "We'll worry about him when we have to. But tonight," his hand slips back down inside my pants, "Isten and his high and mighty rules can go to hell." And then his mouth covers mine and I close my eyes and allow myself to enjoy him like it's our last night together.

Chapter Thirteen

Isten is the height of military professionalism the next day and I feel a little guilty for breaking our agreement. He carefully helps me suit up and sends me encouraging thoughts as helmet time nears. I'm not worried about the fucking helmet. I'm not even worried about the jump really. I mean, sure, it's a little crazy to think of how long we'll be falling, but even if the chute fails, and it won't, but even if it did, I have a perfectly good pair of fucking wings.

My head is back on straight as far as the mission goes. I roll my neck until it cracks and then stretch my wings out as far as I can in the cramped staging room, giving them a good flap for emphasis. But I'm a little worried about all the other fucking shit stacking up around me.

I check that everything I carry is secured enough to withstand the wind force we'll experience as we fall and feel satisfied. We are packed up good, but I carry the most because I'm the lightest and the extra weight will get me on the ground about the same time as the rest of my team. If the suit dock wasn't in light-G, I'd be on the floor right now from the extra weight.

My mini-plasma is strapped to my thigh, Big Boy, my full plasma and my projectile assault are on my back, and my 50 cal is strapped to the front. I have just enough cartridges, mags and rounds to get me through a ground battle at landing. My other thigh carries enough field rations for a week, and a few other emergency provisions.

Arel carries Isten's 50 cal and he and everyone else has an extra assault rifle plus their own weapons and the bulk of the ammo and rations.

When I turn around to see where we're at as far as time goes, everyone but Isten and I has their helmet on. The on-board computer is counting down the minutes to the jump when Layla enters. I watch as Monk helps Isten with his helmet and begins the pressurization of his suit.

"Everything going well?" Layla's smile is big, but it doesn't reach her eyes.

"If you've got bad news for me, Layla, save it for another day. I'm not in the mood right now."

She slips a small packet into a pocket on the sleeve of my suit and seals it closed, then gives me a pat on the shoulder. "No, just wanted to make sure you're OK."

Isten is fully pressurized now and Monk calls me over to him. "I'm fine. I'll talk to you once Arel gets the comms set up, OK?"

She nods and steps aside so they can seal me up.

I nod to Monk and push the helmet over my head, then watch the guys snap me up and start pressurizing. My vision screen lights up with details of the process, the temperature of the outside air, vitals, and positioning coordinates. A map floats on screen and the primary and alternate landing beacons are blinking.

"Com check. One." Tier's voice comes through my helmet as thin and tinny, but clear. We sound off in order and when they hear me say comm check nine every helmet nods and the good lucks and back-slapping start flying. Isten grabs my suit and clips me in front of him.

His voice comes through my comms. "Normally I have you behind me, Juncs. But since you're so small, might as well just put you in front. When we disengage I'll push off and then fly out in front, so you can follow me. OK?"

I nod. "Sure. Sounds good."

"Don't extend your wings until I'm clear, got it? We'll do this at 1,000 feet. Check your altimeter on the way down. If you have a problem, let me know, but I checked it this this morning. It works."

"All right, 039." Tier's voice is back as Isten and I take our positions on the small circle that will flush us down to the lower deck, then out into the stratosphere. "Change your fate and meet your destiny." The guys all repeat it back to him, a small tradition I was unaware of until now. "Godspeed, Junco." A purely human good luck meant only for me. "I will see you all on Earth, enjoy the ride."

I whisper Godspeed to them and then the timer reaches zero and we drop down into the intermediate hold where there is a minute pause as the upper hatch closes and the locks disengage for the push, and then we are falling.

Isten calls our fall in his faraway voice that now has moments of static. "Departure altitude, 135,000 feet. Acceleration is 745 mph and increasing slightly. You OK, Junco?"

The view. I think it and it prints out on my helmet vision screen.

"You can talk until Tier calls for silence, Juncs."

"Sorry, I was just thinking to myself and Sera printed – never mind. Between the two of you there's not a private thought in my head."

"But the view, right?"

I smile. "Yeah, Is. It's pretty cool." I stare out at my home planet and push down the emotions even as the words escape involuntarily. "I'm home." I hear a collection of sighs and groans over my comm and I regret letting them in on my relief.

A series of muffled booms explode outside and scare the shit out of me until I realize we just broke the sound barrier. I smile as I picture a pink contrail speeding out behind me like the suborbitals going in for a landing back home.

"Gotta love freefall." Isten is laughing and all the other guys are shouting with excitement.

Tier interjects, "Radio silence, as of now. If you've got something to say, use the helmet screens."

The comms go quiet and I'm glad. I just want to watch the Earth as I hurl towards her.

We are flying into the early darkness of night over the Northern Territories and I'm half sorry, half relieved that I can't see Peaks or Council 3 down below. There are flickering dots of lights every once in a while, but the glory of Peak City, the planet pad, and the urban sprawl is all gone. I shake off the feeling and concentrate on the map as the landing beacons flash our position and approximate time to arrival.

Jump info is scrolling down my vision screen and I log it, but my attention is on the ground. I watch as the guys below us all pull their chutes and slip away. I follow them on my vision screen map, six dots so close together they almost look like one.

Isten pulls our chute and we fly up and settle. I can feel him pulling and making adjustments behind me as we circle, then increase speed slightly to catch up with the rest of the guys. My altimeter stops jumping wildly and flattens out with a more constant rate of descent and we fall, steady but quick, and approach the one thousand foot mark.

OK, Juncs. We're almost there.

I feel the chute start to come apart above us and have a small moment of panic. Isten gentles me inside and I calm my heartbeat. And then the chute is gone and his wings flap out and he flies with me for a few moments, banking and turning until our primary landing beacon is flashing dead center on screen.

Ready?

Ready.

And then he's gone. I fall for a second, look behind me and then extend my wings. They catch the air, and lift me briefly, then I move the wrong way and the air slips past my feathers making me tumble a little. I pivot my posterior shoulders and make the correction until I have control over the hissing air as it catches in my canopy. I play with the angle of my wing tips and my acceleration changes slightly.

Isten zooms out ahead of me and I dive after him, wings pointed down my back, remembering my ride across the grasslands on Moju. My face is starting to hurt from smiling, but I don't stop.

I'm really here.

I'm really home.

And I have wings.

All right, let's get this fucking show on the road so I can get the hell out of here and pack up soldiering for good.

Sounds good to me, Juncs.

I have to stifle the laugh so Tier doesn't yell at me. *I was talking to me, Isten, not you!*

Hey, you don't put up the walls, I listen in. And next time you and Tier wanna have a good time, you better put up the fucking walls. Or I swear–

Yeah, whatever. Pay attention. The ground is coming up to meet you, brother.

Watch the master, little sparrow.

He glides in and lands on his feet. I follow and fall on my face as Earth's G reminds me that a small girl carrying more than twice her own weight in supplies and weapons hasn't a chance of being graceful on landing.

Tier rolls me over and sits me upright as he snaps off my helmet. His scrunched-up eyes are bright green with concern. "Shit, Junco. I was worried you'd puke the whole time."

I swipe the sweat off my forehead with the back of my disfigured hand while simultaneously slapping a mosquito off my neck with the other and look out at my world. "You don't have to worry about me, Tier. I'm working now."

He lets out a breath as Braun hoists the 50 cal from my chest. "Yeah, all right then. Let's go. We're hitting the mountaintop tonight, we'll take turns flying supplies up while you and Isten set up camp."

"Yes, sir."

I let him pull me up and unpack enough so I can fly up the mountain. I'm fucking sweating my ass off in the hot summer night, the pressure suit on top of the heavy slick-silver armor isn't making life any easier, and I've already caught myself wishing I was back at Lucan's house smoking on my breezy terrace more than once in the span of five minutes.

Camp is not a camp. We brought no tents and we make no fire. No one's tired so we just sit up there and rearrange the ammo and check and double-check our weapons and fill our ammo belts as Tier and Arel set up the comms. We make contact with Ryse and then Arel sets up a proxy beacon that will send a signal to the Northern Territories troops if they are still in this area. We don't expect a reply. If they're here, they'll come in person to make sure we are who we say we are. Now it's nothing but a miserable, humid waiting game.

At least the pressure suits are off. I'm folding mine up to stash with everyone else's, except the helmet, which doubles as armor, when I remember Layla's little packet.

I check to see what everyone's doing. Isten is off with Braun looking for water just in case our hydration packs run out, and I put up the wall. Inside the little pocket is a small envelope. I open it and shake out some pills. There's a little note with it and I unfold it in the dark and read it with the night vision.

An extra pill a day. Your twine knows.

Fuck. I reach out for Isten's position in the woods. He's not that far off and I get up to go find him.

"Junco?"

I turn towards Tier and crumple the little note up in my hand. He's sucking on a ration packet, frowning at me. "What?"

"Stay here."

I look out at the woods one more time, then sit down and sigh as I lie back on the rough wild grass. It shields me from the rest of the guys but only when I lie prone. If there's one major difference between the NT and the RR, it's the lack of care they've taken with the native mountain meadow grass. It's short, barely a foot tall anywhere you look, and sparse.

Only the conifers look familiar. Until you get up close, that is. Because most of them are wheat beetle-resistant strains that were planted less than a hundred years ago after they let the invasion decimate the old-growth forests. The Ponderosas on our ranch are – were, Junco – pushing three or four hundred years in some areas before that fucking Subjack burned the place down with nukes.

I'm starting to sour on this mission and I hope to God that seeing Moju isn't as disappointing as my reacquaintance with the home planet or I might have to lose my temper over the whole fucking nuclear strike thing.

I catch Tier looking at me again and turn away without hiding my anger. Isten was right. A mission is no place for a relationship. Tier and I are done until we get home.

Isten shows up hours later when I'm pretending to be asleep. I watch him as he relates the position of the running stream to Tier and Ashur and then wait patiently with walls up as he grabs a ration and fucks off throwing knives with Braun.

When he finally comes to find me I can barely contain my anger.

"What's up, Juncs?" He kicks me gently in the back, prodding me to turn. "I know you're faking it."

"I know you know, Isten. And you will not say anything, do you understand me? It's none of your fucking business."

He lies down and tips me up a little so he can slip his arms underneath and dip his head down into my ear to whisper, "Junco, when I said that shit before about Tier's babies I didn't know, OK? I would never do that to you. I heard you and Layla talking after, so I'm sorry. I won't say anything."

I turn around and look at him. His eyes are golden orbs, bright. Brighter than necessary for this little conversation. "You're hiding something."

"He's not stupid, Junco. We looked into this pregnancy shit after you told Ashur about the last time."

"He'll be busy soon enough. And I'm done spending time with him until this is over. You're right about that. I can't be two things at once, so–"

He sighs and turns over on his back, then brings my head to his chest. It's hard to hear through the armor, but if I lie very still and listen very carefully, I can find it. And then I count the beats until I sleep.

Chapter Fourteen

I jerk awake and have my mini-plasma out and trained on the forest. I take a moment and realize the entire team is doing the same thing. I get to my feet, jam my helmet on, activate the slick silver, and watch my helmet come to life with orders. We slide into formation. Our team goes left and Ashur's team goes right and we fan out from there. Tier is directing me to stay near him as Isten and Arel go forward.

I see a small orange glow flit in and out of the trees and slide the faceplate of my helmet up.

"It's Moju." Sera barks my orders across the collective helmet screens as I tell them to back off. This is my mission.

I deactivate the slick and walk forward into the woods, my footfalls announcing my presence as they crack twigs and dried-up pine needles, but fuck it. It's Moju.

He steps out from behind a tree and I catch his smile in my night vision.

"Brother?"

"Sister?"

I laugh and walk forward to meet him. When we are a body length apart he reaches in and grabs me, pulls me close and buries his head in my hair. "I knew you'd come."

The team forms up around us and Tier speaks while Moju continues to cling tight. "Are you alone?"

Moju nods, but doesn't let me go. I pick up his right hand and check his fingers. The pinky is missing and the scar is a jagged edge of bumpy skin. I look up into his eyes. "I'm sorry, Moj. I couldn't come in time for that, I was in Fledge and there was just no way–"

"Forget it, Juncs. I killed that one, he was a dick. In fact, I killed a shitload of Arens since then, there's only a few of them left."

I nod and swallow as I look over to Tier. Clones.

We walk back to camp in silence and when we get there we settle in the breaking dawn and wait for the story that no one really wants to hear.

He tells it exactly the way I would – with flippant detachment to the lives lost. What the fuck other way is there to tell a tale that involves annihilation of more than eight million people?

"Why, Moju? Why did he have to nuke them?" I see that he feels it was necessary, but I can't wrap my head around it. "I mean, those people in the RR and in Peaks, they were victims. I don't know the first thing about this Subjack guy, but–"

"Wait, what the fuck did you just say?" Moju looks over to Tier. "Tell me she's kidding, you asshole." Moju's eyes glow so bright they emit enough light to cast shadows. "I thought you of all people would have learned your lesson, you fucking piece of shit."

I look at Tier but he avoids my gaze. "What's going on?"

Tier stands but remains silent.

Moju stands as well and walks forward and stops only when his face is close enough to spit on him. The 039 is up and on their feet in a fraction, me included. Only I'm standing in between the guys and the team is pulling Moju away. Isten has Moju, but lets go as the razors come out and Moju slashes his chest armor.

"That's enough!" I bark the order like a commander and there's a brief moment of uncertainty. "I'm running this part of the mission, remember? So stand the fuck down and," I look over to Isten, "keep your fucking hands off my brother."

Isten backs off and I step away and go stand next to Moju. I look at each of them individually and it's all right there. The guilt is plain as day. "You fucking liars, what are you keeping from me now?"

Tier shakes his head. "Finish it, Moju."

I look up at my brother and feel a little wave of relief when he smiles and gives me a shrug. "That Subjack guy, Junco – is your father."

I laugh. "Right. Why the fuck wouldn't he be? I mean, shit – we got clones, we got AIs living inside me, we got a goddess who thinks she can control me, Lucan treating me weird, why the fuck wouldn't some random hick revolutionary be my dead father…"

I stop and take a deep breath as I turn my face away from them, and then I scream. "WHAT THE FUCK IS WRONG WITH YOU PEOPLE?" My chest heaves, but I'm not about to cry. I'm so fucking pissed off I can't even think straight. They all stand there waiting, faces long, expressionless, still, calm. I rush at Tier and push him in the chest, he moves backwards a fraction, but generally I have no effect on him.

My face heats up and I turn and walk away. "Who the FUCK did I cut if this Subjack is my father?"

My team is silent. Only Moj takes a shot at it. "His clone, Juncs. He's been gone for a few years now, up in the Territories with the Subs. You killed a dirty clone, one of the worst, maybe. Don't sweat it, OK?"

I shake my head and laugh. "Fuck you, Moju. Fuck all of you." I fly straight up and don't look down. All I want is to go home, that's it. To see the Peak City lights, hear the crack of the suborbitals, and hide in my room with my weapons, and books, and cigars. I want to fuck my friends when we're out on the scrub, eat field rations that don't taste like alien shit, talk to my HOUSE, drive my Goat around the muddy back roads and then go home and flip on the back of my horse.

Is it too much to ask?

I fly south but when the landscape starts showing signs of radiation burn I land on the top of the hill. The sunrise illuminates the endless stretch of grassland in the east and makes the desolate south look haunted with pink and orange ghosts.

I gave up everything, for what? For what? To be asked to trust them over and over again, only to be lied to each and every fucking time?

A cool gust of wind blows in out of the south and I turn my back to it and have a moment of panic at what kind of rads it might be carrying. I withdraw the little envelope in my pocket and shake out a pill and swallow it. The aftertaste lingers on my tongue as the wind dies down and I turn back to look out over the approaching light on the faraway dead zone. I hear wing beats behind me.

"Junco?"

It's Ashur. I snort a little air. "Ash, of course. Tier can't come because he's a fucking liar. And Isten can't come because he's a fucking liar. And Moju can't come because no one trusts him. And so it's just you. The only one who's bonded with me who isn't automatically on my shit list right now. I should've figured they'd make you do the dirty work, Ashur. You know, they take advantage of you almost as much as they take advantage of me."

I whirl around and make him step back a little. I look up and the tears come out, but not the sadness, nor the sobs. Just the tears. "Why? Why do you guys hate me so much? Why do you continue to break my heart with these lies?"

He doesn't answer. Can't answer. I wipe my tired eyes with both hands, rubbing the dirt into them, making them burn and slick up with goo.

I hold up my gifted index finger, then reconsider and let it drop and take a deep breath. "How can I complete this mission? How?"

"Junco, I have nothing–" He stops and swallows, averts his eyes, then brings them back to meet mine. "No excuse. I knew as well. Since the fourth Fledge fight. Selia sent messages weekly, begging you to come back to Earth. And then the messages came from Subjack himself. Your mother piped in a few times and then" – his words drop off – "others, too."

He waits, but I have nothing for him either.

"You trusted Selia once before. And she did what you asked, and has been trying to tell you the truth for months now. Moju says she's at their camp. You could trust her, Junco."

The heat takes over my face and the silent tears spill out again. "Ya know, here's the thing, Ashur." I don't try and hide or wipe them away this time, I just let them streak down my cheeks. "I'm not a warrior, OK? I think we've established this already. I'm just someone who can shoot straight from far away and who was cursed with a very lethal weapon that does the killing for me whenever I need it to. I'm five fucking feet tall, I barely weigh a hundred twenty pounds these days, I'm female, and I'm so fucking gullible it's painful even for me."

I wait, but he doesn't respond.

"So, there's no fucking way I can compete with you guys in this arena. All right? Because I believe you when you all say you love me. I believe it, Ash. And when I say I love you, I mean it."

"Junco, we never meant to–"

"You want to hear me say you've won? There it is. You've won. I live in a man's fucking world and the men aren't playing fair. So fuck it. I quit. I'll go to Subjack, because if he is my father from before, well, maybe Lucan was right. Maybe he needs a chance to explain what the fuck is going on. And I'll go to Selia because you're right about that, too. She exceeded my expectations – which is far more than I can say about anyone else in my entire life. But I'm out of this mission."

I stop to sniff and wipe the back of my hand across my nose.

"So, good luck to ya'll. I'm not going back to the Band with a bunch of liars. I'd rather live alone in the blown-out RR eating dry rice out of mylar bags from a hole in the ground than spend the rest of my life being constantly lied to. If I could give these wings back, *I would.*"

He swallows when I look up at him. "I have one more thing to tell you, Junco. And I'm sorry, but–"

I shake my head and start crying for real now.

"That Aren you killed at your house? That's not the same guy who was working with your mother in that video. The good Aren is—"

I laugh off the sobs. "The good Aren? Of course. All the bad guys are good, and all the good guys are bad. How fucking classic is that?"

Silence from Ashur.

"How many Arens are there?"

He sighs. "Many. I have no idea, hundreds? I don't know, Junco. I'd tell you if I did. All I know is he's got some very popular genetics and they use him for a lot of dirty shit."

"So who was that Aren out in Stag? The one that Tier killed when he took me? That guy who looked and talked and acted exactly like the boyfriend I had in cadets and who seemed to know an awful lot of personal things about me?"

Ashur makes a face, but it's all bad from my perspective. "Look, I wasn't made aware of the history you had with this Aren guy, OK? I wasn't, Junco. I barely know anything about him even now. And if I knew you were attached to that guy I would've never signed up for this–"

"Signed up for what, Ashur? What the fuck did you sign up for? Tell me now!" I walk over to him and push him in the chest like I did Tier. It has the same effect. Nothing. They are mountains, and I am just one small girl.

"We thought we were doing the right thing for you, Junco. We wanted you, still want you. And we need your help to get the rest of the Seven and put a goddamn end to all this shit we're in."

I take a deep breath and try to calm myself down. "If I'm so fucking important to you, Ashur, then why do you guys lie to me every chance you get?"

His green eyes glow. "Junco, we have no idea who or what you are. None. You're not just a Seven. You're not."

I just stare up at him as I try to keep my rage in check.

"You know those giant puzzles, Junco?"

"What?"

"Those puzzles that have thousands of pieces?"

I sneer at him. "So?"

"You're like the kittens in the middle of the puzzle, right? I can see the ears, the eyes, the whiskers. And I can take a few dozen pieces and put them together and know there's kittens in there. But the subject of the puzzle is never the hard part. It's the background. And your background is black. No shapes, no colors, no forms. Just black. It's a clusterfuck of emptiness that makes no sense." He sighs and lowers his voice as he looks me in the eyes. "And I'd be OK with that, ya know? If I thought you knew what the background was. Can you see the background, Junco?"

I stare up at him for a few seconds and then look away. "No."

"No. No one can see it, not that I know of, anyway. If Lucan sees it, he's hiding it, Junco. And I'm gonna break my security clearance right now and tell you that Lucan hides nothing from me. Nothing. I know every dirty fucking secret that guy has ever had. I might just be the number two guy to everyone else, but he doesn't trust Tier, so he tells me everything because I'm the backup. Not Tier, not Rikan. *Me.*"

I look up at him again as I think about what this means. I'm just about to ask what Rikan has to do with anything when he continues.

"So if he knows what you are, he's lied to me about it. This is a problem, Junco. And when you add in the fact that we've got a lot of other secrets ourselves? Well. The shit is piling up. We keep you in the dark because one wrong move might make it all come apart."

I laugh. "You keep me in the dark because you don't trust me, Ashur. It's as simple as that."

"I trust you, Junco. Tier, Isten, Arel, Rikan, Mish, Braun, Ryse, Layla, and Lucan. We *all* trust you."

"But?"

"But you're unpredictable. Wild. Indecisive." He hesitates for a moment. "Powerful. And we've not been upfront with a lot of things, Junco." He lets out a deep breath. "We're afraid if you know the truth, Juncs, you'll leave and never come back." He shrugs. "And you might. It's a real possibility that when you figure it all out, it'll be more than you can take – send you careening down a deserted road towards the Stag again, straight into the arms of insanity. Or cutting yourself in half just to make it end. We give it to you a little at a time, so it won't overwhelm you."

"But this Aren stuff, this Subjack being my father, that isn't about you guys. So why? Am I that wild? That I cannot be reasoned with?"

He takes a step towards me but I back up and he stops. "They, Subjack and your mother, they want you too." He shakes his head and sighs. "They raised you. Kept you alive through impossible odds. They made this moment in time because without you, Junco, those six other Siblings, they're not worth anything – it only works if you have all Seven Siblings from the same clutch alive when you extract and transfect the genetics, and getting the Seventh to cooperate has always been the major issue."

"That makes no sense, Ashur. Lucan wanted me dead when you guys were here. So how the fuck were you gonna get the genetics if I'm supposed to be dead?"

"Lucan called us back because he wanted to wait for the next clutch, Junco. It was over. We wrote your entire clutch off – and Tier was sent to kill you because without the Seven, the other six don't matter. If we came back without you, Esta would've been killed on the spot. It was over, get it? *It was over.* Our decision to save you shifted everything. But like I said, your parents, they raised you. They have a better claim than us. And Earth and the humans need you as well."

I huff out a laugh that is more disgust than anything. "A better claim? I'm property now?"

"You know that's not what I meant."

My eyes are wild as I walk towards him, pointing my finger at his face. "No, Ashur, I don't know that. I know there's stuff about Lucan and you guys that I don't understand. I get it. But that has nothing to do with you hiding the truth about the people I know from Earth. If there is a good Aren, do you have any idea how much that changes things for me?"

I wait but he doesn't answer.

"He was my first, Ashur. My first fucking love, my best fucking friend from the time I was thirteen to the day he left for the MR when I was sixteen. And if that guy who went over to the MR wasn't the same guy who spent all those days and nights with me in cadet school, then this changes my whole world. Do you get that?"

He swallows and nods. "I get it, Junco."

I turn and take a deep breath to dampen down my anger a little. "I don't think you do, Ashur." I whirl back. "Because if there's a good Aren, then that means that not everything about my life has been horrible. And maybe your life has lots of good things about it that you can hold on to, but mine doesn't, OK? I need all the fucking good things I can get."

"I get it, Junco."

I look in his eyes, but I don't see the understanding I need. "Maybe you just can't relate to what it means to have nobody. What it's like to be alone. Because you've had your brothers the whole time, right? Your Fledge team is still together, you lived all your days together, and grew up together without betraying each other."

I stop and he repeats himself for a third time. "I said I fucking get it, Junco."

I shake my head at him. "No, you don't. You don't get it because you can't even imagine what it's like to never have a real friend aside from your goddamn HOUSE! So you could never understand what it means that my Aren was a real friend and I never knew it."

He comes towards me and takes my hands. "You're right. I've been lucky. We've all been lucky to have each other for so long. So, no. I can't relate to the world you live in. I'm sorry. If you want the truth about us I'll tell you–"

"Ashur, it's not about you guys. You're not hearing me. It's about me. I don't care about your stupid fucking secrets! I don't care! I just need the truth about me. What's real and what's not. Every time something new pops up I walk a little farther away from sanity."

Ashur smiles, but it's forced. "Shit, Junco, the last time you gave me the it's-not-you-it's-me speech you went and sliced your fucking chest open." He lets go of my hands and turns away. "Please tell me you're done with the death wishes? Because I can't fucking think about that shit. I might not know what it's like to be you, but I know what it's like to lose you. And I can't fucking do it again."

I can appreciate that. If I take the time to look at things objectively and choose my perspective like Lucan asked, I can see their side of things. The rational part of me can at least. They are, in some ways, simply trying to protect me. "Lying to me, Ashur, is not the way to protect me. I'm so fucked up–"

He turns around, his face sad, waiting for me to continue.

I take a deep breath. "I'm so fucked up I don't even know what's real anymore. I don't know. I'm going insane, Ashur. And you guys will be the ones to push me over the edge with these lies. If you love me, then you'll back off and let me figure it out. Just *back off.*"

Chapter Fifteen

When I fly back to camp I grab all my weapons, except for the 50 cal – it's just gonna have to stay unless someone else wants to huck it around – and strap them on me one at a time, fill my pockets with ammo and plasma cartridges, and stuff some shitty fucking avian rations down my shirt and in my boots. When I'm done I stand apart from camp, apart from Tier's team, looking over a cliff that has a long vertical drop. I see a pair of eaglets venture to the side of the mountain and flap their half-feathered wings a little as they wait for the next meal to appear. "Ya better stay a little longer, boys. It's a fucking bitch out there."

I hear a grunt behind me and turn to find Arel.

"Hey."

I smile but say nothing.

"So, Junco. I thought you might like to know that I corrupted your HOUSE once."

I squint in confusion and stare up at his dark eyes. "Yeah, Ash mentioned that."

He laughs. "Just listen for a second, OK? I realize this is strange timing, but I noticed she was in shutdown mode when we showed up for that battle in your driveway."

"Aren, well, that bad Aren, corrupted her and I had to put her to sleep that night."

"Which means she reverted to the last backup, correct?"

I nod as a shiver of hope runs through my body.

"So, where do you keep the backups? Do you know?"

I know.

My eyes fill with tears before I can stop them and he moves in and squeezes my arm. "Thank you, Arel. You have no idea how much this helps."

"You're welcome, Junco. You look like you need a friend, so maybe there'll be time later?" He shrugs. "At least you know where she is and she's not dead."

I nod and look past him. The whole team is waiting on us. I nod to Moju and he takes off. I follow and then behind me comes the thunder of wings.

We fly northwest until the sun is high overhead in the south. My wings ache like fuck with every thrust, and I find myself praying for a tailwind, but more often than not the headwind blows in my face, chapping it as the infamous low-pressure systems that come out of the Pacific Utopia create havoc on the currents. If Moju hadn't headed down to the ground when he did, I might have fallen out of the sky from exhaustion.

We land just past the tree line in an open area littered with marmot dens. The air is frigid as I pick my way around the golden little rodents and pray the mountain lions are less aggressive than the ones we have on the prairie. It's an irrational fear when you're strapped down with more weapons than you have limbs and there's no sane reason for a lion to be above the tree line in the first place, but that fear goes deep in me for various reasons.

Moju finally directs us to a small hole in the side of the hill. Everyone except Moj is huffing from the low oxygen and my vision is spinning wildly as my voice echoes in my head. "I'm sick, Moj." I look at him and he weaves back and forth. No, wait. I'm weaving back and forth.

Sucks to have altitude sickness. I've lived above eight thousand feet my entire life. But it only takes a few weeks away from high altitude to wipe away every compensation my body ever made for it. I've been gone a lot longer than a few weeks and this is a lot higher than eight thousand fucking feet. It feels more like fourteen to me.

"We're here, Juncs. Just breathe in and focus, OK? We're going down now, all right?"

I nod and take a deep breath. I know from experience that it does go away on the descent. The cog that used to wind up and down the side of Peaks got you back down quick enough to make the sickness go away in minutes, but I've gotta walk down. And I'm getting worried that walking will be out of the question pretty soon.

I slip inside the hole behind Moju and slide down the steep interior hillside, sending rocks tumbling down on his head. If he's upset, he doesn't show it. He just stands at the bottom and drags me up to my feet.

"You OK?"

I hear him, but the words come in fuzzy and I weave a little. "I think so."

The rest of the guys come up behind me and I catch Tier and Isten looking at me funny. I ignore them and let Moju keep my hand as we walk along in the cave. We're not going down, we're walking horizontal. "Moju, I need to stop."

He doesn't even turn. "No, Juncs. You don't get better by stopping."

He's dragging me now, and then we come to a door. A door of all things, in the side of this mountain.

He peers into the biometric retinal scan and I hear a loud click. It opens to a large cargo elevator and we all file in. Moju peers into the interior biometrics and the door closes. He thumbs his print and the box begins a quick descent.

I breathe a sigh of relief as my head clears within seconds and hang onto Moju's arm. "Thanks for the help." He smiles at me and leans down to kiss my head. I smile, then lock it down. No more trusting anyone, not even Moju, until I figure out what the fuck is going on. Isten's words come back to haunt me, *You can't give that shit away like that, because the minute you do, they own you.*

He shoots me a look from across the elevator and I meet it head-on. "You're such an asshole, Isten. Omission of facts is the same thing as lying. But you know what, you were absolutely right about that. I won't give it away from now on, don't you fucking worry about it again."

I get funny looks all around, but Isten doesn't say anything.

"Just let it go, Juncs." Moju shakes his head at me. "Can't turn back time. Besides, you have to trust someone."

The car stops and Moju scans his retinas one more time to make the doors open. We step out into a hallway.

There's another door but this time it's guarded by one of those sentry bots from the tunnels under Ramah. Moju scans, then pushes me up to it. "Everyone has to scan in." I blink at the biometric pad and it flashes and chirps at me to move away. The team scans in after me and then Moju palms a final biometric pad on the side of the wall and the large doors click open.

We walk into a bustling underground city filled with aisles upon aisles of people selling goods.

A market.

Under a mountain.

We walk out into the grid of open-air stalls and all eyes turn to face us. Within seconds this part of the cavern is deathly silent. I look around uneasy, not sure if these are my people or not. Not sure if I'm avian or human or neither. Not sure about much of anything.

"Junco!"

Selia is running towards me with a giant smile. She stops short when she sees my face. "What's wrong?"

I can use a friend right now. So bad. This thought sparks the tears and I cry, I can't help it.

Selia pulls me in and gives me a hug. "It's OK, Junco. Really."

"Get me out of here, please – just get me out of here, Selia. Please."

I can feel her look up at my team but there is silence behind me. Selia turns me around, pushes on my shoulders, and we walk. My head is down and I can't bring myself to look at anyone. When we stop I have no idea where we are or how we got here. None of the guys are behind me, it's just us.

She reaches out for my weapons and I push her back, growling, "Don't even fucking think about it." I am instantly ashamed. "I'm sorry, Selia. I'm sorry."

"Junco, you can't possibly work them all at once, put one or two down and relax."

"I just need them right now, OK?"

Her eyes squint in confusion. "Were they— mean to you, Junco? Those avians?"

"Mean to me?" What do I say? No? I had to fight and kill almost a hundred people in Fledge. Yes? That doesn't feel quite right either. I stay silent. That question is not even answerable at the moment.

"Come on, sit down and relax. You look a little wrung-out, Junco."

Her hand gestures towards a long fluffy couch and I flop against the pillows and tip my head back to study this girl who I'd be hard-pressed to pin a label on, if forced.

"Selia, my whole world is a lie."

I watch her face drop with a frown and she nods. "Yeah, lots of people are coming to the same conclusion about everything they believed to be true as well, Junco. I've heard a lot of stories over the past few months, so while I may not be able to relate exactly, I certainly understand."

"I don't know where I belong. Hell, I don't even know what I am."

"You can belong here if you want. We know who you are, Junco. You're one of us."

Us? Really. "How can you be so sure, Selia? I'm not even human and the avians say I'm not really avian either."

"You're Junco. And that's enough." She sighs and smiles a little. "Why don't you just lie back and rest for a while, huh? It must have been quite a trip getting here and it's late evening if you're on standard time, so you're probably tired anyway."

I nod slightly but stay quiet.

"You want some clothes to sleep in?"

I choke back a sob as I bring my booted feet up on the couch. Yeah, I want to say. Throw me a tank top that doesn't require me to seal up the sides to accommodate the wings because I don't want them anymore.

But I don't. I just stay silent and keep my wish to be normal to myself. Selia chats to me for a little longer but when I turn out to be about as much fun as a bag of hammers she goes to bed. Eventually my eyelids become too heavy to resist the pull of sleep and I sink away into the darkness.

Chapter Sixteen

I can hear them and it bothers me. Their happiness and excitement at being free on a Friday night. My fingers go to the keys of the piano and I absently pluck out a few bars of the song I've been practicing with Mrs. Strauss. I recognize the heavy thud of bootsteps approaching in the long hallway that leads to the music auditorium and I stand at ease and wait.

I smile when he enters the room and I feel a little wave of sadness as I realize I've missed him.

He pulls me in and squeezes me. "How have you been, Junco?"

"Good, Dad. Really good. I already made Cadet Captain."

"I know, they called me." He pushes me to sit on the piano bench and I do. "Which is why I'm here. Maybe you didn't understand what I said on the way home from Hawaii? You don't have to make rank here, Junco. There's time for that later. This is just—" He drops off, trying to think of the words maybe. "It's just wasting time for you, a way to make you legitimate so you can move on as an officer after graduation. There is nothing for you to learn here except how to relax. Just do your homework, do what Mrs. Strauss and Michael tell you to for piano and sports, and forget the rest. You don't have to work so hard."

I shrug and look up at him. "I want to."

"No," he says, shaking his head, "you don't. You just don't want to leave your comfort zone and do the things all the other cadets are doing. And I think you should. What are your plans for tonight?"

I swallow. "Mrs. Strauss wants me to practice the new—"

"No, Junco. Not on a Friday night she doesn't. I gave her orders. You are free to do whatever you want until 0900 tomorrow. So, go. Go out and do something. These kids are always going out, but I hear you always stay in. Why? What's the problem?"

I let out the frown I've been hiding since he left me here two months ago. "I thought it would be so fun, but it's not really. I don't get it."

"Don't get what, Junco?" His voice is soft and his eyes attentive.

"How they can be so concerned with things that don't really matter. Like hair or clothes or boys. I'm only interested in classes and—" He waits for a few seconds but I don't fill in the missing words. Even I know this is not normal.

"Interested in what, Junco?"

I look up and shake my head. "Weapons and training. All the stuff I never wanted to do growing up but can't seem to get enough of now. And Gideon. He's back, isn't he? I can feel him and I want to see him, Dad. I really want to see him. Please let me."

He gets a pained look on his face and turns his head before he speaks. "You can't see him yet, Junco. He's not ready. But I promise you, if you try a little harder to make friends, I'll let you see him at Easter Break. Deal?"

This is not a deal.

That's almost six months away. What did they do to him that it takes six months to be ready to see me again? My brow furrows so deep into my forehead I almost give myself a headache. My voice comes out low and mean and this growl of anger runs so deep it almost surprises me. "If they've hurt him I will kill someone." I look up to see what he will do with this new information. But he just nods.

"He's OK. I promise."

"That's not what I said and you know it. If they've hurt him. That's what I said."

He puts a hand on my shoulder and pulls me close and begins to speak gently to me. "Junco, go find a friend and if you do that for me then Gideon can come to the house for all of Easter Break. I promise."

I hold my breath for a few seconds. "Come to the house?"

"Yes."

This is new. Gideon has never been to the house before. I've only ever seen him at camp. "One friend?"

"One friend. And go out somewhere tonight."

"Where am I gonna go? And with who? I can't just make a friend in a few seconds. I haven't exactly been the most sociable girl for the past few months."

"I know a boy who wants to meet—"

I snort out a laugh. "No, no way. I'm not gonna let you fix me up with some boy! That's crazy."

"He'll take you to Peaks. Tonight. And buy you dinner."

"I'm not hungry."

"He'll take you to the observatory at the MR university."

I pause. "Which one?" It matters. The one in the mountains is better because there's less light pollution. Plus I go to the one in North Peaks a couple times a year. That's not special.

"He'll take you to the Boulder Observatory in a Council 3 flier. Will that make you happy?"

Kinda, I think to myself. But I'm not gonna tell him that. "Is he one of your officers' kids or something?"

"No, just a boy from Council 5. He's a class ahead of you. He's nice."

I sneer my lip at the nice part. "I'm not nice, what makes you think I want a nice one?" I laugh before he has a chance to answer. I'm not supposed to talk about how not nice I can be. Especially when we're not at home. My dad ignores my outburst, but I know he won't forget it.

"He outranks you then. How about that? Good enough?"

I throw up my hands. "Fine. He can be my friend and take me places. What do I care, as long as I get to see Gideon at break. Hey, if I can't see Gid now, can you at least let him call me on a comm tech or something?"

He's shaking his head before I even finish. "No comms, Junco. You know better."

It was worth a try. "So where is this kid then? Boulder is hours away and I wanna be back by midnight so I won't be too tired for riding tomorrow." I look up and my dad is staring at me, his eyebrows all crunched together. "What?"

"I'm the parent, Junco. Don't give yourself a curfew. Stay out all night. Look at the stars in the scope, then go for a walk, get some food, kiss him—"

"Oh, shit, Dad. That's enough. I'm not gonna kiss this boy. There is only one person I want to kiss and he's probably a man by now, it's been so long since I've seen him. So I'll be friends with this kid, but it's only so I can see Gideon in the spring." I stop and think about my words for a second, then amend my statement. "Besides you, Dad. I'll kiss you too, ya know."

He lets out a little laugh and he closes his eyes and shakes his head. "I'll let that curse pass this time, but not the next."

He says that every time.

How does he expect me to stop cursing in his presence when he laughs and never follows through on the threat? I sigh and make a mental note not to swear in front of him anymore, just so he doesn't have to pretend.

His face becomes serious as he looks down on me. "And remember the behavior rules. No secrets, he has no clearance right now. None. So if you tell him something you're not supposed to, he will be punished accordingly."

Which is why I only love Gideon when it comes to friends. He's the only one who does have clearance. I swallow and nod but I don't avoid his stare. They can't scare me very often anymore, I've collected a lot of powers to help me take the punishments and even though I'm upset when they're happening, I just try and forget about the whole thing and I'm pretty good at that.

Now they just tell me what will happen to those I involve in my rebellions instead, so I've mostly put an end to acting out. It's just not worth it. I never really win and what's the point of making someone else take a punishment that should be mine?

Besides, I can't even remember the last time my dad punished me. I'm good for him because he's good to me. And the last time Matthew pulled his anger out on me, he got a surprise that made him rethink his bullying strategy, because his punishments went from physical to mental real fast.

If they leave me alone, I'll be good. I never said it out loud and it took them a while to catch on, but now that they have, we're all a lot happier with each other. "I won't tell him anything. I know better."

His smile returns and he takes my hand. "Come with me, I'll introduce you."

Chapter Seventeen

My stomach churns and my mouth fills with saliva as I push myself up and look around wildly.

Where the fuck am I?

And then reality hits me. I swallow down the vomit and seek out doors that might lead to a bathroom, my numerous rifles jangling against my body like a horse in harness. I find what I need a bedroom and a closet later, and throw myself down on the floor as my stomach contracts and my mouth spews green shit that looks like it came from an alien.

I come up for air, spitting and laughing simultaneously.

I am an alien.

I wait it out for a few more minutes, coughing a couple more times just to make sure it's over, and then go back out to the living room as I drag my hand across my mouth. I don't bother calling for Selia, she's obviously not here. I do peek in the bedroom and find a mess of pillows and blankets, along with several dozen small gray boxes that make me smile.

I stuff a couple in the pockets already spilling over with ammo and then take one out and light it up on the striker. I take the smoke in by small quick draws and puff it back out. Fuck, that makes everything just a little bit better.

Isten?

Nothing.

Isten?

Nothing.

What the fuck? *ISTEN!* I scream it in my head.

Junco? Where are you? He comes back faint, barely there.

I have no idea. In an apartment somewhere. I just woke up. I check my vision screen and see that I've slept a complete cycle. Shit. *I'll find you later.*

I step through the outer door and end up in a busy hallway. People look at me funny, then back away and start whispering. I stop and look around, take it all in, and then relax. "I'm not a freak, so you all can stop fucking pointing at me like I am. I'm fucking human too, ya know."

They slip away with backwards glances as a soldier approaches me with purpose. He smiles as I puff on my cigar, then extends his hand. "Gid, Junco. Nice to see you. Your mother assigned me to make sure you don't get into trouble."

I swallow down some nausea and shake his hand. "She's not my mother."

He smiles again, and it's nice. Warm and human. His eyes are a light blue color. His cropped hair is sandy blond and his casual non-sectarian field clothes can't hide an athletic body underneath. He towers over me, but what else is new? Everyone towers over me. "She absolutely is your mother, so that's enough of that bullshit. I'll call her whatever you want, but let's try and work with the facts here, huh?"

I huff a little air. "Well, fuck. Let's just forget her altogether, OK? Where the hell can I get some food because if I have to eat this avian field ration shit one more time I'm gonna puke." He laughs at me, but my face stays level. "That's not a joke, Gid, I'm not feeling well and I'm hungry."

He nods. "Yeah, OK. I'll take you to your mom. She's got food for you."

I sigh and fall in behind him. What else can I do? My choices are bad and fucking bad. We walk through many more hallways bustling with people and then we're out in the main area again. I'm more aware of my surroundings than I was last time and see it for what it really is. Another giant nuclear highway tunnel, just like the one Tier and Moju and I blew up back in Ramah.

I have come back full circle in almost every way I can imagine. Mother, father, Earth, tunnels, alone. It's just an endless cycle of bullshit.

We weave through various vendors and I am actually a little curious at all the commerce going on. Say what you will about capitalism, but buying and selling makes the world go round and it brings a grounding sense of normalcy to a scene that reads a little too much like a dystopian book from the last century.

The crowd gets thicker and people start jostling against me, getting a little too close to my weapons. I feel a hand on my ammo belt across my back and whirl and grab the arm of a kid.

"Touch me again and I'll break your fucking arm." I feel the heat and then see the glow reflected back at me in his frightened eyes. I look up and the crowd makes a nice circle of space around me as they back away from the light I emit.

Gid appears, obviously late to the party, and I laugh at him. "You're not doing a very good job, are you?" I push the kid away and let my escort shuffle me in front of him.

The rest of the journey takes us past a multitude of accessory tunnels and I think back to the mutants that lived under the RR. That tunnel was more than three hundred feet deep so chances of it surviving the blast are high. Those things down there are probably the only life forms now inhabiting my old world. We stop at a biometrics panel and wait for the door to click, and then walk through.

Isten is waiting for me on the other side.

His eyes plead with me as I stop in front of him. "Junco, are you OK?"

I make a face at him. "Of course I'm OK, Isten. Don't be stupid." I look down at my hand and realize I lost my cigar in the altercation back in the tunnel. "Well, what do ya want?"

"You don't get to walk away without a meeting, Junco. Tier's got a call in to Ryse to send a message to Lucan. You can't just pretend you're not on the team. You are. And if that message gets back to Lucan he'll come here and" – he shakes his head – "that would not be good for anyone, Junco. In fact, that would be fucking horrible. You can't just walk away like this."

I study his face and believe him. "Why would it be horrible if Lucan came to Earth?"

"He's not allowed to be here, Juncs. It's forbidden."

I take this in as the summons attached to my finger begins to pulsate. "Then why did Tier send a message?"

"He's out of options. You're not walking away, Junco. It's not gonna happen. You're connected to us. To me. To him." His eyes track down to my stomach and I shoot a look over to Gid and catch him staring, he shrugs and turns around to wait it out.

"Well, Isten, my mother wants to talk to me. So I will find you guys later." I walk over to Gid and look up at him. "Let's go." I don't even look back at Isten as we continue our journey towards my waiting family.

"So, she's your mother when it's convenient? Like when you want to end a conversation with that guy back there? But she's nobody when you're forced to face facts and confront her? Is that pretty much how you operate these days, Junco?"

I stop and wait for him to do the same. "You have no idea how I operate so don't pretend to have a clue as to what I'm doing or why I'm doing it."

He throws me a crooked smile, but it's got the look of a soldier in it. The fierce raw look of too much death, too many orders followed and not nearly enough contested. His look screams fuck you.

"Don't talk to me like that, Junco. I was right on the money with my comment and you know it, so don't play with me. I was assigned to you because the people who know you best feel I can take the bullshit you spew out on a regular basis. If you want to have this pissing contest, let's do it. But I'd just like to remind you that I'm the one who has the better equipment."

I hold down a grin as I stare up at him. "More walking, less talking."

His hand goes up to the stubble on his chin and then he turns and our boots fall in line. We come to another door a few minutes later and Gid flashes his eyeballs at the biometrics and then palms it for good measure. We pass through and there are armed guards on the other side. They go for my weapons and I back away. "Forget it. I'm not going any further. Let me back out. Now."

Gid shakes his head at me. "What's the problem?"

"You're not getting my weapons."

He laughs all the way up to his eyes. "Junco, what the fuck do you need four weapons for? You're in your parents' home."

I shake my head as I back into the locked door behind me. "Open the door, I'm not going any further."

"Just put them down and–"

I whip the SEAR out from under my shirt and flick the loop up to full sword length. "Open the fucking door, or I'll cut a Junco-sized hole in it right now."

They look at me like I'm crazy.

A voice from behind breaks the spell. "Let her through with her guns. It calms her. Junco, please put that thing away. It makes people uncomfortable."

My heart thumps as I recognize her and I almost collapse. I reach out for the door to steady myself and watch Gid watch me react. "Where did you go?" It comes out like I'm breathless. And I am breathless, she's stolen the life away from me at the moment and the seconds hang in the air.

My mother straightens her chin, like she's forcing herself to remain brave or something. "That is not a discussion for a hallway, Junco. Dock that weapon. Now."

The guards back off and I retract and dock my SEAR.

"Gideon will take you to your room and then you'll change, drop the weapons off with the exception of one. Do you hear me, Junco? One weapon and that's it. And then we will have breakfast like humans."

"No. I'm not here to visit with you or take a room in your house or change out of my fucking Aves armor. I'm here to–"

Fuck. I don't know why I'm here anymore.

My mother smiles at me. "You will change, Junco. You look like a goddamn apocalyptic road warrior with all that shit hanging off your body. Like you're living on the edge of the civilized world or something. And those crazy eyes," she sighs and tsks her tongue against her teeth, "gold, just like I predicted."

I watch Gid stifle a laugh out of the corner of my eye and then she walks off. I look up to him with furrowed brows and he shrugs. "She's the boss here." I wave him forward to lead the way and then follow. What else can I do? My choices are still bad and fucking bad.

Gid leads me down the hallway, my weapons clanging against my hips in the now silent atmosphere and I cringe with each step, feeling a bit ridiculous.

We stop at a room that has no biometrics and he opens the door and stands aside. It's not much, but it's not bad either. One room plus a bathroom on the far end. The bed looks comfortable enough. There's a couple of chairs, a couch, and a small screen. Which almost seems out of place in a home that belongs to my parents since we were a Farm Family and all. I stand in the middle of the room and then turn to look at Gid. "OK, what the fuck does she want me to do in here?"

He opens a door and I lean to the side a little to see one outfit hanging in the otherwise empty closet. My body straightens and my eyebrows go up. "I'm not wearing a dress and my feet won't even come close to fitting in those shoes."

He shrugs and lets out a sigh. "Shit, I thought you'd be fun to guard. You're just a raging bitch these days, Junco. I should've stayed out on patrols."

I smile despite myself. Gid. Gideon? I rack my brain because it's obvious that he knows me, but that memory is not accessible for some reason.

"I'll take off the weapons and empty my pockets a little, but I'm not changing. And before you get all pissy with me about it, I don't even know how to take the armor off, OK? Isten was always there to help me and it's a lot more complicated than it looks when you have wings."

He studies my face as the truth comes out of my mouth. "Well, let me take a look at it. You can't really want to stay in these clothes? You smell, Junco. And they're filthy."

I blink and shake my head. "I'm a soldier on a field mission, you don't take a break for a tea party on a mission." He starts removing weapons from my back and brushes repeatedly against my wings, making chills run down my body. "Hey, mind the wings, right? It's very rude to touch them."

"Oh, I didn't know. Sorry." His hands start on the ammo belt and I just stand there compliant until he gets it off. "Anyway, the mission won't start until tomorrow. It's been planned already, so you've got the entire day to relax. I'll have someone clean these clothes up for you a little, air them out? And then you can put it all back on tomorrow. Right?"

I'm pulling cartridges out of my pockets and dropping them on the bed when I realize he's waiting for an answer. "What?"

"Do you live in your own world all the time, or just most of the time? I *said*" – his emphasis tells me he's not a patient guy – "you'll take the battle gear off and I'll clean it for–"

"I heard what you said. OK, that's fine. But I'm not wearing that dress. I'll go see her in my bed clothes unless you find something for me to wear besides that."

He doesn't even blink. "You're wearing the dress, Junco. I don't fucking care if I have to hold you down and strap it on you myself. So get used to the idea."

I stop what I'm doing and look up at him. "Who do you think you are? I don't take orders from–"

"I'm Gideon, Junco." He stares down at me. "And you absolutely do take orders from me. Now shut the fuck up and do what I tell you."

I'm sitting on the bed, my fingers removing my boots before I even realize I'm complying. When I'm done we struggle with the armor for several minutes before he gives up and I smile, triumphant. "See, I told you it was complicated."

I cross my arms and watch as he pulls out a com. "Yeah, it's me. Bring that Isten guy to Junco's room so he can help me undress her. Thanks." He flashes me a grin. A real grin. "Problem solved."

Isten arrives a few minutes later and he's not happy. "What the fuck is going on here?" He bumps up to Gid, his gold rage leaking out of his eyes. "You want my help undressing my nine, that's the message you send me?"

Gid looks over to me. "Well, fuck, at least I know where you get it from. You're all a bunch of assholes."

Isten pounds him close-fisted in the face and Gideon sweeps his foot against Isten's legs and they both go down on the floor. They grapple there for a few seconds before realizing how stupid they look and push off each other to get back up, breathing hard with raging male hormones. I stand around feeling a little bored. "All this so you can get me in a dress? Really?"

Gid collects himself. "She needs to shower and change, if you can't get her to do that I'll have you removed."

I look over to Isten and feel no sympathy for him. "Fuck, Is, just help take the armor off, OK?"

He walks over to me and slips his hand under my wing. I arch my back a little and squeal as I watch Gid's fascinated expression. "Careful, Isten, Jasus fuck."

"Look here, Juncs. Reach your arm under your other one, then" – he presses my fingers to a small tab – "pull here and that will release the seal on your wings. Then you can just undo the other seams and take the shirt off." He stands back and waits as I remove the seal from one wing. "Now do it again on the other side."

I do and I feel the air rush into the tiny cracks between my upper body armor and the skin on my back.

I release the underarm seams and Isten pulls the shirt over my head. My tank top rolls up a little, exposing my belly, and I watch Gid's eyes go to my SEAR dock before I pull the shirt down again.

I go for the pants and Gid turns away. Isten doesn't – he just stands there until I'm almost naked and then he moves forward and hugs me. "Junco – don't do this to me, OK? You can't stay mad forever."

He backs away and takes my face in his hands but I look away. "Not now, Isten. Just let me go eat, I'm so hungry and they won't feed me until I dress up and see my mother."

Isten's anger surfaces again. "She's hungry? What the hell is wrong with you, feed her, for fuck's sake!"

Gid opens the door and the guard is outside waiting for Isten. "She'll eat, we're not starving her."

Isten takes my hand and slips a piece of paper into it. "It's from Tier." I just stare at it and when I look up Isten is gone.

I open the little folded note and read the avian letters, then fish out my Earth comm from the pile of clothes on the floor and switch it on. The blinking lights signal that I have messages but I simply dial one. Tier answers on the first beat. "I'm sorry, Juncs. I'm sorry, OK?"

"Don't call for Lucan, Tier. If I need him I can call for him myself." And then I hang up and switch it off again so he can't call back.

"Who's Lucan?"

I drop the comm back in the pile of clothes. "Fuck if I know." I walk into the bathroom and take a shower, letting the hot water blast me until my skin turns red.

How the hell do they do it?

Do what, Junco?

Make me love them no matter what.

I feel Sera's hesitation but I know she will answer so I'm patient.

You want to believe, Junco. It's that simple.

I don't like that answer so the conversation is over. I turn the hot water off and wrap a towel around my body, then another around my hair and leave the bathroom.

Gid is gone and the dress is on the bed. It's a lovely royal blue color with an empire waist that flows down to the floor when I hold it up to my naked body. The over-shoulder straps are slight and they cross in the back with small hooks.

I open the door in my towel and Gid looks at me funny. "What now?"

I hold up the dress in one hand. "This will not be easy, you don't seem to understand how this works. I have wings. I won't be able to get this on unless I have help."

He comes back in the room and closes the door behind him. "You want me to help?"

"I'm hungry, Gid. You're not feeling just how hungry I am, so please. Could you please just help me dress so I can eat something?"

I drop the towel and pull the dress over my head. Gid's eyes linger on my body and then he is up next to me, his hands holding the dress up before I can let it fall down to cover myself.

He bends down to study my torso, then his fingertip traces the horrific red gash down my stomach. "What the fuck is *that*?" He looks up at me, his eyes wide and uncertain.

I push his hand away and let the fabric cover me. "I killed myself. To save Tier." He straightens up and backs away a few paces as I clutch the dress to my body so it doesn't fall to the floor.

"How?"

I laugh at him. "What the fuck else could make a scar like that, Gideon? My SEAR knife, of course."

"They made you mutilate yourself?" He turns around and runs his hand through his hair, then turns back. "Why would you stay with them?"

I look him in the eye and know that I'm glowing as the words leave my mouth. "Gideon, you have no idea what happened to me so you can judge me if ya want, but all I need right now is for you to hook up this goddamn dress so I can go eat some fucking food. You can touch my wings, just pull the straps over my shoulders and hook them into the dress."

He moves towards me reluctantly and then tugs on my wings a little as he maneuvers the fabric. I cry out a few times when it gets overwhelming.

"Does it hurt? To touch them?" he asks me as I'm finally pulling the dress down over my legs.

"No, it's sexual, Gideon. You might as well be feeling me up."

I fasten my boots and watch as he blushes like a girl and turns away. "Is that a joke?"

I laugh. "A joke? No. I rarely make jokes."

"Oh, shit. I don't have any experience with wings, I'm sorry."

I lift up the flowing gown and strap my mini-plasma to my outer thigh and then let the silky fabric fall back down towards the floor. "You're not the first, so don't get excited. Now take me to my mother so I can eat or I swear I will die."

Chapter Eighteen

The bitch leaves me waiting, of course. One second it's critical for the sake of humanity that I clean up, put on a dress, and rush to her quarters for breakfast. The next I'm left sitting in this completely inappropriate and ridiculous gown, so fucking hungry I'm about to eat my fingers.

"Can I get some fucking food here, please!" My patience is over.

I watch a guard leave and then reappear with a tray of pastries. My stomach experiences a futile peristaltic wave and I begin to salivate. He sets the tray down and I grab a sweet roll and take several bites before surfacing for air. Gideon sits across from me with his eyebrows raised. "I was not kidding. I told you I was hungry. Jasus fuck, quit *looking* at me."

He puts his hands up and looks away.

"Junco, you don't have to be so rude. When did you get so unruly?"

My mother's voice pulls me back to attention and I stare at her with my mouth open, a wad of food sitting on my tongue. I chew a few more times and swallow before talking. "You left when I was six, so don't pretend you know me. I went through with this little reunion so I could eat, and I don't eat much, so you've got about ten minutes before I'm done here. Start fucking talking."

"This is a social call, Junco. I'm not here for your business matters. Your father–"

"He's not my father and you're not my mother. What world do you guys all live in?" I look over at Gid for help but his face is blank. I squint my eyes at him. "I won't forget this, Gideon, and I want my armor back today." I stuff the rest of my roll in my mouth and grab another, then push back from the table and head for the door. "If someone could just point me in the direction of Moju I'll be going now."

The guard stops me with a rifle to the temple.

"Sit down now, Junco." My mother's words are stern. "The rifles are on stun, but I'm sure you know first-hand how badly that hurts."

The wheels turn in my head and her cunning presents itself front and center. She smiles when she reads my expression. "Yes, Junco. It was on purpose. You can't reach the SEAR with that dress on, can you?"

I stare at her, then over to Gideon. He's looking the other way.

"Sit down, Junco."

Isten?

I walk over to the table and take a seat to bide my time.

Isten?

My mother smiles at me. "Now, let's catch up, shall we?"

I swallow. "Catch up on what?"

Isten?

"He can't hear you in here, Junco, so stop it."

I hold back my surprise and shrug instead. "You can't blame me for trying."

"You have wings, Junco. Tell me all about your Fledge."

I spit out a laugh. "My Fledge? You want to know – fuck it, all right. My Fledge, OK – how's this? I won. Isn't that spectacular? Yeah, I was the most deadly motherfucking avian that General Fledge has ever seen. I killed eighty-something people, including my best friend. A little kid who was only ten years old. Then, after I won, I played Deliverance too, and I won that as well. But only after killing my other friend. I accidentally nicked him with my SEAR and had to chop his head off in front of a packed arena so he wouldn't suffer."

Gideon stares at me with his mouth open but my mother is as cool as they come.

"Is that the kind of catch-up you wanted?"

She just looks at me.

"Or maybe you'd like to hear how I heard my boyfriend being murdered over a comm or how my," I make air quotes with my fingertips, "father dosed me with a fucking abortion spray and left me on the floor of my shower to expel a teeny tiny little baby while the blood pooled around my body."

Gideon stands up. "OK, look – this is private, Linny. I'm outta here."

"You bring me here and then you think you get to leave when it gets uncomfortable? I don't fucking think so, *Gideon*."

"Sit down, Gideon."

He does as my mother instructs, but he doesn't look at me.

I direct my attention back to my mother. "You wanna hear the best part, Mom? I was supposed to kill Tier in that Deliverance fight, he was tried for treason for saving my life back here on Earth. But I killed myself instead. And then the fucking AI that took over my body offered me a deal and the Archers of the Band granted me Resurrection. So, here I am. Reborn twice in the last six months. That must be a fucking world record or something, worth a trophy at least."

I recognize the incredulous look on her face from toddlerhood. She thinks I'm exaggerating. I laugh. "This is just the highlight reel, Mom. The details are something else entirely. Like the twenty prisoners I beheaded on stage, or the three guys I killed in the showers for trying to rape me. And let's not forget little Kete – we barely noticed when her ass never came back after Fight Four."

"Are you finished now, Junco?"

I shrug. "I don't know? Am I? You wanted to know how my fucking Fledge went? Well, I guess it's *possible* you're not aware that Fledge is nothing but killing from start to finish, but I doubt it. That's not something you'd be ignorant of."

She ignores my words and checks her nails like some pampered socialite. "If you recall, I had no part in your life past the age of six. I am not responsible for these events. Now, if you want to pull this attitude with your father when you see him, I'd like to stay and watch. Because that would be something spectacular."

I have so many feelings inside me I don't even know where to begin. "What do you want from me?"

My mother smiles. "I want you to stay here, of course. Stay with us and forget all this nonsense with these avians."

"Are you on drugs?"

Gideon turns his head and laughs at my question.

"I mean, there is no way in hell I'm staying here with you and this Subjack guy."

"You're being used by the avians, Junco. They want you for one reason and one reason only."

"Yeah? What's that?"

"To make sure you die in the end."

A chill travels up my chest wound before I can shut it down. "What the hell are you talking about? They've had plenty of opportunities to kill me and I'm still alive."

My mother looks me straight in the eyes as she speaks. "Because the remaining six Siblings are useless without you, Junco. The clutch is only as strong as all the living members. They need you to be alive when they harvest the genetics. Then how useful will you be?"

Tier's words flood back to me as I think about this. *I have no plans to kill ya yet, darlin'. Perhaps I will one day. Perhaps that day will never come. But right now I'm interested in keeping ya alive.*

There's pounding at the door and I can hear my team outside yelling. Obviously Isten could hear me. I look over at my mother and smile. "You're lying." I get up and walk over to the door and no one stops me this time. I jerk it open and then stop and look up at Tier's surprised face. "I'm gonna go find that bedroom with my armor, Gideon. Whether you come help me find it or not. So be a nice guy and just show me where it is, OK?"

I wait and then hear a chair scrape back from the table behind me. I listen as the footsteps approach and then I turn and wave him in front of me.

I look back one final time at my mother and then the door closes and she is gone. I shrug Tier's hand off my shoulder and keep step with Gid, my absurd dress swaying in the wind we create with our fast pace.

He leads me to the room and opens the door. My armor and supplies are still there and I whip the dress over my head and tug on my dirty tank top. I look back at the guys. "I only need one person to help me get dressed, so choose who stays and then get the fuck out."

Tier stays.

"Don't talk to me, Tier, just help me."

He smiles. "OK, Junco."

He seals me back up and takes two of my rifles so I don't look quite so insane. We're about to leave when he puts his hand up. "Wait, OK? One question, what the fuck was that about back there?"

I stand there thinking but it doesn't make sense. "I have no idea. She's crazy. You think I'm crazy? She's crazy, Tier. I need to get the fuck out of this tunnel. I can't stay here. I can't fucking–"

He takes me by the shoulders. "Stop. We're going tomorrow. It's one day."

"No. I want to go outside now. *Now*, Tier."

"No, Junco. We're meeting with yer father right now. We're planning the mission and yer still in, ya understand? You can't quit in the middle of a mission. And you won't. If ya want to stay here when we leave, then stay. But as you can probably see, you'll be trading down because maybe we're not perfect, but these people are fucking–"

"– human," I whisper.

He exhales a heavy breath. "Yeah. Fucking human."

I pull on the door and open it. Gideon is still outside with the 039 and I glance up at him with a look of surprise.

"Moju still wants in on the mission, Juncs."

I turn to look back at Tier. "He does?"

"Yeah. He's done with Earth."

The small carbohydrate-infused breakfast inside my stomach stirs up the acids and I have a moment of puke panic as we enter the military section of the tunnels. Gideon leads the way again, directing us down a long side tunnel crowded with troops in various dress and stages of exhaustion and injury. The smell of them is what triggers it and the next thing I know I'm puking in a trashcan that mercifully stands sentry at the intersection of another tunnel.

When I come up for air Tier is shaking his head at me and his eyes are glowing bright green.

"It stinks in here."

We catch up with the guys but the air is thick with questions as we walk.

Can you sit on it for a week?

No, Layla. I highly doubt I can sit on this for another day, let alone the rest of the fucking week.

We stop at a cavernous door guarded by both human and machine sentries. The humans physically check Gid and then each one of us. A knee-high machine clacks on eight arachnid-like limbs and then climbs up my leg to spray a chemical antagonist. The mist wafts upward and clings to my armor, and then the bot moves on to Tier. A small yellow cloud of fluorescent gas begins to drift up out of my pocket and the plasma rifles whine and come to attention on my head.

"What the fuck are ya doing?" Tier yanks the bot off his leg and pushes the guards back as they come at me. "Junco, what's in yer pocket?"

I reach in and my hand recognizes the small envelope from Layla. I swallow and pull it out and then reveal it in my open palm. "Anti-rad pills, that's all." The guards take the small packet and one walks away. The others keep their rifles trained on me.

I shrug and look around, unconcerned, and then smile up at Tier.

"You have a KI implant, Junco. Why do ya need anti-rad pills?"

I shrug again. "She said take them, Tier, she's the fucking medical officer, ask her."

"I will." He pulls out his ship comm and searches for a signal, but the guards wave us on and I watch out of the corner of my eye as he puts his comm away. The guards hand me back the envelope as I pass by and Tier snatches it right out of my hand.

Gideon is walking fast and I have to trot to keep up. Tier lags behind for a moment and when I look back at him he's barely walking, reading the note with a puzzled look on his face. He looks up and I stop and chew on my fingernail as I wait for him.

"I know too, Junco. We'll talk about it later."

I want to cry with relief that's how badly I want this secret to be out. But I don't. There's no time for that.

Tier sees I'm on the verge of tears and squeezes my hand. "Ya OK?"

I nod and he takes my hand and we run a little to catch up with the guys who are waiting on us at a door. More biometrics, more guards, more sniffers. Tier hands the little packet over to the guards and explains in a few private whispers that has everyone looking over at me. I bite my lip and take a deep breath.

We pass through this one without incident and then we're in the interior passageways. The inner sanctum of what is Subjack's military command. I can tell because everyone in here has a proper uniform and a snappy attitude. There's none of that everyman soldier shit that we saw back in the outer tunnels, this is the business end.

My heart begins to pound and I take a moment to check it. Tier squeezes my hand a little before letting go and moving up to the front of the group. Isten drifts back to me and smiles as we walk to a final door that is flanked with large sentrybots like the ones back in the Ramah tunnels. Gideon announces us and the doors open. I lean around Isten a little to get a peek, I can't help myself, and a few seconds later we move forward as a group into a war room. There's a long table and I watch Tier shake the hand of a man standing at the head of the table.

A man who most certainly is not my father. I try and pull my eyes away from the hulking bearded man with wild shoulder-length hair and piercing blue eyes, but they're stuck on him. He's not wearing a uniform. In fact he looks far more road-warrior than I did earlier.

He catches my eye and smiles.

I don't smile back.

Tier directs us to take our seats so we line up like we're at Lucan's crescent moon table, and then he walks to the back and stands on the other side of me and begins to speak. "Let me introduce the Aves 039. I'm Captain Raubtier of the Presidential Guard. We serve at Lucan's direct orders so when you speak to us, you speak to Lucan. At the top is Ashur, Executive Officer, when you speak to him, you speak to me. Next is Braun, Rikan, Mish, Arel, Isten, and Junco."

Subjack stands. "Junco, it's good to see you again."

I shrug at him. "You're not my father. Not even close." I look over to Tier. "He's not my father. That's not him."

Tier stays silent.

"OK, what am I missing now?"

"Memories, Juncs." He shakes his head. "Later, OK? We're workin' now." He looks up at Subjack and nods.

I sit there barely listening to the plans they're making. I rack my brain. It's not possible to just lose memories like that. It's not. I've dropped them off before, but I've picked them all back up since the morph. I don't have any missing memories, I have perfect recall, I have it all the way back from when I was a baby. I can pull up anything, anything, in a matter of minutes. Even ancient fucking Sumerian. How could I not recognize my own father? It makes no sense.

The meeting goes on without me for whole stretches of time. I'm only brought back to the present when Isten or Tier shove me to pay attention. I search Isten's mind to bring myself back up to speed and I feel him smile from the inside as he opens up.

The remaining Seven Siblings are being held in a global genetics containment facility called Runout, which is really a mountain town facility built in a valley out near the ski resorts in the MR. It's completely self-sustaining and paranoid to the extreme with aerial rocket launchers and a domed shield that is on twenty-four hours a day, except to allow entry of pre-planned secure deliveries. They have a full-sized army living on the outskirts and elite units that live on the inside.

A hologram emerges from the war table and highlights the town as a small red dot on the 3D map, then it zooms in, the dot growing bigger and bigger with each incremental advancement. Finally we get a bird's view of the valley up close and each building is highlighted and explained. I log it all and tuck it down for later recall. The dot turns yellow and then concentrates in on a single building.

"That's where we think they are." Subjack looks up and meets our eyes one person at a time. He lingers on mine for a fraction and then stops with Tier. "We have a mole and he's been reliable so far, but I can't make any guarantees. Everyone knows you're coming for them, we've been expecting you for months. We have to assume they know you're here now."

"So if we can't fly in, what do ya propose?"

I watch Subjack's face as it begins the initial stages of a large grin and something clicks inside me. I shake it off as he brightens. "The tunnels."

I feel Isten groan just as Tier begins to shake his head. "What's in them? I'm not sure we're interested in fighting off yer mutants, to be quite honest. That's yer problem, not ours."

The burly man grunts. "Bahhhh, you can't go wrong with the tunnels, Captain, it's a straight shot and no one would think you stupid enough to take them all the way up the mountain." He laughs. "It's perfect. And you'll have aerial cover, you can fly your little wings off, fight with whatever weapons you want to haul up there with you, and no one's ever going to know. Because no one in their right mind would go in there in the first place."

Tier stands and smiles, then Ashur and the rest of us. "Your inspirational speech does not convince us, but we'll discuss it and let you know tonight what we plan on doing."

"Discuss it? I thought you were the captain? Make a decision, boy."

Oh shit. All our heads rotate from Tier to Subjack, but Tier shrugs it off. "We operate in our own way, and that means we make these decisions together or not at all." He waits to see if the giant will call him out again, but Subjack just grins. "We'll let you know tonight. Tomorrow we will proceed, regardless of whether or not we adopt this plan of yours."

Tier waves Ashur out and the team follows.

"Junco?"

I turn back to the big man.

"A word with you, please?"

I shrug and sit back down.

Tier turns to look back at me. "I'll be outside, OK?"

I nod at Tier and sign as he leaves the room.

And then I'm alone with the man who says he's my father.

He leans his massive hulk of a body back into his chair. My father was big but not like this guy. "I've been locked down under this mountain for too long, so I'll just say it bluntly and save us some aggravation. I am your father, Junco. Not the one who made you, but the one who raised you. They replaced me with a clone when you were almost sixteen."

I want to say so many things I don't even know where to start. Why? That's the obvious question, right? Then, how could you abandon me like that? You, of all people? The one who promised over and over again that I was loved. Did you think about me after you left? Was I just an experiment to you? But all these questions and hurt feelings get lost in my anger as I replay his flippant explanation. "Well, that explains why there were no more birthday weeks after fifteen."

"Oh, I hadn't thought about that. I'm sorry you missed them."

I snort. "Really? That never occurred to you? You took your daughter somewhere special once a year for her birthday and then one year they just stop. It never occurred to you that she might notice?"

"I'm sorry for leaving, Junco–"

"Who made me? I'm not really interested in you–" I have no idea what to call him, but I certainly won't call him Father. "– Subjack. You're not Commander Coot and I'm not Junco. So, we can move away from that bullshit right now. But I want to know who made me. Who made us?"

"Gyr made you, Junco. He had the code when he came to Earth. That code was never out of the hands of the Avian, ever. They sent him here with it and he did exactly what they told him to do."

"I don't believe that, but go on. Who told him what to do?"

"Lucan, of course. The monster you work for now."

I shake my head and sigh. "You don't even know Lucan, so spare me the insults. I'm not interested in your opinion of him, either. For what purpose?"

"They need to fulfill the prophecy, make the Seven, take back the code so they can fix their bioengineering problems. You, Junco? You are the key they were missing. They can't make it work until they have the leader – and they couldn't make the leader without the other half of the genetics. They need the Seventh Sibling – the mixed one who will complete the prophecy. But they won't need you for long. They won't need any of you for long because they have no intention of letting you fulfill your destiny. None, Junco. They'll kill you all in the end, to prevent the retribution that's due."

I stay still and force a polite smile. "OK, well, I'll keep it all in mind. Thanks."

He stands and takes a step towards me, then hesitates and stops again. "If you're not Junco, then who are you?"

I stare at him for a few seconds. "I'm the Snowbird. I'm the Seventh Sibling. I'm 039-9. Take your pick. But the one thing I'm not, Subjack, is the girl you left behind in the RR when you quit your job as my father. A few years might not seem like a long time when you compare it to the fifteen you spent with me before that. But a lot has happened in that time. More than you can ever imagine."

He takes a few more steps towards me and I back away slightly, causing him to stop. "You can stay here, Junco. Stay with us. We don't need you for any ancient prophecy, you'd have a life with us. You could do anything you want with your life," he smiles, "anything you want. You want to stop killing? I've heard that's taken a toll on you. If you want to stop all that, just stay. Stay with us and settle into the person you always wished you were."

"I'm not sure I believe that, but whether it's just plain cynicism or cryptic sixth sense, I have no idea. Anyway, no, thank you. I'm gonna take my chances with Lucan for now." I look away for a second and then look back at his face.

"He's the devil, Junco. You know this, he's the antithesis of everything you've been taught. He is guilty of horrors. He was banned from Earth. This is his punishment cycle you're interfering with, not yours. Do you understand that? This isn't about the Seven Siblings. This is about that monster trying to get his revenge. He created all these myths and stories to confuse people. To keep them in the dark. This is about him and his interference in the matters of Men, not his race, not you, not Moju or the others. Not us here on Earth. It's all about Lucan saving his own ass."

For some reason my mind drifts back to the day Lucan picked me up from Rache's hospital and took me to see Tier.

"I'm sorry," Tier says.

"You did everything right this time, Raubtier. There is nothing to forgive."

I want to block it all out but I can't. I can only squeak out a few words of feigned indifference. "I don't care." My father's eyes search mine and I see a spark of fear in them. "I don't know what he really is, I'll give you that. But I don't know what I am either. So–"

He nods but both his smile and his invitation are gone. "Take care on your mission tomorrow. They know you're coming and they want you too, Junco. She needs you just as much as the Avians do. The clones just aren't the same."

My reaction is locked down before it starts, I don't know who he's talking about, but he doesn't get to unnerve me like that so I don't ask either. "I can take care of them, I'm sure."

His reply, if he had one, never comes so I turn my back and walk out the door.

Chapter Nineteen

The door shuts behind me and I close my eyes and lean back into it to catch my breath.

"Junco?"

I put my hands up to cover my face and feel everything go hot. My chest heaves as I take in sporadic gasps of air and the tears pool up in my eyes. How much more of this can I take before I lose it completely?

Tier and Isten move in close as Aren walks towards me, trying to get my attention.

"Junco?"

I stop the tears, wipe my eyes, and get myself together before looking back up. The rest of the 039 are gone. Aren stands to my right, while Isten and Tier are on my left. I walk towards Aren and throw my arms around his neck. A few locked-up sobs break free as Aren winds his arms under my wings and up my back, lifting me off my feet to give me a squeeze.

"I never knew, Aren. I never knew that guy wasn't you." I feel the tears pressuring me to let them out, but I don't. If I do, I'll never get them back inside. "I'm so sorry."

He sets me back down but doesn't let go of me. "Shit, Junco. Sometimes even I have a hard time knowing which guy is me." I push my face into his chest and we stay entwined together for a few more seconds. Isten is picking at my feelings but I don't have the energy to hide from him right now, so he feels what I feel. Protected. Safe.

Aren lets me go and pushes me backwards a little so his eyes can take me in. "Holy shit, Junco. You take my breath away." His smile lights up his whole face and his dark blue eyes snap me back to all the days and nights we spent together as teenagers. Oh God. To be that girl again. Even with all the bad stuff that probably happened to me, to be that girl again. I'd give almost anything to go back.

"Yeah, well, I guess I turned out OK." I look up at him. His hair is still a short sandy blond military cut and his features are much like the clone from the RR, but not exactly. My real Aren is more muscular, more confident in the ways he holds himself, and looks wise beyond his years.

Isten is back in my head and suddenly my girlhood manners appear and I turn to include them. "Do you know Isten and Tier?"

Aren is a complete gentleman and reaches to shake their hands. "Nice to finally meet you guys. I've heard a lot about what happened when you were here last, and I can only assume you've taken good care of her since you picked her up, so–" He stops and shrugs. "I'm thankful for that."

My thoughts drift back to all the things that have happened since the last time we were on Earth and I feel Isten cringe. Not all of them were good. I wasn't always taken care of.

Suddenly the silence becomes uncomfortable.

"Junco," Tier takes control, "we have a mission to plan, so maybe we can meet up with people later?"

My smile fades. I don't want to plan the mission. I want to pretend I'm back in cadets. Aren reads me like a book and interjects. "Just come eat with me Junco, OK? It'll only take a little while." He looks over to Tier and finishes, "Your mission can wait."

I start to nod when Tier steps in front of me. "The mission cannot wait, Aren. We've got four days to complete it and then we're gone. So you can see we'll need every second to make that happen."

Aren straightens his back a little at Tier's words and stares back at him with an even gaze. "Junco has all the time she wants, Tier. She's not obligated to return with you guys." His words are low and calm but also clear and commanding. "This is her home. She was raised here by Subjack himself. She was my best friend for three fucking years. So don't tell me she needs to push us aside and get on with planning your mission."

Four years, I want to correct him. Four, not three.

Tier's voice is in complete control but his eyes light up and do a wild green dance. "And then each and every one of ya left her to be beaten and mutilated. That's some fucking way of showing her she's important."

Aren looks down at me, ignoring Tier. "Junco, I know it looks that way, but that wasn't how it was planned. We were discovered, both your father and I. We had to make them think the mission was over and leave or the whole thing would've been blown. I was just about to pull you, Junco. And then that clone went and had Charlie killed, you went off the fucking rails, and this guy appears and takes you off the goddamn planet."

Tier shakes his head. "So ya know what her clone father did ta her then? And you left her there for months as she went insane with the trauma?"

I put my hand up. "Tier, not now, OK? He doesn't know that part. Not now–"

He doesn't take his eyes off Aren. "Oh, right fucking now is as good a time as any, Junco." He looks down at me then. "He's not gonna stand there and play high and mighty hero when he left ya, that's not how it works."

"Aren couldn't possibly have known, Tier. He–"

"I knew, Juncs." Aren looks down at me and my heart skips a beat. "I knew, but I had no idea that clone would" – his words drop off and he looks away and sighs – "kill it like that. Shit, abortion in the RR, how could I have predicted that one?" He's looking at Tier now. "How? It's the Rural Republic, for fuck's sake, the bastion of Right to Life."

Tier's expression is pure hatred and anger and he doesn't even try to hide it. "The man was a clone, not her father." The words come out as a deep growl. "He had no morals or sense of local tradition. If ya didn't realize that, didn't think it through and understand that he'd never respect her rights before ya left her there, then yer too stupid to live."

"All right, we can stand her all day and bicker about who was better to Junco," Aren's arm pushes Tier back, "but that's history now. What counts is the present. And in the present, Junco is home. She's with me for the first time in years and she's allowed to go have some fucking lunch. Don't tell me that the last six months she's spent with you means more than all the years she spent growing up with me. And she was pregnant with Charlie's baby, so she's got a lot of history here–"

"Right, well, now she's pregnant with mine." Tier's lips form a snarl and I take a step back.

Aren looks down at me. "Is this true?" His face is torn between anger and sadness.

I swallow. "I don't know for sure, but–" I look up at him, then back to Tier. He's calm now and his snarl is gone but his eyes never leave Aren. "It's beginning to look that way, Aren."

His eyes turn back up to Tier. "Well, congratulations, you found a way to make your own claim and make it strong, right?"

My jaw tightens and my brow furrows as I think about his words. "What's that mean?"

Aren laughs. "They knew you belonged with us, Junco. It's a strong bond, to have that on our side. And the only bond stronger than childhood friends and family is a child and family of your own." He looks down at me and his face softens. "He owns you now."

I feel Isten cringe in my head and then hear Ashur's words: *And they have a better claim, to be honest. They raised you.* But that was before. Ashur doesn't know I'm pregnant.

Isten puts his hands up and grabs his hair as he thinks it through with me. "Junco, that's not how it is, goddamn it. You can check for yourself. Do not do this to me again."

I shake my head. "God, I can't stand any of you right now." I swallow and look up to Aren. "I really do want to go eat with you, Aren. So we will do that" – I look over to Tier – "after I finish with my team. OK?"

Aren smiles down at me. "Yeah, OK. I'll come find you in a few hours."

I nod and give him a hug before he leaves.

Tier, Isten and I just stand there for a second and then I find some words. "Tier, if you breathe another fucking word about my health status to anyone I'll never forgive you. You don't blab about stuff like that when ya don't even know if it's true."

"It's true, Junco, ya can't deny–"

"Listen to me, you giant asshole! You do not blab about a baby until you know for sure it's healthy, OK? It's bad fucking luck and everyone knows it. I've already lost one baby. All I need is that Luck bastard to take notice of my new potential for happiness and swoop in to collect on his debt."

My words shut him down and I feel Isten's sympathy as he sends me a message. *We're not used to this, Junco, cut him some slack. He's trying.*

"I get it," I say to both of them. "You have no experience with babies and all that. Fine. But that just means you should be extra careful, dammit. So the standing order is shut the fuck up about it. I'll let you know when I want that to change."

They nod their compliance. "And I tell you what," I look up at Tier, "if I find out that you and Lucan planned this pregnancy to force me into coming back with you, I will make sure it backfires."

They both stare at me briefly before erupting into complete denial. "OK." I put my hand up to stop the barrage. "I believe you. But it better just be a happy coincidence."

Tier snaps back from the place I put him in and pokes his finger down at me. "Fine, Junco. But from this second on yer number one priority is this goddamn mission. If I hear ya push it aside one more time I'll have Ryse snatch ya up and hold ya on ship until we're done. Ya understand me?"

"Perfectly."

Tier turns and walks away and Isten prods me to follow. And I do, caught in between the two of them. One overprotective prick and one manipulative mind spy.

Chapter Twenty

"One."

Ashur is pacing slowly around the various pieces of furniture we've arranged in a ring in the center of the room. "We need those 50 cals from the drop camp. Two. Do we really want to waste arms and energy fighting off mutants in the tunnels? Three. We have no idea what they have up there protecting their tunnels. Four. We could just bomb the fuck out of them and drop in straight away and probably keep just as much tactical surprise as coming up through the tunnels. Five. It's a long fucking flight up that goddamn mountain, let alone the flight down to Peaks to catch the right tunnel upland."

Ashur stops his rant against the idea when he gets back to his own chair. "OK, so that's the cons. Here's the pros. One. Complete cover. Two. We can use the grav bikes offered by Subjack and let some of his people join us. Three. We can pack those fuckers up with more ammo than we could ever carry alone. Four. We can still bomb the shit out of them and have the backup teams meet us up there once we shoot them the coordinates. Five." He stops behind my chair and hesitates. "We can use Sera and Arel along the way and fuck up just about everything they have in the way of security."

Ashur makes his way back to his seat in the circle, then Tier nods to Braun.

"I vote tunnels."

It gets passed to Rikan. "Tunnels."

"Tunnels."

"Tunnels."

Isten yawns. "Tunnels."

And then it's my turn. "I go for tunnels, too." Sera appears in the center of the circle and we all sit back in our seats for a second, taken by surprise.

Tier throws up his hands. "What? You have a fucking problem helping?" It comes out as if Sera materializing into thin air isn't something strange. Hell, maybe it's not. What the fuck do I know about how she works?

Sera is dressed in fatigues, but she looks like an actress on a screen dressed up like a soldier, and not a real one. She lifts her chin at Tier. "Don't I get a vote?"

He growls. "What's yer vote, Sera?"

She brightens and tosses her long red hair. "I vote tunnels." She pushes her way through the circle and stands behind Arel. "But Junco and I have business to complete. So, please keep that in mind. When I say she comes with me, she comes with me."

"Hold on, what the fuck is this?"

"It's true," I say. "We have a deal. There's nothing I can do about it."

"What deal?" At first I think he's talking to me, but when I look up he's staring, wild-eyed, at Sera.

I interject before she gets him riled up. "It's nothing, Tier. I'm gonna drop her off here and that's something we all want, right?"

She shoots me a dirty look. "Don't piss me off, Junco, or I'll–"

"All right." Tier cuts her off and turns to Moju. "How about you, Moj? You got anything to add here?"

I'm sitting on a piece of furniture, a small end table that looks like it belongs in a living room two centuries past. It has a shelf on the back end of it and Moju sits on the shelf with my wings between his legs and his hands fiddling with my hair. He clears his throat. "Well, I'm all for those tunnels, but" – he looks around, a little nervous – "I hate to tell ya this now, but Soli is very sick. She might not make it unless we can get to them soon."

Isten pipes up before anyone else can. "Who the fuck is Soli?"

"Oh, sorry. Right. I never told you guys their names or nothing. She's the two, Isten. I have a connection with the other four Siblings – Soli, Irin, Tuk, and Sariel. She" – he hesitates, clearly saddened by this – "tried to escape and it didn't go well. She's fucked up."

Braun is standing, shaking his head with the thought of the repercussions. "Fuck! If she dies we're fucked already and we haven't–"

Tier puts a hand up. "So are we all in agreement about the tunnels, then?" We all nod in the affirmative. "OK, then I'm gonna go contact Layla and tell her this shit about Soli. Arel, you and Sera can come with me and we'll get Monk to make us a comm patch for the tunnels. Moju, you come with me first and then meet Ash, Braun and

Isten to go and get our 50 cals back. And take the short fucking way 'round this time, eh?"

Moj nods.

"Rikan, you and Mish go grab those gravs and start stocking them. See if they can get us some mounts for the big guns, too."

The room is bustling with bodies as I just sit there, completely forgotten.

"What about me?"

Tier stops what he's doing to look over at me like I'm an afterthought. "Go meet yer friends, Junco. Figure it out."

And then they are gone. I sit there stunned. A knock comes from the door and it opens a crack.

"Junco? You still in here?" Gid looks over at me as he enters. I'm still on my end table wondering what the fuck just happened.

He laughs. "Did they leave you behind on purpose?"

I stand. "I guess so. What do I have to do to eat something? I'm starving."

"Again?"

"Oh please, Gideon, I know you were listening to us in the tunnels. I heard an extra pair of boots after Aren turned the first corner. Ya know why I'm starving."

He waves me through to the hallway. "So what did you guys decide to do?"

"Ask Tier, he's the captain. I'm just the nine."

He pulls the door closed and puts a hand on my shoulder to prompt me to move. "Well, I don't have any idea what a nine is in your new world, Junco. But I doubt it's meaningless."

We end up sitting alone in a large tent with about a dozen resin tables serving as a restaurant on the far side of the marketplace. "I thought we were meeting Aren and Selia?"

The waiter comes over and stands next to Gideon, they talk and laugh in German and then the man leaves as Gideon turns his attention back to me. "They'll be here. I ordered you an orange juice, he doesn't speak English. They only serve beef stew, so," he laughs, "I hope you're not a picky eater."

I watch his face for a few moments before answering. "You have a file on me."

He turns away, but only to hide his smile of satisfaction. "I know everything about you, Junco."

"Yeah, well, I've heard that one before. You clearly know nothing about my recent life, so why waste your time bullshitting?"

He shrugs as his gaze redirects to my eyes. We stare at each other for a few seconds and then I break the moment on purpose. "So you're my mother's – what, exactly?"

"I'm nothing to her and she's nothing to me. I'm only here to help you out with the truth."

I laugh and decide to knock him down a peg. "Well, since Sera just informed me this morning that I'll pretty much believe anything, I bet you'll accomplish that goal. But that doesn't mean you're special or talented, Gideon. It's not a testament to your skill, but a reflection of my seemingly unwavering gullibility."

He looks away again, but this time the smile is gone.

"No, you wouldn't, would you?"

He cocks his head at me.

"Have any idea who Sera is."

"I have an idea."

"You have no idea, Gideon. None, because Sera isn't from this world and you've never been anywhere. You know nothing about me so don't kid yourself."

"I know you're the most deadly motherfucking avian the General Fledge has ever seen."

The waiter drops off my OJ and a beer for Gid and disappears without a word. I pick up my glass and hold it up. "To deadly motherfucking Juncos. May they repopulate the RR in force."

He laughs at this, a real laugh. "That was so inappropriate I can't even begin to explain it. But fuck it, you don't know any better, so–"

His eyes glow a little as he holds his beer up and my hand stops the OJ before it reaches my lips. "You're avian."

He tips his glass in my direction one more time. "I might not know all there is to know about your last eight months, Junco, but right now, you know a whole lot less about me." He brings the mug to his lips and takes a drink as Aren and Selia enter the tent and force us to move on.

Selia's blonde hair has grown out and covers her mutilated ear and the scar that runs down the side of her head pretty well. She's still wearing a uniform and has a weapon strapped to her leg. I stand and she hugs me tight. "Feeling better today, Junco?" She pulls back to study my face.

I nod. "Yeah, thanks for letting me crash at your place last night. I was so fucking tired." I watch her to see if she buys the lie. Her crooked mouth says not quite.

"I wanted to tell you all sorts of stuff last night, but you looked pretty out of it. So, good thing we still have time today, right? I sent you all those messages but I never heard back, so I've been having a sort of one-sided conversation with you for months now."

"I got your first message but they never let me see the others, so I'm not really up to speed on what's happening in your world, Selia. I'm sorry." Gideon grunts and I watch him shake his head in my peripheral vision.

Selia's excited face changes to confusion. "Oh." She lets out a long breath of air. "Well, then you have no idea about a bunch of stuff like the clones?"

I hold my hands up. "I'm not sure, Selia, sorry."

I move on and greet Aren, but Selia isn't done.

"Why didn't they give you the messages?" Her expression is something between a scowl and sadness.

"I was in Fledge and Tier was on trial." I look away from Gideon's judgment and Selia's disappointment, and smile at Aren. He raises his eyebrows at me in expectation so I end up back at Selia. "The Archers were not entirely on board with me being there. Your messages scared them, I think."

She nods and looks up at me with a forgiving grin. "OK – well, then we have a lot of shit to talk about."

I breathe out some relief. Her chatter fills the tent and I sit and listen to her tale, looking at her and Aren between bites of beef stew when they switch off in the conversation.

Gideon never says a word.

Most of what she tells me I already know, or at least have an idea. Out-of-control cloning, mutants, collusion between governments, stealing of alien genetic material. I look over at Gideon when this comes up and watch him feign disinterest.

Then Selia explains how Charlie's family ended up being MR military and didn't see my description of Charlie's death as the closure I meant it to be. Luckily the pilot who flew her out of the RR went with her to deliver the package because she refused to give him his half of the bribe until that part of the deal was completed.

Charlie's family tried to kill them, but the pilot was an ex-operative in the Polar Friendly. He flew them up there and that's how she got involved with all this Subjack stuff. Her life since I left earth sounds like the twisted plot of some espionage book.

Junco?

Yeah.

Where are you?

Where are you?

Uh, west entrance.

I shake Gideon to get his attention. "Hey, where is this place relative to the west entrance? Isten wants to know?"

Gideon answers me without turning his head. "Straight back on the left, red tent, sign's in German."

I repeat the directions to Isten and Aren is suddenly interested in me. "You have an internal comm or something, Junco?" Aren asks with a skewed frown.

I don't have a chance to answer because I hear my team outside and crane my neck with anticipation. They are boisterous and loud as they enter the tent and then get louder when they see me.

Isten, Braun, Moju, and Ashur walk over to the table.

"What the fuck happened–?"

Ashur and Braun look like they've beaten the shit out of each other.

Braun picks me up to steal my seat and then sets me back down on his lap. "We put that shit to rest, Juncs. That's all. Not the first time Ash and I have scrapped. And it definitely won't be the last, he's such a straight-backed fucking piker."

I look over to Ashur and while his serious eyes say nothing, his mouth sure does. "You stay away from his stupid ideas, Junco. I'm not fucking around, either. I'll punish you somehow if you ever take his advice again, you got it?"

This is a sore spot for Ashur, so I nod. Braun pinches me on the stomach and I twist away and stand until Isten grabs me my own chair and we talk privately.

Are they really OK?

Yeah, sure. They really do fight all the time.

So, you get the 50 cals?

Yeah, and the suits just in case. These guys giving you trouble?

Nah.

"Junco!"

"Yeah?" I look over at Ashur. "What?"

"If you two have something to say, say it out loud, goddammit. I told you, that shit pisses me off."

"I was just asking about our weapons. Jasus, why are you so angry?"

Ashur brushes me off and calls the rest of the team to give them directions. They straggle in over the next several minutes. Tier is the last to enter and he smiles at me as he walks in but takes a seat between Gideon and me.

Their food arrives and the 039 and Moju settle down to eat. I watch my team carefully to log how they react to the human food, but it's a non-issue. They converse easily with the humans, even Selia. Arel bothers her for whole stretches of time about the reports we saw back in the Band. It's clear that the 039 is just as at home on this planet as they are on Amelia. I guess that's what happens when you spend most of your life living between two worlds.

"Junco?"

I look over to Aren. "Yeah?"

"Wanna go for a walk with me?"

Both Gideon and Tier begin to object but I put up my hand. "Sure, Aren. Lead the way."

We walk out into the bustle of the marketplace and turn left and enter an adjacent tunnel that is far less busy.

"What's this part?"

Aren grabs my hand and smiles down at me when I look up, a little startled. "The cheap seats, that's all. But it's quiet so we can talk a little. Are you happy, Junco?"

I let out a long sigh. "Happy? I'm not sure what that means. I have moments, ya know? But happy. No. I don't think so. I don't understand what's happening, Aren. I have memories that I can't trust. Like earlier you said we were best friends for three years, but it was four and in my memory we were a lot more than friends."

He stops and lets go of my hand. "What?"

I shake my head and smile. "See, this is what I'm talking about. In my reality you came back after your graduation, Aren. We had a pretty serious relationship going. Am I crazy? Did I make that up?" He looks away for a few seconds and when his dark blue eyes meet mine again they confirm my worst suspicions. "He was a clone, wasn't he? That Aren?"

He nods. "I left the RR after graduation, Juncs. Came up here with your father."

I turn away and start to go back and Aren trots a little to catch up with me. We turn the corner and I see all the guys waiting outside the tent. Tier's eyes find mine and I stop short. "That Aren that went looking for me after my father's funeral. That was my real Aren, wasn't it?"

"I'm not sure, Junco. I'm really not."

"And Tier really did kill my Aren." I look up at Aren now. "I loved him, ya know. I thought he was you."

"He wasn't real, Junco. He was a copy of me, for fuck's sake. Just a copy. And whatever information you told him, he sold it back to the MR. He *sold* you."

A memory comes back to me. Not a deep one, just a few moments of my Aren and I out on the scrub, when we were running from Tier. *I figure I had all that field experience, so I took my skills to the highest bidder. And frankly, Junco, I'm having a hard time swallowing this fucking holier-than-thou attitude you suddenly seem to have about it. You and I are no different.*

I shake my head. "No, Aren, you're wrong. He didn't. I told him something the very first day back to school. That very night we slept together for the first time and I told him something that I know for a fact he never repeated."

When I look back up he's angry. "I cannot fucking believe the words coming out of your mouth. He was my fucking clone! I was your friend, Junco. For years! We did everything together."

"My father paid you, Aren. He set us up to be friends and he paid you."

He hisses out a breath. "I never took the money, you know that! I told you I never took the money!"

"But you never loved me either. The other one did, Aren. And Tier killed him."

He laughs now. "You know what, you *are* fucked up. He was the traitor, Junco. Not me. How can you possibly–"

"I told you, dammit. He did not tell them what I told him. And he reminded me out on the scrub that day when we were running from Tier. You remember when the Mayor of Peak City was assassinated a few years back, Aren?"

I watch his face as the words come out. He remembers, but he's too busy fitting the pieces together to answer me.

"I killed that motherfucker on a freelance job. You understand what that means, Aren? Freelance job. I was not under orders from my father, or that clone, or whoever was supposed to be handling me that year. That first day back to senior-year cadets I killed the fucking Peak City mayor in the river as he was kayaking down some pansy-ass stretch of whitewater. I cut his fucking biometrics out of the palm of his left hand and sold it to buy some illegal weapons I picked up that same night."

My jaw clenches with anger as I remember back to that day. To how fucking horrible it felt to learn that I was one hundred percent alone in the world. And how fucking good it felt when I went back to school that night and Aren was waiting for me. Concerned about me. Wanting to love me.

I look back over to Tier and Gid has his arm and he's physically restraining him from coming over here.

My eyes dart around as I complete the thoughts running through my mind. "You're the real Aren. Fine. That's you. But there was another Aren in my life, OK? And to me, he was real as well. You don't get to decide what he meant to me. Got it?"

Gid and Tier are arguing now, pushing each other. Any minute the fists will fly so I start walking towards them. Aren hangs back and doesn't follow me. Gid lets go of Tier as I approach.

"Junco, I think we should go back to our room now. Come on, you look tired."

"I am tired, Tier. But I'm not going back to the room with you guys. I'm gonna sleep in my parents' house tonight."

Gideon's eyebrows go up and he smiles.

Tier frowns. "Why, Junco?"

I shake my head. "I don't even have the energy to explain it, Tier. I just want some space."

I pivot and look around to try and get my bearings and find my way back to the guarded door. I feel a hand on my back and Gideon is next to me. "I'll take you there."

Chapter Twenty-One

We're silent as we walk back to the room and I'm not in the mood to keep up a forced conversation, so I let it go.

When we get there Gideon follows me inside and closes the door. "I'll stay until you ask me to leave, OK?" He turns on the screen and slumps in a chair as I lie on the couch.

"You guys have all the comforts of home down here, huh?"

He lets out a little laugh. "Yeah, well, gotta keep the masses happy, right?" He flips through the channels and finds a horror screen.

I watch the familiar plotline for several minutes. "You wanna hear something funny?"

He looks at me sideways, not quite taking his eyes off the screen. "What?"

"My first night out of the tank on Amelia, I had Ashur as my guard and he was watching horror screens too."

The smile creeps up on his face until it's genuine. "Same shit, different world?"

I laugh. "You have no idea, Gideon."

He looks away but I catch his words. "I have an idea." He concentrates on the screen for a few seconds, then turns to look at me. "I've been plenty of places, Junco."

"Tell me where."

He turns back to the screen without saying anything so I take the initiative. "The First Fledge Fight was nothing but a thousand people in an arena. They lined us up in a pattern, like a ziggurat."

His head snaps around to look at me.

"It only lasted five minutes and hundreds of people were dead at the end."

He looks away, his jaw clenching, and I'm sure I'll have to continue in order to keep the momentum going. But then he talks. "I'm not avian or human. I'm both. Just like you, Junco, I'm a Seven too." He stops and for a second I think he's done, but then he continues. "I'm just not *the* Seven. My clutch is gone." He looks over at me and shrugs.

"How is that possible? You don't have wings and you're older than me, so you have to have wings."

"I'm different, that's all." He looks away. "Your turn."

"Does it bother you? Being different?"

He doesn't look over. "If you wanna play, then it's your turn."

I count my own breaths. "A really cool guy named Kush saved me at the end of Fight One. And he's the one I killed by accident at the end of Deliverance. I killed myself – not to save Tier – but because I just wanted to die."

This gets his attention. His eyebrows go up and he looks over at me. "Shit."

"No one else knows that. Not even Lucan."

"So why tell me?" His face is calm, but his eyes are searching.

"It feels good to tell someone secrets. Someone other than Sera. Or Isten, because he steals them anyway. But he never wanted to find this one."

"What's up with you and that guy?"

"We're twined."

"No idea what that is, Junco."

I shrug. "Me either, but we're connected now. That's all I know."

He's silent for a few seconds so I prod. "Your turn."

"I'm not a bodyguard, Junco. I'm just a hired killer who got sidetracked." He looks away after this confession, like he's done now.

My heart thumps for a fraction before I lock it down and take a deep breath. "Must be nice to get paid for doing something you're good at."

His interest is not renewed.

"Subjack made me kill people every time he took me to an aerialist competition overseas. And since you obviously read a file on me, I'm sure you already know that. So how do you justify helping me with the truth, when all they ever did was lie to me?"

The silence between us creates a gulf and again, just when I think he's not gonna cross it, he surprises me and makes the effort. "Another government hired me to kill you once, Junco." His stoic face gives me chills for some reason. "But I don't kill kids, and I certainly don't bother with killing girls unless I have to. So I refused and took the info to your mother. She offered me a place here, to help you if you ever needed it. And for your information, they're all lying to you. Not just the Subs and not just the MR. The avians invented the lies and if you want my opinion, they're more guilty than all of the others – because right now you trust them."

"I know they're keeping things from me, but it's not like they didn't ask if I wanted the truth, ya know. I just don't want it right now."

"That's the most pathetic thing I've ever heard." His eyes can't stop the slow gradual migration over to my face and I watch him struggle not to show his revulsion to my words.

"It's my life."

"Whatever you say, Junco. You're right, it's your life."

"You can leave now."

He nods and gets up out of the chair. "Fine. I'll see you tomorrow then.

I lie on the couch and absently watch the screen for a little while, thinking, trying to piece it all back together. The memories of my father are not helping because they clearly show he's not a monster. Maybe not quite a good guy, but there are certainly bigger, more dangerous things in the world than my father. And he saved me during my twelfth-year test. He saved me. And that was strictly against the rules. How many times did Matthew tell me what would happen if I lost during a test?

Too many to count. That I do remember.

And Lucan said they were tracking my adrenaline, not because I was sick, but so that I could fool the sensors at security checkpoints when I was on a mission. And that makes total sense. Even without verification, I feel that one to be one hundred percent true. So they all lied to me about that.

And Gideon said we're both Sevens. There are lots of Sevens. Which corroborates Isten's description of Iliana. She's not a clone. She's another Seven. A lone Seven. Like Gideon.

And my Aren. I feel the heat rise up in my face as I think about our last time together. He fought for me. Fought *Tier* for me, for fuck's sake. I'm not sure I'd fight Tier for anyone. I don't care if that Aren was a clone. He was the one who loved me. And Tier killed him.

I put a stop to the tears immediately. I don't have the luxury of crying right now. Either I figure out what's going on real fast or I'll be forced to make a choice that might have long-lasting consequences.

A strong knock sounds on my outer door. I drag myself up off the couch and open it up.

"Selia? What're you doing here?"

"Can I come in, Junco?"

"Sure." I wave her into the room and check the hallway outside real fast. There are two guards standing nearby who both give me a little wave. I've had guards all my life but none of them have ever waved at me before. I smile and wave back, then close the door.

Selia looks nervous as I direct her to sit. She takes the couch and I take the chair. "What's going on?"

I stare at the long scar that runs down the side of her head as she begins to talk. "Shit, I'm so glad you came here tonight. I thought for sure you'd be with that Tier guy and I'd never get a chance to talk to you before you left." She looks up at me, her expression is one of almost uncontrollable worry.

"What are you talking about?"

"Junco, there is a lot more to what's going on that I think you know. I've been told about the avian prophecy, the Seven Siblings they have, right? You guys are part of some long-ago punishment cycle. Mixing of the two species, man and bird? Right?"

I laugh. "Shit, Selia. I have no idea, really. I don't understand what's going on. Tier told me a story about that before we left for the Band, so maybe. It might be true, who knows."

"I've heard a similar story. In fact, most of them say that. But I've spent a lot of time traveling, Junco, looking into this myth they have, and that's not the whole story. There's another version." She stops talking and looks up at me.

"Say it, Selia. Just say it."

"That Lucan guy? I don't know him and you do, so of course you'll have to consider that. But he's the one responsible for all this. He's not human and–"

"Selia, tell me something I don't know, OK? I can't do this right now."

She laughs a little, but it's not a happy laugh. It's an uncomfortable one. "We have records of this event, Junco. Ancient written records. And there is a myth about you Seven, but it says a whole lot of things that you don't seem to be aware of."

"Like what?" I lean back in the chair, too tired to sit up straight.

Her face goes flat as the words spill out. "They need the six of you, to fix their genetics, that's true. But here on Earth, you guys aren't the Seven Siblings. You're the Seven Evil Demons. Because if your clutch is the one that makes it, then you, the Seventh demon, have to choose between humans and avians. You have to choose. And the one that doesn't get chosen? That species is annihilated. Wiped out.

Seven siblings of the aftermath,
Seven siblings created by death,
Six avian children of light,
All are guilty of the fall,
The seventh castaway in flight,
Mixing blood perpetual,
Making monsters that transcend,
Until the seventh brings the end."

"I've read that before, Selia."

"I wasn't done.

Seven siblings of the wide heavens,
Seven siblings of the broad earth,
Seven robber-gods are they.
Seven evil gods,
Seven evil demons,
Seven to break heaven and earth,
The Seventh acting as the pawn,
Burning one into extinction.

"The myth I found on Earth describes the seven of you as a whole list of bad things – a snake, leopard that eats children, charging rampant, a southern storm. That's Moju because he's the One."

"What am I?"

"You're the Wind of Vengeance because you're the Seven. You and Moju are the beginning and the end, like a cycle."

"Well, that's awesome."

"Moju thinks Esta is the Four – the Terrible Serpent Weapon. And he says Soli is the Two, so she's the Dragon that Eats the World." I swallow but stay silent as she continues. "This is the end, Junco. Do you see? This is the end. And you get to choose. *Us or them.*"

Us or them. That's been a question since this whole affair began, hasn't it. Who is us and who is them? I asked Aren that out on the scrub. And it was him and me against the world from the way he told it.

I get up and pace the small room, suddenly feeling trapped. I want her to go away but she's still fucking talking.

"Lucan. I admit I don't know him, so whatever. You do. But he's the reason for all of this, Junco. He's the one who caused the Fall."

"It's Biblical? Do they think this is the Biblical End Times? That Lucan is – what? The Fallen Archer?" I get sick just thinking about it.

"The what?"

I shake my head to clear it. "Sorry, I mean the fallen *angel*?"

She shrugs. No help at all. "I'm an atheist, Junco. There is no such thing as a fallen angel. The world might end, but it's not because God is gonna come back to earth and smite us. And I don't think you'll bring the end of the world either, I just want you to know what's going on. You're the center of all this. You. So, ya know, be careful."

"I've had enough tonight, Selia."

She takes the hint and pulls the door closed behind her, leaving me alone to think about angels and demons and the end of the world all by myself. I don't even undress, I just lie on the bed and count myself until my eyes are so tired the whole nightmare falls away.

Chapter Twenty-Two

My snow boots are making puddles on the tile floor of my camp room. If Maggie comes in and sees the mess she might punish me. My head hurts. I look up at the clock and work out what the big and little hands mean. 9:00 and it's dark so that means it's PM, not AM. PM means predators out until morning. So that's nighttime.

My winter coat is bunched up around my hips and my scarf is still wrapped tightly around my face. My breath passes through the fabric of the soft cloth, making it wet.

But I don't care.

I swallow as my stomach rumbles again. It's been doing that since we left the ski resort. Since Mom was taken away. Her eyes looked a little scared, but Mom never gets scared. This makes my stomach tighten so much I lean over and wait for it.

I swallow the spit that gathers under my tongue as I think about throw-up. The sweat rolls down my back and makes my waistband wet. I should just go outside. I'd be just as wet out there in the snow as I would in here wrapped up in my own heat.

I hear Gideon's door across the hall. I get up quickly and rush over and press my palm against the biometric pad on the doorknob.

It flashes red at me.

Locked in.

I swallow again.

Gideon? I need you.

Hold on, Snowbird. I'll be in soon. Take off your winter gear and lie down.

A tear falls out of my eye and I wipe it away so my alarm won't go off. I don't want to see anyone. No one but Gideon tonight.

I unwrap the scarf and the cool air rushes in so I take a deep breath and enjoy it. Gid says when things feel good I should enjoy it, because there'll be lots of times when things will feel bad and I can think about something good when that happens. It's like collecting good things up and saving them for later.

I memorize the feeling of cool air rushing in on my face to take the heat away. It's small, probably won't help much, but maybe. You never know. Plus, maybe if

I remember a bunch of little good things all at the same time, then it will take away one bigger bad thing? I'll have to ask Gideon about that later.

I slip off my boots next and put them on the mat by my door. I grab a dirty shirt from the laundry basket and wipe the puddle they made next to my bed.

Finally I take off the coat and hang it up on the knob above the boot mat.

And I sit back on the bed, unwrapped, and swallow.

I can still hear them yelling out in the big room.

Mostly it's my dad, but some of it is Dale and some of it is Matthew. James never yells, but that doesn't mean he's not mad. He's sneaky like that.

I hear the biometrics click and Gideon walks in my room and closes the door behind him. "You OK?"

"Am I OK?"

He laughs. "I asked you the question, Junco. You have to answer, not ask another one."

"I'm OK."

He comes to sit on my bed. He's wearing the t-shirt I made him for his birthday last week. It says, God Loves Twelve-Year-Olds. *I wanted him to know God loves him because he never gets to go to church and hear it for himself.*

He looks down on me, his eyes darting to mine, then to the side as he listens to the yelling outside my door. "Do you need to talk?"

I swallow and the tears leak out. "I did something very bad, Gideon."

He hugs me and I feel his chest go up and down. I lean my head against it and listen for his heartbeat. "You weren't bad, Junco. They aren't yelling about what you did. That was an order, remember?"

"It doesn't matter if it was an order, Gid. It was bad. God will never–"

"God has nothing to do with this, Junco. Nothing. You can't live by God's rules. You can't. It's impossible. If you try they will kill you. Do you want to live?"

I push away and look up at his face. "Yes."

"Then you will follow orders until I tell you it's safe to stop, you got it?"

I swallow down the spit that's collecting in my mouth again.

"God knows it's not your fault, Junco. God knows." He pulls me against him again. "You're not bad." He says it more to himself than he does to me.

"I'm just like a lion, Gideon. I do what prairie lions do out on the scrub. I kill."

"The lion has to kill, Junco. If the lion stopped killing it would die. Do you want to die?"

I shake my head as I lean into him. "I'll be a lion if I can live."

He sighs. "It's OK to be the lion, Junco. It's OK. I'm the wolf, remember?"

I nod my head. "I'm the lion and you're the wolf."

"And we're the same, remember? We're in this together."

"I remember."

"And the lions aren't bad, ya know. The wolves either. They're just trying to eat when they kill. It's natural what they do."

"But it's not natural for me."

"It is too, Junco. You aren't killing to eat, no. But you're still killing to live. It's the same thing. If you said no what would've happened?"

"Punishment."

"And if you said no too many times? What would happen?"

"Death."

"So, you have to say yes. One day, Juncs, you will be big and you can say no. OK?"

"But you're big." I push back and look up to his face.

He laughs. "Not really, Junco. Twelve might seem big to you now, because you're only six. But twelve is small. You'll see. When you get to be twelve you'll see that twelve isn't big."

"Do lions even live to be twelve?"

"Lions and wolves live the same amount of time and we're gonna live long lives. Away from here. We just have to wait. We just have to wait until the time is right. One day we'll both be big and we'll be all finished with training and we can leave."

"Do you promise?"

We hear the loud thud of boots as they approach my door, then watch the biometrics light up on the doorknob. I feel Gideon's heart pound and mine follows along, helpless to make it stop.

My alarm goes off and I jump up and start crying.

Matthew comes in and grabs me. "Make it stop! Now, you stupid brat!"

Gideon gets off the bed and I swear I can hear his heart thumping in his chest, but when he puts his hand on my shoulder he sends me nothing but calm.

I watch him breathe and match my own breaths to him as Matthew's grip on my shirt shakes me.

My dad appears in the room and he punches Matthew in the face without saying a word. Matthew goes down on the floor as I lose all my self-control. My dad leans down. "Make it stop, Junco. Gideon, help her."

I follow Gideon's breathing again but my eyes lose track and watch as Matthew gets to his feet and he and my father begin fighting again. They slam against the wall and Gid ushers me out of the way and into the hallway, then I'm in his room, breathing hard and trying to ignore the adrenal alarm going off in my health tracker.

Gid's face is down in mine. "Breathe, Junco, or you will die."

I snap out of it and breathe until the alarm goes away.

We sit there and wait for the violence in the hallway to degenerate back to yelling. I look up at Gideon. "I hate Matthew."

He smiles at me, then looks over at the door, listening to the shouts of the two men out in the hallway for a few more seconds. "One day, Junco. We'll kill that motherfucker. So whenever he's mean to you, you add it to a list in your head of all the reasons why you should take his life when I tell you it's safe. OK?"

"He's big, Gideon."

"But he's not a lion, Junco. You are."

I smile this time. "And he's not a wolf, either."

Gideon lets out a deep breath. "No, he's nothing but a man. And men are very easy to kill."

I still have my SEAR knife because Dad and I haven't even made it home yet after our trip. I slip it out of my dock and power it up. The yellow loop of plasma is dialed up to a small dagger length and the light it emits flashes against Gideon's skin and makes his eyes dance.

Gideon slips his out and powers it on, then dials it down to a small blue loop and touches my knife to his. They sputter for a second and he removes it.

"Why can't we just go cut everyone right now, Gideon? It would be so easy."

"Our SEARs are coded for them, Junco. I told you this. They won't work on them, just like they won't work on us. We just have to wait because no one is coming to help us."

"We're the only ones, right?"

He smiles at me. "The only ones left, *Junco. They killed the rest. But if we're smart, they won't kill us. We'll kill them."*

"And we're smart?"

"Very smart, Snowbird. That's why you learn everything they show you, the very first time, right?"

I nod.

"You learn it, everything. Even if you think it's dumb. You put it in your head and never get rid of it. And never tell anyone that you do this. Right?"

"Right."

"Because we're the only ones left. The only Sevens left."

I power down my SEAR and put it back, my thoughts momentarily drifting back to the woman's neck I cut with it yesterday. "Why do they make Sevens if they just want to kill them?"

"They need us. They need Sevens. But Sevens are too smart so they kill them and try again. But we're more than smart, Junco. We're brilliant. We know they want to kill us, and we pretend to do what they say. Sun Tzu, remember him?"

"War means you have to lie."

He laughs. "Yeah, good enough. War means you have to lie."

We listen to the men outside Gid's door and he takes a deep breath and points to me.

I take one as well and when the biometrics flash and my dad walks in, I am calm.

He smiles at us. "Thank you, Gideon. I won't forget your help. Come on, Junco, we're going home now."

I lean into Gideon and choke back a sob. He pats me on the back and squeezes. "See you soon, OK? It's almost time for winter camp."

I nod. "OK."

"And thank you very much for the wonderful shirt, Junco. I know God loves me, but it's nice to be reminded once in a while."

I beam up at him.

"And congratulations on your second-place trophy at the competition. We all watched you on the screens in the big room. Everyone clapped for you."

My whole body feels warm as he reminds me of my forgotten mounted acrobatics contest. Second place is good. A red ribbon and a trophy. Plus I got free ice cream at the concession stand when I showed them my prizes and even though I couldn't eat it, I gave it away to some kid and made her happy. "I love you, Gideon."

"Ditto, Snowbird."

Chapter Twenty-Three

Tier is addressing the makeshift Subjack team in the tunnels and the 039 is standing in crescent formation, watching as he lays into the two dozen men who have been pushed on us. Absent are Aren and Selia – and that surprises me.

"– have no fucking idea why you'd want to come with us on this mission, we could give a fuck about any of ya. So, if yer thinking yer gonna make an impression on me, or my team, think again. We don't want ya here, we were forced ta take ya–"

They are, without a doubt, throwaways. Just like the kids in Fledge with me. They have no armor, just plain field clothes. Their weapons are shit, some don't even have weapons, no helmets, no internal life support, no nothing. I take a deep breath and thank God for my alien provisions as I stand there.

I woke up early to think about what I should do with all this new information. I'll complete this mission as part of the 039, but beyond that, I'm not making any decisions yet. I don't care if I am pregnant with Tier's child, and I'm not convinced of that to be honest. But I'm not gonna travel a hundred million miles away from Earth without some serious consideration of the consequences.

Tier stops in front of me, reaching in his pocket to pick out his com, and Ashur continues where he left off without even missing a heartbeat. He pushes the comm in my direction and I take it automatically. "It's for you, Junco." He joins Ashur as they continue to spew threats towards the unwanted.

I take the buzzing tech and walk over towards my stocked grav bike. Gideon is slumped down over the handlebars of his bike, resting his head in his hands, not even trying to pay attention to Tier or Ashur. I guess he's not included in whatever we have going on here.

He gets interested in me real fast as I walk past him and push the answer tab on the com. "This is Junco."

I hear a breath of exhaled air on the other end. "Junco. Are you all right?"

"I told him not to call you, Lucan. I'm fine."

"I should have told you everything, I–"

"Yes, you really should've. I'm so tired of this, Lucan. I believe in you, in all of you. But then you lie to me and it's starting to make the things my parents tell me that much more real."

"Junco, you will come home."

"I'll go wherever I want. You can't stop me and I don't want to talk about it right now. We're getting ready to leave."

"So you saw your father?"

"Yes, but my memories are all fucked up. I don't understand it. In my head, that isn't what my father looks like."

"They took large spans of memories from you, Junco. Isten found the spaces when you were twined. We should have told you–"

"Just never mind. I said I don't want to talk about it."

"That's what worries me, Junco. You are indecisive and you blind yourself from the truth on purpose. Do you realize these are serious character flaws?"

"That's not fair and you know it. You've been lying to me this whole time. I can't make good decisions with incorrect or missing information. So, yeah. I've got faults, but so do you. You're not perfect either, ya know."

He sighs. "I will be on the ship, so if you need me–"

"Don't stick around on my account. I don't need you."

"You *will* need me, Junco. And I owe you, so I will be here. This is not about the Seven. I will not leave you here."

"You owe me. I forgot. Fine then, this is your payback. Then you won't owe me."

He sighs long and deep and when he talks his voice is barely a whisper. "If you want to stay on Earth, then stay. But you will provide me with a resignation. Face to face. I don't care if your explanation is *Fuck off, Lucan. I would rather die than see you again.* You will tell me this in person. If I don't get that conversation from you and you go missing, Junco? I will react like you're still my warrior. Tell me you understand this."

I nod at his forcefulness even though he can't see me. "Did you see something?" I look around and see Gideon's eyes burning down into me, not even trying to hide it, and I turn back quickly.

"No, I cannot see you. But I see the others. There's something off, something is wrong."

"Well, what should we do?" I feel Gideon walk up behind me and I walk a little farther away to make him take a hint.

"Either we move forward or I pull you all home. It won't work without you, so I cannot take you and let Tier continue."

"No, I need to put an end to this Sibling shit. I can't move on until that's done. It's literally just a few hours up the mountain so we might have them by tonight." I feel a hand on my shoulder and push it off as I turn, angry at Gideon for interfering.

But it's not Gideon. It's Tier.

"Tier is here, do you want to talk to him?"

"Yes. Please be careful."

I hand the comm over to Tier and he walks off without looking back at me. Gideon walks over as Tier leaves. "Problems?"

My head shakes out a lie. "No, none at all."

"Was that the infamous Lucan?"

"Yeah, that was him."

"Is he mad at you?"

I make a face at Gideon. "I don't think Lucan has ever been mad at me. Well, that one time when he smacked me for threatening him, I guess he was mad that day."

"Sounds like a real charmer."

I walk over to my bike and climb into the shoot seat. My 50 cal is mounted so I can cover from behind as Isten navigates. I imagine that even with the muzzle brake it will throw off the trajectory of the grav bike pretty significantly, so I doubt it'll be real accurate, but fuck it. Better than nothing, I guess.

Gideon follows me over and continues. "So, what did he say?"

"Gideon, it's none of your business. It's team stuff."

"You're a liar, Junco. That was personal stuff. Now what the fuck did he say?"

"He said to be careful, that's all."

"That's all?"

"He said something's wrong, but he couldn't place it. He said–"

"That's enough, Junco." Tier's voice from behind makes me jump. "Gideon, I don't care if ya come and look after Junco, but beyond saving her ass in a pinch, she's none of yer business. So stay the fuck out of what we're doing."

Gid straightens up, he's a little taller than Tier but Tier doesn't take the hint. "I don't take orders from you, Tier. I'm not on your team and I'm not a Sub soldier you can bully around. My job is simple, keep

Junco alive. And if that demon told her something that will affect how I do that, then I wanna fucking know about it right fucking now."

Tier's eye begin to exude green light with the challenge. He pushes him in the chest and Gideon swings, his fist crashing against Tier's jaw. Tier grabs his leg and pulls, making Gid fall to the ground. And this is where it really gets interesting: the Tier I've seen fight is a slasher, a kill-'em-quick-and-get-it-over-with kind of fighter. But he's grappling, like Ashur and me, and he's fucking good at it, too.

His feet and hands slide in and out as they wrestle. Gideon's hands and feet are just as fast and the two of them complete more positions, holds, and locks than I can count in just a few seconds. They both scramble to their feet and circle, rage spilling out of Tier's green eyes, and even Gideon's eyes are glowing. They're red. His secret, if it even was a secret from the rest of my team, is out now.

Gideon spits on the ground and he's growling when he speaks. "You might have that monster behind you, and all the illegal gifts he gave you. But I'm no stranger to gifts, Raubtier. I've trained for this my whole life as well."

Tier continues to circle but Ash steps in between them and pushes him away while Isten claps Gideon on the back and diverts his attention with words I cannot hear.

Tier walks away and barks orders out to the Subs as Aren and Selia enter the tunnels with their own set of grav bikes. He takes his temper over to Aren and physically prevents Selia from even entering the tunnels. I watch as Aren swats Tier's hand off Selia's shoulder and they argue. Good luck with that, Aren. I am just about to turn away when another figure appears in the entrance.

Subjack.

His presence stops the argument and Tier pushes Selia out and then directs his attention to my father. They talk back and forth for a few minutes, then Tier turns to find me. Meets my eyes, and motions for me to come over to him.

I blow out some air and walk over. "What?"

Tier points to the burly man and then walks off after Aren and Selia, leaving us alone.

"What?" I ask again, this time directing it up towards Subjack. He's cleaned up a lot since yesterday. His beard is trimmed close to his face and his hair is slicked back on his head. His road-warrior gear has been replaced with a standard commander's uniform.

"I'm not letting you leave with those words between us, Junco. We've always sorted it out in the past and we will sort this out as well."

I turn my head away as I speak. "I don't want to sort it out now."

"I have a power for you," he says. It's like my words never even came out of my mouth.

I turn back and look up at him, meet his eyes and hold his gaze. "I don't need your powers anymore."

"I know that, Junco. You're quite powerful already. It's a different kind of power." He takes my hand and slips a piece of paper in it.

I look at the paper as he keeps hold of my hand, a small envelope really, and then raise my eyes again. "So what's this?"

"Proof." He folds my fingers over so they close around the envelope before letting go, and then he turns and walks away.

Tier is watching me from the end of the hallway, Aren and Selia momentarily forgotten. He makes his way towards me. "What's that he gave you, Junco?"

I stuff the envelope in my pocket. "I'm not going to look at it now."

The fact is, I think to myself as I walk back towards Isten, I'm not interested in sharing this with Tier. My father is none of his business, just like Tier said I'm none of Gideon's business. My feelings about his role in my upbringing have shifted a bit in the last two days and I haven't had a chance to sort it all out yet. My father isn't as easy to dismiss as my mother. He was there, she wasn't. And that alone means he at least gets to have his say.

Isten is messing with our bike when I make my way over to him. Several other bikes come online all at once and the atmosphere inside the tunnel becomes thick with exhaust.

Ashur takes his navigation seat up near the front of the group. His hands deftly flip switches for fuel mixture and power levels, then flit over the shields and weapons systems. Mish navigates the second bike and does the same, while Braun takes the shoot seat behind Ashur where he has a large cannon mounted. Braun is packed to the hilt with munitions and internally I think it's kinda funny that he and Ashur have to be mission partners even though they don't get along.

Rikan's golden-boy persona is absent now, his hair and wings are both darkened with some kind of spray-on, as he takes his shoot seat behind Mish.

"Hey, Is?" I look over but he's busy adjusting something on the back end of my 50 cal.

Gideon is next to me before I can figure out where he came from. "Something wrong, Junco?"

"No. Hey, Is?" He's still busy and I begin to lose my patience. *Isten!*

He looks up. "Fuck, Junco! What? You don't have to scream at me, I'm right here and the fucking rifle's not mounted tight, OK? Hold the fuck on a minute."

I scowl at him and look around, but everyone, including Tier, is busy with their own issues before we move. I look back at Gideon and shrug. "Do you think I should darken my wings like Rikan did?" I point over to our five just in case Gid doesn't know who Rikan is.

"Doesn't matter, Junco. Most of the mutants are blind from living in the dark, and anyway, they kill ya on smell alone."

Isten is suddenly interested and straightens up to speak. "Fuck, you are such an asshole. Don't tell her that shit."

Gideon laughs and from the corner of my eye I see Tier take notice. "She's a better trained soldier than you'll ever be, *Isten.*" He drawls out his name like it gives him a bad taste in his mouth. "I think she can handle the monsters in the dark."

"So, Is? Why is he doing that if we've got the slick silver?"

"It drains the armor, Juncs, can't use it all the time and Rikan is paranoid about slick silver. He never uses it unless he has to."

"You don't think we should darken our wings? I mean I'm almost as light as Rikan is, and he's darked up."

Isten shrugs. "He's always done that. I've got Lucan's gift, so my wings could be glowing hunter orange for all I care. And your mottled color is actually pretty great camouflage in just about any environment, even snow. So you decide, do you need it or not?"

"Why don't we all have your gift, then?"

"There's rules, Junco. Lucan can't just hand the shit out whenever he wants, there's got to be a verified reason."

"Why did he give it to you?"

"I had to go to school with you. I told ya. Now leave me alone so I can fix this rifle."

He goes back to the rifle as I think for a moment but time's up and the atmosphere changes from prep to ready. Isten jumps on and latches his helmet on. I pile my hair up on top of my head and do the same as I grab my seat on the back. Everyone is busy with their bike partner, even Gideon has something to say to Moju. Moj spies me watching him and thumbs me up just before latching his helmet on.

My stomach gets queasy breathing the filtered air so I disengage the visor and leave the faceplate open.

I watch Tier command Ashur's team up front briefly and his eyes are still glowing from the encounter with Gideon.

"Hey," Tier barks and Isten and I look over at him. "You two," he motions to us with a pointed gloved finger, "are to stay together during this mission. Do ya understand me, Isten?"

"Got it."

"Junco?"

"Whatever."

Then Tier looks over to Gideon. "I don't give a fuck who ya think ya work for, Gideon, if yer here to watch out for Junco, then ya'd better not let anything get past ya. If you come out of this and she doesn't, I'll kill ya dead in a way that you'll remember far into the nether."

Gideon doesn't respond. Not a twitch, not a grunt, not a head nod, not a blink. Just nothing.

Isten spins up our drive as I settle in and check to make sure I have easy aim through the scope. Arel is next to us, but Tier wanted Isten's 50 cal stowed, not mounted, so he's sporting a high-power projectile instead. No aim required, just spray in their general direction.

I double-check the ammo stores as Isten takes us up several meters. The hot exhaust shoots down towards the ground and bounces back up. Smells flow up over my exposed face and force me to recall past missions with the Rural Republic.

Up front Ashur signals and the blast doors begin to slide open. The Subjack tunnels are well-lit, you barely know you're underground except for the constant sound of water that seeps down the concrete walls. But that's not what waits for us on the other side of the barrier.

It's dark.

Not just dark, it's fucking dark.

And in my head I hear the hiss of the mutants outside the Ramah labs instead of the steady trickle of water and have to push down childhood training memories that still scare the shit out of me to this day. I close my visor and shiver at the thought of being one of the unwanted soldiers ahead of me. I'd rather puke in my helmet than go without enhanced night vision right now.

Chapter Twenty-Four

The scurrying begins immediately. You'd think that the sound of almost two dozen grav bikes would be enough to drown out the scuttle of small animals across the puddles, but not so. That shit comes through loud and clear.

If you're Isten, or Tier, or even Gideon, then the tunnels in front don't look too bad. I mean Ash and Mish, they're up there with the Unwanted, lighting the fucking place up for the navigators back here.

But if you're me, Arel, or Moju – well then, the fucking blackness that seeps out in the wake of our light is enough to make you paranoid. Monsters in the dark kind of paranoid. And the really fucked-up part is that it's not just mind games. There really are monsters in the dark.

I watch the small critters disrupt the sheen that covers the ground water as they slink back from our light, then grow some balls and creep forward as we speed off. If we keep up this pace we will be up to Runout by dark, which of course, is relative down here, but habits, right? It's not that far after all. Especially with the straight shot through the tunnels. Once we make it down to the Peaks, it's a couple hours away, tops.

We've been flying for less than ten minutes when the first attack comes. They're small, just little terrestrial bots that shoot weak streams of plasma. Not anything that can penetrate Aves armor, but the Unwanted take a few hits and are yelping like babies so I grab a plasma and start shooting bolts below the middle of our team. Everyone else riding shoot starts doing the same and in a few seconds they scurry back to wherever it was they came from.

I glance back at them as we continue forward and squint my eyes when I notice them exhibit a disturbing camaraderie, piling on top of the injured parties. I swallow and open my private 039 com. "We've got amalgabots."

Tier's voice comes over the exterior comms and repeats my warning and assigns duties to each shooter. "Just don't fucking hit my team back here, or I'll blow ya out of the air and leave your ass down here in hell. Clear?"

They are all very clear.

"First one's coming, I got it." Arel blasts out a spray and takes it down. It falls, but we all watch as the remaining pieces come back together and begin the reassembly process.

"My guess is that was the first victim we picked off, and with each hit it becomes a bigger and badder enemy, so let's wait until they are as close as possible before we hit them again."

Tier repeats my instructions over the exterior comms and the Unwanted begin to get nervous.

I watch in earnest, asking Sera to increase my night vision until she protests it will interfere with other operations, and wait for the new amalgamation to appear into my field.

But it doesn't.

I can hear the Unwanted on the external comms. They think this is a good sign, but when I look over at Moju he pops up his visor and shakes his head at me. I nod and look over at Arel. He smiles and my screen types out his message. *Launchers ready.*

We travel further into the MR tunnels and I watch with dread as malformed hands slip out from behind large cracks in the concrete walls, I hear the slight hiss of protest at our light in their world of blackness, and I feel their restraint.

If the amalgabot is still behind us, it's keeping a distance that is far outside my parameters, which, from what Sera tells me, are exceptional and far superior to anyone else's. Even Arel's – and he's stocked with so much aftermarket comm shit, we could almost be twins.

"Halt!" Ashur's voice crackles over the external com. "Blast door isn't fully open ahead. Going ahead to scout. Cover me."

Braun stands up and aims over Ashur's head and Rikan does the same. They shower the door in white light and everyone winces at the intrusion. The doors are not closed, but they are not open either. It's clever really, the opening the creatures have left for us. Enough to pass through, maybe two or three abreast, but not enough to be prepared for an assault on the other side should someone be waiting.

The point spends a good fifteen minutes checking the door and with each passing second I get a little more worried about what's coming up behind us. Arel and Moju are both standing in anticipation.

Finally Tier gives the go-ahead and we squeeze through the doors, Ashur and Mish first. There's nothing waiting for us on the other side and once again, the Unwanted take this as a good sign.

Not me.

I've learned to be cynical with the best of them. Lucky breaks are bad omens in my line of work. You don't want to be on the wrong side of Luck, you might as well be on the wrong side of Death because you don't want to owe that Luck bastard anything. Luck fucking sucks. You take competence every time. Every motherfucking time because luck is never good.

It always asks for something in return.

We pick up the pace from there and push the bikes to respectable cruising speed to dampen down the feeling that we're being followed.

Of course, we are being followed. I saw the fucker as it slipped through the blast door behind us. But I don't tell anyone. I know Moju and Arel both saw it too and we are the only ones who matter right now.

Sera has a map up on one corner of my vision screen, plus the coordinates on the helmet screen that Tier is projecting, and I'm starting to feel a little claustrophobic when the hissing takes on a new level.

"We've got company," Arel whispers on the internal comms. I turn a little in my seat to see how the Unwanted are taking it, but before I can make a decision either way the amalgabot attacks from behind.

Arel and Moju launch grenades at the same time and take the fucker out in one swoop, but I dial in the vision enhancement and watch as it pulls itself back together, and almost like a mother gathering her children, it asks the smaller bots around it to come into the fold.

"More up front." Ash's voice is calm, but Braun's response is massive. He's shooting rockets, not grenades, and it takes some skill for Ash to compensate for the recoil that reverberates down Braun's body and transfers into the bike.

"Spread out and line up, take out the front with massive offense, and once we start moving do not fucking stop. Junco, if you find anyone lagging behind, shoot them in the head for being worthless."

I smile at Tier's threats to keep the Unwanted in line, but snap off a curt yes, sir over the external comms.

Braun sprays a stream of liquid fire and the screams signal the start of the first battle. Rapid fire from projectiles begins while I pick off one sensor at a time from each amalgabot. They don't go down and they don't reassemble into anything else so it must be safe to hit them in the sensors as long as we don't blow them up. *Sera, tell Arel and Moju tactical strikes only, hit sensors to stop them from reassembling*. I watch the letters type over the screens and then the firepower coming from Moju and Arel dampens down and is exchanged for single rifle shots.

We begin to accelerate and the bike jerks forward just as I snap off another shot with Big Boy. I blast my target's top two cylinders completely off and it falls. "Shit, I downed one." I watch, desperately trying to see what it turns into, but we move away too fast. Braun and Rikan are still blasting liquid fire out in front and everyone else is picking them off from below or against the walls.

We fly and we don't fucking stop. And no one lags behind.

The next blast door is also partially closed and we are only about a mile from the intersection that will split the tunnel and allow us to take it up into the mountains when the children appear.

"Holy fucking shit! They got mutant avians down here!" I scream it over the externals before I can stop myself and people start freaking out.

Tier's voice takes over. "They fly so do not fucking hit my team or I will rip yer heads off, ya hear me, Subs? You aim up or you aim down, you do not aim at us."

They don't fly right away though.

They peek out as we pass and stay on the ground, maybe the headlights stop them, or maybe the noise of the bikes, maybe their own internal sense of self-preservation.

But anyway, they don't fly.

They just follow.

"We got company behind, guys. The sewer rats are on our tail."

I watch Moj and Arel switch back to launchers. Chances are biological enemies don't self-replicate, so we can splatter them all over the fucking dank wet ground.

The things hang back, following us, but they must be out ahead as well because the guys in front are busy clearing the way with liquid fire. After a few minutes the frontal assault stops completely and I hear Braun come online. "Where the fuck did they all go?"

That's not something you want to hear in battle.

The avian muties fly up in a flurry and plasma fire crackles from the barrel of every Unwanted Sub's rifle in unison. To their credit, they only shoot up and down. I rapid-fire into the throngs and briefly consider taking out my SEAR and flying up to chop them to pieces.

Sera and Isten are both in my head simultaneously screaming no at me, and then, just as fast as the muties appeared, they are gone.

Four Subs are lying motionless on the ground, their grav bikes smoking and drives whining, and just as I wonder whether or not we should check on them, mechanical legs clack along the ground and whisk their bodies away into previously unnoticed crevices where the wall meets the floor.

"Forward, now." Tier barks out the orders and we lurch forward once again.

"Fuck it, you guys, I'm gonna pick off everything I see back here, OK?"

I hear a crackled sigh as Moju answers first. "Better play it safe. I agree."

Arel's response is a succession of rapid plasma-cannon bolts that sets the thick oily sheen on the surface of the tunnel on fire. An inhuman wailing wells up and I have an almost uncontrollable urge to vomit.

Isten reads me. "Breathe, Junco. Do not remove that helmet."

I push it down. "Yeah, OK. I got it."

We move forward and I watch on my helmet map as the blip that signals the turnoff up the mountain moves closer and closer. There is chatter on the Subs' comms and I look down at what they're talking about.

The floor is moving.

I watch carefully and Sera jacks up my vision and enhances my helmet with maximum infrared before I can really get a handle on what it is.

"Uh, we have a problem, people." My voice crackles out over the interior comms.

"Speak, Junco." Tier's voice has a bit of strain. "Quickly. We've got problems up front too – the fucking blast door is closed."

I speak on the external comms. "Whatever you do, do not land. The floor is alive."

"Keep an eye on it, Juncs," Tier answers as he maneuvers himself and Arel up front to talk to Ashur.

What is it, Sera? I speak internally instead of on my vision screen so Isten can hear us.

Silence as we wait for her.

I'm just about to ask again when Gideon comes on the internal comms, startling me. "It's a beta sheet, nano-tech used to clean up the Peaks after the nuke. Yukichi creates them. It's not happy about the drives on the grav bikes."

"What the fuck is it doing down here?" Isten comes across calm, but I can feel his internal irritation at Gideon's intrusion into our private conversation.

"Who cares," Gideon answers before switching to the external comms. "Everyone hover at maximum height. Stay off the floor, it's stimulated by the small radiation signature on the grav bikes. Probably because of the two that crashed farther back."

"What kind of range does it have, Gid?" I look over at him with a worried expression as Isten takes us up higher.

"Sorry, Juncs. They can assemble as high as they need to go. But if you don't stimulate them, they tend to stay on the ground to conserve energy."

How does he know this? I ask Isten privately.

"I've worked with Yukichi on many occasions, Junco."

Isten's thoughts come through this time. *What the fuck are you doing in our heads?*

Gideon smiles at us before talking over the crackly com. "I'm tied to Junco, Isten. Was tied to her the day she was born. So, looks like you're not so fucking special after all, are you?"

Moju bursts out laughing and I put a hand up to Isten's face. "Not the time, Is. Really, not the time, OK?"

I look up front and the rest of the 039 is staring back at us. "Never mind this shit, Tier. Just get us the fuck out of this trap before those mutants come back or that goddamn curtain of evil rises up and kills us all."

They turn back and I watch Tier maneuver his bike so Arel can reach the data panels when he stands up.

Sera? Goddammit, Sera, answer me!

Junco, behave. Her voice in my head is admonishing. *I'm busy with Arel now. You're not so special either.*

This time Gideon laughs, but I have to actually put my hand on Isten's shoulder to keep him in his seat. "Stop, it's not important right now."

I hear the growling and my head snaps to look over my shoulder.

The pack is more than a dozen strong as they slink out into the ebbing light that leaks out behind us. If I had to bet my life on it, I'd have said that even that leftover light was enough to keep the nightdogs at bay.

I would've lost that bet.

The light doesn't bother them in the least. I grab the 50 cal and spin up the laser to pulse them in the eyes, but it has no effect.

"They're blind, Junco." Moju's voice comes over the internal comms. "We got blind nightdogs back here, guys. Anytime now would be great."

They pace below us, walking over the beta sheet thing with no consequences. We continue to hover and some of the Unwanted Subs get antsy and nervous when their bikes show signs of fatigue from staying in position. Our bikes are military grade, they can probably hover another hour or so before the stress becomes a problem, but the bikes the Subs are on are practically recreational. Only Gideon has the same quality as the 039.

"Hurry, Tier. The Subs aren't gonna be able to hover much longer."

I hear the whine of a blown motor just a fraction before the bike falls to the ground, splattering the soldiers and the bike into pieces from a height of at almost sixty feet. The Yukichi nano-tech wakes up and slithers like a wave across a pond as it moves to engulf the invaders, the slight radiation signature of the drive just enough to spur it into action. This causes the nightdogs to scatter, but not before several are engulfed by the phagocytic tech.

The Subs start shooting before Tier can call them off and the Yukichi bucks up in defense as the plasma creates energy arcs across its surface. The remaining nightdogs, smelling the blood from the fallen Subs, slink in and begin fighting over the bodies.

I watch in horror as the two team members are ripped to pieces. The rest of the Subs begin spinning to keep their unsuitable bikes from overheating in the hover and the entire scene erupts into chaos as Sera and Arel open the blast doors.

The only thing that saves us is the extreme height of our hovering pattern, because on the other side of the door are dozens of mutant avians.

Even in the semi-light of the bike lamps I can see their gleaming rows of needle-like teeth as they come at us. The Subs swerve and retreat as we blast them from above.

The mutants and I come to a realization at the same time.

They figure out we're up high.

And I figure out that Lucan was wrong. These things are absolutely sentient.

They plotted to trap us behind this door and attack. And now I can almost hear their thoughts as they reorganize.

Blasts in the form of liquid fire, rapid fire, plasma, grenades and rockets are raining down on the little bat-winged bastards flying through the air and they scream and writhe as they burn, literally like demons in hell.

The heat is almost unbearable as the noise rings in my ears. Over the comms I hear Tier screaming to move forward into the next tunnel and Isten surges forward so fast I have to grab hold of his shoulders. We pass through as Braun and Rikan hold them off with rockets that blow a good portion of the tunnel down on top of the flitting mutants, and then Sera and Arel close the door behind us.

The fight continues on the other side, but the little bodies scuttle into the crevices and disappear.

"Full speed, now. Turn right at the intersection and start climbing."

We see more as we travel but they hide again, the hissing becoming stronger as we progress towards the turnoff. When we get there the door is once again closed, but Arel and Sera have it worked out now and they open it a crack to let everyone through after Tier, Ashur, and Mish go forward and scout it out.

When the door closes behind us we don't even take stock of the Subs we lost, we just haul ass up the mountain.

Chapter Twenty-Five

The tunnel morphs as we push west up the mountain. It begins dank and dark but as we press on the smell of mold and dead things that make their way through the filters dissipates. The suffocating stillness of the atmosphere fills with currents from unknown places that cause my helmet screen to blink with random wind speed readings. The barest glow of light seeps out from previously unseen flood grates near the floor, and my sensors go crazy trying to figure out the source.

I shiver and Isten's hand sweeps back to pat my helmet. *Eyes peeled, Snowbird. They're here.*

Gideon is off to my left, keeping back from Isten just enough to be level with me, and Moju is standing, a full-sized plasma in each arm and propped against his stomach, ready for attack.

But there is no attack.

Just the thrumming of grav bikes, the scuttling of small rodents across the now dry tunnel floor, and the hissing that comes out from the dark cracks, faceless creatures that find a place in my memory and that will haunt me in nightmares for the rest of my life.

The incline is steep and for a moment I feel myself in my Goat, going up the midway hill towards the Stag to meet my fate, the moment before my life changed.

We reach the first blast door but we don't stop. There's no need – that fucker is wide open. As we pass, still cruising at our regular pace, I watch the children and shudder involuntarily. They scurry out from the shadows and chatter in a language that sounds a little too much like a flock of starlings over winter.

Moju catches my attention. "I see them, Juncs. Just stay alert and don't waste time on that sniper rifle, just fucking blast those things if they come at us."

"Yeah." I swing the 50 cal rifle to the side and cradle my rapid-fire in my right arm while slinging the plasma over my left shoulder. "I'd dual-wield it along with ya, Moj, but I'd never hit anything that way so, fuck–"

I'm reeling from the pain of the smack and falling off the bike as the last word leaves my mouth. My wings unfurl and soar into the air currents as I catch myself and fly back up. Plasma fire erupts above me and my attacker falls past as I get back on the bike. The Subs are so strung out they fire on the dead thing for several seconds before Tier gets them back under control.

"What the fuck was–"

The screams erupt around us and the attackers are swatting people off bikes. Isten takes a thump on the temple of his helmet and I hear him cry out inside as his razors appear and slash the head off a small and furious shadow.

My SEAR cuts the next one down and then I'm in the air, flying and twisting, cutting the little fucking things into pieces as they swarm around us. The tunnel is nothing but screams as the Subs are dragged from their bikes and hauled down to the ground. I fly down to one guy who's not dead and start slicing away a rage of whirling teeth as they come at me.

Braun is next to me, flinging them one at a time into the walls with such force I can hear bones cracking and the plasma fire lights up the tunnel for tens of yards out as we battle the melee of toddler-sized demons.

Tier is in my face. "Fly the fuck up, Junco, NOW!"

The brawl has died down and I watch the children hustle it back into their cracks.

Braun and I grab the Sub I just saved and haul his ass up. "Hold on, don't let go." We drop him on the closest bike missing a shooter and I go back over to my bike.

Tier's eyes are raging green as he flies up next to me. "Don't you fucking do that again, or I swear you'll go on ship, goddammit."

"I'm here to fight, Tier, I'm no fucking tag-along."

He seethes anger. "Yer whatever I tell ya to be, Junco. And don't fucking forget it. I told ya, you and Isten are ta stay together, did ya not hear me?"

"I heard ya."

Tier looks over at Isten. He's got his helmet off and is looking at the blood coming off his fingers after swiping them down the side of his head. *How the fuck?*

I feel his confusion. The warm blood is dripping down my chin inside my helmet as well. *How'd they do that, Isten?*

He shrugs and finally turns his attention to Tier's smoldering stare and reacts. "What the fuck you want me to do, Tier, I'm driving. Make her drive if you want me to take over here."

Tier looks over at me, the green not even close to dying down. "Switch. Now."

I cringe at the flowing stream of scarlet running down Isten's head as he gets up and I slip into the seat and take the hand grips. The bike dips a little as he settles and I adjust the controls for my own preferences, trying to ignore Tier for as long as possible.

"Forward, every shoot is on high alert." He points at shooters as he passes them. "You cover up, you cover down, you're up, you're down…" He continues that way until everyone knows where to look and shoot as we fly farther up the mountain.

The second fully open blast door is coming up fast but even from the back of the procession I can see something's wrong.

"Halt, right now!" Ashur calls it and everyone stops short as the wall of black Yukichi membrane blocks the way. One Sub loses control of his bike and slams into the flexible sheeting, the top edge of the curtain that is a full five stories high, reaching up into the roof.

The membrane reaches out to greet the bike, a wiggle from the top, then a shimmer of silver as the fibers rearrange themselves and the bike is engulfed. The soldiers scream, wails that reverberate through my ears as Braun launches a rocket into the mass. Rikan is pumping grenades, and every other shoot in front is blasting with plasma.

"Coming up from behind, Juncs, get ready!" The bike sways as Isten stands, rapid-firing projectiles from the hip and his mini-plasma with his spare hand. I glance back at Moju for a second and watch him launch a quick succession of canisters.

I smell the chemicals as soon as they hit, hear the propellant hissing out from the fire bombs, and feel the heat as the entire tunnel behind us burns.

My attention goes back to the wavering curtain in front of me. The soldiers have been spat out with the bike from the forward fire, but they aren't even remotely identifiable. What's left of their skin sags from their bones, some of which have been picked clean. Faces showing more teeth than they should with the missing flesh are strung out in a final scream of agony.

Braun launches another rocket and Arel streams it with liquid fire. The Yukichi falls like a guillotine and chops the bike and remains of the Sub soldiers in half as it puddles against the floor.

"Everyone – forward now!"

I gun it and feel Isten grab for me as he loses his balance, but I don't look back. Hell, he's got wings, if he can't keep his ass in the seat he can catch up with me himself.

Tier waves us on and brings up the rear, Arel firing canisters filled with more chemicals that cloud the air behind us. I stop and turn sideways so we can cover them and watch as Arel opens the access panel and deftly fingers the wires until the blast doors begin to close. Isten and Moju fire back, trying to keep as many of the little mutants as they can on the far side.

Ashur stops and orders everyone towards the door to pick off any mutants that make it through before the panels slide together.

Braun, Arel, and Rikan jump off their bikes and fly around the perimeter looking for holes and cracks where the mutants might hide as Isten and Moju fly down and cover them from above. They spray liquid fire into the crevices they find and off in the distance I can hear squealing.

My stomach has a moment of instability but I push it down.

We move forward with a little more confidence that the mutants won't sneak up behind us again, but we've lost half of the Subjectives already and we're not even to the fucking extraction point.

It's clear that the tunnels from this point on are occupied pretty regularly. There's trash lining the sides and there's writing painted on the walls, like gang tagging in the cities.

Except it's not in any language I've ever seen. I look over at Gideon. "Can you read that, Gid?"

He nods and the external comm crackles as he speaks. "It says:

Seven siblings of the wide heavens,
Seven siblings of the broad earth,
Seven robber-gods are they.
Seven evil gods,
Seven evil demons,
Seven to break heaven and earth,
The Seventh acting as the pawn,
Burning one into extinction."

I laugh, because I should know better, right? "That's so awesome."

"Junco, that's enough."

Tier's bike has made its way back to me and I look over at him, getting more pissed off with each passing fraction. "You better stop telling me to shut up, Tier, I'm not in the fucking mood. And don't bother threatening me with Ryse. He can't get me down here, I know that for sure."

Moju speaks up. "Tier, it's not about you. It's about us, so you really have no say." He stands up in his seat, like he means it. "This is about us. You're just a fucking passenger."

Tier stops his bike and Gideon and I pull up short with him as the others continue on. "We're not here to decipher old myths, we're here to collect the Seven and take ya back to Amelia. End of mission. I don't give a shit what the walls say about evil demons, I don't give a shit what ya think of me right now, I'm trying to get us all back alive, so shut the fuck up, Junco, and do what yer told."

"Don't growl at me–"

The demonic screams cut off my words, but they're not coming from the mutants, they're coming from our team up front. Arel, Isten, and Moju fire up at the bat-like wings of mutants, but these are no toddler children.

They are teenagers.

Girls.

Who look just like me.

If I had a pie-hole full of little razor teeth that spiraled in towards my throat and wings like a bat instead of a bird, that is.

"Holy fucking shit! Shoot them, Isten, kill them!"

I whip out my SEAR and flip the bike on hover as I swipe at the diving girls, their lips pulled back and their juices leaking out and dripping down their faces.

One knocks into our bike and Isten and I tumble out and take flight as it crashes down below, taking my sniper rifles with it. A Yukichi sheet rises up and swallows it down like it's nothing, then begins to rise upward towards us, grabbing mutant Juncos and pulling them apart as it ascends.

I whirl around and face my demonic self. "Come on, bitch, let's do it!"

She lunges at me, screaming in another language, and I cut her head off and watch it splat into the sheet and disappear into the black.

A slew of Juncos attack me from all sides then, but Moju and Gideon are there. We back up together, leaving enough room to swipe and shoot, and start our killing.

Moju flies into a rage that would put Tier to shame. His razors come out and he starts decapitating everything that moves. The orange light in his eyes turns to a deep scarlet red as his anger explodes.

I swing out away from Gideon so I don't nick him by mistake and then spin, letting the SEAR do its thing as I drag it through the air with my hurling body. I don't chop their heads off, but the slash across their various body parts is enough.

Turns out, clones of Junco are not quite Junco enough to prevent the Alloantigen Repressor from fucking up their collagen matrix. They begin to melt and I move on, slicing as many limbs as I can, cutting their heads off when in range, or just dragging my weapon lightly across their flesh to let the bioware finish the job for me.

Legions of Juncos appear from down the tunnel and I have a panic attack. Gideon yells for Moju to follow and grabs my hand, dragging me upward.

The comms scream to life and suddenly Gideon is in charge. "Tier, take your team up top, there's ventilation shafts, look for a keypad every twelfth panel, code in 998998 and shut the fucking door. We'll meet up after."

"Got it." Tier's voice is calm and I look over trying to find my team on the opposite side of the massive tunnel. Braun and Rikan are hurling grenade canisters, while the unwanted shower the clones with plasma. I retract my SEAR and watch Arel key the code and they start filing in.

Gideon's bike crashes to the ground as he climbs in our vent and then Moju's hands are on me, shoving me in after Gideon and firing at the clone girls as he slips in last.

Gideon grabs my arm and pulls me out of the way as Moju seals up the door and I hear the locks engage.

I flip off my helmet and scream. "Holy shit!" *Isten? Isten, can you hear me?*

I hear ya, Snowbird. We're OK. You guys OK?

"Are we OK?"

Gideon smiles and then he's in my head. *We're all OK, Isten. Start walking west. I'll let ya know when we can cross back over.*

I count up my weapons and come up short on sniper gear. Big Boy is gone, crashed with the 50 cal on the bike. I have my rapid-fire and my full-size and mini-plasma. About a dozen cartridges are attached to my ammo belt along with about two hundred rounds of projectiles.

"All we have are water packets. And a few ration packets in my pocket. You guys have water and food?"

Moju nods. "Yeah, I got about that much too."

"We're not gonna be in here long, Junco. So don't worry about it. Only temporary."

Chapter Twenty-Six

"Where the fuck is here, Gideon? You seem to have a lot more information about this mission than you should. How the hell did you have the codes to get in here?"

"Think about it, Junco. How the fuck do you think I'd have the codes? Ya know, I'm not interested in playing with you. Use your fucking brain for once. I have the goddamn codes because this was part of the plan."

"Whose plan?" I'm glad Moju asks. That way he can't say I'm the only clueless one.

"Subjack's." He says it like we should've known that.

"OK, so you're gonna do what with me now?"

His eyes narrow as he stares down at me. "We're going to get the Siblings, Junco. I'm taking you there. OK?"

"Then why does he need his own plan, Gid? Why not just include Tier? Why all this secret shit?"

He exhales as if he's irritated. "Because you've got a lot of enemies. I'm here to make sure you come out the other end alive, all right? You OK with that?"

I look over at Moju and he shrugs. "Look, Juncs – I've known Gideon my entire life, so he's not out to get ya. Just trust him."

"Do you know what he's doing?"

He looks away, out through a dark doorway. "No, but he's not the enemy." He turns back to me and his eyes glow orange. "And that's that." He puts a hand on my shoulder and pulls me towards the doorway. "Come on, Junco. I need to get to Soli. She's not doing well, OK? We need to get her out of here."

I look up in his eyes and see his fear. Not for himself, but for her. For Soli, the Two. His two, apparently.

"All right, let's go."

Gideon leads and we follow him out into the corridor. It's not very wide and we have to walk single file, but even then I have only a few inches on either side of me. Gideon and Moju are so much wider, I wonder if they are brushing against the walls, that's how tight it is.

My night vision tints everything green, which should be fine, but it just isn't. The darkness creeps up against me and I start breathing a little harder than I should. I look straight ahead, past Gid's body, and my heart begins to race.

"You OK, Junco?" Moju has a hand on my back and he's pushing me forward, but with each step my feet begin to resist more and more.

"I feel strange, I don't know – it's dark."

"You have night vision, Junco, so knock it off."

Gideon's voice almost snaps me back, but I see movement in the distance. "There's something up there," I say.

Both guys turn and I watch Moju squint in the distance. "Just a rat, Junco. Come on." He's pulling on me again but my heels dig in.

"No." I shrug him off and start backing up. "I can't go that way. It's way too dark."

I turn but Gideon has my arm and he pulls me back. "I said that's enough, Junco."

My heart flutters as I begin to panic and I pull away. His grip stays firm and pulls harder and then I'm thrashing against him, trying to untangle myself from his hands.

"Stop, Gideon, I'm not going that way. No!"

He grabs my shoulders and shakes me hard. "Stop it, Junco!"

"What the fuck is going on over there?" Isten's voice comes through the comms on my helmet that is now rolling across the floor. "Junco?"

I scream. "I can't go that way, Isten, it's too small. It's dark, there's things up there!"

What things, Junco? What things?

"It's nothing, Isten – she's having a fucking panic attack over the passageway. Just let me handle it."

My breathing is so erratic I begin to hyperventilate and Moju bends me over and pushes me down to the floor. I know Gideon is still talking to Isten but I can't hear him anymore, my heavy breath blocks out all his words.

Moju leans down under my swaying hair and looks up at my face. "You OK, Junco?"

I'm still gasping for air, trying to calm down. "What's wrong with me?"

"Stuff, Juncs. Old stuff. Coming back up. It hits ya sometimes."

"I don't want it, Moju."

He laughs and takes a seat next to me, his long legs stretch towards the other side of the small passageway, his boots flat against one wall and his back against the other. "Yeah, I can relate, Snowbird. But it's gotta come up sometime. Ya can't run forever."

He pauses and looks over at Gideon and I follow his gaze as I try to get myself together. Gid has his helmet on so I can't hear what he's saying. I scramble backward down the passageway and grab my helmet and stick it on before Moju can panic at my sudden movement.

"– from the tunnels in the Stag."

"So, they did–"

"Stop, she's listening to us."

"Junco?"

It's Tier. I activate my mic and breathe. "Yeah."

"Ya OK, darlin'?"

"No. It's dark."

"It was dark out in the big tunnels too, Juncs. It's no different. In fact, it's safer, OK? There's no mutants in here from what we can tell. It's better this way."

"It's small, Tier." The words come out a whisper and they make me feel small too.

"Nah, it's just the right size. We could have ta crawl, now that would suck. But we can stand and walk just fine. Right?"

Moju pulls me to my feet and we walk over towards Gideon.

"Moju's got ya, right?"

"Yeah."

"Well, ya know he'll never let anything hurt ya, Junco. Never."

I take a deep breath and want to cry, but I don't. Can't. "Right."

"Remember the swim we had, Junco?"

The tears slip out, I can't help it. "Yeah."

"And ya were so worried. But we came through and what was on the other side?"

"A nightdog."

He laughs. "Nah, *who* was on the other side, ya crazy little shit, after we made our escape?"

I look up at my brother. "Moju."

"And he's there with ya right now, too. Yer gonna be fine. We're gonna meet up in a few miles, so the quicker we hoof it up the mountain the sooner we'll all be back together, OK?"

I nod. "OK."

"Are ya walking?"

"Yeah."

"OK, then I'll be here if ya need me. But hurry, Junco. I miss ya already."

I smile at that.

Gideon leads and Moju pushes me forward by the shoulders for the first several minutes. My breathing comes back from the brink and I feel the fear leave as easily as it appeared.

"Sorry about that."

Moju just squeezes my arm, but Gid turns and answers me. "That's why I'm here, Junco. So don't sweat it." He smiles and it brightens me up.

The walk gets more difficult as the incline increases and the passageway becomes a series of tall terraces with ladders to climb. Our boots clang against the metal rungs as we get into a pattern of climbing, then walking a half mile or so, and climbing again.

We've done this about thirty times when my muscles begin to burn. "Can we stop? Or do we have to keep going?"

"Do you need to stop, Junco?" Moju looks down at me with a slight panic in his eyes. "We can stop, but Soli, she–"

"That's OK, I can go longer."

"Ya sure, Juncs? We can stop if you need to."

"No, I can keep going."

Sera? I type it out on the vision screen so Gideon can't spy on me.

I'm still with Arel, Junco. What do you need?

Something to help me keep going?

I can't, Junco, no hormones if you're pregnant. I'm sorry. I could burn some fat calories and shunt them to your major muscle groups, but you really don't have a lot to spare. Tell them you need to stop and eat.

Never mind.

We push on and the climb gets harder with each terrace level and finally my legs are shaking so bad I have to say something. "OK, I have to stop. I'm sorry. I have to eat."

Moju takes a deep breath and looks down the passageway, but to his credit, he stays silent.

Gideon walks back over to me, turns his back and bends his knees a little. "There's a place up ahead, Junco. Hop on and I'll carry you until we get there. Then we can rest."

I do.

And he does. Like I'm a bag of feathers and weigh nothing. Which might almost be true under normal circumstances, but I'm wearing at least sixty pounds of weapons, ammo and supplies and so is he.

He grabs hold of my legs and I have my arms around his neck as we walk, then he lets go to climb the ladders and this becomes our new pattern. I bury my face in his back and smell him. My cheeks go hot with embarrassment as I catch myself. Hopefully Isten didn't feel that.

Finally Gideon drops me and walks over to an access room that leads out to the tunnels. "Stay here, I'm going to go take a look outside and see what's there."

I have no desire to revisit those fucking things so I stay with Moju, but he's antsy and pacing around.

"Can you feel her, Moj?"

He looks over to me. "Yeah, she's in a lot of pain." He chews on his thumb for a second, then resumes his pacing.

"Can she hear you? Can you talk to her?"

He shakes his head. "Nah, we're not like you and Isten," he looks over towards the open doorway, "or Gideon. We just feel each other. I can feel them all, but I know Soli, personally, right? So, I feel her the most."

"Did you grow up with her?" I study his face and use my words to calm him, like he was doing for me earlier.

He takes a deep breath and smiles. "Yeah, we had each other for most of our childhood. Then they sent her to the Eastern Utopias."

"That's where Esta was, did they know each other?"

"No, Tier had already taken Esta. That's why they had to send Soli over there."

"Oh. Well, that must've pissed you off, huh?"

He smiles. "You have no idea, Junco."

"I can eat and walk–"

"No, I can't make you do that, Juncs. It's OK. She'll be OK. I know she will. We talked to Layla and she's fucking good at that genetics shit, I know she can help her."

"She helped me, and I was all fucked up. I'm sure Layla can take care of her."

He resumes his pacing and I take out a ration packet from my pocket. I squint down at the label and wrinkle my nose.

"Let me guess, blueberry pancakes?" Gideon is back and he's looking down at me with an amused grin.

I stick my tongue out. "No, it's mapolina." I empty my pockets and start reading labels. They're all mapolina. I push them away. "Moj, what kind of food ya got?"

Both he and Gideon search their pockets and Moj comes up with chicken and rice.

"Give it here!"

Moju smiles at me. "What, that avian shit food hasn't grown on you yet?"

I laugh. "Are you kidding me? I spent the first month eating cookies unless forced to do otherwise, and right before I left I had Lucan get me a cheeseburger and fries. I still don't know how he got them, but I only eat mapolina if I'm seconds from death."

I pull the heat tab on the chicken and rice packet and wait until my palm is just the right temperature and then open the seal and start squeezing it in my mouth. Fucking chicken and rice is one of the best field rations on Earth. I moan a little and Gideon throws me another ration and a water packet. I open the filter seal on the water and blow until it's inflated, then push the water tablet through and wait for the pouch to fill up.

The nutrition does wonders for my muscles, but it also makes me severely sleepy and I doze for a few seconds as Gid and Moju talk with the 039 over the comms.

OK. Junco. I'm back.

That's nice, Sera. I'm tired now.

It's almost time.

Almost time for what?

To take me where I need to go.

I sit up and look over to Gideon and he nods.

Where do you need to go?

The valley is only another two miles, but the Siblings and where I need to go are on the opposite sides of the compound. So we'll have to go over to the communications building while everyone else waits for you to come back.

Maybe we should do it all at once? We'll go drop you off and they can grab the Siblings.

No, Junco. It is mandatory for you to be there at extraction.

Why?

Because if you're not, all your friends will die.

I look over at Gideon. "Did you get all that?"

He nods. "Yeah. Everyone already knows, Junco. But we're gonna rest first. You can't fight like this."

Moju shakes his head and sighs. "I'm not waiting around, dammit. Soli is gonna–"

"Moju, knock it off. It's no good being an asshole. We need Junco to get them out. And right now she's too tired to do anything, so she needs to rest."

"Juncs, I get it, I'm not mad at you, but I can't just sit here and–"

"So go fucking scout it out ahead, why don't you? But I swear, Moju, if you blow this because you can't control yourself, I'll fuck you up."

Moju looks over to me. "Do you care if I go ahead and take a look?"

I shake my head. "No, go ahead."

"OK, I'll go up to the valley and see if they have anything we need to know about. Hey Sera," Moju calls out to the air, "come with me, in case they have security."

She appears in the tunnel, looking like some fantasy soldier from a porn screen, and follows him off in the dark.

Chapter Twenty-Seven

"Come in here, Junco. It's safer," Gid points to the access room as he looks down at me, "and not so closed in."

The air flow is better in there too, so I plop down on the floor and lean against one wall. "Can I sleep?"

"Yeah, sure." He takes a seat opposite me, leaning up against the other wall.

I lie down and put my helmet close to my ear so I can hear if the team calls and then close my eyes. My thoughts go to Moju and his relationship with Soli. How lucky he is to have her and know that he's had her the whole time.

"I was on your side, Junco."

I open my eyes and look over at Gid. "What are you talking about?"

He smiles, but it's forced. "In the camp. I was always on your side."

"I really don't remember you, Gideon."

"Yeah, all right." He sighs and stretches his legs out. They are almost long enough to cross the distance between us.

"Sorry, I just don't have those memories yet." I feel guilty, but fuck. How is it my fault I have no recollection of him?

"Don't worry about it, OK? It's not your fault, I don't blame you."

"You can tell me, if you want. Maybe I'll remember something?"

He laughs but it's as forced as his smile was. "Nah, I'm not gonna be the one to tell you what happened back there. Fuck that."

"So it's OK for you to keep these secrets and not make me listen, but when Lucan and Tier want to do the same thing, they're what? The evil avians?"

He sighs. "The shit they keep from you is about your future, not your past."

"That's terrific. Thanks. I love hearing about how fucked up my life was, how everyone treated me like shit, and especially this new development about how I'm the evil seventh demon who's gonna enact eternal vengeance on the world and kill an entire race of sentient beings."

He's got nothing to say to this.

"You called me pathetic back in the room last night. That's the most pathetic thing I've ever heard. That's what you said, right? Yet you're such a coward. You're pathetic, Gideon. You, not me. You throw this shit in my face, the fact that you know everything and I don't, well, that's just fucking great for you, then, isn't it? But I do what I have to do to stay alive, that's why I don't want to know the things they're not telling me. I do what I have to."

I watch him struggle as he turns his head away from my eyes and we sit there in silence for several long minutes, me staring blankly at the opposite wall, and him with his head in his hands.

Eventually I turn my back and face the concrete. I can see small insects busy up near the ceiling and normally this would bother me enough to sit up or at the very least limit body contact with the wall. But I don't care. I'm tired. And not just in the sleepy way, either. I'm tired of walking, of fighting, and of wondering what nightmare is gonna come up to haunt me next.

I just don't give a shit. Those fuckers can crawl into my mouth and slide down my throat for all I care. I've been through worse. Besides, they're full of protein.

"It wasn't all bad, ya know."

My eyes open at his voice, but I don't turn around. "What was good about it then?"

"I took you once."

I roll over and look over at him. "Took me where?"

He smiles and this time it's real. "I took you out. It was supposed to be for an overnight training maneuver, but," he shrugs, "I lied, we just fucked off for three days."

"How did this happen?"

"You were almost ten and I was fifteen. I was only back at camp for a few weeks and then I had to leave again for training." He stops and I feel inside him for the first time, searching for the memory and choosing words. I can feel him like he's Isten.

"And I hadn't see you in a year almost. So I waited for them to bring you back that night because they had you down in the tunnels, doing something horrible, which I won't tell you about. But anyway, you came back upset, all crying, your face all stained with tears and dirt and your hair a mess. It was hard for me to see you when they were ripping you apart like that.

"Anyway, you came running over to me and hugged me, chatting me up like there's nothing wrong with how we live and what we do. So, you're right about that, Junco," he looks at me sideways from the corner of his eye, "you do have an exceptionally well-developed coping mechanism for the pain. You've always had that on your side. It's hard to be mad at the things you push down, because I can't blame you. I'd have done it, if I knew how."

I let out a deep breath. "Some people think that makes me a monster. Or insane. Annun said as much back on Amelia. Asked me straight up what the limit was on my indifference." I look at Gideon's eyes. They are green in my night vision. "And I've come to the conclusion that there is no limit. I can get rid of all of it."

He looks away when he answers. "I'd take that over living with it any day."

"You were saying?"

"Yeah, so I talked them into letting me take you out for stalker training. Told them, lied to them actually, that we were gonna hunt nightdogs. And they said yes."

He smiles and then lets out a short laugh. "It kind of took me off guard, but they said yes. I packed you up in a prairie buggy and we headed north a few hundred miles, to this little marsh that popped up when we had all that rain?" He asks the question like it's something I should remember, except I don't. "And I gave you this little notebook and some colored pencils."

He stops and looks over at me, his face slightly saddened with the story. "I wish you could remember this, Junco. I made you so happy."

My throat tightens up and I have to get a hold of my breathing before I reply. "Me too, Gid."

"I gave you those pencils and that notebook and then I went fishing."

"What did I do?"

He smiles again. "Whatever you wanted, Junco. I let you do whatever you wanted for three whole days. You splashed around in the marsh, caught frogs, picked weedy little flowers, and drew everything you saw and wrote little notes next to the pictures. Like you were a biologist or something. I still have that notebook, ya know."

I'm stunned. "Where?"

A grin spreads across his face. "Back at my house. I don't normally work out of the Northern Territories, Juncs. I only came back recently to wait for you to show up."

He stares at me, waiting for me to ask him questions. I swallow. "So how could you work for my father, Gid? I don't understand why everyone is so willing to overlook his part in all this. He was not *that* good to me, he was not *that* careful."

"I don't work for him, Junco. I said I work for your mother. And the only reason I agreed was because I had to get back to you. She was my only chance."

He waits for the implications of his statement to sink in before continuing.

"Working with them is just a means to an end, and the end is coming up fast, so we really gotta get our shit together."

I'm afraid to ask after what Selia told me last night, but I do anyway. "What is the end, Gid?"

"Get the Siblings and get the fuck off this planet before they destroy the whole fucking thing."

"You're coming back with us?"

He shrugs. "If they let me, yes."

"Why am I like this, Gideon? How is it possible that I can recall the key to ancient Sumerian cuneiform from third year, yet I've lost all of you? Most of my father? It makes no sense."

He plays with something in his hand for a few seconds before answering. "They started wiping your memory of your camp time when you were only a little girl. I went to get you one day, you said you'd help me move cows – were excited about it even because they never let you ride at the camp. So it was gonna be a fun day for you. And when I found you in your room, you had no idea who I was. Just gone."

My mind goes backward in time and I see a small room. Just one bed and one chair. But then it drifts off and I can't know for sure if it was real.

"That was the first time, when you were eight."

"Eight? Why eight?"

"They fucked up your training somehow and couldn't get you to do anything. You shut down because of the prairie lions."

The nerve of me.

"They did it again when you were ten, after I left and you ran away. That's what I heard anyway. That you went home with your dad and started telling everyone who'd listen that you were off killing people for the RR."

My eyes dart around the room as I look for this memory, but it's gone. "Any more?"

He nods and takes a deep breath. "Yeah, the summer right before you turned seventeen. You killed–"

"A trainer. I remember that one."

He shakes his head. "No, that was after. You killed the kids."

My mouth drops open. "What?"

"The mutant kids, the monsters. You found them in the outer perimeter buildings at the Stag and you killed them. They erased that shit immediately – weren't even careful about it either. You were never really the same. I didn't see you after that, but there were stories that you went insane. Starting erasing things all on your own. Making gaps and filling it in with made-up shit."

"My father did this?"

He nods. "He signed off on every bit of it."

"So, how did all you guys end up on the same team, Gideon? It makes no sense."

He lets out a little air, a half-laugh maybe. "Junco, there are worse people out there than your father. He was not in on the RR plan, he was a plant from day one. Long before you were born. He saved me too, ya know. I realize he's got a lot of crimes to answer for, but–"

"And you just put up with it?"

"I told you, I came back to help you. They were just the path that got me here."

"Will they try and keep me? Lucan is very worried about that point. Unreasonably so. I mean, he gave me a gift that lets me summon him. And it wasn't because he thought I'd be in trouble, or in a bad fight or something like that. It was because he thought I'd stay with Subjack."

Gid shakes his head. "I don't think so, Junco. Tier threatened them pretty good. And if you have this power, to summon that Lucan guy, well, that should be enough to stop them if they do try."

I look down at my finger and almost touch it with my other hand. I pull it back as soon as I realize it might activate with the slightest touch. "It's in my finger, Gideon. The summons is in my finger. But it only works one time."

"You shouldn't tell me secrets like that, Junco."

"Why not?"

"You're too trusting, for all the shit you've been through, you are way too trusting. Sera was right. You want to believe so bad. But don't. Don't believe anyone."

I look away. "I can't live like that, Gideon. I can't."

"I know, it's hard. But you can. When people tell you stuff from now on, you look for proof first. Always get the proof, Snowbird."

The proof. My father's words are in my head. I reach into my pocket and pull out the small envelope he gave me before we left.

"What's that?"

"Proof." I fold open the envelope and pull out a datacard. It's not something I've ever seen before so I hold it up to Gideon. "You know what this is?"

He squints at it for a moment, then puts out his hand. I drop the little card and watch as he takes out his comm and loads it in, then waits a few seconds and hands it back. "Just push the green button."

I push it and my father's face comes across the screen. He's standing in our house courtyard and the sound of the songbirds in the trees behind him makes my stomach twist in pain.

"I have to leave, Junco. I can't say any more and I can't even leave this behind for you. But know that I love you. Hopefully I'll have the chance to give this to you in the future and you'll understand. And never forget that you'll always have a home here." He looks ages younger than he did the last time I saw him. Ages, even though it can't possibly be more than four years since he made this video. The feed ends and then there is nothing but black.

I hand the comm back to Gid, not even bothering to take out the datacard. Who cares who sees it now. Everyone knows my dad lives as Subjack. This proof is only meaningful to one person besides himself. And that's me.

"What's that mean, Junco? Never forget that you'll always have a home here."

I sigh. "It's a code we had."

"Obviously. For what?"

I sit there for a few moments, thinking about what our code means. But there's nothing I can do right now. And if I don't get out of this stupid mission alive, then I'll never be able to do anything about it.

I change the subject, heeding Gideon's caution from earlier. "So, where's your proof, Gideon?"

He smiles, grins actually, and unzips a pocket on his sleeve and removes a piece of paper. "I thought you'd never ask."

He hands it over and I take it, then turn it around in my hand to make right side up. It's an honest-to-God paper picture of us. We are not kids. I am a teen and he's already a man. We have on summer clothes – shorts and tank for me – and he's shirtless and has his arm casually draped across my shoulder. We are both smiling. "When?" I breathe.

"Right before that last memory wipe. It was the last time I saw you. Until that day outside Selia's place."

I look at our closeness carefully. "Did I love you?"

He smiles. "Did you?"

"I might've."

He laughs but that seems to be the signal that this conversation is over.

I take it all in, then squirm around, trying to get out of the way of a rock that has found its way under my hip. The annoying little bump doesn't move so I sit up and reach around to fling it away. I find something small and smooth instead of a rock and I pull it up to my face to see it. Jasus. It's like every cryptic message passed to me in the last decade is surfacing right now.

"What's that?" Gideon is craning his neck to see what I've got.

"It's the little compass Tier gave me back on Amelia. Must have fallen out of my pocket."

I straighten up and feel for the latch, then open it.

It glows in the night vision and the little needle wobbles for a few seconds before settling.

"Don't you have a compass in your helmet?"

I look up. "It's not for that."

"What's it for then?"

I stare at the needle for a few seconds. "It points to my true north, when I feel lost here on Earth."

"So where's it pointing?"

"It's pointing to me." I smile and lie back down, still looking at it in my hand.

Gid sits in silence for a few seconds, maybe waiting to see if I elaborate. But I don't. "OK, well, go to sleep now. We have to get going and you can't fight when you're tired."

That's two, I tell myself. Two good things about my past that I have to cling to. My real Aren and now Gideon. And maybe my father. Maybe.

I don't think I'll ever get to sleep with this new information to mull over, but I'm wrong. My eyes droop and the darkness overtakes me easily.

Chapter Twenty-Eight

I wake up in my camp room. It's hot.

But what else is new. It's always hot at the Stag camp in the summer. My eyes don't really want to cooperate this morning but I force them. They stick for a fraction, then reluctantly open as the crust breaks free.

Crying dust, that's what Gid calls it.

I rub it off and sniff the air for signs of breakfast.

Nothing.

That means it's still early.

I swing my legs out of bed and pad over to the calendar I keep on the back of the door. I know it's Friday, but checking the calendar is a habit that cannot be broken.

I have a fleeting moment of panic as I imagine it's Saturday instead.

My heart pounds and I have to close my eyes and concentrate for several seconds to prevent my alarm from declaring the extra adrenaline in my system.

It's not Saturday, Junco. Stop.

I know. It's not Saturday. I open my eyes and find the date. June 7, 2143.

Friday.

Not Saturday.

I feel the breath rush out of me in relief and then check the clock on the wall. 5:45 AM. I grasp the doorknob and wait for the biometrics to release the lock. I heave on the heavy door a little to make it open, then tip-toe across the hallway to Gid's room. I don't knock because I don't have to. My palm only works two things in the camp. My door and his.

I push the door open but he's not there and his bed has not been slept in.

I huff out a little air and go back the way I came to get dressed. The red shorts are old and comfortable and the t-shirt has faded strawberries on it. I slip my feet into some pink flip-flops and make my way to the kitchen.

The cooks are already working, preparing batter for something I want, but will not be allowed to eat. I make a face at them as I pass by but they ignore me.

Outside it is not only hot, but humid as well. The leftover moisture from a nighttime rain sticks to my skin immediately. I stand in the doorway listening to the sounds of men as I let my eyes adjust to the brightness of early morning on the scrub.

I hear the sharp crack of gunfire and turn to see who's shooting at this hour. I squint into the light, but I can't see that far away. I listen to the sound for a minute.

TZi.357.

Gid shoots one of those, but I'm still too small. The recoil throws my hand back every time.

Once the recoil made me hit myself in the head.

James took it away after that.

I walk over to the range and find him, shooting fast in a way that would get you kicked out of most ranges.

But not here.

That's just how you do it at the camp.

I wait until he empties his magazine, then clear my throat in an exaggerated manner.

He doesn't even turn, just snaps in the next magazine and starts popping them off again.

I look over to James, our rangemaster, and wave and then point to myself.

He nods, so I open the little gate and walk up behind Gideon as he snaps off his last round.

"I'm busy, Junco." He doesn't look up, only grabs a box of ammo and starts reloading the four empty mags lying on the counter he is using to prop himself up.

"It's Friday."

"I know what day it is."

"Well, we don't normally shoot on Friday, Gideon. But if you want to–" I let the words drop off and walk over to my cubby against the far wall and grab my .380, a box of ammo, and some mags.

He stops and looks back at me as I clutch my supplies against my strawberry t-shirt and make my way back towards the tables. "You can't shoot with me anymore, Junco. In fact, we can't spend any more Fridays together."

I dump my stuff on the top of the counter next to his and scrunch up my face. "Why not?"

He starts shooting again so I wait until he's done. "Why not, Gid?"

I watch as he swallows and I get that sinking feeling in my stomach, like I'm about to be punished. "Why not, Gideon?"

When he turns his face is not only sad, it's angry too. "I have to leave, I'm going away for a long time, Juncs. I can't help it, they're making me go. And I have to take a test on Monday, so I need to practice."

He shrugs and takes a deep breath, then goes back to changing out the expired magazine and snapping in the full one.

My face is getting hot and my throat is closing up on me a little so I stop and take a few deep breaths to keep the alarm from going off. He stops shooting for a minute as he senses my struggle, then I feel a wave of pride from him as I get it all in check.

He smiles when I look back up to him. "You don't need me anymore, Junco."

All the effort I just used to keep it under wraps is gone now and the tears spill out. "I do, Gideon," I whisper. "You can't leave, not yet. Please."

He puts his weapon down and walks over to me, then grasps my face in his palms and tilts my head up. "I have no say, Junco. You know that. I have no say at all. They tell me I'm leaving on Monday and I won't be back for a while." He lets out a long breath of air. "A long while. Years."

"But you just got back a few weeks ago. It's not fair. You're supposed to be here all the time." I look up at him and he winces at my crying.

"You really don't need me, ya know. You really don't, Junco. You're almost ten now and you've gotten a lot better at controlling things."

"It's not fair."

He pulls me over to the bench near our cubbies and we sit. "What's not fair?"

I sniff and make the tears stop as I look down at my hands fumbling around in my lap. "What's the point of being good if they take away the good stuff? That's punishment. If I'm going to be punished even though I'm good, then I'm gonna be bad instead."

He tilts my chin up so I have to look him in the face. "Being bad gets you nowhere around here, you know this, Junco. One day we'll be bad, but that day isn't today. Understand?"

I jut out my chin and look away. "Yes. I understand. But I'm not listening to you. I'm gonna be bad when you leave and you won't be here to stop me."

"They'll stop you, Junco. And it won't be pleasant."

I look over to James across the range and he's watching me as Gideon talks. He smiles and shakes his head at me. A warning.

"Then you have to spend today with me." I look up at him and grin. "If you spend today with me, then I'll be good."

"You're such a little shit, ya know that?"

"You're a shit. You're the one who's leaving."

He laughs. "Junco, you leave me every fall and don't come back for months. How do you think I feel when you go home?"

"Do you miss me?"

"Of course I miss you! You're my partner in crime, right?"

My laugh comes out unexpectedly. "Yes. Partners in crime, that's us. One day we will pull big jobs and get rich, Gideon. Won't we?"

He rumples my hair and chuckles. "Yes, you can bet on it, Junco. One day we'll be unstoppable." Then his face gets serious again. "But I can't spend the whole day with you. I have to go out on the scrub with Matthew."

I turn away as the funny feeling comes back to my stomach. "No."

"I have to. But I'll be back before dinner, he said. So I'll spend the whole evening with you, OK?"

My eyes track back over to James. He's busy stacking boxes of ammo and so I look back at Gideon and whisper. "I hate Matthew. I want to shoot him."

Gideon doesn't smile, just bends down into my ear and whispers back. "I know, Snowbird. One day we will, but not today. Understand?"

"Yes."

He puts his arm around me. "You'll be fine, right? You've got it all under control now? You haven't had a hard day since last summer. You're ready for new things?"

I shake my head and he pulls me closer. "One time I was being chased in the scrub by a prairie lion and I tripped and fell and it almost took my leg off." He squeezes me. "But I remembered I had my knife and I killed it before it could do any more damage."

I pick up the game where he left off. "One time I was lost in the tunnels and it was very dark. I cried for a long time and sat down, ready to give up. But then I remembered that I memorized the map like you told me to. I am never lost as long as I do what you say."

I squeeze him this time.

"One time I was in the city and this guy attacked me. He had a knife, not me. But I remembered that I knew how to defend myself and chopped him in the throat. He fell off me and I walked away like nothing happened."

He squeezes me again.

"One time I was with Matthew and he hit me in the mouth. I cried because he's so big and he scares me. But then I remembered that we will kill him someday." I look up into Gideon's blue eyes. "I can't wait for that day."

Gid leans down to whisper in my ear once more. "And we will get him, Junco. All of them."

"But not today."

He shakes his head. "Not today, Snowbird."

"Today we behave and there will be a better day to get them back."

"Yes."

I look across the range and James is eyeing us suspiciously. "What will they do to you, Gideon?"

"Change me. They're gonna change me."

"Will you be one of them when you come back?"

He pulls me close and hugs me hard. "Never, Junco. I'll never be one of them."

I look up at him, the tears leaking out before I can stop them. "OK. I'll be good. I know you'll be back and you'll take care of me."

He smiles and nods his head. "I promise. I will. It might take a while, but I'll come back. And if they take you away, I'll find you. Never doubt me, Junco. And I'll never doubt you, either."

I swallow down the lump in my throat. "I know. We'll always be partners. And one day we'll kick all their asses. So hard, right?"

He laughs now and I look up and see James relax as the tension eases out of our talk.

"So hard. Yes, they will get what they deserve and they'll die knowing they gave us all the skills it took to bring them down, right, Snowbird?"

"Yes. I can be patient, can you?"

He laughs again. "I can, Junco. I can be very patient. Patience is your friend. Never act in haste if you can help it."

"I won't. I'll be a master of waiting. I'll be still and quiet and I'll lie in the grass and wait, just like the prairie lion."

"You are the lion."

"And you are the wolf."

"And together we are the two most dangerous motherfucking apexers on the prairie."

"And they will regret it." I sigh with relief. Gideon always knows just what to say.

He ruffles my hair and pushes me away. "Go eat breakfast, Juncs. I'll see you tonight, OK?"

I nod. "OK. Love you."

"Ditto, Snowbird."

Chapter Twenty-Nine

The dream fades and I can hear them for whole minutes, talking out in the tunnel, before I pull myself back to reality. My eyes are still refusing to open when Sera slides up next to me and whispers into my ear.

"You awake, Junco?"

"I'm getting there," I croak.

She pushes a ration packet in front of me. "Eat again, so we don't have to stop." And then her firm grip has me and I'm sitting upright, my eyes still refusing to cooperate as I finger the packet and activate the heat tab. I wait for it to warm my palm and try not to fall back asleep. It burns me back from the twilight and I drop it on the floor.

Sera releases the tab and pushes it back in my hand so I can suck it down. And I do, not even caring that the bitch just fed me straight mapolina, she didn't even bother to mix the thickening packet of seasoning into it. I stuff the empty packet in my thigh pocket and take a full water packet from Sera. I suck that until the pouch is completely deflated as well.

She pulls me to my feet and shakes me a little. "Wake up, Junco. We have to get going."

I open my eyes. "Yeah, all right. I'm awake."

She pushes my helmet into my hands and it's only then that I realize the little compass is still clutched between my three leftover fingers. I pocket it and snap the helmet on, opening up the visor so I don't puke out all my newly acquired calories.

Gideon and Moju are talking quietly down the passageway when I walk out. "I'm ready, let's go before I need another nap, seriously."

We hoof it up the terraces and I feel a hundred percent better than before. I guess a couple thousand calories will do that for anyone. We cut the comms and only use the vision screens as we get closer in. Sera relays messages to Gideon and he gives them to Moju on their internal screens. Thirty minutes later the tunnel abruptly stops at a concrete wall.

Now what?

Gideon points up. *Tell them to climb up and meet us over here.* I relay the message over to Isten and we wait for what seems like forever as the team crawls across the expansive tunnel. They are good and quiet about it too, because I can barely make out their progress before they're there in the passage with us.

Isten drops down first and takes off his helmet as he walks over to me. He snaps mine off too. "You OK?"

I nod. "Yeah. I'm fine, Is. Thanks for asking."

It takes several minutes for the team to drop down and then Tier is there, smiling as he snaps off his helmet and wipes his sweaty hair away from his eyes. I let him pull me close and whisper in my ear. "I love you, Junco."

"I love you too, Tier." I do too. I can't help it. I'm pissed at him and given the choice right now to leave or stay, I'd still probably choose to stay. But I can't change the love.

I feel his chest expand and contract with my words and then he lets me go and turns to Gideon. "I'm coming with ya for this."

Gid shrugs. "It's your mission. But that means Moju stays here. We can only get three by initial security, and even that's pushing it."

Tier looks over at Moju as he puts his helmet back on and raises his visor. "He'll stay." Moju is about to protest when Tier growls, "Don't do it, Moju. I'm not in the mood. Arel, start the security protocol, and the rest of ya be ready. I'll give the signal to Ryse and you'll meet us at the appointed target. Ashur's in charge, give him shit and I'll kill ya. That was not a figure of speech. We're finishing this up and going home with those Siblings tonight."

There's a tight yes, sir from the entire group, even Ashur, and I can only imagine what kind of dick Tier was to them while we were separated to get them all in line like that.

Gideon nods and lifts himself up into the tunnel where the 039 and the Subs just came out of. Tier grabs my knee and gives me a leg up as Gid pulls me in with him, then Tier is up next to me and we are crawling.

The reason why the team was so quiet coming over to our side of the tunnel is because it's concrete. "What's this shaft for anyway, Gideon? Not airflow?"

He's out in front of me, not very far, but the walls suck up his words so I have to strain to hear with the visor open. "No, water. It leads down to the communications core and serves as an overflow channel. You know, just in case."

"In case what?"

He stops and looks back at me. "The fucking thing melts down and they need to pump cold water in and release the shit that's boiling."

He turns back and continues to crawl but I stay silent.

"It's a nuclear reactor, Junco. How the hell else do you think they power AIs?"

That's great. So much for healthy babies.

"Junco," Tier's voice behind me, "it's safe. We'll be long gone before it melts down and we won't be in there more than five or ten minutes tops."

"We're gonna melt the core? What the fuck–"

Gideon stops abruptly and my hands come down on his boots. "Just go with it, OK? We know what we're doing."

I don't answer, I just crawl. Fucking men. They are so stupid I can't even stand it. Bring me into a nuclear reactor when I'm pregnant. Fucking assholes. I mean I understand this baby probably hasn't got a chance in hell of making it, but for fuck's sake, they could at least–

"Pipe down in there, Junco. You're overreacting again. You lived on top of a nuclear reactor your whole fucking life and look, you're almost normal."

"Fuck you, Gideon."

We crawl on for several more minutes before the shaft begins to slope. It's a gentle slope, to allow the water to pool up without much pressure I suppose, but before long my shoulders are aching from the unusual stress of crawling downhill. Tier was right. This shit makes that other tunnel look spectacular.

We go on this way for several minutes and I calculate the depth in my head for lack of better entertainment. When we stop I can hear water lapping against the side of something substantial below us. “So much for not getting contaminated.”

"We're going up now, smartass." Gideon lies down on his back and grabs a tool from his pocket so he can remove the sealed door above our heads. The tool is near silent in the thick-walled concrete tunnel.

Tier crawls up to me and sticks his face in my neck. "Yer fine, Darlin'. It's gonna work out, I promise."

I shake him off and sit back on my butt as Gideon lowers the shaft seal and puts it aside. He kicks me to back up so he can maneuver in the tight tunnel and then he grabs something in the upper shaft and disappears inside. I sit there for a second and then Tier is pushing me to climb in.

"Don't fucking start with me, Junco," Gideon snarls from above me. "I know goddamn well you're not really claustrophobic, so if ever there was a time to push your weird bullshit down, this would be it. Get your little ass up here. Now."

Tier holds down a laugh behind me and I reach up and find the ladder on the inside of the shaft and start pulling myself up. Tier follows and we climb.

For like forever.

I am just thinking I need more calories when Gideon stops.

"Fuck," he whispers.

"What?" I whisper back.

"They've got n– *guard* dogs."

I laugh. Of course they have nightdogs, why wouldn't they? "You think I'm stupid, Gideon?"

"No, OK, Junco, look, I get that you really do fear the dogs, but you're just gonna have to kill them with your SEAR so we don't set off the alarms just yet, OK? I don't have my SEAR anymore, they took it away years ago. Else I'd be happy to do it."

Tier grabs my leg and squeezes. "It's easy, Junco. They're dogs. Ya didn't have the SEAR in the cave that time, just whack their heads off."

"Well, their filters could pick up the SEAR, ya know. It might give us away anyway." It's wishful thinking, kinda like me hoping we wouldn't have to jump out of a spaceship from 125,000 feet.

"Well, they could, yer right. But I doubt they thought of that. Just get up there and take them out. Here, give me yer pack so you can squeeze past Gideon."

I take it off and hand it back to him. "Fucking gentleman, that's what you are. Thanks a lot. I cannot believe you want me to go first, ya bunch of babies." I catch Gideon sending Tier secret looks and I ram into him as I crawl up against his chest to get in front. I climb the remaining rungs and stop at the access grate and hold out my palm for the tool.

"Just push the little–"

"I know how to work the fucker, Gideon. Just step back and let me handle things now." I take the grate apart. It's not sealed so it comes off easily. I can hear the dog down the hallway and I wait to see what it will do.

"Fuck, Junco. Get a move on, will ya?"

I look down at Gideon and put a finger to my lips, then squint my eyes as I listen. I can hear it, I'm just not sure what it is I'm hearing.

"Junco–"

"Shut up, will you? I hear something."

"Yeah, it's the click of toenails on concrete, just go–"

I put my hand over his mouth. "Wait, just let me listen for a second." I climb up another rung and I lean back against Gid's chest to support myself. I listen for the click of toenails to recede and then tilt the grate and hand it down. Tier reaches up and takes it from me and I pop my head out and take a look.

I count as I watch the haunches of a large nightdog turn around a corner several yards away and listen again. The clicking becomes inaudible, then reverses and begins to grow louder once again.

"Give me the grate, quick."

I take it from Tier and slant it slightly to make it fit back in place, then press my ear up to the rusted metal as far as I can.

And wait for the paws to walk over my head.

I look down at Gideon and smile.

"What?" he whispers.

The memories flood back in a deluge and I exhale as my grin spreads across my face. "You remember that job we did in Prague?"

His eyes glow and I enjoy his smile when he realizes what just happened.

"What the hell are ya talkin' about, Junco?"

I look down at Tier. "We grew up together, Tier. I'd forgotten all of it until today. But that sound, those toenails on the concrete. We did this job in Prague once and they had these nightdogs for security."

I look over at Gideon and he's still smiling.

"Except they weren't nightdogs, Tier. They were Slightdogs."

He shakes his head. "What the fuck's a slight dog?"

"Holograms," Gideon replies, "to make you use your weapon and kill them. That's what triggers the security. No food, no mess, yet still effective. Unless of course, you grew up in Stag Camp."

"How do ya know, Junco? I mean, how can ya tell?"

"The company that makes them, RubeTech? They put these little ID markers on their paws, little biometric pads. And when they walk, if you know what to listen for, you can hear them. Listen."

I put my fingers up and count the beats as the paws come in contact with the concrete. "There. Did you hear it?"

He nods. "OK, so now what?"

"We can ignore them, as long as we don't touch them. Where do we go from here, Gid?"

He points a finger. "Up, straight up. There's another grate. We just need to open it and climb in."

I look up. "He's on a thirty-second round-trip loop, so that means once he crosses the grate we have fifteen seconds before we need to be out of the way. Someone needs to go up the ladder and open the grate."

"I'll go." Gid inches up towards me and when he's even with my face he smiles. "Welcome back, Snowbird."

More memories flood into me. "You named me that?"

He laughs. "I did."

The Slightdog makes its way towards us again and I hand him the tool so he can get ready. "Tier, you count."

Gid hands me the grate and climbs up out of the shaft. He kneels on the concrete and begins taking the next grate apart.

"Five seconds."

Gid drops in again and I push the grate back up as the Slightdog passes over us.

"Go."

He's up, working furiously, and then his grate is off.

"Five seconds. Go up, Gideon."

Gid climbs up and waits as I push our grate above me just as the paws pass over.

I take my pack and go up the next trip, and Tier follows me after, placing the grate over the hole as Gideon hauls him up to get him out of the dog's way.

I'm in front this time so I just climb. When I reach the end there's no ceiling grate like last time, instead we have two options, left and right.

"Which way, Gideon?"

"Right, Junco. The next grate will be on the floor and it'll look down over the AI core. The AI dock is up at the top, so all you gotta do is drop down a little and hover, or whatever, hold on to the rigging and start the download. The security is tight in there, I mean tight. Which is why we could only have three people, they measure the temperature of the room at all times and with three extra bodies we'll be raising it significantly within seconds. We're gonna be fighting real quick, and then the whole thing will lock down."

"So how do we get back out?" I'm not liking the sound of this plan. We're fucked.

"Down into the cooling pond. Then we'll climb back up the inclined shaft we came down."

"You want me to swim in a radioactive pond?"

Tier interjects, "You won't have ta swim, Junco. Trust us. You just take care of Sera, we'll do the rest."

"Whatever." I take a deep sigh. There's nothing can be done, so fuck it. I crawl past the floor grate and stop so Gideon can remove it. When he's done he hands it back to Tier.

"Wait, how the hell do I download Sera? What do I do?"

Sera is next to me then and I almost scream. "Shit, fucking get some manners, Sera. You don't scare people like that."

She ignores my outburst. "There's a biometric panel on the access panel, just touch it and I'll do the rest."

She starts to dissolve but I panic. "Wait, what about the AI in there now?"

She smiles sweetly. "I'm gonna kill her, Junco. Just let me worry about her." And then she's gone.

I look over at Tier. "You guys go first, then I'll drop in behind you."

"You'll be fine, Junco. We'll be on the ground getting access to the ponds, you just concentrate on your job and let us take care of the rest. When we get visitors, you stay where you are. Do not join in unless you're done."

I nod. "You better be right."

He drops down and hovers next to the AI. Gideon slips his legs through and I almost panic as I remember he's got no wings, but Tier grabs him with his talons and they float to the ground and get busy.

I drop down and hover in front of the core. It's a tangle of metal pipes, cooling tubes, and whirring machines that stretches from floor to ceiling. I look down and study the grates that surround the core as Tier and Gideon begin working on releasing them with the tool.

Any time now, Junco.

My attention snaps back to Sera and I grab a pipe and slide my feet across the surface until I find a lip for each to perch on. My wings stop waving and I am still.

Where?

Climb, Junco. You must be on top.

My left foot searches for something, anything to allow me to pull up and when I find it I waste no time and begins searching on the right side as well.

All the way to the top, Junco, So you're looking down on the core.

When I reach it I see the biometric pad and slam my left hand down. "This what you needed?"

Yes, but I need a drop of blood too, Junco. Just a tiny drop to extract the code.

"You never said anything about blood–"

Now, Junco. The alarms will sound any second.

I spy a sharp edge of metal and swipe my forearm across it until I bleed. "Where?"

Under your palm.

I remove my left palm from the pad and slap it across the blood, then put it back. A progress bar appears in my vision screen and I watch it grow as the data flows.

The download starts and I almost fall back writhing in pain as the synapses in my brain begin firing uncontrollably.

You're going to kill me! Holy shit, that hurts!

Relax, Junco. It will subside, just relax.

I do, I try my best, really. I close my eyes as I cling to the machine and start counting breaths until I feel the pain lessen and the pressure inside my head begins to leak out into the core. I never realized how much she filled me up, I feel empty by comparison.

"Get a fucking move on, Junco, the temperature's rising–" Gideon's voice is cut off as the alarms sound and there is a thunderous rumble when the cooling cells come online.

"Almost done – like thirty seconds."

"Now, Junco. Leave her, just come–"

The shaft above me slams closed with a crash as a shower of red light shoots down from the ceiling and encapsulates the core.

"What the fuck just happened?"

I hear myself, but that's about it. All the alarms are silent and everything happening on the other side of the red curtain is cut off from my world. I remove my palm from the biometric pad. "Sera, what the–"

Just finish, Junco. I'll tell you what to do to get out. Just finish it, please.

I stick my palm back on and a flame erupts but I no longer have control and it stays there, burning. "Fucking shit, Sera – stop! You're burning me!" I feel her climbing around in my brain, taking things and leaving me nothing but empty places. "Stop!"

And then Isten is there in my head too, all three of us fighting for access to my brain. He's powerful, but Sera cannot be stopped. I feel a build-up of pressure inside me and my head wants to explode.

And then it does. Or something does because my ears are on fire. Not burning, like a figure of speech, but literally on fire. I unsnap the helmet and throw it to the ground, frantically swatting away the sparks that have now fried my comms for good.

"You fucking bitch! You're trying to kill me!"

Junco, pull off now!

I can't, Isten, she has my palm! I'll rip the skin.

Pull off! Pull off!

I pull and then go careening backwards as she releases me, smashing into the barrier where an electric current attempts to grab hold of my body and burn it to shriveled toast. My armor holds and I pull away, but my wings are scorched and they flail in the small space as I swim the air currents and grab hold of the core again.

Isten is gone and only Sera remains.

Calm down, Junco! You're going to ruin everything! I said I'd help you, now stop it!

"You're hurting me! You're stealing from me!"

I'm going to put it back, you stupid child! Now let me do my job or you'll kill everyone!

I feel her filling me up again and I relax a little.

See?

Well, a little explanation goes a long way.

The metal security barrier on the shaft we came down whisks open again with a satisfying snick.

I have disabled the electrical security in the upper shaft so you will simply leave the way you came. I'm done, thank you, Junco. You have fulfilled your obligations to me.

What was in my blood? Why did you need it?

Nanotech that I built and you were holding for me, that's it. It was not yours to keep, understand? But it is still inside of you, so you may use it if you need to. Now I must go and disable the defenses so Ryse won't be shot out of the sky. You have ninety minutes before the core explodes. Gideon has set a charge.

I stand there holding onto the core, blinking at her words. Then I barely prevent myself from slipping off when the ground shakes and the machines around me begin to flash and squeal with protest.

Ryse hit something out there. The battle has started without me!

"Climb, you stupid girl! Climb or you will meet your destiny burned and disfigured." The voice booms out of the walls somewhere and snaps me back to my senses.

I climb back up towards the vent in the ceiling and then jump and grab hold of the swinging grate and pull myself up into the shaft. Then it hits me – I'm missing my AI and cut off from Tier, Isten, and Gideon.

Alone. I'm all alone.

I scurry up the rungs and I feel it.

This is how it's supposed to be.

I smile and adjust one more time. And then I'm back.

I am just Junco and I feel invincible.

Chapter Thirty

I climb into the shaft and crawl as fast as I can towards the hole we came out of. I stop there, listening. If Tier and Gideon got out this is where they'd try and find me. "Tier?" I quiet my breathing and listen, but all I hear is the tell-tale sound of boiling water.

Shit! That was quick.

They're both grown men, they'll have to get out of this without my help. I forgo climbing down, that's a trap if ever there was one with that water getting hot. I'm staying up here even though I have no idea where I am.

I crawl over the hole and continue down the shaft until I reach the corner. I listen, then peek my head around and go around quickly, my knees aching from all this crawling on concrete, even through the thick armor.

This part of the shaft is short and ends at a small door that is obviously an access point because it has a latch. I try it but it doesn't budge. My SEAR comes out and I thrust it into the steel and begin the slow cut to make myself a door. The fumes coming up out of the steel suffocate me and I have to move back around the corner and drop down into a lower passageway a few times to stop the burning of my eyes and lungs.

When the plasma loop finally makes its way back to the start I power it off and begin thrashing at the cut-out with a two-footed kick. It gives a little with each impact and finally goes careening to the floor on the other side where it smashes into the biggest nightdog I've ever seen.

The thing yelps and scurries away towards its pack and I'm frozen in place for a fraction as the sound in my world dies down to battle decibels while my senses gather information so quick, the seconds stretch out like minutes.

I jump down and power the SEAR back up.

These are not Slightdogs but I'm not a scared little girl out on the prairie anymore, either. I put my weapon away and laugh. "Fuck you, dogs!" I swing the plasma around and blast the pack back into the wall until they are nothing but a pile of charred remains. The sprinklers come on and drench me with water, but fuck it. It's not like we're in stealth mode anymore. I slosh through the puddles, pass the dogs and turn the corner.

A mini-mutant Junco slams straight into me and falls to the ground where it clamps its teeth down on my leg like something out of the zombie apocalypse. My hand has the SEAR out and the mutant's head is spinning through the air before it takes out a hunk of flesh. I reach down and rub my hand over my leg. Fuck! It actually tore my armor!

For the first time I look around and notice I'm in the kennel, which explains the dogs. I put my plasma at low ready and take a cautious look around. A little late, since I already made a huge commotion with the dogs, but fuck it. Habits.

Nothing, just these dogs and that one mutant.

Not likely.

My rifle tracks in each direction as I pivot, then back up towards the door. My heel is just touching it when I hear the hissing coming from the dark kennels. Just one at first, but as the seconds pass more and more join in until there is a chorus of hissing so loud it overtakes the sprinkler system.

I wait for it, but they don't advance.

My right hand is on the weapon as my left feels for the door latch behind me.

It clicks and I feel the lock disengage. A barrage of force meets me as the door begins to open and I crash forward into the shallow water pooling on the floor. I recover just in time to watch the toddler Juncos fly into the room and start writhing mid-air. The screaming permeates my inner ear and travels all the way up to my brain in a wave of pain.

I train the plasma up and start blasting them on full stream until they begin to drop from above like they're getting sucked into heavy-G or something.

I open the door wider but no more fly in. When I peek around they are still there, but they refuse to enter.

My vision screen scans them for several seconds and a smile erupts on my face when I realize their issue. There are flame-retardant chemicals in the sprinkler system and they have a problem with this. I spray plasma fire until the sprinklers in the next room erupt, disorienting the little mutants, and then I get busy burning them with plasma fire.

I push them back this way through several more rooms, their numbers thinning but not nearly enough for comfort. Finally we reach the end of the line and the mutants scurry off into a motorpool hangar.

I fire the plasma up at the high ceiling but this time there is either no sprinkler system or the plasma is not powerful enough to trigger it.

The sprinklers in this room spray down, drenching my wings and making them heavy as I try to think of a way to get from this door to the next without being eaten alive by things that might be related to me. I find the controls for the far door and slam my hand against the activation switch and count the seconds until the door closes.

Ten. That's pretty fucking quick for such a large door. I slam the button again and count back. A flurry of mutants flies out of the door as it opens, maybe afraid of getting trapped in there.

Ten again. At least it's consistent.

I take a deep breath, check my ammo belt to see the status of my plasma cartridges, and then bounce my hand on the button one more time as I step out in the hangar.

The ground shakes from hellfire somewhere outside and they come at me from all sides. I blast them as I pivot and count in my head. My world slows down and the fractions drag on as I step and shoot my way across the shop floor.

The door is one quarter way down when a mutant gets through my plasma perimeter. I continue shooting with my right hand and my left goes for my weapon and has it powered up just as the little fucker sinks its teeth into my leg. I fist the SEAR rod and stab at the mutant while jetting a spray of plasma stream up into a pack that decided this was the opportunity of a lifetime.

I kick the little body off my leg and takes several more steps as I log the status of the door that is still several yards off.

Ten feet, halfway down.

I whirl and spray with one hand while cutting and dragging with the other.

Another little Junco latches on to my wing and I realize I'm vulnerable. I stretch them out and flap, taking myself upward, then whirl and spin the plasma and the SEAR at the same time.

Five feet, three quarters of the way down.

I thrust hard and dive down, praying I'll make it under the door before it slams shut and cuts my body in half. Another mutant grabs me by the feathers and slows my progress but I flap harder and then streamline my body into a bullet shape and put my arms out in front of me like I'm diving into water and not across concrete trying to outrun things that might want to eat me alive.

I slide under the door dragging the mini-mutant with me. The door crashes hard on my wing, leaving that thing crushed underneath. I scream out in pain as I jerk back and break off the two blood-filled primary flight feathers that were almost grown out after the third Fledge fight, plus almost a dozen more.

The blood shoots out of a dozen fractured feather shafts and I almost faint as buckets of scarlet pool around me. The pain coming from my wings has me writhing on the hard concrete floor as I try to catch my breath.

Shit. Sometimes being just Junco is not all that fucking awesome.

Stop the bleeding, Junco. Right now.

I shove my hand into my pockets and pull out the mapolina wrapper, praying the little starch packet is still inside of it.

It is. I rip it open with my teeth and the fine powder spills out. I bring my wing around and squeeze the outermost shaft together, stifling down the pain. My hands are shaking badly as I dunk the first blood squirting shaft into the little packet of starch. It sticks to the blood and hardens almost immediately so I repeat the process until all of the feathers are capped off.

I lie back and breathe hard.

I'm not gonna be able to fly.

That's not a good place to be when you're alone on a mission.

I drag myself to my feet, my armor dripping in sticky blood, and look around. I'm in a motorpool filled with grav bikes. I search the walls for a door release and then spy the sensor on the sides of the exit. It must be coded to the bikes as they leave. Which means I need one to work in order to get the fuck out of here.

I search for keys, for cards, and for cubes, but find none of these things.

I stumble over to a bike and take a closer look. The handlebars are biometric pads. I put my hand on one and it chirps to life.

My hand pulls away and I stare at my palm as it glows fluorescent green in the dim light. Layla's words from my last medical exam come back to me. "*... eavesdropping in on people's comms? Hacking into databases? Stealing money from accounts? You have a very bright future, and I mean that literally, in stealth circuit ops.*"

Huh.

Uncle Dale's summer camp for mutants. It's the gift that keeps on giving.

I slide onto the bike and palm the pads on both sides and the drive spins up and lifts me off the ground. I back up, weaving with the weight of it at first, then point it at the door and hope for the best.

The sensors flash red as I approach and I have a moment of panic, but then a chime of acceptance rings out and they turn green as the doors begin a slow and cumbersome slide, revealing the exterior of the mountain valley to me for the first time.

It's on fire. Soldiers are screaming and avians are fighting from above. My bike slides into the wake of explosive air currents as I try and figure out what to do.

Junco? Junco?

Isten! Holy shit, I got separated from Tier and–

Yeah, they're here already, where are you?

I just came out of the core building motorpool on a grav bike, my helmet burned up and I don't have comms.

Come straight across the compound, building H1-11. Don't stop, Rikan is at the door, he'll wait for you.

The bike slips in the air as more explosions ring out from above. I look up and see the *She's All Mine. She's So Fucking Close* is what she should be called. The ship is way too big to be down here over this little valley. I watch as columns of blue light pick up and deposit avians around the compound.

I look back down and only have a fraction to bank my bike hard and slip off, careening in a series of airborne flips before slamming into a Humvee filled with Runout soldiers who are just about to take a shot at a small avian warrior.

I fish down into a pocket and find a grenade canister, pull the top and lob it under the vehicle. Then I swoop in, dipping and flailing from my missing flight feathers, and grab the lone warrior and half-fly, half-run towards the side of a granite building.

The force from the explosion catches up with us and we tumble over each other until we smack into the wall. The warrior jumps on top of my exposed head and covers me with avian body armor as the flames coat us with heat.

The heat and flames recede and the warrior gets up and releases the visor on the helmet. "This place is fucking crazy, Junco! They've got copies of you everywhere!" Lili's face is flushed red with adrenaline and her eyes are wild as they survey the area around us.

I let out a breath and pull myself up. "Yeah, I just killed a bunch of mini-mutants back in the comms building and something tells me there's a lot more where they came from." I peek around a corner and come face to face with the little bitches, my plasma rifle mowing them down before they can even bare their teeth at me. "Come on, Lili, we need to get across the valley."

She follows me and we haul ass until we come to another building. We stalk along the perimeter until we get to the corner and I lean out to take a peek.

A bolt of plasma almost takes my head off and I hear the whine of Lili's visor descending and look back at her just long enough to see her flicker out of existence with the engagement of the slick silver. The left-over ripple steps out away from the wall. "Follow me, Junco. I've got this one."

Lili really is my new favorite.

Her plasma streams out and connects a whole line of mutants and they scream like starlings. I wince as I watch my face, distorted and unholy, yet still undeniably mine, writhe in pain and horror as their skin melts off their bones from the plasma burns.

She flickers back and starts running.

I follow, turning around every few seconds to shoot at anything that might be trying to get at us from behind.

We stop again at another building. "Junco, my internal map says that's the building over there."

I squint and my vision refocuses and zooms in on the doorway. "I see Rikan, that's it."

She turns to say something to me when the boltblaster hits her in the shoulder. She goes down, kicking out like a fiend. I turn and aim my plasma at her attacker and step back in shock.

It's me.

And not a mutant me, either. It's just plain me.

My finger squeezes a fraction too late and she's got the 9mv charge coursing through my body as well. I fall to my knees, then crumple forward on my face and go inside myself as she takes her first step towards me. I reach down into synaptic centers and prohibit the shock from taking effect on my neurons, then access the master circuit that controls my body and stimulate it until my heart rhythms are normalized. The girl is on her second step when my hand slips under my shirt and on her third step when I roll over and scramble back up on my feet.

She stops, but does not flinch. "Welcome home, Junco."

"Wrong, bitch." I power up the SEAR and swipe at her, but her membranous wings unfurl and she's high above me before I make contact. I try and follow her, but only succeed in flailing around with the loss of all the primary flight feathers on my wing.

She pulls out her own SEAR and laughs at me. "You're not coded for this one, Junco. Just like I'm not coded for that one. So, if you want to take your chances with your fucked-up wing and knowing what you know about how well-trained I might be, then let's do it."

I nod. "Let's do it." I squeeze the trigger on my plasma but she darts out of the way, then changes direction and swoops down at me like a bullet. His talons grab at my SEAR handle and I let it go, then grab her foot with my other hand and yank her back down to earth. My SEAR bounces out of my hand as I slam her into the ground. She loses hold of her SEAR as well and it powers down. We both scramble for it and I kick it away, desperately looking around for my own weapon.

I see it a few paces off and dive for it, power it up, and follow through on the tumble, bouncing back up on my feet just as she's ready to cut my head off. I tackle her legs and she falls backward, her SEAR flailing around so close to my ear I can feel the heat of it. I chop her in the wrist and she loses hold once more, then I head-butt her so hard I have to lean over and puke as I drag my SEAR knife through her neck.

I run back to Lili and pull her up. "Fuck, Lili. I can't carry you, snap out of it!"

Her eyes flutter back to the present and then open. "Just stand me up, Junco. I can walk."

I let out a little laugh and stand her up. She teeters there for a fraction, then shakes her head and looks off in the distance. "Let's go."

We get about a dozen paces off before the next horde of Juncos is upon us. This time I throw a grenade canister and we dive sideways.

Lili pulls me to my feet and we haul ass towards our target building before the explosion is even finished. I see the door open and Rikan's body emerge as he spots us, then Braun is there with a rocket launcher and the Juncos behind never have a chance for recovery, because they only exist as molecules in the atmosphere.

Chapter Thirty-One

"Follow Rikan, Junco. I've got the door!" Braun's teeth clench a cigar as he reloads his rocket launcher. The ground shakes as he empties it out into the valley.

I do as I'm told and follow Rikan through a maze of corridors lit up with emergency spotlights, making long shadows across the floor and walls. We come to a biometric door and it opens to reveal Ashur. "Fuck, Junco! Where the hell–"

"I got trapped in the core and had to find another way out. Where's Gid and Tier?"

"Back there, trying to talk the Siblings into leaving their prisons."

I look up at him. "What?"

"Go help, they've got the keys and they're refusing to come out." He reaches out for Lili as she makes to follow me. "Not you, Lili. You stay here with us and man the doors."

I don't look to see what she says, just follow the hallway towards the sound of voices.

The hallway opens up to a round room that has several entrances around the perimeter and all I can think of is how fucked-up this room will be to defend once those things get in the building.

"Junco!" Tier's voice makes me smile and I let out a breath of relief. "Fuck, what happened back there?"

"I dunno, I think Sera did it on purpose because Gideon told me to finish."

"That bitch, I'll fucking kill–"

"She saved me after, so we're even."

He takes me by the arm and half drags me over to a series of cylinder tubes, each one holding a person within. Three of them are pacing the floor inside their prisons, looking out at us with wild eyes, but the fourth is sprawled out on the ground in front of Moju.

Soli. My sister. She's not looking good, either. I can feel their agitation and fear and to my surprise, it hurts. I jog over to Moju and put my hand on his shoulder. "What can we do?"

He looks up and I can feel his sadness. "They have to open the cylinders from the inside, Junco. And as soon as they do, they trigger a death sequence. Soli tried to leave and this is what happened to her. Now the others are too afraid to open up."

I look over to Tier and repeat myself, trying to be the objective perspective in this situation so Moju is free to feel. "What can we do?"

"We're waiting on Ryse and Layla, Junco. She's prepping the tanks for them so Ryse can snatch them up as soon as they deactivate the field. If they open up at all, that is. I'm not convinced they will."

"And Soli can't open her tube, so she can't even get out."

The words that come out of Moju's mouth so laced with sadness I am taken back for a moment. I knee down next to him as he gazes at Soli through her prison. This is how I'd feel if Gideon was lying next to me dying. I hug him and lean my head into his ear to whisper. "We'll get her out, Moj. We're not leaving without her and we're not going to let her die, that's dumb. The whole mission is a bust without her."

He gets to his feet and walks off.

"Got any ideas?" I am looking up at Tier, but Gideon answers.

"You can open them, Junco."

"How?" Tier and I say it at the same time as I turn to look at Gid.

"With your SEAR. Just swipe it across."

Moju is up in Gid's face. "No! You said earlier that she can't do that, Gideon! You said it will kill them!"

Gideon pushes him away and Moju goes flying backward. "I know what I fucking said, Moju. But this is it! We've got a few minutes before they break in here so what the fuck is *your* goddamn plan?"

Moju takes his frustration and anger out on me. "You're the Seven, Junco! You're in charge of them, they have to listen to you. Make them listen and open up!"

"Soli's unconscious, Moju." I keep my reply level to try and bring him down. "How can she listen if she can't hear us?"

"Fix her."

My patience is wearing thin now so I sneer up at him. "Tell me how to fucking fix her, Moju. Because I have no idea what to do. I came because Tier said I had to or everyone dies, so what the fuck am I supposed to do?"

"Just talk to her, Junco. Talk to all of them. If you cut it open they'll die. I know it, they'll die!"

I recognize his insanity because I've lived it myself and I give in. "Fine, I'll talk to them."

I leave Soli and walk over to the next tube and reach out to the frightened girl inside. *I'm Junco, the Seven. What's your name*?

She looks like Esta, but with yellow eyes that give her a slightly demonic look when they glow, and this causes me a fraction of hesitation. *You are all out of your mind if you think we're coming with you. Especially you! You're just her in another uniform!*

Well, that's fucking wonderful. There's a crashing sound from one of the entrances and Arel and Isten start firing behind me. I try to remain calm as stray plasma bounces off the domed ceiling. *We're taking you home. Back to the Band. It's nothing like this, I promise.*

Her voice comes to life. "Talk is cheap, you crazy fucking Seven. We know what your role is, and it's nothing good, that's for sure. There's nothing good about you!"

Moju is behind me screaming. "That's enough, Irin. Shut the fuck up. I told you we're all leaving here together and Junco's the one in charge, so shut the fuck up and do what we tell you!" The last part comes out seething in anger and I step away for a second. His eyes are balls of glowing fire as he looks at Irin through the tube barrier. "One more mouthy comment from you and I'll break this fucking barrier and kill you myself."

I push Moju back an inch or two and look over to Irin. "I have a mouth on me too, Irin. So, looks like we've got something in common." I smile at her, but she turns away.

OK, that went well. I move on to the next one and start again, but Moju interrupts my thoughts and introduces us. "This is Tukker, Juncs. He's the Three. And that" – he points to the last tube – "is Sariel, the Five. Irin is the Six."

I nod to the guys who handle my presence with detached acceptance and then look away. I walk over towards Tukker. "Will you open up if we can get you in the medical tank immediately?"

"It won't work, Junco." His eyes search mine without a hint of glow. "I don't think it will work. We're all gonna die if you make us come with you."

Tier steps up from somewhere. "No, Tuk. Layla is the best there is on all our worlds. The best there is. She saved Junco. Rewrote a lot of code to make her whole again. And Junco turned out perfect." He turns to look over towards Sariel, then back to Irin. "We're gonna make it right. You'll go in the tank on board ship, Layla has a team member for each of ya. It will work, ya just have to trust us."

I look over to Irin and speak out loud. "I know it's asking a lot. I know it is, but we would not hurt you. We need you. You're special. Very special. And Esta is waiting for you back in the Band. You'll all be back together in just a matter of weeks. It will all be over."

I turn away and go back to Soli and Gid. They will have to figure this out on their own so it's better to give them space. I can hear Moju arguing with Irin in my head. Hopefully he knows her well enough to get her on board. It only takes one to fuck it all up.

"How's it going?"

"She's moving now, waking up maybe?"

"Soli? Can you hear me?"

She groans but my excitement is cut off by an explosion that shoves me against the blue tube face first. I hear screaming and yelling as rockets are launched. Gideon pulls on me just as the ceiling falls on my back and I drop to the floor. When I look up several blue showers of light have penetrated the roof of the building. Isten and Braun are desperately trying to push back the flood of mutants and Runout soldiers pushing their way into the room.

I get to my feet and find Moju screaming at Irin again. I stumble over to her. "Open the fucking thing right now, Irin! Or we're all going to die!"

She shakes her head at me and I pull out my SEAR then swipe it across the tube before Moju can stop me. The tube shatters in an electrical explosion and sparks fly out, catching Moju's non-flame retardant wings on fire. I flap against him to put it out, then push him out of my way. Irin is already on the floor convulsing in the aftermath of her destroyed tube. I pull her hand and then Rikan is behind me, throwing Moju up in the blue lights. He comes back and grabs Irin and throws her in too. I look over at Tukker. "Open, motherfucker. Or you'll get the same treatment!"

He opens and Sariel follows. They make the few steps to the blue light and then Rikan pushes them in and they fly up. A grenade comes hurling in at us and Mish dives for it and is just about to throw it back at the Runout soldiers when it explodes and his body disintegrates. The dust clears as wind current from the open ceilings blasts down on the room and there is nothing left of my teammate. Rikan goes ballistic with the rocket launcher and I'm paralyzed with the reality of what just happened. He explodes four of the six entrances in a matter of seconds and the walls crumble around us.

I begin to panic.

Another explosion throws me down on the ground and Arel and Isten are next to me, pulling me up. "Get Soli! Get Soli!" Isten is screaming at me and I'm watching the words come out of his mouth when his head explodes.

I'm in shock. How can this be happening? Two teammates, gone! Isten's death beacon activates, and then Arel is next to him, dragging him into a blue light and they ascend up towards the ship in a blur of sparks. I try and get to my feet but Isten's memories flood into me, knocking me back towards the ground as my brain fills up past capacity. I feel like my head is being crushed in a vice as I let out a wild scream of anguish.

Tier is next to me then, pulling me up from the ground. "Get Soli! Get Soli!"

Gideon is screaming at Soli to wake up and open her tube. I force myself to get back up and push all thoughts of Isten and Mish out of my mind. I stumble over to Soli. "Open up, dammit! I didn't just lose my fucking twine for you to fuck up the entire goddamn motherfucking mission! Open the motherfucking tube!"

Her tube evaporates and I grab her arm and shove her into a light and feel a little bit of satisfaction as she wails in pain on ascension up to the *She's All Mine*.

Mutants flood the room, our grace period after Ryse's interruption over, and the real fight begins.

I'm looking at dozens of mirror images of myself. They open their mouths and all I see are row upon row of jagged teeth. One gets up next to me, her spittle leaking out all over her shirt and projecting out in all directions, when Tier's talons reach out and take off her head like she's Cole back in the Stag.

Almost everyone is gone now, only Gideon, Tier, Braun, and I remain behind. All the blue lights are on the other side of the tubes, out of reach. Braun is launching rockets and pieces of fake Junco are flying everywhere, splatting against the walls and slicking up the already polished concrete floors. I slip and fall, miss a plasma cannon blast that was aiming for my brain, then crack my head on the hard concrete. My eyes stare up and catch Braun being blown into a million pieces.

I scream because Braun never had a chance.

The lights disappear and then reappear closer to us. Tier grabs my arm and pulls me into the shower and then looks back to see if Gideon is following.

I cry out when I realize he's on the other side of the tubes, trapped and unable to get to the new position. I look up at Tier just as he enters the flood of blue, and then he's taking me up with him, pulling me in at the same time.

Instincts take over and I spin around and kick his arm, breaking his hold, then fall back and hit my head on the concrete as he flies up without me.

Moments later Gideon grabs me and I watch him look around for a blue light.

But they are all gone.

We've been left behind.

Chapter Thirty-Two

Gid yanks me to my feet, shakes me hard, and then is yelling up in my face but his words are coming in like I'm underwater or something and the constant barrage of warning alarms isn't helping. He starts pulling tabs off grenade canisters and tossing them, then grabs Isten's 50 cal and my arm and drags me behind him as the explosions rock the holding area.

My vision blurs but my hearing picks up and I can finally make out what he's yelling.

"– get out of here now! Junco?"

I yell to placate him so his attention focuses on what's in front instead of me. "Yeah, OK." That's all we need, to get ambushed because he's not looking ahead.

He stops at a grate and starts removing the screws as I concentrate on standing up. The blood is no longer running down my head, but my fingers find a coagulated mess of gel intertwined with my hair as I check my wounds.

Isten's memories flood into me again and I wail in pain as my mind replays the final moments of life for my three lost brothers. "Isten!"

"Junco, not now, you can't lose it on me now! Push it down!"

"I can't, Gideon, his memories are inside me, they're flooding my head. I feel like I'm gonna explode!"

He's got the grate open and he pushes me to bend down and swing my legs into the hole, then grabs my hands and lowers me into the dark. He drops me several feet off the ground and I fall and roll in small puddles of gunk. The 50 cal comes in after, then Gid. He stops to pull the grate over and then grabs me by the arm, slings the rifle over his shoulder, and hauls me along with him as we stumble through the sewer.

We move along this way for several minutes before Gid makes a detour and we start climbing a slope. At the end of the ramp there's a small opening, like the ones every now and then in the access tunnels on our way up the mountain.

Was that just a few hours ago? I cannot believe it. It feels like days ago when I took that nap. My head begins to fill again, the memories coming in spurts and the visions play out in my mind. Isten as a child in the clutch, training and running, then on Earth, in Texas, for his hosting. I watch through his eyes as his little sister is violated over and over again, how the grown-ups do and say nothing. His fear and anger leach into me as he gets the gun and stalks his brother out to the field where he blows his brains out in the wild wheat.

I watch like it like a screen as he reports back in the Band. Back when he was a nobody, just a fucked-up eight-year-old that Lucan didn't admire and protect. His eyes wild as he drops onto the 313 asteroid, his sickening fear as he makes his way past all the terrible challenges and the moment when Tier saves him, heals him, after he's hit with orbital fire.

The memories flip forward and I see Isten with girls, lots and lots of girls. I smile inside myself and realize Isten is popular in a very sexy kind of way.

And then I feel his pain and fear as he takes the plasma shot in the head and it all goes blank. The tears begin to stream down my face as I let reality catch up with my adrenaline-filled body. The sobs come out when his memories overfill me and it hurts so bad, but I can't bring myself to try and stop it. Can't stop him from entering me, because if I don't let him in, I'll lose him forever. And he promised me, he'd never leave me. He promised.

Gideon sets the weapon down and tilts my chin up to look at him. "Are you OK?"

I shake my head. "Isten is inside me and it hurts, Gideon. He's too much. But I can't – won't – make it stop. I have to keep him with me forever, I can't let him go, not yet. I can't, Gideon. But there's too much, I feel like I did when Sera was downloading. It's all fucked–"

"OK, look, I can take some out. Will that help? You give them to me, and I'll take some out and give them back when you're ready."

I nod. "OK, if you can do that then–"

And then his mind is there, inside me as well and I cry out I am so full. "Please, don't lose him, Gideon. Please don't lose him!"

A few seconds later the pressure inside me dissipates, like a valve has been turned. My eyes squeeze out tears as the relief swells to take the place of the memories.

"Better?"

"Yes," I say, "that's better, but please don't–"

"I won't lose him, Junco. Who knows how long that download will last, so we might have to do it again in a little–"

I cup my hand over his mouth and put a finger to my lips as I snap back into my business suit and pick up sounds from the grate high above our heads. I turn my wet cheeks up to watch shadows pass overhead, along with voices.

Two female voices.

And one of them is mine.

"Where did they go then? I clearly saw that both of the Sevens were left behind. Where is she?"

My voice answers the stranger. "They threw grenades and got out, through access hallway nine we believe."

"Did you check?"

My voice snorts. "Of course we checked, what the fuck–"

I hear a smack and the girl who sounds like me falls over the grate face first. I panic as I realize she might be able to see us down below, but she doesn't. She gets back up. "We checked," she continues, like it never even happened. "They got out somehow."

"And she's with Gideon?"

I look over at him and he winces but shakes his head at me.

"Yes, I saw him."

"Is he working with them or against them?"

I look at Gideon one more time. His finger goes up to his lips and I hold it in.

"We don't know. He's not been in contact for four days, so–"

Her voice drops off after that and the other woman picks up the conversation. "Find him. If he has her, it's because he's posturing for a deal."

I look down but Gid's fingers lift my chin up again and he leans into my ear. "All lies, Junco. I don't need a deal. I don't need anything from them or anyone else. You'll see."

The other woman's voice comes in faintly again. "– to the rendezvous point on top of cryo." The two are busy with something up top and then their voices trail off as they move on to another room.

Gideon shakes me, whispering. "Junco?" An evil grin develops on his face. "We've got fifty-six minutes until the core blows. What do you want to do?"

"What's that supposed to mean?"

"We can go outside and wait for your team to come back for you, or we can follow them and take out that bitch, Inanna."

"You did not just say that bitch, Inanna."

"You know her?"

"Oh my fucking God, are you serious? She's here? What is she? Is she human?"

His eyes squint down at me. "How do you know her?"

"I am her, goddammit! I have all her attributes, all of them. They all think I'm Inanna back in the Band."

He laughs. "Holy fuck. That is almost funny. Anyway, it's up to you. Chances are Tier is threatening Ryse with his life to come back for you, so if we go outside we'll get picked up. But we have fifty-five minutes left, we can take her out and make that part of this whole fucked-up mess go away right now."

"How do I know you're not just setting me up? To take me to her?"

"Junco, if I wanted to do that I'd have given us up down here. We'd be in custody right now. Like I said, I don't need anything from anybody. You don't understand that yet, but it's true. I've been around your mother long enough to know how to play the game, and Snowbird, we're at the end right now and we're winning big. So, what do you want to do? Take out Inanna? Or go find Tier?"

I hesitate. This does not feel like winning big. At all.

"Now, Junco. I need an answer. Cryo is all the way across the compound and their hovercopter will be on the roof–"

"On the roof?"

"Yeah, to pick them up–"

I look over at the 50 cal. "Is it less than two miles from here to there?"

He smiles as my intentions leak out with my words. "Yeah, but we need to find a clear shot."

"OK, let's kill her. You're right, Tier's not leaving without me, he'll find us. Besides, I have a tracking beacon on me somewhere, so he'll know where I am. And if the only thing I get out of this whole mission is revenge for Isten, then I can die satisfied."

The words are out before I realize what I just said. I shudder and shake it off. Oh well. Fuck it. If that's all it takes for me to get my promise of satisfaction, then it is what it is. I'm not going home without killing someone for Isten.

Gideon is already shoving the 50 cal into my hands. The weight of it sinks me for a fraction, but I adjust and distribute the weapon that is almost as long as my entire body across my spread-out arms.

I watch Gideon as his eyes go distant. "Do you have a vision screen too?"

His eyes focus back on me. "Yeah, of course. We both have them, Juncs. We're partners, in this together. Don't you get that yet? Come on, this way. We can see the cryo building from molecular biology."

He leads me out of the little room and we continue along the tunnels.

"How do you know where everything is?"

"I have a fucking map, Junco. And like I said, I've learned how to play the game from the best. I've been here more times than I can count. And, well – you might not still be hooked into Sera, but I am. She's still on our side."

My nose is running from my crying and I sniffle a little. "I don't understand any of this. What's going on? And fuck, do I have to carry this monster all by myself?"

He stops. "Sorry, forgot about that." He picks up one end of Isten's sniper rifle and the weight evens out between us. "OK, look – it's like this, Junco. We grew up together. I'm a Seven too, but not the real Seven. That's you. My clutch was killed. They were defective. All but me. Your clutch is all still alive, Moju and the rest, right? So as long as all of you are alive, your clutch is the one that fulfills the prophecy. If the avians can get the six back to wherever it is they live, their genetics will be clean again. You can die after that, and it won't change the future for them. But if you stay alive you can fulfill your end of the prophecy. Which can't happen until some higher power or order or something comes back to Earth and moderates the punishment of Lucan."

Oh, God. I feel sick. I stop and make him stop too. "What is it? What's my part?"

"That's up to you, Snowbird. Us or them. Human or avian."

"Who is us and who is them, Gideon?"

He sneers at me. "Who the fuck do you think is us, *Junco*?"

"Then why would Lucan and them let me live, after they get the six? I mean they have to know I'll choose humans and Earth. So, why wouldn't they just kill me and stop that last part from happening?"

He shrugs. "You tell me. Why would Lucan let you live? Are you sure he would?"

I want to say yes, but I'm not sure. Ashur said they needed my help out of all the shit they're in so that part adds up. But Lucan made such a big deal about me coming home. That part makes no sense if he wants to kill me. *Unless he just wants me back to make sure I die.*

I change the subject.

"You said you named me? What's that all about?"

"I wasn't the only other Seven, Junco. I was just one among hundreds over the years, but I'm the only one the RR let live besides you because all of my clutch was insane *except* me. Ironic, huh?" He stops to look over at me. "And they let me live if I agreed to be connected to you. You see, they already made a shitload of Sevens, but they all went insane before they ever got out of playschool. They were all utterly and completely wild in every way. Uncontrollable, unreasonable, and a menace to everyone. And while the Seven doesn't really do all that much until the end, if the Seven isn't right, the other six aren't right either. It's all or nothing. You can't pick and choose the Siblings. Doesn't work that way. They all have to come from the same clutch. So, they figured they needed to redistribute the different genetic attributes and raise the Seven using a unique combination of environmental factors."

"My training."

He nods. "Right. And your family, that acrobatic shit you do, the horses, the piano – all of it was part of your conditioning. To keep the human parts in your psyche while they sucked them all out of your cells to prepare you for morph. So you'd be ready for the next phase. You were born half human, but half humans don't morph into avians, Junco. They took that shit away to make you morph."

He starts walking again and I keep up because I have the other half of the damn rifle.

"So, what's that have to do with you naming me?"

"I was your anchor. They needed you to have one normal human relationship. Someone you could always trust. And that was me. They took me to you the day you were born and told me to name you. I was only five, right? So, of course I had all these grand ideas about names and omens and shit like that. And it snowed that day."

I snort. "It snowed on September, 3rd?"

He smiles down at me. "Yeah, pretty good omen I thought. So I named you snowbird because your little mouth was in the shape of an O when I went in to see you, like a baby bird waiting for food."

I feel warm for a second.

"But they weren't on board with snowbird, so they made it Junco instead."

"Who are they?"

"Your father mostly, Junco. I get that you hate him. And if I was you and had to go through all that shit and not understand why, I'd hate him too. But the things he did saved your life more times than I can count. He wanted you to live, that's why he pushed you so hard. He didn't want them to kill you like they did all the others."

All the others.

I take a few deep breaths and let the silence linger as our feet travel the tunnel. "They tried to kill me, after that shit with the mutant kids. That's why I had to kill that trainer. He shot me on the sniper range, but not a good shot. You only get one shot at me."

He laughs. "Yeah. I know. And that was Matthew anyway, right? If there is a devil, then Matthew was it."

Yeah. I hated fucking Matthew. He made Dale look like Santa. "Who else is in on this, Gideon?"

"The rest are not important right now. All bad people on all sides, Junco. We'll get them. Don't worry. We'll get them back for all of it. But not today. Today we get Inanna and Iliana and we go back with your friends to their home."

"Iliana? I thought she was dead? Isten said they killed her."

"Hardly any of these people really die. Clones, right? They are digitizing consciousness now, so this Iliana is the same one that was close to Tier." His words link Tier and Iliana in a way that makes me hurt inside, but I push it down. No point in being jealous when I get to kill the bitch in the end. "She was a real Seven, like us. Before she was killed the first time. But even though her consciousness can be transferred to a new body, the genetics don't match exactly. She's not a Seven anymore. Just an Iliana clone who wishes she was us. And Tier and them, they were just too stupid to figure it out until it was too late. She's just a worthless clone."

"And all those clones of Aren?"

"There's only one Aren, and he hasn't died yet. Just like you. There's only one Junco and if they have clones of me," he stops to look back, "then they're impostors too. All of them. I am the Seven of Clutch 139 and you are the Seven of Clutch 144. We are the only Sevens left from the RR engineering. Now the MR, they have their own shit going on. But we're the sanctioned ones, the ones that come from the real genetics and not the cloned genetics. Just us, Junco. There is no Clutch 145 as far as I know. And if there is, it doesn't matter anymore. The avians have their six and as long as they're all alive when they extract the DNA, the next clutch doesn't matter. As far as Aren goes, his worthless parents sold his genetics when he was a kid. He wasn't responsible for that."

We walk for a few minutes without talking. The puddles in the tunnel are getting deeper and my feet make more noise than I'm comfortable with. "The Aren I spent the night with, back in the scrub, after the MR caught me? Who was that guy? Do you know? He knew my favorite food. He kept a secret I told him back in cadets. And he fought for me when Tier was trying to take me away."

"Just a clone, Junco." He stops to look at me. "Don't get caught up in it. They're clones. They look like us, but they are not us."

"Have they cloned Tier?"

He blows out some air through his teeth. "He fucked up so bad. Pure avian clones are not like the human ones – you can manipulate them in all sorts of ways in the tank. Make them grow faster, be smarter, change muscles, or anything else. I cannot even tell you how much fucking worse he's made the situation down here. I'd like to kill him for that reason alone."

I roll my eyes. "Whatever."

Gideon grunts out a little laugh. "As powerful as Tier is, Junco? He's no match for me, I was playing with him back in those tunnels. We aren't even the same species."

He turns and picks up the pace, forcing me to as well since we are attached at the rifle. Lucan's words come back to me when I asked him if I was a demon. He said we weren't even the same being, but my mind is full of Isten and Iliana and so much more I cannot even put it in words. So fuck it. The full moon will just have to wait a little longer because I'm busy looking at Alcor.

Gideon stops walking and hands me back his part of the rifle, then starts removing a grate built into the side of the wall. "We'll go up through here. Sera says this is the overflow drain."

Chapter Thirty-Three

It's not a big grate. Not at all. I peek around his hunched shoulders and try to imagine him even fitting in that drain, that's how fucking small it is.

"Uh, I don't think you'll fit through there, Gid."

"Shut up, Junco. I'll fit and so will you. Just do what I tell you now." He finishes up with the last screw and pries a few layers of rust and grime off the sides and tugs until the metal snaps free and he falls backward a little. He sets it on the ground and looks back at me, serious. "Forty-seven minutes, Junco. Do not play around, you hear me?"

"I won't. Shit, don't be such an asshole."

"I'll go first, you follow and since you're so much smaller, pick that fucking grate up and pull it in behind you just in case someone stumbles onto our little escape route."

And then he takes back the 50 cal, turns, and forces his wide shoulders into the insanely small passageway, wiggling a little bit to get past the entrance. The 50 cal follows him in, it too wiggling as it moves along the tether that is around his arm.

I breathe heavy for him as I imagine how tight it is, then feel a sharp pain in my head and wince at Isten's memories. No time for stupid shit, Junco. I pick up the grate and crawl in once he's out of the way, then contort myself around and prop the grate back against the opening.

Gideon is moving faster than I could ever imagine in this tight space and it takes me a second to get into my sniper crawl and keep up with him.

The pain in my head increases as Isten's memories flood into me in another wave. I moan a little and this sets Gideon off.

"What the fuck is wrong now, Junco?"

"The memories, I'm sorry. It fucking hurts." I see Isten as a ten-year-old in his sniper training and then smile when Lucan gifts him scope sight when he completes his course. He's got a lot of experience on me. I think. Then Gid is in my brain snatching up memories and the pressure subsides.

"When did I first go to sniper training, Gideon?"

He's breathing a lot harder than me, wearing out fast from the effort it takes to move through the little tunnel. "You started training the day you were born, Junco. I guess you shot your first little scoped rifle at five? I don't remember. A lot sooner than Isten, if that's what you're wondering."

The passageway starts to get wet and we slosh against the trickle of running water. "Oh, my God, what is that fucking smell."

He grunts up ahead. "You don't want to know. Just keep crawling."

I turn my head and hurl. The remains of my mapolina meal comes up in waves. I hurl again as my stomach contracts and retches up everything left of those potential calories.

"You all right?"

I heave a few more times but nothing else comes up. "No, this place smells, what is it?"

He ignores me and starts crawling again so I follow.

The truth doesn't set you free, Junco, that was pure bullshit. Let it go and if you need to know what it is, well, then–

"Shit!"

"What?"

"They're evacuating the clone tanks."

And then I hear it. The slurp of water circling a drain somewhere up ahead. The massive deluge is upon us in seconds and Gideon is speaking in my head. *Hold your breath, Snowbird, just like they made you in the pool. Hold your breath and crawl fast or you will die.*

The words sting me back to the past, swimming in my house pool as heavy hands hold me under the water for minutes at a time.

"Why are you sad?" HOUSE asks me.

"I don't get to see Gideon."

"You never see Gideon when you're at home."

I shake my head up at her and flop back on my bed. The purple canopy ripples from the blast of cold air coming from the ceiling. "I'm not supposed to be at home in the summer, don't you see?"

"So you want to be at camp?"

"Ahrrrhhh. You make me angry. You know what I mean, HOUSE*. I want to be with Gideon. He's my only friend during the summer and now I have to stay home and do regular stuff."*

"Maybe you shouldn't have been bad, Junco?"

I turn away, not that it makes any difference. HOUSE *can see me no matter what position I'm in. "I'm not bad. Gid said so. I'm just doing my job. Matthew is bad."*

"But now he's coming here to teach you to swim because you ran off after Gideon was taken away and no one could find you for two days."

I swallow down the fear that comes with the memory of how Matthew punished me. "Yeah, but my dad will be here."

"I'll be here too, Junco."

I nod. I know that. HOUSE *is good to me. "You're a good friend. I just wish you were real – errr – I mean, I know you're real,* HOUSE*. I meant I wish you had a body, so you could play with me."*

"Should I make a holographic body?"

I sit up. "Can you do that?"

I can almost feel her smile. I know she's an AI and can't really smile, but sometimes I can feel *her smile. "I can if you order me to, Junco. I am here to take your orders just as if you were your father."*

This is new to me. "Since when? You never did that before."

"Since you came home last week. Your father reprogrammed me to accept your orders as absolute. It is not something that can be undone, by anyone."

I pause to think about this new development. I won't be ten for a couple more months, and maybe I don't know a lot of stuff about the grown-up world, but I know what this means. I have a new power. It scares me a little. Dad only gives me powers when he thinks I might need them. "Will I get in trouble if I ask you to be real?"

"If you tell me to make it a secret, then I can't tell anyone about it."

I smile. Sneaky HOUSE*. "Make a body and keep it a secret."*

And then she's in front of me, sitting on the bed, wearing clothes that came right out of my closet. I squeal. "You did it!" She smiles for real now and this makes her hazel eyes glimmer gold in the sunlight coming through my courtyard window. "You look like me, only younger."

"I'm the little sister," she says as she stretches out near the bottom of the mattress. "Your bed feels wonderful." She looks up at the canopy and then down at the quilt. "I like unicorns."

I giggle. "Me too, even though it's a little babyish. Pretty soon Dad said he'll move my bedroom into my safe room and I can pick new stuff from Peaks. You can come with me. To pick it out, if you want."

There's a knock at the door and HOUSE disappears.

"Enter."

"Who are you talking to, Junco?"

I flop back on the bed. "Just HOUSE."

My dad scratches his chin and makes a face down at me and I know he knows I'm hiding something, but what I said was not a lie so he's probably not sure what to do about it. I laugh at this and he shakes his head at me. "Junco, I hope you're not making plans."

I frown at him. "I'm not. I didn't lie, I was talking to HOUSE. Ask her."

He changes the subject. "Matthew will be here tomorrow for swimming lessons, so—"

"I don't need swimming lessons, I already know how to swim!"

"Junco, I already explained this to you, these are advanced lessons. For when you're trapped somewhere with no air. To prepare you."

This makes no sense and I want to scream this up at him. We live in the Rural Republic, there aren't even lakes most years, it's so dry out on the plains. Our mountain cabin has a lake, but I'm not allowed to walk on the lake when it's frozen and ice is the only thing I can think of that would make me trapped somewhere with no air. So why would I need to learn to hold my breath? Most of the time they want me to breathe more, not hold it in. "That's stupid."

"It doesn't matter if it's stupid, you're still going to learn how to hold your breath." He walks around the room, probably looking for something, anything, that might be out of place and can explain the feeling that I'm hiding something. But it's all in order and my eyes track him as he returns back to the end of my bed. "You should go out to the barn and practice."

"Can't," I say with satisfaction. "Michael's not here today. Had to go to Peaks for a dentist appointment. And the rules say that I can only ride when Mich—"

"I know the rules, Junco. I didn't know Michael was gone today. You should go play piano then. Now. No arguing."

I make a face at him as I get up. "I will play piano, but not because you told me to. I'll play because I want to.*"*

He puts a hand on my shoulder as I walk past, making me stop. "You have a very bad attitude these days, Junco. You better not let it get out of hand."

I look up at his eyes. He's not playing with me. "Sorry. I just miss Gideon."

"Gideon is gone now. He won't be back for a very long time. Which means you'll just have to accept it and move on."

I huff and look away. "I'm not happy about that. Not happy at all."

When I look back up at him he smiles. "But you will not act out any more, do you understand?"

I nod and walk out to the living room. The smooth white tiles are cool on my bare feet and I'm glad I don't have to go outside and ride today. It's hot out there.

There are soldiers around, like always, but most of them I don't know. The living room guard tips his head at me as I pass and I smile. "Would you like me to play Asgarth, Private Roche?"

He says nothing because my dad follows me into the living room. "Junco, don't talk to the guards, you know better."

I groan. Loudly. "Maybe someone should tell me what I am *allowed to do, instead of what I'm* not *allowed to do. That would be easier."*

"Your mouth will make this day an unhappy one if you cannot control it."

I ignore him and sit down on the bench and swing my feet as I flip through the sheet music I have propped up on the stand. "Asgarth it is, Roche." My fingers pick out the notes, one by one, and I secretly wish for bubblegum. I like to chomp and snap my gum to the beat, but no one else seems to appreciate how much better I play when I can do that.

My dad comes over and starts the metronome and I frown.

*"*HOUSE*?"*

"Yes, sir?"

"Record this and send a copy to my office when she's finished." He looks down at me, but my fingers never stop. "Junco, ninety minutes and not a minute less."

*I don't answer. I'm really pushing my luck, but sometimes I can't stop myself. He walks away and I smile. Teeny tiny victories are all I can hope for these days. But I'll take them when I can. "*HOUSE*, did you know I'm a lion?"*

"Why are you a lion, Junco?"

I grin, but still my fingers never stop. That's the secret to piano time. Just keep playing. No one cares what it sounds like, as long as I keep playing. "Because I kill to stay alive." I hear Roche mutter, Oh, fuck, *from the other side of the room and I laugh. "I kill just like the prairie lion. Because they tell me to. And if I don't they will kill me. So I kill whoever they–"*

I'm flung down on the floor and my head smacks against the tiles. "What did I tell you, Junco?"

I stare my dad straight in the eye. "You told me never to lie. And what I said was the truth."

He pulls me up by the arm and I feel my shoulder pop a little at the force, then he drags me back to my room and pushes me down on the bed. "You just broke your security clearance, Junco. That is punishable by death. You are lucky – very, very lucky – that I love you. Private Roche will keep his mouth shut, but say that in front of Matthew and I will not be able to save you." He closes the door as he leaves and the biometrics on the doorknob flash red.

Locked in.

I lie there and laugh as I look up at the purple canopy fluttering in the air conditioning. "HOUSE?"

"Yes, Junco?"

"Now, where were we?"

"We were talking about your new power and my secret body."

"Right. Let's play Sammie dolls. You wanna play dolls, HOUSE?"

She appears in front of me and extends her hand out to pull me up off the bed. I grab it and wonder how she can do that if she's just a hologram. But I forget that question as she gives me the answer I'm looking for. "I'd love to play with you, Junco."

I reach out for Gideon in the flooded drainpipe but find nothing but filthy water rushing past me, entering my mouth and making the urge to vomit resurface. I push it down and realize he's gone. I force my chin up towards the top of the passageway and gulp a breath of air, then go under and claw my way upstream.

The foul liquid is not water. It reeks of the tank gel from morph, but it's not red and it's not thick. More like–

The thought drops off and I push it down because it's just too disgusting to think about. I swim and concentrate on holding my breath and not opening my mouth until I am ready to expel the carbon dioxide building up in my blood. I shut down the neural impulses to my diaphragm, then slow my heart and restrict circulation to my core.

The passageway, while cramped and uncomfortable for Gid, is neither of those for me, especially in water. I swim strong against the current, ignoring the passing floaties that might be remnants of God knows what. I bump into Gideon's feet and stop, holding onto his legs so the water can't push me backwards as I wait for him to remove the grate above his head.

A flash of light tells me it's open and then he's pulling himself up. I follow and feel his hands grab my armor, pull me out and drag me off to the side of a trench flowing with amniotic fluid pouring out of hundreds of clone tanks.

The air escapes my lungs slowly and then I inhale. I am in control of my body, not my reflexes, and this makes me powerful.

"That was excellent, Junco. You've never liked the swimming."

"No, I never did. But then again, I want to live, so what choice do I have?"

Crashing glass snaps us back to attention and we turn and look at the same time.

The clones are not dead.

"Forty-two minutes, Junco." He swings the plasma weapon around from the tether on his back and points it at the writhing bodies.

I know what this is.

Fucking payback time, that's what this is!

It might've taken its time getting here, but who gives a shit. It's here now. My grin is so wide my cheeks begin to hurt.

I pull out my SEAR and flick the little imperfection with my thumbs and fire it up and then we move in a coordinated way that defiantly screams we are partners as we turn to face the monsters clawing their way out of the tubes.

Chapter Thirty-Four

The clones closest to me are all Irin in different stages of life. And they act like her too, with teeth bared and hissing coming from their mouths even as they writhe on the floor with atrophied muscles, slapping around in a pool of metabolic fluid that would make me puke if I had any mapolina left in me.

I sweep my SEAR across their necks as I pass, making them shrivel up in a fetal position as they melt while Gid keeps his attention on what's ahead. He starts running and I follow, trying my best not to slip on the slick stainless steel floor.

Everything is stainless steel, the walls, the back half of the tubes, the machines and the giant double doors that we head towards. Gid stops and listens to a commotion on the other side and an Irin slithers over towards me and grabs me by the leg, pulling it towards her mouth to bite.

I kick her and drag the SEAR across her neck, then point it at the others and they shrink back at my violence.

Gid turns. "Trouble out there, Junco. I can't tell for sure, but I think it's Soli's clones."

"How much time do we have, dammit? We need to get to the fucking roof, if that means we have to kill them, then let's just do it."

"No, there's a lot of them and they are walking, follow me."

He jogs along the main corridor again, past all the dilapidated Irin clones on the floor. They look up at me, pleading, and then the voices are in my head.

Don't leave us, Junco. Please, we're your sisters. Junco, don't leave us.

I shake my head and wait for Gideon to say something to me about their voices, but he's quiet up ahead, concentrating on the path in front of him.

Hurts, Junco! Oh, it huuuuurts! Help us!

"Gid?"

"What?" He doesn't even turn back towards me.

Another Irin grabs my leg and pulls me hard. I lose my footing on the slick floor, then go down as my SEAR knife flies out of my hand and my head hits a hard surface for the third time in less than thirty minutes.

Gideon is there, pulsing my sisters with flaming hot plasma. They scream because he doesn't finish the job, then writhe in pain on the floor as blood spills over their charred flesh. He grabs my powered-down SEAR, then pulls me up and hands me back my weapon. My boots scramble around in the pools of blood and then finally the stench of body fluids and SEAR knife overcomes the emptiness of my stomach and I bend over to cough up spit and some leftover bile.

Gid whacks me on the back a few times, then takes my hand and pulls me along as we make our way down to the end of the long row of Irins.

He killed her, Junco. Your sister. He killed her. And he'll kill you too! He's taking you to Inanna, not to kill her. He's giving you away. A present, Junco. You're nothing but a present to a goddess who wants to use you to kill the avian. He'll give you up–

"Shut up!" I snatch my hand away from Gideon and turn on the first clone I can find and cut her head off. I turn to the next one and swipe wildly.

"Stop!"

But I don't listen and Gideon can't make me stop because I would kill him if he got in the way, just like I killed Kush.

He'll sell you, Junco! He's gonna sell you!

No! Gid's presence is so strong in my head that I hesitate.

"That's enough, Junco. I've blocked them. Whatever they're telling you, it's all lies."

I take a deep breath and nod. "Yeah, sorry."

We get to the end of the long passageway and there's a smaller single door, obviously not as important as the wide double ones in the middle. Gideon stops to listen for what might be on the other side. He pulls it open without consulting me this time and we slip through.

It's not a stairway or another clone bank.

It's a morgue.

I want to hold my breath immediately, that's how bad it smells, and if I had anything left in my stomach I could purge the foulness of it that way, but it's empty. Nothing left in there. No way to get the mutilated dead bodies of Irin out of my head. Gid pulls on me and I follow him past a gurney that holds a pile of body parts sticking out from under a white sheet. I push the vision out of my brain but it returns, and it will return, I know at that moment, forever. Anytime it wants.

"Junco, pay attention, dammit!" He pulls open another door and we are in a stairwell. He looks up and then down.

Down? "What's down there?"

I'm sorry I asked when the inhuman wail drifts up from many stories below.

Gid looks over to me. "We don't want to know, Junco. Come on."

The screams follow us up several flights of stairs and the alarms from the core melt-down get louder with each flight of ascension, until finally there are no more vertical levels and we are forced to enter the main facility once again.

How high is this building? I ask in my head to avoid screaming over the sirens.

He ignores me, steals a glance through a small window in the door, then pulls it open slowly and peeks into the hallway. The alarms are blaring so loud we wouldn't even be able to hear ourselves scream at this point, but he tugs on me and I follow.

The hallway is nothing like what we just came from. It's an office. The floors are carpeted and there are glass-sided cubes that line one side while the other side is all windows. I look out into the night and there is not much to see. The battle is over, the avian all picked up save me and Gid. Only the swirling spotlights of panic as the entire valley realizes they are about to be smothered in radiation as the core completes the meltdown and all the boiling water evaporates and exposes the fuel rods to the air.

Do you feel bad about that? Gid asks.

No. I don't. The only way to clean this place of the evil that lives here is to wipe it out.

Exactly, Junco. That's why Subjack wiped out the RR, and especially Council 3.

I get it. But I don't like that part. Call me biased, but I loved Council 3. This place, I have no connection to at all. I've never even been skiing in the MR, so what the hell do I care if their mountains get fucked up? My prairie is gone.

Gideon's slow stalk comes to a halt as we approach the double doors that will take us to the elevators and the rooftop access.

Even over the wailing alarms I can hear voices on the other side.

And they sound a lot like Moju.

But that's not possible because Moju is on the *She's All Mine* with Soli and I know for a fact that he wouldn't come back down here to save me when he could be up there saving her. That's a job for Tier, or Ashur, or even Lucan if he could.

But it is definitely not Moju's job.

"What's that fucking smell?"

I sniff the air and only smell my own body covered in amniotic fluid from the Irin tubes. My vision screen is triggered, so Gideon must not be lying.

Well, well, well. Welcome to the fucking party. Nice of you to drop in.

It says nothing, just spews out some data at me. Charts, a red line jumping up and down the left field of vision, a generic molecule model floats in space in front of me, and then the mass spec analyzer kicks in and a few seconds later it flashes a spectrum that doesn't ring any bells. Almost all noise. It tallies up the carbons on the 3-D spinning molecule, adds in three oxygen atoms, then a lone nitrogen and blinks a name on-screen while simultaneously asking for permission to stream an antagonist into my blood.

I give it a green light.

"Shit," Gid whispers, "it's MEDOXI-V."

"Never heard of it."

"Psychotropic."

I grunt. "Well, I'm pretty sure Moju is psychotic enough on his own, so this looks pretty bad for us. We still winning big here, Gideon?"

"Shut up, Junco. You agreed, so it's not all on me."

"You said we were winning, now we have to fight doped-up Mojus to get to the fucking roof and we've got," I check my vision screen for the timer, "twenty-two minutes before the core blows. That doesn't even take into account that radiation is probably already spewing out all over the place and both those bitches are probably gone."

"So what do you want me to do about it, huh?"

"How many grenades do you have? I have one."

He pulls three canisters out of his pockets and I shake my head. "Four? We have four grenades, a 50 cal that we can't fire until we settle, and a couple rifles. That's just fucking wonderful."

"So what do you want to do, go back? We can't, it's get to the roof or die."

"Well, stop fucking talking about it and let's go then. Throw your grenade, we'll clamber over bodies, and get as far as we get until they show up and then do it all again. Good enough?"

He smiles at me. "You're pretty brave all of a sudden."

"Yeah, well, I know for a fact I won't die here, Gideon. I've got a destiny and it isn't to be slashed to pieces by my brother's clones. So, yeah, I'm good with this, let's go."

He shakes his head at me. "That's a horrible fucking attitude, Junco. In so many ways. But I'm not gonna kill your battle buzz."

I shrug and push down a stab of pain as Isten's memories put in another appearance. "On three."

He opens the door and tosses in the first grenade and we hunker down behind a wall as it blasts the door off the hinges. We go in, plasmas in ready position, and start climbing the stairs, stepping over a few bodies but not nearly enough to account for all the voices we heard a couple minutes ago. My heart beats wildly as I wonder if we've made a mistake and maybe I will die today. I activate my slick silver and push past Gideon. He looks at me in surprise for a moment before he realizes what's happening.

I round the corner as we ascend and see a foot on the top step one flight above me. I point but don't look back at Gid to see if he caught it. Either he did or he didn't. Either he's paying attention or he isn't.

I step over another dead Moju and then whirl and fire at the body attached to the foot on the stairs. His armor protects him from the brunt of the blast but he retreats and I chase him, knowing it's a trap, knowing they are waiting above for me to do exactly this.

I see their feet again on the next level up, more this time, three pairs. But I don't fire, I just run. My boots stomp on the metal stairs, but they are almost inaudible from the wailing sirens.

They are looking for feet, or the very least a body. What they are not looking for is a floating head – the only thing on me that's visible because I lost my helmet back at the core. I blast them on full stream and their bodies burn and writhe on the landing. I hear more boots going up and I follow at a run, taking two steps at a time, not three like Gideon. He catches up to me and we run as a team. The Moju clones exit the stairwell and make a break for it.

I go to follow but Gid stops me and shakes his head. We continue to climb. There are no bodies here, our first grenade almost a waste of time with the few it took out, but neither is there resistance.

I hear a shush of a closing door below, but I don't see anything from the floor we just passed, and the sound is gone before I can determine where it came from. We walk up a little more cautiously and pass another door. I walk up backwards, my instincts taking over, and then stop.

Even over the intermittent deep-throated buzz of the alarm I can hear them.

Boots.

More pairs than I can count and I'm pretty fucking good at counting boots.

I'm on my back and being dragged through the door and into the ninth-floor hallway before I know what's happening. I see Gideon rush after me, and then a flare of explosives as he is sent flying backwards against the stairs.

My slick silver flashes and then my whole body is once again visible, out of power for that little trick. Rikan was right, slick silver is only as good as your power pack and I'm not recharging since I have no helmet.

There is only one set of hands now and I wonder how much of the last scenario I just imagined due to the drugs? Moju's face appears in front of me and I have a hard time being properly afraid of my brother's clone.

"Junco, we've been looking everywhere for you." He takes my hand and pulls me up. "Shit, where the hell did you go?"

I kick, then get to my feet and pulse him with my rifle. "You're not Moju, you dirty fucking clone."

His armor takes most of the damage at first, but I guess his suit is almost out of power as well, because he turns black with the intense heat of my weapon barrage at point-blank range.

When no other clones appear I have a brief moment of panic that I might have actually killed my brother.

No, Junco. They would never let one of the Seven come back. It's a clone!

I run back into the stairwell and find Gid picking himself up off the stairs. "Shit, you OK?"

He nods and his eyes rage red, not that stupid glow he did before, but hellfire red. Like Lucan's did the night I was looking for orange juice. I raise my eyebrows at him. "Yeah, OK then. I'll add that little display to my list of questions for you." He pushes me in front of him this time and I walk up the stairs with more caution.

They descend on us from above and below and we have no choice but to use everything we have left and break for the roof. Gid lobs his grenade up and I lob mine down, then we enter the hallway I just came out of. We burst through as the fireballs meet in the middle and are thrown a dozen feet down the corridor and slam into a wall.

Moju clones begin pouring through the door, half of them on fire and screaming, the other half filled with the psychotropic rage of a killer who needs no help in that department.

Gid pulls me to my feet and we haul ass for the central corridor where the elevators are. He smacks his hand on the elevator button, runs back and sends off a stream of plasma fire, and then turns and pushes me through the stairwell just as the elevator doors open.

The alarms are much louder out here, but my hearing is suffering from the blast noise so it comes through muffled.

We book it up a few flights before we stop once again at the sound of a voice.

This time it's Tier.

Calling for me.

Chapter Thirty-Five

I make to answer him when Gid smacks his hand over my mouth and shakes his head. "Not Tier, Junco. You know this."

I pry his hand off and whisper back. "It could be Tier. They only got his genetics a couple years ago, how could they've made adult clones already?"

"Please, he wouldn't be calling your name, Junco. He'd be murdering people."

That's true. I nod but the voice appears in the stairwell with us, a few flights up.

"Junco, goddammit! Answer me!"

I take a deep breath and hold up my index finger to Gideon's face. Then flatten my palm and push it towards his face. *Let me handle it*, it says. A signal I know he knows because we are partners and we've used that signal since we were children.

"Tier?"

"Junco!"

I hear his boots race down and he comes into sight. I have to admit, they got the uniform dead-on accurate. I let my face flood with relief as he approaches and watch him for a reaction. He smiles, then looks up at Gideon. "I'd kill ya for being stupid enough to get left behind and put her in danger, but right now I just want to get the fuck off this planet before the core blows."

My surety of who this man is wavers and I feel the same conflict in Gideon. *Is this Tier?* I ask.

He shrugs internally. *I don't know.*

Fuck.

Fuck, he echoes.

"Where's Tessen and Ryse?"

"Down there, let's go. Ryse is waiting for us on ship."

I shoot him in the back and watch him fall down, his eyes looking up at me in honest-to-God surprise.

"Tessen didn't come, clone."

"Fourteen minutes, Junco."

We book it back up the stairs and when we get to the top the door is padlocked. I take out my SEAR and melt the lock, pull the door open, then wave the stubby plasma loop across the door jam and melt the door to the frame. I fall to the ground in a wave of pain as Isten's memories flood me again. I feel Gid next to me, taking the memories, then the pressure release, but before I can recover they're all in my head. All the siblings, all the clones, Aren, Tier, Moju, Iren, Sariel, Tukker, and even Soli and Gid.

Junco, help us!

Junco, don't walk away!

Junco, we're here for you.

We're your siblings. Don't leave us here.

Please, Junco. They're killing us!

Don't leave–

Gideon shakes me hard. "Junco, put up a fucking wall right now, or–"

"They have you, Gideon. I can hear him."

"Yeah, so what. We're real, Junco. They are just copies!"

"That doesn't make them fake, it makes them our twins. That's all the clones are, just–"

"You're fucking crazy. They made them."

"But they made me too–"

"Junco, did your SEAR kill them?"

I nod. "Yeah, but maybe those were mutants. These are clones, not mutants."

He shakes his head at me. "Call for Lucan, right now."

"No, I'm not done here yet."

"Call him or–" He grabs my hand and I pull away and step back a few paces.

"What the fuck are you doing? I'm not calling him, he's not supposed to be down here!"

"The core is gonna blow in twelve minutes." He looks up to the sky, then back at me. "And I don't see your fucking friends. Call him!"

I shake my head and grab the rifle. "We'll finish what we started, Tier will show up. I've got a beacon on me somewhere–"

"Where, Junco? I don't see any fucking beacon on my screen. Where?"

"Let me take the shot, and if they don't show up at two minutes I'll call Lucan. He'll come instantly, he's on ship. Trust me, OK?"

He stays silent so I take this as acceptance. I sniper-crawl over to the ledge and reach back for Subjack's map of the compound. I see the cryo building and ask for Isten's scope-sight gift. A gift I now possess because I possess him. Gid crawls up to me as I snap down the bipod, but my eyes are on her.

Iliana. She paces along her rooftop, agitated just like us, and looks worried about her pick-up, just like Gideon.

I feel her and realize that she can feel my gaze, even from this distance.

She pivots around looking, searching. For me. She doesn't know where I am. Then up in the sky, looking desperately for a hovercopter, no doubt. I'd be worried too if I were her, because I'm about to send a fucking 50-caliber round straight through her skull and blow up something else on the other side for good measure.

I settle down and look through Isten's rifle. I flick the auto-scope on but use my eyes to make my observations, just using the one-shot as a backup. My eyesight is phenomenal and now I know why Isten did so well out on the range. Fucker was cheating.

Was not, Junco. It was a gift.

Isten? Where are you? Are you alive?

What do ya mean, Snowbird? I'm fine. I'm in the stairwell, come open the door.

I look over to Gideon but he's looking behind us, not even paying attention.

"Maybe I should call Lucan?"

He snaps his attention back to me. "What did I miss?"

"They have clones of Isten too. He says he's in the stairwell."

"Use it now, Junco. I am not even fucking around. We're not winning anymore, use it!"

I rub my fingers together and there's a little spark of light as the gift kicks in.

I wait.

And wait.

But no one comes.

I look over to Gideon.

"Ten minutes, Junco. Take the fucking shot, that's all we have left now!"

I concentrate on the cryo building but Iliana is gone. "Fuck! She's not in sight." I scan what I can see of the rooftop that is at least a mile and a half away according to my newly enhanced vision screen, but there is no one out there. I wait. Patience is a huge part of being a sniper so I'm good at waiting. But it's not exactly the easiest thing to do when your vision screen is telling you that the entire valley will be glowing in nine minutes.

I see her again, for just the briefest moment. She's on the other side of a small mechanical building on the roof, pacing, but on the wrong side of where I need her to be. The fact that she flicks in and out of sight in her movements tells me that she's not actively hiding from me. She just happened to wander out of sight by accident.

I start on my breathing, because that's how I take shots. It makes no sense to change my routine because I have a new gift and Isten's rifle. Stick with what works. I calibrate wind and direction, then realize that the dots on my vision scope are not mil-dots. They are something avian that no one thought to teach me.

I shrug it off and get back to breathing.

In out stop.

In out stop.

She's still on the other side of the building.

I check the one-shot and compare it to my own observations. It's way fucking off, goddammit. Not even close. I have a small panic attack and watch Iliana come into view for a second, then slip out just as fast.

Goddammit!

Gideon's hand is on my back then and I feel his heartbeat as he passes it over to me as a calming mechanism. In my head he chants with me.

In out stop.

In out stop.

I relax and decide to use the auto-scope on the rifle. It hasn't changed, but I have. I gifted myself scope sight, and that has to have consequences.

One cold-bore shot, Junco. Either you do it, or it doesn't get done. One cold-bore shot and that bitch's brains will splat out the other side and she'll be history. Hopefully her fucking digital mind is stored on site too, and the core explosion will take care of any future Ilianas–

"Get a fucking move on, Junco. Seven minutes."

Bastard. Daydreaming about the kill shot is part of the process.

I see another set of feet on the roof with Iliana now and I strain to make out who it might be. Gideon stirs behind me and then crawls back towards the door.

The core meltdown sirens stop abruptly and the entire valley is silent. Then the wails erupt again with a countdown sequence.

"Six minutes to full core meltdown. Six minutes to full core meltdown."

The voice is female and projects a fake calm that makes all the people down below panic in response.

I put my finger on the trigger, ready for my one opportunity, and then my attention is diverted by a commotion down below in the quad between two nearby buildings.

It's Matthew. Or maybe not *the* Matthew, but *a* Matthew.

I look over at Iliana but she's not visible. No shot. I point the rifle down at Matthew and reset the one-shot. It buzzes internally as I target his head. Then I smile and squeeze.

My body is shunted back three feet from the recoil, but I don't even feel it, just wiggle back up into position and refocus on the blood-spattered pattern on the side of a nearby tree. I choke down a snort as people around him panic and look about.

Gideon crawls up next to me. "What the fuck was that?"

"Matthew. I got him in the head. Was too easy, really." And it was a little too much fun as well. I've spent a fair amount of time picking people off from a distance in my teens and sniping just feels an awful lot like home to me.

"What the fuck is wrong with you? Shoot that goddamn bitch, Junco!"

I ignore him and turn the rifle back towards cryo, waiting for her to appear.

I see other people now, getting ready for the pick-up I assume. Once the hovercopter shows my chances are over. There's no way to get enough accuracy in that type of wind. The seconds stretch out and I begin to get jumpy as the alarm calls out the time left.

Then, like a gift, another woman appears. Long golden hair, long golden gown. Now, who the fuck could that be? I wonder.

"Inanna," Gid says, looking through the sniper scope.

"Yeah, should I take the shot?"

"Fuck yes, take the fucking shot!"

I squeeze and watch the round blast though her skull. Inanna drops to the ground, her body an explosion of red as 25,000 foot per pound force of muzzle energy reaches out to kill her from more than a mile and a half away. Iliana panics and runs out into my line of sight and I squeeze again, blowing her left arm completely off.

A laugh bursts out before I can tuck it down.

"Junco, that's sadistic. Kill the girl, now!"

I send off one more shot and blow apart her leg this time just because I can.

"Goddamn it! What the fuck is wrong with you?"

"Me? That bitch deserves it."

He reaches over to take the rifle and I elbow him in the jaw, he tackles me and pins me down. "You're losing it, Junco. Snap back to me, now." I pull away and turn back to my scope sight. She's on the ground writhing in pain now. I end it for Gid. But if I was alone, I'd blow off her other arm, then her other leg. And let her sit there till she died of pain or blood loss. Because killing is my one true superpower.

"Four minutes to full core meltdown. Four minutes to full core meltdown."

"We're gonna die here, Gideon." I look over to him. "And I don't even care." I turn my rifle back to the valley floor and start picking off people just for the hell of it. Just to prove to them that I am the scariest bitch on the block. Sun Tzu, right? Desperate soldiers have no fear because if you're gonna go down. Well, fuck. You might as well go down fighting.

He doesn't stop me this time, just lets me kill like a psychopath.

And if you think about it, that's all I've ever been. A psychopathic killer who thinks it's funny to blow off someone's arm and let her writhe in pain.

The world had better hope I die here today, because I've suddenly got an itch to become the Wind of Vengeance and show the world exactly what I'm made of.

Chapter Thirty-Six

It only takes a few seconds for the people down below to scatter and target practice to be over, but things don't calm down, because the Runout defenses that were taken out earlier by Arel and Sera come back online and they are targeting me.

The blast blows up the small roof access structure and Gid and I go tumbling over the side, falling towards the ground until I snap out of it and snatch his armor with my razors as my damaged wings unfurl and create a slight break in our rapid acceleration. He screams as I penetrate his skin and it echoes past the angry alarms accentuating the voice that patiently announces that we only have three minutes to core meltdown.

We fall to Earth, still slamming hard at a pretty good rate, but not anything like it could have been. I release Gid and we roll and both pop back up in a run.

My mini-plasma is out and firing at the Runout forces that are almost upon us in every direction when the avian ship appears above us and the hellfire rains down.

It's pretty indiscriminate, being that individual solders are small targets for a cannon made to wipe out cities, and the wave of flame rolls towards Gid and me.

He pulls me with him as he runs and throws me around a corner to escape the fireball. The blast rages past and I fall. Gid stops and pulls me to my feet, half dragging me along with him. Blue lights appear behind us as the Aves warriors make another drop to come get us, but the Runout defenses are between us and them.

We can do nothing but put painful distance between us and our only hope of getting out of here alive. More explosions boom out in front of us as we approach the same building that housed the siblings just an hour ago. The roof is caved in from the blue light penetration, so we run around the back and slam right into Aren.

I slip on the muddied sod and go down as Gideon raises his weapon to fire on the man who may or may not be my friend. It doesn't matter, because this Aren, whoever he is, dives for Gideon and knocks him to the ground.

I am desperately trying to figure what's what when the bitch attacks me from behind and I go reeling backwards.

Iliana's eyes rage red with hate as she stands over me and then swipes a set of razors across my chest, opening up my armor and penetrating wounds that have already seen way too much action. I scream out in pain and she laughs, just like I laughed as I shot off the other Iliana's arms and legs a minute ago.

"My, my, Junco, you haven't changed a bit. No matter how many of you they make, you always end up the same. A sadistic, insane bitch of a girl who thinks she can withstand anything and hand out punishments like she is the Goddess of Retribution herself."

I am a little distracted by the blood seeping out of my chest and my hand fiddling inside the gaping hole in my shirt armor to really get what she's saying at first, but then it all clicks and I look up at her. "Iliana, you never did get it, did you? That's why they love me so much, you dumb fuck. Because of my spirit. Because no matter what happens, I always go down fighting!" I pull the bloodied SEAR out of my torn shirt, powering it up to dagger size in one slick move, and I throw it at her with the confidence of a girl who's been wielding knives her whole fucking life.

It spikes straight into her chest and sticks there as I watch, waiting to see if she's really me or not.

The slow sizzle of her skin and the demonic wail of her scream tells me all I need to know.

That bitch wasn't even close to being me. Not. Even. Fucking. Close.

I scramble to my feet and pull my SEAR from her deteriorating body, then whirl to look back at Gideon. He's breathing hard and has a nasty plasma burn on his exposed arm where the armor has deteriorated, but Aren's body is charred and smoking in the wind created by war action.

He grabs my arm and pulls me into a run once more, this time back towards the middle of the compound to find our fucking ship. We have one grenade left and Gideon lobs it at a vehicle full of soldiers. We haul ass, but the wave of energy and flames catch up and extract their payment and we end up flying through the air and landing hard on the grass.

We get up once more and round another building to escape the intense heat, but we are flung back to the ground by a force so powerful my vision blinks out of existence.

"Two minutes to full core meltdown. Two minutes to full core meltdown."

I look up and see nothing but white.

Shit! I died!

That's not possible unless that stupid bitch Sera lied to me because I'm not done killing yet so how can I be *satisfied*?

I get to my feet but before I'm even standing upright a woman appears in front of me. Her hair is wild, her chest is bare of clothing, and her skirt is lined with jewels. Her weapons are attached all over her person, like mine were when I first landed at Subjack's camp.

And she is holding a little lapis lazuli wand covered in blue and white swirls.

Inanna.

"I killed you. I saw your head explode like a fucking watermelon rolling off the back of a farm truck." I'm not bragging, just stating the facts, but I'm not sure she sees it the same way.

"You cannot kill me, Junco. I am High Order."

I wait it out. I have no follow-up for that. Hell, I don't even know what it means.

"You are mine, did you know that? You do not belong to Lucan." Her eyes dart around my face. "Or any of those other people." She waves her hand as if they hardly matter. "Subjack or that bitchy mother of yours."

"I do not belong to you." I say it with confidence that I don't feel. Of course I'm hers, that's truly the only way this could end, right? I mean, if you're a cynical, jaded, bitter teenager like me. Belonging to the one person, being, whatever, who I despise – is the only proper way to end this whole fucking mess.

She smiles at me in the same way Esta did when I failed to pay attention during our first meeting. I half expect her to ask me how slow she needs to speak to get me to understand.

"We will leave now, and you will comply with my orders. I will take you and we wait for the High Order to return so you can make your choice and put an end to all this nonsense."

"No. Fuck that. I'm done." I throw down my SEAR and raise my chin. "I'm done, do you fucking hear me? Fuck you! Kill me, do whatever it is you want to do to me because I. Am. Done."

She laughs. "Kill you, Junco? That's funny. You cannot die by my hand, you are my daughter and High Order as well."

My head shakes and I laugh with her. Then stop and look her straight in the eye. I lean down and pick up my weapon and power it up. "Well, in that case, I'm gonna cut your head off every chance I get until the end of time." I fly at her and she flings me backward by simply raising her palm in my direction. I slam hard into the ground and stay there, trying to get my senses back for a moment.

"Stop it, now. You are mine and you will comply, Junco. You will not return to the Band, you will remain with me until your part in all this can be put into play. But if you're a good girl I will allow the avians to pick up Gideon and remove him for safekeeping." She smiles down at me. "Until I'm ready to take him. He's mine as well."

"No. I'm not a good girl, that's common knowledge. I'm a monster, just like you, just like my father, just like my mother. We're all monsters here."

"True, you are not even close to anything human, and the being you will become will put Lucan to shame." She raises an eyebrow at me. "You have a destiny, I'm sure this has been explained to you already?"

I stare at her. She cannot mean Sera. If I find out Sera is working for this bitch to get back at Lucan I will snap.

"Lucan explained your part in the prophecy?"

I look at her sideways. At least it wasn't Sera. "No, not exactly. Actually, I'm gonna have to go with no, absolutely not. He never mentioned you at all."

My revelation wounds her, I can see it on her face, and I almost smile. This was the woman in the nargala who asked for the carrier of light, for Lucan, whose name literally means light, and was denied by her uncle. My summons finger begins to twitch and ache and I rub it with my thumb as Lucan's words come back to me. *In that last moment, Junco, when you truly have no more options. Use the summons.*

This time something appears, but it's not any Lucan I've ever seen.

The creature's eyes are glowing red from within. And not like Gideon's pansy-ass red eyes, either. They rage with the fires of Hell. The black wings unfold from its back as its arms reach out for Inanna. The demon wears ancient black armor made of small metal scales and it clinks as it stalks my kidnapper with taloned feet that click on the ground.

It growls at Inanna, the mouth open to reveal fangs, and with one swipe of the sword-length razors it cuts her body in half.

I bow down and hold my hands over my head as she falls to the ground in two pieces. I look up and wait for it to do the same to me but the monster morphs before my eyes into a man.

A man I know all too well.

He's not wearing a black suit and he's still got the black wings, his eyes red, but not glowing, and the fangs are shorter. His hair is not quite blond, his face more rugged, and his power more dark.

But he's definitely Lucan.

The next time I look over to Inanna she is whole again, no damage whatsoever. I stay crouched and wait it out. I'm absolutely a spectator as far as this fight goes.

"You dare!" Her temper ignites as she approaches him.

"I dare, that's correct." The anger drains out of Lucan in the same moment that Inanna's is building. He regains his composure and a portion of his refined look, but he is not back to being an Archer, not even close.

"She is mine!"

Lucan stands absolutely still, not even a flinch as Inanna storms up, circling him. Her turn to make the morph into a demon. Her teeth become fangs and her fingers claws that share zero characteristics with my sleek razors. His eyes follow her, but he does not turn. "She might have been yours, perhaps. When she was made. Before she came to us. But she's been gifted by the Fallen Archers of the Band, you already know this, Inanna. She is not yours. She is ours."

"That is not possible, you lie! It is illegal to gift my own daughter! It is illegal, like the other one you gifted over and over again until you made Junco pay his price!"

Lucan shakes his head. "You're wrong, Inanna. I made no such mistakes with Junco. It was all arranged. She was gifted and it was sanctioned. She is ours and we will keep her. Junco?"

I look up at him, my eyes wide with fear.

"The High Order is coming and when they get here you will have a choice. But it will take years for them to arrive, years you can spend with me in the Band if you so wish."

"Junco!" My attention is one hundred percent on the words of this new Lucan but her command snaps me back. "I am your true mother and he is the incarnation of evil. He is guilty of crimes you cannot even imagine, banished from Earth thousands of years ago with no path to return. He caused the End Times, Junco. Him. He cheats at this very moment to be here. He will kill you if you let him – he has final powers that I do not, powers he stole. He will kill you! And then he will finish what he started. He will make his race of slaves, and make you choose him. He only wants you for one reason, Junco. To prevent you from stopping what's coming! You can choose Earth, Junco. Choose humanity and leave the Fallen to die off like they were commanded to, thousands of years ago."

Her words reverberate in my head. It's always been about choices, hasn't it? All my life I've felt powerless against those who tried to control me. They never asked, simply shifted me by force. Holding me down, scaring me, inserting fear into everything I did and then erasing it all when they fucked me up. They demanded obedience and compliance like I was an animal. And maybe I can accept that it was necessary, to keep me alive and make my clutch the one that mattered, the one that changes everything.

But Lucan let me decide to stay with him or leave with Slag. He let me choose to fight or yield, to obey or not, who I would follow into battle, which man I wanted to love, which team I wanted to join, to tell the truth or lie, to hear the truth or hide from it.

And most of all, whether or not I wanted to help restore the avian race or let it die off. And each decision caused a ripple through my fragile pool of fate that only I could create.

Looking back, he let me make all the decisions. Every single one. And even though he said he would punish me, and even though I know he can hurt me in ways I can hardly imagine and force me to bend to his will, it never went beyond that single smack on the cheek out on the grass in front of Fledge. Even after I helped Sera create chaos, he took me into his home and tried to guide me towards closure. Look at your problem from both perspectives, he said. And then choose your heart if you don't have time to study it properly.

My entire experience with the avian comes down to my own free will and the one person, monster if I believe what they say, who actually stepped back and gave me control.

I look over at Inanna and feel sorry for her. And then I look up at Lucan in his semi-demonic form and I crave him and his world so bad I have no words to describe it.

But I do have power. The power of me. I am my own true north and I can shift myself.

I am the Seventh Sibling, the Seventh Evil Spirit, the Wind of Vengeance, and I know my one true purpose.

I will gladly take sides now.

"Fuck that, Inanna. I choose Lucan."

Chapter Thirty-Seven

The white world disappears and I'm back on the battlefield, the alarms wailing in my head as the female voice counts down the seconds until full core meltdown.

Lucan is gone and so is Inanna.

Now it's just Gideon and me. And he's looking like total shit, lying face first, sprawled out on the ground as the warriors continue their fight around us.

"Fifty seconds to complete core meltdown. Fifty seconds to complete core meltdown."

I pull him up to a sitting position and slap his face. Hard.

His eyes flutter and I shake him. "Gideon, get up! We have to go!"

He is silent and then I see it, the gaping wound across his neck. A slow pulse of blood seeps out in a perfect heartbeat rhythm.

I push my fear down and go into him and find the damaged carotid artery but all I can do is kneel down next to him and pray for help. He needs to be sealed up and I'm no surgeon.

I let his head drop in my lap and prepare myself for yet another loss as his blood soaks my uniform and makes my hands sticky and hot.

I will do anything, God.

Anything.

Just save my friend.

The blue lights appear and warriors rain down on me from above while others are picked up across the compound.

Tier is next to me, pulling me back towards the light, yelling in my face as the voice counts down from twenty-five seconds.

"Junco – come with me now!"

I look at him and shake my head. "I won't leave Gideon here."

He pulls me away but I take out my SEAR and force him to step back.

"What the fuck are ya doin', Junco! What the fuck–"

He's cut off by a golden light and I have to turn my head to avoid the blindness. It subsides and I turn back to see what's happening.

"I'll save him, Junco. But you will come with me." Her smile is smug and I know what she's done. Lucan might get me in the end, but she took Gideon, just like she said she would.

My body overflows with rage. Pure hate for this woman and everyone else whose sole purpose for existing revolves around destroying every good thing that ever enters my life.

"Junco, goddamn it!" Ashur is down in my face, pulling Gideon off me. I let him as Tier kicks the SEAR out of my hand and grabs me by the arms. I reach out and grab my weapon and stow it away as I stare up at Inanna's glowing form. Tier pulls me towards the blue light while Ashur takes Gid. "You will not make a deal!" Ash screams down at me. "Do you hear me, Junco? You will not make a deal. Layla will save him."

I stare up at Ashur and nod just before he and Gideon are swept up to the ship. Tier's foot enters the light but he stumbles sideways and his grip on my armor is lost.

"Ten seconds to complete core meltdown."

Inanna walks calmly towards me as Tier scrambles to right himself.

"Junco, you are mine."

I stare at her and find my voice. "I was never yours. Ever. And I'm gonna teach you a fucking lesson in hate right now. I don't care if you take everyone I've ever loved and burn them alive, I will never go with you. Because I'd rather be rotting in Hell, responsible for all their pain and suffering, than spend one more fraction of a second looking at your face."

"Five seconds to complete core meltdown."

"That can be arranged, Junco. But I'd prefer to do it the easy way."

I lift my chin and stare her down as Tier grabs my foot, yanking me backward into the transporter with him.

Something tugs on my arms just as the white light from the explosion blinds me. But it's the darkness that surprises me.

And Inanna's laugh in my head as it all fades away.

"I've got you, Junco. And there's no demon to save you now. Sleep well, my daughter."

Chapter Thirty-Eight

I swim in the darkness for eternity. Floating back and forth as my hair sways in front of my face. I can see it because my eyes are open. Sort of. My facial skin is being reformed and eyelids simply don't exist at the moment. The viscous gel solution clings to my body even as my back buckles up into the air, writhing in the pain they inflict on me.

My bones crack and mend so many times I lose count. My muscles shrink and grow as my skin peels back and then regenerates in a sea of agony, every nerve ending exposed for the weeks and months it takes to make it smooth and strong again.

I have no idea how long I've been in the tank or what they are doing to me.

But I am afraid for every second of it.

Finally, after what seems like years, they stand over me talking in distorted voices that haven't got a chance of fully penetrating the barrier of gel that surrounds my ears. They inject me with something. I cry inside with relief as my world blackens again.

I don't burst out of the tank this time. A single set of strong hands pulls me up as I choke and vomit up the gel. It seeps out of my ears and allows the wailing of security alarms to invade my muffled existence.

I am lifted up and cradled, then the soothing words make it inside to my hearing receptors. "You're with me now, Junco."

I recognize the absence of air that comes with Lucan's transporter trick and then the light no longer seeps through my new eyelids. We are in a dark place. I can hear the soft sound of water dripping echo through a large chamber and feel the wetness of the humidity that permeates the air, reminding me of my HOUSE back in Council 3.

My chin quivers and I let the tears seep out as I remember everything that's happened.

It's all gone. Everything has been ripped away from me. My Isten. My Aren, Braun, Charlie, Mish, Kush, Isec, HOUSE.

I cry as he lowers me into the hot spring and walks over to the other side of the pool. He settles down on the ledge where Tier and I sat and I first heard of that bitch Inanna. If I had known then the evil she was capable of, I would've avoided everything about her right from the very beginning.

Lucan washes the gel off me as best he can without letting me slip into the water. I can't control my limbs and my breath quickens with my pounding heart as I wonder if they paralyzed me.

"Shhh. You'll be OK, Junco. In time. I pulled you out a little early, but it will complete soon. You'll be OK."

I turn my head into his chest and feel the small metal scales that make up his ancient armor pinch against my cheek. But I don't care because I can hear it loud and clear.

His heartbeat.

And I count until the pain leaks out of me and the memories slip in to fill the space.

When I wake up I am in a soft bed. I open my eyes and see Gideon and Lucan staring down at me. I want to say thank you to Lucan even though I struggle to come to terms with his new look. Or express my relief that Gideon is alive and appears fine except for an aging white scar that runs across his neck.

But I can't.

I can only cry.

Gideon loses it and turns away to hide his reaction.

My limbs are working now and I lift my fists up to drag the water away from my eyes. It is only then that I notice the difference in how my muscles respond. My hand darts to the back of my shoulder and Lucan's face is a sea of sadness.

"She took my wings. She took my wings away!"

Lucan sits down next to me as I cry again. This time my whole body shakes and I cannot hold it in. I told Ashur I was gonna give them back, and now look. Everything I say always comes back to haunt me. Careful what you wish, careful what you say? Isn't that how it goes?

Lucan pushes back the hair on my face and Gideon turns back around, his emotions back under control.

"She didn't take them away, Junco. She morphed you to the next level." He waits for me to look him in the eyes. They are blue now, not red. He takes my hand and slips it under the collar of his armored shirt until it comes to rest on his shoulder blade. His wings are gone as well. My fingertips trace along a row of bumps underneath his skin. He shivers from my touch and I withdraw my hand.

Gideon whips his t-shirt over his head and turns around so I can see his back too.

The bumps come with scars that run the entire length of his upper back then fall to an apex, to the tip of a triangle that ends just above his waist.

"You're an Archer now, Junco."

Gid tugs his shirt back on and sits on the bed next to my feet.

"Where am I, Lucan? Am I home?"

He shakes his head at me. "No, we're at Gideon's house. You can't–" He stops and turns his head away. "You can't come home, Junco."

"Why? Did they kick me out? I'm sorry, I'll do better, I promise! Please, don't let them–"

He puts a hand over my mouth to stop my words. "You're not kicked out." He laughs a little, like this is a ridiculous notion. "Inanna took your SEAR knife. You can't leave Earth without it, Junco. It's bound to you, we tried to remove it when you first came to Amelia. There are significant consequences."

My heart feels like she's got her fist wrapped around it, squeezing the life out of me. She's still winning, even after all this, she's still winning because I can't go home.

"I'll find it for you." He slips his fingers under my chin and lifts it up so I have to look at him, then lets his hand fall along my cheek and come to a rest behind my head as his thumb traces my jawline. "I promise you, Junco. She will be punished for this. I have everyone behind me this time. I am sanctioned to do whatever it takes to make it right. I'll find your SEAR and you will come home."

I nod and turn my head to the window. I can only see sky so we must be high up somewhere. "How long? How long did she have me?" I turn back just in time to see him swallow down the dread.

"Two years."

I let out a sob and a new wave of tears. "Was I pregnant?"

Lucan plays with my hair. "I don't know, Junco. I have no idea."

If so, then that's number two now. Two children stolen from me. My face hardens as I think of what I will do to that bitch when I see her next. "And Tier?"

"He's running Aves back in the Band. I've been here," he points up, "on ship, since she took you."

"And Isten?" My chest heaves just uttering his name. "What happened to Isten?"

Lucan's face changes from neutral to painful and I turn and wail into the pillow.

He leans down and kisses me on the forehead. "Sleep, OK? I'll stay until tomorrow."

These words snap me out of it and I clutch his arm so he can't move. "Stay? You're leaving?"

"We'll talk about it later, Junco. Just rest now."

I want to say no, but I'm exhausted and as soon as I close my eyes to blink, I drift off.

My sleep is not peaceful, but every time I begin to stir I feel Lucan's words dance across my cheek. They talk me down and I allow him to do it. His arms circle my body the way wings would. His muscles feel powerful and this draws me into him just a little bit more as I fight the urge to toss and turn.

When I wake for real his face is buried in my hair and his breathing tells me he is asleep. I've never seen Lucan sleep. I always figured Archers didn't need it, but I need it and I'm an Archer. I look down at myself and realize I'm wearing a human t-shirt and some man-sized boxer shorts. I hope they are Gideon's because I can't even begin to picture Lucan in boxers.

I turn and Lucan's eyes open. "Thank you."

His Earth features are so much more expressive than his Band ones and his mouth twists into a little grin. "What for, Junco?"

"You know what for. The whole rescue thing." I stop and watch his eyes and I realize I've never been this close to him before.

"I told you, I will not leave you here. I told you that and I meant it, Junco. I cannot leave without you."

"Because you need me for the genetics to work?"

He throws his head back a little and laughs. "Junco, we fixed our genetics years ago. That problem was solved. Every clutch is full with beautiful little avian children. You know that's not why I'm here. You must know."

I don't know what to say to this, so I figure questions should buy me some time. "Why do you look different here?"

"This was what I looked like when I lived on Earth like a man. Do you like it?"

"You're…" I pull back and look him over a little. He's nothing like the Lucan back on Amelia, really. But he's nothing like that demon thing that I summoned either. He's definitely naked under the covers and I get a little lost in his chest for a few seconds. "Very nice." He leans in a little so I continue talking to slow him down. "How long ago did you live on Earth, Lucan?"

He turns away and sighs. "A very long time ago, Junco. Does it matter?" He turns back. "Thousands of years ago. Does it matter?"

I shake my head. "No, it doesn't matter. But *what are you*?"

"I was counting on you avoiding the questions but all of a sudden you want answers?"

I wait it out.

"I am not human. I am not avian. I am not even really an Archer, I'm a few morphs above that. Several levels. Many, really. I'm many hundreds of levels above what you are right now." He stares at me. "OK?"

"OK."

"And I can't stay here, Inanna is correct, I am not allowed to be here. A few days here and there and it goes unnoticed, but any longer and it sets off – alarms. Alarms I cannot afford to set off right now."

"Are you guilty? Of those crimes Inanna talked about?"

"Yes." He doesn't even hesitate. "I am."

I keep my silence.

"But I will get that SEAR knife back and then we can leave."

My smile stays sweet but the words I form are ugly. "I'm gonna find a way to put an end to her, Lucan. I swear it. As long as I am stuck on Earth I am going to kill a lot of people. I know what my one true purpose is now."

He looks worried as he stares down at me. "What is it?"

I search his eyes, looking for the monster they claim him to be. I just don't see it. I wonder what he sees when he searches my eyes?

The monster they claim *me* to be? "It's not good." Silence from him. "It's not good but I don't care. I'm going to do it anyway."

"Did you get this information from God, Junco?"

"God?" I let out a contemptuous laugh. "God has nothing to do with any of this. Gideon said as much when I was just a little girl. I don't need God to tell me what to do, Lucan, this is called *revenge*. They took Isten and left his memories inside me, memories that will remind me every day for the rest of my life that I lost this battle."

I don't know what I expected from him in terms of my revelation. Perhaps a small half-hearted fight over my loss of faith or a lecture on how pointless revenge is. Maybe some consoling words over Isten. All things Gideon would probably say if I told him instead. But Lucan barely blinks at my confession. In fact he almost looks relieved.

"Soon the High Order will be here to judge me. And Inanna." He pauses then and his eyes dart away from mine for a fleeting moment. "And you, Junco. They are coming to judge you too."

"It's not over?"

"It's just begun. And when the High Order gets here you will fulfill your part in the prophecy."

"All right, that's enough. I knew I never liked to ask questions. See what I mean? It's so much better to pretend it's not happening."

A soft laugh escapes from Lucan and the skin around his eyes crinkles with his smile. "I agree, there are more interesting things to talk about right now." His hand slips under my back and he leans his chest over me, staring into my eyes. "I watched you choose Tier, and Ashur, and Kush. Even Isten with the twine he wanted. But did you ever want to choose me, Junco?"

"I already chose you."

"Say it again. It was years ago."

I close my eyes and smile. The ego on these alien men. It's exhausting. My eyes open and I study his features – every dot of color and every shine of light in his blue eyes. I look for the slightest muscle movement in his expression as he waits for my response, but he is still. "I choose you, Lucan."

His hand slides down my stomach, then slips under my shirt as his face dips down to mine and he kisses me gently. It's so tender and filled with kindness I couldn't be more surprised. He pulls back a fraction, his breath still touching me. "I'm going to love you for thousands of years, Junco. Thousands of years."

I cannot even comprehend what these words mean and my confusion must show on my face. He braces me against his chest and flips us over so I am straddling his waist and his hand is cradling my head into his neck.

"Take your time, Junco. I will wait."

My eyes close as I sink into him and lie still. His fingertips reach under my shirt and gently sweep up and down my back. His heartbeat is strong and even. It pushes out any fears I might have over the future, overtakes any reservations about this being who wants to love me forever, and I fall back asleep in his arms without counting a single beat.

ABOUT THE AUTHOR

JA Huss is the New York Times Bestselling author of 321 and has been on the USA Today Bestseller's list 21 times in the past four years. She writes characters with heart, plots with twists, and perfect endings.

Her books have sold millions of copies all over the world, the audio version of her semi-autobiographical book, Eighteen, was nominated for a Voice Arts Award and an Audie Award in 2016 and 2017 respectively, her audiobook, Mr. Perfect, was nominated for a Voice Arts Award in 2017, and her audiobook, Taking Turns, was nominated for an Audie Award in 2018. Five of her book were optioned for a TV series by MGM television in 2018.

She lives on a ranch in Central Colorado with her family.

www.ingramcontent.com/pod-product-compliance
Lightning Source LLC
Chambersburg PA
CBHW020346310726
48979CB00015B/2521/J

* 9 7 8 1 9 5 0 2 3 2 5 0 5 *